SUSPENSE

GRAHAM GREENE

SUSPENSE

GRAHAM GREENE

ORIENT EXPRESS

THIS GUN FOR HIRE

THE MINISTRY OF FEAR

OUR MAN IN HAVANA

GALAHAD BOOKS

CONTENTS

Orient Express

PART ONE

Ostend

1

T he purser took the last landing-card in his hand and watched the passengers cross the grey wet quay, over a wilderness of rails and points, round the corners of abandoned trucks. They went with coat-collars turned up and hunched shoulders; on the tables in the long coaches lamps were lit and glowed through the rain like a chain of blue beads. A giant crane swept and descended, and the clatter of the winch drowned for a moment the pervading sounds of water, water falling from the overcast sky, water washing against the sides of channel steamer and quay. It was half-past four in the afternoon.

"A spring day, my God," said the purser aloud, trying to dismiss the impressions of the last few hours, the drenched deck, the smell of steam and oil and stale Bass from the bar, the shuffle of black silk, as the stewardess moved here and there carrying tin basins. He glanced up the steel shafts of the crane, to the platform and the small figure in blue dungarees turning a great wheel, and felt an unaccustomed envy. The driver up there was parted by thirty feet of mist and rain from purser, passengers, the long lit express. I can't get away from their damned faces, the purser thought, recalling the young Jew in the heavy fur coat who had complained because he had been allotted a two-berth cabin; for two God-forsaken hours, that's all.

He said to the last passenger from the second class: "Not that way, miss. The customs-shed's over there." His mood relaxed a little at the unfamiliarity of the young face; this one had not complained. "Don't you want a porter for your bag, miss?"

"I'd rather not," she said. "I can't understand what they say. It's not heavy." She wrinkled her mouth at him over the top of her cheap white mackintosh. "Unless you'd like to carry it—Captain." Her impudence delighted him. "Ah, if I were a young man now you wouldn't be wanting a porter. I don't know what they are coming to." He shook his head as the Jew left the customs-shed, picking his way across the rails in grey suède shoes, followed by two laden porters. "Going far?"

"All the way," she said gazing unhappily past the rails, the piles of luggage, the lit lamps in the restaurant-car, to the dark waiting coaches.

"Got a sleeper?"

"No."

"You ought to 'ave a sleeper," he said, "going all the way like that. Three nights in a train. It's no joke. What do you want to go to Constantinople for anyway? Getting married?''

"Not that I know of." She laughed a little through the melancholy of departure and the fear of strangeness. "One can't tell, can one?''

"Work?"

"Dancing. Variety."

She said good-bye and turned from him. Her mackintosh showed the thinness of her body, which even while stumbling between the rails and sleepers retained its self-consciousness. A signal lamp turned from red to green, and a long whistle of steam blew through an exhaust. Her face, plain and piquant, her manner daring and depressed, lingered for a moment in his mind. "Remember me," he called after her. "I'll see you again in a month or two." But he knew that he would not remember her; too many faces would peer during the following weeks through the window of his office, wanting a cabin, wanting money changed, wanting a berth, for him to remember an individual, and there was nothing remarkable about her.

When he went on board, the decks were already being washed down for the return journey, and he felt happier to find the ship empty of strangers. This was how he would have liked it always to be: a few dagoes to boss in their own tongue, a stewardess with whom to drink a glass of ale. He grunted at the seamen in French and they grinned at him, singing an indecent song of a "cocu" that made his plump family soul wither a little in envy. "A bad crossing," he said to the head steward in English. The man had been a waiter in London and the purser never spoke a word more French than was necessary. "That Jew," he said, "did he give you a good tip?''

"What would you believe? Six francs."

"Was he ill?"

"No. The old fellow with the moustaches—he was ill all the time. And I want ten francs. I win the bet. He was English."

"Go on. You could cut his accent with a knife."

"I see his passport. Richard John. Schoolteacher."

"That's funny," the purser said. And that's funny, he thought again, paying the ten francs reluctantly and seeing in his mind's eye the tired grey man in the mackintosh stride away from the ship's rail, as the gangway rose and the sirens blew out towards a rift in the clouds. He had asked for a newspaper, an evening newspaper. They wouldn't have been published in London as early as that, the purser told him, and when he heard the answer, he stood in a dream, fingering his long grey moustache. While the purser poured out a glass of Bass for the stewardess, before going through the accounts, he thought again of the schoolteacher, and wondered momentarily whether something dramatic had passed close by him, something weary and hunted and the stuff of stories. He too had made no complaint, and for that reason was more easily forgotten than the young Jew, the party of Cook's tourists, the sick woman in mauve who had lost a ring, the old man who had paid twice for his berth. The girl had been forgotten half an hour before. This was the first thing she shared with Richard John—below the tramp of feet, the smell of oil, the winking light of signals, worrying faces, clink of glasses, rows of numerals—a darkness in the purser's mind.

The wind dropped for ten seconds, and the smoke which had swept backwards and forwards across the quay and the metal acres in the quick gusts stayed for that time in the middle air. Like grey nomad tents the smoke seemed to Myatt, as he picked his way through the mud. He forgot that his suède shoes were ruined, that the customs officer had been impertinent over two pairs of silk pyjamas. From the man's rudeness and his contempt, the syllables "Juif, Juif," he crept into the shade of those great tents. Here for a moment he was at home and required no longer the knowledge of his fur coat, of his suit from Savile Row, his money or his position in the firm to hearten him. But as he reached the train the wind rose, the tents of steam were struck, and he was again in the centre of a hostile world.

But he recognised with gratitude what money could buy. It could not always buy courtesy, but it had bought celerity. He was the first through the customs, and before the other passengers arrived, he could arrange with the guard for a sleeping compartment to himself. He had a hatred of undressing before another man, but the arrangement, he knew, would cost him more because he was a Jew; it would be no matter of a simple request and a tip. He passed the lit windows of the restaurant car, small mauve-shaded lamps shining on the linen laid ready for dinner. "Ostend—Cologne—Vienne—Belgrade—Istanbul." He passed the rows of names without a glance; the route was familiar to him; the names travelled back at the level of his eyes, like the spires of minarets, cupolas or domes of the cities themselves, offering no permanent settlement to one of his race.

The guard, as he had expected, was surly. The train was very full, he said, though Myatt knew he lied. April was too early in the year for crowded carriages, and he had seen few first-class passengers on the Channel steamer. While he argued, a bevy of tourists scrambled down the corridor, middle-aged ladies clutching shawls and rugs and sketch-books, an old clergyman complaining that he had mislaid his *Wide World Magazine*—"I always read a *Wide World* when I travel"—and in the rear, perspiring, genial under difficulties, their conductor wearing the button of an agency. "Voilà," the guard said and seemed to indicate with a gesture that his train was bearing an unaccustomed, a cruel burden. But Myatt knew the route too well to be deceived. The party, he guessed from its appearance of harassed culture, belonged to the slip-coach for Athens. When he doubled the tip, the guard gave way and pasted a reserved notice on the window of the compartment. With a sigh of relief Myatt found himself alone.

He watched the swim of faces separated by a safe wall of glass. Even through his fur coat the damp chill of the day struck him, and as he turned the heating-wheel, a mist from his breath obscured the pane, so that soon he could see of those who passed no more than unrelated features, a peering angry eye, a dress of mauve silk, a clerical collar. Only once was he tempted to break this growing solitude and wipe the glass with his fingers in time to catch sight of a thin girl in a white mackintosh disappearing along the corridor towards the second class. Once the door was opened and an elderly man glanced in. He had a grey moustache and wore glasses and a shabby soft hat. Myatt told him in French that the compartment was taken.

"One seat," the man said.

"Do you want the second class?" Myatt asked, but the man shook his head and moved away.

Mr. Opie sank with conscious luxury into his corner and regarded with curiosity and disappointment the small pale man opposite him. The man was extraordinarily commonplace in appearance; ill-health had ruined his complexion. Nerves, Mr. Opie thought, watching the man's moving fingers, but they showed no other sign of acute sensibility. They were short, blunt and thick.

"I always think," Mr. Opie said, wondering whether he had been very unfortunate in his companion, "that as long as one can get a sleeper, it is so unnecessary to travel first class. These second-class carriages are remarkably comfortable."

"Yes—that's so—yes," the other answered with alacrity. "But 'ow did you know I was English?"

"I make a practice," Mr. Opie said with a smile, "of always thinking the best of people."

"Of course," the pale man said, "you as a clergyman——"

The newsboys were calling outside the window, and Mr. Opie leant out. "*Le Temps de Londres.* Qu'est que c'est que ça? Rien du tout? *Le Matin* et un *Daily Mail.* C'est bon. Merci." His French seemed to the other full of copybook phrases, used with gusto and inaccurately. "Combien est cela? Trois francs. Oh la-la."

To the white-faced man he said: "Can I interpret for you? Is there any paper you want? Don't mind me if you want *La Vie.*"

"No, nothing, nothing, thank you. I've a book."

Mr. Opie looked at his watch. "Three minutes and we shall be away."

She had been afraid for several minutes that he would speak, or else the tall thin woman his wife. Silence for the time being she desired more than anything else. If I could have afforded a sleeper, she wondered, would I have been alone? In the dim carriage the lights flickered on, and the plump man remarked, "Now we shan't be long." The air was full of dust and damp, and the flicker of light outside reminded her for a moment of familiar things: the electric signs flashing and changing over the theatre in Nottingham High Street. The stir of life, the passage of porters and paper-boys, recalled for a moment the goose market, and to the memory of the market she clung, tried to externalise it in her mind, to build the bricks and lay the stalls, until they had as much reality as the cold rain-washed quay, the changing signal lamps. Then the man spoke to her, and she was compelled to emerge from her hidden world and wear a pose of cheerfulness and courage.

"Well, miss, we've got a long journey together. Suppose we exchange names. Mine's Peters, and this is my wife Amy."

"Mine's Coral Musker."

"Get me a sandwich," the thin woman implored. "I'm so empty I can hear my stomach."

"Would you, miss? I don't know the lingo."

And why, she would have liked to cry at him, do you suppose I do? I've never been out of England. But she had so schooled herself to accept responsibility wherever and in whatever form it came, that she made no protest, opened the door and would have run down the slippery dusky road between the rails in search of what he wanted if she had not seen a clock. "There's no time," she said, "only one minute before we go." Turning back she caught sight at the corridor's end of a face and figure that made her catch her breath with longing: a last dab of powder on the nose, a good-night to the door-keeper, and outside in the bright glittering betrayal of the dark, the young waiting Jew, the chocolates, the car round the corner, the rapid ride and the furtive dangerous embrace. But it was no one she knew; she was back in the unwanted, dreaded adventure of a foreign land, which could not be checked by a skilful word; no carefully-measured caress would satisfy the approaching dark.

The train's late, Myatt thought, as he stepped into the corridor. He felt in his waistcoat pocket for the small box of currants he always carried there. It was divided into four sections and his fingers chose one at random. As he put it into his mouth, he judged it by the feel. The quality's going off. That's Stein and Co. They are getting small and dry. At the end of the corridor a girl in a white mackintosh turned and gazed at him. Nice figure, he thought. Do I know her? He chose another currant and without a glance placed it. One of our own. Myatt, Myatt and Page. For a moment with the currant upon his tongue he might have been one of the lords of the world, carrying destiny with him. This is mine and this is good, he thought. Doors slammed along the line of coaches, and a horn was blown.

Richard John, with his mackintosh turned up above his ears, leant from the corridor window and saw the sheds begin to move backwards towards the slow wash of the sea. It was the end, he thought, and the beginning. Faces streamed away. A man with a pickaxe on his shoulder swung a red lamp; the smoke from the engine blew round him, and obscured his light. The brakes ground, the clouds parted, and the setting sun flashed on the line, the window and his eyes. If I could sleep, he thought with longing, I could remember more clearly all the things that have to be remembered.

The fire-hole door opened and the blaze and the heat of the furnace for a moment emerged. The driver turned the regulator full open, and the footplate shook with the weight of the coaches. Presently the engine settled smoothly to its work, the driver brought the cut-off back, and the last of the sun came out as the train passed through Bruges, the regulator closed, coasting with little steam. The sunset lit up tall dripping walls, alleys with stagnant water radiant for a moment with liquid light. Somewhere within the dingy casing lay the ancient city, like a notorious jewel, too stared at, talked of, trafficked over. Then a wilderness of allotments opened through the steam, sometimes the monotony broken by tall ugly villas, facing every way, decorated with coloured tiles, which now absorbed the evening. The sparks from the express became visible, like hordes of scarlet beetles tempted into the air by night; they fell and smouldered by the track, touched leaves and twigs and cabbage-stalks and turned to soot. A girl riding a cart-horse lifted her face and laughed; on the bank beside the line a man and woman lay embraced. Then darkness fell outside, and passengers through the glass could see only the transparent reflection of their own features.

2

P remier Service, Premier Service.'' The voice went echoing down the corridor, but Myatt was already seated in the restaurant-car. He did not wish to run the danger of sharing a table, of being forced into polite openings, of being, not improbably, snubbed. Constantinople, for many of the passengers the end of an almost interminable journey, approached him with the speed of the flying climbing telegraph-poles. When the journey was over, there would be no time to think; a waiting car, the rush of minarets, a dingy stair, and Mr. Eckman rising from behind his desk. Subtleties, figures, contracts would encoil him. Here beforehand, in the restaurant-car, in the sleeping-berth, in the corridor, he must plan every word and rehearse every inflection. He wished that his dealings were with Englishmen or Turks, but Mr. Eckman, and somewhere in the background the enigmatic Stein, were men of his own race, practised in reading a meaning into a tone of voice, the grip of fingers round a cigar.

Up the aisle the waiters came carrying the soup. Myatt felt in his breast-pocket and again he nibbled a currant, one of Stein's, small and dry, but, it had to be admitted, cheap. The eternal inevitable war between quality and quantity was fought out to no issue in his mind. Of one thing he had been as nearly certain as possible while tied to a desk in London, meeting only Stein's representatives and never Stein, hearing at best Stein's voice over the long-distance telephone, a ghost of a voice from whose inflections he could tell nothing: Stein was on the rocks. But what rocks? In mid-ocean or near shore? Was he desperate or only resigned to uncomfortable economies? The affair would have been simple if Myatt and Page's agent in Constantinople, the invaluable Mr. Eckman, had not been suspected of intricate hidden relations with Stein skirting the outer fringe of the law.

He dipped his spoon into the tasteless Julienne; he preferred his food rich, highly seasoned, but full of a harsh nourishment. Out in the dark nothing was visible, except for the occasional flash of lights from a small station, the rush of flame in a tunnel, and always the transparent likeness of his own face, his hand floating like a fish through which water and weeds shine. He was a little irritated by its ubiquity and was about to pull down the blind when he noticed, behind his own reflection, the image of the shabby man in the mackintosh who had looked into his compartment. His clothes, robbed of colour and texture and opacity, the ghosts of ancient tailoring, had still a forced gentility; the mackintosh thrown open showed the high stiff collar, the over-buttoned jacket. The man waited patiently for his dinner—so Myatt at first thought, allowing his mind to rest a little from the subtleties of Stein and Mr. Eckman—but before the waiter could reach him, the stranger was asleep. His face for a moment disappeared from view as the lights of a station turned the walls of the coach from mirrors to windows, through which became visible a throng of country passengers waiting with children and packages and string bags for some slow cross-country train. With the darkness the face returned, nodding into sleep.

Myatt forgot him, choosing a medium Burgundy, a Chambertin of 1923, to drink with the veal, though he knew it a waste of money to buy a good wine, for no bouquet could survive the continuous tremor. All down the coach the whimper and whine of shaken glass was audible as the express drove on at full steam towards Cologne. During the first glass Myatt thought again of Stein, waiting in Constantinople for his arrival with cunning or despair. He would sell out, Myatt felt sure, for a price, but another buyer was said to be in the field. That was where Mr. Eckman was suspected of playing a double part, of trying to put up the price against his own firm with a fifteen per cent commission from Stein as the probable motive. Mr. Eckman had written that Moult's were offering Stein a fancy price for his stock and goodwill; Myatt did not believe him. He had lunched one day with young Moult and casually introduced into their talk the name of Stein. Moult was not a Jew; he had no subtlety, no science of evasion; if he wished to lie, he would lie, but the lie would be confined to the words; he had no knowledge how the untrained hand gives the lie to the mouth. In dealing with an Englishman Myatt found one trick enough; as he introduced the important theme or asked the leading question, he would offer a cigar; if the man was lying, however prompt the answer, the hand would hesitate for the quarter of a second. Myatt knew what the Gentiles said of him: "I don't like that Jew. He never looks you in the face." You fools, he would triumph secretly, I know a trick worth two of that. He knew now for example that young Moult had not lied. It was Stein who was lying, or else Mr. Eckman.

He poured himself out another glass. Curious, he thought, that it was he, travelling at the rate of sixty miles an hour, who was at rest, not Mr. Eckman, locking up his desk, picking his hat from the rack, going downstairs, chewing, as it were, the firm's telegram between his sharp prominent teeth. "Mr. Carleton Myatt will arrive Istanbul 14th. Arrange meeting with Stein." In the train, however fast it travelled, the passengers were compulsorily at rest; useless between the walls of glass to feel emotion, useless to try to follow any activity except of the mind; and that activity could be followed without fear of interruption. The world was beating now on Eckman and Stein, telegrams were arriving, men were interrupting the threads of their thought with speech, women were holding dinner-parties. But in the rushing reverberating express, noise was so regular that it was the equivalent of silence, movement was so continuous that after a while the mind accepted it as stillness.

Only outside the train was violence of action possible, and the train would contain him safely with his plans for three days; by the end of that time he would know quite clearly how to deal with Stein and Mr. Eckman.

The ice and the dessert over, the bill paid, he paused beside his table to light a cigar and thus faced the stranger and saw how again he had fallen into sleep between the courses; between the departure of the veal, *au Talleyrand*, and the arrival of the iced pudding he had fallen victim to what must have been a complete exhaustion.

Under Myatt's gaze he woke suddenly. "Well?" he asked. Myatt apologised. "I didn't mean to wake you." The man watched him with suspicion, and something in the sudden change from sleep to a more accustomed anxiety, something in the well-meaning clothes betrayed by the shabby mackintosh, touched Myatt to pity. He presumed on their earlier encounter. "You've found a compartment all right?" "Yes."

Myatt said impulsively: "I thought perhaps you were finding it hard to rest. I have some aspirin in my bag. Can I lend you a few tablets?" The man snapped at him, "I have everything I want. I am a doctor." From habit Myatt watched his hands, thin with the bones showing. He apologised again with a little of the excessive humility of the bowed head in the desert. "I'm sorry to have troubled you. You looked ill. If there is anything I can do for you——"

"No. Nothing. Nothing." But as Myatt went, the other turned and called after him, "The time. What is the right time?" Myatt said, "Eight-forty. No, forty-two," and saw the man's fingers adjust his watch with care for the exact minute.

As he reached the compartment the train was slowing down. The great blast furnaces of Liège rose along the line like ancient castles burning in a border raid. The train lurched and the points changed. Steel girders rose on either side, and very far below an empty street ran diagonally into the dark, and a lamp shone on a café door. The rails opened out, and unattached engines converged on the express, hooting and belching steam. The signals flashed green across the sleepers, and the arch of the station roof rose above the carriage. Newsboys shouted, and a line of stiff sedate men in black broadcloth and women in black veils waited along the platform; without interest, like a crowd of decorous strangers at a funeral, they watched the line of first-class coaches pass them, Ostend—Cologne—Vienne—Belgrade—Istanbul—the slip coach for Athens. Then with their string bags and their children they climbed into the rear coaches, bound perhaps for Pepinster or Verviers, fifteen miles down the line.

Myatt was tired. He had sat up till one o'clock the night before discussing with his father, Jacob Myatt, the affairs of Stein, and he had become aware as never before, watching the jerk of the white beard, of how affairs were slipping away from the old ringed fingers clasped round the glass of warm milk. "They never pick off the skin," Jacob Myatt complained, allowing his son to take the spoon and skim the surface clear. There were many things he now allowed his son to do, and Page counted for nothing; his directorship was a mere decoration awarded for twenty years' faithful service as head clerk. I am Myatt, Myatt and Page, he thought without a tremor at the idea of responsibility; he was the first born and it was the law of nature that the father should resign to the son.

They had disagreed last night over Eckman. Jacob Myatt believed that Stein had deceived the agent, and his son that the agent was in league with Stein. "You'll see," he promised, confident in his own cunning, but Jacob Myatt only said, "Eckman's clever. We need a clever man there."

It was no use, Myatt knew, settling down to sleep before the frontier at Herbesthal. He took out the figures that Eckman proposed as a basis for negotiation with Stein, the value of the stock in hand, the value of the goodwill, the amount which he believed Stein had been offered by another purchaser. It was true that Eckman had not named Moult in so many words; he had only hinted at the name and he could deny the hint. Moult's had never previously shown interest in currants; the nearest they had come to it was a brief flirtation with the date market. Myatt thought: I can't believe these figures. Stein's business is worth that to us, even if we dumped his stock into the Bosphorus, because we should gain a monopoly; but for any other firm it would be the purchase of a rocky business beaten by our competition.

The figures began to swim before his eyes in a mist of sleep. Ones, sevens, nines became Mr. Eckman's small sharp teeth; sixes, fives, threes reformed themselves as in a trick film into Mr. Eckman's dark polished eyes. Commissions in the form of coloured balloons floated across the carriage, growing in size, and he sought a pin to prick them one by one. He was brought back to full wakefulness by the sound of footsteps passing and re-passing along the corridor. Poor devil, he thought, seeing a brown mackintosh disappear past the window and two hands clasped.

But he felt no pity for Mr. Eckman, following him back in fancy from his office to his very modern flat, into the shining lavatory, the silver-and-gilt bathroom, the bright cushioned drawing-room where his wife sat and sewed and sewed, making vests and pants and bonnets and socks for the Anglican Mission: Mr. Eckman was a Christian. All along the line the blast furnaces flared.

The heat did not penetrate the wall of glass. It was bitterly cold, an April night like an old-fashioned Christmas card glittering with frost. Myatt took his fur coat from a peg and went into the corridor. At Cologne there was a wait of nearly forty-five minutes; time enough to get a cup of hot coffee or a glass of brandy. Until then he could walk, up and down, like the man in the mackintosh.

While there was nothing worth his notice in the outside air he knew who would be walking with him in spirit the length of the corridor, in and out of lavatories, Mr. Eckman and Stein. Mr. Eckman he thought, trying to coax some hot water into a gritty basin, kept a chained Bible by his lavatory seat. So at least he had been told. Large and shabby and very "family" amongst the silver-and-gilt taps and plugs, it advertised to every man and woman who dined in his flat Mr. Eckman's Christianity. There was no need of covert allusions to Church-goings, to the Embassy chaplain, merely a "Would you like a wash, dear?" from his wife, his own hearty questions to the men after the coffee and the brandy. But of Stein, Myatt knew nothing.

"What a pity you are not getting out at Buda, as you are so interested in cricket. I'm trying—oh, so hard—to get up two elevens at the embassy." A man with face as bleak and white and impersonal as his clerical collar was speaking to a little rat of a man who crouched opposite him, nodding and becking. The voice, robbed of its characteristic inflections by closed glass, floated out into the corridor as Myatt passed. It was the ghost of a voice and reminded Myatt again of Stein speaking over two thousand miles of cable, hoping that he would one day soon have the honour of entertaining Mr. Carleton Myatt in Constantinople, agreeable, hospitable and anonymous.

He was passing the non-sleeping compartments in the second class; men with their waistcoats off sprawled along seats, blue about the chin; women with hair in dusty nets, like the string bags on the racks, tucked their skirts tightly round them and fell in odd shapes over the seats, large breasts and small thighs, small breasts and large thighs hopelessly confused. A tall thin woman woke for a moment to complain, "That beer you got me. Shocking it was. I can't keep my stomach quiet." On the seat opposite, the husband sat and smiled; he rubbed one hand over his rough chin, squinting sideways at the girl in the white mackintosh, who lay along the seat, her feet against his other hand. Myatt paused and lit a cigarette. He liked the girl's thin figure and her face, the lips tinted enough to lend her plainness an appeal. Nor was she altogether plain; the smallness of her features, of her skull, her nose and ears, gave her a spurious refinement, a kind of bright prettiness, like the window of a country shop at Christmas full of small lights and tinsel and coloured common gifts. Myatt remembered how she had gazed at him down the length of the corridor and wondered a little of whom he had reminded her. He was grateful that she had shown no distaste, no knowledge of his uneasiness in the best clothes that money could buy.

The man who shared her seat put his hand cautiously on her ankle and moved it very slowly up towards her knee. All the time he watched his wife. The girl woke and opened her eyes. "How cold it is," Myatt heard her say and knew from her elaborate and defensive friendliness that she was aware of the hand withdrawn. Then she looked up and saw him watching her. She was tactful, she was patient, but to Myatt she had little subtlety; he knew that his qualities, the possibilities of annoyance which he offered, were being weighed against her companion's. She wasn't looking for trouble: that was the expression she would use; and he found her courage, quickness and decision admirable. "I think I'll have a cigarette outside," she said, fumbling in her bag for a packet; then she was beside him.

"A match?"

"Thanks." And moving out of view of her compartment they stared together into the murmuring darkness.

"I don't like your companion," Myatt said.

"One can't pick and choose. He's not too bad. His name's Peters."

Myatt for a moment hesitated. "Mine's Myatt."

"Mine's Coral—Coral Musker."

"Dancing?"

"Sure."

"American?"

"No. Why did you think so?"

"Something you said. You've got a bit of the accent. Ever been there?"

"Ever been there? Of course I have. Six nights a week and two afternoons. The

Garden of the Country Club, Long Island; Palm Beach: A Bachelor's Apartment on Riverside Drive. Why, if you can't talk American you don't stand a chance in an English musical comedy.''

"You're clever,'' said Myatt gravely, releasing Eckman and Stein from his consideration.

"Let's move,'' the girl said, "I'm cold.''

"Can't you sleep?''

"Not after that crossing. It's too cold, and that fellow's fingering my legs the whole time.''

"Why don't you smack his face?''

"Before we've reached Cologne? I'm not making trouble. We've got to live together to Buda-Pesth.''

"Is that where you are going?''

"Where he is. I'm going all the way.''

"So am I,'' said Myatt, "on business.''

"Well, we are neither of us going for pleasure, are we?'' she said with a touch of gloom. "I saw you when the train started. I thought you were someone I knew.''

"Who?''

"How do I know? I don't trouble to remember what a boy calls himself. It's not the name the post-office knows him by.'' There seemed to Myatt something patient and courageous in her quiet acceptance of deceit. She flattened against the window a face a little blue with cold; she might have been a boy avidly examining the contents of a shop, the clasp-knives, the practical jokes, plate lifters, bombs that smell, buns that squeak, but all that was offered her was darkness and their own features. "Do you think it will get any warmer,'' she asked, "as we go south?'' as though she thought herself bound for a tropical climate. "We don't go far enough for it to make much difference,'' he said. "I've known snow in Constantinople in April. You get the winds down the Bosphorus from the Black Sea. They cut round the corners. The city's all corners.''

"I hope the dressing-rooms are warm,'' she said. "You don't wear enough on the stage to keep the chill out. How I'd like something hot to drink.'' She leant with blue face and bent knees against the window. "Are we near Cologne? What's the German for coffee?'' Her expression alarmed him. He ran down the corridor and closed the only open window. "Are you feeling all right?''

She said slowly with half-closed eyes, "That's better. You've made it quite stuffy. I'm warm enough now. Feel me.'' She lifted her hand; he put it against his cheek and was startled by the heat. "Look here,'' he said. "Go back to your carriage and I'll try and find some brandy for you. You are ill.'' "It's only that I can't keep warm,'' she explained. "I was hot and now it's cold again. I don't want to go back. I'll stay here.''

"You must have my coat,'' he began reluctantly, but before he had time to limit his unwilling offer with "for a while'' or "until you are warm,'' she slid to the floor. He took her hands and chafed them, watching her face with helpless anxiety. It seemed to him suddenly of vital necessity that he should aid her. Watching her dance upon the stage, or stand in a lit street outside a stage-door, he would have regarded her only as game for the senses, but helpless and sick under the dim unsteady lamp of the corridor, her body shaken by the speed of the train, she woke a painful pity. She had not complained of the cold; she had commented on it as a kind of necessary evil, and in a flash of insight he became aware of the innumerable necessary evils of which life for her was made up. He heard the monotonous tread of the man whom he had seen pass and re-pass his compartment and went to meet him. "You are a doctor? There's a girl fainted." The man stopped and asked reluctantly, "Where is she?" Then he saw her past Myatt's shoulder. His hesitation angered the Jew. "She looks really ill," he urged him. The doctor sighed. "All right, I'm coming." He might have been nerving himself to an ordeal.

But the fear seemed to leave him as he knelt by the girl. He was tender towards her with the impersonal experienced tenderness of a doctor. He felt her heart and then lifted her lids. The girl came back to a confusing consciousness; she thought that it was she who was bending over a stranger with a long shabby moustache. She felt pity for the experience which had caused his great anxiety, and her solicitude went out to the friendliness she imagined in his eyes. She put her hands down to his face. He's ill, she thought, and for a moment shut out the puzzling shadows which fell the wrong way, the globe of light shining from the ground. "Who are you?" she asked, trying to remember how it was that she had come to his help. Never, she thought, had she seen a man who needed help more.

"A doctor."

She opened her eyes in astonishment and the world cleared. It was she who was lying in the corridor and the stranger who bent over her. "Did I faint?" she asked. "It was very cold." She was aware of the heavy slow movement of the train. Lights streamed through the window across the doctor's face and on to the young Jew behind. Myatt, My'at. She laughed to herself in sudden contentment. It was as though, for the moment, she had passed to another all responsibility. The train lurched to a standstill, and the Jew was thrown against the wall. The doctor had not stirred. If he had swayed it was with the movement of the train and not against it. His eyes were on her face, his finger on her pulse; he watched her with a passion which was trembling on the edge of speech, but she knew that it was not passion for her or any attribute of her. She phrased it to herself: If I'd got Mistinguett's legs, he wouldn't notice. She asked him, "What is it?" and lost all his answer in the voices crying down the platform and the entrance of blue uniformed men but "my proper work."

"Passports and luggage ready," a foreign voice called to them, and Myatt spoke to her, asking for her bag: "I'll see to your things." She gave him her bag and helped by the doctor sat up against the wall.

"Passport?"

The doctor said slowly, and she became aware for the first time of his accent: "My bags are in the first class. I can't leave this lady. I am a doctor."

"English passport?"

"Yes."

"All right." Another man came up to them. "Luggage?"

"Nothing to declare." The man went on.

Coral Musker smiled. "Is this really the frontier? Why, one could smuggle anything in. They don't look at the bags at all."

"Anything," the doctor said, "with an English passport." He watched the man out of sight and said nothing more until Myatt returned. "I could go back to my carriage now," she said.

"Have you a sleeper?"

"No."

"Are you getting out at Cologne?"

"I'm going all the way."

He gave her the same advice as the purser had done. "You should have had a sleeper." The uselessness of it irritated her and made her for a moment forget her pity for his age and anxiety. "How could I have a sleeper? I'm in the chorus." He flashed back at her with astonishing bitterness, "No, you have not the money."

"What shall I do?" she asked him. "Am I ill?"

"How can I advise you?" he protested. "If you were rich, I should say: Take six months' holiday. Go to North Africa. You fainted because of the crossing, because of the cold. Oh yes, I can tell you all that, but that's nothing. Your heart's bad. You've been overstraining it for years."

She implored him, a little frightened, "But what shall I do?" He opened his hands: "Nothing. Carry on. Take what rest you can. Keep warm. You wear too little."

A whistle blew, and the train trembled into movement. The station lamps sailed by them into darkness, and the doctor turned to leave her. "If you want me again, I'm three coaches farther up. My name is John. Dr. John." She said with intimidated politeness, "Mine's Coral Musker." He gave her a little formal foreign bow and walked away. She saw in his eyes other thoughts falling like rain. Never before had she the sensation of being so instantly forgotten. "A girl that men forget," she hummed to keep up her courage.

But the doctor had not passed out of hearing before he was stopped. Treading softly and carefully along the shaking train, a hand clinging to the corridor rail, came a small pale man. She heard him speak to the doctor, "Is anything the matter? Can I help?" He was a foot shorter and she laughed aloud at the sight of his avid face peering upwards. "You mustn't think me inquisitive," he said, one hand on the other's sleeve. "A clergyman in my compartment thought someone was ill." He added with eagerness, "I said I'd find out."

Up and down, up and down the corridor she had seen the doctor walking, clinging to its emptiness in preference to a compartment shared. Now, through no mistake on his part, he found himself in a crowd, questions and appeals sticking to his mind like burrs. She expected an outbreak, some damning critical remark which would send the fellow quivering down the corridor.

The softness of his reply surprised her. "Did you say a priest?"

"Oh no," the man apologised, "I don't know yet what sect, what creed. Why? Is somebody dying?"

Dr. John seemed to become aware of her fear and called down the corridor a reassurance before he brushed by the detaining hand. The little man remained for a moment in happy possession of a situation. When he had tasted it to the full, he approached. "What's it all about?"

She took no notice, appealing to the only friendly presence she was left with. "I'm not sick like that, am I?"

"What intrigues me," the stranger said, "is his accent. You'd say he was a foreigner, but he gave an English name. I think I'll follow him and talk."

Her mind had worked clearly since she fainted; the sight of a world reversed, in which it had been the doctor who lay beneath her needing pity and care, had made the old images of the world sharp with unfamiliarity; but words lagged behind intuition, and when she appealed, "Don't bother him," the stranger was already out of hearing.

"What do you think?" Myatt asked. "Is he right? Is there a mystery?"

"We've all got some secrets," she said.

"He might be escaping from the police."

She said with absolute conviction, "He's good." He accepted the phrase; it dismissed the doctor from his thoughts. "You must lie down," he said, "and try to sleep," but it did not need her evasive reply, "How can I sleep with that woman and her stomach?" to remind him of Mr. Peters lurking in his corner for her return and the renewal of his cheap easy harmless satisfactions. "You must have my sleeper."

"What? In the first class?" Her disbelief and her longing decided him. He determined to be princely on an Oriental scale, granting costly gifts and not requiring, not wanting, any return. Parsimony was the traditional reproach against his race, and he would show one Christian how undeserved it was. Forty years in the wilderness, away from the flesh pots of Egypt, had entailed harsh habits, the counted date and the hoarded water; nor had a thousand years in the wilderness of a Christian world, where only the secret treasure was safe, encouraged display; but the world was altering, the desert was flowering; in stray corners here and there, in western Europe, the Jew could show that other quality he shared with the Arab, the quality of the princely host, who would wash the feet of beggars and feed them from his own dish; sometimes he could cease to be the enemy of the rich to become the friend of any poor man who sought a roof in the name of God. The roar of the train faded from his consciousness, the light went out in his eyes, while he built for his own pride the tent in the oasis, the well in the desert. He spread his hands before her. "Yes, you must sleep there. I'll arrange with the guard. And my coat—you must take that. It will keep you warm. At Cologne I'll find you coffee, but it will be better for you to sleep."

"But I can't. Where will you sleep?"

"I shall find somewhere. The train's not full." For the second time she experienced an impersonal tenderness, but it was not frightening as the first had been; it was a warm wave into which she let herself down, not too far, if she felt afraid, for her feet to be aware of the sand, but only far enough to float her without effort on her own part where she wanted to go—to a bed and a pillow and a covering and sleep. She had an impression of how grace came back to him with confidence, as he ceased to apologise or to assert and became only a ministering shadow.

Myatt did not go to find the guard but wedged himself between the walls of corridor and compartment, folded his arms and prepared to sleep. But without his coat it was very cold. Although all the windows of the corridor were shut, a draught blew past the swing door and over the footboard joining coach to coach. Nor were the noises of the train regular enough now to be indistinguishable from silence. There were many tunnels between Herbesthal and Cologne, and in each the roar of the express was magnified. Myatt slept uneasily, and the rush of the loosed steam and the draught on his cheek contributed to his dream. The corridor became the long straight Spaniards Road with the heath on either side. He was being driven slowly by Isaacs in his Bentley, and they watched the girls' faces as they walked in pairs along the lamp-lit eastern side, shopgirls offering themselves dangerously for a drink at the inn, a fast ride, and the fun of the thing; on the other side of the road, in the dark, on a few seats, the prostitutes sat, shapeless and shabby and old, with their backs to the sandy slopes and the thorn bushes, waiting for a man old and dumb and blind enough to offer them ten shillings. Isaacs drew up the Bentley under a lamp and they let the anonymous young beautiful animal faces stream by. Isaacs wanted someone fair and plump and Myatt someone thin and dark, but it was not easy to pick and choose, for all along the eastern side were lined the cars of their competitors, girls leaning across the open doors laughing and smoking; on the other side of the road a single two-seater kept patient watch. Myatt was irritated by Isaacs' uncompromising taste; it was cold in the Bentley with a draught on the cheek, and presently when he saw Coral Musker walking by, he jumped from the car and offered her a cigarette and after that a drink and after that a ride. That was one advantage with these girls, Myatt thought; they all knew what a ride meant, and if they didn't care for the look of you, they just said that they had to be going home now. But Coral Musker wanted a ride; she would take him for her companion in the dark of the car, with the lamps and the inns and the houses left behind and trees springing up like paper silhouettes in the green light of the head-lamps, and then the bushes with the scent of wet leaves holding the morning's rain and a short barbarous enjoyment in the stubble. As for Isaacs, he must just put up with his companion, although she was dark and broad and lightly clothed, with a great nose and prominent pointed teeth. But when she was seated next Isaacs in the front of the car she turned and gave him a long smile, saying, "I've come out without a card, but my name's Stein." And then in the teeth of the wind he was climbing a great stair with silver and gilt handrails, and she stood at the top wearing a small moustache, pointing to a woman who sat sewing, sewing, sewing, and called out to him, "Meet Mrs. Eckman."

Coral Musker flung her hand away from the blankets in protest, as she danced and danced and danced in the glare of the spot-light, and the producer struck at her bare legs with a cane, telling her she was no good, that she was a month late, that she'd broken her contract. And all the time she danced and danced and danced, taking no notice of him while he beat at her legs with the cane.

Mrs. Peters turned on her face and said to her husband, "That beer. My stomach won't be quiet. It makes so much noise, I can't sleep."

Mr. Opie dreamed that in his surplice with cricket bat under his arm and batting-glove dangling from his wrist he mounted a great broad flight of marble steps towards the altar of God.

Dr. John asleep at last with a bitter tablet dissolving on his tongue spoke once in German. He had no sleeper and sat bolt upright in the corner of his compartment, hearing outside the slow singing start, "Köln, Köln. Köln."

PART TWO

Cologne

1

But of course, dear, I don't mind your being drunk," said Janet Pardoe. The clock above Cologne station struck one, and a waiter began to turn out the lights on the terrace of the Excelsior. "Look, dear, let me put your tie straight." She leant across the table and adjusted Mabel Warren's tie.

"We've lived together for three years," Miss Warren began to say in a deep melancholy voice, "and I have never yet spoken to you harshly."

Janet Pardoe put a little scent behind her ears. "For heaven's sake, darling, look at the time. The train leaves in half an hour, and I've got to get my bags, and you've got to get your interview. Do drink up your gin and come along."

Mabel Warren took her glass and drank. Then she rose and her square form swayed a little; she wore a tie and a stiff collar and a tweed "sporting" suit. Her eyebrows were heavy, and her eyes were dark and determined and red with weeping.

"You know why I drink," she protested.

"Nonsense, dear," said Janet Pardoe, making certain in her compact mirror of the last niceties of appearance, "you drank long before you ever met me. Have a little sense of proportion. I shall only be away a week."

"These men," said Miss Warren darkly, and then as Janet Pardoe rose to cross the square, she gripped her arm with extraordinary force. "Promise me you'll be careful. If only I could come with you." Almost on the threshold of the station she stumbled in a puddle. "Oh, see what I've done now. What a great clumsy thing I am. To splash your beautiful new suit." With a large rough hand, a signet ring on the small finger, she began to brush at Janet Pardoe's skirt.

"Oh, for God's sake, come on, Mabel," Janet said.

Miss Warren's mood changed. She straightened herself and barred the way. "You say I'm drunk. I am drunk. But I'm going to be drunker."

"Oh, come on."

"You are going to have one more drink with me or I shan't let you on the platform."

Janet Pardoe gave way. "One. Only one, mind." She guided Mabel Warren across a vast black shining hall into a room where a few tired men and women were snatching cups of coffee. "Another gin," said Miss Warren, and Janet ordered it.

In a mirror on the opposite wall Miss Warren saw her own image, red, tousled, very shoddy, sitting beside another and far more familiar image, slim, dark, and beautiful. What do I matter? she thought, with the melancholy of drink. I've made her, I'm responsible for her, and with bitterness, I've paid for her. There's nothing she's wearing that I haven't paid for, sweated for, she thought (although the bitter cold defied the radiators in the restaurant), getting up at all hours, interviewing brothel-keepers in their cells, the mothers of murdered children, "covering" this and "covering" that. She knew with a certain pride what they said in the London office: "When you want sob-stuff, send Dizzy Mabel." All the way down the Rhine was her province; there wasn't a town of any size between Cologne and Mainz where she hadn't sought out human interest, forcing dramatic phrases onto the lips of sullen men, pathos into the mouths of women too overcome with grief to speak at all. There wasn't a suicide, a murdered woman, a raped child who had stirred her to the smallest emotion; she was an artist to examine critically, to watch, to listen; the tears were for paper. But now she sat and wept with ugly grunts because Janet Pardoe was leaving her for a week.

"Who is it you are interviewing?" Janet Pardoe asked. She was not at all interested, but she wanted to distract Mabel Warren from thoughts of separation; her tears were too conspicuous. "You ought to comb your hair," she added. Miss Warren wore no hat and her black hair, cut short like a man's, was hopelessly dishevelled.

"Savory," said Miss Warren.

"Who's he?"

"Sold a hundred thousand copies. *The Great Gay Round.* Half a million words. Two hundred characters. The Cockney Genius. Drops his aitches when he can remember to."

"What's he doing on the train?"

"Going East to collect material. It's not my job, but as I was seeing you off, I took it on. They've asked me for a quarter of a column, but they'll cut it down to a couple of sticks in London. He's chosen the wrong time. In the silly season he'd have got half a column among the mermaids and sea-horses." The flare of professional interest guttered as she looked again at Janet Pardoe: no more of a morning would she see Janet in pyjamas pouring out coffee, no more of an evening come in to the flat and find Janet in pyjamas mixing a cocktail. She said huskily, "Darling, which pair will you be wearing tonight?" The feminine question sounded oddly in Miss Warren's deep masculine voice.

"What do you mean?"

"Pyjamas, darling. I want to think of you tonight just as you are."

"I don't suppose I shall even undress. Look, it's a quarter past one. We must go. You'll never get your interview."

Miss Warren's professional pride was touched. "You don't think I need to ask him questions?" she said. "Just a look at him and I'll put the right words in his mouth. And he won't complain either. It's publicity."

"But I must find the porter with my bags." Everyone was leaving the restaurant. As the door opened and closed the cries of porters, the whistle of steam, came faintly down to where they sat. Janet Pardoe appealed again to Miss Warren. "We

must go. If you want any more gin I shall leave you to it.'' But Miss Warren said
nothing, Miss Warren ignored her; Janet Pardoe found herself attending one of the
regular rites of Mabel Warren's journalistic career, the visible shedding of her
drunkenness. First a hand put the hair into order, then a powdered handkerchief,
her compromise with femininity, disguised the redness of her cheeks and lids. All
the while she was focusing her eyes, using whatever lay before her, cups, waiter,
glasses and so to the distant mirrors and her own image, as a kind of optician's
alphabetic scroll. On this occasion the first letter of the alphabet, the great black
A, was an elderly man in a mackintosh, who was standing beside a table brushing
away his crumbs before leaving to catch the train.

"My God," said Miss Warren, covering her eyes with her hand, "I'm drunk.
I can't see properly. Who's that there?"

"The man with the moustache?"

"Yes."

"I've never seen him before."

"I have," said Miss Warren, "I have. But where?" Something had diverted her
effectually from the thought of separation; her nose was on a scent and leaving half
a finger of gin in the bottom of her glass, she strode in the man's wake to the door.
He was out and walking quickly across the black shining hall to a flight of stairs
before Miss Warren could extricate herself from the swing door. She crashed into
a porter and fell on her knees, swaying her head, trying to free it from the benev-
olence, the melancholy, the vagueness of drink. He stopped to help her and she
seized his arm and stayed him until she could control her tongue. "What train
leaves platform five?" she asked. "Vienna," the man said.

"Belgrade?" "Yes."

It had been pure chance that she had said Belgrade and not Constantinople, but
the sound of her own voice brought her light. She called out to Janet Pardoe: "Take
two seats. I'm coming with you as far as Vienna."

"Your ticket?"

"I've got my reporter's pass." It was she who was now impatient. "Hurry.
Platform five. It's twenty-eight past. Only five minutes." She still kept the porter
to her side with a muscular grip. "Listen. I want you to take a message for me.
Kaiser Wilhelmstrasse 33."

"I can't leave the station," he told her.

"What time do you come off duty?"

"Six."

"That's no good. You must slip out. You can do that, can't you? No one will
notice."

"I'd get the sack."

"Risk it," said Miss Warren. "Twenty marks."

The man shook his head. "The foreman would notice."

"I'll give you another twenty for him."

The foreman wouldn't do it, he said; there was too much to lose; the head foreman
might find out. Miss Warren opened her bag and began to count her money. Above
her head a clock struck the half-hour. The train left in three minutes, but not for

a moment did she allow her desperation to show; any emotion would frighten the man. "Eighty marks," she said, "and give the foreman what you like. You'll only be away ten minutes."

"It's a big risk," the porter said, but he allowed her to press the notes into his hand. "Listen carefully. Go to Kaiser Wilhelmstrasse 33. You'll find the offices of the London *Clarion*. Somebody's sure to be there. Tell him that Miss Warren has taken the Orient Express for Vienna. She won't be letting him have the interview tonight; she'll telephone it from Vienna tomorrow. Tell him she's on to a bill page lead. Now repeat that." While he stumbled slowly through the message she kept an eye on the clock. One-thirty. One-thirty-one and a half. "Right. Off with it. If you don't get it to them by one-fifty I'll report you for taking bribes." She grinned at him with malicious playfulness, showing great square teeth, and then ran for the stairs. One-thirty-two. She thought that she heard a whistle blown and took the last three steps in one stride. The train was moving, a ticket-collector tried to block her way but she knocked him to one side and roared "Pass" at him over her shoulder. The last third-class coaches were slipping by with increasing speed. My God, she thought, I'll give up drink. She got her hand on the bar of the last coach, while a porter shouted and ran at her. For a long ten seconds, with pain shooting up her arm, she thought that she would be dragged off the platform against the wheels of the guard's van. The high step daunted her. I can't make it. Another moment and her shoulder would give. Better drop on the platform and risk concussion than break both legs. But what a story to lose, she thought with bitterness, and jumped. She landed on her knees on the step just in time as the edge of the platform fell away. The last lamp vanished, the door under the pressure of her body opened inwards, and she fell on her back into the corridor. She propped herself up against the wall with care for her aching shoulder and thought with a wry triumph, Dizzy Mabel comes on board.

Morning light came through the slit in the blind and touched the opposite seat. When Coral Musker woke it was the seat and a leather suitcase that she first saw. She felt listless and apprehensive, thinking of the train which had to be caught at Victoria, the dry egg and the slices of the day before yesterday's loaf awaiting her downstairs. I wish I'd never taken the job, she thought, preferring now when the moment of departure was upon her the queue on the stairs of Shaftesbury Avenue, the forced cheerfulness of long waits outside the agent's door. She lifted the blind and was for a moment astonished by a telegraph-pole flashing past, a green river running by, touched with orange by the early sun, and wooded hills. Then she remembered.

It was still early, for the sun was low, only just emerging above the hills. A village on the opposite bank glittered with little lights; a few thin streams of smoke lay in the windless air above the small wooden houses, where early fires were being lit, breakfasts for labourers prepared. The village was so far from the line that it remained still, to be stared at, while the trees and cottages on the near bank, the tethered boats, fled backwards. She raised the other blind and in the corridor saw Myatt sleeping with his back against the wall. Her first instinct was to wake him;

her second to let him sleep and lie back herself in the luxury of another's sacrifice. She felt tender towards him, as though he had given her new hope of a life which was not a continuous struggle for one's own hand; perhaps the world, she thought, was not so hard. She remembered how the purser had spoken to her kindly and called to her, "Remember me"; it seemed not unlikely now, with the young man sleeping outside the door, ready to suffer some hours' discomfort for a stranger, that the purser might still remember her. She thought for the first time, with happiness: Perhaps I have a life in people's minds when I am not there to be seen or talked to. She looked out of the window again, but the village was gone, and the particular green hills she had stared at; only the river was the same. She fell asleep.

Miss Warren staggered down the train. She could not bear to hold the rail with her right hand, for her shoulder pained her still, although she had sat for nearly two hours in the third-class corridor. She felt battered, faint and drunk, and with difficulty arranged her thoughts, but her nose held yet the genuine aroma of the hunt. Never before in ten years of reporting, ten years of women's rights, rapes and murders, had she come so close to an exclusive bill page story, not a story which only the penny papers would trouble to print, but a story which *The Times* correspondent himself would give a year of life to know. It was not everyone, she thought with pride, who would have been capable of seizing the moment as she had done when drunk. As she lurched along the line of first-class compartments triumph sat oddly on her brow like a tip-tilted crown.

Luck favoured her. A man came out of a compartment and made his way towards the lavatory and, as she leant back against a window to let him by, she saw the man in the mackintosh dozing in a corner, for the moment alone. He looked up to see Miss Warren swaying a little forward and back in the doorway. "Can I come in?" she asked. "I got on the train at Cologne, and I can't find a seat." Her voice was low, almost tender; she might have been urging a loved dog towards a lethal chamber.

"The seat's taken."

"Only for a moment," said Miss Warren. "Just to rest my legs. I am so glad that you speak English. I am always so afraid of travelling on a train with nothing but a lot of foreigners. One might want anything almost in the night, mightn't one?" She grinned at him playfully. "I believe that you are a doctor."

"I was once a doctor," the man admitted.

"And you are travelling out to Belgrade?" He looked at her sharply with a sense of uneasiness, and he caught her unawares, the square tweeded form leaning a little forward, the flash of the signet ring, the flushed hungry face. "No," he said, "no. Not so far."

"I am only going to Vienna," said Miss Warren.

He said slowly, "What made you think—?" wondering whether he did right to question her; he was unused to danger in the form of an English spinster a little drunk with gin; he could smell her all across the carriage. The risks he had faced before required only the ducked head, the quick finger, the plain lie. Miss Warren also hesitated, and her hesitation was like a breath of flame to an imprisoned man. She said, "I thought I had seen you in Belgrade."

"I have never been there."

She came roughly into the open, tossing subterfuge aside. "I was at Belgrade," she said, "for my paper at the Kamnetz trial." But she had given him all the warning he needed and he faced her with a complete lack of interest.

"The Kamnetz trial?"

"When General Kamnetz was charged with rape. Czinner was the chief evidence for the prosecution. But of course, the general was acquitted. The jury was packed. The Government would never have allowed a conviction. It was sheer stupidity on Czinner's part to give evidence."

"Stupidity?" His polite interest angered her. "Of course you've heard of Czinner. They had tried to shoot him a week before while he sat in a café. He was the head of the Social Democrats. He played into their hands by giving evidence against Kamnetz; they had a warrant out for his arrest for perjury twelve hours before the trial ended. They simply sat and waited for the acquittal."

"How long ago was all this?"

"Five years." He watched her narrowly, judging what reply would most irritate her. "An old story now then. Is Czinner out of prison?"

"He got away from them. I'd give a lot to know how. It would make a wonderful story. He simply disappeared. Everyone assumed he'd been murdered."

"And hadn't he?"

"No," said Mabel Warren, "he got away."

"A clever man."

"I don't believe it," she said furiously. "A clever man would never have given evidence. What did Kamnetz or the child matter to him? He was a quixotic fool." A cold breath of air blew through the open door and set the doctor shivering. "It's been a bitter night," he said. She brushed the remark on one side with a square worn hand. "To think," she said with awe, "that he never died. While the jury were away he walked out of the court before the eyes of the police. They sat there unable to do anything till the jury came back. Why, I swear that I saw the warrant sticking out of Hartep's breast pocket. He disappeared; he might never have existed; everything went on exactly as before. Even Kamnetz."

He could not disguise a bitter interest. "So? Even Kamnetz?" She seized her advantage, speaking huskily with unexpected imagination. "Yes, if he went back now, he would find everything the same; the clock might have been put back. Hartep taking the same bribes; Kamnetz with his eye for a child; the same slums; the same cafés with the same concerts at six and eleven. Carl's gone from the Moscowa, that's all, the new waiter's a Frenchman. There's a new cinema, too, near the Park. Oh yes, there's one change. They've built over Kruger's beer garden. Flats for civil servants." He remained silent, quite unable to meet this new move of his opponent. So Kruger's was gone with its fairy lights and brightly-coloured umbrellas and the gipsies playing softly from table to table in the dusk. And Carl had gone too. For a moment he would have bartered with the woman all his safety, and the safety of his friends, to know the news of Carl; had he gathered up his tips and retired to a new flat near the Park, folding up the napkins for his own table, drawing the cork for his own glass? He knew that he ought to interrupt the drunken dangerous woman opposite him, but he could not say a word, while she gave him news of Belgrade, the kind of news which his friends in their weekly coded letters never sent him.

There were other things, too, he would have liked to ask her. She had said the slums were the same, and he could feel under his feet the steep steps down into the narrow gorges; he bent under the bright rags stretched across the way, put his handkerchief across his mouth to shut out the smell of dogs, of children, of bad meat and human ordure. He wanted to know whether Dr. Czinner was remembered there. He had known every inhabitant with an intimacy which they would have thought dangerous if they had not so implicitly trusted him, if he had not been by birth one of themselves. As it was, he had been robbed, confided in, welcomed, attacked and loved. Five years was a long time; he might already be forgotten.

Mabel Warren drew in her breath sharply. "To come to facts. I want an exclusive interview for my paper. 'How I escaped?' or 'Why I am returning home?' "

"An interview?" His repetitions annoyed her; she had a splitting headache and felt "wicked." It was the term she used herself; it meant a hatred of men, of all the shifts and evasions they made necessary, of the way they spoiled beauty and stalked abroad in their own ugliness. They boasted of the women they had enjoyed; even the faded middle-aged face before her had in his time seen beauty naked, the hands which clasped his knee had felt and pried and enjoyed. And at Vienna she was losing Janet Pardoe, who was going alone into a world where men ruled. They would flatter her and give her bright cheap objects, as though she were a native to be cheated with Woolworth mirrors and glass beads. But it was not their enjoyment she most feared, it was Janet's. Not loving her at all, or only for the hour, the day, the year, they could make her weak with pleasure, cry aloud in her enjoyment. While she, Mabel Warren, who had saved her from a governess's buried life and fed her and clothed her, who could love her with the same passion until death, without satiety, had no means save her lips to express her love, was faced always by the fact that she gave no enjoyment and gained herself no more than an embittered sense of insufficiency. Now with her head aching, the smell of gin in her nostrils, the knowledge of her flushed ugliness, she hated men with a wicked intensity and their bright spurious graces.

"You are Doctor Czinner." She noted with an increase of her anger that he did not trouble to deny his identity, proffering her carelessly the name he travelled under, "My name is John."

"Doctor Czinner," she growled at him, closing her great teeth on her lower lip in an effort at self-control.

"Richard John, a schoolmaster, on holiday."

"To Belgrade."

"No." He hesitated a moment. "I am stopping at Vienna." She did not believe him, but she won back her amiability with an effort. "I'm getting out at Vienna, too. Perhaps you'll let me show you some of the sights." A man stood in the doorway and she rose. "I'm so sorry. This is your seat." She grinned across the compartment, lurched sideways as the train clattered across a point, and failed to hold a belch which filled the compartment for a few seconds with the smell of gin and shaken motes of cheap powder. "I'll see you again before Vienna," she said, and moving down the corridor leant her red face against the cold smutty glass in a spasm of pain at her own drunkenness and squalor. "I'll get him yet," she thought, blushing at her belch as though she were a young girl at a dinner-party. "I'll get him somehow. God damn his soul."

A tender light flooded the compartments. It would have been possible for a moment to believe that the sun was the expression of something that loved and suffered for men. Human beings floated like fish in golden water, free from the urge of gravity, flying without wings, transparent, in a glass aquarium. Ugly faces and misshapen bodies were transmuted, if not into beauty, at least into grotesque forms fashioned by a mocking affection. On that golden tide they rose and fell, murmured and dreamed. They were not imprisoned, for they were not during the hour of dawn aware of their imprisonment.

Coral Musker woke for the second time. She stood up at once and went to the door; the man dozed wearily, his eyes jerking open to the rhythm of the train. Her mind was still curiously clear; it was as if the golden light had a quality of penetration, so that she could understand motives which were generally hidden, movements which as a rule had for her no importance or significance. Now as she watched him and he became aware of her, she saw his hands go out in a gesture which stayed half-way; she knew that it was a trick of his race which he was consciously repressing. She said softly, "I'm a pig. You've been out there all night." He shrugged his shoulders deprecatingly; he might have been a pawnbroker undervaluing a watch or vase. "Why not? I didn't want you to be disturbed. I had to see the guard. Can I come in?"

"Of course. It's your compartment."

He smiled and was unable to resist a spread of the hands, a slight bow from the hips. "Pardon *me*. It's yours." He took a handkerchief from his sleeve, rolled up his cuffs, made passes in the air. "Look. See. A first-class ticket." A ticket fell from his handkerchief and rolled on the floor between them.

"Yours."

"No, yours." He began to laugh with pleasure at her consternation.

"What do you mean? I couldn't take it. Why, it must have cost pounds."

"Ten," he said boastfully. "Ten pounds." He straightened his tie and said airily, "That's nothing to me."

But his confidence, his boastful eyes, alienated her. She said with a deep suspicion, "What are you getting at? What do you think I am?" The ticket lay between them; nothing would induce her to pick it up. She stamped her foot as the gold faded and became no more than a yellow stain upon the glass and cushions. "I'm going back to my seat."

He said defiantly, "I don't think about you. I've got other things to think about. If you don't want the ticket you can throw it away." She saw him watching her, his shoulders raised again boastfully, carelessly, and she began to cry quietly to herself, turning to the window and the river and a bridge that fled by and a bare beech pricked with early buds. This is my gratitude for a calm long sleepy night; this is the way I take a present; and she thought with shame and disappointment of early dreams of great courtesans accepting gifts from princes. And I snap at him like a tired waitress.

She heard him move behind her and knew that he was stooping for the ticket; she wanted to turn to him and express her gratitude, say: "It would be like heaven to sit on these deep cushions all the journey, sleep in the berth, forget that I'm on the way to a job, think myself rich. No one has ever been so good to me as you are," but her earlier words, the vulgarity of her suspicion, lay like a barrier of class between them. "Lend me your bag," he said. She held it out behind her, and she felt his fingers open the clasp. "There," he said, "I've put it inside. You needn't use it. Just sit here when you want to. And sleep here when you are tired." I am tired, she thought. I could sleep here for hours. She said in a voice strained to disguise her tears, "But how can I?"

"Oh," he said, "I'll find another compartment. I only slept outside last night because I was anxious about you. You might have needed something." She began to cry again, leaning the top of her head against the window, half shutting her eyes, so that her lashes made a curtain between herself and the hard admonishments of old dry women of experience: "There's only one thing a man wants." "Don't take presents from a stranger." It was the size of the present she had been always told that made the danger. Chocolates and a ride, even in the dark, after a theatre, entailed no more than kisses on the mouth and neck, a little tearing of a dress. A girl was expected to repay, that was the point of all advice; one never got anything for nothing. Novelists like Ruby M. Ayres might say that chastity was worth more than rubies, but the truth was it was priced at a fur coat or thereabouts. One couldn't accept a fur coat without sleeping with a man. If you did, all the older women would tell you the man had a grievance. And the Jew had paid ten pounds.

He put his hand on her arm. "What's the matter? Tell me. Do you feel ill?" She remembered the hand that shook the pillow, the whisper of his feet moving away. She said again, "How can I?" but this time it was an appeal for him to speak and to deny the accumulated experience of poverty. "Look," he said, "sit down and let me show you things. That's the Rhine." She found herself laughing. "I guessed that." "Did you see the rock we passed jutting out into the stream? That's the Lorelei rock. Heine."

"What do you mean, Heine?" He said with pleasure, "A Jew." She began to forget the decision she was forced to make and watched him with interest, trying to find a stranger behind the too familiar features, the small eyes, the large nose, the black oiled hair. She had seen this man too often, like a waiter in a dinner-jacket sitting in the front row at provincial theatres, behind a desk at agents' offices, in the wings at rehearsal, outside the stage door at midnight; the world of the theatre vibrated with his soft humble imperative voice; he was mean with a commonplace habitual meanness, generous in fits and starts, never to be trusted. Soft praise at a rehearsal meant nothing, in the office afterwards he would be saying over a glass of whisky, "That little girl in the front row, she's not worth her keep." He was never angered or abusive, never spoke worse of anyone than as "that little girl," and dismissal came in the shape of a typewritten note left in a pigeon-hole. She said gently, partly because none of these qualities prevented her liking Jews for their very quietness, partly because it was a girl's duty to be amiable, "Jews are artistic, aren't they? Why, almost the whole orchestra at *Atta Girl* were Jewish boys."

"Yes," he said with a bitterness which she did not understand.

"Do you like music?"

"I can play the violin," he said, "not well." For a moment it was as if behind the familiar eyes a strange life moved.

"I always wanted to cry at 'Sonny Boy,' " she said. She was aware of the space which divided her understanding from her expression; she was sensible of much and could say little, and what she said was too often the wrong thing. Now she saw the strange life die.

"Look," he said sharply. "No more river. We've left the Rhine. Not long before breakfast."

She was a little pained by a sense of unfairness, but she was not given to argument. "I'll have to fetch my bag," she said, "I've got sandwiches in it."

He stared at her. "Don't tell me you've brought provisions for three days."

"Oh, no. Just supper last night and breakfast this morning. It saves about eight shillings."

"Are you Scotch? Listen to me. You'll have breakfast with me."

"What more do you expect me to have with you?"

He grinned. "I'll tell you. Lunch, tea, dinner. And tomorrow——" She interrupted him with a sigh. "I guess you're a bit rocky. You haven't escaped from anywhere, have you?" His face fell and he asked her with sudden humility, "You couldn't put up with me? You'd be bored?"

"No," she said, "I shouldn't be bored. But why do you do all this for me? I'm not pretty. I guess I'm not clever." She waited with longing for a denial. "You are lovely, brilliant, witty," the incredible words which would relieve her of any need to repay him or refuse his gifts; loveliness and wit were priced higher than any gift he offered, while if a girl were loved, even old women of hard experience would admit her right to take and never give. But he denied nothing. His explanation was almost insulting in its simplicity. "I can talk so easily to you. I feel I know you." She knew what that meant. "Yes," she said with the dry trivial grief of disappointment, "I seem to know you too," and what she meant were the long stairs, the agent's door, and the young friendly Jew, explaining gently and without interest that he had nothing to offer her, nothing to offer her at all.

Yes, she thought, they knew each other; they had both admitted the fact, and it had left them beggared of words. The world shifted and changed and passed them by. Trees and buildings rose and fell against a pale-blue clouded sky, beech changed to elm, and elm to fir, and fir to stone; a world, like lead upon a hot fire, bubbled into varying shapes now like a flame, now like a leaf of clover. Their thoughts remained the same and there was nothing to speak about, because there was nothing to discover.

"You don't really want me to have breakfast with you," she said, trying to be sensible and break the embarrassment of their silence. But he would have nothing to do with her solution. "I do," he said, but there was a weakness in his voice which showed her that she had only to be masterful, to get up and leave him and go to her carriage, and he would make no resistance. But in her bag there were stale sandwiches and some of yesterday's milk in a wine bottle, while down the corridor came the smell of boiling coffee and fresh white loaves.

Mabel Warren poured out her coffee, black and strong with no sugar. "It's the best story I've ever been after," she said. "I saw him five years ago walk out of court, while Hartep watched with the warrant in his pocket. Campbell, of the *News*, was after him at once, but he missed him in the street. He never went home, and no more was heard of him from that day to this. Everyone thought he had been murdered, but I never understood why, if they meant to murder him, they took out a warrant for his arrest."

"Suppose," said Janet Pardoe, without much interest, "that he won't speak."

Miss Warren broke a roll. "I've never failed yet."

"You'll invent something?"

"No, that's good enough for Savory, but not for him." She said viciously, "I'll make him speak. Somehow. Between here and Vienna. I've got nearly twelve hours. I'll think of a way." She added thoughtfully, "He says he's a schoolteacher. It may be true. That would be a good story. And where is he going? He says that he's getting out at Vienna. If he does I'll follow him. I'll follow him to Constantinople if necessary. But I don't believe it. He's going home."

"To prison?"

"To trial. He's trusting the people perhaps. He was always popular in the slums. But he's a fool if he thinks they'll remember him. Five years. No one's ever remembered for so long."

"Darling, how morbid you are."

Mabel Warren came back with difficulty to her immediate surroundings, the coffee swaying in her cup, the gently-rocking table, and Janet Pardoe. Janet Pardoe had pouted and protested and grieved, but now she was squinting sideways at a Jew who shared a table with a girl, common to Miss Warren's eyes, but with a bright attraction. As for the man, his only merits were youth and money, but they were enough, Mabel Warren thought with bitter knowledge, to catch Janet's eye. "You know it's true," she said with useless anger. She tore at another roll with her square worn hand, while her emotion grew, how grotesquely she was aware. "You'll have forgotten me in a week."

"But of course I shan't, darling. Why, I owe you everything." The words did not satisfy Mabel Warren. When I love, she thought, I do not think of what I owe. The world to her was divided into those who thought and those who felt. The first considered the dresses which had been bought them, the bills which had been paid, but presently the dresses went out of fashion and the wind caught the receipt from the desk and blew it away, and in any case the debt had been paid with a kiss or another kindness, and those who thought forgot; but those who felt remembered;

they did not owe and they did not lend, they gave hatred or love. I am one of those, thought Miss Warren, her eyes filling with tears and the bread drying in her throat, I am one of those who love and remember always, who keep faith with the past in black dresses or black bands, I don't forget, and her eyes dwelt for a moment on the Jew's girl, as a tired motorist might eye with longing the common inn, the scarlet curtains and the watered ale, before continuing his drive towards the best hotel, with its music and its palms. She thought: "I'll speak to her. She has a pretty figure." For after all one could not live always with a low voice like music, with a tall figure like a palm. Faithfulness was not the same as remembrance; one could forget and be faithful and one could remember and be faithless.

She loved Janet Pardoe, she would always love Janet Pardoe, she protested inwardly; Janet had been a revelation to her of what love could mean ever since the first evening of their meeting in a cinema in Kaiser Wihelmstrasse, and yet, and yet . . . They had come together in a mutual disgust of the chief actor; at least Mabel Warren had said aloud in English to relieve her feelings in the strained hush of the dark theatre, "I can't bear these oiled men," and had heard a low musical agreement. Yet even then Janet Pardoe had wished to stay till the end, till the last embrace, the final veiled lechery. Mabel Warren urged her to come and have a drink, but Janet Pardoe said that she wanted to see the news and they both stayed. That first evening seemed now to have revealed all of Janet's character that there was to reveal, the inevitable agreement which made no difference to what she did. Sharp words or disagreements had never ruffled her expressionless mood until the evening before, when she had thought herself rid of Mabel Warren. Miss Warren said viciously, not troubling to lower her voice at all, "I don't like Jews," and Janet Pardoe, turning her large luminous eyes back to Mabel Warren's, agreed, "Nor do I, darling."

Mabel Warren implored her with sudden desperation, "Janet, when I've gone, you'll remember our love for each other? You won't let a man touch you?" She would have welcomed dissent, the opportunity to argue, to give reasons, to fix some kind of seal upon that fluid mind, but again all she got was an absent-minded agreement. "But of course not, darling. How could I?" If she had faced a mirror she would have received more sense of an alien mind from the image there, but not, Miss Warren thought, the satisfaction of something beautiful. It was no good thinking of herself, her coarse hair, red lids, and obstinately masculine and discordant voice; there was no one, even the young Jew, who was not her physical rival. When she was gone, Janet Pardoe would remain for a little while a beautiful vacancy, hardly existing at all, save for the need of sleep, the need of food, the need of admiration. But soon she would be sitting back crumbling toast, saying, "But of course I agree. I've always felt that." The cup shook in Mabel Warren's hand, and the coffee trickled over the brim and drops fell to her skirt, already stained with grease and beer. What does it matter, she asked herself, what Janet does so long as I don't know? What does it matter to me if she lets a man take her to bed as long as she comes back? But the last qualification made her wince with mental pain, for would Janet, she wondered, ever return to an ageing plain infatuated woman? She'll tell him about me, Mabel Warren thought, of the two years she has lived with me, of the times when we have been happy, of the scenes I've made, even of the poems I've written her, and he'll laugh and she'll laugh and they'll go to bed laughing. I had better make up my mind that this is the end, that she will never come back from this holiday. I don't even know whether it's really her uncle she's visiting. There are as many fish in the sea as ever came out of it, Miss Warren thought, crumbling a roll, desperately aware of her uncared-for hands, the girl with the Jew, for instance. She was as poor as Janet was that evening in the cinema; she was not lovely as Janet was, so that it was happiness to sit for an hour and watch every motion of Janet's body, Janet doing her hair, Janet changing her dress, Janet pulling on her stockings, Janet mixing a drink, but she probably had twice the mind, common and shrewd though it might be.

"Darling," Janet Pardoe asked with amusement, "are you getting a pash for that little thing?" The train rocked and roared into a tunnel and out again, eliminating Mabel Warren's answer, taking it, as an angry hand might take a letter, tearing it across and scattering the pieces, only one phrase falling face upwards and in view: "For ever," so that no one but Mabel Warren could have said what her protest had been, whether she had sworn to remember always or had declared that one could not be faithful for ever to one person. When the train came out again into the sunlight, coffee-pots glimmering and white linen laid between an open pasture, where a few cows grazed, and a deep wood of firs, Miss Warren had forgotten what she had wished to say, for she recognised in a man who entered the restaurant-car Czinner's companion. At the same moment the girl rose. She and the young man had spoken so seldom Miss Warren could not decide whether they were acquainted; she hoped that they were strange to each other, for she was forming a plan which would not only give her speech with the girl but would help her to nail Czinner once and for all to the bill page of the paper, an exclusive crucifixion.

"Good-bye," the girl said. Mabel Warren, watching them with the trained observer's eye, noted the Jew's raised shoulders, as of the ashamed habitual thief who leaning forward from the dock protests softly, more from habit than any real sense of injustice, that he has not had a fair trial. The casual observer might have read in their faces the result of a lover's quarrel; Mabel Warren knew better. "I'll see you again?" the man asked, and she replied, "If you want me, you'll know where to find me."

Mabel Warren said to Janet, "I'll see you later. There are things I must do," and she followed the girl out of the car over the rocking bridge between the coaches, stumbling and grasping for support, but with the ache in her head quite gone in the warmth and illumination of her idea. For when she said there were things to do, "things" meant nothing vague, but a throned triumphant concept for which her brain was the lit hall and a murmuring and approving multitude. Everything fitted, that she felt above all things, and she began to calculate what space they were likely to allow her in London; she had never led the paper before. There was the Disarmament Conference and the arrest of a peer for embezzlement and a baronet had married a Ziegfeld girl. None of these stories was exclusive; she had read them on the News Agency tape, before she went to the station. They will put the Disarmament Conference and the Ziegfeld girl on a back page, she thought. There's no doubt, short of a European war or the King's death, that my story will lead the paper, and with her eyes on the girl in front, she considered the image of Dr. Czinner, tired and shabby and old-fashioned in the high collar and the little tight tie, sitting in the corner of his compartment with his hands gripped on his knee, while she told him a lot of lies about Belgrade. "Dr. Czinner Alive," she thought, working at the headlines, but that would not do at the top, for five years had passed and not many people would remember his name. "Mystery Man's Return. How Dr. Czinner Escaped Death. Exclusive Story."

"My dear," she gasped, holding to the rail, apparently daunted by the second bridge, the shaking metal and the sound of the linked coaches straining. Her voice did not carry, and she had to repeat her exclamation in a shout, which fitted ill with the part she was assuming—an elderly woman struggling for breath. The girl turned and came back to her, her unschooled face white and miserable, with nothing hidden from any stranger. "What's the matter? Are you ill?"

Miss Warren did not move, thinking intensely on the other side of the overlapping plates of steel. "Oh, my dear, how glad I am that you are English. I feel so sick. I can't cross. I'm a silly old thing, I know." Bitterly but of necessity she played upon her age. "If you would give me your hand." She thought: for this game I ought to have long hair, it would be more womanly. I wish my fingers weren't yellow. Thank God I don't still smell of drink. The girl came back. "Of course. You needn't be afraid. Take my arm." Miss Warren gripped it with strong fingers as she might have gripped the neck of a fighting dog.

When they reached the next corridor she spoke again. The noise of the train was softened, and she was able to subdue her voice to a husky whisper. "If only there was a doctor on the train, my dear. I feel so ill."

"But there is one. His name's Dr. John. I came over faint last night and he helped me. Let me find him."

"I'm so frightened of doctors, dear," said Miss Warren with a glint of triumph; it was extraordinarily lucky that the girl knew Czinner. "Talk to me a little first till I'm calmer. What's your name, my dear?"

"Coral Musker."

"You must call me Mabel, Mabel Warren. I have a niece just like you. I work on a newspaper at Cologne. You must come and see me one day. The darlingest little flat. Are you on a holiday?"

"I dance. I'm off to Constantinople. A girl's ill in an English show there." For a moment with the girl's hand in hers Mabel Warren felt flustered with a longing to be generous in an absurd obvious way. Why not give up the hope of keeping Janet Pardoe and invite the girl to break her contract and take Janet's place as her paid companion? "You are so pretty," she said aloud.

"Pretty," said Coral Musker. No smile softened her incredulity. "You're pulling my leg."

"My dear, you are so kind and good."

"You bet I am." She spoke with a touch of vulgarity that spoiled for a moment Mabel Warren's vision. Coral Musker said with longing, "Leave out the goodness. Say that again about my being pretty." Mabel Warren acquiesced with complete conviction, "My dear, you are lovely." The astonished avidity with which the girl watched her was touching; the word "virginity" passed through the urban darkness of Mabel Warren's mind. "Has no one said that to you?" Eager and unbelieving Mabel Warren implored her: "Not your young friend in the restaurant-car?"

"I hardly know him."

"I think you are wise, my dear. Jews are not to be trusted."

Coral Musker said slowly, "Do you think he thought that? That I didn't like him because he was a Jew?"

"They are used to it, dear."

"Then I shall go and tell him that I like him, that I've always liked Jews." Mabel Warren began to swear with a bitter obscene venom beneath her breath.

"What did you say?"

"You won't leave me like this until you've found the doctor? Look. My compartment's at the end of the corridor with my niece. I'll go there if you'll fetch him." She watched Coral Musker out of sight and slipped into the lavatory. The train came to a sharp halt and then began to move backwards. Miss Warren recognised through the window the spires of Würzburg, the bridge over the Main; the train was shedding its third-class coaches, shunting backwards and forwards between the signal boxes and the sidings. Miss Warren left the door a little open, so that she could see the corridor. When Coral Musker and Dr. Czinner appeared she closed the door and waited for the sound of their footsteps to pass. They had quite a long walk to the end of the corridor; now, if she hurried, she would have time enough. She slipped out. Before she could close the door the train started with a lurch and the door slammed, but neither Coral Musker nor Dr. Czinner looked back.

She ran awkwardly, flung from one side to the other of the corridor by the motion of the train, bruising a wrist and a knee. Passengers returning from breakfast flattened themselves against the windows to let her by, and some of them complained of her in German, knowing her to be English, and imagining that she could not understand them. She grinned at them maliciously, uncovering her great front teeth, and ran on. The right compartment was easy to find, for she recognised the mackintosh hanging in a corner, the soft stained hat. On the seat lay a morning paper that Czinner must have bought a minute or two before Würzburg station. In the brief pursuit of Coral Musker along the corridor she had thought out every move; the stranger who shared the compartment was at breakfast, Dr. Czinner, seeking her at the other end of the train, would be away for at least three minutes. In that time she must learn enough to make him speak.

First there was the mackintosh. There was nothing in the pockets but a box of matches and a packet of Gold Flake. She picked up the hat and felt along the band and inside the lining; she had sometimes found quite valuable information concealed in hats, but the doctor's was empty. Now she reached the dangerous moments of her search, for the examination of a hat, even of the mackintosh pockets, could be disguised, but to drag the suitcase from the rack, to lever the lock open with her pocket-knife and lift the lid, laid her too obviously open to the charge of theft. And one blade of her knife broke while she still laboured at the lock. Her purpose was patent to anyone who passed the compartment, and she sweated a little on the forehead, growing frenzied in her haste. If I am found it means the sack, she thought: the cheapest rag in England could not stand for this; and if I'm sacked, I lose Janet, I lose the chance of Coral. But if I succeed, she thought, prying, pushing, scraping, there's nothing they won't do for me in return for such a story; another four pounds a week wouldn't be too much to demand. I'll be able to take a larger flat; when Janet knows of it, she'll return, she'll never leave me. It is happiness, security, she thought, I'll be getting in return for this, and the lock gave and the lid lifted and her fingers were on the secrets of Dr. Czinner. A woolen stomach-belt was the first of them.

She lifted it with care and found his passport. It gave his name as Richard John and his profession as teaching. His age was fifty-six. That proves nothing, she thought, these shady foreign politicians know where to buy a passport. She put it back where she had found it and began to slip her fingers between his suits, half-way down in the centre of the suitcase, the spot the customs officers always miss when they turn up the contents of a bag at the bottom and at the sides. She hoped to find a pamphlet or a letter, but there was only an old Baedeker published in 1914: *Konstantinopel und Kleinasien, Balkanstaaten, Archipel, Cypern*, slipped inside a pair of trousers. But Mabel Warren was thorough: she calculated that she had about one minute of safety left, and as there was nothing else to examine she opened the Baedeker, for it was curious to find it so carefully packed away. She looked at the fly-leaf and read with disappointment the name of Richard John written in a small fussy hand with a scratching nib, but under it was an address, The School House, Great Birchington-on-Sea, which was worth remembering; the *Clarion* could send a man down to interview the headmaster. A good story might be hidden there.

The guide-book seemed to have been bought second-hand, the cover was very worn and there was the label of a bookseller in Charing Cross Road on the fly-leaf. She turned to Belgrade. There was a one-page map, which had worked loose, but it was unmarked; she examined every page dealing with Belgrade and then every page dealing with Serbia, every page on any of the states which were now part of Yugo-Slavia. There was not so much as a smudge of ink. She would have given up the search if it were not for the position in which she had found the book. Obstinately and against the evidence of her eyes she believed that it had been hidden there and that therefore there must be something to hide. She skimmed the pages against her thumb, they ran unevenly because of the many folded maps, but on one of the early pages she found some lines and circles and triangles drawn in ink over the text. But the text dealt only with an obscure town in Asia Minor and the drawings might have been a child's scribble with ruler and compasses. Certainly, if the lines belonged to a code only an expert could decipher them. He's defeated me, she thought, with hatred, smoothing the surface of the suitcase, there's nothing here; but she felt unwilling to put back the Baedeker. He had hidden it, there must be something to find. She had risked so much already that it was easy to risk a little more. She closed the suitcase and put it back on the rack, but the Baedeker she slipped down her shirt and so under her armpit, where she could hold it with one arm pressed to her side.

But it was no use going back to her own seat, for she would meet Dr. Czinner returning. It was then that she remembered Mr. Quin Savory, whom she had come to the station to interview. His face was well known to her from photographs in the *Tatler*, cartoons in the *New Yorker*, pencil drawings in the *Mercury*. She looked cautiously down the corridor, her eyes blinking a little in a short-sighted manner, and then walked rapidly away. Mr. Quin Savory was not to be found in the first-class carriages, but she ran him to earth in a second-class sleeper. With his chin buried in his overcoat, one hand round the bowl of a pipe, he watched with small glittering eyes the people who passed in the corridor. A clergyman dozed in the opposite corner.

Miss Warren opened the door and stepped inside. Her manner was masterful; she sat down without waiting for an invitation. She felt that she was offering this man something he wanted, publicity, and she was gaining nothing commensurate in return. There was no need to speak softly to him, to lure him into disclosures, as she had tried to lure Dr. Czinner; she could insult him with impunity, for the Press had power to sell his books. "You Mr. Quin Savory?" she asked, and saw out of the corner of her eye how the clergyman's attitude changed to one of respectful attention; poor mutt, she thought, to be impressed by a 100,000 sale, we sell two million, twenty times as many people will have heard of Dr. Czinner tomorrow. "I represent the *Clarion*. Want an interview."

"I'm a bit taken aback," said Mr. Savory, raising his chin, pulling at his overcoat.

"No need to be nervous," said Miss Warren mechanically. She fetched her notebook from her bag and flipped it open. "Just a few words for the English public. Travelling incognito?"

"Oh, no, no," Mr. Savory protested. "I'm not royalty."

Miss Warren began to write. "Where are you going?"

"Why, first of all," said Mr. Savory brightly, as if pleased by Miss Warren's interest, which had already returned to the Baedeker and the scrawl of geometrical figures, "to Constantinople. Then I may go to Ankara, the Far East. Baghdad. China."

"Writing a travel book?"

"Oh, no, no, no. My public wants a novel. It'll be called *Going Abroad*. An adventure of the Cockney spirit. These countries, civilisations," he made a circle in the air with his hand, "Germany, Turkey, Arabia, they'll all take second pew to the chief character, a London tobacconist. D'you see?"

"Quite," said Miss Warren, writing rapidly. " 'Dr. Richard Czinner, one of the greatest revolutionary figures of the immediate post-war period, is on his way home to Belgrade. For five years the world has thought him dead, but during that time he has been living as a schoolmaster in England, biding his time.' " But for what? Miss Warren wondered. "Your opinion of modern literature?" she asked. "Joyce, Lawrence, all that?"

"It will pass," Mr. Savory said promptly with the effect of an epigram.

"You believe in Shakespeare, Chaucer, Charles Reade, that sort of thing?"

"They will live," Mr. Savory declared with a touch of solemnity.

"Bohemianism? You don't believe in that? Fitzroy Tavern?" ("A warrant for his arrest has been issued," she wrote, "but it could not be served till the trial was over. When the trial was over Dr. Czinner had disappeared. Every station had been watched by the police, every car stopped. It was little wonder that the rumour of his murder by government agents spread rapidly.") "You don't believe it's necessary to dress oddly, big black hat, velvet jacket and what not?"

"I think it's fatal," Mr. Savory said. He was now quite at his ease and watched the clergyman covertly while he talked. "I'm not a poet. A poet's an individualist. He can dress as he likes; he depends only on himself. A novelist depends on other men; he's an average man with the power of expression. 'E's a spy," Mr. Savory added with confusing drama, dropping aitches right and left. " 'E 'as to see everything and pass unnoticed. If people recognised 'im they wouldn't talk, they'd pose before 'im; 'e wouldn't find things out." Miss Warren's pencil raced. Now that she had got him started, she could think quickly: no need to press him with questions. Her pencil made meaningless symbols, which looked sufficiently like shorthand to convince Mr. Savory that his remarks were being taken down in full, but behind the deceiving screen of squiggles and lines, circles and squares, Miss Warren thought. She thought of every possible aspect of the Baedeker. It had been published in 1914, but was in excellent condition; it had never been much used, except for the section dealing with Belgrade; the map of the city had been so often handled that it was loose.

"You do follow these views?" Mr. Savory asked anxiously. "They're important. They seem to me the touchstone of lit'ry integrity. One can 'ave that, you know, and yet sell one hundred thousand copies." Miss Warren, annoyed at the interruption, only just prevented herself retorting, "Do you think we should sell two million copies if we told the truth?" "Very interesting," she said. "The public will be interested. Now what do you consider your contribution to English literature?" She grinned at him encouragingly and poised her pencil.

"Surely that's for somebody else to state," said Mr. Savory. "But one 'opes, one 'opes, that it's something of this sort, to bring back cheerfulness and 'ealth to modern fiction. There's been too much of this introspection, too much gloom. After all, the world is a fine adventurous place." The bony hand which held the pipe beat helplessly against his knee. "To bring back the spirit of Chaucer," he said. A woman passed along the corridor, and for a moment all Mr. Savory's attention was visibly caught up to sail in her wake, bobbing, bobbing, bobbing, like his hand. "Chaucer," he said, "Chaucer," and suddenly, before Miss Warren's eyes he gave up the struggle, his pipe fell to the floor, and stooping to find it, he exclaimed irritably, "Damn it all. Damn." He was a man overworked, harassed by a personality which was not his own, by curiosities and lusts, a man on the edge of a nervous breakdown. Miss Warren gloated over him. It was not that she hated him, but that she hated any overpowering success, whether it meant the sale of a hundred thousand copies or the attainment of three hundred miles an hour, which made her an interviewer and a man the condescending interviewed. Failure of the same overwhelming kind was another matter, for then she was the avenging world, penetrating into prison cells, into hotel lounges, into mean back parlours. Then with a man at her mercy between the potted palms and the piano, when he was backed against the wedding photograph and the marble clock, she could almost love her victim, asking him little intimate questions, hardly listening to the answers. Well, not so great a gulf lay, she thought with satisfaction, between Mr. Quin Savory, author of *The Great Gay Round*, and such a failure.

She harped on his phrase. "Health," she said. "That's your mission? None of this 'adults only' stuff. They give you as school prizes."

Her irony had been a little too obvious. "I'm proud of it," he said. "The younger generation's being brought up on 'ealthy traditions." She noticed his dry lips, the squint towards the corridor. I'll put that in about healthy traditions, she thought, the public will like it, James Douglas will like it, and they will like it still better when he's a Hyde Park case, for that's what he'll be in a few years. I'll be alive to remind them. She was proud of her power of prophecy, though she had not yet lived to see any of her prophecies fulfilled. Take an expression in the present, a line of ill-health, a tone of voice, a gesture, no more illuminating to the average unobservant person than the lines and circles in the Baedeker, and fit them to what one knew of the man's surroundings, his friends and furniture, the house he lived in, and one saw the future, his shabby waiting fate. "My God!" said Miss Warren, "I've got it."

Mr. Savory jumped. "What have you got?" he asked. "Toothache?"

"No, no," said Miss Warren. She felt grateful to him for the illumination which now flooded her mind with light, leaving no dark corners left in which Dr. Czinner might hide from her. "Such an excellent interview, I meant. I see the way to present you."

"Do I see a proof?"

"Ah, we are not a weekly paper. Our public can't wait. Hungry, you know, for its lion's steak. No time for proofs. People in London will be reading the interview while they eat their breakfast tomorrow." She left him with this assurance of the public interest, when she would far rather have sown in his overworked mind, grappling already with the problem of another half million popular words, the suggestion of how people forget, how they buy one day what they laugh at the next. But she could not afford the time; bigger game called, for she believed that she had guessed the secret of the Baedeker. It had been the consideration of her own prophecies which had given her the clue. The map was loose, the paper in a Baedeker she remembered was thin and insufficiently opaque; if one fitted the map against the pen drawings on the earlier page, the lines would show through.

My God, she thought, it's not everyone who would think of that. It deserves a drink. I'll find an empty compartment and call the steward. She did not even want Janet Pardoe to share this triumph; she would rather be alone with a glass of Courvoisier where she could think undisturbed and plan her next move. But when she had found the empty compartment she still acted with circumspection; she did not pull the Baedeker from under her shirt until the steward had fetched her the brandy. And not at once even then. She held the glass to her nostrils, allowing the fumes to reach that point at the back of her nose where brain and nose seemed one. The spirit she had drunk the night before was not all dissipated. It stirred like ground vapour on a wet hot day. Swimmy, she thought, I feel quite swimmy.

Through the glass and the brandy she saw the outer world, so flat and regular that it never seemed to alter, neat fields and trees and small farms. Her eyes, short-sighted and flushed already with the mere fume of the brandy, could not catch the changing details, but she noticed the sky, grey and cloudless, and the pale sun. I shouldn't be surprised at snow, she thought, and looked to see whether the heating wheel was fully turned. Then she took the Baedeker from under her shirt. It would not be long before the train reached Nuremberg, and she wanted everything settled before fresh passengers came on board.

She had guessed right, that at least was certain. When she held the map and the marked page to the light the lines ran along the course of streets, the circles enclosed public buildings: the post office, the railway station, the courts of justice, the prison. But what did it all mean? She had assumed that Dr. Czinner was returning to make some kind of personal demonstration, perhaps to stand his trial for perjury. The map in that context had no meaning. She examined it again. The streets were not marked haphazardly, there was a pattern, a nest of squares balanced on another square and the balancing square was the slum quarter. The next square was made on one side by the railway station, on another by the post office, on a third by the courts of justice. Inside this the squares became rapidly smaller, until they enclosed only the prison.

A bank mounted steeply on either side of the train and the sunlight was shut off; sparks, red in the overcast sky, struck the windows like hail, and darkness swept the carriages as the long train roared into a tunnel. Revolution, she thought, it means nothing less, with the map still raised to catch the first light returning.

The roar diminished and light came suddenly back. Dr. Czinner was standing in the doorway, a newspaper under his arm. He was wearing the mackintosh again, and she regarded with contempt the glasses, the grey hair and shabby moustache, the small tight tie. She laid down the map and grinned at him. "Well?"

Dr. Czinner came in and shut the door. He sat down opposite her without a sign of hostility. He knows I've got him fixed, she thought; he's going to be reasonable? He asked her suddenly, "Would your paper approve?"

"Of course not," she said. "I'd be sacked tomorrow. But when they get my story, that'll be a different matter." She added with calculated insolence, "I reckon that you are worth four pounds a week to me."

Dr. Czinner said thoughtfully, without anger, "I don't intend to tell you any-thing." She waved her hand at him. "You've told me a lot already. There's this." She tapped the Baedeker. "You were a foreign master at Great Birchington-on-Sea. We'll get the story from your headmaster." His head dropped. "And then," she said, "there's this map. And these scrawls. I've put two and two together." She had expected some protests of fear or indignation, but he was still brooding over her first guess. His attitude puzzled her and for an anguished moment she wondered, Am I missing the best story? Is the best story not here at all, but at a south-coast school among the red-brick buildings and the pitch-pine desks and ink-stands and cracked bells and the smell of boys' clothes? The doubt made her less certain of herself and she spoke gently, more gently than she had intended, for it was difficult to modulate her husky voice. "We'll get together," she growled in a winning way. "I'm not here to let you down. I don't want to interfere with you. Why, if you succeed, my story's all the more valuable. I'll promise not to release anything at all until you give the word." She said plaintively, as if she were an artist accused of deprecating paint, "I wouldn't spoil your revolution. Why, it'll be a grand story."

Age was advancing rapidly on Dr. Czinner. It was as if he had warded off with temporary success five years of pitch-pine smells and the whine of chalk on blackboards, only to sit now in a railway carriage and allow the baulked years to come upon him, together and not one by one. For the moment he was an old man nodding into sleep, his face as grey as the snow sky over Nuremberg. "Now first," said Miss Warren, "what are your plans? I can see you depend a good deal on the slums."

He shook his head. "I depend on no one."

"You are keeping absolute control?"

"Least of all myself."

Miss Warren struck her knee sharply. "I want plain answers," but she got the same reply, "I shall tell you nothing." He looks more like seventy than fifty-six, she thought; he's getting deaf, he doesn't understand what I've been saying. She was very forbearing; she felt certain that this was not success she faced, it resembled failure too closely, and failure she could love; she could be tender and soft-syllabled towards failure, wooing it with little whinnying words, as long as in the end it spoke. A weak man had sometimes gone away with the impression that Miss Warren was his best friend. She leant forward and tapped on Dr. Czinner's knee, putting all the amiability of which she was capable into her grin. "We are in this together, doctor. Don't you understand that? Why, we can even help you. Public opinion's just another name for the *Clarion*. I know you are afraid we'll be indiscreet, that we'll publish your story tomorrow and the government will be warned. But I tell you we won't breathe so much as a paragraph on the book page until you begin your show. Then I want to be able to put right across the middle page, 'Dr. Czinner's Own Story. Exclusive to the *Clarion*.' Now, that's not unreasonable."

"There's nothing I wish to say."

Miss Warren withdrew her hand. Did the poor fool, she wondered, think that he would stand between her and another four pounds a week, between her and Janet Pardoe? He became, old and stupid and stubborn on the opposite seat, the image of all the men who threatened her happiness, who were closing round Janet with money and little toys and laughter at a woman's devotion to a woman. But the image was in her power; she could break the image. It was not a useless act of mischief on Cromwell's part to shatter statues. Some of the power of the Virgin lay in the Virgin's statue, and when the head was off and a limb gone and the seven swords broken, fewer candles were lit and the prayers said at her altar were not so many. One man like Dr. Czinner ruined by a woman, and fewer stupid girls like Coral Musker would believe all strength and cunning to reside in a man. But she gave him, because of his age, and because he reeked to her nose of failure, one more chance. "Nothing?"

"Nothing."

She laughed at him angrily. "You've said a mouthful already." He was unimpressed and she explained slowly as if to a mental defective, "We reach Vienna at eight-forty tonight. By nine I shall be telephoning to the Cologne office. They'll get my story through to London by ten o'clock. The paper doesn't go to press for the first London edition till eleven. Even if the message is delayed, it's possible to alter the bill page for the last edition up to three o'clock in the morning. My story will be read at breakfast tomorrow. Every paper in London will have a reporter round at the Yugo-Slavian Ministry by nine o'clock in the morning. Before lunch tomorrow the whole story will be known in Belgrade, and the train's not due there till six in the evening. And there won't be much left to the imagination either. Think what I shall be able to say. Dr. Richard Czinner, the famous Socialist agitator, who disappeared from Belgrade five years ago at the time of the Kamnetz trial, is on his way home. He joined the Orient express at Ostend on Monday and his train is due at Belgrade this evening. It is believed that his arrival will coincide with a Socialist outbreak based on the slum quarters, where Doctor Czinner's name has never been forgotten, and an attempt will probably be made to seize the station, the post office and the prison." Miss Warren paused. "That's the story I shall telegraph. But if you'll say more I'll tell them to hold until you give the word. I'm offering you a straightforward bargain."

"I tell you that I am leaving the train at Vienna."

"I don't believe you."

Dr. Czinner sucked in his breath, staring through the window at the grey luminous sky, a group of factory chimneys, and a great black metal drum. The compartment filled with the smell of gas. Cabbages were growing in the allotments through the bad air, gross bouquets sprinkled with frost. He said so softly that she had to lean forward to catch the words, "I have no reason to fear you." He was subdued, he was certain, and his calmness touched her nerves. She protested uneasily and with anger, as if the criminal in the dock, the weeping man beside the potted fern, had been endowed suddenly with a mysterious reserve of strength, "I can play hell with you."

Dr. Czinner said slowly, "There's going to be snow." The train was creeping into Nuremberg, and the great engines that ranged themselves on either side reflected the wet steel aspect of the sky. "No," he said, "there's nothing you can do which will harm me." She tapped the Baedeker and he remarked with a flash of humour: "Keep it as a souvenir of our meeting." She was certain then that her fear was justified; he was escaping her, and she stared at him with rage. If I could do him an injury, she thought, watching in the mirror behind him success, in the likeness of Janet Pardoe, wandering away, lovely and undeserving and vacant, down long streets and through the lounges of expensive hotels, if I could do him an injury.

It angered her the more to find herself speechless and Dr. Czinner in control. He handed her the paper and asked her, "Do you read German? Then read this." All the while that the train stood in Nuremberg station, a long twenty minutes, she stared at it. The message it contained infuriated her. She had been prepared for news of some extraordinary success, of a king's abdication, a government's overthrow, a popular demand for Doctor Czinner's return, which would have raised him into the position of the condescending interviewed. What she read was more extraordinary, a failure which put him completely out of her power. She had been many times bullied by the successful, never before by one who had failed.

"Communist outbreak in Belgrade," she read. "An attempt was made late last night by a band of armed Communist agitators to seize the station and the prison at Belgrade. The police were taken by surprise and for nearly three hours the revolutionaries were in undisturbed possession of the general post office and the goods-yards. All telegraphic communication with Belgrade was interrupted until early this morning. At two o'clock, however, our representative at Vienna spoke to Colonel Hartep, the Chief of Police, by telephone and learned that order had been restored. The revolutionaries were few in number and lacked a proper leader; their attack on the prison was repulsed by the warders, and for some hours afterwards they stayed inactive in the post office, apparently in the hope that the inhabitants of the poorer quarters of the capital would come to their help. Meanwhile the government was able to muster police reinforcements, and with the help of a platoon of soldiers and a couple of field-guns, the police recaptured the post office after a siege lasting little more than three-quarters of an hour." This summary was printed in large type; underneath in small type was a more detailed account of the outbreak. Miss Warren sat and stared at it; she frowned a little and was conscious of the dryness of her mouth. Her brain felt clear and empty. Dr. Czinner explained, "They were three days too early."

Miss Warren snapped at him, "What more could you have done?"

"The people would have followed me."

"They've forgotten you. Five years is the hell of a time. The young men were children when you ran away."

Five years, she thought, seeing them fall on her inevitably through future days, like the endless rain of a wet winter, watching in mind Janet Pardoe's face as it worried over the first wrinkle, the first greyness, or else the smooth tight lifted skin and dark dyed hair every three weeks whitening at the roots.

"What are you going to do now?" she asked, and the promptitude and plainness of his answer, "I've told you. I'm getting out at Vienna," filled her with suspicion. "That's nice," she said, "we'll be together. We can talk. You'll have no objection to an interview now. If you are short of money, our Vienna office will advance you some." She was aware that he was watching her more closely than ever before. "Yes," he said slowly, "perhaps we can talk," and she was certain this time that he was lying. He's going to double, she thought, but it was difficult to see his motive. He had no choice but to get out at Vienna or at Buda-Pesth; it would be unsafe to travel farther. Then she remembered him at the Kamnetz trial, fully aware that no jury would convict and yet giving his dangerous useless evidence while Hartep waited with the warrant. He's fool enough to do anything, she thought, and wondered for a moment whether, behind the quietness, he was already standing in the dock with his companions, uttering his defence with an eye to the packed gallery. If he goes on, she thought, I'll go, I'll stick to him, I'll have his story, but she felt curiously weak and undecided, for she had no threat left. He was beaten, leaning back in his corner old and hopeless, with the newspaper gathering dust on the floor between them, and he was triumphant, watching her leave the carriage, the Baedeker forgotten on the seat, with nothing but silence for her exclamation: "I'll see you again at Vienna."

When Miss Warren had gone, Dr. Czinner stooped for the paper. His sleeve caught an empty glass and it fell and shattered on the floor. His hand rested on the paper and he stared at the glass, unable to concentrate his thought, unable to decide what it was he had to do, pick up the paper or gather the dangerous sharp scraps. Presently he laid the paper carefully folded across his knees and closed his eyes. He was haunted in his personal darkness by the details of the story that Miss Warren had read; he knew every turn in the stairs in the post office, he could see the exact spot where the barricade had been built. The muddling fools, he thought, and tried to feel hate for the men who had destroyed his hopes. They had ruined him with them. They had left him in an empty house which could not find a tenant because old ghosts were sometimes vocal in the rooms, and Dr. Czinner himself now was not even the latest ghost.

If a face peered from a window or a voice was heard upstairs or a carpet whispered, it might have been Dr. Czinner seeking to return to a sentient life after five years of burial, working his way round the corners of desks, exposing his transparency before the blackboard and the insubordinate children, crouched in chapel at a service in which the living man had never believed, asking God with the breathing discordant multitude to dismiss him with His blessing.

And sometimes it seemed as if a ghost might return to life, for he had learned that as a ghost he could suffer pain. The ghost had memories; it could remember the Doctor Czinner who had been so loved that it was worth while for a hired murderer to fire a revolver at his head. That was the proudest memory of all, of how Dr. Czinner sat in the beer-house at the poor corner of the park and heard the shot shatter the mirror behind him and knew it for the final proof of how dearly the poor loved him. But the ghost of Czinner, huddled in a shelter while the east wind swept the front and the grey sea tossed the pebbles, had learned to weep at the memory before returning to the red-brick building and tea and to the children who fashioned subtle barbs of pain. But after the final service and the customary hymns and handshakes the ghost of Czinner found itself again touching the body of Czinner; a touch was all the satisfaction it could get. Now there was nothing left but to leave the train at Vienna and return. In ten days the voices would be singing: "Lord receive us with Thy blessing, Once again assembled here."

Dr. Czinner turned a page of the paper and read a little. The nearest he could attain to hate of these muddled men was envy; he could not hate when he remembered details no newspaper correspondent thought it worth while to give, that the man who, after firing his last shot, was bayoneted outside the sorting-room had been left-handed and a lover of Delius's music, the melancholy idealistic music of a man without a faith in anything but death. And that another, who leapt from the third-floor window of the telephone exchange, had a wife scarred and blinded in a factory accident, whom he loved and to whom he was sadly and unwillingly faithless.

But what is left for me to do? Dr. Czinner put down the paper and began to walk the compartment, three steps one way to the door, three steps the other way to the window, up and down. A few flakes of snow were falling, but the wind blew the smoke of the engine back across the window, and if the flakes touched the glass at all, they were already grey like scraps of paper. But six hundred feet up, on the hills which came down to the line at Neumarkt, the snow began to lie like beds of white flowers. If they had waited, if they had waited, thought Dr. Czinner, and as his mind turned from the dead to the men who lived to be tried, the impossibility of his own easy escape presented itself with such force that he exclaimed in a whisper, "I must go to them." But what was the use? He sat down again and began to argue with himself that the gesture would have practical value. If I give myself up and stand my trial with them, the world will listen to my defence as it would never listen to me, safe in England. The strengthening of his resolution encouraged him; he grew more hopeful; the people he thought, will rise to save me, though they did not rise for the others. Again the ghost of Czinner felt close to life, and warmth touched its frozen transparency.

But there were many things to be considered. First he had to avoid the reporter. He must give her the slip at Vienna; it ought not to be difficult, for the train did not arrive till nearly nine, and by that hour of the evening, surely, he thought, she will be drunk. He shivered a little with the cold and the idea of any further contact with that hoarse dangerous woman. Well, he thought, picking up the Baedeker and letting the newspaper drop to the floor, her sting is drawn. She seemed to hate me; I wonder why; some strange pride of profession, I suppose. I may as well go back to my compartment. But when he reached it, he walked on, hands behind back and Baedeker under arm, absorbed by the idea that the ghostly years were over. I am alive again, he thought, because I am conscious of death as a future possibility, almost a certainty, for they will hardly let me escape again, even if I defend myself and others with the tongue of an angel. Faces which were familiar to him looked up as he passed, but they failed to break his absorption. I am afraid, he told himself with triumph, I am afraid.

2

Not *the* Quin Savory?" asked Janet Pardoe.

"Well," said Mr. Savory, "I don't know of another."

"The Great Gay Whirl?"

"Round," Mr. Savory corrected her sharply. *"Great Gay Round."* He put his hand on her elbow and began to propel her down the corridor. "Time for a sherry. Fancy your being related to the woman who's been interviewing me. Daughter? Niece?"

"Well, not exactly related," said Janet Pardoe. "I'm her companion."

"Better not." Mr. Savory's fingers closed more firmly on her arm. "Get another job. You are too young. It's not 'ealthy."

"How right you are," said Janet Pardoe, stopping for a moment in the corridor and turning to him eyes luminous with admiration.

Miss Warren was writing a letter, but she saw them go by. She had laid her writing-pad upon her knee, and her fountain-pen spluttered across the paper, splashing ink and biting deep holes. *Dear Cousin Con*, she wrote, *I'm writing to you because I've nothing better to do. This is the Orient Express, but I'm not going on to Constantinople. I'm getting out at Vienna. But that's another story. Could you get me five yards of ring velvet? Pink. I'm having my flat done up again, while Janet's away. She's on the same train, but I'm leaving her at Vienna. A job of work really, chasing a hateful old man half across Europe.* The Great Gay Round *is on board, but of course you don't read books. And a rather charming little dancer called Coral, whom I think I shall take as my companion. I can't make up my mind whether to have my flat redecorated. Janet says she'll only be away a week. You mustn't on any account pay more than eight-ar.d-eleven a yard. Blue, I think, would suit me, but of course, not navy. This man I was telling you about,* wrote Miss Warren, following Janet Pardoe with her eyes, digging the pen into the paper, *thinks himself too clever for me, but you know as well as I do, don't you, Con, that I can play hell with anyone who thinks that. Janet is a bitch. I'm thinking of getting a new companion. There's a little actress on this train who would suit me. You should see her, the loveliest figure, Con. You'd admire her as much as I do. Not very pretty, but with lovely legs. I really think I must get my flat done up. Which reminds me. You can go up to ten-and-eleven with that ring velvet. I may be going to Belgrade, so wait till you hear from me again. Janet seems to be getting a pash for this Savory man. But I can play hell with him too if I want to. Goodbye. Look after yourself. Give my love to Elsie. I hope she looks after you better than Janet does me. You've always been luckier, but wait till you see Coral. For God's sake don't forget that ring velvet. Much love. Mabel. P.S. Did you hear that Uncle John died suddenly the other day almost on my doorstep?*

Miss Warren's pen ended the letter in a large pool of ink. She enclosed it in a thick line and wrote *Sorry*. Then she wiped the pen on her skirt and rang the bell for a steward. Her mouth was terribly dry.

Coral Musker stood for a little while in the corridor, watching Myatt, wondering whether what Mabel Warren had suggested was true. He sat with head bent over a pile of papers, running a pencil up and down a row of figures, always returning it to the same numeral. Presently he laid down the pencil and put his head in his hands. Pity for a moment touched her, as well as gratitude. With the knowing eyes hidden he might have been a schoolboy, despairingly engaged on homework which would not come right. She could see that he had taken off his gloves the better to grip the pencil and his fingers were blue with cold; even the ostentation of his fur coat was pathetic to her, for it was hopelessly inadequate. It could not solve his sums or keep his fingers warm.

Coral opened the door and came in. He raised his face and smiled, but his work absorbed him. She wanted to take the work away from him and show him the solution and tell him not to let his master know that he had been helped. Who by? she wondered. Mother? Sister? Nothing so distant as a cousin, she thought, sitting down in the easy silence which was the measure of their familiarity.

Because she grew tired of watching through the window the gathering snow she spoke to him: "You said that I could come in when I wanted to."

"Of course."

"I couldn't help feeling a beast," she said, "going away so suddenly and never thanking you properly. You were good to me last night."

"I didn't like the idea of your staying in the compartment with that man when you were ill," he said impatiently, tapping with his pencil. "You needed proper sleep."

"But why were you interested in me?" She received the fatal inevitable answer: "I seemed to know you quite well." He would have gone back to his calculations if it had not been for the unhappy quality of her silence. She could see how he was worried and surprised and a little harassed; he thinks I want him to make love to me, she thought, and wondered, do I? Do I? It would complete the resemblance to other men she had known if he rumpled her hair a bit and pulled her dress open in getting his lips against her breast. I owe him that, she thought, and the accumulated experience of other women told her again that she owed him a good deal more. But how can I pay, she asked herself, if he doesn't press for payment? And the mere thought of performing that strange act when she was not drunk as she supposed some women were, or passionate, but only grateful, chilled her more than the falling snow. She was not even certain how one went about it, whether it would be necessary to spend a whole night with him, to undress completely in the cold carriage. But she began to comfort herself with the thought that he was like other men she had known and was satisfied with very little; the only difference was that he was more generous.

"Last night," he said, watching her closely while he spoke, and his attitude of attention and his misunderstanding of her silence told her that after all they did not know everything of each other, "last night I dreamed about you." He laughed nervously. "I dreamed that I picked you up and took you for a ride and presently you were going to . . ." He paused and evaded the issue. "I felt excited by you."

She became frightened, as if a moneylender were leaning across his desk and approaching very gently and inexorably to the subject of repayment. "In your dream," she said. But he took no notice of her. "Then the guard came along and woke me up. The dream was very vivid. I was so excited that I bought your ticket."

"You mean that you thought—that you wanted——"

The moneylender raised his shoulders, the moneylender sat back behind his desk, and the moneylender rang the bell for a servant to show her out to the street and strangers and the freedom of being unknown. "I just told you this," he said, "so that you needn't feel you owe me anything. It was the effect of a dream, and when I'd bought the ticket, I thought you might as well use it," and he picked up his pencil and turned back to his papers. He added formally, without thought, "It was brash of me to think that for ten pounds——"

Those words did not at first reach her. She was too confused by her relief, even by the shame of being desirable only in a dream, above all by her gratitude. And then pursuing her out of the silence came the final words with their hint of humility—this was unfamiliar. She faced her terror of the bargain, putting out her hand and touching Myatt's face with a gratitude which had borrowed its gesture from an unknown love. "If you want me to," she said. "I thought that you were bored with me. Shall I come tonight?" She laid her fingers across the papers on his knee, small square hands with powder lying thick in the hollow of the knuckles, nails reddened at the tip, hiding the rows of numerals, Mr. Eckman's calculations and subterfuges and cunning concealments, offering herself with an engaging and pathetic dubiety. He said slowly, half his mind still following Mr. Eckman in and out of hidden rooms, "I thought that you disliked me"; he lifted her hands from his papers and said absentmindedly: "Perhaps because I was Jewish."

"You're tired."

"There's something here I can't get straight."

"Leave it," she said, "until tomorrow."

"I haven't the time. I've got to get this done. We are not sitting still." But in fact all sense of motion had been rapt from them by the snow. It fell so heavily that the telegraph-poles were hidden. She took her hands away and asked him with resentment, "Then you don't want me to come?" The calmness and familiarity with which he met her proposal chilled her gratitude.

"Yes," he said, "come. Come tonight." He touched her hands. "Don't think me cold. It's because we seem to know each other so well." He appealed to her, "Be a little strange."

But before she could gather her wits for a pretence, she had admitted to him, "Yes, I feel that too," so that there was nothing else to say, and they sat on in silence like old friends, thinking without excitement of the night before them. Her brief passion of gratitude was over, for now it seemed as unnecessary as it was unwanted. You were not grateful to an acquaintance of so long standing; you took favors and gave favors and talked a little of the weather, not indignant at a caress or embittered by an indifference; and if you saw him in the stalls, you smiled once or twice as you danced, because something had to be done with your face which was a plain one, and a man liked to be recognised from the stage.

"The snow's getting worse."

"Yes. It'll be cold tonight." And you smiled in case a joke was intended and said as enticingly as possible to so old a friend, "We'll be warm," unable to forget that night was coming, remembering all that friends had said and advised and warned, puzzled and repelled that a man should feel indifference and lust at the same time. All that morning and all through lunch the snow continued to fall, lying deep at Passau on the roof of the customs-shed, melted on the line by the steam from the engine into grey icy streams, and the Austrian officials picked their way in gum-boots and swore a little, searching the luggage perfunctorily.

PART THREE

Vienna

1

Josef Grünlich moved to the sheltered side of the chimney, while the snow piled itself all round him on the roof. Below the central station burned like a bonfire in the dark. A whistle screamed and a long line of lights came into view, moving slowly; he looked at his watch as a clock struck nine. That's the Istanbul Express, he thought, twenty minutes late; it may have been held up by snow. He adjusted his flat silver watch and replaced it in his waistcoat pocket, smoothing the creases over the curve of his belly. Well, he considered, it is lucky to be fat on a night like this. Before buttoning his overcoat he ran his hands between pants and trousers and adjusted the revolver which hung between his legs by a piece of string twisted around a button. Trust Josef for three things, he reminded himself comfortably, for a woman, a meal and a fat crib. He emerged from the shelter of the chimney.

It was very slippery on the roof and there was some danger. The snow beat against his eyes and caked into ice on the heels of his shoes. Once he slipped and saw for a moment rising like a fish through dark water to meet him the lit awning of a café. He whispered, "Hail Mary, full of grace," digging his heels into the snow, clutching with his fingers. Saved by the rim of a gutter, he rose to his feet and laughed softly; it was no good being angry with nature. A little later he found the iron arms of the fire-escape.

The climb that followed he considered the most dangerous part of the whole business, for although the escape ran down the back of the flats, out of sight of the street, it faced the goods-yard, and the yard was the limit of a policeman's beat. He appeared every three minutes, the dim lamp at the corner of a shed gleaming on his black polished gaiters, his leather belt, his pistol holster. The deep snow quietened the sound of feet, and Josef could expect no warning of his approach, but the ticking of his watch kept him in mind of danger. He waited at the head of the ladder, crouched low, uneasily conscious of his white background, until the policeman had come and gone again. Then he began his climb. He had only to pass one unoccupied storey, but as he reached the top window a light flashed on him and a whistle blew. I can't be caught, he thought incredulously, I've never been caught, it doesn't happen to me, and waited with his back to the yard for a word or a bullet, while his brain began to move like the little well-oiled wheels of a watch, one thought fitting into another and setting a third in motion. When nothing happened he turned his face from the ladder and the blank wall; the yard was empty, the light glowed from a lamp someone had carried into the loft of the goods-shed, and the whistle had been one of the many noises of the station. His mistake had wasted precious seconds, and he continued his descent with a reckless disregard of his icy shoes, two steps at a time.

When he came to the next window he tapped. There was no reply, and he murmured a mild imprecation, keeping his head turned to the corner of the yard where the policeman would very soon appear. He tapped again and this time heard the shuffle of loose slippers. The lock of the window was lifted, and a woman's voice said, "Anton. Is that you?" "Yes," said Josef, "this is Anton. Let me in quickly." The curtain was drawn back and a thin hand pulled and pulled at the top pane. "The bottom," Josef whispered, "not the top. You think me an acrobat." When the window was raised he showed great agility for a man so fat in stepping from the escape to the sill, but he found it difficult to squeeze into the room. "Can't you raise it another inch?" An engine hooted three times and his brain automatically noted the meaning of the signal: a heavy goods train on the down line. Then he was in the room, the woman had closed the window and the noise of the station faded.

Josef brushed the snow off his coat and his moustache and looked at his watch; nine-five; the train to Passau would not leave for another forty minutes, and he had his ticket ready. With his back to the window and the woman he took in the room casually, but every detail marched to its ordered place in his memory, the ewer and basin on the liver-coloured washstand, the chipped gilt mirror, the iron bedstead, the chamber-pot, the holy picture. He said, "Better leave the window open. In case your master returns."

A thin shocked voice said, "I couldn't. Oh, I couldn't." He turned to her with amiable mockery, "Modest Anna," and watched her with sharp knowledgeable eyes. She shared his age, but not his experience, standing lean and flustered and excited by the window; her black skirt lay across the bed, but she still wore her black blouse, her white domestic collar, and she held a towel before her legs to hide them.

He regarded her quizzically, "Pretty Anna." Her mouth fell open and she stared back at him, silent and fascinated. Josef noted with distaste her uneven and discoloured teeth: whatever else I have to do, he thought, I will not kiss her, but it was evident that she expected an embrace; her modesty was transformed into a horrible middle-aged coquetry, to which he was forced to respond. He began to talk to her in baby language, sitting down on the edge of her bed and keeping its width between them. "What had the pretty Anna got now then? A great big man? Oh, how he will rumple you." He wagged a finger at her playfully, "You and I, Anna. We'll have a good time by and by. Eh?" He squinted sideways at the door and saw with relief that it was unlocked; it would have been just like the old bitch to have locked him in and hidden the key, but no reflection of his anxiety or his distaste ruffled the plump pink face. "Eh?"

She smiled and let out a long whistling breath. "Oh, Anton." He jumped to his feet, and she dropped the towel and came towards him, with the thin tread of a bird, in her black cotton stockings. "One moment," he said, "one moment," raising his hand defensively, aghast at the antique lust he had aroused. Neither of us are beauties, he thought, and the presence of a pink-and-white Madonna gave the whole situation a kind of conscious blasphemy. He stopped her by his urgent whisper, "Are you sure there's no one in the flat?" Her face reddened as if he had made a crude advance. "No, Anton, we are quite alone." His brain began to work again with precision; it was only personal relationships that confused him; when there was danger, or the need of action, his mind had the reliability of a tested machine. "Have you the bag I gave you?"

"Yes, Anton, here under the bed." She drew out a small black doctor's bag, and he chucked her under the chin and told her that she had pretty eyes. "Get undressed," he said, "and into bed. I'll be with you again in a moment." Before she could argue or ask him to explain, he had skipped gaily through the door on his toes and closed it behind him. Immediately he looked round for a chair and wedged it under the handle, so that the door could not be opened from inside.

He was familiar from a previous visit with the room he was in. It was a cross between an office and an old-fashioned drawing-room. There was a desk, a red velvet sofa, a swivel-chair, several occasional tables, a few large nineteenth-century engravings of children playing with dogs and ladies bending over garden walls. One wall was almost covered by a large roller map of the central station, with its platforms and goods-sheds, points and signal-boxes marked in primary colours. The shapes of furniture were dimly visible now in the half-dark, shadows falling like dust-sheets over the chairs from the street lights reflected on the ceiling and the glow of a reading-lamp on the desk. Josef struck his shin against an occasional table and nearly overturned a palm. He swore mildly, and Anna's voice called out from the bedroom, "What is it, Anton? What are you doing?"

"Nothing," he said, "nothing. I'll be with you in a moment. Your master's left a light on. Are you sure he won't be back?"

She began to cough, but between the paroxysms she let him know, "He's on duty till midnight. Anton, you won't be long?" He made a grimace. "Just taking off a few things, Anna darling." Through the open window the sounds of the road beat up into the room; there was a constant blowing of horns. Josef leant out and examined the street. Taxis sped up and down with luggage and passengers, but he ignored them and the flicker of sky signs, and the clinking café immediately below, questing down the pavements; few people were passing, for it was the hour of dinner, theatre, or cinema. There was no policeman to be seen.

"Anton."

He snapped, "Be quiet," and drew the blinds lest he should be seen from one of the buildings opposite. He knew exactly where the safe was built into the wall; only a meal, a cinema, and a few drinks had been required to get the information from Anna. But he had feared to ask her for the combination; she might have realised that her charm was insufficient to bring him in the dark across an icy roof to her bedroom. From a small book-case behind the desk he drew six heavy volumes of *Railway Working and Railway Management*, which hid a small steel door. Josef

Grünlich's mind was now clear and concentrated; he moved without hurry or hesitation. Before he set to work he noted the time, nine-ten, and calculated that he need not leave for half an hour. Ample time, he thought, and pressed a wet thumb on the safe door, the steel is not half an inch thick. He laid the black bag on the desk and unpacked his tools. His chisels were in beautiful condition, highly polished, with a sharp edge; he took a pride in the neatness of his tools as well as in the speed of his work. He might have broken the thin steel with a jemmy, but Anna would hear the blows and he could not trust her to keep silent. He therefore lit his smallest blow-pipe, first putting on smoked glasses to shield his eyes from the glare. The details of the room started out of the shadows at the first fierce jab of flame, the heat scorched his face, and the steel door began to sizzle like melting butter.

"Anton." The woman shook the handle of the bedroom door. "Anton. What are you doing? Why have you shut me in?" Through the low roar of the flame, he cried to her, "Be quiet." He heard her feeling at the lock and twisting the handle. Then she spoke again urgently, "Anton, let me out." Every time he removed his lips from the pipe to answer her, the flame shrank. Trusting to her timorous stupidity, he addressed her ferociously, "Be quiet, or I'll twist your neck." For a moment there was silence, the flame waxed, the steel door turned from a red to a white heat, then Anna called quite loudly, "I know what you are doing, Anton." Josef pressed his lips to the pipe and paid her no attention, but Anna's next cry startled him: "You are at the safe, Anton." She began to rattle the handle again, until he was forced to let the flame sink and shout at her, "Be quiet. I meant what I said. I'll twist your ugly neck for you, you old bitch." Her voice sank, but he could hear her quite distinctly; her lips must have been pressed to the key-hole. "Don't, don't say that, Anton. Listen. Let me out. I've got something to tell you, to warn you." He did not answer her, blowing the flame and the steel back to a white heat. "I lied to you, Anton. Let me out. Herr Kolber is coming back." He lowered the pipe and sprang round. "What's that? What do you mean?"

"I thought you wouldn't come if you knew. There would have been time to love each other. Half an hour. And if he came in earlier, we could have lain quiet." Josef's brain worked quickly, he wasted no time in cursing the woman, but blew out the pipe and packed it back in his bag with the chisels and the jemmy and the skeleton-key and the pot of pepper. He surrendered without a second thought one of the easiest hauls of his career, but it was his pride that he took no avoidable risks. He had never been caught. Sometimes he had worked with partners and the partners had been caught, but they bore no malice. They recognised the extraordinary nature of Josef's record and went to prison with pride that he had escaped, and afterwards to their friends they would point him out: "That's Josef. Five years now and never jugged."

He closed his bag and jumped a little at a strange sound outside like the twanging of a bow. "What's that?"

Anna whispered through the door, "The lift. Someone has rung it down." He picked up a volume of *Railway Management*, but the safe glowed red with heat and he put it back on the desk. From below came the clang of a gate closing, the high hum of the lift. Josef stepped towards the curtain and drew the string on which the revolver dangled a couple of inches higher. He wondered whether it would be possible to escape through the window, but he remembered that there was a straight drop of thirty feet to the awning of the café. Then the gates opened and closed. Anna whispered through the key-hole: "The floor below."

That's all right, then, Josef thought, I can take my time. Back into Anna's bedroom and then over the roof. I shall have to wait twenty minutes for the Passau train. The chair under the handle was tightly wedged. He had to put down his bag and use both hands. The chair slid along the hardwood floor and crashed over. At the same moment the light went on.

"Stay where you are," said Herr Kolber, "and put your hands up."

Josef Grünlich obeyed at once. He turned round very slowly, and during those seconds formed his plan. "I'm not armed," he said gently, scanning Herr Kolber with mild reproachful eyes. Herr Kolber wore the blue uniform and the round peaked cap of an assistant station-master; he was small and thin with a brown crinkled face, and the hand holding the revolver shook a little with excitement and age and fury. For a moment Josef's mild eyes were narrowed and focused on the revolver, calculating the angle at which it would be fired, wondering whether the bullet would go astray. No, he thought, he will aim at my legs and hit my stomach. Herr Kolber had his back to the safe and could not yet have seen the disarranged books. "You don't understand," Josef said.

"What are you doing at that door?"

Josef's face was still red from the glow of the flame. "Me and Anna," he said.

Herr Kolber shouted at him, "Speak up, you scoundrel."

"Me and Anna are friends. I'm very sorry, Herr Superintendent, to be found like this. Anna invited me in."

"Anna?" Herr Kolber said incredulously. "Why?"

Josef's hips wriggled with embarrassment. "Well, Herr Kolber, you see how it is. Me and Anna are friends."

"Anna, come here." The door opened slowly, and Anna came out. She had put on her skirt and tidied her hair. "It's true, Herr Kolber." She gazed with horror past him at the exposed safe. "What's the matter with you? What are you staring at now? This is a fine kettle of fish. A woman of your age."

"Yes, Herr Kolber, but——" She hesitated and Josef interrupted her before she could defend herself, or accuse him. "I'm very fond of Anna." She accepted his words with a pitiable gratitude. "Yes, he told me that."

Herr Kolber stamped his foot. "You were a fool, Anna. Turn out his pockets. He's probably stolen your money." It still did not occur to him to examine his safe, and Josef played up to the part assigned to him of an inferior thief. He knew the type to the last bluster and the last whine. He had worked with them, employed them, and seen them depart to gaol without regret. Pickpennies, he called them, and he meant by the term that they were men without ambition or resource. "I haven't stolen her money," he whined. "I wouldn't do such a thing. I'm fond of Anna."

"Turn out his pockets." Anna obeyed, but her hands moved in his clothes like a caress. "Now his hip pocket."

"I don't carry a gun," Josef said.

"His hip pocket," Herr Kolber repeated, and Anna turned out the lining. When he saw that that pocket too was empty, Herr Kolber lowered his revolver, but he still quivered with elderly rage. "Making my flat a brothel," he said. "What have you got to say for yourself, Anna? This is a fine kettle of fish."

Anna, with her eyes on the floor, twisted her thin hands. "I don't know what came over me, Herr Kolber," but even while she spoke she seemed to learn. She looked up and Josef Grünlich saw in her eyes affection turn to distaste and distaste to anger. "He tempted me," she said slowly. All the while Josef was conscious of his black bag on the desk behind Herr Kolber's back, of the pile of books and the exposed safe, but uneasiness did not hamper thought. Sooner or later Herr Kolber would discover what had brought him to the flat, and already he had noticed close to the station-master's hand a bell which probably rang in the porter's flat.

"Can I put my hands down, Herr Superintendent?"

"Yes, but don't move an inch." Herr Kolber stamped his foot. "I'm going to have the truth of this if I keep you here all night. I won't have men coming here seducing my maid." The word "men" took Josef for a second off his guard; the idea of the middle-aged Anna as an object of pursuit amused him, and he smiled. Anna saw the smile and guessed the reason. She said to Herr Kolber, "Be careful. He didn't want me. He——" but Josef Grünlich took the accusation out of her mouth. "I'll confess. It was not Anna I came for. Look, Herr Kolber," and he waved his left hand towards the safe. Herr Kolber turned with his revolver pointing to the floor, and Josef shot him twice in the small of the back.

Anna put her hand to her throat and began to scream, looking away from the body. Herr Kolber had fallen on his knees with his forehead touching the floor; he wriggled once between the shots, and then the whole body would have fallen sideways if it had not been propped in its position by the wall. "Shut your mouth," said Josef, and when the woman continued to scream, he took her by the throat and shook her. "If you don't keep quiet for ten minutes, I'll put you underground too—see?" He saw that she had fainted and threw her into a chair; then he shut and locked the window and the bedroom door, for he was afraid that if she returned to the bedroom, her screams might be heard by the policeman when his beat took him to the goods-yard. The key he pushed down the lavatory pan with the handle of a scrubbing-brush. He made a last survey of the study; but he had already decided to leave the black bag on the desk; he always wore gloves, and the bag would bear only Anna's finger-prints. It was a pity to lose such a fine set of tools, but he was prepared to sacrifice anything which might endanger him, even he thought, looking at his watch, the ticket to Passau. The train would not leave for another quarter of an hour, and he could not linger in Vienna so long. He remembered the express he had seen from the roof, the express to Istanbul, and wondered: Can I make it without buying a ticket? He was unwilling to leave the trail of his features behind him, and it even crossed his mind to blind Anna with one of the chisels so that she might not be able to identify him. It was a passing thought; unnecessary violence was abhorrent to him, not because he disliked violence, but because he liked to be precise in his methods, omitting nothing which was necessary and adding nothing which was superfluous. Now with great care to avoid the blood he searched Herr Kolber's pockets for the study key, and when he had found it, he paused for a moment before a mirror to tidy his hair and brush his hat. Then he left the room, locking the door behind him and dropping the key into an umbrella-stand in the hall: he intended to do no more roof-climbing that night.

His only hesitation was when he saw the lift waiting with open door, but he decided almost at once to use the staircase, for the noise of the lift would blaze his trail past other flats. All the way down the stairs he listened for Anna's screams, but only silence followed him. The snow was still falling outside, quietening the wheels of cars, the tread of feet; but the silence up the stairs seemed to fall faster and more thickly and to disguise the signs he had left behind, the pile of books, the black bag, the scorched safe. He had never before killed a man, but as long as silence lasted, he could forget that he had taken the final step which raised him to the dangerous peak of his profession.

A door on the first floor was open, and as he passed he heard a petulant woman's voice, "Such drawers, I tell you. Well, I'm not the President's daughter, and I said to her, give me something respectable. Thin! You've never seen——"

Josef Grünlich twisted his thick grey moustache and stepped boldly out into the street, glancing this way, glancing that, as if he were expecting a friend. There was no policeman in sight, and as the pavements had been swept clear of snow, he left no prints. He turned smartly to the left towards the station, his ears pricked for the sound of screams, but he heard nothing but the hoot of taxi-cabs and the rustle of the snow. At the end of the street the great arch of the station enticed him like the lit façade of a variety theatre.

But it would be dangerous, he thought, to hang about the entrance like a seller of lottery tickets, and suddenly with the sense of dropping all the tenement's height, floor by floor, from Herr Kolber's flat, with the sense renewed of his own resource, the hand pointing to the safe, the quick pull on the string, and the revolver levelled and fired in one moment, pride filled him. I have killed a man. He let his overcoat flap open to the night breeze; he smoothed his waistcoat, fingered his silver chain; to an imaginary female friend he raised his soft grey hat, made by the best maker in Vienna, but a little too small for him, because it had been lifted from a lavatory peg. I, Josef Grünlich, have killed a man. I am clever, he thought, I'll be too much for them. Why should I hurry like a sneak thief to the station, slip inconspicuously through doorways, hide in the shadow of sheds? There's time for a cup of coffee, and he chose a table on the pavement, at the edge of the awning, which he had seen rise towards him when he slipped on the roof. He glanced upwards through the falling snow, one floor, two floors, three floors, and there was the lighted window of Herr Kolber's study; four floors, and the shadow of the building vanished in the grey loaded sky. It would have been an ugly fall.

"Der kaffee mit milch," he said. He stirred the coffee thoughtfully, Josef Grünlich, the man of destiny. There was nothing else to be done, he didn't hesitate. A shadow of discontent passed across his features when he thought: But I can tell no one of this. It would be too dangerous. Even his best friend, Anton, whose Christian name he had used, must remain in ignorance, for there might be a reward offered for information. Nevertheless, sooner or later, he assured himself, they would guess, and they will point me out: "There's Josef. He killed Kolber at Vienna, but they never caught him. He's never been caught."

He put down his glass and listened. Had it been a taxi or a noise from the station or a woman's scream? He looked round the tables; no one had heard anything odd, they were talking, drinking, laughing, and one man was spitting. But Josef Grünlich's thirst was a little dulled while he sat and listened. A policeman came down the street; he had probably been relieved from traffic duty and was on his way home, but Josef, lifting his glass, shielded his face and watched him covertly over the brim. Then quite certainly he heard a scream. The policeman stopped, and Josef, glancing anxiously round for the waiter, rose and laid some coins upon the table; the revolver between his legs had rubbed a small sore.

"Guten Abend." The policeman bought an evening paper and went down the street. Josef put his gloved fingers to his forehead and brought them down damp with sweat. This won't do, he thought, I mustn't get nervous; I must have imagined that scream, and he was about to sit down and finish his coffee when he heard it again. It was extraordinary that it should have passed unnoticed in the café. How long, he wondered, before she unlocks the window? Then they'll hear her. He left his table and out in the street heard the screams more clearly, but the taxis went hooting by, a few hotel porters staggered down the slippery pavement carrying bags; no one stopped, no one heard.

Something struck the pavement with the clink of metal, and Josef looked down. It was a copper coin. That's curious, he thought, a lucky omen, but stooping to pick it up, he saw at intervals, all the way from the café, copper and silver coins lying in the centre of the pavement. He felt in his trouser pocket and found nothing but a hole. My goodness, he thought, have I been dropping them ever since I left the flat? And he saw himself standing at the end of a clear trail that led, paving stone by paving stone, and then stair by stair, to the door of Herr Kolber's study. He began to walk rapidly back along the pavement, picking up the coins and cramming them into his overcoat pocket, but he had not reached the café when the glass of a window broke high up above his head and a woman's voice screamed over and over again: "Zu Hülfe! Zu Hülfe!" A waiter ran out of the café and stared upwards; a taxi-driver put on his brakes and ground his machine to a halt by the kerb; two men who had been playing chess left their pieces and ran into the road. Josef Grünlich had thought it very quiet under the falling snow, but only now was he confronted by real silence, as the taxi stopped and everyone in the café ceased speaking, and the woman continued to scream: "Zu Hülfe! Zu Hülfe!" Somebody said, "Die Polizei," and two policemen came running down the street with clinking holsters. Then everything became again as usual, except that a small knot of idle people gathered at the entrance to the flats. The two chess players went back to their game; the taxi-driver pressed his self-starter, and then because the cold had already touched his engine, climbed out to wind the handle. Josef Grünlich walked, not too rapidly, towards the station, and a newspaper seller began to pick up the coins he had left on the pavement. Certainly, Josef thought, I cannot wait for the

Passau train. But neither, he began to think, could he risk arrest for travelling without a ticket. But I haven't the money to get another; even my small change has gone. Josef, Josef, he abjured himself, don't make difficulties. You must get more. You are not going to give in now: Josef Grünlich, five years and never jugged. You've killed a man: surely for once you, the head of your profession, can do something which any pickpenny finds easy, steal a woman's handbag.

He kept his eyes alert as he went up the steps into the station. He must take no risks. If he was caught, he would have to face a life sentence, not a week in gaol. He must choose carefully. Several bags were almost thrust into his hands in the crowded hall, so carelessly were they guarded, but the owners looked too poor or too gad-about. The first would have only a few shillings; the others, as like as not, would keep in their bags not even small change, only a powder-puff, a lipstick, a mirror, perhaps some French letters.

At last he found what he wanted, something indeed better than he had hoped. A foreign woman, English probably, with short uncovered hair and red eyes, struggling with the door of a telephone-booth. Her bag had fallen at her feet while she put both hands to the handle. She was, he thought, a little drunk, and as she was foreign, she would have plenty of money in her bag. For Josef Grünlich the whole affair was child's play.

The door came open and Mabel Warren faced the black shining instrument which for ten years now had taken her best time and her best phrases. She stooped for her bag, but it was gone. Strange, she thought, I could have sworn—did I leave it in the train? She had eaten a farewell dinner on the train with Janet Pardoe. There had been a glass of sherry, the larger part of a bottle of hock, and two liqueur brandies. Afterwards she had been a little dazed. Janet had paid for the dinner and she had given Janet a cheque and taken the change; she had more than two pounds of small Austrian change in the pocket of her tweed jacket now, but in the bag were nearly eighty marks.

She had some difficulty in making the long distance exchange understand the number she wanted in Cologne, because her voice was a little muzzled. While she waited, balancing her top-heavy form on the small steel seat, she watched the barrier. Fewer and fewer passengers came from the platforms: there was no sign of Dr. Czinner. And yet, when she looked into his compartment ten minutes from Vienna, he was wearing his hat and mackintosh and he had answered her, "Yes, I am getting out." She had not trusted him, and when the train drew up, she waited until he left his compartment, watched him fumbling on the platform for his ticket, and would not then have let him out of her sight if it had not been necessary to telephone the office. For if he was lying she was determined to follow him to Belgrade and she would have no further opportunity to telephone that night. Did I leave my bag in the train? she wondered again, and then the telephone rang.

She looked at her wrist-watch: I've got ten minutes. If he doesn't come out in five, I'll go back to the train. It won't pay him to lie to me. "Hello. Is that the London *Clarion*? Edwards? Right. Get this down. No, my lad, this isn't the Savory story. I'll give you that in a moment. This is your bill-page lead, and you've got to hold it for half an hour. If I don't ring up again, shoot it off. The Communist outbreak at Belgrade, which was put down with some loss of life on Wednesday night, as reported in our later editions yesterday, was planned by the notorious agitator, Dr. Richard Czinner, who disappeared during the Kamnetz trial (no Kamnetz, K for Kaiser, A for Arse, M for Mule, N for Navel, no not that kind. It doesn't matter; it's the same letter. E for Erotic, T for Tart, Z for Zebra. Got it?), Kamnetz trial. Note to sub-editor. See press cuttings, August, 1927. He was believed to have been murdered by Government agents, but although a warrant was out for his arrest, he escaped, and in an exclusive interview with our special correspondent described his life as a schoolmaster at Great Birchington-on-Sea. Note to news-editor: Can't get him to speak about this; get the dope from the headmaster. His name's John. The outbreak at Belgrade was untimely; it had been planned for Saturday night, by which time Dr. Czinner, who left England on Wednesday evening, would have arrived in the capital and taken control. Dr. Czinner learnt of the outbreak and its failure when the express by which he was travelling reached Würzburg and immediately decided to leave the train at Vienna. He was heart-broken and could only murmur over and over again to our special correspondent: 'If only they had waited.' He was confident that if he had been present in Belgrade, the whole working class of the city would have supported the rising. In broken accents he gave our correspondent the amazing tale of his escape from Belgrade in 1927 and described the plans now prematurely ruined. Got that? Now listen carefully. If you don't get the rest of the dope in half an hour cancel everything after 'reaching Würzburg' and continue as follows: And after long and painful hesitation decided to continue his journey to Belgrade. He was heart-broken and could only murmur: 'Those fine brave fellows. How can I desert them?' When he had a little recovered he explained to our special correspondent that he had decided to stand his trial with the survivors, thus living up to the quixotic reputation he gained for himself at the time of the Kamnetz trial. His popularity with the working classes is an open secret, and his action may prove a considerable embarrassment to the Government.''

Miss Warren took a long breath and looked at her watch. Only five minutes now before the train left. ''Hello. Don't run away. Here's the bromide about Savory. You've got to be quick in getting this down. They've asked for half a column, but I haven't the time. I'll give you a few sticks. Mr. Quin Savory, author of *The Great Gay Round*, is on his way to the Far East in search of material for his new novel, *Going Abroad*. Although the book will have an eastern setting, the great novelist will not have quite deserted the London he loves so well, for he will view these distant lands through the eyes of a little London tobacconist. Mr. Savory, a slim bronzed figure, welcomed our correspondent on the platform at Cologne. He has a curt (don't be funny. I said curt. C.U.R.T.) manner which does not hide a warm and sympathetic heart. Asked to estimate his place in literature he said: 'I take my stand with sanity as opposed to the morbid introspection of such writers as Lawrence and Joyce. Life is a fine thing for the adventurous with a healthy mind in a healthy body.' Mr. Savory, who dresses quietly and without eccentricity, does not believe in the Bohemianism of some literary circles. 'They give up to sex,' he said, amusingly adapting Burke's famous phrase, 'what is meant for mankind.' Our correspondent pointed out the warm admiration which had been felt by countless readers for Emmy Tod, the little char in *The Great Gay Round* (which incidentally is now in its hundredth thousand). 'You have a wonderful knowledge of the female heart, Mr. Savory,' he said. Mr. Savory, who is unmarried, climbed back into his carriage with a debonair smile. 'A novelist,' he laughed, 'is something of a spy,' and he waved his hand gaily as the train carried him off. It is an open secret, by the way, that the Hon. Carol Delaine, the daughter of Lord Garthaway, will play the part of Emmy Tod, the chargirl, in the British film production of *The Great Gay Round*. Got that? Of course it's a bromide. What else can one do with the little swine?''

Miss Warren clapped down the receiver. Dr. Czinner had not appeared. She was angry, but satisfied. He had thought to leave her behind in Vienna station, and she pictured with pleasure his disappointment when he looked up from his paper to find her again in the doorway of his compartment. Closer than mud, she whispered to herself, that's what I'll be.

The official at the barrier stopped her: ''Fahrkarte, bitte.'' He was not looking at her, for he was busy collecting the tickets of passengers who had just arrived in some small local train, women with babies in arms and one man clasping a live hen. Miss Warren tried to brush her way through: ''Journalist's pass.'' The ticket collector turned to her suspiciously. Where was it?

''I've left my bag behind,'' said Miss Warren.

He collected the last ticket, shuffled the pasteboard into an even pile, round which with deliberation he twisted an india-rubber ring. The lady, he explained with stubborn courtesy, had told him when she came from the platform that she had a pass; she had waved a piece of card at him and brushed by before he could examine it. Now he would like to see that piece of card.

''Damn,'' said Miss Warren. ''Then my bag has been stolen.''

But the lady had just said that it was in the train.

Miss Warren swore again. She knew that her appearance was against her; she wore no hat, her hair was rumpled, and her breath smelt of drink. ''I can't help it,'' she said. ''I've got to get back on that train. Send a man with me and I'll give him the money.''

The ticket-collector shook his head. He could not leave the barrier himself, he explained, and it would be out of order to send any of the porters who were in the hall on to the platform to collect money for a ticket. Why should not the lady buy a ticket and then claim reimbursement from the company? ''Because,'' said Miss Warren furiously, ''the lady hasn't enough money on her.''

''In that case,'' the ticket-collector said gently, with a glance at the clock, ''the lady will have to go by a later train. The Orient Express will have gone. As for the bag, you need not worry. A telephone message can be sent to the next station.''

Somebody in the booking-hall was whistling a tune. Miss Warren had heard it before with Janet, the setting of a light voluptuous song, while hand in hand they listened in darkness, and the camera panned all the length of a studio street, picking a verse from this man's mouth as he leant from a window, from this woman who sold vegetables behind a barrow, from that youth who embraced a girl in the shadow of a wall. She put one hand to her hair. Into her thoughts and fears, into the company of Janet and Q. C. Savory, Coral and Richard Czinner, a young pink face was for a moment thrust, soft eyes beamed helpfully behind horn-rimmed glasses. "I guess, ma'am, you're having some trouble with this man. I'd be vurra proud to interpret for you."

Miss Warren spun round with fury. "Go and eat corn," she said and strode to the telephone box. The American had turned the scale between sentiment and anger, between regret and revenge. He thinks that he's safe, she thought, that he's shaken me off, that I can't do anything to him just because he's failed. But by the time the bell rang in the box she was quite calm. Janet might flirt with Savory, Coral with her Jew; Mabel Warren for the time being did not care. When there was a choice between love of a woman and hate of a man, her mind could cherish only one emotion, for her love might be a subject for laughter, but no one had ever mocked her hatred.

2

Coral Musker stared with bewilderment at the menu. "Choose for me," she said, and was glad that he ordered wine, for it will help, she thought, tonight. "I like your ring." The lights of Vienna fled by them into the dark, and the waiter leant across the table and pulled down the blind. Myatt said, "It cost fifty pounds." He was back in familiar territory, he was at home, no longer puzzled by the inconsistency of human behaviour. The wine list before him, the napkin folded on his plate, the shuffle of waiters passing his chair, all gave him confidence. He smiled and moved his hand, so that the stone glinted from different facets on the ceiling and on the wine glasses. "It's worth nearly twice that."

"Tell me about her," said Mr. W. C. Savory; "she's an odd type. Drinks?" "So devoted to me." "But who wouldn't be?" He leant forward crumbling bread and asked with caution: "I've never been able to understand. What can a woman like that *do*? . . ."

"No, I won't have any more of this foreign beer. My stomach won't stand it. Ask them, haven't they got a Guinness. I'd just fancy a Guinness."

"Of course you are having a great sports revival in Germany," said Mr. Opie. "Splendid types of young men, one sees. But still it's not the same as cricket. Take Hobbs and Sutcliffe . . ."

* * *

"Kisses. Always kisses."

"But I don't speak the lingo, Amy."

"Do you always say what a thing's worth? Do you know what I'm worth? Her perplexity and fear broke into irritation. "Of course you do. Ten pounds for a ticket."

"I explained," Myatt said, "all about that."

"If I was that girl there . . ." Myatt turned and saw the slender woman in her furs and was caught up and judged and set down again by her soft luminous eyes. "You are prettier," he said with open insincerity, trying again to catch the woman's gaze and learn the verdict. It's not a lie, he told himself, for Coral at her best is pretty, while with the stranger one could never use the insignificant measure of prettiness. But I should be dumb before her, he thought. I could not talk to her easily as I can to Coral; I should be conscious of my hands, of my race; and with a wave of gratitude he turned to Coral, "You're good to me."

He leant across the soup, the rolls and the cruet: "You *will* be good to me."

"Yes," she said, "tonight."

"Why only tonight? When we get to Constantinople why shouldn't you, why shouldn't we . . ." He hesitated. There was something about her which puzzled him: one small unvisited grove in all the acres of their familiarity.

"Live with you there?"

"Why not?" But it was not the reasons against his proposal which thronged her mind, which so coloured her thoughts that she had to focus her eyes more clearly on reality, the swaying train, men and women as far as she could see eating and drinking between the drawn blinds, the scraps of other people's talk.

"Yes, that's all. Kisses. Just kisses."

"Hobbs and Zudgliffe?"

It was all the reasons in favour: instead of the chill return at dawn to a grimy lodging and a foreign landlady, who would not understand her when she asked for a hot-water-bottle or a cup of tea, and would offer for a tired head some alien substitute for aspirin, to go back to a smart flat with shining taps and constant hot water and a soft bed with a flowered silk coverlet, that indeed would be worth any pain, any night's discomfort. But it's too good to be true, she thought, and tonight when he finds me cold and frightened and unused to things, he won't want me any longer. "Wait," she said. "You may not want me."

"But I do."

"Wait till breakfast. Ask me at breakfast. Or just don't ask me."

"No, not crickett. Not crickett," said Josef Grünlich, wiping his moustache. "In Germany we learn to run," and the quaintness of his phrase made Mr. Opie smile. "Have you been a runner yourself?"

"In my day," said Josef Grünlich, "I was a great runner. Nobody runned as well as I. Nobody could catch me."

* * *

"Heller."

"Don't swear, Jim."

"I wasn't swearing. It's the beer. Try some of this. It's not gassy. What you had before they call Dunkel."

"I'm so glad you liked it."

"That little char. I can't remember her name, she was lovely."

"Come back and talk a little after dinner."

"You won't be silly now, Mr. Savory?"

"I shall ask you."

"Don't promise. Don't promise anything. Talk about something else. Tell me what you are going to do in Constantinople."

"That's only business. It's tricky. The next time you eat spotted dog, think of me. Currants. I am currants," he added with a humorous pride.

"Then I'll call you spotted dog. I can't call you Carleton, can I? What a name."

"Look, have a currant. I always carry a few with me. Have one of these in this division. Good, isn't it?"

"Juicy."

"That's one of ours, Myatt, Myatt and Page. Now try one of these. What do you think of that?"

"Look through there in the first class, Amy. Can't you see her? Too good for us, that's what she is."

"With that Jew? Well, one knows what to think."

"I have the greatest respect of course, for the Roman Catholic Church," said Mr. Opie. "I am not bigoted. As an example of organisation . . ."

"So?"

"I am silly now."

"Juicy."

"No, no, that one's not juicy."

"Have I said the wrong thing?"

"That was one of Stein's. A cheap inferior currant. The vineyards are on the wrong side of the hills. It makes them dry. Have another. Can't you see the difference?"

"Yes, this is dry. It's quite different. But the other was juicy. You don't believe me, but it really was. You must have got them mixed."

"No, I chose the sample myself. It's odd. It's very odd."

All down the restaurant-cars fell the sudden concerted silence which is said to mean that an angel passes overhead. But through the human silence the tumblers tingled on the table, the wheels thudded along the iron track, the windows shook and sparks flickered like match heads through the darkness. Late for the last service Dr. Czinner came down the restaurant-car in the middle of the silence, with knees a little bent as a sailor keeps firm foothold in a stormy sea. A waiter preceded him, but he was unaware of being led. Words glowed in his mind and became phrases. You say that I am a traitor to my country, but I do not recognise my country. The dark downward steps, the ordure against the unwindowed wall, the starving faces. These are not Slavs, he thought, who owe a duty to this frock-coated figure or to that: they are the poor of all the world. He faced the military tribunal sitting under the eagles and the crossed swords: It is you who are old-fashioned with your machine-guns and your gas and your talk of country. Unconsciously as he walked the aisle from table to table he touched and straightened the tightly-knotted tie and fingered the Victorian pin: I am of the present. But for a moment into his grandiloquent dream obtruded the memory of long rows of malicious adolescent faces, the hidden mockery, the nicknames, the caricatures, the notes passed in grammars, under desks, the ubiquitous whispers impossible to place and punish. He sat down and stared without comprehension at the bill of fare.

Yes, I wouldn't mind being that Jew, Mr. Peters thought during the long angelic visitation, he's got a nice skirt all right, all right. Not pretty. I wouldn't say pretty, but a good figure, and that, said Mr. Peters to himself, watching his wife's tall angularity, remembering her murmurous stomach, that's the most important thing.

It was odd. He had chosen the samples with particular care. It was natural of course that even Stein's currants should not all be inferior, but when so much was suspected, a further suspicion was easy. Suppose, for example, Mr. Eckman had been doing a little trade on his own account, had allowed Stein some of the firm's consignment of currants, in order temporarily to raise the quality, had, on the grounds of that improved quality, indeed, induced Moults' to bid for the business. Mr. Eckman must be having uneasy moments now, turning up the time-table, looking at his watch, thinking that half Myatt's journey was over. Tomorrow, he thought, I will send a telegram and put Joyce in charge; Mr. Eckman shall have a month's holiday. Joyce will keep an eye on the books, and he pictured the scurryings to and fro, as in an ants' nest agitated by a man's foot, a telephone call from Eckman to Stein or from Stein to Eckman, a taxi ordered here and dismissed there, a lunch for once without wine, and then the steep office steps and at the top of them the faithful rather stupid Joyce keeping his eye upon the books. And all the time, at the modern flat, Mrs. Eckman would sit on her steel sofa knitting baby clothes for the Anglican mission, and the great dingy Bible, Mr. Eckman's first deception, would gather dust on its unturned leaf.

Q. C. Savory pushed the button of the spring blind and moonlight touched his face and his fish knife and turned the steel rails on the quiet up-line to silver. The snow had stopped falling and lay piled along the banks and between the sleepers, lightening the darkness. A few hundred yards away the Danube flickered like mercury. He could see tall trees fly backwards and telegraph-poles, which caught the moonlight on their metal arms as they passed. While silence held the carriage, he put the thought of Janet Pardoe away from him; he wondered what terms he could use to describe the night. It is all a question of choice and arrangement; I must show not all that I see but a few selected sharp points of vision. I must not mention the shadows across the snow, for their colour and shape are indefinite, but I may pick out the scarlet signal lamp shining against the white ground, the flame of the waiting-room fire in the country station, the bead of light on a barge beating back against the current.

Josef Grünlich stroked the sore on his leg where the revolver pressed and wondered: How many hours to the frontier? Would the frontier guards have received notice of the murder? But I am safe. My passport is in order. No one saw me take the bag. There's nothing to connect me with Kolber's flat. Ought I to have dropped the gun somewhere? he wondered, but he reassured himself: it might have been traced to me. They can tell miraculous things nowadays from a scratch on the bore. Crime grew more unsafe every year; he had heard rumours of a new finger-print stunt, some way by which they could detect the print even when the hand had been gloved. But they haven't caught me yet with all their science.

One thing the films had taught the eye, Savory thought, the beauty of landscape in motion, how a church tower moved behind and above the trees, how it dipped and soared with the uneven human stride, the loveliness of a chimney rising towards a cloud and sinking behind the further cowls. That sense of movement must be conveyed in prose, and the urgency of the need struck him, so that he longed for paper and pencil while the mood was on him and repented his invitation to Janet Pardoe to come back with him after dinner and talk. He wanted to work; he wanted for an hour or two to be free from any woman's intrusion. I don't want her, he thought, but as he snapped the blind down again, he felt again the prick of desire. She was well-dressed; she "talked like a lady"; and she had read his books with admiration; these three facts conquered him, still aware of his birthplace in Balham, the fugitive Cockney intonation of his voice. After six years of accumulative success, success represented by the figures of sales, 2,000, 4,000, 10,000, 25,000, 100,000, he was still astonished to find himself in the company of well-dressed women, and not divided by a thick pane of restaurant glass or the width of a counter. One wrote, day by day, with labour and frequent unhappiness, but with some joy, a hundred thousand words; a clerk wrote as many in an office ledger, and yet the words which he, Q. C. Savory, the former shop assistant, wrote had a result that the hardest work on an office stool could not attain; and as he picked at his fish and watched Janet Pardoe covertly, he thought not of current accounts, royalties and shares, nor of readers who wept at his pathos or laughed at his Cockney humour, but the long stairs to London drawing-rooms, the opening of double doors, the announcement of his name, faces of women who turned towards him with interest and respect.

Soon in an hour or two he will be my lover; and at the thought and the touch of fear at a strange relationship the dark knowing face lost its familiarity. When she fainted in the corridor he had been kind, with hands that pulled a warm coat round her, a voice that offered her rest and luxury; gratitude pricked at her eyes, and but for the silence all down the car she would have said: "I love you." She kept the words on her lips, so that she might break their private silence with them when the public silence passed.

The Press will be there, Czinner thought, and saw the journalists' box as it had been at the Kamnetz trial full of men scribbling and one man who sketched the general's likeness. It will be my likeness. It will be the justification of the long cold hours on the esplanade, when I walked up and down and wondered whether I had done right to escape. I must have every word perfect, remember clearly the object of my fight, remember that it is not only the poor of Belgrade who matter, but the poor of every country. He had protested many times against the national outlook of the militant section of the Social-Democratic party. Even their great song was national, "March, Slavs, march"; it had been adopted against his wishes. It pleased him that the passport in his pocket was English, the plan in his suitcase German. He had bought the passport at a little paper-shop near the British Museum, kept by a Pole. It was handed to him over the tea-table in the back parlour, and the thin spotty man, whose name he had already forgotten, had apologised for the price. "The expense is very bad," he complained, and while he helped his customer into his coat had asked mechanically and without interest: "How is your business?" It was quite obvious that he thought Czinner a thief. Then he had to go into the shop to sell an *Almanach Gaulois* to a furtive schoolboy. "March, Slavs, march." The man who had written the music had been bayoneted outside the sorting-room.

"Braised chicken! Roast veal . . ." The waiters called their way along the carriage and broke the minute's silence. Everyone began talking at once.

"I find the Hungarians take to cricket quite naturally. We had six matches last season."

"This beer's no better. I *would* just like a glass of Guinness."

"I do believe these currants——" "I love you." "Our agent—what did you say?" "I said that I loved you." The angel had gone, and noisily and cheerfully with the thud of wheels, the clatter of plates, voices talking and the tingle of mirrors, the express passed a long line of fir-trees and the flickering Danube. In the coach the pressure gauge rose, the driver turned the regulator open, and the speed of the train was increased by five miles an hour.

3

Coral Musker paused on the metal plates between the restaurant-car and the second-class coaches. She was jarred and shaken by the heave of the train, and for the moment she could not go on to fetch her bag from the compartment where Mr. Peters sat with his wife Amy. Away from the rattling metal, the beating piston, she stepped in thought, wrapping a fur coat round her, up the stairs to her flat. On the drawing-room table was a basket of hot-house roses and a card "with love from Carl," for she had decided to call him that. One could not say: "I love you, Carleton," but "I adore you, Carl" was easy. She laughed aloud and clapped her hands with the sudden sense that love was a simple affair, made up of gratitude and gifts and familiar jokes, a flat, no work, and a maid.

She began to run down the corridor, buffeted from one side to the other, but caring not at all. I'll go into the theatre three days late, and I shall say: "Is Mr. Sidney Dunn to be found?" But of course the door-keeper will be a Turk and only mutter through his whiskers, so I'll have to find my own way along the passage to the dressing-rooms, over a litter of firehoses, and I shall say "Good afternoon" or "Bong jour," and put my head into the general dressing-room and say "Where's Sid?" He'll be rehearsing in front, so I'll pop out of the wings at him, and he'll say, "Who the hell are you?" beating time while Dunn's Babies dance and dance and dance. "Coral Musker." "You're three days late. What the hell do you mean by it?" And I'll say, "I just looked in to give notice." She repeated the sentence aloud to hear how it would sound: "I just looked in to give notice," but the roar of the train beat her bravado into a sound more like a tremulous wail.

"Excuse me," she said to Mr. Peters, who was drowsing in his corner a little greasy after his meal. His legs were stretched across the compartment and barred her entry. "Excuse me," she repeated, and Mr. Peters woke up and apologised. "Coming back to us? That's right."

"No," she said, "I'm fetching my bag."

Amy Peters folded along a seat with a peppermint dissolving in her mouth said with sudden venom, "Don't speak to her, Herbert. Let her get her bag. Thinks she's too good for us."

"I only want my bag. What's getting your goat? I never said a word——"

"Don't get fussed, Amy," said Mr. Peters. "It's none of our business what this young lady does. Have another peppermint. It's her stomach," he said to Coral. "She's got indigestion."

"Young lady, indeed. She's a tart."

Coral had pulled her bag from beneath the seat, but now she set it down again firmly on Mr. Peters' toes. She put her hands on her hips and faced the woman, feeling very old and confident and settled, because the nature of the quarrel brought to mind her mother, arms akimbo, exchanging a few words with a neighbour, who had suggested that she was "carrying on" with the lodger. For that moment she was her mother; she had sloughed her own experiences as easily as a dress, the feigned gentility of the theatre, the careful speech. "Who do you think you are?" She knew the answer: shopkeepers on a spree, going out to Budapest on a Cook's tour, because it was a little farther than Ostend, because they could boast at home of being travellers, and show the bright labels of a cheap hotel on their suitcases. Once she would have been impressed herself, but she had learnt to take things casually, never to admit ignorance, to be knowing. "Who do you think you are talking to? I'm not one of your shopgirls. Not that you have any in your back street."

"Now, now," said Mr. Peters, touched on the raw by her discovery, "there's no call to get angry."

"Oh, isn't there. Did you hear what she called me? I suppose she saw you trying to get off with me."

"We know he wasn't good enough for you. Easy money's what you want. Don't think we want you in this carriage. I know where you belong."

"Take that stuff out of your mouth when you talk to me."

"Arbuckle Avenue. Catch 'em straight off the train at Paddington."

Coral laughed. It was her mother's histrionic laugh to call the neighbours to come and see the fight. Her fingers tingled upon her hips with excitement; she had been good so long, never dropped an aitch, or talked of a boy friend, or said "pleased to meet you." For years she had been hovering indecisively between the classes and belonged nowhere except to the theatre, with her native commonsense lost and natural refinement impossible. Now with pleasure she reverted to type. "I wouldn't be a scarecrow like you, not if you paid me. No wonder you've got a belly-ache with a face like that. No wonder your old man wanted a change."

"Now, now, ladies," said Mr. Peters.

"He wouldn't soil his hands with you. A dirty little Jew, that's all you're good for."

Coral suddenly began to cry, although her hands still flaunted battle, and she had voice enough to reply, "Keep off him," but Mrs. Peters' words remained smudged, like the dissolving smoke of an aerial advertisement, across the fair prospect.

"Oh, we know he's your boy."

"My dear," said a voice behind her, "don't let them worry you."

"Here's another of your friends."

"So?" Dr. Czinner put his hand under Coral's elbow and insinuated her out of the compartment.

"Jews and foreigners. You ought to be ashamed."

Dr. Czinner picked up the suitcase and laid it in the corridor. When he turned back to Mrs. Peters, he showed her not the harassed miserable face of the foreign master, but the recklessness and the sarcasm which the journalists had noted when he took the witness-box against Kamnetz. "So?" Mrs. Peters took the peppermint out of her mouth; Dr. Czinner, thrusting both hands into the pockets of his mackintosh, swayed backwards and forwards upon his toes. He appeared the master of the situation, but he was uncertain how to speak, for his mind was still full of grandiloquent phrases, of socialist rhetoric. He was made harsh by the signs of oppression, but he lacked for the moment words with which to contest it. They existed, he was aware, somewhere in the obscurity of his mind, glowing phrases, sentences as bitter as smoke. "So?"

Mrs. Peters began to find her courage. "What are you barging your head in about? It's a bit too much. First one Nosey Parker, then another. Herbert, you do something."

Dr. Czinner began to speak. In his thick accent the words assumed a certain ponderous force that silenced, though they did not convince, Mrs. Peters. "I am a doctor." He told them how useless it was to expect from them the sense of shame. The girl last night had fainted; he had ordered her for her health to have a sleeper. Suspicion only dishonoured the suspicious. Then he joined Coral Musker in. the corridor. They were out of sight of the compartment, but Mrs. Peters' voice was clearly audible, "Yes, but who pays? That's what I'd like to know." Dr. Czinner pressed the back of his head against the glass and whispered with hatred, "Bourgeois."

"Thank you," Coral said, and added, when she saw his expression of disappointment, "Can I do anything? Are *you* ill?"

"No, no," he said. "But I was useless. I have not the gift of making speeches." He leant back against the window and smiled at her. "You were better. You talked very well."

"Why were they such beasts?" she asked.

"They are always the same, the bourgeois," he said. "The proletariat have their virtues, and the gentleman is often good, just and brave. He is paid for something useful, for governing or teaching or healing, or his money is his father's. He does not deserve it perhaps, but he has done no one harm to get it. But the bourgeois —he buys cheap and sells dear. He buys from the worker and sells back to the worker. He is useless."

Her question had not required an answer. She stared at him, bewildered by the flood of his explanation and the strength of his conviction, without understanding a word of what he said. "I didn't do them any harm."

"Ah, but you've done them great harm. So have I. We have come from the same class. But we earn our living honestly, doing no harm but some good. We are an example against them, and they do not like that."

Out of this explanation she picked the only phrase she understood. "Aren't you a gentleman?"

"No, and I am not a bourgeois."

She could not understand the faint boastfulness of his reply, for ever since she left her home it had been her ambition to be mistaken for a lady. She had studied to that end with as much care as an ambitious subaltern studies for the staff college: every month her course included a new number of *Woman and Beauty*, every week a *Home Notes*; she examined in their pages the photographs of younger stars and of the daughters of the obscurer peers, learning what accessories were being worn and what were the powders in favour.

He began to advise her gently, "If you cannot take a holiday, try to keep as quiet as possible. Do not get angry for no reason——"

"They called me a tart." She could see that the word meant nothing to him. It did not for a moment ruffle the surface of his mind. He continued to talk gently about her health, not meeting her eyes. He's thinking of something else, she thought, and stooped impatiently for her bag, intending to leave him. He forestalled her by a spate of directions about sedatives and fruit juices and warm clothes. Obscurely she realised a change in his attitude. Yesterday he had wanted solitude, now he would seize any excuse to keep her company a minute longer. "What did you mean," she asked, "when you said 'My proper work'?"

"When did I say that?" he asked sharply.

"Yesterday when I was faint."

"I was dreaming. I have only one work." He said no more, and after a moment she picked up her bag and went.

Nothing in her experience would have enabled her to realise the extent of the loneliness to which she had abandoned him. "I have only one work." It was a confession which frightened him, for it had not been always true. He had not lived beside and grown accustomed to the idea of a unique employment. His life had once been lit by the multitude of his duties. If he had been born with a spirit like a vast bare room, covered with the signs of a house gone down in the world, scratches and peeling paper and dust, his duties, like the separate illuminations of a great candelabra too massive to pawn, had adequately lit it. There had been his duty to his parents who had gone hungry that he might be educated. He remembered the day when he took his degree, and how they had visited him in his bed-sitting-room and sat quiet in a corner watching him with respect, even with awe, and without love, for they could not love him now that he was an educated man; once he heard his father address him as "Sir." Those candles had blown out early, and he had hardly noticed the loss of two lights among so many, for he had his duty to his patients, his duty to the poor of Belgrade, and the slowly growing idea of his duty to his own class in every country. His parents had starved themselves that he might be a doctor, he himself had gone hungry and endangered his health that he might be a doctor, and it was only when he had practised for several years that he realised the uselessness of his skill. He could do nothing for his own people; he could not recommend rest to the worn-out or prescribe insulin to the diabetic, because they had not the money to pay for either.

He began to walk the corridor, muttering a little to himself. Small flakes of snow were again falling; they were blown against the windows like steam.

There had been his duty to God. He corrected himself: to a god. A god who had swayed down crowded aisles under a bright moth-worn canopy, a god the size of a crown-piece enclosed in a gold framework. It was a two-faced god, a deity who comforted the poor in their distress as they raised their eyes to his coming between the pillars, and a deity who had persuaded them, for the sake of a doubtful future, to endure their pain, as they bowed their heads, while the surge of the choristers and the priests and the singing passed by. He had blown that candle out with his own breath, telling himself that God was a fiction invented by the rich to keep the poor content; he had blown it out with a gesture, with a curious old-fashioned sense of daring, and he sometimes felt an unreasoning resentment against those who nowadays were born without religious sense and were able to laugh at the seriousness of the nineteenth-century iconoclast.

And now there was only one dim candle to light the vast room. I am not a son, he thought, nor a doctor, nor a believer, I am a Socialist; the word mouthed by politicians on innumerable platforms, printed in bad type on bad paper in endless newspapers rang cracked. I have failed even there. He was alone, and his single light was guttering, and he would have welcomed the company of anyone.

When he reached his compartment and found a stranger there he was glad. The man's back was turned, but he spun quickly round on short stout legs. The first thing which Dr. Czinner noticed was a silver cross on his watch-chain, the next that his suitcase was not in the same spot where he had left it. He asked sadly, "Are you, too, a reporter?"

"Ich spreche kein Englisch," the man replied. Dr. Czinner said in German, while he barred the way into the corridor, "A police spy? You are too late." His eyes were still on the silver cross, which swung backwards and forwards with the man's movement; it might have been lurching to the human stride, and for a moment Dr. Czinner flattened himself against the wall of a steep street to let the armoured men, the spears and the horses pass, and the tired tortured man. He had not died to make the poor contented, to bind the chains tighter; his words had been twisted.

"I am not a police spy."

Dr. Czinner paid the stranger small attention as he faced the possibility that, if the words had been twisted, some of the words might have been true. He argued with himself that the doubt came only from the approach of death, because when the burden of failure was almost too heavy to bear, a man inevitably turned to the most baseless promise. "I will give you rest." Death did not give rest, for rest could not exist without the consciousness of rest.

"You misunderstand me, Herr——"

"Czinner." He relinquished his name to the stranger without hesitation; the time was past for disguises, and in the new veracious air he had to doff not only the masks of identity. There were words which he had not inquired into closely, common slogans which he had accepted because they helped his cause: "Religion is the rich man's friend." He said to the stranger: "If you are not a police spy, who are you? What have you been doing here?"

"My name," and the fat man bobbed a little from the waist, while a finger twisted the bottom button of his waistcoat, "is——" The name was tossed into the bright snow-lit darkness, drowned by the roar of the train, the clatter of steel piles, an echoing bridge; the Danube, like a silver eel, slipped from one side to the other of the line. The man had to repeat his name, "Josef Grünlich." He hesitated and then continued, "I was looking for money, Herr Czinner."

"You've stolen——"

"You came back too soon." He began slowly to explain. "I have escaped from the police. Nothing disgraceful, Herr Czinner, I can assure you." He twisted and twisted his waistcoat button, an unconvincing alien talker in the newly-lit air of Dr. Czinner's brain, populated only by incontestable truths, by a starving face, a bright rag, a child in pain, a man staggering up the road to Golgotha. "It was a political offence, Herr Czinner. An affair of a newspaper. A great injustice has been done me, and so I had to fly. It was for the sake of the cause that I opened your suitcase." He blew out the word "cause" with a warm intense breath, cheapening it into a shibboleth, an easy emotion. "You will call the guard?" He fixed his knees, and his finger tightened on the button.

"What do you mean by your cause?"

"I am a Socialist." The realisation came sharply to Dr. Czinner that a movement could not be judged by its officers; socialism was not condemned by the adherence of Grünlich, but he was anxious, none the less, to forget Grünlich. "I will let you have some money." He took out his pocket-book and handed the man five English pounds. "Good night."

It was easy to dismiss Grünlich and it had cost him little, for money would be of no value to him in Belgrade. He did not need a lawyer to defend him: his defence was his own tongue. But it was less easy to evade the thought which Grünlich had left behind, that a movement was not condemned by the dishonesty of its officers. He himself was not without dishonesty, and the truth of his belief was not altered because he was guilty of vanity, of several meannesses; once he had got a girl with child. Even his motives in travelling first class were not unmixed; it was easier to evade the frontier police, but it was also more comfortable, more fitted to his vanity as a leader. He found himself praying: "God forgive me." But he was shut off from any assurance of forgiveness, if there existed any power which forgave.

The guard came and looked at his ticket. "Snowing again," he said. "It is worse up the line. It will be lucky if we get through without delay." He showed an inclination to stay and talk. Three winters ago, he said, they had had a bad time. They had been snowed up for forty-eight hours on one of the worst patches of the line, one of the bare Balkan patches; no food to be got, and the fuel had to be saved.

"Shall we reach Belgrade to time?"

"One can't tell. My experience is—snow this side of Buda, twice as much snow before Belgrade. It's a different case before we reach the Danube. It can be snowing in Munich and like summer at Buda. Good night, Herr Doktor. You'll be having patients in this cold." The guard went down the corridor beating his hands together.

Doctor Czinner did not stay long in his compartment; the man who had shared it had left the train at Vienna. Soon it would be impossible to see even passing lights through the window; the snow was caked in every crevice and ice was forming on the glass. When a signal-box or a station lamp went by its image was cut into wedges by the streaks of opaque ice, so that for a moment the window of the train became a kaleidoscope in which the jumbled pieces of coloured glass were shaken. Dr. Czinner wrapped his hands for warmth in the loose folds of his mackintosh and began again to walk the corridor. He passed through the guard's van and came out into the third-class carriages which had been attached to the train at Vienna. Most of the compartments were in darkness except for a dim globe burning in the roof. On the wooden seats the passengers were settling themselves for the night with rolled coats under their heads; some of the compartments were so full that the men and women slept bolt upright in two rows, their faces green and impassive in the faint light. There was a smell of cheap red wine from the empty bottles under the seats, and a few scraps of sour bread lay on the floor. When he came near the lavatory he turned back, the smell was too much for him. Behind him the door blew open and shut with the shaking of the express.

I belong there, he thought without conviction; I should be travelling third class. I do not wish to be like a constitutional Labour member taking his first-class ticket to cast his vote in a packed parliament. But he comforted himself with the thought of how he would have been delayed by frequent changes and how he might have been held up at the frontier. He remained aware nevertheless of the mixture of his motives; they had only begun to worry him since his knowledge of failure; all his vanities, meannesses and small sins would have been swept to darkness in the thrill and unselfishness of victory. But he wished, now that all depended on his tongue, that he could make his speech from the dock with a conscience perfectly clear. Small things in his past, which his enemies would never know, might rise in his own mind to clog his tongue. I failed utterly with those two shopkeepers; shall I succeed any better in Belgrade?

Because his future had an almost certain limit, he began to dwell, as he was not accustomed to do, on the past. There had been a time when a clear conscience could be bought at the price of a moment's shame: "since my last confession, I have done this or that." If, he thought with longing and a little bitterness, I could get back my purity of motive so easily, I should be a fool not to take the chance. My regret for what I have done is not less now than then, but I have no conviction of forgiveness; I have no conviction that there is anyone to forgive. He came near to sneering at his last belief: Shall I go and confess my sins to the treasurer of the Social-Democratic party, to the third-class passengers? The priest's face turned away, the raised fingers, the whisper of a dead tongue, seemed to him suddenly as beautiful, as infinitely desirable and as hopelessly lost as youth and first love in the corner of the viaduct wall.

It was then that Dr. Czinner caught sight of Mr. Opie alone in a second-class compartment, writing in a notebook.

He watched him with a kind of ashamed greed, for he was about to surrender to a belief which it had been his pride to subdue. But if it gives me peace, he protested, and at the still darkling associations of the word he pulled the door back and entered the compartment. The long pale face and pale eyes, the impression of inherited culture, embarrassed him; by his request he would admit the priest's superiority; and he was again for a moment the boy with grubby hands blushing in the dark of the confessional at his commonplace sins. He said in his stiff betraying English, "Will you excuse me? Perhaps I am disturbing you. You want to sleep?"

"Not at all. I get out at Buda. I don't suppose I shall sleep," he laughed deprecatingly, "until I am safe ashore."

"My name is Czinner."

"And mine is Opie." To Mr. Opie his name had conveyed nothing; perhaps it was kept in mind only by journalists. Dr. Czinner drew the door to and sat down in the opposite seat. "You are a priest?" He tried to add "father," but the word stuck on his tongue; it meant too much, it meant a grey starved face, affection hardening into respect, sacrifice into suspicion of a son grown like an enemy. "Not of the Roman persuasion," said Mr. Opie. Dr. Czinner was silent for several minutes, uncertain how to word his request. His lips felt dry with a literal thirst for righteousness, which was like a glass of ice-cold water on a table in another man's room. Mr. Opie seemed aware of his embarrassment and remarked cheerfully, "I am making a little anthology." Dr. Czinner repeated mechanically, "Anthology?"

"Yes," said Mr. Opie, "a spiritual anthology for the lay mind, something to take the place in the English church of the Roman books of contemplation." His thin white hand stroked the black wash-leather cover of his notebook. "But I intend to strike deeper. The Roman books are, what shall I say? too exclusively religious. I want mine to meet all the circumstances of everyday life. Are you a cricketer?"

The question took Dr. Czinner by surprise; he had again in memory been kneeling in darkness, making his act of contrition. "No," he said, "no."

"Never mind. You will understand what I mean. Suppose that you are the last man in; you have put on your pads; eight wickets have fallen; fifty runs must be made; you wonder whether the responsibility will fall upon you. You will get no strength for that crisis from any of the usual books of contemplation; you may indeed be a little suspicious of religion. I aim at supplying that man's need."

Mr. Opie had spoken rapidly and with enthusiasm, and Dr. Czinner found his knowledge of English failing him. He did not understand the words "pad," "wickets," "runs"; he knew that they were connected with the English game of cricket; he had become familiar with the words during the last five years and they were associated in his mind with salty wind-swept turf, the supervision of insubordinate children engaged on a game which he could not master; but the religious significance of the words escaped him. He supposed that the priest was using them metaphorically: "responsibility," "crisis," "man's need," these phrases he understood, and they gave him the opportunity he required to make his request.

"I wished to speak to you," he said, "of confession." At the sound of the word he was momentarily young again.

"It's a difficult subject," said Mr. Opie. He examined his hands for a moment and then began to speak rapidly. "I am not dogmatic on the point. I think there is a great deal to be said for the attitude of the Roman church. Modern psychology is working on parallel lines. There is a similarity in the relationship between the confessor and the penitent and that between the psycho-analyst and the patient. There is, of course, this difference, that one claims to forgive the sins. But the difference," Mr. Opie continued hurriedly, as Dr. Czinner tried to speak, "is not after all very great. In the one case the sins are said to be forgiven and the penitent leaves the confessional with a clear mind and the intention of making a fresh start; in the other the mere expression of the patient's vices and the bringing to light of his unconscious motives in practising them are said to remove the force of the desire. The patient leaves the psycho-analyst with the power, as well as the intention, of making a fresh start." The door into the corridor opened, and a man entered. "From that point of view," said Mr. Opie, "confession to the psycho-analyst seems to be more efficacious than confession to the priest."

"You are discussing confession?" the newcomer asked. "May I draw a red 'erring across your argument? There's a literary aspect to be considered."

"Let me introduce you to each other," said Mr. Opie. "Dr. Czinner—Mr. Q. C. Savory. We really have here the elements of a most interesting discussion; the doctor, the clergyman, and the writer."

Dr. Czinner said slowly: "Have you not left out the penitent?"

"I was going to introduce him," Mr. Savory said. "In a way surely *I* am the penitent. In so far as the novel is founded on the author's experience, the novelist is making a confession to the public. This puts the public in the position of the priest and the analyst."

Mr. Opie countered him with a smile. "But your novel is a confession only in so far as a dream is a confession. The Freudian censor intervenes. The Freudian censor," he had to repeat in a louder voice as the train passed under a bridge. "What does the medical man say?" Their polite bright attentive gaze confused Dr. Czinner. He sat with head a little bent, unable to bring the bitter phrases from his mind to his lips; speech was failing him for a second time that evening; how could he depend on it when he reached Belgrade?

"And then," said Mr. Savory, "there's Shakespeare."

"Where is there not?" said Mr. Opie. "He strides this narrow world like a colossus. You mean——"

"What was his attitude to confession? He was born, of course, a Roman Catholic."

"In *Hamlet*," began Mr. Opie, but Dr. Czinner waited no longer. He rose and made two short bows. "Good night," he said. He wanted to express his anger and disappointment, but all he found to say was: "So interesting." The corridor, lit only by a chain of dim blue globes, sloped grey and vibrating towards the dark vans. Somebody turned in his sleep and said in German, "Impossible. Impossible."

When Coral left the doctor she began to run, as fast as was possible with a suitcase in a lurching train, so that she was out of breath and almost pretty when Myatt saw her pulling at the handle of his door. He had put away the correspondence from Mr. Eckman and the list of market prices ten minutes ago, because he found that always, before the phrases or the figures could convey anything to his mind, he heard the girl's voice: "I love you."

What a joke, he thought, what a joke.

He looked at his watch. No stop now for seven hours and he had tipped the guard. He wondered whether they got used to this kind of affair on long-distance trains. When he was younger he used to read stories of king's messengers seduced by beautiful countesses travelling alone and wonder whether such good fortune would ever happen to him. He looked at himself in the glass and pressed back his oiled black hair. I am not bad-looking if my skin were not so sallow; but when he took off his fur coat, he could not help remembering that he was growing fat and that he was travelling in currants and not with a portfolio of sealed papers. Nor is she a beautiful Russian countess, but she likes me and she has a pretty figure.

He sat down, and then looked at his watch and got up again. He was excited. You fool, he thought, she's nothing new; pretty and kind and common, you can find her any night on the Spaniards road, and yet in spite of these persuasions he could not but feel that the adventure had in it a touch of freshness, of unfamiliarity. Perhaps it was only the situation: travelling at sixty miles an hour in a berth little more than two feet across. Perhaps it was her exclamation at dinner; the girls he had known were shy of using that phrase; they would say "I love you" if they were asked, but their spontaneous tribute was more likely to be "You're a nice boy." He began to think of her as he had never thought before of any woman who was attainable: she is dear and sweet, I should like to do things for her. It did not occur to him for several moments that she had already reason for gratitude.

"Come in," he said, "come in." He took the suitcase from her and pushed it under the seat and then took her hands.

"Well," she said with a smile, "I'm here, aren't I?" In spite of her smile he thought her frightened and wondered why. He loosed her hands in order to pull down the blinds of the corridor windows, so that they seemed suddenly to become alone in a small trembling box. He kissed her and found her mouth cool, soft, uncertainly responsive. She sat down on the seat which had become converted into a berth and asked him, "Did you wonder whether I'd come?"

"You promised," he reminded her.

"I might have changed my mind."

"But why?" Myatt was becoming impatient. He did not want to sit about and talk; her legs, swinging freely without touching the floor, excited him. "We'll have a nice time." He took off her shoes and ran his hands up her stockings. "You know a lot, don't you?" she said. He flushed. "Do you mind that?"

"Oh, I'm glad," she said, "so glad. I couldn't bear it if you hadn't known a lot." Her eyes large and scared, her face pale under the dim blue globe, first amused him, then attracted him. He wanted to shake her out of aloofness into passion. He kissed her again and tried to slip her frock over her shoulder. Her body trembled and moved under her dress like a cat tied in a bag; suddenly she put her lips up to him and kissed his chin. "I do love you," she said, "I do."

The sense of unfamiliarity deepened round him. It was as if he had started out from home on a familiar walk, past the gas works, across the brick bridge over the Wimble, across two fields, and found himself not in the lane which ran uphill to the new road and the bungalows, but on the threshold of a strange wood, faced by a shaded path he had never taken, running God knows where. He took his hands from her shoulders and said without touching her: "How sweet you are," and then with astonishment: "How dear." He had never before felt the lust rising in him checked and increasing because of the check; he had always spilt himself into new adventures with an easy excitement.

"What shall I do? Shall I take off my clothes?" He nodded, finding it hard to speak, and saw her rise from the berth and go into a corner and begin to undress slowly and very methodically, folding each garment in turn and laying it neatly on the opposite seat. He was conscious as he watched her calm movements of the inadequacy of his body. He said, "You are lovely," and his words stumbled with an unfamiliar excitement. When she came across the carriage he saw that he had been deceived; her calm was like a skin tightly drawn; her face was flushed with excitement and her eyes were scared; she looked uncertain whether to laugh or cry. They came together quite simply in the narrow space between the seats. "I wish the light would go right out," she said. She stood close against him while he touched her with his hands, both swaying easily to the motion of the train. "No," he said.

"It would be more becoming," she said and began to laugh quietly to herself. Her laughter lay, an almost imperceptible pool of sound, beneath the pounding and the clatter of the express, but when they spoke, instead of whispering, they had to utter the intimate words loudly and clearly.

The sense of strangeness survived even the customary gestures; lying in the berth she proved awkward in a mysterious innocent fashion which astonished him. Her laughter stopped, not coming gradually to an end, but vanishing so that he wondered whether he had imagined the sound or whether it had been a trick of the glancing wheels. She said suddenly and urgently, "Be patient, I don't know much," and then she cried out with pain. He could not have been more startled if a ghost had passed through the compartment dressed in an antique wear which antedated steam. He would have left her if she had not held him to her with her hands, while she said in a voice of which snatches only escaped the sound of the engine, "Don't go. I'm sorry. I didn't mean . . ." Then the sudden stopping of the train lurched them apart. "What is it?" she said. "A station." She protested with pain, "Why must it now?"

Myatt opened the window a little way and leant out. The dim chain of lights lit the ground for only a few feet beside the line. Snow already lay inches thick; somewhere in the distance a red spark shone intermittently, like a revolving light between the white gusts. "It isn't a station," he said. "Only a signal against us." The stilling of the wheels made the night very quiet with one whistle of steam to break it; here and there men woke and put their heads out of windows and spoke to each other. From the third-class carriages at the rear of the train came the sound of a fiddle. The tune was bare, witty, mathematical, but in its passage through the dark and over the snow it became less determinate, until it picked from Myatt's mind a trace of perplexity and regret: "I never knew. I never guessed." There was such warmth in the carriage now between them that, without closing the window, he knelt beside the berth and put his hand to her face, touching her features with curious fingers. Again he was overwhelmed with the novel thought, "How sweet, how dear." She lay quiet, shaken a little by quick breaths of pain or excitement.

Somebody in the third-class carriages began to curse the fiddler in German, saying that he could not sleep for the noise. It seemed not to occur to him that he had slept through the racket of the train, and that it was the silence surrounding the precise slow notes which woke him. The fiddler swore back and went on fiddling, and a number of people began to talk at once, and someone laughed.

"Were you disappointed?" she asked. "Was I awfully bad at it?"

"You were lovely," he said. "But I never knew. Why did you agree?"

She said in a tone as light as the fiddle's, "A girl's got to learn some time." He touched her face again. "I hurt you."

"It wasn't a picnic," she said.

"Next time," he began to promise, but she interrupted with a question which made him laugh by its gravity: "There'll be another time? Did I pass all right?"

"You want another time?"

"Yes," she said, but she was thinking not of his embrace, but of the flat in Constantinople and her own bedroom and going to bed at ten. "How long will you stay out there?"

"Perhaps a month. Perhaps longer." She whispered with so much regret, "So soon," that he began to promise many things he knew very well he would regret in daylight. "You can come back with me. I'll give you a flat in town." Her silence seemed to emphasise the wildness of his promises. "Don't you believe me?"

"Oh," she said in a voice of absolute trust, "it's too good to be true."

He was touched by the complete absence of coquetry, and remembered again with sudden force that he had been her first lover. "Listen," he said, "will you come again tomorrow?" She protested with real apprehension that he would tire of her before they reached Constantinople. He ignored her objection. "I'd give a party to celebrate."

"Where? In Constantinople?"

"No," he said, "I've no one to invite there," and for a moment the thought of Mr. Eckman cast a shadow over his pleasure.

"What, in the train?" She began to laugh again, but this time in a contented and unfrightened way.

"Why not?" he became a little boastful. "I'll invite everyone. It'll be a kind of wedding dinner."

She teased him, "Without the wedding," but he became the more pleased with his idea. "I'll invite everyone: the doctor, that person in the second class, the inquisitive fellow (do you remember him?)" He hesitated for a second. "That girl." "What girl?" "The niece of your friend." But his grandiloquence was a little dashed by the thought that she would never accept his invitation; she is not a chorus girl, he thought with shame at his own ingratitude, she is not pretty and easy and common, she is beautiful, she is the kind of woman I should like to marry; and for a moment he contemplated with a touch of bitterness her inaccessibility. Then he recovered his spirits. "I'll get the fiddler," he boasted, "to play to us while we eat."

"You wouldn't dare to invite them," she said with shining eyes.

"I will. They'll never refuse the kind of dinner I'll pay for. We'll have the best wine they can give us," he said, making rapid calculations of cost and choosing to forget that a train reduces all wine to a common mediocrity. "It'll cost two pounds a head."

She beat her hands together in approval. "You'll never dare to tell them the reason."

He smiled at her. "I'll tell them it's to drink the health of my mistress." For a long time then she lay quiet, dwelling on the word and its suggestion of comfort and permanence, almost of respectability. Then she shook her head, "It's too good to be true," but her expression of disbelief was lost in the whistle of steam and the grinding of the wheels into motion.

While the couplings between the carriages strained and the signal burning a green light lurched slowly by, Josef Grünlich was saying, "I am the President of the Republic." He woke as a gentleman in a tailcoat was about to present him with a golden key to open the new city safe deposits; he woke at once to a full knowledge of his surroundings and to a full memory of his dream. Leaning his hands upon his fat knees he began to laugh. President of the Republic, that's good, and why not? I can spin a yarn all right. Kolber and that doctor both deceived in one day. Five English pounds he gave me, because I was sharp and spotted what he was when he said, "Police spy." Quick, that's Josef Grünlich all over. "Look over there, Herr Kolber." Flick at the string, aim, fire, all in one second. And I've got away with it too. They can't catch Josef. What was it the priest said? Josef began to laugh deep down in his belly. "Do you play cricket in Germany?" And I said, "No, they teach us to run. I was a great runner in my time." That was quick if you like, and he never saw the joke, said something about "Sobs and Hudglich."

But it was a bad moment all the same, thought Josef, staring out into the falling snow, when the doctor spotted that his bag had been moved. I'd got my finger on the string. If he'd tried to call the guard I'd have shot him in the stomach before he could shout a word. Josef laughed again happily, feeling his revolver rub gently against the sore on the inside of his knee: I'd have spilt his guts for him.

PART FOUR

Subotica

1

The telegraph receiving set in the station-master's office at Subotica flickered; dots and dashes were spilt into the empty room. Through the open door Lukitch, the clerk, sat in a corner of the parcels office and cursed the importunate sounds. But he made no effort to rise. "It can't be important at this hour," he explained to the parcels clerk and to Ninitch, a young man in a grey uniform, one of the frontier guards. He shuffled a pack of cards and at the same time the clock struck seven. Outside an indeterminate sun was breaking over grey half-melted snow, the wet rails glinted. Ninitch sipped his glass of *rakia*; the heavy plum wine brought tears to his eyes; he was very young.

Lukitch went on shuffling. "What do you think it's all about?" asked the parcels clerk. Lukitch shook his grimy tousled head. "One can't tell of course. But I shouldn't be surprised all the same. It will serve her right." The parcels clerk began to giggle. Ninitch raised his dark eyes, that could contain no expression save simplicity, and asked: "Who is she?" To his imagination the telegraph began to speak in an imperious feminine way.

"Ah, you soldiers," said the parcels clerk. "You don't know half of what goes on."

"That's true," Ninitch said. "We stand about for hours at a time with our bayonets fixed. There's not going to be another war, is there? Up to the barracks and down to the station. We don't have time to see things." Dot, dot, dot, dash, went the telegraph. Lukitch dealt the pack into three equal piles; the cards sometimes stuck together and he licked his fingers to separate them. He ranged the three piles side by side in front of him. "It's probably the station-master's wife," he explained. "When she goes away for a week she sends him telegrams at the oddest times, every day. Late in the evening or early in the morning. Full of tender expressions. In rhyme sometimes: 'Your little dove sends all her love,' or 'I think of you faithfully and ever so tenderly.' "

"Why does she do it?" asked Ninitch.

"She's afraid he may have one of the servants in bed with him. She thinks he'll repent if he gets a telegram from her just at the moment."

The parcels clerk giggled. "And of course the funny part is, he wouldn't look at his servants. His inclinations, if she only knew it, are all the other way."

"Your bets, gentlemen," said Lukitch and he watched them narrowly, while they put copper coins on two of the piles of cards. Then he dealt out each pack in turn. In the third pack, on which no money had been placed, was the knave of diamonds. He stopped dealing and pocketed the coins. "Bank wins," he said, and passed the cards to Ninitch. It was a very simple game.

The parcels clerk stubbed out his cigarette and lit another, while Ninitch shuffled. "Was there any news on the train?"

"Everything quiet in Belgrade," said Lukitch.

"Is the telephone working?"

"Worse luck." The telegraph had stopped buzzing, and Lukitch sighed with relief. "That's over, anyway."

The soldier suddenly stopped shuffling and said in a puzzled voice, "I'm glad I wasn't in Belgrade."

"Fighting, my boy," said the parcels clerk hilariously.

"Yes," said Ninitch shyly, "but they were, weren't they, our own people? It was not as if they were Bulgars."

"Kill or be killed," said the parcels clerk. "Come, deal away, Ninitch, my boy."

Ninitch began to deal; several times he lost count of the cards; it was obvious that something was on his mind. "And then, what did they want? What did they want to get by it all?"

"They were Reds," said Lukitch.

"Poor people? Make your bets, gentlemen," he added mechanically. Lukitch piled all the coppers he had won on the same heap as the parcels clerk; he caught the clerk's eye and winked; and the other man increased his bet. Ninitch was too absorbed in his slow clumsy thoughts to realise that he had shown the position of the knave when he dealt. The parcels clerk could not restrain a giggle. "After all," said Ninitch, "I am poor, too."

"We've made our bets," said Lukitch impatiently, and Ninitch dealt out the cards. His eyes opened a little wider when he saw that both bets had been successful; for a moment a faint suspicion affected his manner; then he counted out the coins and rose. "Are you going to stop?" asked Lukitch.

"Must be getting back to the guard-room."

The parcels clerk grinned. "He's lost all his money. Give him some more *rakia* before he goes, Lukitch." Lukitch poured out another glass and stood with bottle tipped. The telephone-bell was ringing. "The devil," he said. "It's that woman." He put the bottle down and went into the other room. A pale sun slanted through the window and touched the crates and trunks piled behind the counter. Ninitch raised his glass, and the parcels clerk sat with one finger on the pack of cards listening. "Hello, hello!" bellowed Lukitch in a rude voice. "Who do you want? The telegraph? I've heard nothing. I can't hang over it the whole time. I've got a lot to do in this station. Tell the woman to send her telegrams at a reasonable hour. What's that?" His voice suddenly changed. "I'm very sorry, sir. I never dreamed . . ." The parcels clerk giggled. "Of course. Immediately, sir, immediately. I'll send at once, sir. If you would not mind holding the line for two minutes, sir . . ."

Ninitch sighed and went out into the bitter air of the small platformless station.

He had forgotten to put on his gloves, and before he could huddle them on, his fingers were nipped by the cold. He dragged his feet slowly through the first half-melted and then half-frozen mud and snow. No, I am glad I was not in Belgrade, he thought. It was all very puzzling; they were poor and he was poor; they had wives and children; he had a wife and a small daughter; they must have expected to gain something by it, those Reds. The sun getting up above the roof of the customs-shed touched his face with the ghost of warmth; a stationary engine stood like a stray dog panting steam on the up-line. No train would be passing through to Belgrade before the Orient express was due; for half an hour there would be clamour and movement, the customs-officers would arrive and the guards be posted conspicuously outside the guard-room, then the train would steam out, and there would be only one more train, a small cross-country one to Vinkovce, that day. Ninitch buried his hands in his empty pockets: then would be the time for more *rakia* and another game of cards: but he had no money. Again a slight suspicion that he had been cheated touched his stubborn mind.

"Ninitch. Ninitch." He looked round and saw the station-master's clerk plunging after him through the slush without overcoat or gloves. Ninitch thought: He has robbed me, his heart has been touched by God, he is going to make restitution. He stopped and smiled at Lukitch, as much as to say: Have no fear, I am not angry with you. "You fool, I thought I should never make you hear," said the clerk, panting at his side, small and grimy and ill-natured. "Go at once to Major Pet-kovitch. He's wanted on the telephone. I can't make the guard-room answer."

"The telephone went out of order last night," Ninitch explained, "while the snow fell."

"Incompetence," fumed the clerk.

"A man was coming from the town to see to it today." He hesitated. "The major won't come out in the snow. He has a fire in his room so high."

"Fool. Imbecile," said the clerk. "It's the Chief of Police speaking from Belgrade. They were trying to send through a telegram, but you were talking so hard, how could anyone hear? Be off." Ninitch began to walk on towards the guard-room, but the clerk screamed after him, "Run, you fool, run." Ninitch broke into a trot, handicapped by his heavy boots. It's curious, he thought, one's treated like a dog, but a moment later he thought: After all, it's good of them to play cards with me; they must earn in a day what I earn in a week; and they get paid, too, he said to himself, considering the deductions from his own pay for mess, for quarters, for fires. "Is the major in?" he asked in the guard-room and then knocked timidly on the door. He should have passed the message through the serjeant, but the serjeant was not in the room, and in any case one never knew when an opportunity for special service might arise, and that might lead to promotion, more pay, more food, a new dress for his wife.

"Come in."

Major Petkovitch sat at his desk facing the door. He was short, thin, sharp-featured, and wore pince-nez. There was probably some foreign blood in his family, for he was fair-haired. He was reading an out-of-date German book on strategy and feeding his dog with pieces of sausage. Ninitch stared with envy at the roaring fire. "Well, what is it?" the major asked irritably, like a schoolmaster disturbed while going through his pupils' exercises.

"The Chief of Police has rung up, sir, and wants you on the telephone in the station-master's office."

"Isn't our own telephone working?" the major asked, trying, not very successfully, as he laid down the book, to hide his curiosity and excitement; he wanted to give the impression of being on intimate terms with the Chief of Police.

"No, sir, the man hasn't come from the town yet."

"How very trying. Where is the serjeant?"

"He's gone out for a moment, sir."

Major Petkovitch plucked at his gloves and smoothed them. "You had better come with me. I may need a messenger. Can you write?"

"A very little, sir." Ninitch was afraid that the major would choose another messenger, but all he said was, "Tut." Ninitch and the dog followed at the major's heels across the guard-room and over the rails. In the station-master's office Lukitch was making a great show of work in a corner, while the parcels clerk hung round the door totting up entries on a folio sheet. "The line is quite clear, sir," said Lukitch and scowled at Ninitch behind the major's back; he envied his proximity to the instrument.

"Hello, hello, hello," called Major Petkovitch acidly. The private soldier leant his head a little towards the telephone. Over the long miles between the frontier and Belgrade came the ghost of a cultured insolent voice with an intonation so clear that even Ninitch, standing two feet away from the instrument, could catch the measured syllables. They fell, like a succession of pins, into a deep silence: Lukitch and the parcels clerk held their breath in vain; the stationary engine across the track had stopped panting. "Colonel Hartep speaking." It is the Chief of Police, Ninitch thought, I have heard him speak: how proud my wife will be this evening: the story will go all around the barracks, trust her for that. She has not much reason to be proud of me, he considered simply, without self-depreciation, she makes the very most of what she has.

"Yes, yes, this is Major Petkovitch."

The insolent voice was a little lowered; Ninitch caught the words only in snatches. "On no account . . . Belgrade . . . search the train."

"Should I take him to the barracks?"

The voice rose a little in emphasis. "No. As few people must see him as possible. . . . On the spot."

"But really," Major Petkovitch protested, "we haven't the accommodation here. What can we do with him?"

". . . a few hours only."

"By court-martial? It's very irregular." The voice began to laugh gently. "Myself . . . with you by lunch . . ."

"But in the event of an acquittal?"

". . . myself," said the voice indistinctly, "you, Major, Captain Alexitch." It fell lower still. "Discreet . . . among friends," and then more clearly, "He may not be alone . . . suspects . . . any excuse . . . the customs. No fuss, mind."

Major Petkovitch said in a tone of the deepest disapproval, "Is there anything else, Colonel Hartep?" The voice became a little animated. "Yes, yes. About lunch. I suppose you haven't got much choice up there. . . . At the station . . . a good fire . . . something hot . . . cold things in the car and wine." There was a pause. "Remember, you're responsible."

"For something so irregular," began Major Petkovitch. "No, no, no," said the voice, "I was referring, of course, to lunch."

"Is everything quiet in Belgrade?" Major Petkovitch asked stiffly. "Fast asleep," the voice said.

"May I ask one more question?"

Major Petkovitch called, "Hello. Hello. Hello," in an irritated voice and then slammed down the receiver. "Where's that man? Come with me," and again followed by Ninitch and his dog he plunged into the cold, crossed the rails and the guard-room, and slammed the door of his room behind him. Then he wrote a number of notes very briefly and handed them to Ninitch for delivery: he was so hurried and irritated that he forgot to seal two of them. These, of course, Ninitch read; his wife would be proud of him that evening. There was one to the chief customs officer, but that was sealed; there was one to the captain at the barracks telling him to double the station guard immediately and to serve out twenty rounds of ammunition per man. It made Ninitch uneasy; did it mean war, that the Bulgars were coming? Or the Reds? He remembered what had happened at Belgrade and was very much disturbed. After all, he thought, they are our own people, they are poor, they have wives and children. Last of all there was a note for the cook at the barracks, containing detailed instructions for a lunch for three, to be served hot in the major's room at one-thirty; "Remember, you're responsible," it ended.

When Ninitch left the room, Major Petkovitch was again reading the out-of-date German book on strategy, while he fed his dog with pieces of sausage.

2

Coral Musker had fallen asleep long before the train reached Budapest. When Myatt drew a cramped arm from under her head, she woke to a grey morning like the swell of a leaden sea. She scrambled quickly from the berth and dressed; she was hurried and excited and she mislaid things. She began to sing light-heartedly under her breath: *I'm so happy, Happy-go-lucky me.* The motion of the train flung her against the window, but she gave the grey morning only a hurried glance. Lights came out here and there, one after the other, but there was not yet day enough to see the houses by; a lamp-lit bridge across the Danube gleamed like the buckle of a garter. *I just go my way, Singing every day.* Somewhere down by the river a white house glowed; it might have been mistaken for a tree trunk in an orchard, but for two lights in ground-floor rooms; as she watched, they were turned out. They've been celebrating late; she wondered, what's been going on there? and laughed a little, feeling herself at one with all daring, scandalous and youthful things. *Things that worry you Never worry me. Summer follows Spring. I just smile and . . .* Quite dressed now except for her shoes, she turned towards the berth and Myatt.

He was uneasily asleep and needed a shave; he lay in rumpled clothes, and she could connect him with the excitement and pain of the night only with difficulty. This man was a stranger; he would disclaim responsibility for words spoken by an intruder in the dark. So much had been promised her. But she told herself that that kind of good fortune did not come her way. The words of elderly experienced women were brought again to mind: "They'll promise anything beforehand," and the strange moral code of her class warned her: "You mustn't remind them." Nevertheless she approached him and with her hand tried gently to arrange his hair into some semblance of her lover's. As she touched his forehead he woke, and she faced with courage the glance which she feared to see momentarily blank with ignorance of who she was and what they had done together. She fortified herself with maxims: "There's as good fish in the sea," but to her glad amazement he said at once without any struggle to remember, "Yes, we must have the fiddler."

She clapped her hands together in relief: "And don't forget the doctor." She sat down on the edge of the berth and slipped on her shoes. *I'm so happy.* He remembers, he's going to keep his promise. She began to sing again: *Living in the sunlight, loving in the moonlight, Having a wonderful time.* The guard came down the corridor knocking on the door: "Budapest." The lights were clustering together; above the opposite bank of the river, apparently dropped half-way from the heavy sky, shone three stars. "What's that? There. It's going. Quick."

"The castle," he said.

"Budapest." Josef Grünlich, nodding in his corner, started awake and went to the window. He had a flashing glimpse of water between tall grey houses, of lights burning in upper rooms, cut off abruptly by the arch of the station, and then the train slid to rest in a great echoing hall. Mr. Opie at once emerged, brisk and cheerful and laden, dumping two suitcases upon the ground, and then a golf bag, and a tennis racket in its case. Josef grinned and blew out his chest; the sight of Mr. Opie reminded him of his crime. A man in Cook's uniform came by leading a tall crumpled woman and her husband; they stumbled at his heels, bewildered, and unhappy through the whistling steam and the calling of strange tongues. It seemed to Josef that he might leave the train. Immediately, because this was something which concerned his safety, he ceased to think either humorously or grandiloquently; the small precise wheels of his brain went round and like the auditing machine in a bank began to record with unfailing accuracy the debits and credits. In a train he was virtually imprisoned; the police could arrange his arrest at any point of his journey; therefore the sooner he was at liberty the better. As an Austrian he would pass unnoticed in Budapest. If he continued his journey to Constantinople, he would run the risk of three more customs examinations. The automatic machine ran again through the figures, added, checked and passed on to the debit side. The police in Budapest were efficient. In the Balkan countries they were corrupt and there was nothing to fear from the customs. He was farther from the scene of his crime. He had friends in Istanbul. Josef Grünlich decided to go on. The decision made, he again leant back in a dream of triumph; images of revolvers quickly drawn flashed through his mind, voices spoke of him: "There's Josef. Five years now and never jugged. He killed Kolber at Vienna."

"Budapest." Dr. Czinner ceased writing for a little more than a minute. That small pause was the tribute he paid to the city in which his father had been born. His father had left Hungary when a young man and settled in Dalmatia; in Hungary he had been a peasant, toiling on another man's land; in Split and eventually in Belgrade he had been a shoemaker working for himself; and yet the previous more servile existence, the inheritance of a Hungarian peasant's blood, represented to Dr. Czinner the breath of a larger culture blowing down the dark stinking Balkan alleys. It was as if an Athenian slave, become a freed man in barbarian lands, regretted a little the statuary, the poetry, the philosophy of a culture in which he had had no share. The station began to float away from him; names slipped by in a language which his father had never taught him: "Restoracioj," "Pôsto," "Informoj." A poster flapped close to the carriage window: "Teatnoj Kaj Amuzejoj," and mechanically he noted the unfamiliar names, the entertainments which would be just opening as the train arrived at Belgrade, the Opera, the Royal Orfeum, the Tabarin, and the Jardin de Paris. He remembered how his father had often commented, in the dark basement parlour behind his shop: "They enjoy themselves in Buda." His father, too, had once enjoyed himself in the city, pressing his face against the glass of restaurants, watching, without envy, the food carried to the tables, the fiddlers moving from group to group, making merry himself in a simple vicarious way. He had been angered by his father's easy satisfaction.

He wrote for ten minutes more and then folded the paper and slipped it into the pocket of his mackintosh. He wished to be prepared for any eventuality; his enemies he knew had no scruples; they would rather see him quickly murdered in a back street than alive in the dock. The strength of his position lay in their ignorance of his coming; he had to proclaim his voluntary presence in Belgrade before they knew that he was there, for then there could be no quick assassination of an unidentified stranger; they would have no choice but to put him upon his trial. He opened his suitcases and took out the Baedeker. Then he lit a match and held it to the corner of the map; the shiny paper burned slowly. The railway shot up in a little lick of flame, and he watched the post office square turn into tough black ash. Then the green of the park, the Kalimagdan, turned brown. The streets of the slum quarter were the last to burn, and he blew the flame to hasten it.

When the map was quite burned he threw the ash under the seat, put a bitter tablet on his tongue, and tried to sleep. He found it difficult. He was a man without humour or he would have smiled at the sudden lightness of his heart, as he recognised, fifty miles beyond Buda, a sudden break in the great Danube plain, a hill shaped like a thimble and shaggy with fir trees. A road made a great circle to avoid it and then shot straight towards the city. Road and hill were both white now under the snow, which hung in the trees in great lumps like the nests of rooks. He remembered the road and the hill and the wood because they were the first things he had noted with a sense of full security after escaping across the frontier five years before. His companion who drove the car had broken silence for the first time since they left Belgrade and called to him: "We shall be in Buda in an hour and a quarter." Dr. Czinner had not realised till then that he was safe. Now his lightness of heart had opposite cause. He thought not that he was only fift miles from Budapest, but that he was only seventy miles from the frontier. He was nearly home. Instinct for the moment was stronger in him than opinion. It was no use telling himself that he had no home and that his destination was a prison; for that one moment of light-hearted enjoyment it was to Kruger's beer-garden, to the park at evening swimming in green light, to the steep streets and the bright rags that he was journeying. After all, he told himself, I shall see all this again; they'll drive me from the prison to the court. It was then that he remembered with unreasoning melancholy that the beer-garden had been turned into flats.

Across the breakfast table Coral and Myatt faced each other with immeasurable relief as strangers. At dinner they had been old friends with nothing to say to one another. All through breakfast they talked fast and continuously as if the train was consuming time, not miles, and they had to fill the hours with talk sufficient for a life together.

"And when I get to Constantinople, what shall I do? My room's been booked."

"Never mind that. I've taken a room at an hotel. You'll come with me and we'll make it a double room."

She accepted his solution with breathless pleasure, but there was no time for silence, for sitting back. Rocks, houses, bare pastures were receding at fifty miles an hour, and there was much to be said. "We get in at breakfast time, don't we? What shall we do all day?"

"We'll have lunch together. In the afternoon I'll have to go to the office and see to things there. You can go shopping. I'll be back in the evening and we'll have dinner and go to the theatre."

"Yes, and what theatre?" It was extraordinary to her, the transformation which the night had caused. His face no longer resembled that of all the Jewish boys she had known with half intimacy; even the gesture with which he gave and gave, the instinctive spreading of the hands, was different; his emphasis on how much he would spend, on what a good time he would give her, was unique because she believed him.

"We'll have the best seats at your theatre."

"Dunn's Babies?"

"Yes, and we'll take them all out to dinner afterwards, if you like."

"No." She shook her head; she could not risk losing him now, and many of Dunn's Babies would be prettier than she. "Let's go back to bed after the theatre." They began to laugh over their coffee, spilling brown drops upon the tablecloth.

There was no apprehension in her laugh; she was happy because pain was behind her. "Do you know how long we've sat at breakfast?" she asked. "A whole hour. It's a scandal. I've never done it before. A cup of tea in bed at ten o'clock is my breakfast. And two pieces of toast and some orange juice if I've got a nice landlady."

"And when you haven't any work?"

She laughed. "I leave out the orange juice. Are we near the frontier now?"

"Very near." Myatt lit a cigarette. "Smoke?"

"Not in the morning. I'll leave you to it." She got up and at the same moment the train ground across a point and she was flung against him. She caught his arm to steady herself and over his shoulder saw a signal-box sway dizzily out of sight and a black shed against which the snow had drifted. She held his arm a moment till her giddiness passed. "Darling, come soon. I'll be waiting for you." Suddenly she wanted to say to him, "Come now." She felt afraid at being left alone when the train was in a station. Strangers might come in and take his seat, and she would be unable to make them understand. She would not know what the customs men said to her. But she told herself that he would soon tire if she made demands on him; it wasn't safe to trouble a man; her happiness was not so secure that she dared take the smallest risk with it. She looked back; he sat with head a little bent, caressing with his fingers a gold cigarette-case. She was glad later that she had taken that last glance, it was to serve as an emblem of fidelity, an image to carry with her, so that she might explain, "I've never left you."

The train stopped as she reached her seat, and she looked out of the window at a small muddy station. Subotica was printed in black letters on a couple of lamps; the station buildings were little more than a row of sheds, and there was a platform. A group of customs-officers in green uniforms came down between the lines with half a dozen soldiers; they seemed in no hurry to begin their search. They laughed and talked and went on towards the guard's van. A row of peasants stood watching the train, and one woman suckled a child. There were a good many soldiers about with nothing to do; one of them shooed the peasants off the rails, but they scrambled over them again twenty yards down the line. The passengers began to grow impatient; the train was half an hour late already, and no attempt had yet been made to search the luggage or examine the passports. Several people climbed on to the line and crossed the rails in hope of finding a refreshment-room; a tall thin German with a bullet head walked up and down, up and down. Coral Musker saw the doctor leave the train, wearing his soft hat and mackintosh and a pair of grey wool gloves. He and the German passed and repassed and passed again, but they might have been walking in different worlds for all the notice they took of each other. Once they stood side by side while an official looked at their passports, but they still belonged to different worlds, the German was fuming and impatient, and the doctor was smiling to himself.

When she came near him she could see the quality of his smile, vacuous and sentimental. It seemed out of place. "Excuse me speaking to you," she said humbly, a little frightened by his stiff respectful manner. He bowed and put his grey gloved hands behind him; she caught a glimpse of a hole in the thumb. "I was wondering

. . . we were wondering . . . if you would have dinner with us tonight.'' The smile had been tidied away, and she saw him gathering together a forbidding weight of words. She explained, ''You have been so kind to me.'' It was very cold in the open air and they both began to walk; the frozen mud crackled round the tops of her shoes and marked her stockings. ''It would have given me great pleasure,'' he said, marshalling his words with terrible correctness, ''and it is my sorrow that I cannot accept. I am leaving the train tonight at Belgrade. I should have enjoyed . . .'' He stopped in his stride with creased brows and seemed to forget what he was saying; he put the hand in the worn glove into his mackintosh pocket. ''I should have enjoyed . . .'' Two men in uniform were walking up the line towards them.

The doctor put his hand on her arm and swung her gently round, and they began to walk back along the train. He was still frowning and he never finished his sentence. Instead, he began another, ''I wonder if you would mind—my glasses are frosted over—what do you see in front of us?''

''There are a few customs-officers coming down from the guard's van to meet us.''

''Is that all? In green uniform?''

''No, in grey.''

The doctor stopped. ''So?'' He took her hand in his, and she felt an envelope folded into her palm. ''Go quickly back to your carriage. Hide this. When you get to Istanbul post it. Go now quickly. But don't seem in a hurry.'' She obeyed without understanding him; twenty steps brought her up to the men in grey and she saw that they were soldiers; they carried no rifles, but she guessed it by their bayonet sheaths. They barred her way, and for a moment she thought they would stop her; they were talking rapidly among themselves, but when she came within a few feet of them, one man stepped aside to let her by. She was relieved but still a little frightened, feeling the letter folded in her hand. Was she being made to smuggle something? A drug? Then one of the soldiers came after her; she heard his boots cracking the mud; she reassured herself that she was imagining things, that if he wanted her he would call, and his silence encouraged her. Nevertheless, she walked more rapidly. Her compartment was only one carriage away, and her lover would be able to explain in German to the man who she was. But Myatt was not in the compartment; he was still smoking in the restaurant. For a second she hesitated. I will go to the restaurant and tap on the window, but her second's hesitation had been too long. A hand touched her elbow, and a voice said something to her gently in a foreign tongue.

She swung round to protest, to implore, ready, if need be, to break away and run to the restaurant-car, but her fears were a little quietened by the soldier's large gentle eyes. He smiled at her and nodded his head and pointed to the station buildings. She said, ''What do you want? Can't you speak English?'' He shook his head and smiled again and pointed, and she saw the doctor meet the soldiers and walk with them towards the buildings. There could be nothing wrong, he was walking in front of them, they were not using force. The soldier nodded and smiled and then with a great effort brought out three words of English. "All quite good," he said and pointed again to the buildings.

"Can I just tell my friend?" she asked. He nodded and smiled and took her arm, leading her gently away from the train.

The waiting-room was empty except for the doctor. A stove burnt in the middle of the floor, and the view from the windows was broken by lines of frost. She was conscious all the while of the letter in her hand. The soldier ushered her in gently and politely and then closed the door without locking it. "What do they want?" she asked. "I mustn't miss the train."

"Don't be frightened," he said. "I'll explain to them; they'll let you go in five minutes. You must let them search you if they want to. Have they taken the letter?"

"No."

"Better give it to me. I don't want to get you into trouble." She held out her hand and at the same moment the door opened. The soldier came in and smiled encouragingly and took the letter from her. Dr. Czinner spoke to him, and the man talked rapidly; he had simple unhappy eyes. When he had gone again Dr. Czinner said, "He doesn't like it. He was told to look through the key-hole and see if anything passed between us."

Coral Musker sat down on a wooden seat and stuck her feet out towards the stove. Dr. Czinner noted with amazement, "You are very calm."

"It's no use getting shirty," she said. "They can't understand, anyway. My friend'll be looking for me soon."

"That's true," he said with relief. He hesitated for a moment. "You must wonder why I do not apologise to you for this—discomfort. You see there's something I hold more important than any discomfort. I expect you don't understand."

"Don't I, though," she said, thinking with wry humour of the night. A long whistle shivered through the cold air and she sprang up apprehensively. "That's not our train, is it? I can't miss it." Dr. Czinner was at the window. He freed the inner surface from steam with the palm of his hand and peered between the ridges of frost. "No," he said, "it's an engine on the other line. I think they are changing engines. It will take them a long time. Don't be frightened."

"Oh, I'm not scared," she said, settling herself again on the hard seat. "My friend'll be along soon. *They'll* be scared then. He's rich, you know."

"So?" said Dr. Czinner.

"Yes, and important too. He's the head of a firm. They do something with currants." She began to laugh. "He told me to think of him when I eat spotted dog."

"So?"

"Yes. I like him. He's been sweet to me. He's quite different from other Jews. They're generally kind, but he—well, he's quiet."

"I think that he must be a very lucky young man," said Dr. Czinner. The door was opened and two soldiers pushed a man in. Dr. Czinner moved quickly forward and put his foot in the door. He spoke to them softly. One of them replied, the other thrust him back and closed and locked the door. "I asked them," he said, "why they were keeping you here. I told them you must catch the train. One of them said it was quite all right. An officer wants to ask you a question or two. The train doesn't go for half an hour.''

"Thank you,'' Coral said.

"And me?'' said the newcomer in a furious voice. "And me?''

"I know nothing about you, Herr Grünlich.''

"The customs they came and they search me. They take my cannon. They say: 'Why haven't you declared that you keep a cannon in possession?' I say: 'No one would travel in your country without a cannon.' '' Coral Musker began to laugh: Josef Grünlich glared at her wickedly, then he smoothed his rumpled waistcoat, glanced at his watch, and sat down. With his hands on his fat knees he stared straight in front of him, considering.

He must have finished his cigarette by now, Coral thought. He'll have gone back to the compartment and found I'm not there. Perhaps he'll wait ten minutes before he asks one of the men at the station whether they've seen me. In twelve minutes he'll have found me. Her heart leapt when a key turned in the lock, wondering at the speed with which he had traced her, but it was not Myatt who entered, but a fair fussed officer. He snapped an order over his shoulder and two soldiers came in behind him and stood against the door.

"But what's it all about?'' Coral asked Dr. Czinner. "Do they think we've smuggled something?'' She could not understand what the foreigners said to each other, and suddenly she felt lost and afraid, knowing that however much these men might wish to help her, they could not understand what she said or what she wanted. She implored Dr. Czinner, "Tell them I must catch this train. Ask them to tell my friend.'' He took no notice, but stood stiffly by the stove with his hands in his pockets answering questions. She turned to the German in the corner, staring at the toes of his shoes. "Tell them that I've done nothing, please.'' He raised his eyes for a moment and looked at her with hatred.

At last Dr. Czinner said, "I have tried to explain that you know nothing of the note I passed you. But he says he must keep you a little longer until the Chief of Police has questioned you.''

"But the train?'' she implored, "the train?''

"I think it will be all right. It will be here for another half an hour. I have asked him to let your friend know and he says that he will see what can be done.'' She went to the officer and touched his arm. "I must go by this train,'' she said, "I must. Do understand me, please.'' He shook his arm free, and rebuked her in a sharp precise tone, his pince-nez nodding, but what the terms of the rebuke were she could not tell. Then he left the waiting-room.

Coral pressed her face to the window. Between two fronds of frost the German passed, walking up and down the track; she tried to see as far as the restaurant-car. "Is he in sight?'' Dr. Czinner asked.

"It's going to snow again,'' she said, and left the window. Suddenly she could bear her perplexity no longer. "Why do they want me? What are they keeping me here for?''

He assured her, "It's a mistake. They are frightened. There has been rioting in Belgrade. They want me, that's all.''

"But why? You're English, aren't you?"

"No, I'm one of them," he said with some bitterness.

"What have you done?"

"I've tried to make things different." He explained with an air of distaste for labels: "I am a Communist."

At once she exclaimed, "Why? Why?" watching him fearfully, unable to hide that she felt her faith shaken in the only man, except Myatt, able and willing to help her. Even the kindness he had shown her on the train she now regarded with suspicion. She went to the bench and sat down as far as she could from the German.

"It would take a long time to tell you why," he said. She took no notice, shutting her mind to the meaning of any words he uttered. She thought of him now as one of the untidy men who paraded on Saturday afternoons in Trafalgar Square bearing hideous banners: "Workers of the World, Unite," "Walthamstow Old Comrades," "Balham Branch of the Juvenile Workers' League." They were the kill-joys, who would hang the rich and close the theatres and drive her into dismal free love at a summer camp, and afterwards make her walk in procession down Oxford Street, carrying her baby behind a banner: "British Women Workers."

"Longer than I've got," he said.

She took no notice. She was, for the moment in her thoughts, immeasurably above him. She was a rich man's mistress, and he was a workman. When she at last took notice of him it was with contempt: "I suppose you'll go to gaol."

"I think they'll shoot me," he said.

She stared at him in amazement, forgetting their difference in class: "Why?" He smiled with a touch of conceit: "They're afraid."

"In England," she said, "they let the Reds speak as much as they like. The police stand round."

"Ah, but there's a difference. We do more than speak."

"But there'll be a trial?"

"A sort of trial. They'll take me to Belgrade."

Somewhere a horn was blowing, and the cold air was split by a whistle. "They must be shunting," Dr. Czinner said to reassure her. A film of smoke was blown across the windows, darkening the waiting-room, and voices called and feet began to run along the track outside. Links between coaches groaned and pushed and strained, and then the thin walls shook to the grinding of pistons, the beat of heavy wheels. When the smoke cleared, Coral Musker sat quite still on the wooden bench. There was nothing to be said and her feet were stone cold. But after a while she began to read in Dr. Czinner's silence an accusation, and she spoke with warmth, "He'll come back for me," she said. "You wait and see."

Ninitch let his rifle fall into the crook of his arm and beat his gloved hands together. "That new engine's noisy," he said, as he watched the train stretch like elastic round a bend and disappear. The points groaned back into place, and the signal on the passenger up-line rose. A man came down the steps from the box, crossed the line and disappeared in the direction of a cottage.

"Gone for lunch," Ninitch's companion said enviously.

"I've never heard an engine as noisy as that," Ninitch said, "all the time I've been here.'' Then his companion's remark reached him. ''The major's having a hot meal down from the barracks,'' he said. But he did not tell his friend that the Chief of Police was coming from Belgrade; he kept the news for his wife.

''You are a lucky one,'' his companion said. ''You'll be having a meal all right. I've often thought it must be good to be married when I see your wife come down of a morning.''

''It's not too bad,'' said Ninitch modestly.

''Tell me, what does she bring you?''

''A loaf of bread and a piece of sausage. Sometimes a bit of butter. She's a good girl.'' But his thoughts were not so temperate. I am not good enough for her; I should like to be rich and give her a dress and a necklace and take her to Belgrade to the theatre. He thought at first with envy of the foreign girl locked in the waiting-room, of her clothes which seemed to him very costly and of her green glass necklace, but in comparing her with his wife he soon forgot his envy and began to regard the foreigner, too, with affection. The beauty and fragility of women struck him with pathos, as he beat his great clumsy hands together.

''Wake up,'' his friend whispered, and both men straightened and stood ''at ease'' in a stiff attitude as a car plunged up the road to the station, breaking through the frozen surface and scattering water. ''Who the devil?'' his friend whispered, hardly moving his lips, but Ninitch proudly knew; he knew that the tall ribboned officer was the Chief of Police, he even knew the name of the other officer who bounded out of the car like a rubber ball and held the door open for Colonel Hartep to alight.

''What a place,'' said Colonel Hartep with amused distaste, looking first at the mud and then at his polished boots.

Captain Alexitch blew out his round red cheeks. ''They might have laid some boards.''

''No, no, we are the police. They don't like us. God knows what sort of a lunch they'll give us. Here, my man,'' he beckoned to Ninitch, ''help the chauffeur out with these cases. Be careful to keep the wine steady and upright.''

''Major Petkovitch, sir . . .''

''Never mind Major Petkovitch.''

''Excuse me,'' said a precise angry voice behind Ninitch.

''Certainly, Major,'' Colonel Hartep smiled and bowed, ''but I am sure that there is no need to excuse you.''

''This man is on guard over the prisoners.''

''You have captured a number of them. I congratulate you.''

''Two men and a girl.''

''In that case I should imagine a good lock, a guard, a bayonet, a rifle, and twenty rounds of ammunition will meet the case.''

Major Petkovitch licked his lips. ''The police, of course, know best how to guard a prison. I bow to superior knowledge. Take the things out of the car,'' he said to Ninitch, ''and bring them to my room.'' He led the officers round the corner of the waiting-room and out of sight. Ninitch stared after them, until the chauffeur called out to him, ''I can't wait here in the car all day. Look lively. You soldiers aren't used to a spot of work.'' He began to take the boxes out of the car, telling over their contents as he did so: "A half case of champagne. A cold duck. Fruit. Two bottles of sherry. Sausage. Wine biscuits. Lettuce. Olives."

"Well," Ninitch's friend called out, "is it a good meal?"

Ninitch stood and stared for a moment in silence. Then he said in a low voice, "It's a feast."

He had carried the sherry and champagne and the duck to the major's room when he saw his wife coming up the road bringing his own lunch wrapped in a white cloth. She was small and dark with her shawl twisted tightly round her shoulders; she had a malicious humorous face and big boots. He put down the case of fruit and went to meet her. "I shall not be long," he told her in a low voice, so that the chauffeur might not hear. "Wait for me. I've something to tell you," and very seriously he went back to his task. His wife sat down by the side of the road and watched him, but when he came back from the major's office, where the table was already spread and the officers were making headway with the wine, she was gone. She had left his lunch by the side of the road. "Where is she?" he asked the other guard.

"She talked to the chauffeur and then she went back to the barracks. She seemed excited about something."

Ninitch suffered a pang of disappointment. He had looked forward to telling his wife the story of Colonel Hartep's coming, and now the chauffeur had anticipated him. It was always the same. A soldier's life was a dog's life. It was the civilians who got high wages and robbed the soldiers at cards and abused them and even interfered between a soldier and his wife. But his resentment was brief. There were secrets he could yet discover for his wife, if he kept ears and eyes open. He waited for some time before he carried the last case to the major's room. The champagne was bubbling low; all three men spoke at once, and Major Petkovitch's glasses had fallen in his lap. "Such bobbles," Captain Alexitch was saying, "such thighs. I said to His Excellency if I was in your place . . ." Major Petkovitch drew lines on the tablecloth with a finger dipped in wine. "The first maxim is, never strike at the wings. Crumple the centre." Colonel Hartep was quite sober. He leant back in his chair smoking. "Take just a trifle of French mustard; two sprigs of parsley," but neither of his juniors paid him any attention. He smiled gently and filled their glasses.

The snow was falling again, and through the windblown drifts Dr. Czinner saw the peasants of Subotica straggling across the line, thrusting their inquisitive twisted bodies towards the waiting-room. One man got close enough to the window to stare in and examine the doctor's face. They were separated by a few feet and a sheet of glass and the lines of frost and the vapour of their breath. Dr. Czinner could count his wrinkles, name the colour of his eyes and examine with brief professional interest a sore upon his cheek. But always the peasants were driven back by the two soldiers, who struck at them with the butts of their rifles. The peasants gave way and moved on to the line, but presently they swarmed back, obstinate, stupid and hopeless.

There had been silence in the waiting-room for a very long while. Dr. Czinner went back to the stove. The girl sat with her thumbs joined and her head a little bent. He knew what she was doing; she was praying that her lover would come back for her soon, and from her secrecy he guessed that she was not accustomed to prayer. She was very frightened, and with a cold sympathy he was able to judge the measure of her fear. His experience told him two things, that prayers were not answered and that so casual a lover would not trouble to return.

He was sorry that he had involved her, but he regretted it only as he might have regretted a necessary lie. He had always recognised the need of sacrificing his own integrity; only a party in power could possess scruples; scruples in himself would be a confession that he doubted the overwhelming value of his cause. But the reflection for some reason made him bitter; he found himself envying virtues which he was not rich or strong enough to cherish. He would have welcomed generosity, charity, meticulous codes of honour to his breast if he could have succeeded, if the world had been shaped again to the pattern he loved and longed for. He spoke to her angrily: "You are lucky to believe that that will do good," but he found to his amazement that she could instinctively outbid his bitterness, which was founded on theories laboriously worked out by a fallible reason. "I don't," she said, "but one must do something."

He was shocked by the ease of her disbelief, which did not come from the painful reading of rationalist writers and nineteenth-century scientists, she had been born to disbelief as securely as he had been born to belief. He had sacrificed security in order to reach the same position, and for a moment he longed to sow in her some dry plant of doubt, a half-belief which would make her mistrust her judgment. He allowed the inclination to pass and encouraged her. "He'll come back for you from Belgrade."

"Perhaps he can't afford the time."

"He'll telegraph to the British Consul."

She said, "Of course," without conviction. The events of the night, the experience of Myatt's tenderness, swam back from her, like a lit pier, into darkness. She strained her memory in the effort to recover sight of him, but he soon became an indistinguishable member of a crowd gathered to say good-bye. It was not long before she began to question his difference from all the other Jews she had known. Even her body, rested now and healed, but the deep peace gone with the pain, was aware of no difference. She repeated, "Of course," because she was ashamed at her lack of faith, because it was no use grumbling anyway, because at any rate she was no worse off except for being a day late for the show. There's as good fish in the sea, she told herself, but feeling none the less strangely tied to a memory which lacked all conviction.

The German sat bolt upright in his corner, sleeping; his eyelids twitched, ready to rise at the least unfamiliar sound. He was accustomed to rest in strange places and to take advantage of any respite. When the door opened, his eyes were at once attentive.

A guard entered and waved his hand at them and shouted. Dr. Czinner repeated what he said in English. "We are to come out." The snow blew in at the open door, making a grey tidemark on the threshold. They could see the peasants huddled on the line. Josef Grünlich stood up and smoothed his waistcoat, and pressed his elbow in Dr. Czinner's side. "If we runned now, eh, through the snow, all together?" "They would shoot," Dr. Czinner said. The guard shouted again and waved his hand. "But they shoot anyway, eh? What do they want outside?"

Dr. Czinner turned to Coral Musker. "I don't think there's anything to fear. Are you coming?"

"Of course." Then she implored him, "Wait one moment for me. I've lost my handkerchief." The tall thin form bent like a pair of grey compasses, went down on the knees and fetched it from beneath the seat. His awkwardness made her smile; she forgot her distrust and thanked him with disproportionate gratitude. Outside he walked with bent head to avoid the snow, smiling to himself. One guard led them and one walked behind with his rifle unslung and his bayonet fixed. They called to each other in a language she could not understand over the prisoners' heads, and she was being taken she did not know where. There was a scramble and splashing of feet over the rails and the mud as the peasants came nearer, hungry for a sight of them, and she was a little daunted by the olive faces and her own ignorance of what it was all about. She asked Dr. Czinner, "Why are you smiling?" and hoped to hear that he had seen a way to release them all, to catch the express, to put back the hands of the clock. He said, "I don't know. Was I smiling? It is perhaps because I am home again." For a moment his mouth was serious, then it fell again into a loose smile, and his eyes as they peered this way and that through his frosted glasses seemed moist and empty of anything but a kind of stupid happiness.

3

Myatt, with his eye on the lengthening ash of his cigar, thought. These were the moments he cherished, when he felt alone with himself and feared no rebuff, when his body was satisfied and his emotions stilled. The night before he had tried in vain to work; the girl's face had come between him and the figures; now she was relegated to her proper place. Presently, as evening came on, he might need her and she would be there, and at the thought he felt tenderness and even gratitude, not least because her physical presence gone, she had left no importunate ghost. He could remember now without looking at his papers the figures he had been unable to arrange. He multiplied, divided, subtracted, seeing the long columns arrange themselves down the window, across which the transparent bodies of customs-officials and porters passed unnoticed. Presently somebody asked to see his passport, and then the ash fell from his cigar and he went back to his compartment to open his luggage. Coral was not there, but he supposed that she was in the lavatory. The customs-officer tapped her bag. "And this?"

"It's unlocked," he said. "The lady is not here. You will find nothing." When he was alone again he lay back in his corner and closed his eyes, the better to consider the affairs of Mr. Eckman, but by the time the train drew out of Subotica he was asleep. He dreamed that he was mounting the stairs to Mr. Eckman's office. Narrow, uncarpeted and unlit, they might have led to a disreputable flat off Leicester Square, instead of to the headquarters of the biggest currant importers in Europe. He did not remember passing through the door; the next moment he was sitting face to face with Mr. Eckman. A great pile of papers lay between them and Mr. Eckman stroked his dark moustache and tapped the desk with his fountainpen, while a spider drew the veins of its web across a dry ink-well. The electric light was dim and the window was sooty and in the corner Mrs. Eckman sat on a steel sofa knitting baby clothes.

"I admit everything," said Mr. Eckman. Suddenly his chair rose, until he sat high overhead, tapping with an auctioneer's hammer. "Answer me these questions," said Mr. Eckman. "You are on oath. Don't prevaricate. Say yes or no. Did you seduce the girl?"

"In a way."

Mr. Eckman drew a sheet of paper from the middle of the pile, and another and another, till the pile tottered and fell to the floor with the noise of falling bricks. "This affair of Jervis. Slim work I call it. You had contracted with the trustees and had only delayed to sign."

"It was legal."

"And this £10,000 to Stavrog when you'd already had an offer of £15,000."

"It's business."

"And the girl on the Spaniards Road."

"And the £1,000 to Moults' clerk for information."

"What have I done that you haven't done? Answer me quick. Don't prevaricate. Say yes or no. My lord and gentlemen of the jury, the prisoner at the bar . . ."

"I want to speak. I've got something to say. I'm not guilty."

"Under what clause? What code? Law of Equity? Law of Tithes? Admiralty Court or the King's Bench? Answer me quick. Don't prevaricate. Say yes or no. Three strokes of the hammer. Going, going. This fine flourishing business, gentlemen."

"Wait a moment. I'll tell you. George. Cap. III. Section 4. Vic. 2504. Honour among Thieves."

Mr. Eckman, suddenly very small in the dingy office, began to weep, stretching out his hands. And all the washerwomen who paddled in the stream knee-deep lifted up their heads and wept, while a dry wind tore up the sand from the sea-beaches and flung it rattling against the leaves of the forest, and a voice which might have been Mrs. Eckman's implored him over and over again, "Come back." Then the desert shook under his feet and he opened his eyes. The train had stopped, and the snow was caking on the glass of the window. Coral had not returned.

Presently somebody at the back of the train began to laugh and jeer, and others joined in, whistling and catcalling. Myatt looked at his watch. He had slept for more than two hours, and perhaps because he remembered the voice in his dream, he felt uneasy at Coral's absence. Smoke poured from the engine and a man in dungarees with a blackened face stood apart from it, gazing hopelessly. Several people called to him from the third class and he turned and shook his head and shrugged in a graceful bewildered way. The *chef de train* walked rapidly down the track away from the engine. Myatt stopped him. "What has happened?"

"Nothing. Nothing at all. A little defect."

"Are we stuck here for long?"

"Oh, a mere trifle. An hour, an hour and a half perhaps. We are telephoning for a new engine."

Myatt closed the window and went into the corridor; there was no sign of Coral. He passed down the whole length of the train, looking into compartments, trying the doors of lavatories until he reached the third class. There he remembered the man with the violin and sought him through the hard wooden odorous compartments, until he ran him to earth, a small pinched fellow with a swollen eye.

"I am giving a dinner tonight," Myatt said to him in German, "and I want you to play for me. I'll give you fifty paras."

"Seventy-five, your excellency."

Myatt was hurried; he wanted to find Coral. "Seventy-five, then."

"Something dreamy, melancholy, to bring tears, your excellency?"

"Of course not. I want something light and cheerful."

"Ah, well, of course? That is more expensive."

"What do you mean? Why more expensive?"

His excellency, of course, was a foreigner. He did not understand. It was the custom of the country to charge more for light songs than for melancholy. Oh, an age-old custom. One and a half dinas?—Suddenly, dispelling his impatience and his anxiety, the joy of bargaining gripped Myatt. The money was nothing; there was less than half a crown at stake, but this was business; he would not give in. "Seventy-five paras. Not a para more."

The man grinned at him with pleasure: this was a stranger after his own heart. "One dina thirty paras. It is my last word, your excellency. I should disgrace my profession if I accepted less." The odour of stale bread and sour wine no longer disturbed Myatt; it was the smell of the ancestral market-place. This was the pure poetry of business: gain and loss hardly entered into a transaction fought out in paras, each of which was worth less than a farthing. He came a little way into the carriage, but he did not sit down. "Eighty paras."

"Your excellency, one must live. One dina twenty-five. It would shame me to take less."

Myatt offered the man a cigarette. "A glass of *rakia*, your excellency?" Myatt nodded and took without distaste the thick chipped tumbler. "Eighty-five paras. Take it or leave it." Smoking and drinking together in a close understanding they grew fierce with each other. "You insult me, your excellency. I am a musician."

"Eight-seven paras, that is my last word."

The three officers sat round the table, which had been cleared of the glasses. Two soldiers stood before the door with fixed bayonets. Dr. Czinner watched Colonel Hartep with curiosity; he had last seen him at the Kamnetz trial marshalling his lying witnesses with a graceful disregard of justice. That was five years ago, but the years had done little to alter his appearance. His hair was a fine silver above his ears and there were a few kindly wrinkles at the corners of his eyes. "Major Petkovitch," he said, "will you read the charge against the prisoners? Let the lady have a chair."

Dr. Czinner took his hands from the pockets of his mackintosh and wiped his glasses. He could keep emotion from his voice, but not from his hands, which trembled a little. "A charge?" he said. "What do you mean? Is this a court?"

Major Petkovitch, paper in hand, snapped at him, "Be quiet."

"It's a reasonable question, Major," said Colonel Hartep. "The doctor has been abroad. You see," he said, speaking gently and with great kindness, "measures have had to be taken for your safety. Your life would not be safe in Belgrade. People are angry about the rising."

"I still don't understand your right," Dr. Czinner said, "to make more than a preliminary inquiry."

Colonel Hartep explained. "This is a court martial. Martial Law was proclaimed early yesterday morning. Now, Major Petkovitch."

Major Petkovitch began to read a long document in a manuscript which he found often illegible. "The prisoner, Richard Czinner . . . conspiracy against the Government . . . unserved sentence for perjury . . . false passport. The prisoner, Josef Grünlich, found in possession of arms. The prisoner, Coral Musker, conspiracy with Richard Czinner, against the Government." He laid the paper down and said to Colonel Hartep, "I am uncertain of the legality of this court as it stands. The prisoners should be represented by counsel."

"Dear, dear, that is certainly an oversight. Perhaps you, Major . . . ?"

"No. The court must consist of not less than three officers."

Dr. Czinner interrupted. "Don't trouble yourselves. I will do without counsel. These others cannot understand a word of what you say. They won't object."

"It's irregular," said Major Petkovitch. The Chief of Police looked at his watch. "I have noted your protest, Major. Now we can begin." The fat officer hiccuped, put his hand to his mouth, and winked.

"Ninety paras."

"One dina."

Myatt stubbed out his cigarette. He had played the game long enough. "One dina, then. Tonight at nine." He walked rapidly back to his compartment, but Coral was not there. Passengers were scrambling from the train, talking and laughing and stretching their arms. The engine-driver was the centre of a small crowd to whom he was explaining the breakdown with humour. Although there was no house in sight two or three villagers had already appeared and were offering for sale bottled mineral waters and sweets on the end of sticks. The road ran parallel to the line, separated only by a ridge of snow; the driver of a motor-car honked his horn and shouted again and again. "Quick car to Belgrade. A hundred and twenty dinas. Quick car to Belgrade." It was an exorbitant rate and only one stout merchant paid him attention. A long wrangle began beside the road. "Mineral waters. Mineral waters." A German with cropped head paced up and down muttering angrily to himself. Myatt heard a voice saying behind him in English, "There's going to be more snow." He turned in the hope that it might be Coral, but it was the woman whom he had seen in the restaurant-car.

"It will be no fun to be stuck here," he said. "They may be hours bringing another engine. What about sharing a car to Belgrade?"

"Is that an invitation?"

"A Dutch one," Myatt said hastily.

"But I haven't a sou." She turned and waved her hand. "Mr. Savory, come and share a car. You'll pay my share, won't you?" Mr. Savory elbowed his way out of the group of people round the driver. "I can't make out what the fellow's saying. Something about a boiler," he said. "Share a car?" he went on more slowly. "That'll be rather expensive, won't it?" He eyed the woman carefully and waited, as if he expected her to answer his question; he is wondering, of course, Myatt thought, what he will get out of it. Mr. Savory's hesitation, the woman's waiting silence, aroused his competitive instincts. He wanted to unfurl the glory of wealth like a peacock's tail before her and dazzle her with the beauty of his possessions. "Sixty dinas," he said, "for the two of you."

"I'll just go along," said Mr. Savory, "and see the *chef de train*. He may know how long . . ." The first snow began to fall. "If you would be my guest," said Myatt, "Miss——"

"My name's Janet Pardoe," she said, and drew her fur coat up above her ears. Her cheeks glowed where the snow touched them, and Myatt could follow through the fur the curve of her concealed body and compare it with Coral's thin nakedness. I shall have to take Coral too, he thought. "Have you seen," he said, "a girl in a mackintosh, thin, shorter than you?"

"Oh yes," Janet Pardoe said, "she got out of the train at Subotica. I know whom you mean. You had supper with her last night." She smiled at him. "She's your mistress, isn't she?"

"Do you mean she got out with her bag?"

"Oh no. She had nothing with her. I saw her going across to the station with a customs man. She's a funny little thing, isn't she? A chorus girl?" she asked with polite interest, but her tone conveyed to Myatt a criticism not of the girl but of himself for spending his money to so little advantage. It angered him as much as if she had criticised the quality of his currants; it was a reflection on his discernment and his discretion. After all, he thought, I have spent on her no more than I should spend on you by taking you into Belgrade, and would you pay me back so readily in kind? But the unlikelihood woke desire and bitterness, for this girl was silver polished goods, while Coral was at the best a piece of pretty coloured glass, valued for sentimental reasons; the other had intrinsic worth. She is the kind, he thought, who needs more than money: a handsome body to meet her own lust, and wit and education. I am a Jew, and I have learned nothing except how to make money. But none the less her criticism angered him and made it easier to relinquish the unattainable.

"She must have missed the train. I'll have to go back for her." He did not apologise for his broken promise, but went quickly while it was still easy to go.

The merchant was haggling with the driver. He had brought the price down to a hundred dinas, and his own offer had risen to ninety. Myatt was ashamed of his interruption, and of the contempt both men must feel for his hasty unbusinesslike manner. "I'll give you a hundred and twenty dinas to take me to Subotica and back." When he saw that the driver was ready to begin another argument he raised his offer. "A hundred and fifty dinas if you take me there and back before this train leaves."

The car was old, battered and very powerful. They drove into the face of the storm at sixty miles an hour along a road which had not been mended in a lifetime. The springs were broken and Myatt was flung from side to side, as the car fell into holes and climbed and heeled. It groaned and panted like a human being, driven to the edge of endurance by a merciless master. The snow fell faster; the telegraph-poles along the line seemed glimpses of dark space in the gaps of a white wall. Myatt leant over to the driver and shouted in German above the roar of the ancient engine, "Can you see?" The car twisted and swerved across the road and the man yelled back at him that there was nothing to fear, they would meet nothing on the road; he did not say that he could see.

Presently the wind rose. The road which had before been hidden from them by a straight wall of snow now rose and fell back on them, like a wave of which the snow was the white stinging spume. Myatt shouted to the driver to go slower; if a tyre bursts now, he thought, we are dead. He saw the driver look at his watch and put his foot upon the accelerator and the ancient engine responded with a few more miles an hour, like one of those strong obstinate old men of whom others say, "They are the last. We don't breed that kind now." Myatt shouted again, "Slower," but the driver pointed to his watch and drove his car to its creaking, unsafe, and gigantic limit of strength. He was a man to whom thirty dinas, the difference between catching and losing the train, meant months of comfort; he would have risked his life and the life of his passenger for far less money. Suddenly, as the wind took the snow and blew it aside, a cart appeared in the gap ten yards away and right in front of them. Myatt had just time to see the bemused eyes of the oxen, to calculate where their horns would smash the glass of the windscreen; an elderly man screamed and dropped his goad and jumped. The driver wrenched his wheel round, the car leapt a bank, rode crazily on two wheels, while the others hummed and revolved between the wind and earth, leant farther and farther over till Myatt could see the ground rise like boiling milk, left the bank, touched two wheels to the ground, touched four, and roared down the road at sixty-five miles an hour, while the snow closed behind them, and hid the oxen and cart and the astonished terrified old man.

"Drive slower," Myatt gasped, but the driver turned and grinned at him and waved an untrembling hand.

The officers sitting in a row at the table, the guards at the door, the doctor answering question after question after question receded. Coral Musker fell asleep. The night had tired her; she could not understand a word that was said; she did not know why she was there; she was frightened and beginning to despair. She dreamed first that she was a child and everything was very simple and very certain and everything had an explanation and a moral. And then she dreamed that she was very old and was looking back over her life and she knew everything and she knew what was right and what was wrong, and why this and that had happened and everything was very simple and had a moral. But this second dream was not like the first one, for she was nearly awake and she ruled the dream to suit herself, and always in the background the talking went on. In this dream she began to remember from the safety of age the events of the night and the day and how everything had turned out for the best and how Myatt had come back for her from Belgrade.

Dr. Czinner too had been given a chair. He could tell from the fat officer's expression that the lie was nearly done with, for he had ceased to pay any attention to the questions, nodding and hiccuping and nodding again. Colonel Hartep kept up the appearance of justice from a genuine kindliness. He had no scruples, but he did not wish to give unnecessary pain. If it had been possible he would have left Dr. Czinner until the end some scraps of hope. Major Petkovitch continually raised objections; he knew as well as anyone what the outcome of the trial would be, but he was determined that it should have a superficial legality, that everything should be done in the proper order according to the regulations in the 1929 handbook.

With his hands folded quietly in front of him, and his shabby soft hat on the floor at his feet, Dr. Czinner fought them without hope. The only satisfaction he could expect to gain would be the admission of the hollowness of his trial; he was going to be quietly tucked away in earth at the frontier station after dark, without publicity. "On the ground of perjury," he said, "I have not yet been tried. It's outside the jurisdiction of a court martial."

"You were tried in your absence," Colonel Hartep said, "and sentenced to five years' imprisonment."

"I think you will find that I must still be brought up before a civil judge for sentence."

"He's quite right," said Major Petkovitch. "We have no jurisdiction there. If you look up Section 15——"

"I believe you, Major. We'll waive then the sentence for perjury. There remains the false passport."

Dr. Czinner said quickly, "You must prove that I have not become a naturalised British subject. Where are your witnesses? Will you telegraph to the British Ambassador?"

Colonel Hartep smiled. "It would take so long. We'll waive the false passport. You agree, Major?"

"No," said Major Petkovitch, "I think it would be more correct to postpone trial on the smaller charge until sentence—that is to say, a verdict—has been declared on the greater."

"It is all the same to me," said Colonel Hartep. "And you, Captain?" The captain nodded and grinned and closed his eyes.

"And now," Colonel Hartep said, "the charge of conspiring." Major Petkovitch interrupted, "I have been thinking it over. I think 'treason' should have been the word used in the indictment."

"Treason, then."

"No, no, Colonel. It is impossible to alter the indictment now. 'Conspiracy' will have to stand."

"The maximum penalty——?"

"Is the same."

"Well then, Dr. Czinner, do you wish to plead guilty or not guilty?"

Dr. Czinner sat for a moment considering. Then he said, "It makes little difference." Colonel Hartep looked at his watch, and then touched a letter which lay on the table. "In the opinion of the court this is sufficient to convict." He had the air of a man who wishes politely but firmly to put an end to an interview.

"I have the right, I suppose, to demand that it should be read, to cross-examine the soldier who took it?"

"Without doubt," said Major Petkovitch eagerly.

Dr. Czinner smiled. "I won't trouble you. I plead guilty." But if this had been a court in Belgrade, he told himself, with the pressmen scribbling in their box, I would have fought every step. Now that he had nobody to address, his mind was flooded with eloquence, words which could stab and words which would have brought tears. He was no longer the angry tongue-tied man who had failed to impress Mrs. Peters. "The court adjourns," Colonel Hartep said. In the short silence the wind could be heard wandering like an angry watch-dog round the station buildings. It was a very brief interval, just long enough for Colonel Hartep to write a few sentences on a sheet of paper and push it across the table to his companions to sign. The two guards a little eased their position.

"The court finds all the prisoners guilty," Colonel Hartep read. "The prisoner, Josef Grünlich, is sentenced to a month's imprisonment, after which he will be repatriated. The prisoner, Coral Musker, is sentenced to twenty-four hours' imprisonment and will then be repatriated. The prisoner . . . ."

Dr. Czinner interrupted: "Can I speak to the court before sentence is passed?"

Colonel Hartep glanced quickly at the window: it was shut; at the guards: their disciplined faces were uncomprehending and empty. "Yes," he said.

Major Petkovitch's face flushed. "Impossible," he said. "Quite impossible. Regulation 27a. The prisoner should have spoken before the court adjourned." The Chief of Police looked past the major's sharp profile to where Dr. Czinner sat, bunched up on the chair, his hands folded together in grey woollen gloves. An engine hooted outside and ground slowly down the line. The snow whispered at the window. He was aware of the long ribbons on his coat and of the hole in Dr. Czinner's glove. "It would be most irregular," Major Petkovitch railed on, while with one hand he absent-mindedly felt for his dog under the table and pulled the beast's ears. "I note your protest," Colonel Hartep said, and then he spoke to Dr. Czinner. "You know as well as I do," he said kindly, "that nothing you can say will alter the verdict. But if it pleases you, if it will make you any happier to speak, you may."

Dr. Czinner had expected opposition or contempt and his words would have flown to meet them. Kindness and consideration for a moment made him dumb. He envied again the qualities which only confidence and power could give the possessor. Before Colonel Hartep's kindly waiting silence he was tongue-tied. Captain Alexitch opened his eyes and closed them again. The doctor said slowly, "Those medals you won in the service of your country during the war. I have no medals, because I love my country too much. I won't kill men because they also love their country. What I am fighting for is not new territory but a new world." His words halted; there was no audience to bear him up; and he became conscious of the artificiality of his words which did not bear witness to the great love and the great hate driving him on. Sad and beautiful faces, thin from bad food, old before their time, resigned to despair, passed through his mind; they were people he had known, whom he had attended and failed to save. The world was in chaos to leave so much nobility unused, while the great financiers and the soldiers prospered. He said, "You are employed to bolster up an old world which is full of injustice and muddle. For people like Vuskovitch, who steal the small savings of the poor, and live for ten years fast, full, stupid lives, and then shoot themselves. And yet you are paid to defend the only system which would protect men like him. You put the small thief in prison, but the big thief lives in a palace."

Major Petkovitch said, "What the prisoner is saying has no bearing on the case. It is a political speech."

"Let him go on." Colonel Hartep shaded his face with his hands and closed his eyes. Dr. Czinner thought that he was feigning sleep to mask his indifference, but he opened them again when Dr. Czinner called out to him angrily, "How old-fashioned you are with your frontiers and your patriotism. The aeroplane doesn't know a frontier; even your financiers don't recognise frontiers." Then Dr. Czinner saw that something saddened him and the thought that perhaps Colonel Hartep had no desire for his death made him again at a loss for words. He moved his eyes restlessly from point to point, from the map on the wall to the little shelf below the clock full of books on strategy and military history in worn jackets. At last his eyes reached the two guards; one stared past him, paying him no attention, careful to keep his eyes on one spot and his rifle at the correct angle. The other watched him with wide stupid unhappy eyes. That face joined the sad procession through his brain, and he was aware for a moment that he had a better audience than pressmen, that here was a poor man to be converted from the wrong service to the right, and words came to him, the vague and sentimental words which had once appealed to him and would appeal to the other. But he was cunning now with the guile of his class, staring away from the man at the floor and only letting his gaze flicker back once like a lizard's tail. He addressed him in the plural as "Brothers." He urged that there was no shame in poverty that they should seek to be rich, and that there was no crime in poverty that they should be oppressed. When all were poor, no one would be poor. The wealth of the world belonged to everyone. If it was divided, there would be no rich men, but every man would have enough to eat, and would have no reason to feel ashamed beside his neighbour.

Colonel Hartep lost interest. Dr. Czinner was losing the individuality of the grey wool gloves and the hole in the thumb; he was becoming a tub orator, no more. He looked at his watch and said, "I think I have allowed you enough time." Major Petkovitch muttered something under his breath and becoming suddenly irritable kicked his dog in the ribs and said, "Be off with you. Always wanting attention." Captain Alexitch woke up and said in a tone of great relief, "Well, that's over." Dr. Czinner, staring at the floor five yards to the left of the guard, said slowly, "This wasn't a trial. They had sentenced me to death before they began. Remember, I'm dying to show you the way. I don't mind dying. Life has not been so good as that. I think I shall be of more use dead." But while he spoke his clearer mind told him that the chances were few that his death would have any effect.

"The prisoner Richard Czinner is sentenced to death," Colonel Hartep read, "the sentence to be carried out by the officer commanding the garrison at Subotica in three hours' time." It will be dark by then, the doctor thought. No one will know of this.

For a moment everyone sat still as though they were at a concert and a movement had ended and they were uncertain whether to applaud. Coral Musker woke. She could not understand what was happening. The officers were speaking together, shuffling papers. Then one of them gave a command and the guards opened the door and motioned towards the wind and the snow and the white veiled buildings.

The prisoners passed out. They kept close to each other in the storm of snow which struck them. They had not gone far when Josef Grünlich seized Dr. Czinner's sleeve. "You tell me nothing. What shall happen to me? You walk along and say nothing." He grumbled and panted.

"A month's imprisonment," Dr. Czinner said, "and then you are to be sent home."

"They think that, do they? They think they are damned clever." He became silent, studying with close attention the position of the buildings. He stumbled on the edge of the line and muttered angrily to himself.

"And me?" Coral asked. "What's to happen to me?"

"You'll be sent home tomorrow."

"But I can't. There's my job. I shall lose it. And my friend." She had been afraid of this journey, because she could not understand what porters said to her, because of the strange food, and the uncertainty at the end of it: there had been a moment as the purser called after her across the wet quay at Ostend when she would gladly have turned back. But "things" had happened since then: she would be returning to the same lodgings, to the toast and orange juice for breakfast, the long wait on the agent's stairs with Ivy and Flo and Phil and Dick, all the affectionate people one kissed and called by their front names and didn't know from Adam. Intimacy with one person could do this—empty the world of friendships, give a distaste for women's kisses and their bright chatter, make the ordinary world a little unreal and very uninteresting. Even the doctor did not matter to her as he stalked along in a different world, but she remembered as they reached the door of the waiting-room to ask him, "And you? What's happening to you?"

He said vaguely, forgetting to stand aside for her to enter, "I'm being kept here."

"Where will they take me?" Josef Grünlich asked as the door closed.

"And me?"

"To the barracks, I expect, for tonight. There's no train to Belgrade. They've let the stove out." Through the window he tried to catch a view of the peasants, but apparently they had grown tired of waiting and had gone home. He said with relief, "There's nothing to be done," and with obscure humour, "It's something to be at home." He saw himself for a moment facing a desert of pitch-pine desks, row on row of malicious faces, and he remembered the times when he had felt round his heart the little cold draughts of disobedience, the secret signals and spurts of disguised laughter threatening his livelihood, for a master who could not keep order must eventually be dismissed. His enemies were offering him the one thing he had never known, security. There was no need to decide anything. He was at peace.

Dr. Czinner began to hum a tune. He said to Coral Musker, "It's an old song. The lover says: 'I cannot come in daylight, for I am poor and your father will set the dogs on me. But at night I will come to your window and ask you to let me in.' And the girl says: 'If the dogs bark, stay very still in the shadow of the wall and I will come down to you, and we will go together to the orchard at the bottom of the garden.' " He sang the first verse in a voice a little harsh from lack of use; Josef Grünlich, sitting in the corner, scowled at the singer, and Coral stood by the cold stove and listened with surprise and pleasure because he seemed to be younger and full of hope. "At night I will come to your window and ask you to let me in." He was not addressing a lover: the words had no power to bring a girl's face from his dry purposeful political years, but his parents bobbed at him their humorous wrinkled faces, no longer with awe for the educated man, for the doctor, for the almost gentleman. Then in a lower voice he sang the girl's part. His voice was less harsh and might once have been beautiful; one of the guards came to the window and looked in and Josef Grünlich began to weep in a meaningless Teutonic way, thinking of orphans in the snow and princesses with hearts of ice and not for a moment of Herr Kolber, whose body was borne now through the grey city snow followed by two officials in a car and one mourner in a taxi, an elderly bachelor, a great draughts player. "Stay very still in the shadow of the wall and I will come down to you." The world was chaotic; when the poor were starved and the rich were not happier for it; when the thief might be punished or rewarded with titles; when wheat was burned in Canada and coffee in Brazil, and the poor in his own country had no money for bread and froze to death in unheated rooms; the world was out of joint and he had done his best to set it right, but that was over. He was powerless now and happy. "We will go to the orchard at the bottom of the garden." Again it was no memory of a girl which comforted him, but the sad and beautiful faces of the poor who promised him rest. He had done all that he could do; nothing more was expected of him; they surrendered him their hopelessness, the secret of their beauty and their happiness as well as of their grief, and led him towards the leafy rustling darkness. The guard pressed his face to the window, and Dr. Czinner stopped singing. "It's your turn," he said to Coral.

"Oh, I don't know any songs that you'd like," she told him seriously, searching her memory at the same time for something a little old-fashioned and melancholy, something which would share the quality of a sad idyll with the song he had sung.

"We must pass the time somehow," he said, and suddenly she began to sing in a small clear voice like the tinkle of a musical box:

> *"I was sitting in a car*
> *With Michael;*
> *I looked at a star*
> *With John;*
> *I had a glass of bitter*
> *With Peter*
> *In a bar;*
> *But the pips went wrong; they never go right.*
> *This year, next year*
> *(You may have counted wrong, count again, dear),*
> *Some day, never.*
> *I'll be a good girl for ever and ever."*

"Is this Subotica?" Myatt shouted, as a few mud cottages plunged at them through the storm, and the driver nodded and waved his hand forward. A small child ran out into the middle of the road and the car swerved to avoid it; a chicken squawked and handfuls of grey feathers were flung up into the snow. An old woman ran out of a cottage and shouted after them. "What's she saying?" The driver grinned over his shoulder: "Dirty Jew."

The arrow on the speedometer wavered and retreated: fifty miles, forty miles, thirty miles, twenty. "Soldiers about," the man said.

"You mean there's a speed limit?"

"No, no. These damned soldiers if they see a good car, they commandeer it. Same with the horses." He pointed at the fields through the driving snow. "The peasants, they are all starving. I worked here once, but I thought: no, the city for me. The country's dead, anyway." He nodded towards the line which disappeared into the storm. "One or two trains a day, that's all. You can't blame the Reds for making trouble."

"Has there been trouble?"

"Trouble? You should have seen it. The goods yard all in flames; the post-office smashed to bits. The police were scared. There's martial law in Belgrade."

"I wanted to send a telegram from there. Will it get through?" The car panted its way on second gear up a small hill and came into a street of dingy brick houses plastered with advertisements. "If you want to send a telegram," the driver said, "I should send it from here. There are queues of newspaper men at Belgrade, and the post-office is smashed and they've had to commandeer old Nikola's restaurant. You know what that means; but you don't because you are a foreigner. It's not the bugs, nobody minds a few bugs, it's healthy, but the smells———"

"Have I got time to send a telegram here and catch the train?"

"That train," the driver said, "won't go for hours and hours. They've sent for a new engine, but nobody's going to pay any attention to them in the city. You should see the station, the mess—You had better let me drive you into Belgrade. I'll show you the sights too. I know all the best houses."

Myatt interrupted him, "I'll go to the post-office first. And then we'll try the hotels for the lady."

"There's only one."

"And then the station."

The sending of the telegram took some time; first he had to write the message to Joyce in such a way that no action for libel could be brought by Mr. Eckman. He decided at last on: "Eckman granted a month's holiday to start immediately. Please take charge at once. Arriving tomorrow." That ought to convey what he wanted, but it then had to be put into the office code, and when the coded telegram was handed across the counter, the clerk refused to accept it. All telegrams were liable to censorship, and no coded messages could be transmitted. At last he got away, only to find that nothing was known of Coral at the hotel, which smelt of dried plants and insect powder. She must be still at the station, he thought. He left the car a hundred yards down the road in order to get rid of the driver who was proving too talkative and too helpful and pushed forward alone through the wind and snow.

He passed two sentries outside a building and asked them the way to the waiting-room. One of them said that there was no waiting-room now.

"Where can I make inquiries?"

The tallest of the guards suggested the station-master. "And where is his office?" The man pointed to a second building, but added gently that the station-master was away; he was in Belgrade. Myatt checked his impatience, the man was so obviously good-natured. His companion spat to show his contempt and muttered remarks about Jews under his breath. "Where can I go then to make inquiries?"

"There's the major," the man said doubtfully, "or there's the station-master's clerk."

"You can't see the major. He's gone to the barracks," the other· guard said. Myatt absent-mindedly drew a little nearer to the door; he could hear low voices inside. The surly guard became suddenly angry and brutal; he struck at Myatt's legs with the butt of his rifle. "Go away. We don't want spies round here. Go away, you Jew." With the calm of his race Myatt drew away; it was a superficial calm carried unconsciously like an inherited feature; beneath it he felt the resentment of a young man aware of his own importance. He leant towards the soldier with the intention of lodging in the flushed animal face some barb of speech, but he stopped in time, aware with amazement and horror of the presence of danger; in the small hungry eyes shone hatred and a desire to kill; it was as if all the oppressions, the pogroms, the chains, and the envy and superstition which caused them, had been herded into a dark cup of the earth and now he stared down at them from the rim. He moved back with his eyes on the soldier while the man's fingers felt round the trigger. "I'll see the station-master's clerk," he said, but his instinct told him to walk quickly back to his car and rejoin the train.

"That's not the way," the friendly guard called after him. "Over there. Across the line." Myatt was thankful for the storm that roared along the line and blew gustily between him and the soldiers. Where he stood there was no prevailing wind, for it was trapped in the alleys between the buildings and sent swirling round the corners in contrary directions. He wondered at his own persistence in staying in the empty dangerous station; he told himself that he owed the girl nothing, and he knew that she would agree with him. "We're quits," she would say. "You've given me the ticket, and I've given you a nice time." But he was tied by her agreement, by her refusal to make any claim. Before so complete a humility one could be nothing else but generous. He picked his way across the line and pushed open a door. A tousled man sat at a desk drinking wine. His back was turned, and Myatt said in what he hoped was an intimidating authoritative tone, "I want to make an inquiry." He had no reason to be afraid of a civilian, but when the man turned and he saw the eyes grow cunning and insolent at the sight of him, he despaired. A mirror hung above the desk, and in it Myatt saw the reflection of himself quite clearly for a moment, short and stout and nasal in his heavy fur coat, and it occurred to him that perhaps these people hated him not only because he was a Jew but because he carried the traces of money into their resigned surroundings. "Well?" said the clerk.

"I want to make an inquiry," Myatt said, "about a girl who was left behind here from the Orient express this morning."

"What do you mean?" the clerk asked insolently. "If anybody leaves the train, they leave it. They aren't left behind. Why, the train was waiting here this morning for more than half an hour."

"Well, then, did a girl get out?"

"No."

"Will you just examine your tickets and check that?"

"No. I said no one got out, didn't I? What are you waiting here for? I'm a busy man."

Myatt knew suddenly that he would not be sorry to accept the clerk's word and end his search; he would have done all that lay in his power, and he would be free. He thought of Coral for a moment as a small alley, enticing a man's footsteps, but blind at the end with a windowless wall; there were others, and he thought for a moment of Janet Pardoe, who were like streets lined with shops full of glitter and warmth, streets which led somewhere. He was reaching an age when he wanted to marry and have children, set up his tent and increase his tribe. But his thoughts had been too precise; they roused his conscience on behalf of someone who had not shown the slightest hope of marriage but had been intent only on honest payment and her own affection. It came to him again as a strange and unexpected cry, her exclamation, "I love you." He returned from the doorway to the clerk's desk determined to do all that he could do, to scamp no effort; she might now be somewhere in discomfort, stranded without money, possibly afraid. "She was seen to leave the train."

The clerk groaned at him: "What do you want me to do? Come out in the snow looking for her? I tell you I don't know a thing about her. I haven't seen any girl." His voice trailed off as he watched Myatt take out his note-case. Myatt removed a five-dina note and smoothed it between his fingers. "If you can tell me where she is, you can have two of these." The clerk stammered a little, tears came to his eyes, and he said with poignant regret, "If I could, if I only could. I am sure I should be glad to help." His face lit up and he suggested hopefully, "You ought to try the hotel.'' Myatt put the case back in his pocket; he had done all that he could do; and he went out to find his car.

For the last few hours the sun had been obscured, but its presence had been shown in the glitter of the falling snow, in the whiteness of the drifts; now it was sinking and the snow was absorbing the greyness of the sky; he would not get back to the train before dark. But even the hope of catching the train became faint, for he found when he reached his car that the engine had frozen, in spite of the rugs spread across the radiator.

4

Josef Grünlich said: ''It is all very well to sing.'' Although he complained of their inanition his eyes were red with weeping, and it was with an effort that he put away from him the little match girls and the princesses with hearts of ice. ''They will not catch me so easily.'' He began to walk round the walls of the waiting-room pressing a wet thumb to the woodwork. ''Never have I been imprisoned. It may surprise you, but it is true. At my time of life one cannot start something like that. And they are sending me back to Austria.''

''Are you wanted there?''

Josef Grünlich pulled down his waistcoat and set the little silver cross shaking. ''I do not mind telling you. We are all together, eh?'' He twisted his neck a little in a sudden access of modesty. ''I have slaughtered a man at Vienna.''

Coral said with horror, ''Do you mean that you are a murderer?'' Josef Grünlich thought: I should like to tell them. It's too good to be a secret. Quickness? Why —''Look over there, Herr Kolber,'' flick of the string, aim, fire twice, wriggle, man dead, all in two seconds; but better not. He encouraged himself with the cautious motto of his profession, the poker-work injunction to keep pride in bounds—''One never knows.'' He ran his finger inside his collar and said airily, ''I had to. It was an affair of honour.'' His hesitation was infinitesimal. ''He had—how do you say it?—made my daughter big.'' With difficulty he prevented himself laughing as he thought of Herr Kolber, small and dry, and of his petulant exclamation, ''This is a pretty kettle of fish.''

''You mean you killed him,'' Coral asked with amazement, ''just because he'd played around with your daughter?''

Josef Grünlich raised his hands and asked absent-mindedly, his eyes straying to the window and measuring its height from the ground, ''What could I do? Her honour, my honour . . .''

''Gosh,'' said Coral, ''I'm glad I haven't a father.''

Josef Grünlich said suddenly, ''A hairpin perhaps.''

"What do you mean, a hairpin?"

"Or a pocket knife?"

"I haven't got any hairpins. What would I want hairpins for?"

"I have a paper-cutter," Dr. Czinner said. As he handed it over, he said, "My watch has stopped. Could you tell me how long we have been back here?"

"An hour," said Josef.

"Two hours more then," Dr. Czinner remarked thoughtfully. Neither of the others heard him. Josef tiptoed to the door, paper-cutter in hand, and Coral watched him. "Come here, Fraülein," Josef said, and when she was beside him he whispered to her, "Have you some grease?" She gave him a pot of cold cream from her bag and he spread the cream thickly over the lock of the door, leaving a little space clear. He began to laugh gently to himself, bent almost double, with his eye to the lock. "Such a lock," he whispered jubilantly, "such a lock."

"What do you want the cream for?"

"Quiet," he said. "It will make what I do quieter."

He came back to the cold stove and waved them together. "That lock," he told them in an undertone, "is nothing. If we could send one guard away we could run."

"You'll be shot," Dr. Czinner said.

"They cannot shoot all three at once," Grünlich said. He dropped two suggestions into their silence: "The dark. The snow," and then stood back, waiting for their decision. His own mind worked smoothly. He would be the first out of the door, the first away; he could run faster than an old man and a girl; the guard would fire at the nearest fugitive.

"I should advise you to stay," Dr. Czinner said to Coral. "You aren't in any danger here."

Grünlich opened his mouth to protest, but he said nothing. They all three watched the window and the passing of one of the guards, rifle slung across his shoulder. "How long will it take you to open the door?" Dr. Czinner asked.

"Five minutes."

"Get to work then." Dr. Czinner tapped on the window and the other guard came. His large friendly eyes were pressed close to the glass and he stared into the waiting-room. The room was darker than the open air and he could see nothing but dim shapes moving restlessly here and there for warmth. Dr. Czinner put his mouth close to the glass and spoke to him in his own tongue. "What is your name?" Scratch, scratch, scratch went the paper knife, but when it slipped the whine was hushed by the layer of cream.

"Ninitch," said the ghost of a voice through the glass.

"Ninitch," Dr. Czinner repeated slowly. "Ninitch. I used to know your father, I think, in Belgrade." Ninitch showed no doubt of the easy lie, flattening his nose against the window, but all his view of the waiting-room was cut off by the doctor's features. "He died six years ago," he said.

Dr. Czinner took what was only a small risk to one acquainted with the poor in Belgrade and of the food they eat. "Yes. He was ill when I knew him. Cancer of the stomach."

"Cancer?"

"Pains."

"Yes, yes, in the belly. That was him. They came on at night, and he would get very hot in the face. My mother used to lie beside him with a cloth to dry his skin. Fancy you knowing him, your honour. Shall I open the window so that we can talk better?" Grünlich's knife scratched and scratched and scratched; a screw came out and tinkled like a needle on the floor.

"No," Dr. Czinner said. "Your companion might not like it."

"He's gone up to the town to the barracks to see the major. There's a foreigner been here making inquiries. He thinks there's something wrong."

"A foreigner?" Dr. Czinner asked. His mouth had gone dry with hope. "Has he gone?"

"He's just gone back to his car, down the road." The waiting-room was full of shadows. Dr. Czinner turned for a moment from the window and asked softly, "How is it going? Can you be quick?"

"Two minutes more," Grünlich said.

"There's a foreigner with a car down the road. He's been making inquiries."

Coral put her hands together and said softly, "He's come back for me. You see. You said he wouldn't." She began to laugh gently, and when Dr. Czinner whispered to her to keep calm, she said, "I'm not hysterical. I'm just happy," for it had occurred to her that this frightening adventure had been, after all, for the best; it had shown that he was fond of her, otherwise he would never have troubled to come back. He must have missed the train, she thought, and we shall have to spend the night together in Belgrade, perhaps two nights, and she began to dream of smart hotels, and dinners and his hand on her arm.

Dr. Czinner turned back to the window. "We are very thirsty," he said. "Have you any wine?"

Ninitch shook his head. "No." He added doubtfully, "Lukitch has a bottle of *rakia* across the way." Dusk had already made the way longer; there was no moon to light the steel of the rails and the lamp in the stationmaster's office might have been a hundred yards away and not a hundred feet.

"Be a good fellow and get us a drink."

He shook his head. "I mustn't leave the door."

Dr. Czinner did not offer him money; instead he called through the glass that he had attended Ninitch's father. "I gave him tablets to take when the pain was too bad."

"Little round tablets?" Ninitch asked.

"Yes. Morphia tablets."

Ninitch with his face pressed against the glass considered. It was possible to see the thoughts moving like fish in the translucent eyes. He said, "Fancy your giving him those tablets. He used to take one whenever the pain came, and one at night too. It made him sleep."

"Yes."

"What a lot I shall have to tell my wife."

"The drink," Dr. Czinner prompted him.

Ninitch said slowly, "If you tried to escape while I was gone, I should get into trouble." Dr. Czinner said, "How could we escape? The door's locked and the window is too small."

"Very well, then."

Dr. Czinner saw him go and turned with a sigh of unhappiness to the others. "Now," he said. His sigh was for the loss of his security. The struggle was renewed. It was his distasteful duty to escape if he could.

"One moment," Grünlich said, scratching at the door.

"There's no one outside. The guard's the other side of the line. When you come out of the door turn to the left and turn to the left again between the buildings. The car's down the road."

"I know all that," said Grünlich, and another screw tinkled to the floor. "Ready."

"I should stay here." Dr. Czinner said to Coral.

"But I couldn't. My friend's just down the road."

"Ready," Grünlich said again, scowling at them. They gathered at the door. "If they fire," Dr. Czinner said, "run crookedly." Grünlich pulled the door open and the snow blew in. It was not so dark outside as it had been in the room; the stationmaster's lamp across the rails lit up the figure of the guard in the window. Grünlich dived first into the storm; with head bent almost to his knees he bounced forward like a ball. The others followed. It was not easy to run. The wind and snow were enemies allied to drive them back: the wind broke their speed and the snow blinded them. Coral gasped with pain as she ran into a tall iron pillar with a trunk like an elephant's used for watering engines. Grünlich was far ahead of her; Dr. Czinner was a little behind; she could hear the painful effort of his lungs. Their footsteps made no sound in the snow, and they dared not shout to the driver of the car.

Before Grünlich had reached the gap between the buildings, a door slammed, someone called, and a rifle was fired. Grünlich's first effort had exhausted him. The distance between him and Coral lessened. The guard fired twice, and Coral could hear the buzz of the bullets far overhead. She wondered whether he was deliberately aiming high. Ten seconds more and they would pass the corner out of his sight and be visible from the car. She heard a door open again, a bullet whipped up the snow beside her and she ran the faster. She was almost side by side with Grünlich when they reached the corner. Dr. Czinner exclaimed behind her and she thought he was urging her to run faster, but before she turned the corner she looked back and saw that he was hugging the wall with both hands. She stopped and called out, "Herr Grünlich," but he paid her no attention, bundling round the building and out of sight.

"Go on," Dr. Czinner said.

The light shining from the horizon behind the thinner clouds faded. "Take my arm," she said. He obeyed, but his weight was too much for her, though he tried to ease it with one hand against the wall. They reached the corner. The rear lamp of the car blinked through the dusk and snow a hundred yards away, and she stopped. "I can't do it," she said. He made no answer, and when she took her hand away he slid down to the snow.

For a few seconds she wondered whether to leave him. She told herself with conviction that he would never have waited for her. But then she was in no great danger and he was. She stood hesitating, bent down to watch his pale old face; she noticed that there was blood on his moustache. Voices sounded round the corner, and she found she had no time to decide. Dr. Czinner was sitting with his back to a wooden door which was on the latch, and she pulled him inside and closed it again, but she was afraid to shoot the bolt. Someone ran by, an engine spluttered. Then the car roared into activity and distance took the sound and subdued it to a murmur. The shed had no windows: it was quite dark, and it was too late now for her to leave him.

She felt in Dr. Czinner's pockets and found a box of matches. When she struck one the roof shot above her like a bean-stalk. Something blocked the shed at one end, stacked half-way to the roof. Another match showed her fat sacks piled more than twice the height of a man. In Dr. Czinner's right-hand pocket was a folded newspaper. She tore off a page and made a spill, so that she might have enough light to drag him across the shed, for she was afraid that at any moment the guard would open the door. But his weight was too much for her. She held the spill close to his eyes to see whether he was conscious, and the stinging smoke woke him. He opened his eyes and watched her with perplexity. She whispered to him, "I want to hide you in the sacks." He did not seem to understand and she repeated the sentence very slowly and distinctly.

He said, "Ich spreche kein Englisch."

Oh, she thought, I wish I'd left him; I wish I was in the car now. He must be dying; he can't understand a word I say, and she was terrified at the idea of being left all alone in the shed with a dead man. Then the flame went out, choked in its own ash. She searched for the newspaper again on hands and knees and tore a page and folded it and made another spill. Then she found that she had mislaid the matches, and on hands and knees she felt the floor all round her. Dr. Czinner began to cough, and something moved on the floor close to her hands. She nearly screamed for fear of rats, but when at last she had found the matches and lit a spill, she saw it was the doctor who had moved. He was crawling crookedly towards the end of the shed. She tried to guide him, but he seemed unaware of her. All the slow way across she wondered why no one came to look in the shed.

Dr. Czinner was completely exhausted when he reached the sacks and he lay down with his face buried against them; he had been bleeding from the mouth. Again all the responsibility was hers. She wondered whether he was dying and she put her mouth close to his ear. "Shall I get help?" She was afraid that he would answer her in German, but this time he said quite clearly, "No, no." After all, she thought, he's a doctor; he must know. She asked him, "What can I do for you?" He shook his head and closed his eyes; he was no longer bleeding and she thought him better. She pulled sacks down from the pile and made a kind of cave large enough to shelter them, piling the sacks at the entrance, so that no one could see them from the door. The sacks were heavy with grain, and the work was unfinished when she heard voices. She crouched low in the hole with her fingers crossed for luck, and the door opened, a torch flashed over the sacks above her head. Then the door was shut and quiet returned. It was a long time before she had the courage to finish her work.

"We'll miss the train," Myatt said as he watched the driver turn and turn the starting handle; the self-starter was useless.

"I will take you back quicker," the man said. At last the engine began to wake, grumble, fall asleep and wake again. "Now we're off," he said. He climbed into his seat and turned on the front lamps, but while he was coaxing the engine into a steady roar, there was an explosion in the dusk behind. "What's that?" Myatt asked thinking the car had back-fired. Then it happened again, and a little afterwards there was another sound like the popping of a cork. "They are firing in the station," the driver said, pushing at the self-starter. Myatt knocked his hand away. "We'll wait."

The man repeated, "Wait?" He explained hurriedly, "It's the soldiers. We had better be off." He could not know how closely Myatt echoed his advice. Myatt was frightened; he had seen in the soldiers' attitude the spirit which made pogroms possible; but he remained obstinate; he was not quite satisfied that he had done everything he could to find the girl in Subotica.

"They are coming," the man said. Along the road from the station someone was running. At first he eluded them in the falling snow. Then they could make out a man dodging a little this way and a little that. He was upon them with surprising speed, short and fat, clawing at the door to climb in. "What's up?" Myatt asked him. He spluttered a little at the mouth. "Drive off quick." The door stuck and he bundled himself over the top and collapsed out of breath in the back seat.

"Is there anybody else?" Myatt asked. "Are you alone?"

"Yes, yes, alone," the man assured him. "Drive away quick."

Myatt leant back and tried to see his face. "No girl?"

"No. No girl."

There was a flash of light somewhere by the station buildings and a bullet scraped the mudguard. The driver, without waiting for an order, thrust down his foot and sent the car ricocheting from hole to hole along the road. Myatt again studied the stranger's face. "Weren't you on the Istanbul express?" The man nodded. "And you haven't seen a girl at the station?" The man became voluble. "I will tell you all about it." His speech was indistinct; many phrases were taken from his mouth by the plunging car; he said he had been detained for not declaring a little piece of lace, a very small little piece of lace, and had been badly treated by the soldiers and fired on when he escaped. "And you saw no girl?"

"No. No girl." He met Myatt's gaze with a complete honesty. It would have needed a long inquisition to spy at the back of the blank eyes the spark of malice, the little glint of cunning.

Although the wooden walls trembled with the wind, it was warm among the sacks, in the dark, in the unwindowed shed. Dr. Czinner turned to escape the pain in his chest and turned again, but it pursued him; only in the moment of turning did he gain a few strides; when he was still, the pain was on him. So all through the night he turned and turned. There were times when he became conscious of the wind outside and mistook the rustle of the snow for the movement of the pebbles at the sea's edge. During those moments a memory of his years of exile took shape in the barn, so that he began to recite declensions and French irregular verbs. But his resistance was weakened, and instead of showing an obstinate sarcastic front to his tormentors, he wept.

Coral Musker laid his head in an easier position, but he moved it again, turning it and turning it, muttering rhythmically, tears falling down his cheeks and on to his moustache. She gave up the attempt to help him and tried to escape into the past from her own fear, so that if their thoughts had been given a form visible to each other, a strange medley would have filled the barn. Under coloured lights which spilt out "It's a Baby" a clergyman rumpled his gown across his arm and dived at a black-board with a piece of chalk; several children pursued another with taunts in and out of stage doors, up and down agents' stairs. In a glass shelter on a grey sea-front a woman gave a neighbour a piece of her mind, while a bell tolled for tea or chapel.

"Wasser," Dr. Czinner whispered. "What do you want?" She bent down to him and tried to see his face. "Wasser."

"Shall I fetch someone?" He did not hear her.

"Do you want something to drink?" He paid her no attention, repeating "Wasser" again and again. She knew that he was not conscious, but her nerves were worn and she was irritated by his failure to answer her. "All right then, lie there. I've done all I can, I'm sure." She scrambled as far away from him as she could and tried to sleep, but the trembling of the walls kept her awake, the moaning of the wind made her aware of desolation, and she crept back to Dr. Czinner's side for company and comfort. "Wasser," he whispered again. Her hand touched his face and she was astonished at the heat and dryness of the skin. Perhaps he wants water, she thought, and was at a loss for a minute where to find it until she realised that it was falling all round her and piling itself against the walls of the shed. She was warned by a faint doubt: should somebody in a fever be given water? But remembering the dryness of his skin, she gave way to pity.

Although water was all round her, it was not easily or quickly reached. She had to light two spills and climb from the hole among the sacks without extinguishing them. She opened the door of the shed boldly, for she would half have welcomed discovery now, but the night was dark and there was no one to be seen. She gathered a handful of snow and went back into the shed and closed the door; the draught of the closing door blew out her light.

She called to Dr. Czinner, but he made no reply, and she was frightened at the thought that he might be dead. With one hand held in front of her face she walked forward and was brought up short by the wall. She waited a moment before trying again and was glad to hear a movement. She went to it and was again stopped by the wall. She thought with rising fear: it must have been a rat that moved. The snow in her hand was beginning to melt. She called out again, and this time a whisper answered. She jumped, it was so close to her, and feeling sideways her hand immediately touched the barricade of sacks. She began to laugh, but rebuked herself: Now don't be hysterical. Everything depends on you; and she tried to comfort herself with the assurance that this was her first star part. But it was difficult to play with confidence in the dark without applause.

When she had found the hole among the sacks most of the snow was melted or spilt, but she pressed what was left against the doctor's mouth. It seemed to ease him. He lay still, while the snow upon his lips melted and trickled between his teeth. He was so quiet that she lit a spill to see his face and was astonished at his shrewd conscious gaze. She spoke to him, but he was too full of thought to answer.

He was taking in his position, the force of his second failure. He knew that he was dying; he had been brought to consciousness by the touch of cold upon the tongue; and after a moment of bewilderment, remembered everything. He could tell where he had been shot from the pain; he was aware of his own fever and of the secret fatal bleeding within. For a moment he thought it his duty to brush the snow from his lips, but then he realised that he had no more duties to anyone but himself.

When the girl lit the spill he was thinking: Grünlich has escaped. It amused him to consider how hard it would be for a Christian to reconcile the escape with his own death. He smiled a little, maliciously. But then, his Christian training took an ironical revenge, for he too began to try to reconcile the events of the last few days and to wonder in what he had erred and how it was that others had succeeded. He saw the express in which they had travelled breaking the dark sky like a rocket. They clung to it with every stratagem in their power, leaning this way and leaning that, altering the balance now in this direction, now in that. One had to be very alive, very flexible, very opportunist. The snow on the lips had all melted and its effect was passing. Before the spill had flickered to its end, his sight had dimmed, and the great shed with its cargo of sacks floated away from him into darkness. He had no sense that he was within it; he thought that he was left behind, watching it disappear. His mind became confused; and soon he was falling through endless space, breathless, with a windy vacancy in head and chest, because he had been unable to retain his foothold on what was sometimes a ship and at other times a comet, the world itself, or only a fast train from Ostend to Istanbul. His mother and father bobbed at him their seamed thin faces, followed him through the ether, past the rush of stars, telling him that they were glad and grateful, that he had done what he could, that he had been faithful. He was breathless and could not answer them, tugged downward in great pain by gravity. He wanted to say to them that he had been damned by his faithfulness, that one must lean this way and that, but he had to listen all the way to their false comfort, falling and falling in great pain.

It was impossible to tell in the barn the progress of the dark; when Coral struck a match to see her watch, she was disappointed to find how slowly time went by. After a while the store of matches became low and she did not dare to strike another. She wondered whether to leave the shed and surrender herself, for she began to despair now of seeing Myatt again. He had done more than could have been expected of him by returning; it was unlikely that he would come back again. But she was frightened of the world outside, not of the soldiers, but of the agents, the long stairs, the landladies, the old life. As long as she lay by Dr. Czinner's side, she retained something of Myatt, a memory they both possessed.

Of course, she told herself, I can write to him, but months might pass before he was again in London, and she couldn't expect either his affection or desire to last when she was away. She knew too, that she could make him see her when he returned. He would feel that it was his duty at least to give her lunch, but "I'm not after his money," she whispered aloud in the dark barn beside the dying man. Her sense of desolation, the knowledge that for some reason, God alone knew why, she loved him, made her for a moment protestant. Why not? Why shouldn't I write to him? He might like it; he might want me still, and if he doesn't, why shouldn't I put up a fight? I'm tired of being decent, of doing the right thing. Her thoughts were very close to Dr. Czinner's when she exclaimed to herself that it didn't pay.

But she knew too well that it was her nature, she was born so and she must make the best of it. She would be a fumbler at the other game; relentless when she ought to be weak, forgiving when she ought to be hard. Even now she could not dwell long with envy and admiration at the thought of Grünlich driving away into the dark beside Myatt; her thoughts returned with a stupid fidelity to Myatt himself, to her last sight of him in the restaurant-car with his fingers caressing his gold cigarette case. But she was aware all the time that there was no quality in Myatt to justify her fidelity; it was just that she was like that and he had been kind. She wondered for a moment whether Dr. Czinner's case was not the same; he had been too faithful to people who could have been served better by cunning. She heard his difficult breathing through the dark and thought again without bitterness or criticism, it just doesn't pay.

The fork of roads sprang towards the headlights. The driver hesitated for a fraction too long, then twisted his wheel and sent the car spinning round on two wheels. Josef Grünlich fell from one end of the seat to the other, gasping with fear. He did not dare to open his eyes again until the four wheels were on the ground. They had left the main road, and the car was bounding down the ruts of a country lane, splashing a fierce light on the budding trees and turning them to cardboard. Myatt leaned back from his seat beside the driver and explained, "He's avoiding Subotica and is going over the line by a cattle crossing. You had better hold tight." The trees vanished and suddenly they were roaring downhill between bare snow-draped fields. The lane had been churned by cattle into mud which had frozen. Two red lights sprang up towards them from below, and a short stretch of rail glinted with emerald drops. The lights swung backward and forward and a voice could be heard above the engine, calling.

"Shall I drive through them?" the man asked calmly, his foot ready to fall on the accelerator. "No, no!" Myatt exclaimed. He saw no reason why he should get into trouble for a stranger's sake. He could see the men holding the lanterns. They wore grey uniforms and carried revolvers. The car stopped between them, jumping the first rail and coming to rest tilted like a stranded boat. One of the soldiers said something which the driver translated into German. "He wants to see our papers."

Josef Grünlich leant back quietly against the cushions with his legs crossed. One hand played idly with his silver chain. When one of the soldiers caught his eye he smiled gently and nodded; anyone would have taken him for a rich and amiable business man, travelling with his secretary. It was Myatt who was flurried, sunk in his fur coat, remembering the woman's cry of "Dirty Jew," the sentry's eyes, the clerk's insolence. It was in some such barren quarter of the world, among frozen fields and thin cattle, that one might expect to find old hatreds the world was outgrowing still alive. A soldier flashed his lamp in his face and repeated his demand with impatience and contempt. Myatt took out his passport, the man held it upside down and examined closely the lion and the unicorn; then he brought out his one word of German:

"Englander?"

Myatt nodded and the man threw the passport back on the seat and became absorbed in the driver's papers, which opened out into a long streamer like a child's book. Josef Grünlich leant cautiously forward and took Myatt's passport from the seat in front. He grinned when the red light was flashed on his face and flourished the passport. The guard called his friend, they stood and examined him under the light, speaking together in low voices, paying no attention to his gesture. "What do they want?" he complained without altering his fixed fat smile. One of the men gave an order, which the driver translated. "Stand up."

With Myatt's passport in one hand, the other on his silver chain, he obeyed, and they moved the lights from his feet to his head. He had no overcoat and shivered with the cold. One of the men laughed and prodded him in the stomach with a finger. "They want to see if it's real," the driver explained.

"What's real?"

"Your roundness."

Josef Grünlich had to feign amusement at the insult and smile and smile. His self-esteem had been pricked by two anonymous fools whom he would never see again. Someone else would have to bear the pain of his indignity, for it had been his pride, as it was now his grief, that he never forgot an injury. He did his best by pleading with the driver in German, "Can't you run them down?" and he grinned at the men and waggled the passport, while they discussed him point by point. Then they stood back and nodded, and the driver pressed the starter. The car lifted over the rails, then slowly climbed a long rutted lane, and Josef Grünlich looking back saw the two red lamps bobbing like paper lanterns in the darkness.

"What did they want?"

"They were looking for someone," the driver said. But that Josef knew well. Hadn't he killed Kolber in Vienna? Hadn't he escaped only an hour ago from Subotica under the eyes of a sentry? Wasn't he the cute one, the cunning fellow, who was quick and never hesitated? They had closed every road to cars and yet he slipped through. But like a small concealed draught the thought came to him that if they had been seeking him they would have found him. They were looking for someone else. They thought someone else of more importance. They had circulated the description of the old slow doctor and not of Josef Grünlich, who had killed Kolber and whose boast it was—"five years now and never jugged." The fear of speed left him. As they hurtled through the dark in the creaking antique car, he sat still, brooding on the injustice of it all.

Coral Musker woke with the sense of strangeness, of difference. She sat up and the sack of grain creaked under her. It was the only sound; the whisper of falling snow had stopped. She listened, and realised with fear that she was alone. Dr. Czinner had gone; she could no longer hear his breathing. Somewhere from far away the sound of a car changing gear reached her through the dusk. It came to her side like a friendly dog, fawning and nuzzling.

If Dr. Czinner is gone, she thought, there's nothing to keep me here. I'll go and find that car. If it's the soldiers they won't do anything to me; it may be . . . Longing kept the sentence open like the beak of a hungry bird. She put out a hand to steady herself, while she got upon her knees, and touched the doctor's face. He did not move, and though the face was warm, she could feel the blood as crisp and dry round his mouth as old skin. She screamed once and then was quiet and purposeful, feeling for the matches, lighting a spill. But her hand shook. Her nerves were bending, even though they had not given way, beneath the weight of her responsibilities. It seemed to her that every day for the past week had loaded her with something to decide, some fear which she must disguise. "Here's this job at Constantinople. Take it or leave it. There are a dozen girls on the stairs"; Myatt pressing the ticket into her bag; her landlady advising this and that; the sudden terror of strangeness on the quay at Ostend with the purser calling after her to remember him.

In the light of the spill she was again surprised by the doctor's knowledgeable stare, but it was a frozen knowledge which never changed. She looked away and looked back and it was the same. I never knew he was as bad as that, she thought. I can't stay here. She even wondered whether they would accuse her of his death. These foreigners, whose language she could not understand, were capable of anything. But she delayed too long, while the spill burned down, because of an odd curiosity. Had he too once had a girl? The thought robbed him of impressiveness, he was no longer terrifying dead, and she examined his face more closely than she had ever dared before. Manners went out with life. She noticed for the first time that his face was curiously coarse-featured; if it had not been so thin it might have been repulsive; perhaps it was only anxiety and scant food which had lent it intelligence and a certain sensibility. Even in death, under the shaking blue light of a slip of newspaper, the face was remarkable for its lack of humour. Perhaps, unlike most men, he had never had a girl. If he had lived with somebody who laughed at him a bit, she thought, he would not now be here like this; he wouldn't have taken things so seriously; he'd have learnt not to fuss, to let things slide; it's the only way. She touched the long moustaches. They were comic; they were pathetic; they could never let him seem tragic. Then the spill went out and he might have been buried already for all she could see of him and soon for all she thought of him, her mind swept away by faint sounds of a cruising car and of footsteps. Her scream had not gone unheard.

A narrow wash of light flowed under the ill-fitting door; voices spoke; and the car came humming gently down the road outside. The footsteps moved away, a door opened, and through the thin walls of the barn she heard somebody routing among the sacks next door; a dog snuffled. It brought back the level dull Nottingham fields, on a Sunday, the little knot of miners with whom she once went ratting, a dog called Spot. In and out of barns the dog went while they all stood in a circle armed with sticks. There was an argument going on outside, but she could not recognise any of the voices. The car stopped, but the engine was left softly running.

Then the door of the shed opened and the light leaped upwards to the sacks. She raised herself on an elbow and saw, through a crack of her barricade, the pale officer in pince-nez and the soldier who had been on guard outside the waiting-room. They crossed the floor towards her and her nerves gave way; she could not bear to wait all the slow time till she was discovered. They were half turned from her and when she got to her feet and called out, "Here I am," the officer jumped round, pulling out his revolver. Then he saw who it was, and asked her a question, standing still in the middle of the floor with his revolver levelled. She thought she understood him and said, "He's dead."

The officer gave an order and the soldier advanced and began to pull away the sacks slowly. It was the same man who had stopped her on the way to the restaurant-car, and she hated him for a moment until he raised his face and smiled at her miserably and apologetically, while the officer bombarded him from behind with little barbed impatiences. Suddenly, as he pulled away the last sack at the cave mouth, their faces almost touched, and in that instant she got as much from him as from conversation with a quiet man.

Major Petkovitch, when he saw that the doctor made no movement, crossed the shed and shone the light full on the dead face. The long moustaches paled in the glow and the open eyes cast back the light like plates. The major held out his revolver to the soldier. The good humour, the remnants of simple happiness, which had remained somewhere behind the façade of misery, collapsed. It was as if all the floors of a house fell and left the walls standing. He was horrified and inarticulate and motionless; and the revolver remained lying in the major's palm. Major Petkovitch did not lose his temper; he watched the other with curiosity and determination through his gold pince-nez. He had all the feeling of a barracks at his finger's end; beside the worn books on German strategy there stood on his shelves a little row of volumes on psychology; he knew every one of his privates with the intimacy of a confessor, how far they were brutal, how far kind, how far cunning and how far simple; he knew what their pleasures were—*rakia* and gaming and women; their ambitions, though these might be no more than an exciting or a happy story to tell a wife. He knew best of all how to adjust punishment to character, and how to break the will. He had been impatient with the soldier as he pulled so slowly at the sacks, but he was not impatient now; he let the revolver lie in his palm and repeated his command quite calmly, gazing through the gold rims.

The soldier lowered his head and wiped his nose with his hand and squinted painfully along the floor. Then he took the revolver and put it to Dr. Czinner's mouth. Again he hesitated. He laid his hand on Coral's arm, and with a push sent her face downwards to the floor, and as she lay there, she heard the shot. The soldier had saved her from the sight, but he could not save her from her imagination. She got up and fled to the door, retching as she ran. She had expected the relief of darkness, and the glare of the headlamps outside came like a blow on the head. She leant against the door and tried to steady herself, feeling infinitely more alone than when she woke and found Dr. Czinner dead; she wanted Myatt desperately, with pain. People were still arguing beside the car, and there was a faint smell of liquor in the air.

"What the hell?" a voice said. The knot of people was torn in two, and Miss Warren appeared between them. Her face was red and sore and triumphant. She gripped Coral's arm. "What's happening? No, don't tell me now. You're sick. You're coming with me straight out of this." The soldiers stood between her and the car, and the officer came from the shed and joined them. Miss Warren said rapidly in a low voice, "Promise anything. Don't mind what you say." She put a large square hand on the officer's sleeve and began to talk ingratiatingly. He tried to interrupt her, but his words were swept away. He took off his glasses and wiped them and was lost. Threats would have been idle, she might have protested all night, but she offered him the one bait it would have been against his nature to refuse, reason. And behind the reason she offered she allowed him to catch a glimpse of a different, a more valuable reason, a high diplomatic motive. He wiped his glasses again, nodded, and gave in. Miss Warren seized his hand and squeezed it, imprinting deep on the wincing finger the mark of her signet ring.

Coral slid to the ground. Miss Warren touched her and she tried to shake herself free. After the great noise the earth was swimming up to her in silence. Very far away a voice said, "Your heart's bad," and she opened her eyes again, expecting to see an old face beneath her. But she was stretched along the back seat of a car and Miss Warren was covering her with a rug. She poured out a glass of brandy and held it to Coral's mouth; the car starting shook them together and spilled the brandy over her chin; Coral smiled back at the flushed, tender, rather drunken face.

"Listen, darling," Miss Warren said, "I'm taking you back with me to Vienna first. I can wire the story from there. If any dirty skunk tries to get at you say nothing. Don't even open your mouth to say no."

The words conveyed nothing to Coral. She had a pain in her breast. She saw the station lights go out as the car turned away towards Vienna and she wondered with an obstinate fidelity where Myatt was. The pain made breathing difficult, but she was determined not to speak. To speak, to describe her pain, to ask for help would be to empty her mind for a moment of his face; her ears would lose the sound of his voice whispering to her of what they would do together in Constantinople. I won't be the first to forget, she thought with obstinacy, fighting with all the other images which strove for supremacy, the scarlet blink of the car down the dusky road, Dr. Czinner's stare in the light of the spill; fighting desperately at last against pain, against breathlessness, against a desire to cry out, against a darkness of the brain which was robbing her even of the images she fought.

I remember. I haven't forgotten. But she could not restrain one cry. It was so low that the humming motor drowned it. It never reached Miss Warren's ears any more than the renewed whisper which followed it: I haven't forgotten.

"Exclusive," Miss Warren said, drumming with her fingers on the rugs. "I want it exclusive. It's my story," she claimed with pride, allowing somewhere at the back of her mind, behind the headlines and the leaded type, a dream to form of Coral in pyjamas pouring out coffee, Coral in pyjamas mixing a cocktail, Coral asleep in the redecorated and rejuvenated flat.

PART FIVE

Constantinople

1

H ello, hello. Has Mr. Carleton Myatt arrived yet?"
The small lively Armenian, with a flower in his buttonhole, answered, in an English as trim and well cut as his morning coat, "No. I am afraid not. Is there any message?"

"Surely the train is in?"

"No. It is three hours late. I believe the engine broke down near Belgrade."

"Tell him Mr. Joyce . . ."

"And now," said the reception clerk, leaning confidentially over the counter towards two rapt American girls, who watched him with parted lips, under beautiful plucked brows, "what can I advise for you two ladies this afternoon? You should have a guide for the bazaars."

"Perhaps you, Mr. Kalebdjian," they said almost in the same breath; their wide avaricious virginal eyes followed him as he swung round at the buzz of the telephone: "Hello. Hello. Long-distance personal call? Right. Hello. No, Mr. Carleton Myatt has not arrived yet. We expect him any moment. Shall I take a message? You will ring up again at six. Thank you."

"Ah," he said to the two Americans, "if I could, it would be such a pleasure. But duty keeps me here. I have a second cousin though, and I will arrange that he shall meet you here tomorrow morning and take you to the bazaar. Now this afternoon I would suggest that you take a taxi to the Blue Mosque by way of the Hippodrome, and afterwards visit the Roman cisterns. Then if you took tea at the Russian restaurant in Pera, and came back here for dinner, I would recommend you to a theatre for the evening. Now if that suits you, I'll order you a taxi for the afternoon from a reliable garage."

They both opened their mouths at once and said, "That'll be swell, Mr. Kalebdjian," and while he was ringing up his third cousin's garage in Pera, they moved across the hall to the dusty confectionery stall and wondered whether to buy him a box of candies. The great garish hotel with its tiled floors and international staff and its restaurant in imitation of the Blue Mosque had been built before the war; now that the Government had shifted to Ankara and Constantinople was feeling the competition of the Piraeus, the hotel had sunk a little in the world. The staff had been cut, and it was possible to wander through the great empty lounge without meeting a page and the bells notoriously did not ring. But at the reception counter Mr. Kalebdjian opposed the general inertia in his well-cut coat.

"Is Mr. Carleton Myatt in, Kalebdjian?"

"No, sir, the train's late. Would you care to wait?"

"He's got a sitting-room?"

"Oh, naturally. Here, boy, show this gentleman to Mr. Myatt's room."

"Give him my card when he comes in."

The two Americans decided not to give Mr. Kalebdjian a box of Turkish delight, but he was so sweet and pretty they wanted to do something for him and they stood lost in thought, until he appeared suddenly at their elbow: "Your taxi is here, ladies. I will give the driver full directions. You will find him most reliable." He led them out and saw them safely away. The little stir and bustle subsided like dust, and Mr. Kalebdjian went back into the silent hall. For a moment it had been almost as in the old days at the height of the season.

No one came in for a quarter of an hour; an early fly nipped by the cold died noisily against a window-pane. Mr. Kalebdjian rang up the housekeeper's room to make sure that the heating was turned on in the rooms, and then he sat with his hands between his knees with nothing to think about and nothing to do.

The swing doors turned and turned, and a knot of people entered. Myatt was the first of them. Janet Pardoe and Mr. Savory followed him and three porters with their luggage. Myatt was happy. This was his chosen ground; an international hotel was his familiar oasis, however bare. The nightmare of Subotica faded and lost all reality before Mr. Kalebdjian advancing to meet him. He was glad that Janet Pardoe should see how he was recognised in the best hotels far away from home.

"How are you, Mr. Carleton Myatt? This is a great joy." Mr. Kalebdjian shook hands, bowing from the hips, his incredibly white teeth flashing with genuine pleasure.

"Glad to see you, Kalebdjian. Manager away as usual? These are my friends, Miss Pardoe and Mr. Savory. The whole of this hotel is on Kalebdjian's shoulders," he explained to them. "You are making us comfortable? That's right. See that there's a box of sweets in Miss Pardoe's room."

Janet Pardoe began softly, "My uncle's meeting me," but Myatt swept aside her objection. "He can wait one day. You must be my guest here tonight." He was beginning to unfurl again his peacock tail with a confidence which he borrowed from the palms and pillars and Mr. Kalebdjian's deference.

"There've been two telephone calls for you, Mr. Carleton Myatt, and a gentleman is waiting to see you in your room."

"Good. Give me his card. See to my friends. My room the usual one?" He walked rapidly to the lift, his lips pursed with exhilaration, for there had been in the last few days too much that had been uncertain and difficult to understand, and now he was back at work. It will be Mr. Eckman, he thought, not troubling to look at the card, and suddenly quite certain of what he would say to him. The lift rose uneasily to the first floor and the boy led him down a dusty passage and opened a door. The sunlight poured into the room and he could hear the yapping of cars through the open window. A fair stocky man in a tweed suit got up from the sofa. "Mr. Carleton Myatt?" he asked.

Myatt was surprised. He had never seen this man before. He looked at the card in his hand and read Mr. Leo Stein. "Ah, Mr. Stein."

"Surprised to see me?" said Mr. Stein. "Hope you don't think me precipitate." He was very bluff and cordial. Very English, Myatt thought, but the nose betrayed him, the nose which had been straightened by an operation and bore the scar. The hostility between the open Jew and the disguised Jew showed itself at once in the conjurer's smiles, the hearty handclasp, the avoidance of the eyes. "I had expected our agent," Myatt said.

"Ah, poor Eckman, poor Eckman," Stein sighed, shaking his blond head.

"What do you mean?"

"My business here really. To ask you to come and see Mrs. Eckman. Very worrying for her."

"You mean he's gone?"

"Disappeared. Never went home last night. Very mysterious."

It was cold. Myatt shut the window and with his hands in the pockets of his fur coat walked up and down the room, three paces this way and three paces that. He said slowly, "I'm not surprised. He couldn't face me, I suppose."

"He told me a few days ago that he felt you didn't trust him. He was hurt, very hurt."

Myatt said slowly and carefully, "I never trust a Jew who has turned Christian."

"Oh come, Mr. Myatt, isn't that a little dogmatic?" Stein said with a trace of discomfort.

"Perhaps. I suppose," Myatt said, stopping in the middle of the room, with his back to Stein, but with Stein's body reflected to the knees in a gilt mirror, "he had gone further in his negotiations than he had ever let me know."

"Oh, the negotiations," Stein's image in the mirror was less comfortable than his voice, "they, of course, were finished."

"He had told you we wouldn't buy?"

"He'd bought."

Myatt nodded. He was not surprised. There must have been a good deal behind Eckman's disappearance. Stein said slowly, "I'm really worried about poor Eckman. I can't bear to think he may have killed himself."

"I don't think you need worry. He's just retired from business, I expect. A little hurriedly."

"You see," Stein said, "he had worries."

"Worries?"

"Well, there was the feeling that you didn't trust him. And then he didn't have any children. He wanted children. He had a lot to worry him, Mr. Myatt. One must be charitable."

"But I am not a Christian, Mr. Stein. I don't believe that charity is the chief virtue. Can I see the paper he signed?"

"Of course." Mr. Stein drew a long envelope folded in two from the pocket of the tweed coat. Myatt sat down, spread the pages out on a table, and read them carefully. He made no comment and his expression conveyed nothing. No one could have told how great was his happiness at being back with figures, with something that he could understand and that had no feelings. When he had finished reading, he leant back and stared at his nails; they had been manicured before he left London, but they needed attention already.

Mr. Stein asked gently, "Had a good journey? Trouble in Belgrade didn't affect you, I suppose?"

"No," Myatt said, with an absent mind. It was true. It seemed to him that the whole unexplained incident at Subotica was unreal. Very soon he would have forgotten it because it was isolated from ordinary life and because it had no explanation. He said, "Of course you know we could drive a coach through this agreement."

"I don't think so," Mr. Stein said. "Poor Eckman was your accredited agent. You left him in charge of the negotiations."

"He never had the authority to sign this. No, Mr. Stein, this is no good to you, I'm afraid."

Mr. Stein sat down on the sofa and crossed his legs. He smelt of pipe smoke and tweeds. "Of course, Mr. Myatt," he said, "I don't want to force anything down your throat. My motto is: Never let down a fellow business man. I'd tear that agreement up now, Mr. Myatt, if it was the fair thing to do. But you see, since poor Eckman signed this, Moults' have given up. They won't reopen their offer now."

"I know just how far Moults' were interested in currants," Myatt said.

"Well, you see, under the circumstances, and in all friendliness, Mr. Myatt, if you tear that agreement up, I shall have to fight it. Mind if I smoke?"

"Have a cigar."

"Mind if I have a pipe?" He began to stuff a pale sweet tobacco into the bowl. "I suppose Eckman got a commission on this?"

"Ah, poor Eckman," Mr. Stein said enigmatically. "I'd really like you to come along and see Mrs. Eckman. She's very worried."

"She has no need to worry if his commission was big enough." Mr. Stein smiled and lit his pipe. Myatt began to read the agreement over again. It was true that it could be upset, but courts of law were chancy things. A good barrister might give a lot of trouble. There were figures one would rather not see published. After all Stein's business was of value to the firm. What he disliked was the price and the directorship granted to Stein. Even the price was not out of the question, but he could not bear the intrusion of a stranger into the family business. He said, "I'll tell you what I'll do. We'll tear this up and make you a new offer."

Mr. Stein shook his head. "Come now, that wouldn't be quite fair to me, would it, Mr. Myatt?" Myatt decided what he would do. He did not want to worry his father with a lawsuit. He would accept the agreement on condition that Stein resigned the directorship. But he was not going to show his hand yet; Stein might crumple. "Sleep on it, Mr. Stein," he advised.

"Well, that," Mr. Stein said cheerfully, "I doubt if I shall be allowed to do.

Not if I know the girls of today. I'm meeting a niece here this afternoon. She travelled out on your train from Cologne. Poor Pardoe's child.''

Myatt took out his cigar-case, and while he chose and cut a cigar, decided what he would do. He began to despise Stein. He talked too much and gave away unnecessary information. No wonder his business had not prospered. At the same time Myatt's vague attraction to Stein's niece crystallised. The knowledge that her mother had been a Jewess made him feel suddenly at home with her. She became approachable, and he was ashamed of the stiffness of his company the night before. They had dined together in the train on his return from Subotica, but all the time he had been on his best behaviour. He said slowly, "Oh yes, I met Miss Pardoe on the train. In fact she's down below now. We came from the station together.''

It was Mr. Stein's turn to weigh his words. When he spoke it was at a slight significant tangent. "Poor girl, she's got no parents. My wife thought we ought to have her to stay. I'm her guardian, you see.'' They sat side by side with the table between them. On it lay the agreement signed by Mr. Eckman. They did not mention it; business seemed laid aside, but Stein and Myatt knew that the whole discussion had been reopened. Each was aware of the thought in the other's mind, but they spoke in evasions.

"Your sister,'' Myatt said, "must have been a lovely woman.''

"She got her looks from my father,'' Mr. Stein said. Neither would admit that they were interested in Janet Pardoe's beauty. Even her grandparents were mentioned before her. "Did your family come from Leipzig?'' Myatt asked.

"That's right. It was my father who brought the business here.''

"You found it a mistake?''

"Oh, come now, Mr. Myatt, you've seen the figures. It wasn't as bad as that. But I want to sell out and retire while I can still enjoy life.''

"How do you mean?'' Myatt asked with curiosity. "How enjoy life?''

"Well, I'm not very much interested in business,'' Mr. Stein said.

Myatt repeated with amazement, "Not interested in business?''

"Golf,'' said Mr. Stein, "and a little place in the country. That's what I look forward to.''

The shock passed, and Myatt again noted that Stein gave away too much information. Stein's expansive manner was his opportunity; he flashed the conversation back to the agreement: "Why do you want this directorship then? I think perhaps I could come near to meeting you on the money question if you resigned the directorship.''

"I don't want it for myself necessarily,'' said Mr. Stein, puffing at his pipe between his phrases, squinting sideways at Myatt's lengthening ash, "but I'd like—for the sake of tradition, you know—to have one of the family on the board.'' He gave a long candid chuckle. "But I have no son. Not even a nephew.''

Myatt said thoughtfully, "You'll have to encourage your niece,'' and they both laughed and walked downstairs together. Janet Pardoe was nowhere to be seen.

"Miss Pardoe gone out?'' he asked Mr. Kalebdjian.

"No, Mr. Myatt, Miss Pardoe has just gone to the restaurant with Mr. Savory."

"Ask them to wait lunch twenty minutes, and Mr. Stein and I will join them."

There was a slight tussle to be last through the swing door; the friendship between Myatt and Mr. Stein grew rapidly.

When they were in a taxi on the way to Mr. Eckman's flat, Stein spoke. "This Savory,' he said, "who's he?"

"Just a writer," said Myatt.

"Is he hanging round Janet?"

"Friendly," Myatt said. "They met on the train." He clasped his hands over his knees and sat silent, contemplating seriously the subject of marriage. She is very lovely, he thought, she is refined, she would make a good hostess, she is half Jewish.

"I'm her guardian," said Mr. Stein. "Ought I perhaps to speak to him?"

"He's well off."

"Yes, but a writer," said Mr. Stein. "I don't like it. They are chancy. I'd like to see her married to a steady fellow in business."

"She was introduced to him, I think, by this woman she's been living with in Cologne."

"Oh yes," said Mr. Stein, uncomfortably, "she's been earning her own living since her poor parents died. I didn't interfere. It's good for a girl, but my wife thought we ought to see something of her, so I invited her here. Thought perhaps we could find her a better job near us."

They swerved round a miniature policeman standing on a box to direct traffic and climbed a hill. Below them, between a tall bare tenement and a telegraph-pole, the domes of the Blue Mosque floated up like a cluster of azure soap bubbles.

Mr. Stein was still uneasy. "It's good for a girl," he repeated. "And the firm's been taking up all my time lately. But when this sale is through," he added brightly, "I'll settle something on her."

The taxi drew into a small dark courtyard, containing a solitary dustbin, but the long stair they climbed was lighted by great windows and the whole of Stamboul seemed to flow out beneath them. They could see St. Sophia and the Fire Tower and a long stretch of water up the western side of the Golden Horn towards Eyub. "A fine situation," said Mr. Stein. "There's not a better flat in Constantinople," and he rang the bell, but Myatt was thinking of the cost and wondering how much the firm had contributed to Mr. Eckman's view.

The door opened. Mr. Stein did not trouble to give his name to the maid, but led the way down a white panelled passage which trapped the sun like a tawny beast between its windows. "A friend of the family?" Myatt suggested. "Oh, poor Eckman and I have been quite intimate for some time now," said Mr. Stein, flinging open a door on to a great glassy drawing-room, in which a piano and a bowl of flowers and a few steel chairs floated in primrose air. "Well, Emma," said Mr. Stein, "I've brought along Mr. Carleton Myatt to see you."

There were no dark corners in the room, no shelter from the flow of soft benevolent light, but Mrs. Eckman had done her best to hide behind the piano which stretched like a polished floor between them. She was small and grey and fashionably dressed, but her clothes did not suit her. She reminded Myatt of an old family maid who wears her mistress's discarded frocks. She had a pile of sewing under her arm and she whispered her welcome from where she stood, not venturing any farther on to the sun-splashed floor.

"Well, Emma," said Mr. Stein, "have you heard anything from your husband?"

"No. Not yet. No," she said. She added with bright misery, "He's such a bad correspondent," and asked them to sit down. She began to hide away needles and cotton and balls of wool and pieces of flannel in a large work-bag. Mr. Stein stared uncomfortably from steel chair to steel chair. "Can't think why poor Eckman bought all this stuff," he breathed to Myatt.

Myatt said: "You mustn't worry, Mrs. Eckman. I've no doubt you'll hear from your husband today."

She stopped in the middle of her tidying and watched Myatt's lips.

"Yes, Emma," said Mr. Stein, "directly poor Eckman knows how well Mr. Myatt and I agree, he'll come hurrying home."

"Oh," Mrs. Eckman whispered from her corner, away across the shining floor, "I don't mind if he doesn't come back here. I'd go to him anywhere. This isn't *home*," she said with a small emphatic gesture and dropped a needle and two pearl buttons.

"Well, I agree," Mr. Stein remarked and blew out his cheeks. "I don't understand what your husband sees in all this steel stuff. Give me some good mahogany pieces and a couple of arm-chairs a man can go to sleep in."

"Oh, but my husband has very good taste," Mrs. Eckman whispered hopelessly, her frightened eyes peering out from under her fashionable hat like a mouse lost in a wardrobe.

"Well," Myatt said impatiently, "I'm sure you needn't worry at all about your husband. He's been upset about business, that's all. There's no reason to think that he's—that anything has happened to him."

Mrs. Eckman emerged from behind the piano and came across the floor, twisting her hands nervously. "I'm not afraid of that," she said. She stopped between them and then turned round and went back quickly to her corner. Myatt was startled. "Then what are you afraid of?" he asked.

She nodded her head at the bright steely room. "My husband's so modern," she said with fear and pride. Then her pride went out, and with her hands plunged in her work-basket, among the buttons and the balls of wool, she said, "He may not want to come back for me."

"Well, what do you think of that?" Mr. Stein said as he went downstairs.

"Poor woman," Myatt said.

"Yes, yes, poor woman," Mr. Stein repeated, blowing his nose in an honest emotional way. He felt hungry, but Myatt had more to do before lunch, and Mr. Stein stuck close. He felt that with every taxi they shared, their intimacy grew, and apart altogether from their plans for Janet Pardoe, intimacy with Myatt was worth several thousand pounds a year to him. The taxi rattled down a steep cobbled street out into the cramped square by the general post office, and then down-hill again to Galata and the docks. At the top of a dingy stair they reached the small office, crammed with card indexes and dispatch-boxes, with only one window that looked out on to a high wall and the top of a steamer's funnel. Dust lay thick on the sill. It was the room which had given birth to the great glassy drawing-room, as an elderly mother may bear an artist as her last child. A grandfather clock, which with the desk filled most of the remaining space, struck two, but early as it was Joyce was there. A typist disappeared into a kind of boot cupboard at the back of the room.

"Any news of Eckman?"

"No, sir," said Joyce. Myatt glanced at a few letters and then left him, crouched like a faithful dog over Eckman's desk and Eckman's transgressions. "And now lunch," he said. Mr. Stein moistened his lips. "Hungry?" Myatt asked.

"I had an early breakfast," said Mr. Stein without reproach.

But Janet Pardoe and Mr. Savory had not waited for them. They were drinking coffee and liqueurs in the blue tiled restaurant when Myatt and Mr. Stein exclaimed how lucky it was that his niece and Myatt had met already and were friends. Janet Pardoe said nothing, but watched him with peaceful eyes, and smiled once at Myatt. She seemed to Myatt to be saying, "How little does he know of us," and he smiled back before he remembered that there was nothing to know.

"So I suppose you two," said Mr. Stein, "kept each other company all the way from Cologne."

Mr. Savory asserted himself, "Well, I think your niece saw more of me," but Mr. Stein swept on, eliminating him. "Got to know each other well, eh?"

Janet Pardoe opened her soft pronounced lips a little way and said softly, "Oh, Mr. Myatt had another friend he knew better than me." Myatt turned his head to order lunch, and when he gave his attention again to them, Janet Pardoe was saying with a sweet gentle malice, "Oh, she was his mistress, you know."

Mr. Stein laughed heartily. "Look at the wicked fellow. He's blushing."

"And you know she ran away from him," said Janet Pardoe.

"Ran away from him? Did he beat her?"

"Well, if you ask him he'll try and make a mystery about it. When the train broke down he motored all the way back to the last station and looked for her. He was away ages. And the mystery he tries to make of it. He helped someone to escape from the customs."

"But the girl?" Mr. Stein asked, eyeing Myatt roguishly.

"She ran away with a doctor," Mr. Savory said.

"He'll never admit it," Janet Pardoe said, nodding at Myatt.

"Well, really, I'm a little uneasy about it," Myatt said. "I shall telephone to the consul at Belgrade."

"Telephone to your grandmother," Mr. Savory exclaimed and looked with a bright nervousness from one to the other. It was his habit when he was quite certain of his company to bring out some disarming colloquialism which drew attention to the shop counter, the apprentices' dormitory, in his past. He was still at times swept by an intoxicating happiness at being accepted, at finding himself at the best hotel, talking on equal terms to people whom he had once thought he would never know except across the bales of silk, the piles of tissue paper. The great ladies who invited him to their literary At Homes were delighted by his expressions. What was the good of displaying a novelist who had risen from the bargain counter if he did not carry with him some faint trace of his ancestry, some remnant from the sales?

Mr. Stein glared at him. "I think you would be quite right," he said to Myatt. Mr. Savory was abashed. These people were among the minority who had never read his books, who did not know his claim to attention. They thought him merely vulgar. He sank a little in his seat and said to Janet Pardoe, "The doctor. Wasn't *your* friend interested in the doctor?" but she was aware of the others' disapproval, and did not trouble to search her mind for the long dull story Miss Warren had told her. She cut him short, "I can't keep count of all the people Mabel's interested in. I don't remember anything about the doctor."

It was only the vulgarity of Mr. Savory's expression to which Mr. Stein objected. He was very much in favour of a little honest chaff about the girl. It would seal his valuable intimacy with Myatt. When the first course was on the table, he brought the conversation round again. "Now tell us some more of what Mr. Myatt's been up to."

"She's very pretty," said Janet Pardoe, with audible charity. Mr. Savory glanced at Myatt to see whether he was taking offence, but Myatt was too hungry; he was enjoying his late lunch. "On the stage, isn't she?" he asked.

"Yes. Variety."

"I said she was a chorus girl," Janet Pardoe remarked. "There was something just the faintest bit common. Had you met her before?"

"No, no," Myatt said hurriedly. "Just a chance meeting."

"The things that go on in these long-distance trains," Mr. Stein exclaimed with relish. "Did she cost you much?" He caught his niece's eye and winked. When she smiled back, he was pleased. It would have been tiresome if she had been one of those old-fashioned girls in front of whom one could not talk openly; there was nothing he liked better than a little bit of smut in female company; so long, of course, he thought, with his eye turning with disapproval to Mr. Savory, as it was quite refined.

"Ten pounds," Myatt said, nodding to the waiter.

"My dear, how expensive," said Janet Pardoe, and she watched him with respect.

"I'm joking," Myatt said. "I didn't give her any money. I got her a ticket. Besides, it was just a friendship. She's a good creature."

"Ah, ha," said Mr. Stein. Myatt drained his glass. Across the blue tiles a waiter came, pushing a trolley. "The food's very good here," said Mr. Savory. Myatt expanded in the air of home, faintly aromatic with cooking; in one of the public rooms a Rachmaninoff Concerto was being played. One might have been in London. At the sound of the music a memory swam up into his mind and broke in scarlet light; people stuck their heads out of windows, laughing, talking, jeering at the fiddler. He said slowly to himself, "She was in love with me." He had never meant the words to drop audibly into the bare blue restaurant; he was embarrassed and a little shocked to hear them; they sounded boastful, and he had not meant to boast; there was nothing to boast about in being loved by a chorus girl. He blushed when they all laughed at him.

"Ah, these girls," Mr. Stein said, shaking his head, "they know how to get round a man. It's the glamour of the stage. I remember when I was a young fellow how I'd wait outside the stage door for hours just to see some little hussy from the front row. Chocolates. Suppers." He was stopped for a moment by the sight of a duck's grey breast on his plate. "The lights of London," he said.

"Talking of theatres, Janet," Myatt said, "will you do a show with me tonight?" He used her Christian name, feeling quite at ease now that he knew that her mother was Jewish and that her uncle was in his pocket.

"I should love to, but I've promised Mr. Savory to have dinner with him."

"We could go along to a late cabaret." But he had no intention of allowing her to dine with Mr. Savory. All the afternoon he was too busy to see her; there were hours he had to spend at the office, straightening out all the affairs which Mr. Eckman had so ingeniously tangled; he had visits to pay. At half-past three driving through the Hippodrome he saw Mr. Savory taking photographs in the middle of a group of children; he worked rapidly; three times he squeezed his bulb while the taxi went by, and each time the children laughed at him. It was half-past six when Myatt returned to the hotel.

"Is Miss Pardoe about, Kalebdjian?" Mr. Kalebdjian knew everything that went on in the hotel. Only his restlessness explained the minuteness of his information; he would make sudden dives from the deserted hall, rattle upstairs and down again, penetrate into distant lounges, and then be back at his desk with his hands between his knees, doing nothing. "Miss Pardoe is changing for dinner, Mr. Carleton Myatt." Once when a member of the Government was staying in the hotel, Mr. Kalebdjian had startled a meticulous caller from the British Embassy: "His Excellency is in the lavatory. But he will not be more than another three minutes." Trotting down corridors, listening at bathroom doors, back again with nothing to do but turn over in his mind a little sheaf of information, that was Mr. Kalebdjian's life.

Myatt tapped on Janet Pardoe's door. "Who's that?"

"May I come in?"

"The door's not locked."

Janet Pardoe had nearly finished dressing. Her frock lay across the bed and she sat before her dressing-table powdering her arms. "Are you really going to have dinner with Savory?" Myatt asked.

"Well, I promised to," Janet said.

"We could have had dinner at the Pera Palace, and then gone on to the Petits Champs."

"It would have been lovely, wouldn't it," Janet Pardoe said. She began to brush her eyelashes.

"Who's that?" Myatt pointed at a large photograph in a folding frame of a woman's square face. The hair was bobbed and the photographer had tried to dissolve in mist the rocky outline of the jaw.

"That's Mabel. She came with me on the train as far as Vienna."

"I don't remember seeing her."

"Her hair's cut short now. That's an old photograph. She doesn't like being taken."

"She looks grim."

"I put it up there in case I began to feel naughty. She writes poetry. There's some on the back. It's very bad, I think. I don't know anything about poetry."

"Can I read it?"

"Of course. I expect you think it very funny that anyone should write me poetry." Janet Pardoe stared into the mirror.

Myatt turned the photograph round and read.

"Naiad, slim, water-cool,
Borne for a river,
Running to the sea:
Endure a year longer
Salt, rocky, narrow pool"

"It doesn't rhyme. Or does it?" Myatt asked. "What does it mean, anyway?"

"I think it's meant as a compliment," Janet Pardoe said, polishing her nails.

Myatt sat down on the edge of the bed and watched her. What would she do, he wondered, if I tried to seduce her? He knew the answer: she would laugh. Laughter was the perfect defence of chastity. He said, "You aren't going to have dinner with Savory. I wouldn't be seen dead with a man like that. A counter-jumper."

"My dear," Janet Pardoe said, "I promised. Besides he's a genius."

"You are going to come downstairs with me, jump into a taxi, and have dinner at the Pera Palace."

"Poor man, he'll never forgive me. It would be fun."

And that's that. Myatt thought, pulling at his black tie, everything is easy now that I know her mother was Jewish. It was easy to talk hard all through dinner and to put his arm round her as they walked from the Pera Palace to the Petits Champs near the British Embassy. The night was warm, for the wind had dropped, and the tables in the garden were crowded. Subotica became the more unreal when he remembered the snow driven against his face. On the stage, a Frenchwoman in a dinner jacket pranced up and down with a cane under her arm, singing a song about "Ma Tante," which Spinelli had made popular in Paris more than five years before. The Turkish gentlemen, drinking coffee, laughed and chattered and shook their small dark feathery heads like noisy domestic birds, but their wives, so lately freed from the veil, sat silent and stared at the singer, their faces pasty and expressionless. Myatt and Janet Pardoe walked along the garden's edge, looking for a table, while the Frenchwoman screeched and laughed and pranced, flinging her desperate indecencies towards the inattentive and the unamused. Pera fell steeply away below them, the lights of fishing boats in the Golden Horn flashed like pocket torches, and the waiters went round serving coffee. "I don't believe there's a table. We shall have to go into the theatre." A fat man waved his hand and grinned. "Do you know him?" Myatt thought for a moment, walking on. "Yes, I think. . . . A man called Grünlich." He had seen him clearly only twice, once when he had climbed into the car and once when he had climbed out into the light of the waiting train. His memory therefore was dim, as of someone he had known better a long while ago in another country. When they had passed the table, he forgot him.

"There's an empty one." Under the table their legs touched. The Frenchwoman disappeared, swinging her hips, and a man flung cartwheels on to the stage from the wings. He got to his feet, took off his hat, and said something in Turkish which made everyone laugh.

"What did he say?"

"I couldn't hear," Myatt said. The man threw his hat into the air, caught it, leant forward until he was bent double, and called out a single word. All the Turkish gentlemen laughed again, and even the pasty faces smiled. "What did he say?"

"It must have been dialect. I couldn't understand it."

"I'd like something sentimental," Janet Pardoe said. "I drank too much at dinner. I'm feeling sentimental."

"They give you a good dinner, don't they?" Myatt said with pride.

"Why don't you stay there? People say that it's the best hotel."

"Oh well, you know, ours is pretty good, and I like Kalebdjian. He always makes me comfortable."

"Still the best people——"

A troupe of girls in shorts danced on the stage. They wore guards' caps and they had hung whistles round their necks, but the significance was lost on the Turkish audience, which was not used to guards dressed in shorts. "I believe they are English girls," Myatt said, and he suddenly leant forward.

"Do you know one of them?"

"I thought—I hoped," but he was not sure that it had not been fear he felt at the appearance of Dunn's Babies. Coral had not told him she was going to dance at the Petits Champs, but very likely she had not known. He remembered her staring with brave bewilderment into the noisy dark.

"I like the Pera Palace."

"Well, I did stay there once," Myatt said, "but something embarrassing happened. That's why I never went again."

"Tell me. But don't be silly, you must. Do tell me."

"Well, I had a friend with me. She seemed quite a nice young thing."

"A chorus girl?"

Dunn's Babies began to sing:

> "If you want to express
> That feeling you've got,
> When you're sometimes cold,
>   sometimes hot."

"No, no. She was the secretary of a friend of mine. Shipping."

"*Come up here,*" Dunn's Babies sang. "*Come up here,*" and some English sailors sitting at the back of the garden clapped and shouted: "Wait for us. We're coming." One sailor began to push his way between the tables towards the stage.

> *"If you want to express*
> *That kind of gloom*
> *You feel alone in a double*
> *   room . . ."*

The man fell on his back and everyone laughed. He was very drunk.

Myatt said, "It was terrible. She suddenly went mad at about two o'clock in the morning. Shouting and breaking things. The night porter came upstairs, and everybody stood about in the passage. They thought I was doing something to her."

"And were you?"

"No. I'd been fast asleep. It was terrible. I've never spent a night there since."

"*Come up here. Come up here.*"

"What was she like?"

"I can't remember a thing about her."

Jane Pardoe said softly, "You can't think how tired I am of living with a woman." Accidentally their hands touched on the table and then stayed side by side. The fairy lights hanging in the bushes gleamed back at him from her necklace, and at the very end of the garden, over her shoulder Myatt saw Mr. Stein pressing his way between the tables, pipe in hand. It was a mass attack. He knew that he only had to lean forward now to ask her to marry him and he would have arranged far more than his domestic future; he would have bought Mr. Stein's business at Mr. Stein's figure, and Mr. Stein would have a nephew on the board and be satisfied. Mr. Stein came nearer and waved his pipe; he had to make a detour to avoid the drunk man on the ground, and during that moment's grace Myatt summoned to his assistance any thoughts likely to combat the smooth and settled future. He remembered Coral and the sudden strangeness of their meeting, when he had thought that all was as familiar as cigarette smoke, but her face eluded him, perhaps because the train at that moment had been almost in darkness. She was fair, she was thin, but he could not remember her features. I have done all I can for her, he told himself; we should have said good-bye in any case in a few weeks. It's about time I settled down.

Mr. Stein waved his pipe again, and Dunn's Babies stamped their feet and blew their whistles.

> *"Waiting at the station*
> *For a near relation,*
> *Puff, puff, puff, puff——"*

Myatt said, "Don't go back to her. Stay with me."

"Puff, puff, puff, puff,
The Istanbul train."

She nodded and their hands moved together. He wondered whether Mr. Stein had the contract in his pocket.

This Gun for Hire

1

i

Murder didn't mean much to Raven. It was just a new job. You had to be careful. You had to use your brains. It was not a question of hatred. He had only seen the Minister once: he had been pointed out to Raven as he walked down the new housing estate between the small lit Christmas trees, an old grubby man without friends, who was said to love humanity.

The cold wind cut Raven's face in the wide Continental street. It was a good excuse for turning the collar of his coat well above his mouth. A hare-lip was a serious handicap in his profession; it had been badly sewn in infancy, so that now the upper lip was twisted and scarred. When you carried about so easy an identification you couldn't help becoming ruthless in your methods. It had always, from the first, been necessary for Raven to eliminate a witness.

He carried an attaché case. He looked like any other youngish man going home after his work; his dark overcoat had a clerical air. He moved steadily up the street like hundreds of his kind. A tram went by, lit up in the early dusk: he didn't take it. An economical young man, you might have thought, saving money for his home. Perhaps even now he was on his way to meet his girl.

But Raven had never had a girl. The hare-lip prevented that. He had learnt, when he was very young, how repulsive it was. He turned into one of the tall grey houses and climbed the stairs, a sour bitter screwed-up figure.

Outside the top flat he put down his attaché case and put on gloves. He took a pair of clippers out of his pocket and cut through the telephone wire where it ran out from above the door to the lift shaft. Then he rang the bell.

He hoped to find the Minister alone. This little top-floor flat was the socialist's home; he lived in a poor bare solitary way and Raven had been told that his secretary always left him at half-past six; he was very considerate with his employees. But Raven was a minute too early and the Minister half an hour too late. A woman opened the door, an elderly woman with pince-nez and several gold teeth. She had her hat on and her coat was over her arm. She had been on the point of leaving and she was furious at being caught. She didn't allow him to speak, but snapped at him in German, "The Minister is engaged."

He wanted to spare her, not because he minded a killing but because his employers would prefer him not to exceed his instructions. He held the letter of introduction out to her silently; as long as she didn't hear his foreign voice or see the hare-lip she was safe. She took the letter primly and held it up close to her pince-nez. Good, he thought, she's short-sighted. "Stay where you are," she said, and walked back up the passage. He could hear her disapproving governess voice, then she was back in the passage saying, "The Minister will see you. Follow me, please." He couldn't understand the foreign speech, but he knew what she meant from her behaviour.

His eyes, like little concealed cameras, photographed the room instantaneously: the desk, the easy chair, the map on the wall, the door to the bedroom behind, the wide window above the bright cold Christmas street. A small oil-stove was all the heating, and the Minister was having it used now to boil a saucepan. A kitchen alarm-clock on the desk marked seven o'clock. A voice said, "Emma, put in another egg." The Minister came out from the bedroom. He had tried to tidy himself, but he had forgotten the cigarette ash on his trousers, and his fingers were ink-stained. The secretary took an egg out of one of the drawers in the desk. "And the salt. Don't forget the salt," the Minister said. He explained in slow English, "It prevents the shell cracking. Sit down, my friend. Make yourself at home. Emma, you can go."

Raven sat down and fixed his eyes on the Minister's chest. He thought: I'll give her three minutes by the alarm-clock to get well away: he kept his eyes on the Minister's chest: just there I'll shoot. He let his coat collar fall and saw with bitter rage how the old man turned away from the sight of his hare-lip.

The Minister said, "It's years since I heard from him. But I've never forgotten him, never. I can show you his photograph in the other room. It's good of him to think of an old friend. So rich and powerful too. You must ask him when you go back if he remembers the time——" A bell began to ring furiously.

Raven thought: the telephone. I cut the wire. It shook his nerve. But it was only the alarm-clock drumming on the desk. The Minister turned it off. "One egg's boiled," he said and stooped for the saucepan. Raven opened his attaché case: in the lid he had fixed his automatic fitted with a silencer. The Minister said: "I'm sorry the bell made you jump. You see I like my egg just four minutes."

Feet ran along the passage. The door opened. Raven turned furiously in his seat, his hare-lip flushed and raw. It was the secretary. He thought: my God, what a household. They won't let a man do things tidily. He forgot his lip, he was angry, he had a grievance. She came in flashing her gold teeth, prim and ingratiating. She said, "I was just going out when I heard the telephone," then she winced slightly, looked the other way, showed a clumsy delicacy before his deformity which he couldn't help noticing. It condemned her. He snatched the automatic out of the case and shot the Minister twice in the back.

The Minister fell across the oil stove; the saucepan upset and the two eggs broke on the floor. Raven shot the Minister once more in the head, leaning across the desk to make quite certain, driving the bullet hard into the base of the skull, smashing it open like a china doll's. Then he turned on the secretary; she moaned at him; she hadn't any words; the old mouth couldn't hold its saliva. He supposed she was begging him for mercy. He pressed the trigger again; she staggered under it as if she had been kicked by an animal in the side. But he had miscalculated. Her unfashionable dress, the swathes of useless material in which she hid her body, had perhaps confused his aim. And she was tough, so tough he couldn't believe his eyes; she was through the door before he could fire again, slamming it behind her.

But she couldn't lock it; the key was on his side. He twisted the handle and pushed; the elderly woman had amazing strength; it only gave two inches. She began to scream some word at the top of her voice.

There was no time to waste. He stood away from the door and shot twice through the woodwork. He could hear the pince-nez fall on the floor and break. The voice screamed again and stopped; there was a sound outside as if she were sobbing. It was her breath going out through her wounds. Raven was satisfied. He turned back to the Minister.

There was a clue he had been ordered to leave; a clue he had to remove. The letter of introduction was on the desk. He put it in his pocket and between the Minister's stiffened fingers he inserted a scrap of paper. Raven had little curiosity; he had only glanced at the introduction and the nickname at its foot conveyed nothing to him; he was a man who could be depended on. Now he looked round the small bare room to see whether there was any clue he had overlooked. The suitcase and the automatic he was to leave behind. It was all very simple.

He opened the bedroom door; his eyes again photographed the scene, the single bed, the wooden chair, the dusty chest of drawers, a photograph of a young Jew with a small scar on his chin as if he had been struck there with a club, a pair of brown wooden hairbrushes initialled J.K., everywhere cigarette ash: the home of an old lonely untidy man; the home of the Minister for War.

A low voice whispered an appeal quite distinctly through the door. Raven picked up the automatic again; who would have imagined an old woman could be so tough? It touched his nerve a little just in the same way as the bell had done, as if a ghost were interfering with a man's job. He opened the study door; he had to push it against the weight of her body. She looked dead enough, but he made quite sure with the automatic almost touching her eyes.

It was time to be gone. He took the automatic with him.

ii

They sat and shivered side by side as the dusk came down; they were borne in their bright small smoky cage above the streets; the bus rocked down to Hammersmith. The shop windows sparkled like ice and "Look," she said, "it's snowing." A few large flakes went drifting by as they crossed the bridge, falling like paper scraps into the dark Thames.

He said, "I'm happy as long as this ride goes on."

"We're seeing each other to-morrow—Jimmy." She always hesitated before his name. It was a silly name for anyone of such bulk and gravity.

"It's the nights that bother me."

She laughed, "It's going to be wearing," but immediately became serious, "I'm happy too." About happiness she was always serious; she preferred to laugh when she was miserable. She couldn't avoid being serious about things she cared for, and happiness made her grave at the thought of all the things which might destroy it. She said, "It would be dreadful now if there was a war."

"There won't be a war."

"The last one started with a murder."

"That was an Archduke. This is just an old politician."

She said: "Be careful. You'll break the record—Jimmy."

"Damn the record."

She began to hum the tune she'd bought: "It's only Kew to you"; and the large flakes fell past the window, melted on the pavement: "a snowflower a man brought from Greenland."

He said, "It's a silly song."

She said, "It's a lovely song—Jimmy. I simply can't call you Jimmy. You aren't Jimmy. You're outsize. Detective-sergeant Mather. You're the reason why people make jokes about policemen's boots."

"What's wrong with 'dear,' anyway?"

"Dear, dear," she tried it out on the tip of her tongue, between lips as vividly stained as a winter berry. "Oh no," she decided, "I'll call you that when we've been married ten years."

"Well—'darling'?"

"Darling, darling. I don't like it. It sounds as if I'd known you a long, long time." The bus went up the hill past the fish-and-chip shops: a brazier glowed and they could smell the roasting chestnuts. The ride was nearly over, there were only two more streets and a turn to the left by the church, which was already visible, the spire lifted like a long icicle above the houses. The nearer they got to home the more miserable she became, the nearer they got to home the more lightly she talked. She was keeping things off and out of mind: the peeling wallpaper, the long flights to her room, cold supper with Mrs. Brewer and next day the walk to the agent's, perhaps a job again in the provinces away from him.

Mather said heavily, "You don't care for me like I care for you. It's nearly twenty-four hours before I see you again."

"It'll be more than that if I get a job."

"You don't care. You simply don't care."

She clutched his arm. "Look. Look at that poster." But it was gone before he could see it through the steamy pane. "Europe Mobilising" lay like a weight on her heart.

"What was it?"

"Oh, just the same old murder again."

"You've got that murder on your mind. It's a week old now. It's got nothing to do with us."

"No, it hasn't, has it?"

"If it had happened here, we'd have caught him by now."

"I wonder why he did it."

"Politics. Patriotism."

"Well. Here we are. It might be a good thing to get off. Don't look so miserable. I thought you said you were happy."

"That was five minutes ago."

"Oh," she said out of her light and heavy heart, "one lives quickly these days." They kissed under the lamp; she had to stretch to reach him; he was comforting like a large dog, even when he was sullen and stupid, but one didn't have to send away a dog alone in the cold dark night.

"Anne," he said, "we'll be married, won't we, after Christmas?"

"We haven't a penny," she said, "you know. Not a penny—Jimmy."

"I'll get a rise."

"You'll be late for duty."

"Damn it, you don't care."

She jeered at him, "Not a scrap—dear," and walked away from him up the street to No. 54, praying let me get some money quick, let *this* go on *this* time; she hadn't any faith in herself. A man passed her going up the road; he looked cold and strung-up, as he passed in his black overcoat; he had a hare-lip. Poor devil, she thought, and forgot him, opening the door of 54, climbing the long flights to the top floor, the carpet stopped on the first. She put on the new record, hugging to her heart the silly senseless words, the slow sleepy tune:

> *It's only Kew*
> *To you,*
> *But to me*
> *It's Paradise.*
> *They are just blue*
> *Petunias to you,*
> *But to me*
> *They are your eyes.*

The man with the hare-lip came back down the street; fast walking hadn't made him warm; like Kay in *The Snow Queen* he bore the cold within him as he walked. The flakes went on falling, melting into slush on the pavement, the words of a song dropped from the lit room on the third floor, the scrape of a used needle.

> *"They say that's a snowflower*
> *A man brought from Greenland.*
> *I say it's the lightness, the coolness, the whiteness*
> *Of your hand."*

The man hardly paused; he went on down the street, walking fast; he felt no pain from the chip of ice in his breast.

iii

Raven sat at an empty table in the Corner House near a marble pillar. He stared with distaste at the long list of sweet iced drinks, of *parfaits* and sundaes and *coupes* and splits. Somebody at the next table was eating brown bread and butter and drinking Horlick's. He wilted under Raven's gaze and put up his newspaper. One word "Ultimatum" ran across the top line.

Mr. Cholmondeley picked his way between the tables.

He was fat and wore an emerald ring. His wide square face fell in folds over his collar. He looked like a real-estate man, or perhaps a man more than usually successful in selling women's belts. He sat down at Raven's table and said, "Good evening."

Raven said, "I thought you were never coming, Mr. Chol-mon-deley," pronouncing every syllable.

"Chumley, my dear man, Chumley," Mr. Cholmondeley corrected him.

"It doesn't matter how it's pronounced. I don't suppose it's your own name."

"After all I chose it," Mr. Cholmondeley said. His ring flashed under the great inverted bowls of light as he turned the pages of the menu. "Have a *parfait*."

"It's odd wanting to eat ice in this weather. You've only got to stay outside if you're hot. I don't want to waste any time, Mr. Chol-mon-deley. Have you brought the money? I'm broke."

Mr. Cholmondeley said: "They do a very good Maiden's Dream. Not to speak of Alpine Glow. Or the Knickerbocker Glory."

"I haven't had a thing since Calais."

"Give me the letter," Mr. Cholmondeley said. "Thank you." He told the waitress, "I'll have an Alpine Glow with a glass of kümmel over it."

"The money," Raven said.

"Here in this case."

"They are all fivers."

"You can't expect to be paid two hundred in small change. And it's nothing to do with me," Mr. Cholmondeley said, "I'm merely the agent." His eyes softened as they rested on a Raspberry Split at the next table. He confessed wistfully to Raven, "I've got a sweet tooth."

"Don't you want to hear about it?" Raven said. "The old woman . . ."

"Please, please," Mr. Cholmondeley said, "I want to hear nothing. I'm just an agent. I take no responsibility. My clients . . ."

Raven twisted his hare-lip at him with sour contempt. "That's a fine name for them."

"How long the waitress is with my *parfait*," Mr. Cholmondeley complained. "My clients are really quite the best people. These acts of violence—they regard them as war."

"And I and the old man . . ." Raven said.

"Are in the front trench." He began to laugh softly at his own humour; his great white open face was like a curtain on which you can throw grotesque images: a rabbit, a man with horns. His small eyes twinkled with pleasure at the mass of iced cream which was borne towards him in a tall glass. He said, "You did your work very well, very neatly. They are quite satisfied with you. You'll be able to take a long holiday now.'' He was fat, he was vulgar, he was false, but he gave an impression of great power as he sat there with the cream dripping from his mouth. He was prosperity, he was one of those who possessed things, but Raven possessed nothing but the contents of the wallet, the clothes he stood up in, the hare-lip, the automatic he should have left behind. He said, ''I'll be moving.''

''Good-bye, my man, good-bye,'' Mr. Cholmondeley said, sucking through a straw.

Raven rose and went. Dark and thin and made for destruction, he wasn't at ease among the little tables, among the bright fruit drinks. He went out into the Circus and up Shaftesbury Avenue. The shop windows were full of tinsel and hard red Christmas berries. It maddened him, the sentiment of it. His hands clenched in his pockets. He leant his face against a modiste's window and jeered silently through the glass. A girl with a neat curved figure bent over a dummy. He fed his eyes contemptuously on her legs and hips; so much flesh, he thought, on sale in the Christmas window.

A kind of subdued cruelty drove him into the shop. He let his hare-lip loose on the girl when she came towards him with the same pleasure that he might have felt in turning a machine-gun on a picture gallery. He said, ''That dress in the window. How much?''

She said, ''Five guineas.'' She wouldn't ''sir'' him. His lip was like a badge of class. It revealed the poverty of parents who couldn't afford a clever surgeon.

He said, ''It's pretty, isn't it?''

She lisped at him genteelly, ''It's been vewwy much admired.''

''Soft. Thin. You'd have to take care of a dress like that, eh? Do for someone pretty and well off?''

She lied without interest, ''It's a model.'' She was a woman, she knew all about it, she knew how cheap and vulgar the little shop really was.

''It's got class, eh?''

''Oh yes,'' she said, catching the eye of a dago in a purple suit through the pane, ''it's got class.''

''All right,'' he said. ''I'll give you five pounds for it.'' He took a note from Mr. Cholmondeley's wallet.

''Shall I pack it up?''

''No,'' he said. ''The girl'll fetch it.'' He grinned at her with his raw lip. ''You see, she's class. This is the best dress you have?'' and when she nodded and took the note away he said, ''It'll just suit Alice then.''

And so out into the Avenue with a little of his scorn expressed, out into Frith Street and round the corner into the German café where he kept a room. A shock awaited him there, a little fir tree in a tub hung with coloured glass, a crib. He said to the old man who owned the café, ''You believe in this? This junk?''

''Is there going to be war again?'' the old man said. ''It's terrible what you read.''

''All this business of no room in the inn. They used to give us plum pudding. A decree from Cæsar Augustus. You see I know the stuff, I'm educated. They used to read it us once a year.''

''I have seen one war.''

''I hate the sentiment.''

''Well,'' the old man said, ''it's good for business.''

Raven picked up the bambino. The cradle came with it all of a piece: cheap painted plaster. "They put him on the spot, eh? You see I know the whole story. I'm educated."

He went upstairs to his room. It hadn't been seen to: there was still dirty water in the basin and the ewer was empty. He remembered the fat man saying, "Chumley, my man, Chumley. It's pronounced Chumley," flashing his emerald ring. He called furiously, "Alice," over the banisters.

She came out of the next room, a slattern, one shoulder too high, with wisps of fair bleached hair over her face. She said, "You needn't shout."

He said, "It's a pigsty in there. You can't treat me like that. Go in and clean it." He hit her on the side of the head and she cringed away from him, not daring to say anything but, "Who do you think you are?"

"Get on," he said, "you humpbacked bitch." He began to laugh at her when she crouched over the bed. "I've bought you a Christmas dress, Alice. Here's the receipt. Go and fetch it. It's a lovely dress. It'll suit you."

"You think you're funny," she said.

"I've paid a fiver for this joke. Hurry, Alice, or the shop'll be shut." But she got her own back calling up the stairs, "I won't look worse than what you do with that split lip." Everyone in the house could hear her, the old man in the café, his wife in the parlour, the customers at the counter. He imagined their smiles. "Go it, Alice, what an ugly pair you are." He didn't really suffer; he had been fed the poison from boyhood drop by drop: he hardly noticed its bitterness now.

He went to the window and opened it and scratched on the sill. The kitten came to him, making little rushes along the drain pipe, feinting at his hand. "You little bitch," he said, "you little bitch." He took a small two-penny carton of cream out of his overcoat pocket and spilt it in his soap-dish. She stopped playing and rushed at him with a tiny cry. He picked her up by the scruff and put her on top of his chest of drawers with the cream. She wriggled from his hand, she was no larger than the rat he'd trained in the home, but softer. He scratched her behind the ear and she struck back at him in a preoccupied way. Her tongue quivered on the surface of the milk.

Dinner-time, he told himself. With all that money he could go anywhere. He could have a slap-up meal at Simpson's with the business men; cut off the joint and any number of veg.

When he got by the public call-box in the dark corner below the stairs he caught his name "Raven." The old man said, "He always has a room here. He's been away."

"You," a strange voice said, "what's your name—Alice—show me his room. Keep an eye on the door, Saunders."

Raven went on his knees inside the telephone-box. He left the door ajar because he never liked to be shut in. He couldn't see out, but he had no need to see the owner of the voice to recognise: police, plain clothes, the Yard accent. The man was so near that the floor of the box vibrated to his tread. Then he came down again. "There's no one there. He's taken his hat and coat. He must have gone out."

"He might have," the old man said. "He's a soft-walking sort of fellow."

The stranger began to question them. "What's he like?"

The old man and the girl both said in a breath, "A hare-lip."

"That's useful," the detective said. "Don't touch his room. I'll be sending a man round to take his fingerprints. What sort of a fellow is he?"

Raven could hear every word. He couldn't imagine what they were after. He knew he'd left no clues; he wasn't a man who imagined things; he knew. He carried the picture of that room and flat in his brain as clearly as if he had the photographs. They had nothing against him. It had been against orders to keep the automatic, but he could feel it now safe under his armpit. Besides, if they had picked up any clue they'd have stopped him at Dover. He listened to the voices with a dull anger; he wanted his dinner; he hadn't had a square meal for twenty-four hours, and now with two hundred pounds in his pocket he could buy anything, anything.

"I can believe it," the old man said. "Why, to-night he even made fun of my poor wife's crib."

"A bloody bully," the girl said. "*I* shan't be sorry when you've locked him up."

He told himself with surprise: they hate me.

She said, "He's ugly through and through. That lip of his. It gives you the creeps."

"An ugly customer all right."

"I wouldn't have him in the house," the old man said. "But he pays. You can't turn away someone who pays. Not in these days."

"Has he friends?"

"You make me laugh," Alice said. "Him friends. What would he do with friends?"

He began to laugh quietly to himself on the floor of the little dark box: that's me they're talking about, me: staring up at the pane of glass with his hand on his automatic.

"You seem kind of bitter? What's he been doing to you? He was going to give you a dress, wasn't he?"

"Just his dirty joke."

"You were going to take it, though."

"You bet I wasn't. Do you think I'd take a present from him? I was going to sell it back to them and show him the money, and wasn't I going to laugh?"

He thought again with bitter interest: they hate me. If they open this door, I'll shoot the lot.

"I'd like to take a swipe at that lip of his. I'd laugh. I'd say I'd laugh."

"I'll put a man," the strange voice said, "across the road. Tip him the wink if our man comes in." The café door closed.

"Oh," the old man said, "I wish my wife was here. She would not miss this for ten shillings."

"I'll give her a ring," Alice said. "She'll be chatting at Mason's. She can come right over and bring Mrs. Mason too. Let 'em all join in the fun. It was only a week ago Mrs. Mason said she didn't want to see his ugly face in her shop again."

"Yes, be a good girl, Alice. Give her a ring."

Raven reached up his hand and took the bulb out of the fitment; he stood up and flattened himself against the wall of the box. Alice opened the door and shut herself in with him. He put his hand over her mouth before she had time to cry. He said, "Don't you put the pennies in the box. I'll shoot if you do. I'll shoot if you call out. Do what I say.'' He whispered in her ear. They were as close together as if they were in a single bed. He could feel her crooked shoulder pressed against his chest. He said, "Lift the receiver. Pretend you're talking to the old woman. Go on. I don't care a damn if I shoot you. Say, hello, Frau Groener.''

"Hello, Frau Groener.''

"Spill the whole story.''

"They are after Raven.''

"Why?''

"That five-pound note. They were waiting at the shop.''

"What do you mean?''

"They'd got its number. It was stolen.''

He'd been double-crossed. His mind worked with mechanical accuracy like a ready-reckoner. You only had to supply it with the figures and it gave you the answer. He was possessed by a deep sullen rage. If Mr. Cholmondeley had been in the box with him, he would have shot him: he wouldn't have cared a damn.

"Stolen from where?''

"You ought to know that.''

"Don't give me any lip. Where from?''

He didn't even know who Cholmondeley's employers were. It was obvious what had happened: they hadn't trusted him. They had arranged this so that he might be put away. A newsboy went by outside calling, "Ultimatum. Ultimatum.'' His mind registered the fact, but no more: it seemed to have nothing to do with him. He repeated, "Where from?''

"I don't know. I don't remember.''

With the automatic stuck against her back he even tried to plead with her. "Remember, can't you? It's important. I didn't do it.''

"I bet you didn't,'' she said bitterly into the unconnected 'phone.

"Give me a break. All I want you to do is remember.''

She said, "On your life I won't.''

"I gave you that dress, didn't I?''

"You didn't. You tried to plant your money, that's all. You didn't know they'd circulated the numbers to every shop in town. We've even got them in the café.''

"If I'd done it, why should I want to know where they came from?''

"It'll be a bigger laugh then ever if you get jugged for something you didn't do.''

"Alice,'' the old man called from the café, "is she coming?''

"I'll give you ten pounds.''

"Phoney notes. No thank you, Mr. Generosity.''

"Alice,'' the old man called again; they could hear him coming along the passage.

"Justice,'' he said bitterly, jabbing her between the ribs with the automatic.

"You don't need to talk about justice,'' she said. "Driving me like I was in prison. Hitting me when you feel like it. Spilling ash all over the floor. I've got enough to do with your slops. Milk in the soap-dish. Don't talk about justice.''

Pressed against him in the tiny dark box she suddenly came alive to him. He was so astonished that he forgot the old man till he had the door of the box open. He whispered passionately out of the dark, "Don't say a word or I'll plug you." He had them both out of the box in front of him. He said, "Understand this. They aren't going to get me. I'm not going to prison. I don't care a damn if I plug one of you. I don't care if I hang. My father hanged . . . what's good enough for him . . . Get along in front of me up to my room. There's hell coming to somebody for this."

When he had them there he locked the door. A customer was ringing the café bell over and over again. He turned on them. "I've got a good mind to plug you. Telling them about my hare-lip. Why can't you play fair?" He went to the window; he knew there was an easy way down—that was why he had chosen the room. The kitten caught his eye, prowling like a toy tiger in a cage up and down the edge of the chest of drawers, afraid to jump. He lifted her up and threw her on his bed; she tried to bite his finger as she went; then he got through on to the leads. The clouds were massing up across the moon, and the earth seemed to move with them, an icy barren globe, through the vast darkness.

iv

Anne Crowder walked up and down the small room in her heavy tweed coat; she didn't want to waste a shilling on the gas meter, because she wouldn't get her shilling's worth before morning. She told herself, I'm lucky to have got that job. I'm glad to be going off to work again, but she wasn't convinced. It was eight now; they would have four hours together till midnight. She would have to deceive him and tell him she was catching the nine o'clock, not the five o'clock train, or he would be sending her back to bed early. He was like that. No romance. She smiled with tenderness and blew on her fingers.

The telephone at the bottom of the house was ringing. She thought it was the door-bell and ran to the mirror in the wardrobe. There wasn't enough light from the dull globe to tell her if her make-up would stand the brilliance of the Astoria Dance Hall. She began making up all over again; if she was pale he would take her home early.

The landlady stuck her head in at the door and said, "It's your gentleman. On the 'phone."

"On the 'phone?"

"Yes," the landlady said, sidling in for a good chat, "he sounded all of a jump. Impatient, I should say. Half barked my head off when I wished him good evening."

"Oh," she said despairingly, "it's only his way. You mustn't mind him."

"He's going to call off the evening, I suppose," the landlady said. "It's always the same. You girls who go travelling round never get a square deal. You said *Dick Whittington*, didn't you?"

"No, no, *Aladdin*."

She pelted down the stairs. She didn't care a damn who saw her hurry. She said, "Is that you, darling?" There was always something wrong with their telephone. She could hear his voice so hoarsely vibrating against her ear she could hardly realise it was his. He said, "You've been ages. This is a public call-box. I've put in my last pennies. Listen, Anne, I can't be with you. I'm sorry. It's work. We're on to the man in that safe robbery I told you about. I shall be out all night on it. We've traced one of the notes." His voice beat excitedly against her ear.

She said, "Oh, that's fine, darling. I know you wanted . . ." but she couldn't keep it up. "Jimmy," she said, "I shan't be seeing you again. For weeks."

He said, "It's tough, I know. I'd been thinking . . . Listen. You'd better not catch that early train, what's the point? There isn't a nine o'clock. I've been looking them up."

"I know. I just said . . ."

"You'd better go to-night. Then you can get a rest before rehearsals. Midnight from Euston."

"But I haven't packed . . ."

He took no notice. It was his favourite occupation planning things, making decisions. He said, "If I'm near the station, I'll try . . ."

"Your two minutes up."

He said, "Oh hell, I've no coppers. Darling, I love you."

She struggled to bring it out herself, but his name stood in the way, impeded her tongue. She could never bring it out without hesitation—"Ji——" The line went dead on her. She thought bitterly: he oughtn't to go out without coppers. She thought: it's not right, cutting off a detective like that. Then she went back up the stairs; she wasn't crying; it was just as if somebody had died and left her alone and scared, scared of the new faces and the new job, the harsh provincial jokes, the fellows who were fresh, scared of herself, scared of not being able to remember clearly how good it was to be loved.

The landlady said, "I just thought so. Why not come down and have a cup of tea and a good chat? It does you good to talk. Really good. A doctor said to me once it clears the lungs. Stands to reason, don't it? You can't help getting dust up and a good talk blows it out. I wouldn't bother to pack yet. There's hours and hours. My old man would never of died if he'd talked more. Stands to reason. It was something poisonous in his throat cut him off in his prime. If he'd talked more he'd have blown it out. It's better than spitting."

v

The crime reporter couldn't make himself heard. He kept on trying to say to the chief reporter, "I've got some stuff on that safe robbery."

The chief reporter had had too much to drink. They'd all had too much to drink. He said, "You can go home and read *The Decline and Fall*. . . ."

The crime reporter was a young earnest man who didn't drink and didn't smoke;

it shocked him when someone was sick in one of the telephone-boxes. He shouted at the top of his voice: "They've traced one of the notes."

"Write it down, write it down, old boy," the chief reporter said, "and then smoke it."

"The man escaped—held up a girl—it's a terribly good story," the earnest young man said. He had an Oxford accent; that was why they had made him crime reporter; it was the news-editor's joke.

"Go home and read Gibbon."

The earnest young man caught hold of someone's sleeve. "What's the matter? Are you all crazy? Isn't there going to be any paper or what?"

"War in forty-eight hours," somebody bellowed at him.

"But this is a wonderful story I've got. He held up a girl and an old man, climbed out of a window . . ."

"Go home. There won't be any room for it."

"They've killed the annual report of the Kensington Kitten Club."

"No Round the Shops."

"They've made the Limehouse Fire a News in Brief."

"Go home and read Gibbon."

"He got clean away with a policeman watching the front door. The Flying Squad's out. He's armed. The police are taking revolvers. It's a lovely story."

The chief reporter said, "Armed! Go away and put your head in a glass of milk. We'll all be armed in a day or two. They've published their evidence. It's clear as daylight a Serb shot him. Italy's supporting the ultimatum. They've got forty-eight hours to climb down. If you want to buy armament shares hurry and make your fortune."

"You'll be in the army this day week," somebody said.

"Oh no," the young man said, "no, I won't be that. You see I'm a pacifist."

The man who was sick in the telephone-box said, "I'm going home. There wouldn't be any room in the paper if the Bank of England was blown up."

A little thin piping voice said, "*My* copy's going in."

"I tell you there isn't any room."

"There'll be room for mine. Gas Masks for All. Special Air Raid Practices for Civilians in every town of more than fifty thousand inhabitants." He giggled.

"The funny thing is—it's—it's——" but nobody ever heard what it was: a boy opened the door and flung them in a pull of the middle page: damp letters on a damp grey sheet; the headlines came off on the hands: "Yugo-Slavia Asks for Time. Adriatic Fleet at War Stations. Paris Rioters Break into Italian Embassy." Everyone was suddenly quite quiet as an aeroplane went by; driving low overhead through the dark, heading south, a scarlet tail-lamp, pale transparent wings in the moonlight. They watched it through the great glass ceiling, and suddenly nobody wanted to have another drink.

The chief reporter said, "I'm tired. I'm going to bed."

"Shall I follow up this story?" the crime reporter asked.

"If it'll make you happy, but *That's* the only news from now on."

They stared up at the glass ceiling, the moon, the empty sky.

vi

The station clock marked three minutes to midnight. The ticket collector at the barrier said, "There's room in the front."

"A friend's seeing me off," Anne Crowder said. "Can't I get in at this end and go up front when we start?"

"They've locked the doors."

She looked desperately past him. They were turning out the lights in the buffet; no more trains from that platform.

"You'll have to hurry, miss."

The poster of an evening paper caught her eye and as she ran down the train, looking back as often as she was able, she couldn't help remembering that war might be declared before they met again. He would go to it; he always did what other people did, she told herself with irritation, although she knew it was his reliability she loved. She wouldn't have loved him if he'd been eccentric, had his own opinions about things; she lived too closely to thwarted genius, to second touring company actresses who thought they ought to be Cochran stars, to admire difference. She wanted her man to be ordinary, she wanted to be able to know what he'd say next.

A line of lamp-struck faces went by her; the train was full, so full that in the first-class carriages you saw strange shy awkward people who were not at ease in the deep seats, who feared the ticket-collector would turn them out. She gave up the search for a third-class carriage, opened a door, dropped her *Woman and Beauty* on the only seat and struggled back to the window over legs and protruding suitcases. The engine was getting up steam, the smoke blew back up the platform, it was difficult to see as far as the barrier.

A hand pulled at her sleeve. "Excuse me," a fat man said, "if you've quite finished with that window. I want to buy some chocolate."

She said, "Just one moment, please. Somebody's seeing me off."

"He's not here. It's too late. You can't monopolise the window like that. I must have some chocolate." He swept her on one side and waved an emerald ring under the light. She tried to look over his shoulder to the barrier; he almost filled the window. He called "Boy, Boy!" waving the emerald ring. He said, "What chocolate have you got? No, not Motorist's, not Mexican. Something sweet."

Suddenly through a crack she saw Mather. He was past the barrier, he was coming down the train looking for her, looking in all the third-class carriages, running past the first-class. She implored the fat man: "Please, please do let me come. I can see my friend."

"In a moment. In a moment. Have you Nestlé? Give me a shilling packet."

"Please let me."

"Haven't you anything smaller," the boy said, "than a ten-shilling note?"

Mather went by, running past the first-class. She hammered on the window, but he didn't hear her, among the whistles and the beat of trolley wheels, the last packing cases rolling into the van. Doors slammed, a whistle blew, the train began to move.

"Please. Please."

"I must get my change," the fat man said, and the boy ran beside the carriage counting the shillings into his palm. When she got to the window and leant out they were past the platform, she could only see a small figure on a wedge of asphalt who couldn't see her. An elderly woman said, "You oughtn't to lean out like that. It's dangerous."

She trod on their toes getting back to her seat, she felt unpopularity well up all around her, everyone was thinking, "She oughtn't to be in the carriage. What's the good of our paying first-class fares when . . ." But she wouldn't cry; she was fortified by all the conventional remarks which came automatically to her mind about spilt milk and it will be all the same in fifty years. Nevertheless she noted with deep dislike on the label dangling from the fat man's suitcase his destination, which was the same as hers, Nottwich. He sat opposite her with the *Passing Show* and the *Evening News* and the *Financial Times* on his lap eating sweet milk chocolate.

2

i

Raven walked with his handkerchief over his lip across Soho Square, Oxford Street, up Charlotte Street. It was dangerous but not so dangerous as showing his hare-lip. He turned to the left and then to the right into a narrow street where big-breasted women in aprons called across to each other and a few solemn children scouted up the gutter. He stopped by a door with a brass plate, Dr. Alfred Yogel on the second floor, on the first floor the North American Dental Company. He went upstairs and rang the bell. There was a smell of greens from below and somebody had drawn a naked torso in pencil on the wall.

A woman in nurse's uniform opened the door, a woman with a mean lined face and untidy grey hair. Her uniform needed washing; it was spotted with grease-marks and what might have been blood or iodine. She brought with her a harsh smell of chemicals and disinfectants. When she saw Raven holding his handkerchief over his mouth she said, "The dentist's on the floor below."

"I want to see Dr. Yogel."

She looked him over closely, suspiciously, running her eyes down his dark coat. "He's busy."

"I can wait."

One naked globe swung behind her head in the dingy passage. "He doesn't generally see people as late as this."

"I'll pay for the trouble," Raven said. She judged him with just the same appraising stare as the doorkeeper at a shady nightclub. She said, "You can come in." He followed her into a waiting-room: the same bare globe, a chair, a round oak table splashed with dark paint. She shut him in and he heard her voice start in the next room. It went on and on. He picked up the only magazine, *Good Housekeeping* of eighteen months back, and began mechanically to read: "Bare walls are very popular today, perhaps one picture to give the necessary point of colour . . ."

The nurse opened the door and jerked her hand. "He'll see you." Dr. Yogel was washing his hands in a fixed basin behind his long yellow desk and swivel chair. There was no other furniture in the room except a kitchen chair, a cabinet and a long couch. His hair was jet-black; it looked as if it had been dyed, and there was not much of it; it was plastered in thin strands across the scalp. When he turned he showed a plump hard bonhomous face, a thick sensual mouth. He said, "And what can we do for you?" You felt he was more accustomed to deal with women than with men. The nurse stood harshly behind waiting.

Raven lowered his handkerchief. He said, "Can you do anything about this lip quickly?"

Dr. Yogel came up and prodded it with a little fat forefinger. "I'm not a surgeon."

Raven said, "I can pay."

Dr. Yogel said, "It's a job for a surgeon. It's not in my line at all."

"I know that," Raven said, and caught the quick flicker of glances between the nurse and Dr. Yogel. Dr. Yogel lifted up the lip on each side; his fingernails were not quite clean. He watched Raven carefully and said, "If you come back to-morrow at ten . . ." His breath smelt faintly of brandy.

"No," Raven said. "I want it done now at once."

"Ten pounds," Dr. Yogel said quickly.

"All right."

"In cash."

"I've got it with me."

Dr. Yogel sat down at his desk. "And now if you'll give me your name . . ."

"You don't need to know my name."

Dr. Yogel said gently: "Any name . . ."

"Chumley, then."

"CHOLMO . . ."

"No. Spell it CHUMLEY."

Dr. Yogel filled up a slip of paper and handed it to the nurse. She went outside and closed the door behind her. Dr. Yogel went to the cabinet and brought out a tray of knives. Raven said, "The light's bad."

"I'm used to it," Dr. Yogel said. "I've a good eye." But as he held up a knife to the light his hand very slightly trembled. He said softly, "Lie down on the couch, old man."

Raven lay down. He said, "I knew a girl who came to you. Name of Page. She said you did her trick fine."

Dr. Yogel said, "She oughtn't to talk about it."

"Oh," Raven said, "you are safe with me. I don't go back on a fellow who treats me right." Dr. Yogel took a case like a portable gramophone out of his cabinet and carried it over to the couch. He produced a long tube and a mask. He smiled gently and said, "We don't run to anæsthetists here, old man."

"Stop," Raven said, "you're not going to give me gas."

"It would hurt without it, old man," Dr. Yogel said, approaching with the mask, "it would hurt like hell."

Raven sat up and pushed the mask aside. "I won't have it," he said, "not gas. I've never had gas. I've never passed out yet. I like to see what's going on."

Dr. Yogel laughed gently and pulled at Raven's lip in a playful way. "Better get used to it, old man. We'll all be gassed in a day or two."

"What do you mean?"

"Well, it looks like war, doesn't it?" Dr. Yogel said, talking rapidly and unwinding more tube, turning screws in a soft, shaking, inexorable way. "The Serbs can't shoot a Minister of War like that and get away with it. Italy's ready to come in. And the French are warming up. We'll be in it ourselves inside a week."

Raven said, "All that because an old man . . ." He explained, "I haven't read the papers."

"I wish I'd known beforehand," Dr. Yogel said, making conversation, fixing his cylinder. "I'd have made a fortune in munition shares. They've gone up to the sky, old man. Now lean back. It won't take a moment." He again approached the mask. He said, "You've only got to breathe deep, old man."

Raven said, "I told you I wouldn't have gas. Get that straight. You can cut me about as much as you like, but I won't have gas."

"It's very silly of you, old man," Dr. Yogel said. "It's going to hurt." He went back to the cabinet and again picked up a knife, but his hand shook more than ever. He was frightened of something. And then Raven heard from outside the tiny tinkle a telephone makes when the receiver is lifted. He jumped up from the couch; it was bitterly cold, but Dr. Yogel was sweating; he stood by the cabinet holding his surgical knife, unable to say a word. Raven said, "Keep quiet. Don't speak." He flung the door suddenly open and there was the nurse in the little dim hall with the telephone at her ear. Raven stood sideways so that he could keep his eye on both of them. "Put back that receiver," he said. She put it back, watching him with her little mean conscienceless eyes. He said furiously, "You double-crossing——" He said, "I've got a mind to shoot you both."

"Old man," Dr. Yogel said, "old man. You've got it all wrong," but the nurse said nothing. She had all the guts in their partnership, she was toughened by a long career of illegalities, by not a few deaths. Raven said, "Get away from that 'phone." He took the knife out of Dr. Yogel's hand and hacked and sawed at the telephone wire. He was touched by something he had never felt before: a sense of injustice stammered on his tongue. These people were of his own kind; they didn't belong inside the legal borders; for the second time in one day he had been betrayed by the lawless. He had always been alone, but never so alone as this. The telephone wire gave. He wouldn't speak another word for fear his temper might master him and he might shoot. This wasn't the time for shooting. He went downstairs in a dark loneliness of spirit, his handkerchief over his face, and from the little wireless shop at the street corner heard, "We have received the following notice . . ." The same voice followed him down the street from the open windows of the little impoverished homes, the suave expressionless voice from every house: "New Scotland Yard. Wanted. James Raven. Aged about twenty-eight. Easily recognisable from his hare-lip. A little above the middle height. Last seen wearing a dark overcoat and a black felt hat. Any information leading to the arrest . . ." Raven walked away from the voice, out into the traffic of Oxford Street, bearing south.

There were too many things he didn't understand: this war they were talking of, why he had been double-crossed. He wanted to find Cholmondeley. Cholmondeley was of no account, he was acting under orders, but if he found Cholmondeley he could squeeze out of him . . . He was harassed, hunted, lonely, he bore with him a sense of great injustice and a curious pride. Going down the Charing Cross Road, past the music shops and the rubber goods shops, he swelled with it: after all it needed a man to start a war as he was doing.

He had no idea where Cholmondeley lived; the only clue he had was an accommodation address. It occurred to him there was a faint chance that if he watched the small shop to which Cholmondeley's letters were sent he might see him: a very faint chance, but it was strengthened by the fact of his escape. Already the news was on the air, it would be in the evening papers, Cholmondeley might want to clear out of the way for a while, and there was just a possibility that before he went he would call for letters. But that depended on whether he used that address for other letters besides Raven's. Raven wouldn't have believed there was one chance in a thousand if it were not that Cholmondeley was a fool. You didn't have to eat many ices with him to learn that.

The shop was in a side street opposite a theatre. It was a tiny one-roomed place in which was sold nothing above the level of *Film Fun* and *Breezy Stories*. There were postcards from Paris in sealed envelopes, American and French magazines, and books on flagellation in paper jackets for which the pimply youth or his sister, whoever was in the shop, charged twenty shillings, fifteen shillings back if you returned the book.

It wasn't an easy shop to watch. A woman policeman kept an eye on the tarts at the corner and opposite there was just the long blank theatre wall, the gallery door. Against the wall you were as exposed as a fly against wall-paper, unless, he thought, waiting for the lights to flash green and let him pass, unless—the play was popular.

And it was popular. Although the doors wouldn't open for another hour, there was quite a long queue for the gallery. Raven hired a camp stool with almost his last small change and sat down. The shop was only just across the way. The youth wasn't in charge, but his sister. She sat there just inside the door in an old green dress that might have been stripped from one of the billiard tables in the pub next door. She had a square face that could never have looked young, a squint that her heavy steel spectacles did nothing to disguise. She might have been any age from twenty to forty, a parody of a woman, dirty and depraved, crouched under the most lovely figures, the most beautiful vacant faces the smut photographers could hire.

Raven watched: with a handkerchief over his mouth, one of sixty in the gallery queue, he watched. He saw a young man stop and eye *Plaisirs de Paris* furtively and hurry on; he saw an old man go into the shop and come out again with a brown-paper parcel. Somebody from the queue went across and bought cigarettes.

An elderly woman in pince-nez sat beside him. She said over her shoulder, "That's why I always liked Galsworthy. He was a gentleman. You knew where you were, if you know what I mean."

"It always seems to be the Balkans."

"I liked *Loyalties*."

"He was such a humane man."

A man stood between Raven and the shop holding up a little square of paper. He put it in his mouth and held up another square. A tart ambled by on the other side of the road and said something to the girl in the shop. The man put the second piece of paper in his mouth.

"They say the fleet . . . ."

"He makes you *think*. That's what I like."

Raven thought: if he doesn't come before the queue begins to move I'll have to go.

"Anything in the papers?"

"Nothing new."

The man in the road took the papers out of his mouth and began to tear them and fold them and tear them. Then he opened them out and it was a paper St. George's Cross, blowing flimsily in the cold wind.

"He used to subscribe heavily to the Anti-Vivisection Society. Mrs. Milbanke told me. She showed me one of his cheques with his signature."

"He was really humane."

"And a *really* great writer."

A girl and a boy who looked happy applauded the man with the paper flag and he took off his cap and began to come down the queue collecting coppers. A taxi drew up at the end of the street and a man got out. It was Cholmondeley. He went into the bookshop and the girl got up and followed him. Raven counted his money. He had two and sixpence and a hundred and ninety-five pounds in stolen notes he could do nothing with. He sank his face deeper in his handkerchief and got up hurriedly like a man taken ill. The paper-tearer reached him, held out his cap, and Raven saw with envy the odd dozen pennies, a sixpence, a threepenny bit. He would have given a hundred pounds for the contents of that cap. He pushed the man roughly and walked away.

At the other end of the road there was a taxi rank. He stood there bowed against the wall, a sick man, until Cholmondeley came out.

He said, "Follow that taxi," and sank back with a sense of relief, moving back up Charing Cross Road, Tottenham Court Road, the Euston Road where all the bicycles had been taken in for the night and the second-hand car dealers from that end of Great Portland Street were having a quick one, before they bore their old school ties and their tired tarnished bonhomie back to their lodgings. He wasn't used to being hunted; this was better: to hunt.

Nor did the meter fail him. He had a shilling to spare when Mr. Cholmondeley led the way in by the Euston war memorial to the great smoky entrance and rashly he gave it to the driver: rashly because there was a long wait ahead of him with nothing but his hundred and ninety-five pounds to buy a sandwich with. For Mr. Cholmondeley led the way with two porters behind him to the left-luggage counter, depositing there three suitcases, a portable typewriter, a bag of golf clubs, a small attaché case and a hat-box. Raven heard him ask from which platform the midnight train went.

Raven sat down in the great hall beside a model of Stephenson's "Rocket." He had to think. There was only one midnight train. If Cholmondeley was going to report, his employers were somewhere in the smoky industrial north; for there wasn't a stop before Nottwich. But again he was faced with his wealthy poverty; the numbers of the notes had been circulated everywhere; the booking clerks would almost certainly have them. The trail for a moment seemed to stop at the barrier to Number 3 platform.

But slowly a plan did form in Raven's mind as he sat under the "Rocket" among the bundles and crumbs of sandwich-eaters. He *had* a chance, for it was possible that the ticket-collectors on the trains had not been given the numbers. It was the kind of loophole the authorities might forget. There remained, of course, this objection: that the note would eventually give away his presence on the north-bound train. He would have to take a ticket to the limit of the journey and it would be easy enough to trace him to the town where he alighted. The hunt would follow him, but there might be a time lag of half a day in which his own hunt could get nearer to *his* prey. Raven could never realise other people; they didn't seem to him to live in the same way as he lived; and though he bore a grudge against Mr. Cholmondeley, hated him enough to kill him, he couldn't imagine Mr. Cholmondeley's own fears and motives. He was the greyhound and Mr. Cholmondeley only the mechanical hare; but in this case the greyhound was chased in its turn by another mechanical hare.

He was hungry, but he couldn't risk changing a note; he hadn't even a copper to pass him into the lavatory. After a while he got up and walked the station to keep warm among the frozen smuts, the icy turbulence. At eleven-thirty he saw from behind a chocolate machine Mr. Cholmondeley fetch his luggage, followed him at a distance until he passed through the barrier and down the length of the lit train. The Christmas crowds had begun; they were different from the ordinary crowd, you had a sense of people going home. Raven stood back in the shadow of an indicator and heard their laughter and calls, saw smiling faces raised under the great lamps; the pillars of the station had been decorated to look like enormous crackers. The suitcases were full of presents, a girl had a sprig of holly in her coat, high up under the roof dangled a bough of mistletoe lit by flood-lamps. When Raven moved he could feel the automatic rubbing beneath his arm.

At two minutes to twelve Raven ran forward, the engine smoke was blowing back along the platform, the doors were slammed. He said to the collector at the barrier: "I haven't time to get a ticket. I'll pay on the train."

He tried the first carriages. They were full and locked. A porter shouted to him to go up front, and he ran on. He was only just in time. He couldn't find a seat, but stood in the corridor with his face pressed against the pane to hide his hare-lip, watching London recede from him: a lit signal box and inside a saucepan of cocoa heating on the stove, a signal going green, a long line of blackened houses standing rigid against the coldstarred sky; watching because there was nothing else to do to keep his lip hidden, but like a man watching something he loves slide back from him out of his reach.

ii

Mather walked back up the platform. He was sorry to have missed Anne, but it wasn't important. He would be seeing her again in a few weeks. It was not that his love was any less than hers but that his mind was more firmly anchored. He was on a job; if he pulled it off, he might be promoted; they could marry. Without any difficulty at all he wiped his mind clear of her.

Saunders was waiting on the other side of the barrier. Mather said, "We'll be off."

"Where next?"

"Charlie's."

They sat in the back seat of a car and dived back into the narrow dirty streets behind the station. A prostitute put her tongue out at them. Saunders said, "What about J-J-J-Joe's?"

"I don't think so, but we'll try it."

The car drew up two doors away from a fried-fish shop. A man sitting beside the driver got down and waited for orders. "Round to the back, Frost," Mather said. He gave him two minutes and then hammered on the door of the fish shop. A light went on inside and Mather could see through the window the long counter, the stock of old newspapers, the dead grill. The door opened a crack. He put his foot in and pushed it wide. He said, " 'Evening, Charlie," looking round.

"Mr. Mather," Charlie said. He was as fat as an eastern eunuch and swayed his great hips coyly when he walked like a street woman.

"I want to talk to you," Mather said.

"Oh, I'm delighted," Charlie said. "Step this way, Mr. Mather. I was just off to bed."

"I bet you were," Mather said. "Got a full house down there to-night?"

"Oh, Mr. Mather. What a wag you are. Just one or two Oxford boys."

"Listen. I'm looking for a fellow with a hare-lip. About twenty-eight years old."

"He's not here."

"Dark coat, black hat."

"I don't know him, Mr. Mather."

"I'd like to take a look over your basement."

"Of course, Mr. Mather. There are just one or two Oxford boys. Do you mind if I go down first? Just to introduce you, Mr. Mather." He led the way down the stone stairs. "It's safer."

"I can look after myself," Mather said. "Saunders, stay in the shop."

Charlie opened a door. "Now, boys, don't be scared. Mr. Mather's a friend of mine." They faced him in an ominous line at the end of the room, the Oxford boys, with their broken noses and their cauliflower ears, the dregs of pugilism.

" 'Evening," Mather said. The tables had been swept clear of drink and cards. He plodded down the last steps into the stone-floored room. Charlie said, "Now, boys, you don't need to get scared."

"Why don't you get a few Cambridge boys into this club?" Mather said.

"Oh, what a wag you are, Mr. Mather."

They followed him with their eyes as he crossed the floor; they wouldn't speak to him; he was the Enemy. They didn't have to be diplomats like Charlie, they could show their hatred. They watched every move he made. Mather said, "What are you keeping in that cupboard?" Their eyes followed him as he went towards the cupboard door.

Charlie said, "Give the boys a chance, Mr. Mather. They don't mean any harm. This is one of the best-run clubs——" Mather pulled open the door of the cupboard. Four women fell into the room. They were like toys turned from the same mould with their bright brittle hair. Mather laughed. He said, "The joke's on me. That's a thing I never expected in one of your clubs, Charlie. Good night all." The girls got up and dusted themselves. None of the men spoke.

"Really, Mr. Mather," Charlie said, blushing all the way upstairs. "I do wish this hadn't happened in my club. I don't know what you'll think. But the boys didn't mean any harm. Only you know how it is. They don't like to leave their sisters alone."

"What's that?" Saunders said at the top of the stairs.

"So I said they could bring their sisters and the dear girls sit around . . ."

"What's that?" Saunders said. "G-g-g-girls?"

"Don't forget, Charlie," Mather said. "Fellow with a hare-lip. You'd better let me know if he turns up here. You don't want your club closed."

"Is there a reward?"

"There'd be a reward for you all right."

They got back into the car. "Pick up Frost," Mather said. "Then Joe's." He took his notebook out and crossed off another name. "And after Joe's six more——"

"We shan't be f-f-finished till three," Saunders said.

"Routine. He's out of town by now. But sooner or later he'll cash another note."

"Finger-prints?"

"Plenty. There was enough on his soap-dish to stock an album. Must be a clean sort of fellow. Oh, he doesn't stand a chance. It's just a question of time."

The lights of Tottenham Court Road flashed across their faces. The windows of the big shops were still lit up. "That's a nice bedroom suite," Mather said.

"It's a lot of f-fuss, isn't it," Saunders said. "About a few notes, I mean. When there may be a w-w-w-w. . . ."

Mather said, "If those fellows over there had our efficiency there mightn't be a war. We'd have caught the murderer by now. Then all the world could see whether the Serbs . . . Oh," he said softly, as Heal's went by, a glow of soft colour, a gleam of steel, allowing himself about the furthest limits of his fancy, "I'd like to be tackling a job like that. A murderer with all the world watching."

"Just a few n-notes," Saunders complained.

"No, you are wrong," Mather said, "it's the routine which counts. Five-pound notes to-day. It may be something better next time. But it's the routine which matters. That's how I see it," he said, letting his anchored mind stretch the cable as far as it could go as they drove round St. Giles's Circus and on towards Seven Dials, stopping every hole the thief might take one by one. "It doesn't matter to me if there is a war. When it's over I'll still want to be going on with this job. It's the organisation I like. I always want to be on the side that organises. On the other you get your geniuses, of course, but you get all your shabby tricksters, you get all the cruelty and the selfishness and the pride."

You got it all, except the pride, in Joe's where they looked up from their bare tables and let him run the place through, the extra aces back in the sleeve, the watered spirit out of sight, facing him each with his individual mark of cruelty and egotism. Even pride was perhaps there in a corner, bent over a sheet of paper, playing an endless game of double noughts and crosses against himself because there was no one else in that club he deigned to play with.

Mather again crossed off a name and drove southwest towards Kennington. All over London there were other cars doing the same: he was part of an organisation. He did not want to be a leader, he did not even wish to give himself up to some God-sent fanatic of a leader, he liked to feel that he was one of thousands more or less equal working for a concrete end—not equality of opportunity, not government by the people or by the richest or by the best, but simply to do away with crime which meant uncertainty. He liked to be certain, to feel that one day quite inevitably he would marry Anne Crowder.

The loud speaker in the car said: "Police cars proceed back to the King's Cross area for intensified search. Raven driven to Euston Station about seven p.m. May not have left by train." Mather leant across to the driver, "Right about and back to Euston." They were by Vauxhall. Another police car came past them through the Vauxhall tunnel. Mather raised his hand. They followed it back over the river. The flood-lit clock on the Shell-Mex building showed half-past one. The light was on in the clock tower at Westminster: Parliament was having an all-night sitting as the opposition fought their losing fight against mobilisation.

It was six o'clock in the morning when they drove back towards the Embankment. Saunders was asleep. He said, "That's fine." He was dreaming that he had no impediment in his speech; he had an independent income; he was drinking champagne with a girl; everything was fine. Mather totted things up on his notebook; he said to Saunders, "He got on a train for sure. I'd bet you——" Then he saw that Saunders was asleep and slipped a rug across his knees and began to consider again. They turned in at the gates of New Scotland Yard.

Mather saw a light in the chief inspector's room and went up.

"Anything to report?" Cusack asked.

"Nothing. He must have caught a train, sir."

"We've got a little to go on at this end. Raven followed somebody to Euston. We are trying to find the driver of the first car. And another thing, he went to a doctor called Yogel to try and get his lip altered. Offered some more of those notes.

Still handy too with that automatic. We've got him taped. As a kid he was sent to an industrial school. He's been smart enough to keep out of our way since. I can't think why he's broken out like this. A smart fellow like that. He's blazing a trail.''

"Has he much money besides the notes?''

"We don't think so. Got an idea, Mather?''

Colour was coming into the sky above the city. Cusack switched off his table-lamp and left the room grey. "I think I'll go to bed.''

"I suppose,'' Mather said, "that all the booking offices have the numbers of those notes?''

"Every one.''

"It looks to me,'' Mather said, "that if you had nothing but phoney notes and wanted to catch an express——''

"How do we know it was an express?''

"Yes, I don't know why I said that, sir. Or perhaps—if it was a slow train with plenty of stops near London, surely someone would have reported by this time——''

"You may be right.''

"Well, if I wanted to catch an express, I'd wait till the last minute and pay on the train. I don't suppose the ticket collectors carry the numbers.''

"I think you're right. Are you tired, Mather?''

"No.''

"Well, I am. Would you stay here and ring up Euston and King's Cross and St. Pancras, all of them? Make a list of all the outgoing expresses after seven. Ask them to telephone up the line to all stations to check up on any man travelling without a ticket who paid on the train. We'll soon find out where he stepped off. Good night, Mather.''

"Good morning, sir.'' He liked to be accurate.

iii

There was no dawn that day in Nottwich. Fog lay over the city like a night sky with no stars. The air in the streets was clear. You had only to imagine that it was night. The first tram crawled out of its shed and took the steel track down towards the market. An old piece of newspaper blew up against the door of the Royal Theatre and flattened out. In the streets on the outskirts of Nottwich nearest the pits an old man plodded by with a pole tapping at the windows. The stationer's window in the High Street was full of Prayer Books and Bibles: a printed card remained among them, a relic of Armistice Day, like the old drab wreath of Haig poppies by the War Memorial: "Look up, and swear by the slain of the war that you'll never forget.'' Along the line a signal lamp winked green in the dark day and the lit carriages drew slowly in past the cemetery, the glue factory, over the wide tidy cement-lined river. A bell began to ring from the Roman Catholic cathedral. A whistle blew.

The packed train moved slowly into another morning: smuts were thick on all the faces, everyone had slept in his clothes. Mr. Cholmondeley had eaten too many sweets; his teeth needed cleaning; his breath was sweet and stuffy. He put his head into the corridor and Raven at once turned his back and stared out at the sidings, the trucks heaped with local coal; a smell of bad fish came in from the glue factory. Mr. Cholmondeley dived back across the carriage to the other side trying to make out at which platform the train was drawing in. He said: "Excuse me," trampling on the feet; Anne smiled softly to herself and hacked his ankle. Mr. Cholmondeley glared at her. She said: "I'm sorry," and began to mend her face with her tissues and her powder, to bring it up to standard, so that she could bear the thought of the Royal Theatre, the little dressing-rooms and the oil-heating, the rivalry and the scandals.

"If you'll let me by," Mr. Cholmondeley said fiercely, "I'm getting down here."

Raven saw his ghost in the window-pane getting down. But he didn't dare follow him closely. It was almost as if a voice blown over many foggy miles, over the long swelling fields of the hunting counties, the villa'd suburbs creeping up to town, had spoken to him: "any man travelling without a ticket," he thought, with the slip of white paper the collector had given him in his hand. He opened the door and watched the passengers flow by him to the barrier. He needed time, and the paper in his hand would so quickly identify him. He needed time, and he realised now that he wouldn't have even so much as a twelve-hour start. They would visit every boarding house, every lodging in Nottwich; there was nowhere for him to stay.

Then it was that the idea struck him, by the slot machine on No. 2 arrival platform, which thrust him finally into other people's lives, broke the world in which he walked alone.

Most of the passengers had gone now, but one girl waited for a returning porter by the buffet door. He went up to her and said, "Can I help and carry your bags?"

"Oh, if you would," she said. He stood with his head a little bent, so that she mightn't see his lip.

"What about a sandwich?" he said. "It's been a hard journey."

"Is it open," she said, "this early?"

He tried the door. "Yes, it's open."

"Is it an invitation?" she said. "You're standing treat?"

He gazed at her with faint astonishment: her smile, the small neat face with the eyes rather too wide apart; he was more used to the absent-minded routine endearments of prostitutes than to this natural friendliness, this sense of rather lost and desperate amusement. He said, "Oh yes. It's on me." He carried the bags inside and hammered on the counter. "What'll you have?" he said. In the pale light of the electric globe he kept his back to her; he didn't want to scare her yet.

"There's a rich choice," she said. "Bath buns, penny buns, last year's biscuits, ham sandwiches. I'd like a ham sandwich and a cup of coffee. Or will that leave you broke? If so, leave out the coffee."

He waited till the girl behind the counter had gone again, till the other's mouth was full of sandwich so that she couldn't have screamed if she'd tried. Then he turned his face on her. He was disconcerted when she showed no repulsion, but smiled as well as she could with her mouth full. He said, "I want your ticket. The police are after me. I'll do anything to get your ticket."

She swallowed the bread in her mouth and began to cough. She said, "For God's sake, hit me on the back." He nearly obeyed her; she'd got him rattled; he wasn't used to normal life and it upset his nerve. He said, "I've got a gun," and added lamely, "I'll give you this in return." He laid the paper on the counter and she read it with interest between the coughs. "First class. All the way to——Why, I'll be able to get a refund on this. I call that a fine exchange, but why the gun?"

He said: "The ticket."

"Here."

"Now," he said, "you are going out of the station with me. I'm not taking any chances."

"Why not eat your ham sandwich first?"

"Be quiet," he said. "I haven't the time to listen to your jokes."

She said, "I like he-men. My name's Anne. What's yours?" The train outside whistled, the carriages began to move, a long line of light going back into the fog, the steam blew along the platform. Raven's eyes left her for a moment; she raised her cup and dashed the hot coffee at his face. The pain drove him backwards with his hands to his eyes; he moaned like an animal; this was pain. This was what the old War Minister had felt, the woman secretary, his father when the trap sprang and the neck took the weight. His right hand felt for the automatic, his back was against the door; people were driving him to do things, to lose his head. He checked himself; with an effort he conquered the agony of the burns, the agony which drove him to kill. He said, "I've got you covered. Pick up those cases. Go out in front of me with that paper."

She obeyed him, staggering under the weight. The ticket collector said: "Changed your mind? This would have taken you to Edinburgh. Do you want to break the journey?"

"Yes," she said, "yes. That's it." He took out a pencil and began to write on the paper. An idea came to Anne: she wanted him to remember her and the ticket. There might be inquiries. "No," she said, "I'll give it up. I don't think I'll be going on. I'll stay here," and she went out through the barrier, thinking: he won't forget that in a hurry.

The long street ran down between the small dusty houses. A milk float clattered round a corner out of sight. She said, "Well, can I go now?"

"You think me a fool," he said bitterly. "Keep on walking."

"You might take one of these bags." She dropped one in the road and went on; he had to pick it up. It was heavy, he carried it in his left hand, he needed his right for the automatic.

She said, "This isn't taking us into Nottwich. We ought to have turned right at the corner."

"I know where I'm going."

"I wish I did."

The little houses went endlessly on under the fog. It was very early. A woman came to the door and took in the milk. Through a window Anne saw a man shaving. She wanted to scream to him, but he might have been in another world; she could imagine his stupid stare, the slow working of the brain before he realised anything was wrong. On they went, Raven a step behind. She wondered if he were bluffing her; he must be wanted for something very serious if he was really ready to shoot.

She spoke her thoughts aloud, "Is it murder?" and the lapse of her flippancy, the whispered fear, came to Raven like something familiar, friendly: he was used to fear. It had lived inside him for twenty years. It was normality he couldn't cope with. He answered her without strain, "No. I'm not wanted for that."

She challenged him, "Then you wouldn't dare to shoot," but he had the answer pat, the answer which never failed to convince because it was the truth. "I'm not going to prison. I'd rather hang. My father hanged."

She asked again, "Where are we going?" watching all the time for her chance. He didn't answer.

"Do you know this place?" but he had said his say. And suddenly the chance was there: outside a little stationer's where the morning posters leaned, looking in the window filled with cheap notepaper, pens and ink bottles—a policeman. She felt Raven come up behind her, it was all too quick, she hadn't time to make up her mind, they were past the policeman and on down the mean road. It was too late to scream now; he was twenty yards away; there'd be no rescue. She said in a low voice, "It *must* be murder."

The repetition stung him into speech. "That's justice for you. Always thinking the worst. They've pinned a robbery on to me, and I don't even know where the notes were stolen." A man came out of a public-house and began to wipe the steps with a wet cloth; they could smell frying bacon; the suitcases weighed on their arms. Raven couldn't change his hands for fear of leaving hold of the automatic. He said, "If a man's born ugly, he doesn't stand a chance. It begins at school. It begins before that."

"What's wrong with your face?" she asked with bitter amusement. There seemed hope while he talked. It must be harder to murder anyone with whom you'd had any kind of relationship.

"My lip, of course."

"What's up with your lip?"

He said with astonishment, "Do you mean you haven't noticed——?"

"Oh," Anne said, "I suppose you mean your hare-lip. I've seen worse things than that." They had left the little dirty houses behind them. She read the name of the new street: Shakespeare Avenue. Bright-red bricks and tudor gables and half timbering, doors with stained glass, names like Restholme. These houses represented something worse than the meanness of poverty, the meanness of the spirit. They were on the very edge of Nottwich now, where the speculative builders were running up their hire-purchase houses. It occurred to Anne that he had brought her here to kill her in the scarred fields behind the housing estate, where the grass had been trampled into the clay and the stumps of trees showed where an old wood had been. Plodding on they passed a house with an open door which at any hour of the day visitors could enter and inspect, from the small square parlour to the small square bedroom and the bathroom and water closet off the landing. A big placard said: "Come in and Inspect A Cozyholme. Ten Pounds Down and a House Is Yours."

"Are you going to buy a house?" she said with desperate humour.

He said, "I've got a hundred and ninety pounds in my pocket and I couldn't buy a box of matches with them. I tell you, I was double-crossed. I never stole these notes. A bastard gave them me."

"That was generous."

He hesitated outside "Sleepy Nuik." It was so new that the builder's paint had not been removed from the panes. He said, "It was for a piece of work I did. I did the work well. He ought to have paid me properly. I followed him here. A bastard called Chol-mon-deley."

He pushed her through the gate of "Sleepy Nuik," up the unmade path and round to the back door. They were at the edge of the fog here: it was as if they were at the boundary between night and day; it faded out in long streamers into the grey winter sky. He put his shoulder against the back door and the little doll's house lock snapped at once out of the cheap rotten wood. They stood in the kitchen, a place of wires waiting for bulbs, of tubes waiting for the gas cooker. "Get over to the wall," he said, "where I can watch you."

He sat down on the floor with the pistol in his hand. He said, "I'm tired. All night standing in that train. I can't think properly. I don't know what to do with you."

Anne said, "I've got a job here. I haven't a penny if I lose it. I'll give you my word I'll say nothing if you'll let me go." She added hopelessly, "But you wouldn't believe me."

"People don't trouble to keep their word to me," Raven said. He brooded darkly in his dusty corner by the sink. He said, "I'm safe here for a while as long as you are here too." He put his hand to his face and winced at the soreness of the burns. Anne made a movement. He said, "Don't move. I'll shoot if you move."

"Can't I sit down?" she said. "I'm tired too. I've got to be on my feet all the afternoon." But while she spoke she saw herself, bundled into a cupboard with the blood still wet. She added, "Dressed up as a Chink. Singing." But he wasn't listening to her; he was making his own plans in his own darkness. She tried to keep her courage up with the first song that came into her head, humming it because it reminded her of Mather, the long ride home, the "see you to-morrow."

> *It's only Kew*
> *To you,*
> *But to me*
> *It's Paradise.*

He said, "I've heard that tune." He couldn't remember where: he remembered a dark night and a cold wind and hunger and the scratch of a needle. It was as if something sharp and cold were breaking in his heart with great pain. He sat there under the sink with the automatic in his hand and began to cry. He made no sound, the tears seemed to run like flies of their own will from the corners of his eyes. Anne didn't notice for a while, humming the song. *"They say that's a snowflower a man brought from Greenland."* Then she saw. She said, "What's the matter?"

Raven said, "Keep back against that wall or I'll shoot."

"You're all in."

"That doesn't matter to you."

"Well, I suppose I'm human," Anne said. "You haven't done me any harm yet."

He said, "This doesn't mean anything. I'm just tired." He looked along the bare dusty boards of the unfinished kitchen. He tried to swagger. "I'm tired of living in hotels. I'd like to fix up this kitchen. I learned to be an electrician once. I'm educated." He said: " 'Sleepy Nuik.' It's a good name when you are tired. But they've gone and spelt 'Nook' wrong."

"Let me go," Anne said. "You can trust me. I'll not say a thing. I don't even know who you are."

He laughed miserably. "Trust you. I'd say I can. When you get into the town you'll see my name in the papers and my description, what I'm wearing, how old I am. I never stole the notes, but *I* can't put a description in of the man I want: name of Chol-mon-deley, profession double-crosser, fat, wears an emerald ring . . ."

"Why," she said, "I believe I travelled down with a man like that. I wouldn't have thought he'd have the nerve . . ."

"Oh, he's only the agent," Raven said, "but if I could find him I'd squeeze the names . . ."

"Why don't you give yourself up? Tell the police what happened?"

"That's a great idea, that is. Tell them it was Cholmondeley's friends got the old Czech killed. You're a bright girl."

"The old Czech?" she exclaimed. A little more light came into the kitchen as the fog lifted over the housing estate, the wounded fields. She said, "You don't mean what the papers are so full of?"

"That's it," he said with gloomy pride.

"You know the man who shot him?"

"As well as myself."

"And Cholmondeley's mixed up in it. . . . Doesn't that mean—that everyone's all wrong?"

"They don't know a thing about it, these papers. They can't give credit where credit's due."

"And you know and Cholmondeley. Then there won't be a war at all if you find Cholmondeley."

"I don't care a damn whether there's a war or not. I only want to know who it is who double-crossed me. I want to get even," he explained, looking up at her across the floor, with his hand over his mouth, hiding his lip, noticing that she was young and flushed and lovely with no more personal interest than a mangy wolf will show from the cage in the groomed well-fed bitch beyond the bars. "A war won't do people any harm," he said. "It'll show them what's what, it'll give them a taste of their own medicine. I know. There's always been a war for me." He touched the automatic. "All that worries me is what to do with you to keep you quiet for twenty-four hours."

She said under her breath, "You wouldn't kill me, would you?"

"If it's the only way," he said. "Let me think a bit."

"But I'd be on your side," she implored him, looking this way and that for anything to throw, for a chance of safety.

"Nobody's on my side," Raven said. "I've learned that. Even a crook doctor. . . . You see—I'm ugly. I don't pretend to be one of your handsome fellows. But I'm educated. I've thought things out." He said quickly, "I'm wasting time. I ought to get started."

"What are you going to do?" she asked, scrambling to her feet.

"Oh," he said in a tone of disappointment, "you are scared again. You were fine when you weren't scared." He faced her across the kitchen with the automatic pointed at her breast. He pleaded with her. "There's no need to be scared. This lip——"

"I don't mind your lip," she said desperately. "You aren't bad-looking. You ought to have a girl. She'd stop you worrying about that lip."

He shook his head. "You're talking that way because you are scared. You can't get round me that way. But it's hard luck on you, my picking on you. You shouldn't be so afraid of death. We've all got to die. If there's a war, you'll die anyway. It's sudden and quick: it doesn't hurt," he said, remembering the smashed skull of the old man—death was like that: no more difficult than breaking an egg.

She whispered, "Are you going to shoot me?"

"Oh no, no," he said, trying to calm her, "turn your back and go over to that door. We'll find a room where I can lock you up for a few hours." He fixed his eyes on her back; he wanted to shoot her clean: he didn't want to hurt her.

She said, "You aren't so bad. We might have been friends if we hadn't met like this. If this was the stage-door. Do you meet girls at stage-doors?"

"Me," he said, "no. They wouldn't look at me."

"You aren't ugly," she said. "I'd rather you had that lip than a cauliflower ear like all those fellows who think they are tough. The girls go crazy on them when they are in shorts. But they look silly in a dinner jacket." Raven thought: if I shoot her here anyone may see her through a window; I'll shoot her upstairs in the bathroom. He said, "Go on. Walk."

She said, "Let me go this afternoon. Please. I'll lose my job if I'm not at the theatre."

They came out into the little glossy hall, which smelt of paint. She said, "I'll give you a seat for the show."

"Go on," he said, "up the stairs."

"It's worth seeing. Alfred Bleek as the Widow Twankey." There were only three doors on the little landing: one had ground-glass panes. "Open the door," he said, "and go in there." He decided that he would shoot her in the back as soon as she was over the threshold; then he would only have to close the door and she would be out of sight. A small aged voice whispered agonisingly in his memory through a closed door. Memories had never troubled him. He didn't mind death;

it was foolish to be scared of death in this bare wintry world. He said hoarsely, "Are you happy? I mean, you like your job?"

"Oh, not the job," she said. "But the job won't go on for ever. Don't you think someone might marry me? I'm hoping."

He whispered, "Go in. Look through that window," his finger touching the trigger. She went obediently forward; he brought the automatic up, his hand didn't tremble, he told himself that she would feel nothing. Death wasn't a thing she need be scared about. She had taken her handbag from under her arm; he noticed the odd sophisticated shape; a circle of twisted glass on the side and within it chromium initials, A.C.; she was going to make her face up.

A door closed and a voice said, "You'll excuse me bringing you here this early, but I have to be at the office till late . . ."

"That's all right, that's all right, Mr. Graves. Now don't you call this a snug little house?"

He lowered the pistol as Anne turned. She whispered breathlessly, "Come in here quick." He obeyed her, he didn't understand, he was still ready to shoot her if she screamed. She saw the automatic and said, "Put it away. You'll only get into trouble with that."

Raven said, "Your bags are in the kitchen."

"I know. They've come in by the front door."

"Gas and electric," a voice said, "laid on. Ten pounds down and you sign along the dotted line and move in the furniture."

A precise voice which went with pince-nez and a high collar and thin flaxen hair said, "Of course, I shall have to think it over."

"Come and look upstairs, Mr. Graves."

They could hear them cross the hall and climb the stairs, the agent talking all the time. Raven said, "I'll shoot if you——"

"Be quiet," Anne said. "Don't talk. Listen. Have you those notes? Give me two of them." When he hesitated she whispered urgently, "We've got to take a risk." The agent and Mr. Graves were in the best bedroom now. "Just think of it, Mr. Graves," the agent was saying, "with flowered chintz."

"Are the walls sound-proof?"

"By a special process. Shut the door," the door closed and the agent's voice went thinly, distinctly on, "and in the passage you couldn't hear a thing. These houses were specially made for family men."

"And now," Mr. Graves said, "I should like to see the bathroom."

"Don't move," Raven threatened her.

"Oh, put it away," Anne said, "and be yourself." She closed the bathroom door behind her and walked to the door of the bedroom. It opened and the agent said with the immediate gallantry of a man known in all the Nottwich bars, "Well, well, what have we here?"

"I was passing," Anne said, "and saw the door open. I'd been meaning to come and see you, but I didn't think you'd be up this early."

"Always on the spot for a young lady," the agent said.

"I want to buy this house."

"Now look here," Mr. Graves said, a young-old man in a black suit who carried about with him in his pale face and irascible air the idea of babies in small sour rooms, of insufficient sleep. "You can't do that. I'm looking over this house."

"My husband sent me here to buy it."

"I'm here first."

"Have you bought it?"

"I've got to look it over first, haven't I?"

"Here," Anne said, showing two five-pound notes. "Now all I have to do . . ."

"Is sign along the dotted line," the agent said.

"Give me time," Mr. Graves said. "I like this house." He went to the window. "I like the view." His pale face stared out at the damaged fields stretching under the fading fog to where the slag-heaps rose along the horizon. "It's quiet country," Mr. Graves said. "It'll be good for the children and the wife."

"I'm sorry," Anne said, "but you see I'm ready to pay and sign."

"References?" the agent said.

"I'll bring them this afternoon."

"Let me show you another house, Mr. Graves." The agent belched slightly and apologised. "I'm not used to business before breakfast."

"No," Mr. Graves said, "if I can't have this I won't have any." Pallid and aggrieved he planted himself in the best bedroom of "Sleepy Nuik" and presented his challenge to fate, a challenge which he knew from long and bitter experience was always accepted.

"Well," the agent said, "you can't have this. First come, first served."

Mr. Graves said, "Good morning," carried his pitiful, narrow-chested pride downstairs; at least he could claim that, if he had been always too late for what he really wanted, he had never accepted substitutes.

"I'll come with you to the office," Anne said, "straight away," taking the agent's arm, turning her back on the bathroom where the dark pinched man stood waiting with his pistol, going downstairs into the cold overcast day which smelt to her as sweet as summer because she was safe again.

iv

What did Aladdin say
When he came to Pekin?

Obediently the long shuffling row of them repeated with tired vivacity, bending forward, clapping their knees, "*Chin Chin.*" They had been rehearsing for five hours.

"It won't do. It hasn't got any sparkle. Start again, please."

"*What did Aladdin say . . .*"

"How many of you have they killed so far?" Anne said under her breath. "*Chin Chin.*"

"Oh, half a dozen."

"I'm glad I got in at the last minute. A fortnight of this! No thank you."

"Can't you put some Art into it?" the producer implored them. "Have some pride. This isn't just any panto."

"What did Aladdin say . . ."

"You look washed out," Anne said.

"You don't look too good yourself."

"Things happen quick in this place."

"Once more, girls, and then we'll go on to Miss Maydew's scene."

What did Aladdin say
When he came to Pekin?

"You won't think that when you've been here a week."

Miss Maydew sat sideways in the front row with her feet up on the next stall. She was in tweeds and had a golf-and-grouse-moor air. Her real name was Binns, and her father was Lord Fordhaven. She said in a voice of penetrating gentility to Alfred Bleek, "I said I won't be presented."

"Who's the fellow at the back of the stalls?" Anne whispered. He was only a shadow to her.

"I don't know. Hasn't been here before. One of the men who put up the money, I expect, waiting to get an eyeful." She began to mimic an imaginary man. "Won't you introduce me to the girls, Mr. Collier? I want to thank them for working so hard to make this panto a success. What about a little dinner, missy?"

"Stop talking, Ruby, and make it snappy," said Mr. Collier.

What did Aladdin say
When he came to Pekin?

"All right. That'll do."

"Please, Mr. Collier," Ruby said, "may I ask you a question?"

"Now, Miss Maydew, your scene with Mr. Bleek. Well, what is it you want to know?"

"What *did* Aladdin say?"

"I want discipline," Mr. Collier said, "and I'm going to have discipline." He was rather under-sized with a fierce eye and straw-coloured hair and a receding chin. He was continually glancing over his shoulder in fear that somebody was getting at him from behind. He wasn't a good director; his appointment was due to more "wheels within wheels" than you could count. Somebody owed money to somebody else who had a nephew . . . but Mr. Collier was not the nephew: the chain of causes went much further before you reached Mr. Collier. Somewhere it included Miss Maydew, but the chain was so long you couldn't follow it. You got a confused idea that Mr. Collier must owe his position to merit. Miss Maydew didn't claim that for herself. She was always writing little articles in the cheap women's papers on: "Hard Work the only Key to Success on the Stage." She lit a new cigarette and said, "Are you talking to *me?*" She said to Alfred Bleek, who was in a dinner-jacket with a red knitted shawl round his shoulders, "It was to get away from all that . . . royal garden parties."

Mr. Collier said, "Nobody's going to leave this theatre." He looked nervously over his shoulder at the stout gentleman emerging into the light from the back of the stalls, one of the innumerable "wheels within wheels" that had spun Mr. Collier into Nottwich, into this exposed position at the front of the stage, into this fear that nobody would obey him.

"Won't you introduce me to the girls, Mr. Collier?" the stout gentleman said. "If you are finishing. I don't want to interrupt."

"Of course," Mr. Collier said. He said, "Girls, this is Mr. Davenant, one of our chief backers."

"Davis, not Davenant," the fat man said. "I bought out Davenant." He waved his hand; the emerald ring on his little finger flashed and caught Anne's eye. He said, "I want to have the pleasure of taking every one of you girls out to dinner while this show lasts. Just to tell you how I appreciate the way you are working to make the panto a success. Whom shall I begin with?" He had an air of desperate jollity. He was like a man who suddenly finds he has nothing to think about and somehow must fill the vacuum.

"Miss Maydew," he said half-heartedly, as if to show to the chorus the honesty of his intentions by inviting the principal boy.

"Sorry," Miss Maydew said, "I'm dining with Bleek."

Anne walked out on them; she didn't want to high-hat Davis, but his presence there shocked her. She believed in Fate and God and Vice and Virtue, Christ in the stable, all the Christmas stuff; she believed in unseen powers that arranged meetings, drove people along ways they didn't mean to go; but she was quite determined she wouldn't help. She wouldn't play God or the Devil's game; she had evaded Raven, leaving him there in the bathroom of the little empty house, and Raven's affairs no longer concerned her. She wouldn't give him away; she was not yet on the side of the big organised battalions; but she wouldn't help him either. It was a strictly neutral course she steered out of the changing-room, out of the theatre door, into Nottwich High Street.

But what she saw there made her pause. The street was full of people; they stretched along the southern pavement, past the theatre entrance, as far as the market. They were watching the electric bulbs above Wallace's, the big drapers, spelling out the night's news. She had seen nothing like it since the last election, but this was different, because there were no cheers. They were reading of the troop movements over Europe, of the precautions against gas raids. Anne was not old enough to remember how the last war began, but she had read of the crowds outside the Palace, the enthusiasm, the queues at the recruiting offices, and that was how she had pictured every war beginning. She had feared it only for herself and Mather. She had thought of it as a personal tragedy played out against a background of cheers and flags. But this was different: this silent crowd wasn't jubilant, it was afraid. The white faces were turned towards the sky with a kind of secular entreaty; they weren't praying to any God; they were just willing that the electric bulbs would tell a different story. They were caught there, on the way back from work, with tools and attaché cases, by the rows of bulbs, spelling out complications they simply didn't understand.

Anne thought: can it be true that that fat fool . . . that the boy with the hare-lip *knows*. . . . Well, she told herself, I believe in Fate, I suppose I can't just walk out and leave them. I'm in it up to the neck. If only Jimmy were here. But Jimmy, she remembered with pain, was on the other side; he was among those hunting Raven down. And Raven must be given the chance to finish *his* hunt first. She went back into the theatre.

Mr. Davenant—Davis—Cholmondeley, whatever his name was, was telling a story. Miss Maydew and Alfred Bleek had gone. Most of the girls had gone too to change. Mr. Collier watched and listened nervously; he was trying to remember who Mr. Davis was; Mr. Davenant had been silk stockings and had known Callitrope, who was the nephew of the man Dreid owed money to. Mr. Collier had been quite safe with Mr. Davenant, but he wasn't certain about Davis. . . . This panto wouldn't last forever and it was as fatal to get *in* with the wrong people as to get *out* with the right. It was possible that Davis was the man Cohen had quarrelled with, or he might be the uncle of the man Cohen had quarrelled with. The echoes of that quarrel were still faintly reverberating through the narrow back-stage passages of provincial theatres in the second-class touring towns. Soon they would reach the third companies and everyone would either move up one or move down one, except those who couldn't move down any lower. Mr. Collier laughed nervously and glared in a miserable attempt to be in and out simultaneously.

"I thought somebody breathed the word dinner," Anne said. "I'm hungry."

"First come, first served," Mr. Davis—Cholmondeley said cheerily. "Tell the girls I'll be seeing them. Where shall it be, Miss?"

"Anne."

"That's fine," Mr. Davis—Cholmondeley said. "I'm Willie."

"I bet you know this town well," Anne said. "I'm new." She came close to the floodlights and deliberately showed herself to him; she wanted to see whether he recognised her; but Mr. Davis never looked at a face. He looked past you. His large square face didn't need to show its force by any eye-to-eye business. Its power lay in its existence at all; you couldn't help wondering, as you wondered with an outsize mastiff, how much sheer weight of food had daily to be consumed to keep him fit.

Mr. Davis winked at Mr. Collier, and said, "Oh yes, I know this town. In a manner of speaking I made this town." He said, "There isn't much choice. There's the Grand or the Metropole. The Metropole's more intimate."

"Let's go to the Metropole."

"They have the best sundaes too in Nottwich."

The street was no longer crowded, just the usual number of people looking in the windows, strolling home, going into the Imperial Cinema. Anne thought, where is Raven now? How can I find Raven?

"It's not worth taking a taxi," Mr. Davis said, "the Metropole's only just round the corner. You'll like the Metropole," he repeated. "It's more intimate than the Grand," but it wasn't the kind of hotel you associated with intimacy. It came in sight at once all along one side of the market place, as big as a railway station, of red and yellow stone with a clock-face in a pointed tower.

"Kind of Hôtel de Ville, eh?" Mr. Davis said. You could tell how proud he was of Nottwich.

There were sculptured figures in between every pair of windows; all the historic worthies of Nottwich stood in stiff neo-Gothic attitudes, from Robin Hood up to the Mayor of Nottwich in 1864. "People come a long way to see this," Mr. Davis said.

"And the Grand? What's the Grand like?"

"Oh, the Grand," Mr. Davis said, "the Grand's gaudy."

He pushed her in ahead of him through the swing doors, and Anne saw how the porter recognised him. It wasn't going to be hard, she thought, to trace Mr. Davis in Nottwich; but how to find Raven?

The restaurant had enough room for the passengers of a liner; the roof was supported on pillars painted in stripes of sage-green and gold. The curved ceiling was blue scattered with gold stars arranged in their proper constellations. "It's one of the sights of Nottwich," Mr. Davis said. "I always keep a table under Venus." He laughed nervously, settling in his seat, and Anne noticed that they weren't under Venus at all but under Jupiter.

"You ought to be under the Great Bear," she said.

"Ha, ha, that's good," Mr. Davis said. "I must remember that." He bent over the wine-list. "I know you ladies always like a sweet wine." He confessed, "I've a sweet tooth myself." He sat there studying the card, lost to everything; he wasn't interested in her; he seemed interested at that moment in nothing but a series of tastes, beginning with the lobster he had ordered. This was his chosen home: the huge stuffy palace of food; this was his idea of intimacy, one table set among two hundred tables.

Anne thought he had brought her there for a flirtation. She had imagined that it would be easy to get on terms with Mr. Davis, even though the ritual a little scared her. Five years of provincial theatres had not made her adept at knowing how far she could go without arousing in the other more excitement than she could easily cope with. Her retreats were always sudden and dangerous. Over the lobster she thought of Mather, of security, of loving one man. Then she put out her knee and touched Mr. Davis's. Mr. Davis took no notice, cracking his way through a claw. He might just as well have been alone. It made her uneasy, to be so neglected. It didn't seem natural. She touched his knee again and said, "Anything on your mind, Willie?"

The eyes he raised were like the lenses of a powerful microscope focused on an unmounted slide. He said, "What's that? This lobster all right, eh?" He stared past her over the wide rather empty restaurant, all the tables decorated with holly and mistletoe. He called, "Waiter, I want an evening paper," and set to again at his claw. When the paper was brought he turned first of all to the financial page. He seemed satisfied; what he read there was as good as a lollipop.

Anne said, "Would you excuse me a moment, Willie?" She took three coppers out of her bag and went to the ladies' lavatory. She stared at herself in the glass over the wash basin; there didn't seem to be anything wrong. She said to the old woman there, "Do I look all right to you?"

The woman grinned. "Perhaps he doesn't like so much lipstick."

"Oh no," Anne said, "he's the lipstick type. A change from home. Hubbie on the razzle." She said, "Who is he? He calls himself Davis? He says he made this town."

"Excuse me, dear, but your stocking's laddered."

"It's not his doing, anyway. Who is he?"

"I've never heard of him, dear. Ask the porter."

"I think I will."

She went to the front door. "That restaurant's so hot," she said. "I had to get a bit of air." It was a peaceful moment for the porter of the Metropole. Nobody came in; nobody went out. He said, "It's cold enough outside." A man with one leg stood on the kerb and sold matches; the trams went by; little lighted homes full of smoke and talk and friendliness. A clock struck half-past eight and you could hear from one of the streets outside the square the shrill voices of children singing a tuneless carol. Anne said, "Well, I must be getting back to Mr. Davis." She said, "Who *is* Mr. Davis?"

"He's got plenty," the porter said.

"He says he made this town."

"That's boasting," the porter said. "It's Midland Steel made this town. You'll see their offices in the Tanneries. But they're ruining the town now. They *did* employ fifty thousand. Now they don't have ten thousand. I was a doorkeeper there once myself. But they even cut down the doorkeepers."

"It must have been cruel," Anne said.

"It was worse for him," the porter said, nodding through the door at the one-legged man. "He had twenty years with them. Then he lost his leg and the court brought it in wilful negligence, so they didn't give him a tanner. They economised there too, you see. It was negligence, all right; he fell asleep. If you tried watching a machine do the same thing once every second for eight hours, you'd feel sleepy yourself."

"But Mr. Davis?"

"Oh, I don't know anything about Mr. Davis. He may have something to do with the boot factory. Or he may be one of the directors of Wallace's. They've got money to burn." A woman came through the door carrying a Pekinese; she wore a heavy fur coat. She asked: "Has Mr. Alfred Piker been in here?"

"No, ma'am."

"There. It's just what his uncle was always doing. Disappearing." She said, "Keep hold of the dog," and rolled away across the square.

"That's the Mayoress," the porter said.

Anne went back. But something had happened. The bottle of wine was almost empty and the paper lay on the floor at Mr. Davis's feet. Two sundaes had been laid in place, but Mr. Davis hadn't touched his. It wasn't politeness; something had put him out. He growled at her, "Where have you been?" She tried to see what he had been reading; it wasn't the financial page any more, but she could make out only the main headlines: "Decree *Nisi* for Lady——" the name was too complicated to read upside down; "Manslaughter Verdict on Motorist." Mr. Davis said, "I don't know what's wrong with the place. They've put salt or something in the sundaes." He turned his furious dewlapped face at the passing waiter. "Call this a Knickerbocker Glory?"

"I'll bring you another, sir."

"You won't. My bill."

"So we call it a day," Anne said.

Mr. Davis looked up from the bill with something very like fear. "No, no," he said, "I didn't mean that. You won't go and leave me flat now?"

"Well, what do you want to do, the flickers?"

"I thought," Mr. Davis said, "you might come back with me to my place and have a tune on the radio and a glass of something good. We might foot it together a bit, eh?" He wasn't looking at her; he was hardly thinking of what he was saying. He didn't look dangerous. Anne thought she knew his type, you could pass them off with a kiss or two, and when they were drunk tell them a sentimental story until they began to think you were their sister. This would be the last: soon she would be Mather's; she would be safe. But first she was going to learn where Mr. Davis lived.

As they came out into the square the carol singers broke on them, six small boys without an idea of a tune between them. They wore wool gloves and mufflers and they stood across Mr. Davis's path chanting: "*Mark my footsteps well, my page.*"

"Taxi, sir?" the porter asked.

"No." Mr. Davis explained to Anne, "It saves three-pence to take one from the rank in the Tanneries." But the boys got in his way, holding out their caps for money. "Get out of the way," Mr. Davis said. With the intuition of children they recognised his uneasiness and baited him, pursuing him along the kerb, singing: "*Follow in them boldly.*" The loungers outside the Crown turned to look. Somebody clapped. Mr. Davis suddenly rounded and seized the hair of the boy nearest him; he pulled it till the boy screamed; pulled it till a tuft came out between his fingers. He said, "That will teach you," and sinking back a moment later in the taxi from the rank in the Tanneries, he said with pleasure, "They can't play with me." His mouth was open and his lip was wet with saliva; he brooded over his victory in the same way as he had brooded over the lobster; he didn't look to Anne as safe as she had thought. She reminded herself that he was only an agent. He *knew* the murderer, Raven said; he hadn't committed it himself.

"What's that building?" she asked, seeing a great black glass-front stand out from the Victorian street of sober offices where once the leather-workers had tanned their skins.

"Midland Steel," Mr. Davis said.

"Do you work there?"

Mr. Davis for the first time returned look for look. "What made you think that?"

"I don't know," Anne said and recognised with uneasiness that Mr. Davis was only simple when the wind stood one way.

"Do you think you could like me?" Mr. Davis said, fingering her knee.

"I dare say I might."

The taxi had left the Tanneries. It heaved over a net of tramlines and came out into the Station Approach. "Do you live out of town?"

"Just at the edge," Mr. Davis said.

"They ought to spend more on lighting in this place."

"You're a cute little girl," Mr. Davis said. "I bet you know what's what."

"It's no good looking for eggshell if that's what you mean," Anne said, as they drove under the great steel bridge that carried the line on to York. There were only two lamps on the whole of the long steep gradient to the station. Over a wooden fence you could see the shunted trucks on the side line, the stacked coal ready for entrainment. An old taxi and a bus waited for passengers outside the small dingy station entrance. Built in 1860, it hadn't kept pace with Nottwich.

"You've got a long way to go to work," Anne said.

"We are nearly there."

The taxi turned to the left. Anne read the name of the road: Khyber Avenue, a long row of mean villas showing apartment cards. The taxi stopped at the end of the road. Anne said, "You don't mean you live *here?*" Mr. Davis was paying off the driver. "Number sixty-one," he said (Anne noticed there was no card in this window between the pane and the thick lace curtains). He smiled in a soft ingratiating way and said, "It's really nice inside, dear." He put a key in the lock and thrust her firmly forward into a little dimly lit hall with a hatstand. He hung up his hat and walked softly towards the stairs on his toes. There was a smell of gas and greens. A blue fan of flame lit up a dusty plant.

"We'll turn on the wireless," Mr. Davis said, "and have a tune."

A door opened in the passage and a woman's voice said, "Who's that?"

"Just Mr. Cholmondeley."

"Don't forget to pay before you go up."

"The first floor," Mr. Davis said. "The room straight ahead of you. I won't be a moment," and he waited on the stairs till she passed him. The coins clinked in his pocket as his hand groped for them.

There *was* a wireless in the room, standing on a marble washstand, but there was certainly no space to dance in, for the big double bed filled the room. There was nothing to show the place was ever lived in: there was dust on the wardrobe mirror and the ewer beside the loud speaker was dry. Anne looked out of the window behind the bedposts on a little dark yard. Her hand trembled against the sash: this was more than she had bargained for. Mr. Davis opened the door.

She was badly frightened. It made her take the offensive. She said at once, "So you call yourself Mr. Cholmondeley?"

He blinked at her, closing the door softly behind him: "What if I do?"

"And you said you were taking me home. This isn't your home."

Mr. Davis sat down on the bed and took off his shoes. He said, "We mustn't make a noise, dear. The old woman doesn't like it." He opened the door of the washstand and took out a cardboard box; it spilt soft icing sugar out of its cracks all over the bed and the floor as he came towards her. "Have a piece of Turkish Delight."

"This isn't your home," she persisted.

Mr. Davis, with his fingers half-way to his mouth, said, "Of course it isn't. You don't think I'd take you to my home, do you? You aren't as green as that. I'm not going to lose my reputation." He said, "We'll have a tune, shall we, first?" And turning the dials he set the instrument squealing and moaning. "Lot of atmospherics about," Mr. Davis said, twisting and turning the dials until very far away you could hear a dance band playing, a dreamy rhythm underneath the shrieking in the air; you could just discern the tune: *"Night light, Love light."* "It's our own Nottwich programme," Mr. Davis said. "There isn't a better band on the Midland Regional. From the Grand. Let's do a step or two," and grasping her round the waist he began to shake up and down between the bed and the wall.

"I've known better floors," Anne said, trying to keep up her spirits with her own hopeless form of humour, "but I've never known a worse crush," and Mr. Davis said, "That's good. I'll remember that." Quite suddenly, blowing off relics of icing sugar which clung round his mouth, he grew passionate. He fastened his lips on her neck. She pushed him away and laughed at him at the same time. She had to keep her head. "Now I know what a rock feels like," she said, "when the sea amen—anem—damn, I can never say that word."

"That's good," Mr. Davis said mechanically, driving her back.

She began to talk rapidly about anything which came into her head. She said, "I wonder what this gas practice will be like. Wasn't it terrible the way they shot the old woman through her eyes?"

He loosed her at that, though she hadn't really meant anything by it. He said, "Why do you bring that up?"

"I was just reading about it," Anne said. "The man must have made a proper mess in that flat."

Mr. Davis implored her, "Stop. Please stop." He explained weakly, leaning back for support against the bed-post, "I've got a weak stomach. I don't like horrors."

"I like thrillers," Anne said. "There was one I read the other day . . ."

"I've got a very vivid imagination," Mr. Davis said.

"I remember once when I cut my finger . . ."

"Don't. Please don't."

Success made her reckless. She said, "I've got a vivid imagination too. I thought someone was watching this house."

"What do you mean?" He was scared all right. But she went too far. She said, "There was a dark fellow watching the door. He had a hare-lip."

Mr. Davis went to the door and locked it. He turned the wireless low. He said, "There's no lamp within twenty yards. You couldn't have seen his lip."

"I just thought . . ."

"I wonder how much he told you," Mr. Davis said. He sat down on the bed and looked at his hands. "You wanted to know where I lived, whether I worked . . ." He cut his sentence short and looked up at her with horror. But she could tell from his manner that he was no longer afraid of her; it was something else that scared him. He said, "They'd never believe you."

"Who wouldn't?"

"The police. It's a wild story." To her amazement he began to sniffle, sitting on the bed nursing his great hairy hands. "There must be some way out. I don't want to hurt you. I don't want to hurt anyone. I've got a weak stomach."

Anne said, "I don't know a thing. Please open the door."

Mr. Davis said in a low furious voice, "Be quiet. You've brought it on yourself."

She said again, "I don't know anything."

"I'm only an agent," Mr. Davis said. "I'm not responsible." He explained gently, sitting there in his stockinged feet with tears in his deep selfish eyes, "It's always been our policy to take no risks. It's not my fault that fellow got away. I did my best. I've always done my best. But he won't forgive me again."

"I'll scream if you don't open that door."

"Scream away. You'll only make the old woman cross."

"What are you going to do?"

"There's more than half a million at stake," Mr. Davis said. "I've got to make sure this time." He got up and came towards her with his hands out; she screamed and shook the door, then fled from it because there was no reply and ran round the bed. He just let her run; there was no escape in the tiny cramped room. He stood there muttering to himself, "Horrible. Horrible." You could tell he was on the verge of sickness, but the fear of somebody else drove him on.

Anne implored him, "I'll promise anything."

He shook his head, "He'd never forgive me," and sprawled across the bed and caught her wrist. He said thickly, "Don't struggle. I won't hurt you if you don't struggle," pulling her to him across the bed, feeling with his other hand for the pillow. She told herself even then: it isn't me. It's other people who are murdered. Not me. The urge to life which made her disbelieve that this could possibly be the end of everything for her, for the loving enjoying I, comforted her even when the pillow was across her mouth; never allowed her to realise the full horror, as she fought against his hands, strong and soft and sticky with icing sugar.

v

The rain blew up along the River Weevil from the east; it turned to ice in the bitter night and stung the asphalt walks, pitted the paint on the wooden seats. A constable came quietly by in his heavy raincoat gleaming like wet macadam, moving his lantern here and there in the dark spaces between the lamps. He said, "Good night" to Raven without another glance. It was couples he expected to find, even in December under the hail, the signs of poor cooped provincial passion.

Raven buttoned to the neck went on, looking for any shelter. He wanted to keep his mind on Cholmondeley, on how to find the man in Nottwich. But continually he found himself thinking instead of the girl he had threatened that morning. He remembered the kitten he had left behind in the Soho café. He had loved that kitten.

It had been sublimely unconscious of his ugliness. "My name's Anne." "You aren't ugly." She never knew, he thought, that he had meant to kill her; she had been as innocent of his intention as a cat he had once been forced to drown; and he remembered with astonishment that she had not betrayed him, although he had told her that the police were after him. It was even possible that she had believed him.

These thoughts were colder and more uncomfortable than the hail. He wasn't used to any taste that wasn't bitter on the tongue. He had been made by hatred; it had constructed him into this thin smoky murderous figure in the rain, hunted and ugly. His mother had borne him when his father was in gaol, and six years later when his father was hanged for another crime, she had cut her own throat with a kitchen knife; afterwards there had been the home. He had never felt the least tenderness for anyone; he was made in this image and he had his own odd pride in the result; he didn't want to be unmade. He had a sudden terrified conviction that he must be himself now as never before if he was to escape. It was not tenderness that made you quick on the draw.

Somebody in one of the larger houses on the riverfront had left his garage gate ajar; it was obviously not used for a car, but only to house a pram, a child's playground and a few dusty dolls and bricks. Raven took shelter there; he was cold through and through except in the one spot that had lain frozen all his life. That dagger of ice was melting with great pain. He pushed the garage gate a little further open; he had no wish to appear furtively hiding if anyone passed along the river beat; anyone might be excused for sheltering in a stranger's garage from *this* storm, except, of course, a man wanted by the police with a hare-lip.

These houses were only semi-detached. They were joined by their garages. Raven was closely hemmed in by the red-brick walls. He could hear the wireless playing in both houses. In the one house it switched and changed as a restless finger turned the screw and beat up the wavelengths, bringing a snatch of rhetoric from Berlin, of opera from Stockholm. On the National Programme from the other house an elderly critic was reading verse. Raven couldn't help but hear, standing in the cold garage by the baby's pram, staring out at the black hail:

> *A shadow flits before me,*
> *Not thou, but like to thee;*
> *Ah Christ, that it were possible*
> *For one short hour to see*
> *The souls we loved, that they might tell us*
> *What and where they be.*

He dug his nails into his hands, remembering his father who had been hanged and his mother who had killed herself in the basement kitchen, all the long parade of those who had done him down. The elderly cultured Civil Service voice read on:

> *And I loathe the squares and streets,*
> *And the faces that one meets,*
> *Hearts with no love for me . .*

He thought: give her time and she too will go to the police. That's what always happens in the end with a skirt,

> *—My whole soul out to thee——*

trying to freeze again, as hard and safe as ever, the icy fragment.

"That was Mr. Druce Winton, reading a selection from *Maud* by Lord Tennyson. This ends the National Programme. Good night, everybody."

3

i

Mather's train got in at eleven that night and with Saunders he drove straight through the almost empty streets to the police station. Nottwich went to bed early; the cinemas closed at ten-thirty and a quarter of an hour later everyone had left the middle of Nottwich by tram or bus. Nottwich's only tart hung round the market place, cold and blue under her umbrella, and one or two business men were having a last cigar in the hall of the Metropole. The car slid on the icy road. Just before the police station Mather noticed the posters of *Aladdin* outside the Royal Theatre. He said to Saunders, "My girl's in that show." He felt proud and happy.

The Chief Constable had come down to the police station to meet Mather. The fact that Raven was known to be armed and desperate gave the chase a more serious air than it would otherwise have had. The Chief Constable was fat and excited. He had made a lot of money as a tradesman and during the war had been given a commission and the job of presiding over the local military tribunal. He prided himself on having been a terror to pacifists. It atoned a little for his own home life and a wife who despised him. That was why he had come down to the station to meet Mather: it would be something to boast about at home.

Mather said, "Of course, sir, we don't *know* he's here. But he was on the train all right, and his ticket was given up. By a woman."

"Got an accomplice, eh?" the Chief Constable asked.

"Perhaps. Find the woman and we may have Raven."

The Chief Constable belched behind his hand. He had been drinking bottled beer before he came out and it always repeated itself. The superintendent said, "Directly we heard from the Yard we circulated the number of the notes to all shops, hotels and boarding houses."

"That a map, sir," Mather asked, "with your beats marked?"

They walked over to the wall and the superintendent pointed out the main points in Nottwich with a pencil: the railway station, the river, the police station.

"And the Royal Theatre," Mather said, "will be about there?"

"That's right."

"What's brought 'im to Nottwich?" the Chief Constable asked.

"I wish we knew, sir. Now these streets round the station, are they hotels?"

"A few boarding houses. But the worst of it is," the superintendent said, absent-mindedly turning his back on the Chief Constable, "a lot of these houses take occasional boarders."

"Better circulate them all."

"Some of them wouldn't take much notice of a police request. Houses of call, you know. Quick ten minutes and the door always open."

"Nonsense," the Chief Constable said, "we don't have that kind of place in Nottwich."

"If you wouldn't mind my suggesting it, sir, it wouldn't be a bad thing to double the constables on any beats of that kind. Send the sharpest men you've got. I suppose you've had his description in the evening papers? He seems to be a pretty smart safebreaker."

"There doesn't seem to be much more we can do to-night," the superintendent said. "I'm sorry for the poor devil if he's found nowhere to sleep."

"Keep a bottle of whisky here, super?" the Chief Constable asked. "Do us all good to 'ave a drink. Had too much beer. It returns. Whisky's better, but the wife doesn't like the smell." He leant back in his chair with his fat thighs crossed and watched the inspector with a kind of child-like happiness; he seemed to be saying, what a spree this is, drinking again with the boys. Only the superintendent knew what an old devil he was with anyone weaker than himself. "Just a splash, super." He said over his glass, "You caught that old bastard Baines out nicely," and explained to Mather. "Street betting. He's been a worry for months."

"He was straight enough. I don't believe in harrying people. Just because he was taking money out of Macpherson's pocket."

"Ah," the Chief Constable said, "but that's legal. Macpherson's got an office and a telephone. He's got expenses to carry. Cheerio, boys. To the ladies." He drained his glass. "Just another two fingers, super." He blew out his chest. "What about some more coal on the fire? Let's be snug. There's no work we can do tonight."

Mather was uneasy. It was quite true there wasn't much one could do, but he hated inaction. He stayed by the map. It wasn't such a large place, Nottwich. They ought not to take long to find Raven, but here he was a stranger. He didn't know what dives to raid, what clubs and dance halls. He said, "We think he's followed someone here. I'd suggest, sir, that first thing in the morning we interview the ticket collector again. See how many local people he can remember leaving the train. We might be lucky."

"Do you know that story about the Archbishop of York?" the Chief Constable asked. "Yes, yes. We'll do that. But there's no hurry. Make yourself at 'ome, man, and take some Scotch. You're in the Midlands now. The slow Midlands (eh, super?). We don't 'ustle, but we get there just the same."

Of course, he was right. There *was* no hurry, and there wasn't anything anyone could do at this hour, but as Mather stood beside the map, it was just as if someone were calling him, "Hurry. Hurry. Hurry. Or you may be too late." He traced the main streets with his finger; he wanted to be as familiar with them as he was with central London. Here was the G.P.O., the market, the Metropole, the High Street: what was this? the Tanneries. "What's this big block in the Tanneries, sir?" he asked.

"That'll be Midland Steel," the superintendent said and turning to the Chief Constable he went on patiently, "No, sir. I hadn't heard that one. That's a good one, sir."

"The mayor told me that," the Chief Constable said. "He's a sport, old Piker. Do you know what he said when we had that committee on the gas practice? He said, 'This'll give us a chance to get into a strange bed.' He meant the women couldn't tell who was who in a gas mask. You see?"

"Very witty man, Mr. Piker, sir."

"Yes, super, but I was too smart for him there. I was on the spot that day. Do you know what I said?"

"No, sir."

"I said, 'You won't be able to find a strange bed, Piker.' Catch me meaning? He's a dog, old Piker."

"What are your arrangements for the gas practice, sir?" Mather asked with his finger jabbed on the Town Hall.

"You can't expect people to buy gas masks at twenty-five bob a time, but we're having a raid the day after to-morrow with smoke bombs from Hanlow aerodrome, and anyone found in the street without a mask will be carted off by ambulance to the General Hospital. So anyone who's too busy to stop indoors will have to buy a mask. Midland Steel are supplying all their people with masks, so it'll be business as usual there."

"Kind of blackmail," the superintendent said. "Stay in or buy a mask. The transport companies have spent a pretty penny on masks."

"What hours, sir?"

"We don't tell them that. Sirens hoot. You know the idea. Boy Scouts on bicycles. They've been lent masks. But of course we know it'll be all over before noon."

Mather looked back at the map. "These coal yards," he said, "round the station. You've got them well covered?"

"We are keeping an eye on those," the superintendent said. "I saw to that as soon as the Yard rang through."

"Smart work, boys, smart work," the Chief Constable said, swallowing the last of his whisky. "I'll be off home. Busy day before us all to-morrow. You'd like a conference with me in the morning, I dare say, super?"

"Oh, I don't think we'll trouble you that early, sir."

"Well, if you do need any advice, I'm always at the end of the 'phone. Good night, boys."

"Good night, sir. Good night."

"The old boy's right about one thing." The superintendent put the whisky away in his cupboard. "We can't do anything more to-night."

"I won't keep you up, sir," Mather said. "You mustn't think I'm fussy. Saunders will tell you I'm as ready to knock off as any man, but there's something about this case. . . . I can't leave it alone. It's a queer case. I was looking at this map, sir, and trying to think where I'd hide. What about these dotted lines out here on the east?"

"It's a new housing estate."

"Half-built houses?"

"I've put two men on special beat out there."

"You've got everything taped pretty well, sir. You don't really need us."

"You mustn't judge us by *him*."

"I'm not quite easy in my mind. He's followed someone here. He's a smart lad. We've never had anything on him before, and yet for the last twenty-four hours he's done nothing but make mistakes. The chief said he's blazing a trail, and it's true. It strikes me that he's desperate to get someone.''

The superintendent glanced at the clock.

"I'm off, sir," Mather said. "See you in the morning. Good night, Saunders. I'm just going to take a stroll around a bit before I come to the hotel. I want to get this place clear.''

He walked out into the High Street. The rain had stopped and was freezing in the gutters. He slipped on the pavement and had to push his hand on the lamp standard. They turned the lights very low in Nottwich after eleven. Over the way, fifty yards down towards the market, he could see the portico of the Royal Theatre. No lights at all to be seen there. He found himself humming, "*But to me it's Paradise*," and thought: it's good to love, to have a centre, a certainty, not just to be *in* love floating around. He wanted that too to be organised as soon as possible: he wanted love stamped and sealed and signed and the licence paid for. He was filled with a dumb tenderness he would never be able to express outside marriage. He wasn't a lover; he was already like a married man, but a married man with years of happiness and confidence to be grateful for.

He did the maddest thing he'd done since he had known her: he went and took a look at her lodgings. He had the address. She'd given it him over the 'phone, and it fitted in with his work to find his way to All Saints Road. He learnt quite a lot of things on the way, keeping his eyes open: it wasn't really a waste of time. He learnt, for instance, the name and address of the local papers: the *Nottwich Journal* and the *Nottwich Guardian*, two rival papers facing each other across Chatton Street, one of them next a great gaudy cinema. From their posters he could even judge their publics: the *Journal* was popular, the *Guardian* was "class." He learnt too where the best fish-and-chip shops were and the public-houses where the pitmen went; he discovered the park, a place of dull wilted trees and palings and gravel paths for perambulators. Any of these facts might be of use and they humanised the map of Nottwich so that he could think of it in terms of people, just as he thought of London, when he was on a job, in terms of Charlies and Joes.

All Saints Road was two rows of small neo-Gothic houses lined up as carefully as a company on parade. He stopped outside No. 14 and wondered if she were awake. She'd get a surprise in the morning; he had posted a card at Euston telling her he was putting up at the Crown, the commercial "house." There was a light on in the basement: the landlady was still awake. He wished he could have sent a quicker message than that card; he knew the dreariness of new lodgings, of waking to the black tea and the unfriendly face. It seemed to him that life couldn't treat her well enough.

The wind froze him, but he lingered there on the opposite pavement, wondering whether she had enough blankets on her bed, whether she had any shillings for the gas meter. Encouraged by the light in the basement he nearly rang the bell to ask the landlady whether Anne had all she needed. But he made his way instead towards the Crown. He wasn't going to look silly; he wasn't even going to tell her that he'd been and had a look at where she slept.

ii

A knock on the door woke him. It was barely seven. A woman's voice said, "You're wanted on the 'phone," and he could hear her trailing away downstairs, knocking a broom handle against the banisters. It was going to be a fine day.

Mather went downstairs to the telephone which was behind the bar in the empty saloon. He said, "Mather. Who's that?" and heard the station sergeant's voice, "We've got some news for you. He slept last night in St. Mark's, the Roman Catholic Cathedral. And someone reports he was down by the river earlier."

But by the time he was dressed and at the station more evidence had come in. The agent of a housing estate had read in the local paper about the stolen notes and brought to the station two notes he had received from a girl who said she wanted to buy a house. He'd thought it odd because she had never turned up to sign the papers.

"That'll be the girl who gave up his ticket," the superintendent said. "They are working together on this."

"And the cathedral?" Mather asked.

"A woman saw him come out early this morning. Then when she got home (she was on the way to chapel) and read the paper, she told a constable on point duty. We'll have to have the churches locked."

"No, watched," Mather said. He warmed his hand over the iron stove. "Let me talk to this house agent."

The man came breezily in in plus fours from the outer room. "Name of Green," he said.

"Could you tell me, Mr. Green, what this girl looked like?"

"A nice little thing," Mr. Green said.

"Short? Below five-feet-four?"

"No, I wouldn't say that."

"You said little?"

"Oh," Mr. Green said, "term of affection, you know. Easy to get on with."

"Fair? Dark?"

"Oh, I couldn't say that. Don't look at their hair. Good legs."

"Anything strange in her manner?"

"No, I wouldn't say that. Nicely spoken. She could take a joke."

"Then you wouldn't have noticed the colour of her eyes?"

"Well, as a matter of fact, I did. I always look at a girl's eyes. They like it. 'Drink to me only,' you know. A bit of poetry. That's my gambit. Kind of spiritual, you know."

"And what colour were they?"

"Green with a spot of gold."

"What was she wearing? Did you notice that?"

"Of course I did," Mr. Green said. He moved his hands in the air. "It was something dark and soft. You know what I mean."

"And the hat? Straw?"

"No. It wasn't straw."

"Felt?"

"It might have been a kind of felt. That was dark too. I noticed that."

"Would you know her again if you saw her?"

"Of course I would," Mr. Green said. "Never forget a face."

"Right," Mather said, "you can go. We may want you later to identify the girl. We'll keep these notes."

"But I say," Mr. Green said, "those are good notes. They belong to the company."

"You can consider the house is still for sale."

"I've had the ticket collector here," the superintendent said. "Of course he doesn't remember a thing that helps. In these stories you read people always remember *something*, but in real life they just say she was wearing something dark or something light."

"You've sent someone up to look at the house? Is this the man's story? It's odd. She must have gone there straight from the station. Why? And why pretend to buy the house and pay him with stolen notes?"

"It looks as if she was desperate to keep the other man from buying. As if she'd got something hidden there."

"Your man had better go through the house with a comb, sir. But of course they won't find much. If there was still anything to find she'd have turned up to sign the papers."

"No, she'd have been afraid," the superintendent said, "in case he'd found out they were stolen notes."

"You know," Mather said, "I wasn't much interested in this case. It seemed sort of petty. Chasing down a small thief when the whole world will soon be fighting because of a murderer those fools in Europe couldn't catch. But now it's getting me. There's something odd about it. I told you what my chief said about Raven? He said he was blazing a trail. But he's managed so far to keep just ahead of us. Could I see the ticket collector's statement?"

"There's nothing in it."

"I don't agree with you, sir," Mather said, while the superintendent turned it up from the file of papers on his desk, "the books are right. People generally do remember something. If they remembered nothing at all, it would look very queer. It's only spooks that don't leave any impression. Even that agent remembered the colour of her eyes."

"Probably wrong," the superintendent said. "Here you are. All he remembers is that she carried two suitcases. It's something, of course, but it's not worth much."

"Oh, one could make guesses from that," Mather said. "Don't you think so?" He didn't believe in making himself too clever in front of the provincial police; he needed their co-operation. "She was coming for a long stay (a woman can get a lot in one suitcase) or else, if she was carrying his case too, he was the dominant one. Believes in treating her rough and making her do all the physical labour. That fits in with Raven's character. As for the girl——"

"In these gangster stories," the superintendent said, "they call her a moll."

"Well, this moll," Mather said, "is one of those girls who like being treated rough. Sort of clinging and avaricious, I picture her. If she had more spirit he'd carry one of the suitcases or else she'd split on him."

"I thought this Raven was about as ugly as they are made."

"That fits too," Mather said. "Perhaps she likes 'em ugly. Perhaps it gives her a thrill."

The superintendent laughed. "You've got a lot out of those suitcases. Read the report and you'll be giving me her photograph. Here you are. But he doesn't remember a thing about her, not even what she was wearing."

Mather read it. He read it slowly. He said nothing, but something in his manner of shock and incredulity was conveyed to the superintendent. He said, "Is anything wrong? There's nothing *there*, surely?"

"You said I'd be giving you her photograph," Mather said. He took a slip of newspaper from the back of his watch. "There it is, sir. You'd better circulate that to all stations in the city and to the Press."

"But there's nothing in the report," the superintendent said.

"Everybody remembers something. It wasn't anything you could have spotted. I seem to have private information about this crime, but I didn't know it till now."

The superintendent said, "He doesn't remember a thing. Except the suitcases."

"Thank God for those," Mather said. "It may mean . . . You see he says here that one of the reasons he remembers her—he calls it remembering her—is that she was the only woman who got out of the train at Nottwich. And this girl I happen to know was travelling by it. She'd got an engagement at the theatre here."

The superintendent said bluntly—he didn't realise the full extent of the shock, "And is she of the type you said? Likes 'em ugly?"

"I thought she liked them plain," Mather said, staring out through the window at a world going to work through the cold early day.

"Sort of clinging and avaricious?"

"No, damn it."

"But if she'd had more spirit——" the superintendent mocked; he thought Mather was disturbed because his guesses were wrong.

"She had all the spirit there was," Mather said. He turned back from the window. He forgot the superintendent was his superior officer; he forgot you had to be tactful to these provincial police officers; he said, "God damn it, don't you see? He didn't carry his suitcase because he had to keep her covered. He *made* her walk out to the housing estate." He said, "I've got to go out there. He meant to murder her."

"No, no," the superintendent said. "You are forgetting: she paid the money to Green and walked out of the house with him alone. He saw her off the estate."

"But I'd swear," Mather said, "she isn't in this. It's absurd. It doesn't make sense." He said, "We're engaged to be married."

"That's tough," the superintendent said. He hesitated, picked up a dead match and cleaned a nail, then he pushed the photograph back. "Put it away," he said. "We'll go about this differently."

"No," Mather said. "I'm on this case. Have it printed. It's a bad smudged photo." He wouldn't look at it. "It doesn't do her justice. But I'll wire home for a better likeness. I've got a whole strip of Photomatons at home. Her face from every angle. You couldn't have a better lot of photos for newspaper purposes.''

"I'm sorry, Mather," the superintendent said. "Hadn't I better speak to the Yard? Get another man sent?''

"You couldn't have a better on the case," Mather said. "I know her. If she's to be found, I'll find her. I'm going out to the house now. You see, your man may miss something. I *know* her.''

"There may be an explanation," the superintendent said.

"Don't you see," Mather said, "that if there's an explanation it means—why, that she's in danger, she may even be——''

"We'd have found her body.''

"We haven't even found a living man," Mather said. "Would you ask Saunders to follow me out? What's the address?'' He wrote it carefully down; he always noted facts; he didn't trust his brain for more than theories, guesses.

It was a long drive out to the housing estate. He had time to think of many possibilities. She might have fallen asleep and been carried on to York. She might not have taken the train . . . and there was nothing in the little hideous house to contradict him. He found a plainclothes man in what would one day be the best front room; in its flashy fireplace, its dark brown picture rail and the cheap oak of its wainscoting, it bore already the suggestion of heavy unused furniture, dark curtains and Gosse china. "There's nothing," the detective said, "nothing at all. You can see, of course, that someone's been here. The dust has been disturbed. But there wasn't enough dust to make a footprint. There's nothing to be got here.''

"There's always something," Mather said. "Where did you find traces? All the rooms?''

"No, not all of them. But that's not evidence. There was no sign in this room, but the dust isn't as thick here. Maybe the builders swept up better. You can't say no one was in here.''

"How did she get in?''

"The lock of the back door's busted.''

"Could a girl do that?''

"A cat could do it. A determined cat.''

"Green says he came in at the front. Just opened the door of this room and then took the other fellow straight upstairs, into the best bedroom. The girl joined them there just as he was going to show the rest of the house. Then they all went straight down and out of the house except the girl went into the kitchen and picked up her suitcases. He'd left the front door open and thought she'd followed them in.''

"She was in the kitchen all right. And in the bathroom.''

"Where's that?''

"Up the stairs and round to the left.''

The two men, they were both large, nearly filled the cramped bathroom. "Looks as if she heard them coming," the detective said, "and hid in here.''

"What brought her up? If she was in the kitchen she had only to slip out at the back.'' Mather stood in the tiny room between the bath and the lavatory seat and thought: *she* was here yesterday. It was incredible. It didn't fit in at any point with what he knew of her. They had been engaged for six months; she couldn't have disguised herself so completely: on the bus ride from Kew that evening, humming the song—what was it?—something about a snowflower; the night they sat two programmes round at the cinema because he'd spent his week's pay and hadn't been able to give her dinner. She never complained as the hard mechanised voices began all over again, "A wise guy, huh?" "Baby, you're swell." "Siddown, won't you?" "Thenks," at the edge of their consciousness. She was straight, she was loyal, he could swear that; but the alternative was a danger he hardly dared contemplate. Raven was desperate. He heard himself saying with harsh conviction, "Raven was here. He drove her up at the point of his pistol. He was going to shut her in here—or maybe shoot her. Then he heard voices. He gave her the notes and told her to get rid of the other fellows. If she'd tried anything on, he'd have shot her. Damn it, isn't it plain?" but the detective only repeated the substance of the superintendent's criticism, "She walked right out of the place alone with Green. There was nothing to prevent her going to the police station."

"He may have followed at a distance."

"It looks to me," the detective said, "as if you are taking the most *unlikely* theory," and Mather could tell from his manner how puzzled he was at the Yard man's attitude: these Londoners were a little too ingenious: he believed in good sound Midland common sense. It angered Mather in his professional pride; he even felt a small chill of hatred against Anne for putting him in a position where his affection warped his judgment. He said, "We've no proof that she didn't try to tell the police," and he wondered: do I want her dead and innocent or alive and guilty? He began to examine the bathroom with meticulous care. He even pushed his finger up the taps in case . . . He had a wild idea that if it were really Anne who had stood here, she would have wanted to leave a message. He straightened himself impatiently. "There's nothing here." He remembered there was a test: she might have missed her train. "I want a telephone," he said.

"There'll be one down the road at the agent's."

Mather rang up the theatre. There was no one there except a caretaker, but as it happened she could tell him that no one had been absent from rehearsal. The producer, Mr. Collier, always posted absentees on the board inside the stage door. He was great on discipline, Mr. Collier. Yes, and she remembered that there *was* a new girl. She happened to see her going out with a man at dinner-time after the rehearsal just as she came back to the theatre to tidy up a bit and thought: "that's a new face." She didn't know who the man was. He might be one of the backers. "Wait a moment, wait a moment," Mather said; he had to think what to do next; she *was* the girl who gave the agent the stolen notes; he had to forget that she was Anne who had so wildly wished that they could marry before Christmas, who had hated the promiscuity of her job, who had promised him that night on the bus from Kew that she would keep out of the way of all rich business backers and stage-door loungers. He said: "Mr. Collier? Where can I find him?"

"He'll be at the theatre to-night. There's a rehearsal at eight."

"I want to see him at once."

"You can't. He's gone up to York with Mr. Bleek."

"Where can I find any of the girls who were at the rehearsal?"

"I dunno. I don't have the address book. They'll be all over town."

"There must be *someone* who was there last night——"

"You could find Miss Maydew, of course."

"Where?"

"I don't know where she's staying. But you've only got to look at the posters of the jumble."

"The jumble? What do you mean?"

"She's opening the jumble up at St. Luke's at two."

Through the window of the agent's office Mather saw Saunders coming up the frozen mud of the track between the Cozyholmes. He rang off and intercepted him. "Any news come in?"

"Yes," Saunders said. The superintendent had told him everything, and he was deeply distressed. He liked Mather. He owed everything to Mather; it was Mather who had brought him up every stage of promotion in the police force, who had persuaded the authorities that a man who stammered could be as good a policeman as the champion reciter at police concerts. But he would have loved him anyway for a quality of idealism, for believing so implicitly in what he did.

"Well? Let's have it."

"It's about your g-girl. She's disappeared." He took the news at a run, getting it out in one breath. "Her landlady rang up the station, said she was out all night and never came back."

"Run away," Mather said.

Saunders said, "D-don't you believe it. You t-t-t-told her to take that train. She wasn't going till the m-m-m-m-morning."

"You're right," Mather said. "I'd forgotten that. Meeting him must have been an accident. But it's a miserable choice, Saunders. She may be dead now."

"Why should he do that? We've only got a theft on him. What are you going to do next?"

"Back to the station. And then at two," he smiled miserably, "a jumble sale."

iii

The vicar was worried. He wouldn't listen to what Mather had to say; he had too much to think about himself. It was the curate, the new bright broad-minded curate from a London east-end parish, who had suggested inviting Miss Maydew to open the jumble sale. He thought it would be a draw, but as the vicar explained to Mather, holding him pinned there in the pitch-pine ante-room of St. Luke's Hall, a jumble was always a draw. There was a queue fifty yards long of women with baskets waiting for the door to open; they hadn't come to see Miss Maydew; they had come for bargains. St. Luke's jumble sales were famous all over Nottwich.

A dry perky woman with a cameo brooch put her head in at the door. "Henry," she said, "the committee are rifling the stalls again. Can't you *do* something about it? There'll be nothing left when the sale starts."

"Where's Mander? It's *his* business," the vicar said.

"Mr. Mander, of course, is off fetching Miss Maydew." The perky woman blew her nose and crying "Constance, Constance!" disappeared into the hall.

"You can't really do anything about it," the vicar said. "It happens every year. These good women give their time voluntarily. The Altar Society would be in a very bad way without them. They *expect* to have first choice of everything that's sent in. Of course the trouble is: *they* fix the prices."

"Henry," the perky woman said, appearing again in the doorway, "you *must* interfere. Mrs. Penny has priced that very good hat Lady Cundifer sent at eighteen pence and bought it herself."

"My dear, how can I say anything? They'd never volunteer again. You must remember they've given time and trouble . . ." but he was addressing a closed door. "What worries me," he said to Mather, "is that this young lady will expect an ovation. She won't understand that nobody's interested in *who* opens a jumble sale. Things are so different in London."

"She's late," Mather said.

"They are quite capable of storming the doors," the vicar said with a nervous glance through the window at the lengthening queue. "I must confess to a little stratagem. After all she is our guest. She is giving time and trouble." Time and trouble were the gifts of which the vicar was always most conscious. They were given more readily than coppers in the collection. He went on, "Did you see any young boys outside?"

"Only women," Mather said.

"Oh dear, oh dear. I *told* Troop Leader Lance. You see, I thought if one or two Scouts, in plain clothes, of course, brought up autograph books, it would please Miss Maydew, seem to show we appreciated . . . the time and trouble." He said miserably, "The St. Luke's troop is always the least trustworthy . . ."

A grey-haired man with a carpet bag put his head in at the door. He said, "Mrs. 'Arris said as there was something wrong with the toilet."

"Ah, Mr. Bacon," the vicar said, "so kind of you. Step into the hall. You'll find Mrs. Harris there. A little stoppage, so I understand."

Mather looked at his watch. He said, "I must speak to Miss Maydew directly ——" A young man entered at a rush; he said to the vicar, "Excuse me, Mr. Harris, but will Miss Maydew be speaking?"

"I hope not. I profoundly hope not," the vicar said. "It's hard enough as it is to keep the women from the stalls till after I've said a prayer. Where's my prayer book? Who's seen my prayer book?"

"Because I'm covering it for the *Journal*, and if she's not, you see, I can get away——"

Mather wanted to say: Listen to me. Your damned jumble is of no importance. My girl's in danger. She may be dead. He wanted to do things to people, but he stood there heavy, immobile, patient, even his private passion and fear subdued by his training. One didn't give way to anger, one plodded on calmly, adding fact to fact; if one's girl was killed, one had the satisfaction of knowing one had done one's best according to the standards of the best police force in the world. He wondered bitterly, as he watched the vicar search for his prayer book, whether that would be any comfort.

Mr. Bacon came back and said, "She'll pull now," and disappeared with a clank of metal. A boisterous voice said, "Upstage a little, upstage, Miss Maydew," and the curate entered. He wore suede shoes, he had a shiny face and plastered hair and he carried an umbrella under his arm like a cricket bat; he might have been returning to the pavilion after scoring a duck in a friendly, taking his failure noisily as a good sportsman should. "Here is my C.O., Miss Maydew, on the O.P. side." He said to the vicar, "I've been telling Miss Maydew about our dramatics."

Mather said, "May I speak to you a moment privately, Miss Maydew?"

But the vicar swept her away. "A moment, a moment, first our little ceremony. Constance! Constance!" and almost immediately the ante-room was empty except for Mather and the journalist, who sat on the table swinging his legs, biting his nails. An extraordinary noise came from the next room: it was like the trampling of a herd of animals, a trampling suddenly brought to a standstill at a fence; in the sudden silence one could hear the vicar hastily finishing off the Lord's Prayer, and then Miss Maydew's clear immature principal boy's voice saying, "I declare this jumble well and truly——" and then the trampling again. She had got her words wrong—it had always been foundation stones her mother laid; but no one noticed. Everyone was relieved because she hadn't made a speech. Mather went to the door; half a dozen boys were queued up in front of Miss Maydew with autograph albums; the St. Luke's troop hadn't failed after all. A hard astute woman in a toque said to Mather, "This stall will interest *you*. It's a Man's Stall." and Mather looked down at a dingy array of penwipers and pipe-cleaners and hand-embroidered tobacco pouches. Somebody had even presented a lot of old pipes. He lied quickly, "I don't smoke."

The astute woman said, "You've come here to spend money, haven't you, as a duty? You may as well take *some*thing that will be of use. You won't find anything on any of the other stalls," and between the women's shoulders, as he craned to follow the movements of Miss Maydew and the St. Luke's troop, he caught a few grim glimpses of discarded vases, chipped fruit stands, yellowing piles of babies' napkins. "I've got several pairs of braces. You may just as well take a pair of braces."

Mather, to his own astonishment and distress, said, "She may be dead."

The woman said, "Who dead?" and bristled over a pair of mauve suspenders.

"I'm sorry," Mather said. "I wasn't thinking." He was horrified with himself for losing grip. He thought: I ought to have let them exchange me. It's going to be too much. He said, "Excuse me," seeing the last Scout shut his album.

He led Miss Maydew into the ante-room. The journalist had gone. He said, "I'm trying to trace a girl in your company called Anne Crowder."

"Don't know her," Miss Maydew said.

"She only joined the cast yesterday."

"They all look alike," Miss Maydew said, "like Chinamen. I never can learn their names."

"This one's fair. Green eyes. She has a good voice."

"Not in *this* company," Miss Maydew said, "not in *this* company. I can't listen to them. It sets my teeth on edge."

"You don't remember her going out last night with a man, at the end of rehearsal?"

"Why should I? Don't be so sordid."

"He invited you out too."

"The fat fool," Miss Maydew said.

"Who was he?"

"I don't know. Davenant, I think Collier said, or did he say Davis? Never saw him before. I suppose he's the man Cohen quarrelled with. Though somebody said something about Callitrope."

"This is important, Miss Maydew. The girl's disappeared."

"It's always happening on these tours. If you go into their dressing-rooms it's always *Men* they are talking about. How can they ever hope to act? So sordid."

"You can't help me at all? You've no idea where I can find this man Davenant?"

"Collier will know. He'll be back to-night. Or perhaps he won't. I don't think he knew him from Adam. It's coming back to me now. Collier called him Davis and he said, No, he was Davenant. He'd bought out Davis."

Mather went sadly away. Some instinct that always made him go where people were, because clues were more likely to be found among a crowd of strangers than in empty rooms or deserted streets, drove him through the hall. You wouldn't have known among these avid women that England was on the edge of war. "I said to Mrs. 'Opkinson, if you are addressing me, I said." "That'll look tasty on Dora." A very old woman said across a pile of artificial silk knickers, " 'E lay for five hours with 'is knees drawn up." A girl giggled and said in a hoarse whisper, "Awful. I'd say so. 'E put 'is fingers right down." Why should these people worry about war? They moved from stall to stall in an air thick with their own deaths and sicknesses and loves. A woman with a hard driven face touched Mather's arm; she must have been about sixty years old; she had a way of ducking her head when she spoke as if she expected a blow, but up her head would come again with a sour unconquerable malice. He had watched her, without really knowing it, as he walked down the stalls. Now she plucked at him; he could smell fish on her fingers. "Reach me that bit of stuff, dear," she said. "You've got long arms. No, not that. The pink," and began to fumble for money—in Anne's bag.

iv

Mather's brother had committed suicide. More than Mather he had needed to be part of an organisation, to be trained and disciplined and given orders, but unlike Mather he hadn't found his organisation. When things went wrong he killed himself, and Mather was called to the mortuary to identify the body. He had hoped it was a stranger until they had exposed the pale drowned lost face. All day he had been trying to find his brother, hurrying from address to address, and the first feeling he had when he saw him there was not grief. He thought: I needn't hurry, I can sit down. He went out to an A.B.C. and ordered a pot of tea. He only began to feel his grief after the second cup.

It was the same now. He thought: I needn't have hurried, I needn't have made a fool of myself before that woman with the braces. She must be dead. I needn't have felt so rushed.

The old woman said, "Thank you, dear," and thrust the little piece of pink material away. He couldn't feel any doubt whatever about the bag. He had given it her himself; it was an expensive bag, not of a kind you would expect to find in Nottwich, and to make it quite conclusive, you could still see, within a little circle of twisted glass, the place where two initials had been removed. It was all over forever; he hadn't got to hurry any more; a pain was on its way worse than he had felt in the A.B.C. (a man at the next table had been eating fried plaice and now, he didn't know why, he associated a certain kind of pain with the smell of fish). But first it was a perfectly cold calculating satisfaction he felt, that he had the devils in his hands already. Someone was going to die for this. The old woman had picked up a small bra and was testing the elastic with a malicious grin because it was meant for someone young and pretty with breasts worth preserving. "The silly things they wear," she said.

He could have arrested her at once, but already he had decided that wouldn't do; there were more in it than the old woman; he'd get them all, and the longer the chase lasted the better; he wouldn't have to begin thinking of the future till it was over. He was thankful now that Raven was armed because he himself was forced to carry a gun, and who could say whether chance might not allow him to use it?

He looked up and there on the other side of the stall, with his eyes fixed on Anne's bag, was the dark bitter figure he had been seeking, the hare-lip imperfectly hidden by a few days' growth of moustache.

4

i

Raven had been on his feet all the morning. He had to keep moving; he couldn't use the little change he had on food, because he did not dare to stay still, to give anyone the chance to study his face. He bought a paper outside the post office and saw his own description there, printed in black type inside a frame. He was angry because it was on a back page: the situation in Europe filled the front page. By midday, moving here and moving there with his eyes always open for Cholmondeley, he was dog-tired. He stood for a moment and stared at his own face in a barber's window; ever since his flight from the café he had remained unshaven; a moustache would hide his scar, but he knew from experience how his hair grew in patches, strong on the chin, weak on the lip, and not at all on either side of the red deformity. Now the scrubby growth on his chin was making him conspicuous and he didn't dare go into the barber's for a shave. He passed a chocolate machine, but it would take only six-penny or shilling pieces, and his pocket held nothing but half-crowns, florins, halfpennies. If it had not been for his bitter hatred he would have given himself up; they couldn't give him more than five years, but the death of the old minister lay, now that he was so tired and harried, like an albatross round his neck. It was hard to realise that he was wanted only for theft.

He was afraid to haunt alleys, to linger in culs-de-sac because if a policeman passed and he was the only man in sight he felt conspicuous; the man might give him a second glance, and so he walked all the time in the most crowded streets and took the risk of innumerable recognitions. It was a dull cold day, but at least it wasn't raining. The shops were full of Christmas gifts, all the absurd useless junk which had lain on back shelves all the year was brought out to fill the windows; foxhead brooches, book-rests in the shape of the Cenotaph, woollen cosies for boiled eggs, innumerable games with counters and dice and absurd patent variations on darts or bagatelle, "Cats on a Wall," the old shooting game, and "Fishing for Gold Fish." In a religious shop by the Catholic Cathedral he found himself facing again the images that angered him in the Soho café: the plaster mother and child, the wise men and the shepherds. They were arranged in a cavern of brown paper among the books of devotion, the little pious scraps of St. Theresa. "The Holy Family": he pressed his face against the glass with a kind of horrified anger that that tale still went on. "Because there was no room for them in the inn"; he remembered how they had sat in rows on the benches waiting for Christmas dinner, while the thin precise voice read on about Cæsar Augustus and how everyone went up to his own city to be taxed. Nobody was beaten on Christmas Day: all punishments were saved for Boxing Day. Love, Charity, Patience, Humility—he was educated; he knew all about those virtues; he'd seen what they were worth. They twisted everything; even that story in there, it was historical, it had happened, but they twisted it to their own purposes. They made him a God because they could feel fine about it all, they didn't have to consider themselves responsible for the raw deal they'd given him. He'd consented, hadn't he? That was the argument, because he could have called down "a legion of angels" if he'd wanted to escape hanging there. On your life he could, he thought with bitter lack of faith, just as easily as his own father taking the drop at Wandsworth could have saved himself when the trap opened. He stood there with his face against the glass waiting for somebody to deny *that* reasoning, staring at the swaddled child with a horrified tenderness, "the little bastard," because he was educated and knew what the child was in for, the double-crossing Judas and only one man to draw a knife on his side when the Roman soldiers came for him in the garden.

A policeman came up the street, as Raven stared into the window, and passed without a glance. It occurred to him to wonder how much they knew. Had the girl told them her story? He supposed she had by this time. It would be in the paper, and he looked. There was not a word about her there. It shook him. He'd nearly killed her and she hadn't gone to them: that meant she had believed what he'd told her. He was momentarily back in the garage again beside the Weevil in the rain and dark with the dreadful sense of desolation, of having missed something valuable, of having made an irretrievable mistake, but he could no longer comfort himself with any conviction with his old phrase: "give her time . . . it always happens with a skirt." He wanted to find her, but he thought: what a chance, I can't even find Cholmondeley. He said bitterly to the tiny scrap of plaster in the plaster cradle: "If you were a God, you'd know I wouldn't harm her: you'd give me a break, you'd let me turn and see her on the pavement," and he turned with half a hope, but of course there was nothing there.

As he moved away he saw a sixpence in the gutter. He picked it up and went back the way he had come to the last chocolate slot machine he had passed. It was outside a sweet shop and next a church hall, where a queue of women waited along the pavement for some kind of sale to open. They were getting noisy and impatient; it was after the hour when the doors should have opened, and he thought what fine game they would be for a really expert bag-picker. They were pressed against each other and would never notice a little pressure on the clasp. There was nothing personal in the thought; he had never fallen quite so low, he believed, as picking women's bags. But it made him idly pay attention to them, as he walked along the line. One stood out from the others, carried by an old rather dirty woman, new, expensive, sophisticated, of a kind he had seen before; he remembered at once the occasion, the little bathroom, the raised pistol, the compact she had taken from the bag.

The door was opened and the women pushed in; almost at once he was alone on the pavement beside the slot machine and the jumble-sale poster: "Entrance 6d." It couldn't be her bag, he told himself, there must be hundreds like it, but nevertheless he pursued it through the pitch-pine door. "And lead us not into temptation," the vicar was saying from a dais at one end of the hall above the old hats and the chipped vases and the stacks of women's underwear. When the prayer was finished he was flung by the pressure of the crowd against a stall of fancy goods: little framed amateur water-colours of lakeland scenery, gaudy cigarette boxes from Italian holidays, brass ashtrays and a row of discarded novels. Then the crowd lifted him and pushed on towards the favourite stall. There was nothing he could do about it. He couldn't seek for any individual in the crowd, but that didn't matter, for he found himself pressed against a stall, on the other side of which the old woman stood. He leant across and stared at the bag; he remembered how the girl had said, "My name's Anne," and there, impressed on the leather, was a faint initial A, where a chromium letter had been removed. He looked up, he didn't notice that there was another man beside the stall, his eyes were filled with the image of a dusty wicked face.

He was shocked by it just as he had been shocked by Mr. Cholmondeley's duplicity. He felt no guilt about the old War Minister, he was one of the great ones of the world, one of those who "sat," he knew all the right words, he was educated, "in the chief seats at the synagogues," and if he was sometimes a little worried by the memory of the secretary's whisper through the imperfectly shut door, he could always tell himself that he had shot her in self-defence. But this was evil: that people of the same class should prey on each other. He thrust himself along the edge of the stall until he was by her side. He bent down. He whispered, "How did you get that bag?" but an arrowhead of predatory women forced themselves between; she couldn't even have seen who had whispered to her. As far as she knew it might have been a woman mistaking it for a bargain on one of the stalls, but nevertheless the question had scared her. He saw her elbowing her way to the door and he fought to follow her.

When he got out of the hall she was just in sight, trailing her long old-fashioned skirt round a corner. He walked fast. He didn't notice in his hurry that he in his turn was followed by a man whose clothes he would immediately have recognised, the soft hat and overcoat worn like a uniform. Very soon he began to remember the road they took; he had been this way with the girl. It was like retracing in mind an old experience. A newspaper shop would come in sight next moment, a policeman had stood just there, he had intended to kill her, to take her out somewhere beyond the houses and shoot her quite painlessly in the back. The wrinkled deep malice in the face he had seen across the stall seemed to nod at him: "You needn't worry, we have seen to all that for you."

It was incredible how quickly the old woman scuttled. She held the bag in one hand, lifted the absurd long skirt with the other; she was like a female Rip Van Winkle who had emerged from her sleep in the clothes of fifty years ago. He thought: they've done something to her, but who are "they"? She hadn't been to the police; she'd believed his story; it was only to Cholmondeley's advantage that she should disappear. For the first time since his mother died he was afraid for someone else, because he knew too well that Cholmondeley had no scruples.

Past the station she turned to the left up Khyber Avenue, a line of dingy apartment houses. Coarse grey lace quite hid the interior of little rooms save when a plant in a jardinière pressed glossy green palms against the glass between the lace. There were no bright geraniums lapping up the air behind closed panes: those scarlet flowers belonged to a poorer class than the occupants of Khyber Avenue, to the exploited. In Khyber Avenue they had progressed to the aspidistra of the small exploiters. They were all Cholmondeleys on a tiny scale. Outside No. 61 the old woman had to wait and fumble for her key; it gave Raven time to catch her up. He put his foot against the closing door and said, "I want to ask you some questions."

"Get out," the old woman said. "We don't 'ave anything to do with your sort."

He pressed the door steadily open. "You'd better listen," he said. "It'd be good for you." She stumbled backwards amongst the crowded litter of the little dark hall: he noted it all with hatred: the glass case with a stuffed pheasant, the moth-eaten head of a stag picked up at a country auction to act as a hat-stand, the black metal umbrella-holder painted with gold stars, the little pink glass shade over the gas-jet. He said, "Where did you get that bag? Oh," he said, "it wouldn't take much to make me squeeze your old neck."

"Acky!" the old woman screamed. "Acky!"

"What do you do here, eh?" He opened one of the two doors at random off the hall and saw a long cheap couch with the ticking coming through the cover, a large gilt mirror, a picture of a naked girl knee-deep in the sea; the place reeked of scent and stale gas.

"Acky!" the old woman screamed again. "Acky!"

He said, "So that's it, eh? You old bawd," and turned back into the hall. But she was supported now. She had Acky with her; he had come through to her side from the back of the house on rubber-soled shoes, making no sound. Tall and bald, with a shifty pious look, he faced Raven. "What d'you want, my man?" He belonged to a different class altogether: a good school and a theological college had formed his accent; something else had broken his nose.

"What names!" the old woman said, turning on Raven from under Acky's protecting arm.

Raven said, "I'm in a hurry. I don't want to break up this place. Tell me where you got that bag."

"If you refer to my wife's reticule," the bald man said, "it was given her— was it not, Tiny?—by a lodger."

"When?"

"A few nights ago."

"Where is she now?"

"She only stayed one night."

"Why did she give her bag to you?"

"We only pass this way once," Acky said, "and therefore—you know the quotation?"

"Was she alone?"

"Of course she wasn't alone," the old woman said. Acky coughed, put his hand over her face and pushed her gently behind him. "Her betrothed," he said, "was with her." He advanced towards Raven. "That face," he said, "is somehow familiar. Tiny, my dear, fetch me a copy of the *Journal*."

"No need," Raven said. "It's me all right." He said, "You've lied about that bag. If the girl was here, it was last night. I'm going to search this bawdy house of yours."

"Tiny," her husband said, "go out at the back and call the police." Raven's hand was on his gun, but he didn't move, he didn't draw it, his eyes were on the old woman as she trailed indeterminately through the kitchen door. "Hurry, Tiny, my dear."

Raven said, "If I thought she was going, I'd shoot you straight, but she's not going to any police. You're more afraid of them than I am. She's in the kitchen now hiding in a corner."

Acky said, "Oh no, I assure you she's gone; I heard the door; you can see for yourself," and as Raven passed him he raised his hand and struck with a knuckle-duster at a spot behind Raven's ear.

But Raven had expected that. He ducked his head and was safely through in the kitchen doorway with his gun out. "Stay put," he said. "This gun doesn't make any noise. I'll plug you where you'll feel it if you move." The old woman was where he had expected her to be, between the dresser and the door squeezed in a corner. She moaned, "Oh, Acky, you ought to 'ave 'it 'im."

Acky began to swear. The obscenity trickled out of his mouth effortlessly like dribble, but the tone, the accent never changed; it was still the good school, the theological college. There were a lot of Latin words Raven didn't understand. He said impatiently, "Now where's the girl?" But Acky simply didn't hear; he stood there in a kind of nervous seizure with his pupils rolled up almost under the lids; he might have been praying; for all Raven knew some of the Latin words might be prayers: "*Saccus stercoris,*" "*fauces.*" He said again: "Where's the girl?"

"Leave 'im alone," the old woman said. " 'E can't 'ear you. Acky," she moaned from her corner by the dresser, "it's all right, love, you're at 'ome." She said fiercely to Raven, "The things they did to 'im."

Suddenly the obscenity stopped. He moved and blocked the kitchen door. The hand with the knuckle-duster grasped the lapel of his coat. Acky said softly, "After all, my Lord Bishop, you too, I am sure—in your day—among the haycocks," and tittered.

Raven said, "Tell him to move. I'm going to search this house." He kept his eye on both of them. The little stuffy house wore on his nerves, madness and wickedness moved in the kitchen. The old woman watched him with hatred from her corner. Raven said, "My God, if you've killed her . . ." He said, "Do you know what it feels like to have a bullet in your belly? You'll just lie there and bleed . . ." It seemed to him that it would be like shooting a spider. He suddenly shouted to her husband, "Get out of my way."

Acky said, "Even St. Augustine . . ." watching him with glazed eyes, barring the door. Raven struck him in the face, then backed out of reach of the flailing arm. He raised the pistol and the woman screamed at him, "Stop! I'll get 'im out." She said, "Don't you dare to touch Acky. They've treated 'im bad enough in 'is day." She took her husband's arm; she only came half-way to his shoulder, grey and soiled and miserably tender. "Acky, dear," she said, "come into the parlour." She rubbed her old wicked wrinkled face against his sleeve. "Acky, there's a letter from the bishop."

His pupils moved down again like those of a doll. He was almost himself again. He said, "Tut-tut! I gave way, I think, to a little temper." He looked at Raven with half-recognition. "That fellow's still here, Tiny."

"Come into the parlour, Acky dear. I've got to talk to you." He let her pull him away into the hall and Raven followed them and mounted the stairs. All the way up he heard them talking. They were planning something between them; as like as not when he was out of sight and round the corner they'd slip out and call the police. If the girl was really not here or if they had disposed of her, they had little to fear from the police. On the first-floor landing there was a tall cracked mirror; he came up the stairs into its reflection, unshaven chin, hare-lip and ugliness. His heart beat against his ribs; if he had been called on to fire now, quickly, in self-defence, his hand and eye would have failed him. He thought hopelessly: this is ruin, I'm losing grip, a skirt's got me down. He opened the first door to hand and came into what was obviously the best bedroom, a wide double-bed with a flowery eiderdown, veneered walnut furniture, a little embroidered bag for hair combings, a tumbler of Lysol on the washstand for someone's false teeth. He opened the big wardrobe door and a musty smell of old clothes and camphor balls came out at him. He went to the closed window and looked out at Khyber Avenue, and all the while he looked he could hear the whispers from the parlour: Acky and Tiny plotting together. His eye for a moment noted a large rather clumsy-looking man in a soft hat chatting to a woman at the house opposite; another man came up the road and they strolled together out of sight. He recognised the police at once. They mightn't, of course, have seen him there, they might be engaged on a purely routine inquiry. He went quickly out on to the landing and listened: Acky and Tiny were quite silent now. He thought at first they might have left the house, but when he listened carefully he could hear the faint whistling of the old woman's breath somewhere near the foot of the stairs.

There was another door on the landing. He tried the handle. It was locked. He wasn't going to waste any more time with the old people downstairs. He shot through the lock and crashed the door open. But there was no one there. The room was empty. It was a tiny room almost filled by its double-bed, its dead fireplace hidden by a smoked brass trap. He looked out of the window and saw nothing but a small stone yard, a dust-bin, a high sooty wall keeping out neighbours, the grey waning afternoon light. On the washstand was a wireless set, and the wardrobe was empty. He had no doubt what this room was used for.

But something made him stay: some sense uneasily remaining in the room of someone's terror. He couldn't leave it, and there was the locked door to be accounted for. Why should they have locked up an empty room unless it held some clue, some danger to themselves? He turned over the pillows of the bed and wondered, his hand loose on the pistol, his brain stirring with another's agony. Oh, to know, to know. He felt the painful weakness of a man who had depended always on his gun. I'm educated, aren't I, the phrase came mockingly into his mind, but he knew that one of the police out there could discover in this room more than he. He knelt down and looked under the bed. Nothing there. The very tidiness of the room seemed unnatural, as if it had been tidied after a crime. Even the mats looked as if they had been shaken.

He asked himself whether he had been imagining things. Perhaps the girl had really given the old woman her bag? But he couldn't forget that they had lied about the night she'd stayed with them, had picked the initial off the bag. And they had locked this door. But people did lock doors—against burglars, but in that case surely they left the key on the outside. Oh, there was an explanation, he was only too aware of that, for everything; why should you leave another person's initials on a bag? When you had many lodgers, naturally you forgot which night . . . There were explanations, but he couldn't get over the impression that something had happened here, that something had been tidied away, and it came over him with a sense of great desolation that only he could not call in the police to find this girl. Because he was an outlaw she had to be an outlaw too. *Ah, Christ! that it were possible.* The rain beating on the Weevil, the plaster child, the afternoon light draining from the little stone yard, the image of his own ugliness fading in the mirror, and from below stairs Tiny's whistling breath. *For one short hour to see . . .*

He went back on to the landing, but something all the time pulled him back as if he were leaving a place which had been dear to him. It dragged on him as he went upstairs to the second floor and into every room in turn. There was nothing in any of them but beds and wardrobes and the stale smell of scent and toilet things and in one cupboard a broken cane. They were all of them more dusty, less tidy, more used than the room he'd left. He stood up there among the empty rooms listening; there wasn't a sound to be heard now; Tiny and her Acky were quite silent below him waiting for him to come down. He wondered again if he had made a fool of himself and risked everything. But if they had nothing to hide, why hadn't they tried to call the police? He had left them alone, they had nothing to fear while he was upstairs, but something kept them to the house just as something kept him tied to the room on the first floor.

It took him back to it. He was happier when he had closed the door behind him and stood again in the small cramped space between the big bed and the wall. The drag at his heart ceased. He was able to think again. He began to examine the room thoroughly inch by inch. He even moved the radio on the washstand. Then he heard the stairs creak and leaning his head against the door he listened to someone he supposed was Acky mounting the stairs step by step with clumsy caution; then he was crossing the landing and there he must be, just outside the door waiting and listening. It was impossible to believe that those old people had nothing to fear. Raven went along the walls, squeezing by the bed, touching the glossy flowery paper with his fingers; he had heard of people before now papering over a cavity. He reached the fireplace and unhooked the brass trap.

Propped up inside the fireplace was a woman's body, the feet in the grate, the head out of sight in the chimney. The first thought he had was of revenge; if it's the girl, if she's dead, I'll shoot them both, I'll shoot them where it hurts most so that they die slow. Then he went down on his knees to ease the body out.

The hands and feet were roped, an old cotton vest had been tied between the teeth as a gag, the eyes were closed. He cut the gag away first; he couldn't tell whether she was alive or dead; he cursed her, "Wake up, you bitch, wake up." He leant over her, imploring her, "Wake up." He was afraid to leave her, there was no water in the ewer, he couldn't do a thing; when he had cut away the ropes he just sat on the floor beside her with his eyes on the door and one hand on his pistol and the other on her breast. When he could feel her breathing under his hand it was like beginning life over again.

She didn't know where she was. She said, "Please. The sun. It's too strong." There was no sun in the room; it would soon be too dark to read. He thought: what ages have they had her buried there, and held his hand over her eyes to shield them from the dim winter light of early evening. She said in a tired voice, "I could go to sleep now. There's air."

"No, no," Raven said, "we've got to get out of here," but he wasn't prepared for her simple acquiescence. "Yes, where to?"

He said, "You don't remember who I am. I haven't anywhere. But I'll leave you some place where it's safe."

She said, "I've been finding out things." He thought she meant things like fear and death, but as her voice strengthened she explained quite clearly, "It was the man you said. Cholmondeley."

"So you know me," Raven said. But she took no notice. It was as if all the time in the dark she had been rehearsing what she had to say when she was discovered, at once, because there was no time to waste.

"I made a guess at somewhere where he worked. Some company. It scared him. He must work there. I don't remember the name. I've got to remember."

"Don't worry," Raven said. "It'll come back. But how is it you aren't crazy . . . Christ! you've got nerve."

She said, "I remembered till just now. I heard you looking for me in the room, and then you went away and I forgot everything."

"Do you think you could walk now?"

"Of course I could walk. We've got to hurry."

"Where to?"

"I had it all planned. It'll come back. I had plenty of time to think things out."

"You sound as if you weren't scared at all."

"I knew I'd be found all right. I was in a hurry. We haven't got much time. I thought about the war all the time."

He said again admiringly, "You've got nerve."

She began to move her hands and feet up and down quite methodically as if she were following a programme she had drawn up for herself. "I thought a lot about that war. I read somewhere, but I'd forgotten, about how babies can't wear gas masks because there's not enough air for them." She knelt up with her hand on his shoulder. "There wasn't much air there. It made things sort of vivid. I thought, we've got to stop it. It seems silly, doesn't it, us two, but there's nobody else." She said, "My feet have got pins and needles bad. That means they are coming alive again." She tried to stand up, but it wasn't any good.

Raven watched her. He said, "What else did you think?"

She said, "I thought about you. I wished I hadn't had to go away like that and leave you."

"I thought you'd gone to the police."

"I wouldn't do that." She managed to stand up this time with her hand on his shoulder. "I'm on your side."

Raven said, "We've got to get out of here. Can you walk?"

"Yes."

"Then leave go of me. There's someone outside." He stood by the door with his gun in his hand listening. They'd had plenty of time, those two, to think up a plan, longer than he. He pulled the door open. It was very nearly dark. He could see no one on the landing. He thought: the old devil's at the side waiting to get a hit at me with the poker. I'll take a run for it, and immediately tripped across the string they had tied across the doorway. He was on his knees with the gun on the floor; he couldn't get up in time and Acky's blow got him on the left shoulder. It staggered him, he couldn't move, he had just time to think: it'll be the head next time, I've gone soft, I ought to have thought of a string, when he heard Anne speak: "Drop the poker." He got painfully to his feet; the girl had snatched the gun as it fell and had Acky covered. He said with astonishment, "You're fine." At the bottom of the stairs the old woman cried out, "Acky, where are you?"

"Give me the gun," Raven said. "Get down the stairs, you needn't be afraid of the old bitch." He backed after her, keeping Acky covered, but the old couple had shot their bolt. He said regretfully, "If he'd only rush I'd put a bullet in him."

"It wouldn't upset *me*," Anne said. "I'd have done it myself."

He said again, "You're fine." He nearly forgot the detectives he had seen in the street, but with his hand on the door he remembered. He said, "I may have to make a bolt for it if the police are outside." He hardly hesitated before he trusted her. "I've found a hide-out for the night. In the goods yard. A shed they don't use any longer. I'll be waiting by the wall to-night fifty yards down from the station." He opened the door. Nobody moved in the street; they walked out together and down the middle of the road into a vacant dusk. Anne said, "Did you see a man in the doorway opposite?"

"Yes," Raven said. "I saw him."

"I thought it was like—but how could it——?"

"There was another at the end of the street. They were police all right, but they didn't know who I was. They'd have tried to get me if they'd known."

"And you'd have shot?"

"I'd have shot all right. But they didn't know it was me." He laughed with the night damp in his throat. "I've fooled them properly." The lights went on in the city beyond the railway bridge, but where they were it was just a grey dusk and the sound of an engine shunting in the yard.

"I can't walk far," Anne said. "I'm sorry. I suppose I'm a bit sick after all."

"It's not far now," Raven said. "There's a loose plank. I got it all fixed up for myself early this morning. Why, there's even sacks, lots of sacks. It's going to be like home," he said.

"Like home?" He didn't answer, feeling along the tarred wall of the goods yard, remembering the kitchen in the basement and the first thing very nearly he could remember, his mother bleeding across the table. She hadn't even troubled to lock the door: that was all she cared about him. He'd done some ugly things in his time, he told himself, but he'd never been able to equal that ugliness. Some day he would. It would be like beginning life over again: to have something else to look back to when somebody spoke of death or blood or wounds or home.

"A bit bare for a home," Anne said.

"You needn't be scared of me," Raven said. "I won't keep you. You can sit down a bit and tell me what he did to you, what Cholmondeley did, and then you can be getting along anywhere you want."

"I couldn't go any farther if you paid me." He had to put his hands under her shoulders and hold her up against the tarred wood, while he put more will into her from his own inexhaustible reserve. He said, "Hold on. We're nearly there." He shivered in the cold, holding her with all his strength, trying in the dusk to see her face. He said, "You can rest in the shed. There are plenty of sacks there." He was like somebody describing with pride some place he lived in, that he'd bought with his own money or built with his own labour stone by stone.

ii

Mather stood back in the shadow of the doorway. It was worse in a way than anything he'd feared. He put his hand on his revolver. He had only to go forward and arrest Raven—or stop a bullet in the attempt. He was a policeman; he couldn't shoot first. At the end of the street Saunders was waiting for him to move. Behind, a uniformed constable waited on them both. But he made no move. He let them go off down the road in the belief that they were alone. Then he followed as far as the corner and picked up Saunders. Saunders said, "The d-d-devil."

"Oh no," Mather said, "it's only Raven—and Anne." He struck a match and held it to the cigarette which he had been holding between his lips for the last twenty minutes. They could hardly see the man and woman going off down the dark road by the goods-yard, but beyond them another match was struck. "We've got them covered," Mather said. "They won't be able to get out of our sight now."

"W-will you take them b-b-both?"

"We can't have shooting with a woman there," Mather said. "Can't you see what they'd make of it in the papers if a woman got hurt? It's not as if he was wanted for murder."

"We've got to be careful of your girl," Saunders brought out in a breath.

"Get moving again," Mather said. "We don't want to lose touch. I'm not thinking about *her* any more. I promise you that's over. She's led me up the garden properly. I'm just thinking of what's best with Raven—and any accomplice he's got in Nottwich. If we've got to shoot, we'll shoot."

Saunders said, "They've stopped." He had sharper eyes than Mather. Mather said, "Could you pick him off from here, if I rushed him?"

"No," Saunders said. He began to move forward quickly. "He's loosened a plank. They are getting through."

"Don't worry," Mather said. "I'll follow. Bring up three more men and post one of them at the gap where I can find him. We've got all the gates into the yard picketed already. Bring the rest inside. But keep it quiet." He could hear the slight shuffle of cinders where the two were walking; it wasn't so easy to follow them because of the sound his own feet made. They disappeared round a stationary truck and the light failed more and more. He caught a glimpse of their moving shadows and then an engine hooted and belched a grey plume of steam round him; for a moment it was like walking in a mountain fog. A warm dirty spray settled on his face; when he was clear he had lost them. He began to realise the difficulty of finding anyone in the yard at night. There were trucks everywhere; they could slip into one and lie down. He barked his shin and swore softly; then quite distinctly he heard Anne whisper, "I can't make it." There were only a few trucks between them; then the movements began again, heavier movements as if someone were carrying a weight. Mather climbed on to the truck and stared across a dark desolate waste of cinders and points, a tangle of lines and sheds and piles of coal and coke. It was like a No Man's Land full of torn iron across which one soldier picked his way with a wounded companion in his arms. Mather watched them with an odd sense of shame, as if he were a spy. The thin limping shadow became a human being who knew the girl he loved. There was a kind of relationship between them. He thought: how many years will he get for that robbery? He no longer wanted to shoot. He thought: poor devil, he must be pretty driven by now, he's probably looking for a place to sit down in, and there the place was, a small wooden workman's shed between the lines.

Mather struck a match again and presently Saunders was below him waiting for orders. "They are in that shed," Mather said. "Get the men posted. If they try to get out, nab them quick. Otherwise wait for daylight. We don't want any accidents."

"You aren't s-staying?"

"You'll be easier without me," Mather said. "I'll be at the station to-night." He said gently: "Don't think about me. Just go ahead. And look after yourself. Got your gun?"

"Of course."

"I'll send the men along to you. It's going to be a cold watch, I'm afraid, but it's no good trying to rush that shed. He might shoot his way clear out."

"It's t-t-t-tough on you," Saunders said. The dark had quite come; it healed the desolation of the yard. Inside the shed there was no sign of life, no glimmer of light; soon Saunders couldn't have told that it existed, sitting there with his back to a truck out of the wind's way, hearing the breathing of the policeman nearest him and saying over to himself to pass the time (his mind's words free from any impediment) the line of a poem he had read at night-school about a dark tower: "He must be wicked to deserve such pain." It was a comforting line, he thought; those who followed his profession couldn't be taught a better; that's why he had remembered it.

iii

"Who's coming to dinner, dear?" the Chief Constable asked, putting his head in at the bedroom door.

"Never you mind," Mrs. Calkin said, "you'll change."

The Chief Constable said: "I was thinking, dear, as 'ow——"

"As how," Mrs. Calkin said firmly.

"The new maid. You might teach her that I'm *Major* Calkin."

Mrs. Calkin said, "You'd better hurry."

"It's not the Mayoress again, is it?" He trailed drearily out towards the bathroom, but on second thoughts nipped quietly downstairs to the dining-room. Must see about the drinks. But if it was the Mayoress there wouldn't be any. Piker never turned up; he didn't blame him. While there he might just as well take a nip; he took it neat for speed and cleaned the glass afterwards with a splash of soda and his handkerchief. He put the glass as an afterthought where the Mayoress would sit. Then he rang up the police station.

"Any news?" he asked hopelessly. He knew there was no real hope that they'd ask him down for a consultation.

The inspector's voice said, "We know where he is. We've got him surrounded. We are just waiting till daylight."

"Can I be of any use? Like me to come down, eh, and talk things over?"

"It's quite unnecessary, sir."

He put the receiver down miserably, sniffed the Mayoress's glass (she'd never notice that) and went upstairs. Major Calkin, he thought wistfully, Major Calkin. The trouble is I'm a man's man. Looking out of the window of his dressing-room at the spread lights of Nottwich he remembered for some reason the war, the tribunal, the fun it had all been giving hell to the conchies. His uniform still hung there, next the tails he wore once a year at the Rotarian dinner when he was able to get among the boys. A faint smell of moth-balls came out at him. His spirits suddenly lifted. He thought: my God, in a week's time we may be at it again. Show the devils what we are made of. I wonder if the uniform will fit. He couldn't resist trying on the jacket over his evening trousers. It was a bit tight, he couldn't deny that, but the general effect in the glass was not too bad, a bit pinched; it would have to be let out. With his influence in the county he'd be back in uniform in a fortnight. With any luck he'd be busier than ever in this war.

"Joseph," his wife said, "whatever are you doing?" He saw her in the mirror placed statuesquely in the doorway in her new black and sequined evening dress like a shop-window model of an outsize matron. She said, "Take it off at once. You'll smell of moth-balls now all dinner-time. The Mayoress is taking off her things and any moment Sir Marcus——"

"You might have told me," the Chief Constable said. "If I'd known Sir Marcus was coming. . . . How did you snare the old boy?"

"He invited himself," Mrs. Calkin said proudly. "So I rang up the Mayoress."

"Isn't old Piker coming?"

"He hasn't been home all day."

The Chief Constable slipped off his uniform jacket and put it away carefully. If the war had gone on another year they'd have made him a colonel: he had been getting on the very best terms with the regimental headquarters, supplying the mess with groceries at very little more than the cost price. In the next war he'd make the grade. The sound of Sir Marcus's car on the gravel brought him downstairs. The Lady Mayoress was looking under the sofa for her Pekinese, which had gone to ground defensively to escape strangers; she was on her knees with her head under the fringe saying, "Chinky, Chinky," ingratiatingly. Chinky growled out of sight.

"Well, well," the Chief Constable said, trying to put a little warmth into his tones, "and how's Alfred?"

"Alfred?" the Mayoress said, coming out from under the sofa, "it's not Alfred, it's Chinky. Oh," she said, talking very fast, for it was her habit to work towards another person's meaning while she talked, "you mean how is he? Alfred? He's gone again."

"Chinky?"

"No, Alfred." One never got much further with the Mayoress. Mrs. Calkin came in. She said, "Have you got him, dear?"

"No, he's gone again," the Chief Constable said, "if you mean Alfred."

"He's under the sofa," the Mayoress said. "He won't come out."

Mrs. Calkin said, "I ought to have warned you, dear. I thought of course you would know the story of how Sir Marcus hates the very sight of dogs. Of course, if he stays there quietly . . ."

"The poor dear," Mrs. Piker said, "so sensitive, he could tell at once he wasn't wanted."

The Chief Constable suddenly could bear it no longer. He said, "Alfred Piker's my best friend. I won't have you say he wasn't wanted," but no one took any notice of him. The maid had announced Sir Marcus.

Sir Marcus entered on the tips of his toes. He was a very old, sick man with a little wisp of white beard on his chin resembling chicken fluff. He gave the effect of having withered inside his clothes like a kernel in a nut. He spoke with the faintest foreign accent and it was difficult to determine whether he was Jewish or of an ancient English family. He gave the impression that very many cities had rubbed him smooth. If there was a touch of Jerusalem, there was also a touch of St. James's, if of some Central European capital, there were also marks of the most exclusive clubs in Cannes.

"So good of you, Mrs. Calkin," he said, "to give me this opportunity . . ." It was difficult to hear what he said; he spoke in a whisper. His old scaly eyes took them all in. "I have always been hoping to make the acquaintance . . ."

"May I introduce the Lady Mayoress, Sir Marcus?"

He bowed with the slightly servile grace of a man who might have been pawn-broker to the Pompadour. "So famous a figure in the city of Nottwich." There was no sarcasm or patronage in his manner. He was just old. Everyone was alike to him. He didn't trouble to differentiate.

"I thought you were on the Riviera, Sir Marcus," the Chief Constable said breezily. "Have a sherry. It's no good asking the ladies."

"I don't drink, I'm afraid," Sir Marcus whispered. The Chief Constable's face fell. "I came back two days ago."

"Rumours of war, eh? Dogs delight to bark . . ."

"Joseph," Mrs. Calkin said sharply, and glanced with meaning at the sofa.

The old eyes cleared a little. "Yes. Yes," Sir Marcus repeated. "Rumours."

"I see you've been taking on more men at Midland Steel, Sir Marcus."

"So they tell me," Sir Marcus whispered.

The maid announced dinner; the sound startled Chinky, who growled under the sofa, and there was an agonising moment while they all watched Sir Marcus. But he had heard nothing, or perhaps the noise had faintly stirred his subconscious mind, for as he took Mrs. Calkin in to the dining-room he whispered venomously, "The dogs drove me away."

"Some lemonade for Mrs. Piker, Joseph," Mrs. Calkin said. The Chief Constable watched her drink with some nervousness. She seemed a little puzzled by the taste, she sipped and tried again. "Really," she said, "what delicious lemonade. It has quite an aroma."

Sir Marcus passed the soup; he passed the fish. When the entrée was served, he leant across the large silverplated flower bowl inscribed "To Joseph Calkin from the assistants in Calkin and Calkin's on the occasion . . ." (the inscription ran round the corner out of sight) and whispered, "Might I have a dry biscuit and a little hot water?" He explained, "My doctor won't allow me anything else at night."

"Well, that's hard luck," the Chief Constable said. "Food and drink as a man gets older . . ." He glared at his empty glass: what a life, oh for a chance to get away for a bit among the boys, throw his weight about and know that he was a man.

The Lady Mayoress said suddenly, "How Chinky would love these bones," and choked.

"Who is Chinky?" Sir Marcus whispered.

Mrs. Calkin said quickly, "Mrs. Piker has the most lovely cat."

"I'm glad it isn't a dog," Sir Marcus whispered. "There is something about a dog," the old hand gestured hopelessly with a piece of cheese biscuit, "and of all dogs the Pekinese." He said with extraordinary venom, "Yap, yap, yap," and sucked up some hot water. He was a man almost without pleasures; his most vivid emotion was venom, his main object defence: defence of his fortune, of the pale flicker of vitality he gained each year in the Cannes sun, of his life. He was quite content to eat cheese biscuits to the end of them if eating biscuits would extend his days.

The old boy couldn't have many left, the Chief Constable thought, watching Sir Marcus wash down the last dry crumb and then take a white tablet out of a little flat gold box in his waistcoat pocket. He had a heart; you could tell it in the way he spoke, from the special coaches he travelled in when he went by rail, the Bath chairs which propelled him softly down the long passages in Midland Steel. The Chief Constable had met him several times at civic receptions; after the General Strike Sir Marcus had given a fully equipped gymnasium to the police force in recognition of their services, but never before had Sir Marcus visited him at home.

Everyone knew a lot about Sir Marcus. The trouble was, all that they knew was contradictory. There were people who, because of his Christian name, believed that he was a Greek; others were quite as certain that he had been born in a ghetto. His business associates said that he was of an old English family; his nose was no evidence either way; you found plenty of noses like that in Cornwall and the west country. His name did not appear at all in *Who's Who*, and an enterprising journalist who once tried to write his life found extraordinary gaps in registers; it wasn't possible to follow any rumour to its source. There was even a gap in the legal records of Marseilles where one rumour said that Sir Marcus as a youth had been charged with theft from a visitor to a bawdy house. Now he sat there in the heavy Edwardian dining-room brushing biscuit crumbs from his waistcoat, one of the richest men in Europe.

No one even knew his age, unless perhaps his dentist; the Chief Constable had an idea that you could tell the age of a man by his teeth. But then they probably were *not* his teeth at his age: another gap in the records.

"Well, we shan't be leaving them to their drinks, shall we?" Mrs. Calkin said in a sprightly way, rising from the table and fixing her husband with a warning glare, "but I expect they have a lot to talk about together."

When the door closed Sir Marcus said, "I've seen that woman somewhere with a dog. I'm sure of it."

"Would you mind if I gave myself a spot of port?" the Chief Constable said. "I don't believe in lonely drinking, but if you really won't—Have a cigar?"

"No," Sir Marcus whispered, "I don't smoke." He said, "I wanted to see you—in confidence—about this fellow Raven. Davis is worried. The trouble is he caught a glimpse of the man. Quite by chance. At the time of the robbery at a friend's office in Victoria Street. This man called on some pretext. He has an idea that the wild fellow wants to put him out of the way. As a witness."

"Tell him," the Chief Constable said proudly, pouring himself out another glass of port, "that he needn't worry. The man's as good as caught. We know where he is at this very moment. He's surrounded. We are only waiting till daylight, till he shows himself . . ."

"Why wait at all? Wouldn't it be better," Sir Marcus whispered, "if the silly desperate fellow were taken at once?"

"He's armed, you see. In the dark anything might happen. He might shoot his way clear. And there's another thing. He has a girl friend with him. It wouldn't do if he escaped and the girl got shot."

Sir Marcus bowed his old head above the two hands that lay idly, with no dry biscuit or glass of warm water or white tablet to occupy them, on the table. He said gently, "I want you to understand. In a way it is our responsibility. Because of Davis. If there were any trouble: if the girl was killed: all our money would be behind the police force. If there had to be an inquiry the best counsel . . . I have friends too, as you may suppose . . ."

"It would be better to wait till daylight, Sir Marcus. Trust me. I know how things stand. I've been a soldier, you know."

"Yes, I understand that," Sir Marcus said.

"Looks as if the old bulldog will have to bite again, eh? Thank God for a Government with guts."

"Yes, yes," Sir Marcus said. "I should say it was almost certain now." The scaly eyes shifted to the decanter. "Don't let me stop you having your glass of port, Major."

"Well, if you say so, Sir Marcus, I'll just have one more glass for a nightcap."

Sir Marcus said, "I'm very glad that you have such good news for me. It doesn't look well to have an armed ruffian loose in Nottwich. You mustn't risk any of your men's lives, Major. Better that this—waste product—should be dead than one of your fine fellows.'' He suddenly leant back in his chair and gasped like a landed fish. He said, ''A tablet. Please. Quick.''

The Chief Constable picked the gold box from his pocket, but Sir Marcus had already recovered. He took the tablet himself. The Chief Constable said, ''Shall I order your car, Sir Marcus?''

''No, no,'' Sir Marcus whispered, ''there's no danger. It's simply pain.'' He stared with dazed old eyes down at the crumbs on his trousers. ''What were we saying? Fine fellows, yes, you mustn't risk *their* lives. The country will need them.''

''That's very true.''

Sir Marcus whispered with venom, ''To me this—ruffian—is a traitor. This is a time when every man is needed. I'd treat him like a traitor.''

''It's one way of looking at it.''

''Another glass of port, Major.''

''Yes, I think I will.''

''To think of the number of able-bodied men this fellow will take from their country's service even if he shoots no one. Warders. Police guards. Fed and lodged at his country's expense when other men . . .''

''Are dying. You're right, Sir Marcus.'' The pathos of it all went deeply home. He remembered his uniform jacket in the cupboard: the buttons needed shining: the King's buttons. The smell of moth-balls lingered round him still. He said, ''Somewhere there's a corner of a foreign field that is for ever . . . Shakespeare knew. Old Gaunt when he said that——''

''It would be so much better, Major Calkin, if your men take no risks. If they shoot on sight. One must take up weeds—by the roots.''

''It would be better.''

''You're the father of your men.''

''That's what old Piker said to me once. God forgive him, he meant it differently. I wish you'd drink with me, Sir Marcus. You're an understanding man. You know how an officer feels. I was in the army once.''

''Perhaps in a week you will be in it again.''

''You know how a man feels. I don't want anything to come between us, Sir Marcus. There's one thing I'd like to tell you. It's on my conscience. There *was* a dog under the sofa.''

''A dog?''

''A Pekinese called Chinky. I didn't know as 'ow . . .''

''She said it was a cat.''

''She didn't want you to know.''

Sir Marcus said, ''I don't like being deceived. I'll see to Piker at the elections.'' He gave a small tired sigh as if there were too many things to be seen to, to be arranged, revenges to be taken, stretching into an endless vista of time, and so much time already covered—since the ghetto, the Marseilles brothel, if there had ever been a ghetto or a brothel. He whispered abruptly, ''So you'll telephone now to the station and tell them to shoot at sight? Say you'll take the responsibility. I'll look after you.''

''I don't see as 'ow, as how . . .''

The old hands moved impatiently: so much to be arranged. "Listen to me. I never promise anything I can't answer for. There's a training depot ten miles from here. I can arrange for you to have nominal charge of it, with the rank of colonel, directly war's declared."

"Colonel Banks?"

"He'll be shifted."

"You mean if I telephone?"

"No. I mean if you are successful."

"And the man's dead?"

"He's not important. A young scoundrel. There's no reason to hesitate. Take another glass of port."

The Chief Constable stretched out his hand for the decanter. He thought, with less relish than he would have expected, "Colonel Calkin," but he couldn't help remembering other things. He was a sentimental man. He remembered his appointment: it had been "worked," of course, no less than his appointment to the training depot would be worked, but there came vividly back to him his sense of pride at being head of one of the best police forces in the Midlands. "I'd better not have any more port," he said lamely. "It's bad for my sleep and the wife . . ."

Sir Marcus said, "Well, Colonel," blinking his old eyes, "you'll be able to count on me for anything."

"I'd like to do it," the Chief Constable said imploringly. "I'd like to please you, Sir Marcus. But I don't see as how. . . . The police couldn't do that."

"It would never be known."

"I don't suppose they'd take my orders. Not on a thing like that."

Sir Marcus whispered, "Do you mean in your position—you haven't any *hold*?" He spoke with the astonishment of a man who had always been careful to secure his hold on the most junior of his subordinates.

"I'd like to please you."

"There's the telephone," Sir Marcus said. "At any rate, you can use your influence. I never ask a man for more than he can do."

The Chief Constable said: "They are a good lot of boys. I've been down often to the station of an evening and had a drink or two. They're keen. You couldn't have keener men. They'll get him. You needn't be afraid, Sir Marcus."

"You mean dead?"

"Alive or dead. They won't let him escape. They are good boys."

"But he has got to be dead," Sir Marcus said. He sneezed. The intake of breath seemed to have exhausted him. He lay back again, panting gently.

"I couldn't ask them, Sir Marcus, not like that. Why, it's like murder."

"Nonsense."

"Those evenings with the boys mean a lot to me. I wouldn't even be able to go down there again after doing that. I'd rather stay what I am. They'll give me a tribunal. As long as there's wars there'll be conchies."

"There'd be no commission of any kind for you," Sir Marcus said. "I could see to that.'' The smell of mothballs came up from Calkin's evening shirt to mock him. ''I can arrange too that you shan't be Chief Constable much longer. You and Piker.'' He gave a queer little whistle through the nose. He was too old to laugh, to use his lungs wastefully. ''Come. Have another glass.''

''No. I don't think I'd better. Listen, Sir Marcus, I'll put detectives at your office. I'll have Davis guarded.''

''I don't much mind about Davis,'' Sir Marcus said. ''Will you get my chauffeur?''

''I'd like to do what you want, Sir Marcus. Won't you come back and see the ladies?''

''No, no,'' Sir Marcus whispered, ''not with that dog there.'' He had to be helped to his feet and handed his stick; a few dry crumbs lay in his beard. He said, ''If you change your mind to-night, you can ring me up. I shall be awake.'' A man at his age, the Chief Constable thought charitably, would obviously think differently of death; it threatened him every moment on the slippery pavement, in a piece of soap at the bottom of a bath. It must seem quite a natural thing he was asking; great age was an abnormal condition: you had to make allowances. But watching Sir Marcus helped down the drive and into his deep wide car, he couldn't help saying over to himself, ''Colonel Calkin. Colonel Calkin.'' After a moment he added, ''C.B.''

The dog was yapping in the drawing-room. They must have lured it out. It was highly bred and nervous, and if a stranger spoke to it too suddenly or sharply, it would rush around in circles, foaming at the mouth, crying out in a horribly human way, its low fur sweeping the carpet like a vacuum cleaner. I might slip down, the Chief Constable thought, and have a drink with the boys. But the idea brought no lightening of his gloom and indecision. Was it possible that Sir Marcus could rob him of even that? But he had robbed him of it already. He couldn't face the superintendent or the inspector with this on his mind. He went into his study and sat down by the telephone. In five minutes Sir Marcus would be home. So much stolen from him already, surely there was little more he could lose by acquiescence. But he sat there doing nothing, a small plump bullying henpecked profiteer.

His wife put her head in at the door. ''Whatever are you doing, Joseph?'' she said. ''Come at once and talk to Mrs. Piker.''

iv

Sir Marcus lived with his valet who was also a trained nurse at the top of the big building in the Tanneries. It was his only home. In London he stayed at Claridge's, in Cannes at the Carlton. His valet met him at the door of the building with his Bath chair and pushed him into the lift, then out along the passage to his study.

The heat of the room had been turned up to the right degree, the tape-machine was gently ticking beside his desk. The curtains were not drawn and through the wide double-panes the night sky spread out over Nottwich striped by the searchlights from Hanlow aerodrome.

"You can go to bed, Mollison. I shan't be sleeping."

Sir Marcus slept very little these days. In the little time left him to live a few hours of sleep made a distinct impression. And he didn't really need the sleep. No physical exertion demanded it. Now with the telephone within his reach he began to read first the memorandum on his desk, then the strips of tape. He read the arrangements for the gas drill in the morning. All the clerks on the ground floor who might happen to be needed for outside work were already supplied with gas masks. The sirens were expected to go almost immediately the rush hour was over and work in the offices had begun. Members of the transport staff, lorry drivers and special messengers would wear their masks immediately they started work. It was the only way to ensure that they wouldn't leave them behind somewhere and be caught unprotected during the hours of the practice and so waste in hospital the valuable hours of Midland Steel.

More valuable than they had ever been since November, 1918. Sir Marcus read the tape prices. Armament shares continued to rise, and with them steel. It made no difference at all that the British Government had stopped all export licences; the country itself was now absorbing more armaments than it had ever done since the peak year of Haig's assaults on the Hindenburg Line. Sir Marcus had many friends, in many countries; he wintered with them regularly at Cannes or in Soppelsa's yacht off Rhodes; he was the intimate friend of Mrs. Cranbeim. It was impossible now to export arms, but it was still possible to export nickel and most of the other metals which were necessary to the arming of nations. Even when war was declared, Mrs. Cranbeim had been able to say quite definitely, that evening when the yacht pitched a little and Rosen was so distressingly sick over Mrs. Ziffo's black satin, the British Government would not forbid the export of nickel to Switzerland or other neutral countries so long as the British requirements were first met. The future was very rosy indeed, for you could trust Mrs. Cranbeim's word. She spoke directly from the horse's mouth, if you could so describe the elder statesman whose confidence she shared.

It seemed quite certain now; Sir Marcus read, in the tape messages, that the two governments chiefly concerned would not either amend or accept the terms of the ultimatum. Probably within five days, at least four countries would be at war and the consumption of munitions have risen to several million pounds a day.

And yet Sir Marcus was not quite happy. Davis had bungled things. When he had told Davis that a murderer ought not to be allowed to benefit from his crime, he had never expected all this silly business of the stolen notes. Now he must wait up all night for the telephone to ring. The old thin body made itself as comfortable as it could on the air-blown cushions: Sir Marcus was as painfully aware of his bones as a skeleton must be, wearing itself away against the leaden lining of its last suit. A clock struck midnight; he had lived one more whole day.

5

i

Raven groped through the dark of the small shed till he had found the sacks. He piled them up, shaking them as one shakes a pillow. He whispered anxiously: "You'll be able to rest there a bit?" Anne let his hand guide her to the corner. She said, "It's freezing."

"Lie down and I'll find more sacks." He struck a match and the tiny flame went wandering through the close cold darkness. He brought the sacks and spread them over her, dropping the match.

"Can't we have a little light?" Anne asked.

"It's not safe. Anyway," he said, "it's a break for me. You can't see me in the dark. You can't see *this*." He touched his lip secretly. He was listening at the door; he heard feet stumble on the tangle of metal and cinders and after a time a low voice spoke. He said, "I've got to think. They know I'm here. Perhaps you'd better go. They've got nothing on you. If they come there's going to be shooting."

"Do you think they know I'm here?"

"They must have followed us all the way."

"Then I'll stay," Anne said. "There won't be any shooting while I'm here. They'll wait till morning, till you come out."

"That's friendly of you," he said with sour incredulity, all his suspicion of friendliness coming back.

"I've told you. I'm on your side."

"I've got to think of a way," he said.

"You may as well rest now. You've all the night to think in."

"It *is* sort of—good in here," Raven said, "out of the way of the whole damned world of them. In the dark." He wouldn't come near her, but sat down in the opposite corner with the automatic in his lap. He said suspiciously, "What are you thinking about?" He was astonished and shocked by the sound of a laugh. "Kind of homey," Anne said.

"I don't take any stock in homes," Raven said. "I've been in one."

"Tell me about it. What's your name?"

"You know my name. You've seen it in the papers."

"I mean your Christian name."

"Christian. That's a good joke, that one. Do you think anyone ever turns the other cheek these days?" He tapped the barrel of the automatic resentfully on the cinder floor. "Not a chance." He could hear her breathing there in the opposite corner, out of sight, out of reach, and he was afflicted by the odd sense that he had missed something. He said, "I'm not saying you aren't fine. I dare say you're Christian all right."

"Search me," Anne said.

"I took you out to that house to kill you . . ."

"To kill me?"

"What did you think it was for? I'm not a lover, am I? Girl's dream? Handsome as the day?"

"Why didn't you?"

"Those men turned up. That's all. I didn't fall for you. I don't fall for girls. I'm saved that. You won't find me ever going soft on a skirt." He went desperately on, "Why didn't you tell the police about me? Why don't you shout to them now?"

"Well," she said, "you've got a gun, haven't you?"

"I wouldn't shoot."

"Why not?"

"I'm not all that crazy," he said. "If people go straight with me, I'll go straight with them. Go on. Shout. I won't do a thing."

"Well," Anne said, "I don't have to ask your leave to be grateful, do I? You saved me to-night."

"That lot wouldn't have killed you. They haven't the nerve to kill. It takes a man to kill."

"Well, your friend Cholmondeley came pretty near it. He nearly throttled me when he guessed I was in with you."

"In with me?"

"To find the man you're after."

"The double-crossing bastard." He brooded over his pistol, but his thoughts always disturbingly came back from hate to this dark safe corner; he wasn't used to that. He said, "You've got sense all right. I like you."

"Thanks for the compliment."

"It's no compliment. You don't have to tell me. I've got something I'd like to trust you with, but I can't."

"What's the dark secret?"

"It's not a secret. It's a cat I left back in my lodgings in London when they chased me out. You'd have looked after it."

"You disappoint me, Mr. Raven. I thought it was going to be a few murders at least." She exclaimed with sudden seriousness, "I've got it. The place where Davis works."

"Davis?"

"The man you call Cholmondeley. I'm sure of it. Midland Steel. In a street near the Metropole. A big palace of a place."

"I've got to get out of here," Raven said, beating the automatic on the freezing ground.

"Can't you go to the police?"

"Me?" Raven said. "Me go to the police?" He laughed. "That'd be fine, wouldn't it? Hold out my hands for the cuffs . . ."

"I'll think of a way," Anne said. When her voice ceased it was as if she had gone. He said sharply, "Are you there?"

"Of course I'm here," she said. "What's worrying you?"

"It feels odd not to be alone." The sour incredulity surged back. He struck a couple of matches and held them to his face, close to his disfigured mouth. "Look," he said, "take a long look." The small flames burnt steadily down. "You aren't going to help *me*, are you? Me?"

"You are all right," she said. The flames touched his skin, but he held the two matches rigidly up and they burnt out against his fingers; the pain was like joy. But he rejected it; it had come too late; he sat in the dark feeling tears like heavy weights behind his eyes, but he couldn't weep. He had never known the particular trick that opened the right ducts at the right time. He crept a little way out of his corner towards her, feeling his way along the floor with the automatic. He said, "Are you cold?"

"I've been in warmer places," Anne said.

There were only his own sacks left. He pushed them over to her. "Wrap 'em round," he said.

"Have you got enough?"

"Of course I have. I can look after myself," he said sharply, as if he hated her. His hands were so cold that he would have found it hard to use the automatic. "I've got to get out of here."

"We'll think of a way. Better have a sleep."

"I can't sleep," he said, "I've been dreaming bad dreams lately."

"We might tell each other stories? It's about the children's hour."

"I don't know any stories."

"Well, I'll tell you one. What kind? A funny one?"

"They never seem funny to me."

"The three bears might be suitable."

"I don't want anything financial. I don't want to hear anything about money."

She could just see him now that he had come closer, a dark hunched shape that couldn't understand a word she was saying. She mocked him gently, secure in the knowledge that he would never realise she was mocking him. She said: "I'll tell you about the fox and the cat. Well, this cat met a fox in a forest, and she'd always heard the fox cracked up for being wise. So she passed him the time of day politely and asked how he was getting along. But the fox was proud. He said, 'How dare you ask me how I get along, you hungry mouse-hunter? What do you know about the world?' 'Well, I do know one thing,' the cat said. 'What's that?' said the fox. 'How to get away from the dogs,' the cat said. 'When they chase me, I jump into a tree.' Then the fox went all high and mighty and said, 'You've only one trick and I've a hundred. I've got a sack full of tricks. Come along with me and I'll show you.' Just then a hunter ran quietly up with four hounds. The cat sprang into the tree and cried, 'Open your sack, Mr. Fox, open your sack.' But the dogs held him with their teeth. So the cat laughed at him saying, 'Mr. Know-all, if you'd had just this one trick in your sack, you'd be safe up the tree with me now.' " Anne stopped. She whispered to the dark shape beside her, "Are you asleep?"

"No," Raven said, "I'm not asleep."

"It's your turn now."

"I don't know any stories," Raven said, sullenly, miserably.

"No stories like that? You haven't been brought up properly."

"I'm educated all right," he protested, "but I've got things on my mind. Plenty of them."

"Cheer up. There's someone who's got more."

"Who's that?"

"The fellow who began all this, who killed the old man, you know who I mean. Davis's friend."

"What do you say?" he said furiously. "Davis's friend?" He held his anger in. "It's not the killing I mind; it's the double-crossing."

"Well, of course," Anne said cheerily, making conversation under the pile of sacks, "I don't mind a little thing like killing myself."

He looked up and tried to see her through the dark, hunting a hope "You don't mind that?"

"But there are killings *and* killings," Anne said. "If I had the man here who killed—what was the old man's name?"

"I don't remember."

"Nor do I. We couldn't pronounce it anyway."

"Go on. If he was here . . ."

"Why, I'd let you shoot him without raising a finger. And I'd say 'Well done' to you afterwards." She warmed to the subject. "You remember what I told you, that they can't invent gas masks for babies to wear? That's the kind of thing he'll have on his mind. The mothers alive in their masks watching the babies cough up their insides."

He said stubbornly, "The poor ones'll be lucky. And what do I care about the rich? This isn't a world I'd bring children into." She could just see his tense crouching figure. "It's just their selfishness," he said. "They have a good time and what do they mind if someone's born ugly? Three minutes in bed or against a wall, and then a lifetime for the one that's born. Mother love," he began to laugh, seeing quite clearly the kitchen table, the carving knife on the linoleum, the blood all over his mother's dress. He explained, "You see I'm educated. In one of His Majesty's own homes. They call them that—homes. What do you think a home means?" But he didn't allow her time to speak. "You are wrong. You think it means a husband in work, a nice gas cooker and a double-bed, carpet slippers and cradles and the rest. That's not a home. A home's solitary confinement for a kid that's caught talking in the chapel and the birch for almost anything you do. Bread and water. A sergeant knocking you around if you try to lark a bit. That's a home."

"Well, he was trying to alter all that, wasn't he? He was poor like we are."

"Who are you talking about?"

"Old what's-his-name. Didn't you read about him in the papers? How he cut down all the army expenses to help clear the slums? There were photographs of him opening new flats, talking to the children. He wasn't one of the rich. He wouldn't have gone to war. That's why they shot him. You bet there are fellows making money now out of him being dead. And he'd done it all himself too, the obituaries said. His father was a thief and his mother committed——"

"Suicide?" Raven whispered. "Did you read how she . . ."

"She drowned herself."

"The things you read," Raven said. "It's enough to make a fellow think."

"Well, I'd say the fellow who killed old what's-his-name had something to think about."

"Maybe," Raven said, "he didn't know all the papers know. The men who paid him, they knew. Perhaps if we knew all there was to know, the kind of breaks the fellow had had, we'd see his point of view."

"It'd take a lot of talking to make me see that. Anyway we'd better sleep now."

"I've got to think," Raven said.

"You'll think better after you've had a nap."

But it was far too cold for him to sleep; he had no sacks to cover himself with, and his black tight overcoat was worn almost as thin as cotton. Under the door came a draught which might have travelled down the frosty rails from Scotland, a north-east wind, bringing icy fogs from the sea. He thought to himself: I didn't mean the old man any harm, there was nothing personal. . . . "I'd let you shoot him, and afterwards I'd say, 'Well done'." He had a momentary crazy impulse to get up and go through the door with his automatic in his hand and let them shoot. "Mr. Know-all," she could say then, "if you'd only had this one trick in your sack, the dogs wouldn't . . ." But then it seemed to him that this knowledge he had gained of the old man was only one more count against Chol-mon-deley. Chol-mon-deley had known all this. There'd be one more bullet in his belly for this, and one more for Cholmondeley's master. But how was he to find the other man? He had only the memory of a photograph to guide him, a photograph which the old Minister had somehow connected with the letter of introduction Raven had borne, a young scarred boy's face which was probably an old man's now.

Anne said, "Are you asleep?"

"No," Raven said. "What's troubling you?"

"I thought I heard someone moving."

He listened. It was only the wind tapping a loose board outside. He said, "You go to sleep. You needn't be scared. They won't come till it's light enough to see." He thought: where would those two have met when they were so young? Surely not in the kind of home he'd known, the cold stone stairs, the cracked commanding bell, the tiny punishment cells. Quite suddenly he fell asleep and the old Minister was coming towards him saying, "Shoot me. Shoot me in the eyes," and Raven was a child with a catapult in his hands. He wept and wouldn't shoot and the old Minister said, "Shoot, dear child. We'll go home together. Shoot."

Raven woke again as suddenly. In his sleep his hand had gripped the automatic tight. It was pointed at the corner where Anne slept. He gazed with horror into the dark, hearing a whisper like the one he had heard through the door when the secretary tried to call out. He said, "Are you asleep? What are you saying?"

Anne said: "I'm awake." She said defensively, "I was just praying."

"Do you believe in God?"

"I don't know," Anne said. "Sometimes maybe. It's a habit, praying. It doesn't do any harm. It's like crossing your fingers when you walk under a ladder. We all need any luck that's going."

Raven said, "We did a lot of praying in the home. Twice a day, and before meals too."

"It doesn't prove anything."

"No, it doesn't prove anything. Only you get sort of mad when everything reminds you of what's over and done with. Sometimes you want to begin fresh, and then someone praying, or a smell, or something you read in the paper, and it's all back again, the places and the people." He came a little nearer in the cold shed for company; it made you feel more than usually alone to know that they were waiting for you outside, waiting for daylight so that they could take you without any risk of your escaping or of your firing first. He had a good mind to send her out directly it was day and stick where he was and shoot it out with them. But that meant leaving Chol-mon-deley and his employer free; it was just what would please them most. He said, "I was reading once—I like reading—I'm educated, something about psicko—psicko——"

"Leave it at that," Anne said. "I know what you mean."

"It seems your dreams mean things. I don't mean like tea-leaves or cards."

"I knew someone once," Anne said. "She was so good with the cards it gave you the creeps. She used to have those cards with queer pictures on them. The Hanged Man . . ."

"It wasn't like that," Raven said. "It was—Oh, I don't know properly. I couldn't understand it all. But it seems if you told your dreams. . . . It was like you carry a load around you; you are born with some of it because of what your father and mother were and their fathers . . . seems as if it goes right back, like it says in the Bible about the sins being visited. Then when you're a kid the load gets bigger; all the things you need to do and can't; and then all the things you do. They get you either way." He leant his sad killer's face on his hands. "It's like confessing to a priest. Only when you've confessed you go and do it all over again. I mean you tell these doctors everything, every dream you have, and afterwards you don't *want* to do it. But you have to tell them everything."

"Even the flying pigs?" Anne said.

"Everything. And when you've told everything it's gone."

"It sounds phoney to me," Anne said.

"I don't suppose I've told it right. But it's what I read. I thought that maybe it might be worth a trial."

"Life's full of funny things. Me and you being here. You thinking you wanted to kill me. Me thinking we can stop a war. Your psicko isn't any funnier than that."

"You see it's getting rid of it all that counts," Raven said. "It's not what the doctor does. That's how it seemed to me. Like when I told you about the home, and the bread and water and the prayers, they didn't seem so important afterwards." He swore softly and obscenely, under his breath. "I'd always said I wouldn't go soft on a skirt. I always thought my lip'd save me. It's not safe to go soft. It makes you slow. I've seen it happen to other fellows. They've always landed in gaol or got a razor in their guts. Now I've gone soft, as soft as all the rest."

"I like you," Anne said. "I'm your friend——"

"I'm not asking anything," Raven said. "I'm ugly and I know it. Only one thing. Be different. Don't go to the police. Most skirts do. I've seen it happen. But maybe you aren't a skirt. You're a girl.''

"I'm *someone*'s girl.''

"That's all right with me," he exclaimed with painful pride in the coldness and the dark. "I'm not asking anything but that, that you don't grass on me.''

"I'm not going to the police," Anne said. "I promise you I won't. I like you as well as any man—except my friend.''

"I thought as how perhaps I could tell you a thing or two—dreams—just as well as any doctor. You see I know doctors. You can't trust them. I went to one before I came down here. I wanted him to alter this lip. He tried to put me to sleep with gas. He was going to call the police. You can't trust them. But I could trust you.''

"You can trust me all right," Anne said. "I won't go to the police. But you'd better sleep first and tell me your dreams after if you want to. It's a long night.''

His teeth suddenly chattered uncontrollably with the cold and Anne heard him. She put out a hand and touched his coat. "You're cold," she said. "You've given me all the sacks.''

"I don't need 'em. I've got a coat.''

"We're friends, aren't we?" Anne said. "We are in this together. You take two of these sacks.''

He said, "There'll be some more about. I'll look," and he struck a match and felt his way round the wall. "Here are two," he said, sitting down farther away from her, empty-handed, out of reach. He said, "I can't sleep. Not properly. I had a dream just now. About the old man.''

"What old man?''

"The old man that got murdered. I dreamed I was a kid with a catapult and he was saying, 'Shoot me through the eyes,' and I was crying and he said, 'Shoot me through the eyes, dear child.' ''

"Search *me* for a meaning," Anne said.

"I just wanted to tell it you.''

"What did he look like?''

"Like he did look." Hastily he added, "Like I've seen in the photographs.'' He brooded over his memories with a low passionate urge towards confession. There had never in his life been anyone he could trust till now. He said, "You don't mind hearing these things?" and listened with a curious deep happiness to her reply, "We are friends." He said, "This is the best night I've ever had." But there were things he still couldn't tell her. His happiness was incomplete till she knew everything, till he had shown his trust completely. He didn't want to shock or pain her; he led slowly towards the central revelation. He said, "I've had other dreams of being a kid. I've dreamed I opened a door, a kitchen door, and there was my mother—she'd cut her throat—she looked ugly—her head nearly off— she'd sawn at it—with a bread knife——''

Anne said, "That wasn't a dream.''

"No," he said, "you're right, that wasn't a dream." He waited. He could feel her sympathy move silently towards him in the dark. He said, "That was ugly, wasn't it? You'd think you couldn't beat that for ugliness, wouldn't you? She hadn't even thought enough of me to lock the door so as I shouldn't see. And after that, there was a Home. You know all about that. You'd say that was ugly too, but it wasn't as ugly as *that* was. And they educated me too properly so as I could understand the things I read in the papers. Like this psicko business. And write a good hand and speak the King's English. I got beaten a lot at the start, solitary confinement, bread and water, all the rest of the homey stuff. But that didn't go on when they'd educated me. I was too clever for them after that. They could never put a thing on me. They suspected all right, but they never had the proof. Once the chaplain tried to frame me. They were right when they told us the day we left about it was like life. Jim and me and a bunch of soft kids.'' He said bitterly, "This is the first time they've had anything on me and I'm innocent.''

"You'll get away,'' Anne said. "We'll think up something together.''

"It sounds good your saying 'together' like that, but they've got me this time. I wouldn't mind if I could get that Chol-mon-deley and his boss first.'' He said with a kind of nervous pride, "Would you be surprised if I'd told you I'd killed a man?'' It was like the first fence; if he cleared that, he would have confidence . . .

"Who?''

"Did you ever hear of Battling Kite?''

"No.''

He laughed with a scared pleasure. "I'm trusting you with my life now. If you'd told me twenty-four hours ago that I'd trust my life to . . . but of course I haven't given you any *proof*. I was doing the races then. Kite had a rival gang. There wasn't anything else to do. He'd tried to bump my boss off on the course. Half of us took a fast car back to town. He thought we were on the train with him. But we were on the platform, see, when the train came in. We got round him directly he got outside the carriage. I cut his throat and the others held him up till we were all through the barrier in a bunch. Then we dropped him by the bookstall and did a bolt.'' He said, "You see it was his lot or our lot. They'd had razors out on the course. It was war.''

After a while Anne said, "Yes. I can see that. He had his chance.''

"It sounds ugly,'' Raven said, "Funny thing is, it wasn't ugly. It was natural.''

"Did you stick to that game?''

"No. It wasn't good enough. You couldn't trust the others. They either went soft or else they got reckless. They didn't use their brains.'' He said, "I wanted to tell you about Kite. I'm not sorry. I haven't got religion. Only you said about being friendly and I don't want you to get any wrong ideas. It was that mix-up with Kite brought me up against Chol-mon-deley. I can see now, he was only in the racing game so as he could meet people. I thought he was a mug.''

"We've got a long way from dreams.''

"I was coming back to them,'' Raven said. "I suppose killing Kite like that made me nervous.'' His voice trembled very slightly from fear and hope, hope because she had accepted one killing so quietly and might, after all, take back what she had said: ("Well done,'' "I wouldn't raise a finger''); fear because he didn't really believe that you could put such perfect trust in another and not be deceived. But it'd be fine, he thought, to be able to tell everything, to know that another person knew and didn't care; it would be like going to sleep for a long while. He said, "That spell of sleep I had just now was the first for two—three—I don't know how many nights. It looks as if I'm not tough enough after all."

"You seem tough enough to me," Anne said. "Don't let's hear any more about Kite."

"No one will hear any more about Kite. But if I was to tell you——" he ran away from the revelation. "I've been dreaming a lot lately it was an old woman I killed, not Kite. I heard her calling out through a door and I tried to open the door, but she held the handle. I shot at her through the wood, but she held the handle tight, I had to kill her to open the door. Then I dreamed she was still alive and I shot her through the eyes. But even that—it wasn't *ugly*."

"You are tough enough in your dreams," Anne said.

"I killed an old man too in that dream. Behind his desk. I had a silencer. He fell behind it. I didn't want to hurt him. He didn't mean anything to me. I pumped him full. Then I put a bit of paper in his hand. I didn't have to take anything."

"What do you mean—you didn't have to take?"

Raven said, "They hadn't paid me to take anything. Chol-mon-deley and his boss."

"It wasn't a dream."

"No. It wasn't a dream." The silence frightened him. He began to talk rapidly to fill it. "I didn't know the old fellow was one of us. I wouldn't have touched him if I'd known he was like that. All this talk of war. It doesn't mean a thing to me. Why should I care if there's a war? There's always been a war for me. You talk a lot about the kids. Can't you have a bit of pity for the men? It was me or him. Two hundred pounds when I got back and fifty pounds down. It's a lot of money. It was only Kite over again. It was just as easy as it was with Kite." He said, "Are you going to leave me now?" and in the silence Anne could hear his rasping anxious breath. She said at last, "No. I'm not going to leave you."

He said, "That's good. Oh, that's good," putting out his hand, feeling hers cold as ice on the sacking. He put it for a moment against his unshaven cheek; he wouldn't touch it with his malformed lip. He said, "It feels good to trust someone with everything."

ii

Anne waited for a long time before she spoke again. She wanted her voice to sound right, not to show her repulsion. Then she tried it on him, but all she could think of to say was again, "I'm not going to leave you." She remembered very clearly in the dark all she had read of the crime: the old woman secretary shot through the eyes lying in the passage, the brutally smashed skull of the old Socialist. The papers had called it the worst political murder since the day when the King and Queen of

Serbia were thrown through the windows of their palace to ensure the succession of the war-time hero king.

Raven said again, "It's good to be able to trust someone like this," and suddenly his mouth which had never before struck her as particularly ugly came to mind and she could have retched at the memory. Nevertheless, she thought, I must go on with this, I mustn't let him know, he must find Cholmondeley and Cholmondeley's boss and then. . . . She shrank from him into the dark.

He said, "They are out there waiting now. They've got cops down from London."

"From London?"

"It was all in the papers," he said with pride. "Detective-Sergeant Mather from the Yard."

She could hardly restrain a cry of desolation and horror. "Here?"

"He may be outside now."

"Why doesn't he come in?"

"They'd never get me in the dark. And they'll know by now that *you* are here. They wouldn't be able to shoot."

"And you—you would?"

"There's no one *I* mind hurting," Raven said.

"How are you going to get out when it's daylight?"

"I shan't wait till then. I only want just light enough to see my way. And see to shoot. *They* won't be able to fire first; they won't be able to shoot to kill. That's what gives me a break. I only want a few clear hours. If I get away, they'll never guess where to find me. Only you'll know I'm at Midland Steel."

She felt a desperate hatred. "You'll just shoot like that in cold blood?"

"You said you were on my side, didn't you?"

"Oh yes," she said warily, "yes," trying to think. It was getting too much to have to save the world—*and* Jimmy. If it came to a show-down the world would have to take second place. And what, she wondered, is Jimmy thinking? She knew his heavy humourless rectitude; it would take more than Raven's head on a platter to make him understand why she had acted as she had with Raven and Cholmondeley. It sounded weak and fanciful even to herself to say that she wanted to stop a war.

"Let's sleep now," she said. "We've got a long, long day ahead."

"I think I could sleep now," Raven said. "You don't know how good it seems . . ." It was Anne now who could not sleep. She had too much to think about. It occurred to her that she might steal his pistol before he woke and call the police in. That would save Jimmy from danger, but what was the use? They'd never believe her story; they had no proof that he had killed the old man. And even then he might escape. She needed time and there was no time. She could hear very faintly droning up from the south, where the military aerodrome was, a flight of planes. They passed very high on special patrol, guarding the Nottwich mines and the key industry of Midland Steel, tiny specks of light the size of fireflies travelling fast in formation, over the railway, over the goods yard, over the shed where Anne and Raven lay, over Saunders beating his arms for warmth behind a truck out of the wind's way, over Acky dreaming that he was in the pulpit of St. Luke's, over Sir Marcus sleepless beside the tape machine.

Raven slept heavily for the first time for nearly a week, holding the automatic in his lap. He dreamed that he was building a great bonfire on Guy Fawkes day. He threw in everything he could find: a saw-edged knife, a lot of racing cards, the leg of a table. It burnt warmly, deeply, beautifully. A lot of fireworks were going off all round him and again the old War Minister appeared on the other side of the fire. He said, "It's a good fire," stepping into it himself. Raven ran to the fire to pull him out, but the old man said, "Let me be. It's warm here," and then he sagged like a Guy Fawkes in the flames.

A clock struck. Anne counted the strokes, as she had counted them all through the night; it must be nearly day and she had no plan. She coughed; her throat was stinging; and suddenly she realised with joy that there was fog outside: not one of the black upper fogs, but a cold damp yellow fog from the river, through which it would be easy, if it was thick enough, for a man to escape. She put out her hand unwillingly, because he was now so repulsive to her, and touched Raven. He woke at once. She said, "There's a fog coming up."

"What a break!" he said, "what a break!" laughing softly. "It makes you believe in Providence, doesn't it?" They could just see each other in the pale earliest light. He was shivering now that he was awake. He said, "I dreamed of a big fire." She saw that he had no sacks to cover him, but she felt no pity at all. He was just a wild animal who had to be dealt with carefully and then destroyed. "Let him freeze," she thought. He was examining the automatic; she saw him put down the safety catch. He said, "What about you? You've been straight with me. I don't want you to get into any trouble. I don't want them to think," he hesitated and went on with questioning humility, "to know that we are in this together."

"I'll think up something," Anne said.

"I ought to knock you out. They wouldn't know then. But I've gone soft. I wouldn't hurt you not if I was paid."

She couldn't resist saying, "Not for two hundred and fifty pounds?"

"He was a stranger," Raven said. "It's not the same. I thought he was one of the high and mighties. You're——" he hesitated again, glowering dumbly down at the automatic, "a friend."

"You needn't be afraid," Anne said. "I'll have a tale to tell."

He said with admiration, "You're clever." He watched the fog coming in under the badly fitting door, filling the small shed with its freezing coils. "It'll be nearly thick enough now to take a chance." He held the automatic in his left hand and flexed the fingers of the right. He laughed to keep his courage up. "They'll never get me now in this fog."

"You'll shoot?"

"Of course I'll shoot."

"I've got an idea," Anne said. "We don't want to take any risks. Give me your overcoat and hat. I'll put them on and slip out first and give them a run for their money. In this fog they'll never notice till they've caught me. Directly you hear the whistles blow count five slowly and make a bolt. I'll run to the right. You run to the left."

"You've got nerve," Raven said. He shook his head. "No. They might shoot."

"You said yourself they wouldn't shoot first."

"That's right. But you'll get a couple of years for this."

"Oh," Anne said, "I'll tell them a tale. I'll say you forced me." She said with a trace of bitterness, "This'll give me a lift out of the chorus. I'll have a speaking part."

Raven said shyly, "If you made out you were my girl, they wouldn't pin it on you. I'll say that for them. They'd give a man's girl a break."

"Got a knife?"

"Yes." He felt in all his pockets; it wasn't there; he must have left it on the floor of Acky's best guest-chamber.

Anne said, "I wanted to cut up my skirt. I'd be able to run easier."

"I'll try and tear it," Raven said, kneeling in front of her, taking a grip, but it wouldn't tear. Looking down she was astonished at the smallness of his wrists; his hands had no more strength or substance than a delicate boy's. The whole of his strength lay in the mechanical instrument at his feet. She thought of Mather and felt contempt now as well as repulsion for the thin ugly body kneeling at her feet.

"Never mind," she said. "I'll do the best I can. Give me the coat."

He shivered, taking it off, and seemed to lose some of his sour assurance without the tight black tube which had hidden a very old, very flamboyant check suit in holes at both the elbows. It hung on him uneasily. He looked under-nourished. He wouldn't have impressed anyone as dangerous now. He pressed his arms to his sides to hide the holes. "And your hat," Anne said. He picked it up from the sacks and gave it her. He looked humiliated, and he had never accepted humiliation before without rage. "Now," Anne said, "remember. Wait for the whistles and then count."

"I don't like it," Raven said. He tried hopelessly to express the deep pain it gave him to see her go; it felt too much like the end of everything. He said, "I'll see you again—some time," and when she mechanically reassured him, "Yes," he laughed with his aching despair, "Not likely, after I've killed——" but he didn't even know the man's name.

6

i

Saunders had half fallen asleep; a voice at his side woke him. "The fog's getting thick, sir."

It was already dense, with the first light touching it with dusty yellow, and he would have sworn at the policeman for not waking him earlier if his stammer had not made him chary of wasting words. He said, "Pass the word round to move in."

"Are we going to rush the place, sir?"

"No. There's a girl there. We can't have any sh-sh-shooting. Wait till he comes out."

But the policeman hadn't left his side when he noticed, "The door's opening." Saunders put his whistle in his mouth and lowered his safety catch. The light was bad and the fog deceptive; but he recognised the dark coat as it slipped to the right into the shelter of the coal trucks. He blew his whistle and was after it. The black coat had half a minute's start and was moving quickly into the fog. It was impossible to see at all more than twenty feet ahead. But Saunders kept doggedly just in sight blowing his whistle continuously. As he hoped, a whistle blew in front; it confused the fugitive; he hesitated for a moment and Saunders gained on him. They had him cornered, and this Saunders knew was the dangerous moment. He blew his whistle urgently three times into the fog to bring the police round in a complete circle and the whistle was taken up in the yellow obscurity, passing in a wide invisible circle.

But he had lost pace, the fugitive spurted forward and was lost. Saunders blew two blasts: "Advance slowly and keep in touch." To the right and in front a single long whistle announced that the man had been seen, and the police converged on the sound. Each kept in touch with a policeman on either hand. It was impossible as long as the circle was kept closed for the man to escape. But the circle drew in and there was no sign of him; the short single exploratory blasts sounded petulant and lost. At last Saunders gazing ahead saw the faint form of a policeman come out of the fog a dozen yards away. He halted them all with a whistled signal: the fugitive must be somewhere just ahead in the tangle of trucks in the centre. Revolver in hand Saunders advanced and a policeman took his place and closed the circle.

Suddenly Saunders spied his man. He had taken up a strategic position where a pile of coal and an empty truck at his back made a wedge which guarded him from surprise. He was invisible to the police behind him, and he had turned sideways like a duellist and presented only a shoulder to Saunders, while a pile of old sleepers hid him to the knees. It seemed to Saunders that it meant only one thing, that he was going to shoot it out; the man must be mad and desperate. The hat was pulled down over the face; the coat hung in an odd loose way; the hands were in the pockets. Saunders called at him through the yellow coils of fog, "You'd better come quietly." He raised his pistol and advanced, his finger ready on the trigger. But the immobility of the figure scared him. It was in shadow half hidden in the swirl of fog. It was he who was exposed, with the east, and the pale penetration of early light, behind him. It was like waiting for execution, for he could not fire first. But all the same, knowing what Mather felt, knowing that this man was mixed up with Mather's girl, he did not want much excuse to fire. Mather would stand by him. A movement would be enough. He said sharply without a stammer, "Put up your hands!" The figure didn't move. He told himself again with a kindling hatred for the man who had injured Mather: I'll plug him if he doesn't obey: they'll all stand by me: one more chance. "Put up your hands!" and when the figure stayed as it was with its hands hidden, a hardly discernible menace, he fired.

But as he pressed the trigger a whistle blew, a long urgent blast which panted and gave out like a rubber animal, from the direction of the wall and the road. There could be no doubt whatever what that meant, and suddenly he saw it all—

he had shot at Mather's girl; she'd drawn them off. He screamed at the men behind him, "Back to the gate!" and ran forward. He had seen her waver at his shot. He said, "Are you hurt?" and knocked the hat off her head to see her better.

"You're the third person who's tried to kill me," Anne said weakly, leaning hard against the truck. "Come to sunny Nottwich. Well, I've got six lives left."

Saunders's stammer came back: "W-w-w-w."

"This is where you hit," Anne said, "if that's what you want to know," showing the long yellow sliver on the edge of the truck. "It's only an outer. You don't even get a box of chocolates."

Saunders said, "You'll have to c-c-come along with me."

"It'll be a pleasure. Do you mind if I take off this coat? I feel kind of silly."

At the gate four policemen stood round something on the ground. One of them said, "We've sent for an ambulance."

"Is he dead?"

"Not yet. He's shot in the stomach. He must have gone on whistling——"

Saunders had a moment of vicious rage. "Stand aside, boys," he said, "and let the lady see." They drew back in an embarrassed unwilling way as if they'd been hiding a dirty chalk picture on the wall and showed the white drained face which looked as if it had never been alive, never known the warm circulation of blood. You couldn't call the expression peaceful; it was just nothing at all. The blood was all over the trousers the men had loosened, was caked on the charcoal of the path. Saunders said, "Two of you take this lady to the station. I'll stay here till the ambulance comes."

ii

Mather said, "If you want to make a statement I must warn you. Anything you say may be used in evidence."

"I haven't got a statement to make," Anne said. "I want to talk to you, Jimmy."

Mather said, "If the superintendent had been here, I should have asked him to take the case. I want you to understand that I'm not letting personal—that my not having charged you doesn't mean——"

"You might give a girl a cup of coffee," Anne said. "It's nearly breakfast time."

Mather struck the table furiously. "Where was he going?"

"Give me time," Anne said, "I've got plenty to tell. But you won't believe it."

"You saw the man he shot," Mather said. "He's got a wife and two children. They've rung up from the hospital. He's bleeding internally."

"What's the time?" Anne said.

"Eight o'clock. It won't make any difference your keeping quiet. He can't escape us now. In an hour the air raid signals go. There won't be a soul on the streets without a mask. He'll be spotted at once. What's he wearing?"

"If you'd give me something to eat. I haven't had a thing for twenty-four hours. I could think then."

Mather said, "There's only one chance you won't be charged with complicity. If you make a statement."

"Is this the third degree?" Anne said.

"Why do you want to shelter him? Why keep your word to him when you don't——?"

"Go on," Anne said. "Be personal. No one can blame you. I don't. But I don't want you to think I'd keep my word to him. He killed the old man. He told me so."

"What old man?"

"The War Minister."

"You've got to think up something better than that," Mather said.

"But it's true. He never stole those notes. They double-crossed him. It was what they'd paid him to do the job."

"He spun you a fancy yarn," Mather said. "But *I* know where those notes came from."

"So do I. I can guess. From somewhere in this town."

"He told you wrong. They came from United Rail Makers in Victoria Street."

Anne shook her head. "They didn't start from there. They came from Midland Steel."

"So that's where he's going, to Midland Steel—in the Tanneries?"

"Yes," Anne said. There was a sound of finality about the word which daunted her. She hated Raven now, the policeman she had seen bleeding on the ground called at her heart for Raven's death, but she couldn't help remembering the hut, the cold, the pile of sacks, his complete and hopeless trust. She sat with bowed head while Mather lifted the receiver and gave his orders. "We'll wait for him there," he said. "Who is it he wants to see?"

"He doesn't know."

"There might be something in it," Mather said. "Some connection between the two. He's probably been double-crossed by some clerk."

"It wasn't a clerk who paid him all that money, who tried to kill me just because I knew——"

Mather said, "Your fairy tale can wait." He rang a bell and told the constable who came, "Hold this girl for further inquiries. You can give her a sandwich and a cup of coffee now."

"Where are you going?"

"To bring in your boy friend," Mather said.

"He'll shoot. He's quicker than you are. Why can't you let the others——?" She implored him, "I'll make a full statement. How he killed a man called Kite too."

"Take it," Mather said to the constable. He put on his coat. "The fog's clearing."

She said, "Don't you see that if it's true—only give him time to find his man and there won't be—war."

"He was telling you a fairy story."

"He was telling me the truth—but, of course, you weren't there—you didn't hear him. It sounds differently to you. I thought I was saving—everyone."

"All you did," Mather said brutally, "was get a man killed."

"The whole thing sounds so differently in here. Kind of fantastic. But he believed. Maybe," she said hopelessly, "he was mad."

Mather opened the door. She suddenly cried to him, "Jimmy, he wasn't mad. They tried to kill *me*."

He said, "I'll read your statement when I get back," and closed the door.

7

i

T hey were all having the hell of a time at the hospital. It was the biggest rag they'd had since the day of the street collection when they kidnapped old Piker and ran him to the edge of the Weevil and threatened to duck him if he didn't pay a ransom. Good old Fergusson, good old Buddy, was organising it all. They had three ambulances out in the courtyard and one had a death's-head banner on it for the dead ones. Somebody shrieked that Mike was taking out the petrol with a nasal syringe, so they began to pelt him with flour and soot; they had it ready in great buckets. It was the unofficial part of the programme: all the casualties were going to be rubbed with it, except the dead ones the death's-head ambulance picked up. *They* were going to be put in the cellar where the refrigerating plant kept the corpses for dissection fresh.

One of the senior surgeons passed rapidly and nervously across a corner of the courtyard. He was on the way to a Cæsarian operation, but he had no confidence whatever that the students wouldn't pelt him or duck him; only five years ago there had been a scandal and an inquiry because a woman had died on the day of a rag. The surgeon attending her had been kidnapped and carried all over town dressed as Guy Fawkes. Luckily she wasn't a paying patient, and, though her husband had been hysterical at the inquest, the coroner had decided that one must make allowance for youth. The coroner had been a student himself once and remembered with pleasure the day when they had pelted the Vice-Chancellor of the University with soot.

The senior surgeon had been present that day too. Once safely inside the glass corridor he could smile at the memory. The Vice-Chancellor had been unpopular; he had been a classic which wasn't very suitable for a provincial university. He had translated Lucan's *Pharsalia* into some complicated metre of his own invention. The senior surgeon remembered something vaguely about stresses. He could still see the little wizened frightened Liberal face trying to smile when his pince-nez broke, trying to be a good sportsman. But anyone could tell that he wasn't really a good sportsman. That was why they pelted him so hard.

The senior surgeon, quite safe now, smiled tenderly down at the rabble in the courtyard. Their white coats were already black with soot. Somebody had got hold of a stomach pump. Very soon they'd be raiding the shop in the High Street and seizing their mascot, the stuffed and rather moth-eaten tiger. Youth, youth, he thought, laughing gently when he saw Colson the treasurer, scuttle from door to door with a scared expression: perhaps they'll catch him: no, they've let him by: what a joke it all was, "trailing clouds of glory," "turn as swimmers into cleanness leaping."

Buddy was having the hell of a time. Everyone was scampering to obey his orders. He was the leader. They'd duck or pelt anyone he told them to. He had an enormous sense of power; it more than atoned for unsatisfactory examination results, for surgeons' sarcasms. Even a surgeon wasn't safe to-day if *he* gave an order. The soot and water and flour were his idea; the whole gas practice would have been a dull sober official piece of routine if he hadn't thought of making it a "rag." The very word "rag" was powerful; it conferred complete freedom from control. He'd called a meeting of the brighter students and explained. "If anyone's on the streets without a gas-mask he's a conchie. There are people who want to crab the practice. So when we get 'em back to the hospital we'll give 'em hell."

They boiled round him. "Good old Buddy." "Look out with that pump." "Who's the bastard who's pinched my stethoscope?" "What about Tiger Tim?" They surged round Buddy Fergusson, waiting for orders, and he stood superbly above them on the step of an ambulance, his white coat apart, his fingers in the pockets of his double-breasted waistcoat, his square squat figure swelling with pride, while they shouted, "Tiger Tim! Tiger Tim! Tiger Tim!"

"Friends, Romans and Countrymen," he said and they roared with laughter: Good old Buddy. Buddy always had the right word. He could make any party go. You never knew what Buddy would say next. "Lend me your——" They shrieked with laughter. He was a dirty dog, old Buddy. Good old Buddy.

Like a great beast which is in need of exercise, which has fed on too much hay, Buddy Fergusson was aware of his body. He felt his biceps; he strained for action. Too many exams, too many lectures, Buddy Fergusson wanted action. While they surged round him he imagined himself a leader of men. No Red Cross work for him when war broke: Buddy Fergusson, company commander, Buddy Fergusson, the daredevil of the trenches. The only exam he had ever successfully passed was Certificate A in the school O.T.C.

"Some of our friends seem to be missing," Buddy Fergusson said. "Simmons, Aitkin, Mallowes, Watt. They are bloody conchies, every one, grubbing up anatomy while we are serving our country. We'll pick 'em up in town. The flying squad will go to their lodgings."

"What about the women, Buddy?" someone screamed, and everyone laughed and began to hit at each other, wrestle and mill. For Buddy had a reputation with the women. He spoke airily to his friends of even the super-barmaid at the Metropole, calling her Juicy Juliet and suggesting to the minds of his hearers amazing scenes of abandonment over high tea at his digs.

Buddy Fergusson straddled across the ambulance step. "Deliver 'em to me. In war-time we need more mothers." He felt strong, coarse, vital, a town bull; he hardly remembered himself that he was a virgin, guilty only of a shame-faced unsuccessful attempt on the old Nottwich tart; he was sustained by his reputation, it bore him magically in imagination into every bed. He knew women, he was a realist.

"Treat 'em rough," they shrieked at him, and "You're telling me," he said magnificently, keeping well at bay any thought of the future: the small provincial G.P.'s job, the panel patients in dingy consulting rooms, innumerable midwife cases, a lifetime of hard underpaid fidelity to one dull wife. "Got your gas-masks ready?" he called to them, the undisputed leader, daredevil Buddy. What the hell did examinations matter when you were a leader of men? He could see several of the younger nurses watching him through the panes. He could see the little brunette called Milly. She was coming to tea with him on Saturday. He felt his muscles taut with pride. What scenes, he told himself, *this* time there would be of disreputable revelry, forgetting the inevitable truth known only to himself and each girl in turn: the long silence over the muffins, the tentative references to League results, the peck at empty air on the doorstep.

The siren at the glue factory started its long mounting whistle rather like a lap dog with hysteria and everyone stood still for a moment with a vague reminiscence of Armistice Day silences. Then they broke into three milling mobs, climbing on to the ambulance roofs, fixing their gas-masks, and drove out into the cold empty Nottwich streets. The ambulances shed a lot of them at each corner, and small groups formed and wandered down the streets with a predatory disappointed air. The streets were almost empty. Only a few errand boys passed on bicycles, looking in their gas-masks like bears doing a trick cycle act in a circus. They all shrieked at each other because they didn't know how their voices sounded outside. It was as if each of them were enclosed in a separate sound-proof telephone cabinet. They stared hungrily through their big mica eye-pieces into the doorways of shops, wanting a victim. A little group collected round Buddy Fergusson and proposed that they should seize a policeman who, being on point duty, was without a mask. But Buddy vetoed the proposal. He said this wasn't an ordinary rag. What they wanted were people who thought so little about their country that they wouldn't even take the trouble to put on a gas-mask. "They are the people," he said, "who avoid boat-drill. We had great fun with a fellow once in the Mediterranean who didn't turn up to boat-drill."

That reminded them of all the fellows who weren't helping, who were probably getting ahead with their anatomy at that moment. "Watt lives near here," Buddy Fergusson said, "let's get Watt and debag him." A feeling of physical well-being came over him just as if he had drunk a couple of pints of bitter. "Down the Tanneries," Buddy said. "First left. First right. Second left. Number twelve. First floor." He knew the way, he said, because he'd been to tea several times with

Watt their first term before he'd learned what a hound Watt was. The knowledge of his early mistake made him unusually anxious to do something to Watt physically, to mark the severance of their relationship more completely than with sneers.

They ran down the empty Tanneries, half a dozen masked monstrosities in white coats smutted with soot; it was impossible to tell one from another. Through the great glass door of Midland Steel they saw three men standing by the lift talking to the porter. There were a lot of uniformed police about, and in the square ahead they saw a rival group of fellow-students, who had been luckier than they, carrying a little man (he kicked and squealed) towards an ambulance. The police watched and laughed, and a troop of planes zoomed overhead, diving low over the centre of the town to lend the practice verisimilitude. First left. First right. The centre of Nottwich to a stranger was full of sudden contrasts. Only on the edge of the town to the north, out by the park, were you certain of encountering street after street of well-to-do middle-class houses. Near the market you changed at a corner from modern chromium offices to little cats'-meat shops, from the luxury of the Metropole to seedy lodgings and the smell of cooking greens. There was no excuse in Nottwich for one half of the world being ignorant of how the other half lived.

Second left. The houses on one side gave way to bare rock and the street dived steeply down below the Castle. It wasn't really a castle any longer; it was a yellow brick municipal museum full of flint arrowheads and pieces of broken brown pottery and a few stags' heads in the zoological section suffering from moths and one mummy brought back from Egypt by the Earl of Nottwich in 1843. The moths left that alone, but the custodian thought he had heard mice inside. Mike, with a nasal douche in his breast pocket, wanted to climb up the rock. He shouted to Buddy Fergusson that the custodian was outside, without a mask, signalling to enemy aircraft. But Buddy and the others ran down the hill to number twelve.

The landlady opened the door to them. She smiled winningly and said Mr. Watt was in; she thought he was working; she buttonholed Buddy Fergusson and said she was sure it would be good for Mr. Watt to be taken away from his books for half an hour. Buddy said, "We'll take him away."

"Why, that's Mr. Fergusson," the landlady said. "I'd know your voice anywhere, but I'd never 'ave known you without you spoke to me, not in them respiratororries. I was just going out when Mr. Watt minded me as 'ow it was the gas practice."

"Oh, he remembers, does he?" Buddy said. He was blushing inside the mask at having been recognised by the landlady. It made him want to assert himself more than ever.

"He said I'd be taken to the 'ospital."

"Come on, men," Buddy said and led them up the stairs. But their number was an embarrassment. They couldn't all charge through Watt's door and seize him in a moment from the chair in which he was sitting. They had to go through one at a time after Buddy and then bunch themselves in a shy silence beside the table. This was the moment when an experienced man could have dealt with them, but Watt was aware of his unpopularity. He was afraid of losing dignity. He was a man who worked hard because he liked the work; he hadn't the excuse of poverty.

He played no games because he didn't like games, without the excuse of physical weakness. He had a mental arrogance which would ensure his success. If he suffered agony from his unpopularity now as a student it was the price he paid for the baronetcy, the Harley Street consulting room, the fashionable practice of the future. There was no reason to pity him; it was the others who were pitiable, living in their vivid vulgar way for five years before the long provincial interment of a lifetime.

Watt said, "Close the door, please. There's a draught," and his scared sarcasm gave them the chance they needed, to resent him.

Buddy said, "We've come to ask why you weren't at the hospital this morning?"

"That's Fergusson, isn't it?" Watt said. "I don't know why you want to know."

"Are you a conchie?"

"How old-world your slang is," Watt said. "No. I'm not a conchie. Now I'm just looking through some old medical books, and as I don't suppose they'd interest you, I'll ask you to show yourselves out."

"Working? That's how fellows like you get ahead, working while others are doing a proper job."

"It's just a different idea of fun, that's all," Watt said. "It's my pleasure to look at these folios, it's yours to go screaming about the streets in that odd costume."

That let them loose on him. He was as good as insulting the King's uniform. "We're going to debag you," Buddy said.

"That's fine. It'll save time," Watt said, "if I take them off myself," and he began to undress. He said, "This action has an interesting psychological significance. A form of castration. My own theory is that sexual jealousy in some form is at the bottom of it."

"You dirty tyke," Buddy said. He took the inkpot and splashed it on the wallpaper. He didn't like the word "sex." He believed in barmaids and nurses and tarts, and he believed in love, something rather maternal with deep breasts. The word sex suggested that there was something in common between the two: it outraged him. "Wreck the room!" he bawled and they were all immediately happy and at ease, exerting themselves physically like young bulls. Because they were happy again they didn't do any real damage, just pulled the books out of the shelves and threw them on the floor; they broke the glass of a picture frame in puritanical zeal because it contained the reproduction of a nude girl. Watt watched them; he was scared, and the more scared he was the more sarcastic he became. Buddy suddenly saw him as he was, standing there in his pants marked from birth for distinction, for success, and hated him. He felt impotent; he hadn't "class" like Watt, he hadn't the brains, in a very few years nothing he could do or say would affect the fortunes or the happiness of the Harley Street specialist, the woman's physician, the baronet. What was the good of talking about free will? Only war and death could save Buddy from the confinements, the provincial practice, the one dull wife and the bridge parties. It seemed to him that he could be happy if he had the strength to impress himself on Watt's memory. He took the inkpot and poured it over the open title-page of the old folio on the table.

"Come on, men," he said. "This room stinks," and led his party out and down the stairs. He felt an immense exhilaration; it was as if he had proved his manhood. Almost immediately they picked up an old woman. She didn't in the least know what it was all about. She thought it was a street collection and offered them a penny. They told her she had to come along to the hospital; they were very courteous and one offered to carry her basket; they reacted from violence to a more than usual gentility. She laughed at them. She said, "Well I never, what you boys will think up next!" and when one took her arm and began to lead her gently up the street, she said, "Which of you's Father Christmas?" Buddy didn't like that: it hurt his dignity: he had suddenly been feeling rather noble: "women and children first": "although bombs were falling all round he brought the woman safely . . ." He stood still and let the others go on up the street with the old woman; she was having the time of her life; she cackled and dug them in the ribs: her voice carried a long distance in the cold air. She kept on telling them to "take off them things and play fair," and just before they turned a corner out of sight she was calling them Mormons. She meant Mohammedans, because she had an idea that Mohammedans went about with their faces covered up and had a lot of wives. An aeroplane zoomed overhead and Buddy was alone in the street with the dead and dying until Mike appeared. Mike said he had a good idea. Why not pinch the mummy in the Castle and take it to the hospital for not wearing a gas-mask? The fellows with the death's-head ambulance had already got Tiger Tim and were driving round the town crying out for old Piker.

"No," Buddy said, "this isn't an ordinary rag. This is serious," and suddenly at the entrance to a side street he saw a man without a mask double back at the sight of him. "Quick. Hunt him down," Buddy cried, "Tallyho," and they pelted up the street in pursuit. Mike was the faster runner: Buddy was already a little inclined to fatness, and Mike was soon leading by ten yards. The man had a start, he was round one corner and out of sight. "Go on," Buddy shouted, "hold him till I come." Mike was out of sight too when a voice from a doorway spoke as he passed. "Hi," it said, "you. What's the hurry?"

Buddy stopped. The man stood there with his back pressed to a house door. He had simply stepped back and Mike in his hurry had gone by. There was something serious and planned and venomous about his behaviour. The street of little Gothic villas was quite empty.

"You were looking for me, weren't you?" the man said.

Buddy demanded sharply, "Where's your gas-mask?"

"Is this a game?" the man asked angrily.

"Of course it's not a game," Buddy said. "You're a casualty. You'll have to come along to the hospital with me."

"I will, will I?" the man said, pressed back against the door, thin and undersized and out-at-elbows.

"You'd better," Buddy said. He inflated his chest and made his biceps swell. Discipline, he thought, discipline. The little brute didn't recognise an officer when he saw one. He felt the satisfaction of superior physical strength. He'd punch his nose for him if he didn't come quietly.

"All right," the man said, "I'll come." He emerged from the dark doorway, mean vicious face, hare-lip, a crude check suit, ominous and aggressive in his submission. "Not that way," Buddy said, "to the left."

"Keep moving," the small man said, covering Buddy through his pocket, pressing the pistol against his side. "*Me* a casualty," he said, "that's a good one," laughing without mirth. "Get in through that gate or you'll be the casualty――" (they were opposite a small garage; it was empty; the owner had driven to his office, and the little bare box stood open at the end of a few feet of drive).

Buddy blustered, "What the hell!" but he had recognised the face of which the description had appeared in both the local papers, and there was a control in the man's action which horribly convinced Buddy that he wouldn't hesitate to shoot. It was a moment in his life that he never forgot; he was not allowed to forget it by friends who saw nothing wrong in what he did. All through his life the tale cropped up in print in the most unlikely places: serious histories, symposiums of famous crimes: it followed him from obscure practice to obscure practice. Nobody saw anything important in what he did: nobody doubted that he would have done the same: walked into the garage, closed the gates at Raven's orders. But friends didn't realise the crushing nature of the blow: they hadn't just been standing in the street under a hail of bombs, they had not looked forward with pleasure and excitement to war, they hadn't been Buddy, the daredevil of the trenches one minute, before genuine war in the shape of an automatic in a thin desperate hand pressed on him.

"Strip!" Raven said, and obediently Buddy stripped. But he was stripped of more than his gas-mask, his white coat, his green tweed suit. When it was over he hadn't a hope left. It was no good hoping for a war to prove him a leader of men. He was just a stout flushed frightened young man shivering in his pants in the cold garage. There was a hole in the seat of his pants and his knees were pink and clean-shaven. You could tell that he was strong, but you could tell too in the curve of his stomach, the thickness of his neck, that he was beginning to run to seed. Like a mastiff he needed more exercise than the city could afford him, even though several times a week undeterred by the frost he would put on shorts and a singlet and run slowly and obstinately round the park, a little red in the face but undeterred by the grins of nursemaids and the shrill veracious comments of unbearable children in prams. He was keeping fit, but it was a dreadful thought that he had been keeping fit for this: to stand shivering and silent in a pair of holed pants, while the mean thin undernourished city rat, whose arm he could have snapped with a single twist, put on his clothes, his white coat and last of all his gas-mask.

"Turn round," Raven said, and Buddy Fergusson obeyed. He was so miserable now that he would have missed a chance even if Raven had given him one, miserable and scared as well. He hadn't much imagination; he had never really visualised danger as it gleamed at him under the garage globe in a long grey wicked-looking piece of metal charged with pain and death. "Put your hands behind you." Raven tied together the pink strong ham-like wrists with Buddy's tie: the striped chocolate-and-yellow old boys' tie of one of the obscurer public schools. "Lie down," and meekly Buddy Fergusson obeyed and Raven tied his feet together with a handkerchief and gagged him with another. It wasn't very secure, but it would have to do.

He'd got to work quickly. He left the garage and pulled the doors softly to behind him. He could hope for several hours' start now, but he couldn't count on as many minutes.

He came quietly and cautiously up under the Castle rock, keeping his eye open for students. But the gangs had moved on; some were picketing the station for train arrivals, and the others were sweeping the streets which led out northwards towards the mines. The chief danger now was that at any moment the sirens might blow the "All Clear." There were a lot of police about: he knew why, but he moved unhesitatingly past them and on towards the Tanneries. His plan carried him no further than the big glass doors of Midland Steel. He had a kind of blind faith in destiny, in a poetic justice; somehow when he was inside the building he would find the way to the man who had double-crossed him. He came safely round into the Tanneries and moved across the narrow roadway, where there was only room for a single stream of traffic, towards the great functional building of black glass and steel. He hugged the automatic to his hip with a sense of achievement and exhilaration. There was a kind of lightheartedness now about his malice and hatred he had never known before; he had lost his sourness and bitterness; he was less personal in his revenge. It was almost as if he were acting for someone else.

Behind the door of Midland Steel a man peered out at the parked cars and the deserted street. He looked like a clerk. Raven crossed the pavement. He peered back through the panes of the mask at the man behind the door. Something made him hesitate: the memory of a face he had seen for a moment outside the Soho café where he lodged. He suddenly started away again from the door, walking in a rapid scared way down the Tanneries. The police were there before him.

It meant nothing, Raven told himself, coming out into a silent High Street empty except for a telegraph boy in a gas-mask getting on to a bicycle by the Post Office. It merely meant that the police too had noted a connection between the office in Victoria Street and Midland Steel. It didn't mean that the girl was just another skirt who had betrayed him. Only the faintest shadow of the old sourness and isolation touched his spirits. She's straight, he swore with almost perfect conviction, *she* wouldn't grass, we are together in this, and he remembered with a sense of doubtful safety how she had said, "We are friends."

ii

The producer had called a rehearsal early. He wasn't going to add to the expenses by buying everyone gas-masks. They would be in the theatre by the time the practice started and they wouldn't leave until the "All Clear" had sounded. Mr. Davis had said he wanted to see the new number, and so the producer had sent him notice of the rehearsal. He had it stuck under the edge of his shaving mirror next a card with the telephone numbers of all his girls.

It was bitterly cold in the modern central-heated bachelor's flat. Something, as usual, had gone wrong with the oil engines, and the constant hot water was barely warm. Mr. Davis cut himself shaving several times and stuck little tufts of cotton-wool all over his chin. His eye caught Mayfair 632 and Museum 798. Those were Coral and Lucy. Dark and fair, nubile and thin. His fair and dark angel. A little early fog still yellowed the panes, and the sound of a car back-firing made him think of Raven safely isolated in the railway yard surrounded by armed police. He knew that Sir Marcus was arranging everything and he wondered how it felt to be waking to your last day. "We know not the hour," Mr. Davis thought happily, plying his styptic pencil, sticking the cotton-wool on the larger wounds, but if one knew, as Raven must know, would one still feel irritation at the failure of central heating, at a blunt blade? Mr. Davis's mind was full of great dignified abstractions, and it seemed to him a rather grotesque idea that a man condemned to death should be aware of something so trivial as a shaving cut. But then, of course, Raven would not be shaving in his shed.

Mr. Davis made a hasty breakfast—two pieces of toast, two cups of coffee, four kidneys and a piece of bacon sent up by lift from the restaurant, some sweet "Silver Shred" marmalade. It gave him a good deal of pleasure to think that Raven would not be eating such a breakfast—a condemned man in prison, possibly, but not Raven. Mr. Davis did not believe in wasting anything; he had paid for the breakfast, so on the second piece of toast he piled up all the remains of the butter and the marmalade. A little of the marmalade fell off on to his tie.

There was really only one worry left, apart from Sir Marcus's displeasure, and that was the girl. He had lost his head badly: first in trying to kill her and then in not killing her. It had all been Sir Marcus's fault. He had been afraid of what Sir Marcus would do to him if he learnt of the girl's existence. But now everything would be all right. The girl had come out into the open as an accomplice; no court would take a criminal's story against Sir Marcus's. He forgot about the gas practice, as he hurried down to the theatre for a little relaxation now that everything really seemed to have been tidied up. On the way he got a sixpenny packet of toffee out of a slot machine.

He found Mr. Collier worried. They'd already had one rehearsal of the new number and Miss Maydew, who was sitting at the front of the stalls in a fur coat, had said it was vulgar. She said she didn't mind sex, but this wasn't in the right class. It was music-hall; it wasn't revue. Mr. Collier didn't care a damn what Miss Maydew thought, but it might mean that Mr. Cohen . . . He said, "If you'd tell me what's vulgar . . . I just don't see . . ."

Mr. Davis said, "I'll tell you if it's vulgar. Have it again," and he sat back in the stalls just behind Miss Maydew with the warm smell of her fur and her rather expensive scent in his nostrils, sucking a toffee. It seemed to him that life could offer nothing better than this. And the show was his. At any rate forty per cent of it was his. He picked out his forty per cent as the girls came on again in blue shorts with a red stripe and bras and postmen's caps, carrying cornucopias: the dark girl with the oriental eyebrows on the right, the fair girl with the rather plump legs and the big mouth (a big mouth was a good sign in a girl). They danced between two pillar-boxes, wriggling their little neat hips, and Mr. Davis sucked his toffee.

"It's called 'Christmas for Two'," Mr. Collier said.

"Why?"

"Well, you see, those cornucops are meant to be Christmas presents made sort of classical. And 'For Two' just gives it a little sex. Any number with 'For Two' in it goes."

"We've already got 'An Apartment for Two'," Miss Maydew said, "and 'Two Make a Dream'."

"You can't have too much of 'For Two'," Mr. Collier said. He appealed pitiably, "Can't you tell me what's vulgar?"

"Those cornucopias, for one thing."

"But they are classical," Mr. Collier said. "Greek."

"And the pillar-boxes, for another."

"The pillar-boxes," Mr. Collier exclaimed hysterically. "What's wrong with the pillar-boxes?"

"My dear man," Miss Maydew said, "if you don't know what's wrong with the pillar-boxes, I'm not going to tell you. If you like to get a committee of matrons I wouldn't mind telling *them*. But if you *must* have them, paint them blue and let them be air mail."

Mr. Collier said, "Is this a game or what is it?" He added bitterly, "What a time you must have when you write a letter." The girls went patiently on behind his back to the jingle of the piano, offering the cornucopias, offering their collar-stud bottoms. He turned on them fiercely. "Stop that, can't you? and let me think."

Mr. Davis said, "It's fine. We'll have it in the show." It made him feel good to contradict Miss Maydew, whose perfume he was now luxuriously taking in. It gave him in a modified form the pleasure of beating her or sleeping with her: the pleasure of mastery over a woman of superior birth. It was the kind of dream he had indulged in adolescence, while he carved his name on the desk and seat in a grim Midland board school.

"You really think that, Mr. Davenant?"

"My name's Davis."

"I'm sorry, Mr. Davis." Horror on horror, Mr. Collier thought; he was alienating the new backer now.

"I think it's lousy," Miss Maydew said. Mr. Davis took another piece of toffee. "Go ahead, old man," he said. "Go ahead." They went ahead: the songs and dances floated agreeably through Mr. Davis's consciousness, sometimes wistful, sometimes sweet and sad, sometimes catchy. Mr. Davis liked the sweet ones best. When they sang, "You have my mother's way," he really did think of his mother: he was the ideal audience. Somebody came out of the wings and bellowed at Mr. Collier. Mr. Collier screamed, "What do you say?" and a young man in a pale blue jumper went on mechanically singing:

Your photograph
Is just the sweetest half . . .

"Did you say Christmas tree?" Mr. Collier yelled.

In your December
I shall remember . . .

Mr. Collier screamed, "Take it away." The song came abruptly to an end with the words "*Another mother*." The young man said, "You took it too fast," and began to argue with the pianist.

"I can't take it away," the man in the wings said. "It was ordered." He wore an apron and a cloth cap. He said, "It took a van and two horses. You'd better come and have a look." Mr. Collier disappeared and returned immediately. "My God!" he said, "it's fifteen feet high. Who can have played this fool trick?" Mr. Davis was in a happy dream: his slippers had been warmed by a log fire in a big baronial hall, a little exclusive perfume like Miss Maydew's was hovering in the air, and he was just going to go to bed with a good but aristocratic girl to whom he had been properly married that morning by a bishop. She reminded him a little of his mother. "*In your December . . .*"

He was suddenly aware that Mr. Collier was saying, "And there's a crate of glass balls and candles."

"Why," Mr. Davis said, "has my little gift arrived?"

"*Your*—little——?"

"I thought we'd have a Christmas party on the stage," Mr. Davis said. "I like to get to know all you artistes in a friendly homey way. A little dancing, a song or two," there seemed to be a visible lack of enthusiasm, "plenty of pop." A pale smile lit Mr. Collier's face. "Well," he said, "it's very kind of you, Mr. Davis. We shall certainly appreciate it."

"Is the tree all right?"

"Yes, Mr. Daven—Davis, it's a magnificent tree." The young man in the blue jumper looked as if he was going to laugh and Mr. Collier scowled at him. "We all thank you very much, Mr. Davis, don't we, girls?" Everybody said in refined and perfect chorus as if the words had been rehearsed, "*Rather*, Mr. Collier," except Miss Maydew, and a dark girl with a roving eye who was two seconds late and said, "You bet."

That attracted Mr. Davis's notice. Independent, he thought approvingly, stands out from the crowd. He said, "I think I'll step behind and look at the tree. Don't let me be in the way, old man. Just you carry on," and made his way into the wings where the tree stood blocking the way to the changing rooms. An electrician had hung some of the baubles on for fun and among the litter of properties under the bare globes it sparkled with icy dignity. Mr. Davis rubbed his hands, a buried childish delight came alive. He said, "It looks lovely." A kind of Christmas peace lay over his spirit: the occasional memory of Raven was only like the darkness pressing round the little lighted crib.

"That's a tree all right," a voice said. It was the dark girl. She had followed him into the wings; she wasn't wanted on the stage for the number they were rehearsing. She was short and plump and not very pretty; she sat on a case and watched Mr. Davis with gloomy friendliness.

"Gives a Christmas feeling," Mr. Davis said.

"So will a bottle of pop," the girl said.

"What's your name?"

"Ruby."

"What about meeting me for a spot of lunch after the rehearsal's over?"

"Your girls sort of disappear, don't they?" Ruby said. "I could do with a steak and onions, but I don't want any conjuring. I'm not a detective's girl."

"What that?" Mr. Davis said sharply.

"She's the Yard man's girl. He was round here yesterday."

"That's all right," Mr. Davis said crossly, thinking hard, "you're safe with me."

"You see, I'm unlucky."

Mr. Davis, in spite of his new anxiety, felt alive, vital: this wasn't *his* last day. The kidneys and bacon he had had for breakfast returned a little in his breath. The music came softly through to them: "*Your photograph is just the sweetest half . . .*" He licked a little grain of toffee on a back tooth as he stood under the tall dark gleaming tree and said, "You're in luck now. You couldn't have a better mascot than me."

"You'll have to do," the girl said with her habitual gloomy stare.

"The Metropole? At one sharp?"

"I'll be there. Unless I'm run over. I'm the kind of girl who *would* get run over before a free feed."

"It'll be fun."

"It depends what you call fun," the girl said and made room for him on the packing case. They sat side by side staring at the tree. "*In your December, I shall remember.*" Mr. Davis put his hand on her bare knee. He was a little awed by the tune, the Christmas atmosphere. His hand fell flatly, reverently, like a bishop's hand on a choirboy's head.

"Sinbad," the girl said.

"Sinbad?"

"I mean Bluebeard. These pantos get one all mixed up."

"You aren't frightened of *me*?" Mr. Davis protested, leaning his head against the postman's cap.

"If any girl's going to disappear, it'll be me for sure."

"She shouldn't have left me," Mr. Davis said softly, "so soon after dinner. Made me go home alone. She'd have been safe with me." He put his arm tentatively round Ruby's waist and squeezed her, then loosed her hastily as an electrician came along. "You're a clever girl," Mr. Davis said, "you ought to have a part. I bet you've got a good voice."

"Me a voice? I've got as much voice as a peahen."

"Give me a little kiss?"

"Of course I will." They kissed rather wetly. "What do I call you?" Ruby asked. "It sounds silly to me to call a man who's standing me a free feed Mister."

Mr. Davis said, "You could call me—Willie?"

"Well," Ruby said, sighing gloomily, "I hope I'll be seeing you, Willie. At the Metropole At one. I'll be there. I only hope *you*'ll be there or bang'll go a good steak and onions.'' She drifted back towards the stage. She was needed. *What did Aladdin say* . . . She said to the girl next her. ''He fed out of my hand.'' *When he came to Pekin?* ''The trouble is,'' Ruby said, ''I can't keep them. There's too much of this love-and-ride-away business. But it looks as if I'll get a good lunch, anyway.'' She said, ''There I go again. Saying that and forgetting to cross my fingers.''

Mr. Davis had seen enough; he had got what he'd come for; all that had to be done now was to shed a little light and comradeship among the electricians and other employees. He made his way slowly out by way of the dressing-rooms exchanging a word here and there, offering his gold cigarette-case. One never knew. He was fresh to this backstage theatre and it occurred to him that even among the dressers he might find—well, youth and talent, something to be encouraged, and fed too, of course, at the Metropole. He soon learnt better; all the dressers were old; they couldn't understand what he was after and one followed him round everywhere to make sure that he didn't hide in any of the girls' rooms. Mr. Davis was offended, but he was always polite. He departed through the stage door into the cold tainted street waving his hand. It was about time anyway that he looked in at Midland Steel and saw Sir Marcus.

The High Street was curiously empty except that there were more police about than was usual; he had quite forgotten the gas practice. No one attempted to interfere with Mr. Davis, his face was well known to all the force, though none of them could have said what Mr. Davis's occupation was. They would have said, without a smile at the thin hair, the heavy paunch, the plump and wrinkled hands, that he was one of Sir Marcus's young men. With an employer so old you could hardly avoid being one of the young men by comparison. Mr. Davis waved gaily to a sergeant on the other pavement and took a toffee. It was not the job of the police to take casualties to hospital and no one would willingly have obstructed Mr. Davis. There was something about his fat good nature which easily turned to malevolence. They watched him with covert amusement and hope sail down the pavement towards the Tanneries, rather as one watches a man of some dignity approach an icy slide. Up the street from the Tanneries a medical student in a gas-mask was approaching.

It was some while before Mr. Davis noticed the student and the sight of the gas-mask for a moment quite shocked him. He thought: these pacifists are going too far: sensational nonsense, and when the man halted Mr. Davis and said something which he could not catch through the heavy mask, Mr. Davis drew himself up and said haughtily, ''Nonsense. We're well prepared.'' Then he remembered and became quite friendly again; it wasn't pacifism after all, it was patriotism. ''Well, well,'' he said, ''I quite forgot. Of course, the practice.'' The anonymous stare through the thickened eyepieces, the muffled voice made him uneasy. He said jocularly, ''You won't be taking *me* to the hospital now, will you? I'm a busy man.'' The student seemed lost in thought with his hand on Mr. Davis's arm. Mr. Davis saw a policeman go grinning down the opposite pavement and he found it hard to restrain his irritation. There was a little fog still left in the upper air and a flight of planes drove through it, filling the street with their deep murmur, out towards the south ₂nd the aerodrome. ''You see,'' Mr. Davis said, keeping his temper, "the practice is over. The sirens will be going any moment now. It would be too absurd to waste a morning at the hospital. You know me. Davis is the name. Everyone in Nottwich knows me. Ask the police there. No one can accuse *me* of being a bad patriot."

"You think it's nearly over?" the man said.

"I'm glad to see you boys enthusiastic," Mr. Davis said. "I expect we've met some time at the hospital. I'm up there for all the big functions and I never forget a voice. Why," Mr. Davis said, "it was me who gave the biggest contribution to the new operating theatre." Mr. Davis would have liked to walk on, but the man blocked his way and it seemed a bit undignified to step into the road and go round him. The man might think he was trying to escape: there might be a tussle, and the police were looking on from the corner. A sudden venom spurted up into Mr. Davis's mind like the ink a cuttlefish shoots, staining his thoughts with its dark poison. That grinning ape in uniform . . . I'll have him dismissed . . . I'll see Calkin about it. He talked on cheerily to the man in the gas-mask, a thin figure, little more than a boy's figure on which the white medical coat hung loosely. "You boys," Mr. Davis said, "are doing a splendid work. There's no one appreciates that more than I do. If war comes——"

"You call yourself Davis," the muffled voice said.

Mr. Davis said with sudden irritation, "You're wasting my time. I'm a busy man. Of course I'm Davis." He checked his rising temper with an effort. "Look here. I'm a reasonable man. I'll pay anything you like to the hospital. Say, ten pounds ransom."

"Yes," the man said, "where is it?"

"You can trust me," Mr. Davis said, "I don't carry that much on me," and was amazed to hear what sounded like a laugh. This was going too far. "All right," Mr. Davis said, "you can come with me to my office and I'll pay you the money. But I shall expect a proper receipt from your treasurer."

"You'll get your receipt," the man said in his odd toneless mask-muffled voice and stood on one side to let Mr. Davis lead the way. Mr. Davis's good humour was quite restored. He prattled on. "No good offering you a toffee in that thing," he said. A messenger boy passed in a gas-mask with his cap cocked absurdly on the top of it; he whistled derisively at Mr. Davis. Mr. Davis went a little pink. His fingers itched to tear the hair, to pull the ear, to twist the wrist. "The boys enjoy themselves," he said. He became confiding; a doctor's presence always made him feel safe and oddly important: one could tell the most grotesque things to a doctor about one's digestion and it was as much material for them as an amusing anecdote was for a professional humourist. He said, "I've been getting hiccups badly lately. After every meal. It's not as if I eat fast . . . but, of course, you're only a student still. Though you know more about these things than I do. Then too I get spots before my eyes. Perhaps I ought to cut down my diet a bit. But it's difficult. A man in my position has a lot of entertaining to do. For instance——" he grasped his companion's unresponsive arm and squeezed it knowingly—"it would be no good my promising you that I'd go without my lunch today. You medicos are men of the world and I don't mind telling you I've got a little girl meeting me. At the

Metropole. At one.'' Some association of ideas made him feel in his pocket to make sure his packet of toffee was safe.

They passed another policeman and Mr. Davis waved his hand. His companion was very silent. The boy's shy, Mr. Davis thought, he's not used to walking about town with a man like me: it excused a certain roughness in his behaviour; even the suspicion Mr. Davis had resented was probably only a form of gawkiness. Mr. Davis, because the day was proving fine after all, a little sun sparkling through the cold obscured air, because the kidneys and bacon had really been done to a turn, because he had asserted himself in the presence of Miss Maydew, who was the daughter of a peer, because he had a date at the Metropole with a little girl of talent, because too by this time Raven's body would be safely laid out on its icy slab in the mortuary, for all these reasons Mr. Davis felt kindness and Christmas in his spirit; he exerted himself to put the boy at his ease. He said, ''I feel sure we've met somewhere. Perhaps the house surgeon introduced us.'' But his companion remained glumly unforthcoming. ''A fine sing-song you all put on at the opening of the new ward.'' He glanced again at the delicate wrists. ''You weren't by any chance the boy who dressed up as a girl and sang that naughty song?'' Mr. Davis laughed thickly at the memory, turning into the Tanneries, laughed as he had laughed more times than he could count over the port, at the club, among the good fellows, at the smutty masculine jokes, ''I was tickled to death.'' He put his hand on his companion's arm and pushed through the glass door of Midland Steel.

A stranger stepped out from round a corner and the clerk behind the inquiries counter told him in a strained voice, ''That's all right. That's Mr. Davis.''

''What's all this?'' Mr. Davis asked in a harsh no-nonsense voice, now that he was back where he belonged.

The detective said, ''We are just keeping an eye open.''

''Raven?'' Mr. Davis asked in a rather shrill voice. The man nodded. Mr. Davis said, ''You let him escape? What fools . . .''

The detective said, ''You needn't be scared. He'll be spotted at once if he comes out of hiding. He can't escape this time.''

''But why,'' Mr. Davis said, ''are you here? Why do you expect . . .''

''We've got our orders,'' the man said.

''Have you told Sir Marcus?''

''He knows.''

Mr. Davis looked tired and old. He said sharply to his companion, ''Come with me and I'll give you the money. I haven't any time to waste.'' He walked with lagging hesitating feet down a passage paved with some black shining composition to the glass lift-shaft. The man in the gas-mask followed him down the passage and into the lift; they moved slowly and steadily upwards together, as intimate as two birds caged. Floor by floor the great building sank below them, a clerk in a black coat hurrying on some mysterious errand which required a lot of blotting paper, a girl standing outside a closed door with a file of papers whispering to herself, rehearsing some excuse, an errand boy walking erratically along a passage balancing a bundle of new pencils on his head. They stopped at an empty floor.

There was something on Mr. Davis's mind. He walked slowly, turned the handle of his door softly, almost as if he feared that someone might be waiting for him inside. But the room was quite empty. An inner door opened, and a young woman with fluffy gold hair and exaggerated horn spectacles said, "Willie," and then saw his companion. She said, "Sir Marcus wants to see you, Mr. Davis."

"That's all right, Miss Connett," Mr. Davis said. "You might go and find me an ABC."

"Are you going away—at once?"

Mr. Davis hesitated. "Look me up what trains there are for town—after lunch."

"Yes, Mr. Davis." She withdrew and the two of them were alone. Mr. Davis shivered slightly and turned on his electric fire. The man in the gas-mask spoke and again the muffled coarse voice pricked at Mr. Davis's memory. "Are you scared of something?"

"There's a madman loose in this town," Mr. Davis said. His nerves were alert at every sound in the corridor outside, a footstep, the ring of a bell. It had needed more courage than he had been conscious of possessing to say "after lunch," he wanted to be away at once, clear away from Nottwich. He started at the scrape of a little cleaner's platform which was being lowered down the wall of the inner courtyard. He padded to the door and locked it; it gave him a better feeling of security to be locked into his familiar room, with his desk, his swivel chair, the cupboard where he kept two glasses and a bottle of sweet port, the bookcase, which contained a few technical works on steel, a *Whitaker's*, a *Who's Who* and a copy of *His Chinese Concubine*, than to remember the detective in the hall. He took everything in like something seen for the first time, and it was true enough that he had never so realised the peace and comfort of his small room. Again he started at the creak of the ropes from which the cleaner's platform hung. He shut down his double window. He said in a tone of nervous irritation, "Sir Marcus can wait."

"Who's Sir Marcus?"

"My boss." Something about the open door of his secretary's room disturbed him with the idea that anyone could enter that way. He was no longer in a hurry, he wasn't busy any more, he wanted companionship. He said, "You aren't in any hurry. Take that thing off, it must be stuffy, and have a glass of port." On his way to the cupboard he shut the inner door and turned the key. He sighed with relief, fetching out the port and the glasses, "Now we are *really* alone, I want to tell you about these hiccups." He poured two brimming glasses, but his hand shook and the port ran down the sides. He said, "Always just after a meal . . ."

The muffled voice said, "The money . . ."

"Really," Mr. Davis said, "you are rather impudent. You can trust *me*. I'm Davis." He went to his desk and unlocked a drawer, took out two five-pound notes and held them out. "Mind," he said, "I shall expect a proper receipt from your treasurer."

The man put them away. His hand stayed in his pocket. He said, "Are these phoney notes, too?" A whole scene came back to Mr. Davis's mind: a Lyons' Corner House, the taste of an Alpine Glow, the murderer sitting opposite him trying to tell him of the old woman he had killed. Mr. Davis screamed: not a word, not a plea for help, just a meaningless cry like a man gives under an anæsthetic when the knife cuts the flesh. He ran, bolted, across the room to the inner door and tugged at the handle. He struggled uselessly as if he were caught on barbed wire between trenches.

"Come away from there," Raven said. "You've locked the door."

Mr. Davis came back to his desk. His legs gave way and he sat on the ground beside the waste-paper basket. He said, "I'm sick. You wouldn't kill a sick man." The idea really gave him hope. He retched convincingly.

"I'm not going to kill you yet," Raven said. "Maybe I won't kill you if you keep quiet and do what I say. This Sir Marcus, he's your boss?"

"An old man," Mr. Davis protested, weeping beside the waste-paper basket.

"He wants to see you," Raven said. "We'll go along." He said, "I've been waiting days for this—to find the two of you. It almost seems too good to be true. Get up. Get up," he repeated furiously to the weak flabby figure on the floor.

Mr. Davis led the way. Miss Connett came down the passage carrying a slip of paper. She said, "I've got the trains, Mr. Davis. The best is the three-five. The two-seven is really so slow that you wouldn't be up more than ten minutes earlier. Then there's only the five-ten before the night train."

"Put them on my desk," Mr. Davis said. He hung about there in front of her in the shining modern plutocratic passage as if he wanted to say good-bye to a thousand things if only he had dared, to this wealth, this comfort, this authority; lingering there ("Yes, put them on my desk, May") he might even have been wanting to express at the last some tenderness that had never before entered his mind in connection with "little girls." Raven stood just behind him with his hand in his pocket. Her employer looked so sick that Miss Connett said, "Are you feeling well, Mr. Davis?"

"Quite well," Mr. Davis said. Like an explorer going into strange country he felt the need of leaving some record behind at the edge of civilisation, to say to the next chance comer, "I shall be found towards the north" or "the west." He said, "We are going to Sir Marcus, May."

"He's in a hurry for you," Miss Connett said. A telephone bell rang. "I shouldn't be surprised if that's him now." She pattered down the corridor to her room on very high heels and Mr. Davis felt again the remorseless pressure on his elbow to advance, to enter the lift. They rose another floor and when Mr. Davis pulled the gates apart he retched again. He wanted to fling himself to the floor and take the bullets in his back. The long gleaming passage to Sir Marcus's study was like a mile-long stadium track to a winded runner.

Sir Marcus was sitting in his Bath chair with a kind of bed-table on his knees. He had his valet with him and his back was to the door, but the valet could see with astonishment Mr. Davis's exhausted entrance in the company of a medical student in a gas-mask. "Is that Davis?" Sir Marcus whispered. He broke a dry biscuit and sipped a little hot milk. He was fortifying himself for a day's work.

"Yes, sir." The valet watched with astonishment Mr. Davis's sick progress across the hygienic rubber floor; he looked as if he needed support, as if he was about to collapse at the knees.

"Get out then," Sir Marcus whispered.

"Yes, sir." But the man in the gas-mask had turned the key of the door; a faint expression of joy, a rather hopeless expectation, crept into the valet's face as if he were wondering whether something at last was going to happen, something different from pushing Bath chairs along rubber floors, dressing and undressing an old man, not strong enough to keep himself clean, bringing him the hot milk or the hot water or the dry biscuits.

"What are you waiting for?" Sir Marcus whispered.

"Get back against the wall," Raven suddenly commanded the valet.

Mr. Davis cried despairingly, "He's got a gun. Do what he says." But there was no need to tell the valet that. The gun was out now and had them all three covered, the valet against the wall, Mr. Davis dithering in the middle of the room, Sir Marcus who had twisted the Bath chair round to face them.

"What do you want?" Sir Marcus said.

"Are you the boss?"

Sir Marcus said, "The police are downstairs. You can't get away from here unless I——" The telephone began to ring. It rang on and on and on, and then ceased.

Raven said, "You've got a scar under that beard, haven't you? I don't want to make a mistake. He had your photograph. You were in the home together," and he glared angrily round the large rich office room comparing it in mind with his own memories of cracked bells and stone stairs and wooden benches, and of the small flat too with the egg boiling on the ring. This man had moved further than the old Minister.

"You're mad," Sir Marcus whispered. He was too old to be frightened; the revolver represented no greater danger to him than a false step in getting into his chair, a slip in his bath. He seemed to feel only a faint irritation, a faint craving for his interrupted meal. He bent his old lip forward over the bed-table and sucked loudly at the rim of hot milk.

The valet suddenly spoke from the wall. "He's got a scar," he said. But Sir Marcus took no notice of any of them, sucking up his milk untidily over his thin beard.

Raven twisted his gun on Mr. Davis. "It was him," he said. "If you don't want a bullet in your guts tell me it was him."

"Yes, yes," Mr. Davis said in horrified subservient haste, "he thought of it. It was his idea. We were on our last legs here. We'd got to make money. It was worth more than half a million to him."

"Half a million!" Raven said. "And he paid me two hundred phoney pounds."

"I said to him we ought to be generous. He said: 'Stop your mouth.' "

"I wouldn't have done it," Raven said, "if I'd known the old man was like he was. I smashed his skull for him. And the old woman, a bullet in both eyes." He shouted at Sir Marcus, "That was your doing. How do you like that?" but the old man sat there apparently unmoved: old age had killed the imagination. The deaths he had ordered were no more real to him than the deaths he read about in the newspapers. A little greed (for his milk), a little vice (occasionally to put his old hand inside a girl's blouse and feel the warmth of life), a little avarice and calculation (half a million against a death), a very small persistent, almost mechanical, sense of self-preservation: these were his only passions. The last made him edge his chair imperceptibly towards the bell at the edge of his desk. He whispered gently, "I deny it all. You are mad."

Raven said, "I've got you now where I want you. Even if the police kill me," he tapped the gun, "here's my evidence. This is the gun I used. They can pin the murder to this gun. You told me to leave it behind, but here it is. It would put you away a long, long time even if I didn't shoot you."

Sir Marcus whispered gently, imperceptibly twisting his silent rubbered wheels, "A Colt No. 7. The factories turn out thousands."

Raven said angrily, "There's nothing the police can't do now with a gun. There are experts——" He wanted to frighten Sir Marcus before he shot him; it seemed unfair to him that Sir Marcus should suffer less than the old woman he hadn't wanted to kill. He said, "Don't you want to pray? You're a Jew, aren't you? Better people than you," he said, "believe in a God," remembering how the girl had prayed in the dark cold shed. The wheel of Sir Marcus's chair touched the desk, touched the bell, and the dull ringing came up the well of the lift, going on and on. It conveyed nothing to Raven until the valet spoke. "The old bastard," he said, with the hatred of years, "he's ringing the bell." Before Raven could decide what to do, someone was at the door, shaking the handle.

Raven said to Sir Marcus, "Tell them to keep back or I'll shoot."

"You fool," Sir Marcus whispered, "they'll only get you for theft. If you kill me, you'll hang." But Mr. Davis was ready to clutch at any straw. He screamed to the man outside, "Keep away. For God's sake keep away."

Sir Marcus said venomously, "You're a fool, Davis. If he's going to kill us anyway——" While Raven stood pistol in hand before the two men, an absurd quarrel broke out between them. "He's got no cause to kill me," Mr. Davis screamed. "It's you who've got us into this. I only acted for you."

The valet began to laugh. "Two to one on the field," he said.

"Be quiet," Sir Marcus whispered venomously back at Mr. Davis. "I can put you out of the way at any time."

"I defy you," Mr. Davis screamed in a high peacock voice. Somebody flung himself against the door.

"I have the West Rand Goldfields filed," Sir Marcus said, "the East African Petroleum Company."

A wave of impatience struck Raven. They seemed to be disturbing some memory of peace and goodness which had been on the point of returning to him when he had told Sir Marcus to pray. He raised his pistol and shot Sir Marcus in the chest. It was the only way to silence them. Sir Marcus fell forward across the bed-table, upsetting the glass of warm milk over the papers on his desk. Blood came out of his mouth.

Mr. Davis began to talk very rapidly. He said, "It was all him, the old devil. You heard him. What could I do? He had me. You've got nothing against me." He shrieked, "Go away from that door. He'll kill me if you don't go," and immediately began to talk again, while the milk dripped from the bed-table to the desk drop by drop. "I wouldn't have done a thing if it hadn't been for him. Do you know what he did? He went and told the Chief Constable to order the police to shoot you on sight." He tried not to look at the pistol which remained pointed at his chest. The valet was white and silent by the wall; he watched Sir Marcus's life bleeding away with curious fascination. So this was what it would have been like, he seemed to be thinking, if he himself had had courage . . . any time . . . during all these years.

A voice outside said, "You had better open this door at once or we'll shoot through it."

"For God's sake," Mr. Davis screamed, "leave me alone. He'll shoot me," and the eyes watched him intently through the panes of the gas-mask, with satisfaction. "There's not a thing I've done to you," he began to protest. Over Raven's head he could see the clock: it hadn't moved more than three hours since his breakfast, the hot stale taste of the kidneys and bacon was still on his palate: he couldn't believe that this was really the end: at one o'clock he had a date with a girl: you didn't die before a date. "Nothing," he murmured, "nothing at all."

"It was you," Raven said, "who tried to kill . . ."

"Nobody. Nothing," Mr. Davis moaned.

Raven hesitated. The word was still unfamiliar on his tongue. "My friend."

"I don't know. I don't understand."

"Keep back," Raven cried through the door, "I'll shoot him if you fire." He said, "The girl."

Mr. Davis shook all over. He was like a man with St. Vitus's dance. He said, "She wasn't a friend of yours. Why are the police here if she didn't . . . who else could have known . . . ?"

Raven said, "I'll shoot you for that and nothing else. She's straight."

"Why," Mr. Davis screamed at him, "she's a policeman's girl. She's the Yard man's girl. She's Mather's girl."

Raven shot him. With despair and deliberation he shot his last chance of escape, plugged two bullets in where one would do, as if he were shooting the whole world in the person of stout moaning bleeding Mr. Davis. And so he was. For a man's world is his life and he was shooting that: his mother's suicide, the long years in the home, the race-course gangs, Kite's death and the old man's and the woman's. There was no other way; he had tried the way of confession, and it had failed him for the usual reason. There was no one outside your own brain whom you could trust: not a doctor, not a priest, not a woman. A siren blew up over the town its message that the sham raid was over, and immediately the church bells broke into a noisy Christmas carol: the foxes have their holes, but the son of man. . . . A bullet smashed the lock of the door. Raven, with his gun pointed stomach-high, said, "Is there a bastard called Mather out there? He'd better keep away."

While he waited for the door to open he couldn't help remembering many things. He did not remember them in detail; they fogged together and formed the climate of his mind as he waited there for the chance of a last revenge: a voice singing above a dark street as the sleet fell: *They say that's a snowflower a man brought from Greenland*, the cultivated unlived voice of the elderly critic reading *Maud*:

Oh, that 'twere possible after long grief, while he stood in the garage and felt the ice melt at his heart with a sense of pain and strangeness. It was as if he were passing the customs of a land he had never entered before and would never be able to leave: the girl in the café saying, "He's bad and ugly . . .", the little plaster child lying in its mother's arms waiting the double-cross, the whips, the nails. She had said to him, "I'm your friend. You can trust me." Another bullet burst in the lock.

The valet, white-faced by the wall, said, "For God's sake, give it up. They'll get you anyway. He was right. It *was* the girl. I heard them on the 'phone."

I've got to be quick, Raven thought, when the door gives, I must shoot first. But too many ideas besieged his brain at once. He couldn't see clearly enough through the mask and he undid it clumsily with one hand and dropped it on the floor.

The valet could see now the raw inflamed lip, the dark and miserable eyes. He said, "There's the window. Get on to the roof." He was talking to a man whose understanding was dulled, who didn't know whether he wished to make an effort or not, who moved his face so slowly to see the window that it was the valet who noticed first the painter's platform swinging down the wide tall pane. Mather was on the platform, but the detective had not allowed for his own inexperience. The little platform swung this way and that; he held a rope with one hand and reached for the window with the other; he had no hand free for his revolver as Raven turned. He dangled outside the window six floors above the narrow Tanneries, a defenceless mark for Raven's pistol.

Raven watched him with bemused eyes, trying to take aim. It wasn't a difficult shot, but it was almost as if he had lost interest in killing. He was only aware of a pain and despair which was more like a complete weariness than anything else. He couldn't work up any sourness, any bitterness, at his betrayal. The dark Weevil under the storm of frozen rain flowed between him and any human enemy. *Ah, Christ! that it were possible,* but he had been marked from his birth for this end, to be betrayed in turn by everyone until every avenue into life was safely closed: by his mother bleeding in the basement, by the chaplain at the home, by the shady doctor off Charlotte Street. How could he have expected to have escaped the commonest betrayal of all: to go soft on a skirt? Even Kite would have been alive now if it hadn't been for a skirt. They all went soft at some time or another: Penrith and Carter, Jossy and Ballard, Barker and the Great Dane. He took aim slowly, absent-mindedly, with a curious humility, with almost a sense of companionship in his loneliness: the Trooper and Mayhew. They had all thought at one time or another that their skirt was better than other men's skirts, that there was something exalted in *their* relation. The only problem when you were once born was to get out of life more neatly and expeditiously than you had entered it. For the first time the idea of his mother's suicide came to him without bitterness, as he reluctantly fixed his aim and Saunders shot him in the back through the opening door. Death came to him in the form of unbearable pain. It was as if he had to deliver this pain as a woman delivers a child, and he sobbed and moaned in the effort. At last it came out of him and he followed his only child into a vast desolation.

i

The smell of food came through into the lounge whenever somebody passed in or out of the restaurant. The local Rotarians were having a lunch in one of the private rooms upstairs and when the door opened Ruby could hear a cork pop and the scrap of a limerick. It was five-past one. Ruby went out and chatted to the porter. She said, "The worst of it is I'm one of the girls who turn up on the stroke. One o'clock he said and here I am panting for a good meal. I know a girl ought to keep a man waiting, but what do you do if you're hungry? He might go in and start." She said, "The trouble is I'm unlucky. I'm the kind of girl who daren't have a bit of fun because she'd be dead sure to get a baby. Well, I don't mean I've had a baby, but I did catch mumps once. Would you believe a grown man could give a girl mumps? But I'm that kind of girl." She said, "You look fine in all that gold braid with those medals. You might say something."

The market was more than usually full, for everyone had come out late to do their last Christmas shopping now that the gas practice was over. Only Mrs. Alfred Piker, as Lady Mayoress, had set an example by shopping in a mask. Now she was walking home, and Chinky trotted beside her, trailing his low fur and the feathers on his legs in the cold slush, carrying her mask between his teeth. He stopped by a lamp-post and dropped it in a puddle. "O, Chinky, you bad little thing," Mrs. Piker said. The porter in his uniform glared out over the market. He wore the Mons medal and the Military Medal. He had been three times wounded. He swung the glass door as the business men came in for their lunch, the head traveller of Crosthwaite and Crosthwaite, the managing director of the big grocery business in the High Street. Once he darted out into the road and disentangled a fat man from a taxi. Then he came back and stood beside Ruby and listened to her with expressionless good humour.

"Ten minutes late," Ruby said, "I thought he was a man a girl could trust. I ought to have touched wood or crossed my fingers. It serves me right. I'd rather have lost my honour than that steak. Do you know him? He flings his weight about a lot. Called Davis."

"He's always in here with girls," the porter said.

A little man in pince-nez bustled by. "A Merry Christmas, Hallows."

"A Merry Christmas to you, sir." The porter said, "You wouldn't have got far with him."

"I haven't got as far as the soup," Ruby said.

A newsboy went by calling out a special midday edition of the *News*, the evening edition of the *Journal*, and a few minutes later another newsboy went past with a special edition of the *Post*, the evening edition of the more aristocratic *Guardian*. It was impossible to hear what they were shouting and the north-east wind flapped their posters, so that on one it was only possible to read the syllable ''—gedy' and on the other the syllable ''—der.''

"There are limits," Ruby said, "a girl can't afford to make herself cheap. Ten minutes' wait is the outside limit."

"You've waited more than that now," the porter said.

Ruby said, "I'm like that. You'd say I fling myself at men, wouldn't you? That's what I think, but I never seem to hit them." She added with deep gloom, "The trouble is I'm the kind that's born to make a man happy. It's written all over me. It keeps them away. I don't blame them. I shouldn't like it myself."

"There goes the Chief Constable," the porter said. "Off to get a drink at the police station. His wife won't let him have them at home. The best of the season to you, sir."

"He seems in a hurry." A newspaper poster flapped "Trag——" at them. "Is he the kind that would buy a girl a good rump steak with onions and fried potatoes?"

"I tell you what," the porter said. "You wait around another five minutes and then I shall be going off for lunch."

"That's a date," Ruby said. She crossed her fingers and touched wood. Then she went and sat inside and carried on a long conversation with an imaginary theatrical producer whom she imagined rather like Mr. Davis, but a Mr. Davis who kept his engagements. The producer called her a little woman with talent, asked her to dinner, took her back to a luxurious flat and gave her several cocktails. He asked her what she would think of a West-End engagement at fifteen pounds a week and said he wanted to show her his flat. Ruby's dark plump gloomy face lightened; she swung one leg excitedly and attracted the angry attention of a business man who was making notes of the midday prices. He found another chair and muttered to himself. Ruby, too, muttered to herself. She was saying, "This is the dining-room. And through there is the bathroom. And this—elegant, isn't it?—is the bedroom." Ruby said promptly that she'd like the fifteen pounds a week, but need she have the West-End engagement? Then she looked at the clock and went outside. The porter was waiting for her.

"What?" Ruby said. "Have I got to go out with that uniform?"

"I only get twenty minutes," the porter said.

"No rump steak then," Ruby said. "Well, I suppose sausages would do."

They sat at a lunch counter on the other side of the market and had sausages and coffee. "That uniform," Ruby said, "makes me embarrassed. Everyone'll think you're a guardsman going with a girl for a change."

"Did you hear the shooting?" the man behind the counter said.

"What shooting?"

"Just round the corner from you at Midland Steel. Three dead. That old devil Sir Marcus, and two others." He laid the midday paper open on the counter, and the old wicked face of Sir Marcus, the plump anxious features of Mr. Davis, stared up at them beyond the sausages, the coffee cups, the pepper-pot, beside the hot-water urn. "So that's why he didn't come," Ruby said. She was silent for a while reading.

"I wonder what this Raven was after," the porter said. "Look here," and he pointed to a small paragraph at the foot of the column which announced that the head of the special political department of Scotland Yard had arrived by air and gone straight to the offices of Midland Steel. "It doesn't mean a thing to me," Ruby said.

The porter turned the pages looking for something. He said, "Funny thing, isn't it? Here we are just going to war again, and they fill up the front page with a murder. It's driven the war on to a back page."

"Perhaps there won't be a war."

They were silent over their sausages. It seemed odd to Ruby that Mr. Davis, who had sat on the box with her and looked at the Christmas tree, should be dead, so violently and painfully dead. Perhaps he had meant to keep the date. He wasn't a bad sort. She said, "I feel sort of sorry for him."

"Who? Raven?"

"Oh no, not him. Mr. Davis, I mean."

"I know how you feel. I almost feel sorry too—for the old man. I was in Midland Steel myself once. He had his moments. He used to send round turkeys at Christmas. He wasn't too bad. It's more than they do at the hotel."

"Well," Ruby said, draining her coffee, "life goes on."

"Have another cup."

"I don't want to sting you."

"That's all right." Ruby leant against him on the high stool; their heads touched; they were a little quietened because each had known a man who was suddenly dead, but the knowledge they shared gave them a sense of companionship which was oddly sweet and reassuring. It was like feeling safe, like feeling in love without the passion, the uncertainty, the pain.

ii

Saunders asked a clerk in Midland Steel the way to a lavatory. He washed his hands and thought, "That job's over." It hadn't been a satisfactory job; what had begun as a plain robbery had ended with two murders and the death of the murderer. There was a mystery about the whole affair; everything hadn't come out. Mather was up there on the top floor now with the head of the political department; they were going through Sir Marcus's private papers. It really seemed as if the girl's story might be true.

The girl worried Saunders more than anything. He couldn't help admiring her courage and impertinence at the same time as he hated her for making Mather suffer. He was ready to hate anyone who hurt Mather. "She'll have to be taken to the Yard," Mather said. "There may be a charge against her. Put her in a locked carriage on the three-five. I don't want to see her until this thing's cleared up." The only cheerful thing about the whole business was that the constable whom Raven had shot in the coal-yard was pulling through.

Saunders came out of Midland Steel into the Tanneries with an odd sensation of having nothing to do. He went into a public-house at the corner of the market and had half a pint of bitter and two cold sausages. It was as if life had sunk again to the normal level, was flowing quietly by once more between its banks. A card hanging behind the bar next a few cinema posters caught his eye. "A New Cure for Stammerers." Mr. Montague Phelps, M.A., was holding a public meeting in the Masonic Hall to explain his new treatment. Entrance was free, but there would be a silver collection. Two o'clock sharp. At one cinema Eddie Cantor. At another George Arliss. Saunders didn't want to go back to the police station until it was time to take the girl to the train. He had tried a good many cures for stammering; he might as well try one more.

It was a large hall. On the walls hung large photographs of masonic dignitaries. They all wore ribbons and badges of strange significance. There was an air of oppressive well-being, of successful groceries, about the photographs. They hung, the well-fed, the successful, the assured, over the small gathering of misfits, in old mackintoshes, in rather faded mauve felt hats, in school ties. Saunders entered behind a fat furtive woman and a steward stammered at him, "T-t-t——?" "One," Saunders said. He sat down near the front and heard a stammered conversation going on behind him, like the twitters of two Chinamen. Little bursts of impetuous talk and then the fatal impediment. There were about fifty people in the hall. They eyed each other rather as an ugly man eyes himself in shop windows: from this angle, he thinks, I am really not too bad. They gained a sense of companionship; their mutual lack of communication was in itself like a communication. They waited together for a miracle.

Saunders waited with them: waited as he had waited on the windless side of the coal truck, with the same patience. He wasn't unhappy. He knew that he probably exaggerated the value of what he lacked; even if he could speak freely, without care to avoid the dentals which betrayed him, he would probably find it no easier to express his admiration and his affection. The power to speak didn't give you words.

Mr. Montague Phelps, M.A., came on to the platform. He wore a frock-coat and his hair was dark and oiled. His blue chin was lightly powdered and he carried himself with a rather aggressive sangfroid, as much as to say to the depressed inhibited gathering, "See what you too might become with a little more self-confidence, after a few lessons from me." He was a man of about forty-two who had lived well, who obviously had a private life. One thought in his presence of comfortable beds and heavy meals and Brighton hotels. For a moment he reminded Saunders of Mr. Davis who had bustled so importantly into the offices of Midland Steel that morning and had died very painfully and suddenly half an hour later. It almost seemed as if Raven's act had had no consequences: as if to kill was just as much an illusion as to dream. Here was Mr. Davis all over again; they were turned out of a mould, and you couldn't break the mould, and suddenly over Mr. Montague Phelps's shoulder Saunders saw the photograph of the Grand Master of the Lodge, above the platform: an old face and a crooked nose and a tuft of beard, Sir Marcus.

iii

Major Calkin was very white when he left Midland Steel. He had seen for the first time the effect of violent death. That was war. He made his way as quickly as he could to the police station and was glad to find the superintendent in. He asked quite humbly for a spot of whisky. He said, "It shakes you up. Only last night he had dinner at my house. Mrs. Piker was there with her dog. What a time we had stopping him knowing the dog was there."

"That dog," the superintendent said, "gives us more trouble than any man in Nottwich. Did I ever tell you the time it got in the women's lavatory in Higham Street? That dog isn't much to look at, but every once in a while it goes crazy. If it wasn't Mrs. Piker's we'd have had it destroyed many a time."

Major Calkin said, "He wanted me to give orders to your men to shoot this fellow on sight. I told him I couldn't. Now I can't help thinking we might have saved two lives."

"Don't you worry, sir," the superintendent said, "we couldn't have taken orders like that. Not from the Home Secretary himself."

"He was an odd fellow," Major Calkin said. "He seemed to think I'd be certain to have a hold over some of you. He promised me all kinds of things. I suppose he was what you'd call a genius. We shan't see his like again. What a waste." He poured himself out some more whisky. "Just at a time, too, when we need men like him. War——" Major Calkin paused with his hand on his glass. He stared into the whisky, seeing things, the remount depot, his uniform in the cupboard. He would never be a colonel now, but on the other hand Sir Marcus could not prevent . . . but curiously he felt no elation at the thought of once more presiding over the tribunal. He said, "The gas practice seems to have gone off well. But I don't know that it was wise to leave so much to the medical students. They don't know where to stop."

"There was a pack of them," the superintendent said, "went howling past here looking for the Mayor. I don't know how it is Mr. Piker seems to be like catmint to those students."

"Good old Piker," Major Calkin said mechanically.

"They go too far," the superintendent said. "I had a ring from Higginbotham, the cashier at the Westminister. He said his daughter went into the garage and found one of the students there without his trousers."

Life began to come back to Major Calkin. He said, "That'll be Rose Higginbotham, I suppose. Trust Rose. What did she do?"

"He said she gave him a dressing down."

"Dressing down's good," Major Calkin said. He twisted his glass and drained his whisky. "I must tell that to old Piker. What did you say?"

"I told him his daughter was lucky not to find a murdered man in the garage. You see that's where Raven must have got his clothes and his mask."

"What was the boy doing at the Higginbothams' anyway?" Major Calkin said. "I think I'll go and cash a cheque and ask old Higginbotham that." He began to laugh; the air was clear again; life was going on quite in the old way: a little scandal, a drink with the super, a story to tell old Piker. On his way to the Westminster he nearly ran into Mrs. Piker. He had to dive hastily into a shop to avoid her, and for a horrible moment he thought Chinky, who was some way ahead of her, was going to follow him inside. He made motions of throwing a ball down the street, but Chinky was not a sporting dog and anyway he was trailing a gas-mask in his teeth. Major Calkin had to turn his back abruptly and lean over a counter. He found it was a small haberdasher's. He had never been in the shop before. "What can I get you, sir?"

"Suspenders," Major Calkin said desperately. "A pair of suspenders."

"What colour, sir?" Out of the corner of his eye Major Calkin saw Chinky trot on past the shop door followed by Mrs. Piker. "Mauve," he said with relief.

iv

The old woman shut the front door softly and trod on tiptoe down the little dark hall. A stranger could not have seen his way, but she knew exactly the position of the hat rack, of the what-not table, and the staircase. She was carrying an evening paper, and when she opened the kitchen door with the very minimum of noise so as not to disturb Acky, her face was alight with exhilaration and excitement. But she held it in, carrying her basket over to the draining board and unloading there her burden of potatoes, a tin of pineapple chunks, two eggs and a slab of cod.

Acky was writing a long letter on the kitchen table. He had pushed his wife's mauve ink to one side and was using the best blue-black and a fountain pen which had long ceased to hold ink. He wrote slowly and painfully, sometimes making a rough copy of a sentence on another slip of paper. The old woman stood beside the sink watching him, waiting for him to speak, holding her breath in, so that sometimes it escaped in little whistles. At last Acky laid down his pen. "Well, my dear?" he said.

"Oh, Acky," the old woman said with glee, "what do you think? Mr. Cholmondeley's dead. Killed." She added, "It's in the paper. And that Raven too."

Acky looked at the paper. "Quite horrible," he said with satisfaction. "Another death as well. A holocaust." He read the account slowly.

"Fancy a thing like that 'appening 'ere in Nottwich."

"He was a bad man," Acky said, "though I wouldn't speak ill of him now that he's dead. He involved us in something of which I was ashamed. I think perhaps now it will be safe for us to stay in Nottwich." A look of great weariness passed over his face as he looked down at the three pages of small neat classical handwriting.

"Oh, Acky, you've been tiring yourself."

"I think," Acky said, "this will make everything clear."

"Read it to me, love," the old woman said. Her little old vicious face was heavily creased with tenderness as she leant back against the sink in an attitude of infinite patience. Acky began to read. He spoke at first in a low hesitating way, but he gained confidence from the sound of his own voice, his hand went up to the lapel of his coat. " 'My lord bishop' . . ." He said, "I thought it best to begin formally, not to trespass at all on my former acquaintanceship."

"That's right, Acky, you are worth the whole bunch."

" 'I am writing to you for the fourth time . . . after an interval of some eighteen months.' "

"Is it so long, love? It was after we took the trip to Clacton."

" 'Sixteen months . . . I am quite aware what your previous answers have been, that my case has been tried already in the proper Church Court, but I cannot believe, my lord bishop, that your sense of justice, if once I convince you of what a deeply injured man I am, will not lead you to do all that is in your power to have my case reheard. I have been condemned to suffer all my life for what in the case of other men is regarded as a peccadillo, a peccadillo of which I am not even guilty.' "

"It's written lovely, love."

"At this point, my dear, I come down to particulars. 'How, my lord bishop, could the hotel domestic swear to the identity of a man seen once, a year before the trial, in a darkened chamber, for in her evidence she agreed that he had not allowed her to draw up the blind? As for the evidence of the porter, my lord bishop, I asked in court whether it was not true that money had passed from Colonel and Mrs. Mark Egerton into his hands, and my question was disallowed. Is this justice, founded on scandal, misapprehension, and perjury?' "

The old woman smiled with tenderness and pride. "This is the best letter you've written, Acky, so far."

" 'My lord bishop, it was well known in the parish that Colonel Mark Egerton was my bitterest enemy on the church council, and it was at his instigation that the inquiry was held. As for Mrs. Mark Egerton she was a bitch.' "

"Is that wise, Acky?"

"Sometimes, dear, one reaches an impasse, when there is nothing to be done but to speak out. At this point I take the evidence in detail as I have done before, but I think I have sharpened my arguments more than a little. And at the end, my dear, I address the worldly man in the only way he can understand." He knew this passage off by heart; he reeled it fierily off at her, raising his crazy sunken flawed saint's eyes. " 'But even assuming, my lord bishop, that this perjured and bribed evidence were accurate, what then? Have I committed the unforgivable sin that I must suffer all my life long, be deprived of my livelihood, depend on ignoble methods to raise enough money to keep myself and my wife alive? Man, my lord bishop, and no one knows it better than yourself—I have seen you among the flesh-pots at the palace—is made up of body as well as soul. A little carnality may be forgiven even to a man of my cloth. Even you, my lord bishop, have in your time no doubt sported among the haycocks.' " He stopped, he was a little out of breath; they stared back at each other with awe and affection.

Acky said, "I want to write a little piece, dear, now about you." He took in with what could only have been the deepest and purest love the black sagging skirt, the soiled blouse, the yellow wrinkled face. "My dear," he said, "what I should have done without——'' He began to make a rough draft of yet another paragraph, speaking the phrases aloud as he wrote them. '' 'What I should have done during this long trial—no, martyrdom—I do not know—I cannot conceive—if I had not been supported by the trust and the unswerving fidelity—no, fidelity and unswerving trust of my dear wife, a wife whom Mrs. Mark Egerton considered herself in a position to despise. As if Our Lord had chosen the rich and well-born to serve him. At least this trial—has taught me to distinguish between my friends and enemies. And yet at my trial *her* word, the word of the woman who loved and believed in me, counted—for nought beside the word—of that—that—trumpery and deceitful scandal-monger.' ''

The old woman leant forward with tears of pride and importance in her eyes. She said, ''That's lovely. Do you think the bishop's wife will read it? Oh, dear, I know I ought to go and tidy the room upstairs (we might be getting some young people in), but some'ow, Acky dear, I'd just like to stay right 'ere with you awhile. What you write makes me feel kind of 'oly.'' She slumped down on the kitchen chair beside the sink and watched his hand move on, as if she were watching some unbelievably lovely vision passing through the room, something which she had never hoped to see and now was hers. ''And finally, my dear,'' Acky said, ''I propose to write: 'In a world of perjury and all manner of uncharitableness one woman remains my sheet anchor, one woman I can trust until death and beyond.' ''

''They ought to be ashamed of themselves. Oh, Acky, my dear,'' she wept, ''to think they've treated you that way. But you've said true. I won't ever leave you. I won't leave you, not even when I'm dead. Never, never, never,'' and the two old vicious faces regarded each other with the complete belief, the awe and mutual suffering of a great love, while they affirmed their eternal union.

v

Anne cautiously felt the door of the compartment in which she had been left alone. It was locked, as she had thought it would be in spite of Saunders's tact and his attempt to hide what he was doing. She stared out at the dingy Midland station with dismay. It seemed to her that everything which made her life worth the effort of living was lost; she hadn't even got a job, and she watched, past an advertisement of Horlick's for night starvation and a bright blue-and-yellow picture of the York-shire coast, the weary pilgrimage which lay before her from agent to agent. The train began to move by the waiting-rooms, the lavatories, the sloping concrete into a waste of rails.

What a fool, she thought, I have been, thinking I could save us from a war. Three men are dead, that's all. Now that she was herself responsible for so many deaths, she could no longer feel the same repulsion towards Raven. In this waste through which she travelled, between the stacks of coal, the tumbledown sheds, abandoned trucks in sidings where a little grass had poked up and died between the cinders, she thought of him again with pity and distress. They had been on the same side, he had trusted her, she had given her word to him, and then she had broken it without even the grace of hesitation. He must have known of her treachery before he died: in that dead mind she was preserved for ever with the chaplain who had tried to frame him, with the doctor who had telephoned to the police.

Well, she had lost the only man she cared a damn about: it was always regarded as some kind of atonement, she thought, to suffer too: lost him for no reason at all. For *she* couldn't stop a war. Men were fighting beasts, they needed war; in the paper that Saunders had left for her on the opposite seat she could read how the mobilisation in four countries was complete, how the ultimatum expired at midnight; it was no longer on the front page, but that was only because to Nottwich readers there was a war nearer at hand, fought out to a finish in the Tanneries. How they love it, she thought bitterly, as the dusk came up from the dark wounded ground and the glow of furnaces became visible beyond the long black ridge of slag-heaps. This was war too: this chaos through which the train moved slowly, grinding over point after point like a dying creature dragging itself painfully away through No-Man's Land from the scene of battle.

She pressed her face against the window to keep her tears away: the cold pressure of the frosting pane stiffened her resistance. The train gathered speed by a small neo-Gothic church, a row of villas, and then the country, the fields, a few cows making for an open gate, a hard broken lane and a cyclist lighting his lamp. She began to hum to keep her spirits up, but the only tunes she could remember were "Aladdin" and "It's only Kew." She thought of the long bus-ride home, the voice on the telephone, and how she couldn't get to the window to wave to him and he had stood there with his back to her while the train went by. It was Mr. Davis even then who had ruined everything.

And it occurred to her, staring out at the bleak frozen countryside, that perhaps even if she had been able to save the country from a war, it wouldn't have been worth the saving. She thought of Mr. Davis and Acky and his old wife, of the producer and Miss Maydew and the landlady at her lodging with the bead of liquid on her nose. What had made her play so absurd a part? If she had not offered to go out to dinner with Mr. Davis, Raven probably would be in gaol and the others alive. She tried to remember the watching anxious faces studying the sky-signs in Nottwich High Street, but she couldn't remember them with any vividness.

The door into the corridor was unlocked and staring through the window into the grey fading winter light she thought: more questions. Will they never stop worrying me? She said aloud, "I've made my statement, haven't I?"

Mather's voice said, "There are still a few things to discuss."

She turned hopelessly towards him. "Need *you* have come?"

"I'm in charge of this case," Mather said, sitting down opposite to her with his back to the engine, watching the country which she could see approach flow backwards over her shoulder and disappear. He said, "We've been checking what you told us. It's a strange story."

"It's true," she repeated wearily.

He said: "We've had half the Embassies in London on the 'phone. Not to speak of Geneva. And the Commissioner."

She said with a flicker of malice, "I'm sorry you've been troubled." But she couldn't keep it up; her formal indifference was ruined by his presence, the large clumsy, once friendly hand, the bulk of the man. "Oh, I'm sorry," she said. "I've said it before, haven't I? I'd say it if I'd spilt your coffee, and I've got to say it after all these people are killed. There are no other words, are there, which mean more? It all worked out wrong; I thought everything was clear. I've failed. I didn't mean to hurt you ever. I suppose the Commissioner . . ." She began to cry without tears; it was as if those ducts were frozen.

He said, "I'm to have promotion. I don't know why. It seems to me as if I'd bungled it." He added gently and pleadingly, leaning forward across the compartment, "We could get married—at once—though I dare say you don't want to now, you'll do all right. They'll give you a grant."

It was like going into the manager's office expecting dismissal and getting a rise instead—or a speaking part, but it never had happened that way. She stared silently back at him.

"Of course," he said gloomily, "you'll be the rage now. You'll have stopped a war. I know I didn't believe you. I've failed. I thought I'd always trust—— We've found enough already to prove what you told me and I thought was lies. They'll have to withdraw their ultimatum now. They won't have any choice." He added with a deep hatred of publicity, "It'll be the sensation of a century," sitting back with his face heavy and sad.

"You mean," she said with incredulity, "that when we get in—we can go off straight away and be married?"

"Will you?"

She said, "The taxi won't be fast enough."

"It won't be as quick as all that. It takes three weeks. We can't afford a special licence."

She said, "Didn't you tell me about a grant? I'll blow it on the licence," and suddenly as they both laughed it was as if the past three days left the carriage, were whirled backward down the metals to Nottwich. It had all happened there, and they need never go back to the scene of it. Only a shade of disquiet remained, a fading spectre of Raven. If his immortality was to be on the lips of living men, he was fighting now his last losing fight against extinction.

"All the same," Anne said, as Raven covered her with his sack: Raven touched her icy hand, "I failed."

"Failed?" Mather said. "You've been the biggest success," and it seemed to Anne for a few moments that this sense of failure would never die from her brain, that it would cloud a little every happiness; it was something she could never explain: her lover would never understand it. But already as his face lost its gloom, she was failing again—failing to atone. The cloud was blown away by his voice; it evaporated under his large and clumsy and tender hand.

"Such a success." He was as inarticulate as Saunders, now that he was realising what it meant. It was worth a little publicity. This darkening land, flowing backwards down the line, was safe for a few more years. He was a countryman, and he didn't ask for more than a few years' safety at a time for something he so dearly loved. The precariousness of its safety made it only the more precious. Somebody was burning winter weeds under a hedge, and down a dark lane a farmer rode home alone from the hunt in a queer old-fashioned bowler hat on a horse that would never take a ditch. A small lit village came up beside his window and sailed away like a pleasure steamer hung with lanterns; he had just time to notice the grey English church squatted among the yews and graves, the thick deaths of centuries, like an old dog who will not leave his corner. On the wooden platform as they whirled by a porter was reading the label on a Christmas tree.

"You haven't failed," he said.

London had its roots in her heart: she saw nothing in the dark countryside, she looked away from it to Mather's happy face. "You don't understand," she said, sheltering the ghost for a very short while longer, "I *did* fail." But she forgot it herself completely when the train drew in to London over a great viaduct under which the small bright shabby streets ran off like the rays of a star with their sweet shops, their Methodist chapels, their messages chalked on the paving stones. Then it was she who thought: this is safe, and wiping the glass free from steam, she pressed her face against the pane and happily and avidly and tenderly watched, like a child whose mother has died watches the family *she* must rear without being aware at all that the responsibility is too great. A mob of children went screaming down a street, she could tell they screamed because she was one of them, she couldn't hear their voices or see their mouths; a man was selling hot chestnuts at a corner, and it was on *her* face that his little fire glowed, the sweet shops were full of white gauze stockings crammed with cheap gifts. "Oh," she said with a sigh of unshadowed happiness, "we're home."

The Ministry of Fear

BOOK ONE

The Unhappy Man

1

The Free Mothers

"None passes without warrant."
THE LITTLE DUKE

i

There was something about a fête which drew Arthur Rowe irresistibly, bound him a helpless victim to the distant blare of a band and the knock-knock of wooden balls against coconuts. Of course this year there were no coconuts because there was a war on: you could tell that too from the untidy gaps between the Bloomsbury houses—a flat fireplace half-way up a wall, like the painted fireplace in a cheap dolls' house, and lots of mirrors and green wall-papers, and from round a corner of the sunny afternoon the sound of glass being swept up, like the lazy noise of the sea on a shingled beach. Otherwise the square was doing its very best with the flags of the free nations and a mass of bunting which had obviously been preserved by somebody ever since the Jubilee.

Arthur Rowe looked wistfully over the railings—there were still railings. The fête called him like innocence: it was entangled in childhood, with vicarage gardens and girls in white summer frocks and the smell of herbaceous borders and security. He had no inclination to mock at these elaborately naïve ways of making money for a cause. There was the inevitable clergyman presiding over a rather timid game of chance; an old lady in a print dress that came down to her ankles and a floppy garden hat hovered officially, but with excitement, over a treasure-hunt (a little plot of ground like a child's garden was staked out with claims), and as the evening darkened—they would have to close early because of the blackout—there would be some energetic work with trowels. And there in a corner, under a plane tree, was the fortune-teller's booth—unless it was an impromptu outside lavatory. It all seemed perfect in the late summer Sunday afternoon. "My peace I give unto you. Not as the world knoweth peace . . ." Arthur Rowe's eyes filled with tears, as the small military band they had somehow managed to borrow struck up again a faded song of the last war: *Whate'er befall I'll oft recall that sunlit mountainside.*

Pacing round the railings he came towards his doom: pennies were rattling down a curved slope on to a chequer-board—not very many pennies. The fête was ill-attended; there were only three stalls and people avoided those. If they had to spend money they would rather try for a dividend—of pennies from the chequer-board or savings-stamps from the treasure-hunt. Arthur Rowe came along the railings, hesitantly, like an intruder, or an exile who has returned home after many years and is uncertain of his welcome.

He was a tall stooping lean man with black hair going grey and a sharp narrow face, nose a little twisted out of the straight and a too sensitive mouth. His clothes were good but gave the impression of being uncared for; you would have said a bachelor if it had not been for an indefinable married look . . .

"The charge," said the middle-aged lady at the gate, "is a shilling, but that doesn't seem quite fair. If you wait another five minutes you can come in at the reduced rate. I always feel it's only right to warn people when it gets as late as this."

"It's very thoughtful of you."

"We don't want people to feel cheated—even in a good cause, do we?"

"I don't think I'll wait, all the same. I'll come straight in. What exactly is the cause?"

"Comforts for free mothers—I mean mothers of the free nations."

Arthur Rowe stepped joyfully back into adolescence, into childhood. There had always been a fête about this time of the year in the vicarage garden, a little way off the Trumpington Road, with the flat Cambridgeshire field beyond the extemporised bandstand, and at the end of the fields the pollarded willows by the stickleback stream and the chalk-pit on the slopes of what in Cambridgeshire they call a hill. He came to these fêtes every year with an odd feeling of excitement—as if anything might happen, as if the familiar pattern of life that afternoon might be altered forever. The band beat in the warm late sunlight, the brass quivered like haze, and the faces of strange young women would get mixed up with Mrs. Troup, who kept the general store and post office, Miss Savage the Sunday School teacher, the publicans' and the clergy's wives. When he was a child he would follow his mother round the stalls—the baby clothes, the pink woollies, the art pottery, and always last and best the white elephants. It was always as though there might be discovered on the white elephant stall some magic ring which would give three wishes or the heart's desire, but the odd thing was that when he went home that night with only a second-hand copy of *The Little Duke*, by Charlotte M. Yonge, or an out-of-date atlas advertising Mazawattee tea, he felt no disappointment: he carried with him the sound of brass, the sense of glory, of a future that would be braver than to-day. In adolescence the excitement had a different source; he imagined he might find at the vicarage some girl whom he had never seen before, and courage would touch his tongue, and in the late evening there would be dancing on the lawn and the smell of stocks. But because these dreams had never come true there remained the sense of innocence. . . .

And the sense of excitement. He couldn't believe that when he had passed the gate and reached the grass under the plane trees nothing would happen, though now it wasn't a girl he wanted or a magic ring, but something far less likely—to mislay the events of twenty years. His heart beat and the band played, and inside the lean experienced skull lay childhood.

"Come and try your luck, sir?" said the clergyman in a voice which was obviously baritone at socials.

"If I could have some coppers."

"Thirteen for a shilling, sir."

Arthur Rowe slid the pennies one after the other down the little inclined groove and watched them stagger on the board.

"Not your lucky day, sir, I'm afraid. What about another shilling's-worth? Another little flutter in a good cause?"

"I think perhaps I'll flutter further on." His mother, he remembered, had always fluttered further on, carefully dividing her patronage in equal parts, though she left the coconuts and the gambling to the children. At some stalls it had been very difficult to find anything at all, even to give away to the servants. . . .

Under a little awning there was a cake on a stand surrounded by a small group of enthusiastic sightseers. A lady was explaining, "We clubbed our butter rations —and Mr. Tatham was able to get hold of the currants."

She turned to Arthur Rowe and said, "Won't you take a ticket and guess its weight?"

He lifted it and said at random, "Three pounds five ounces."

"A very good guess, I should say. Your wife must have been teaching you."

He winced away from the group. "Oh no, I'm not married."

War had made the stall-holders' task extraordinarily difficult: second-hand Penguins for the Forces filled most of one stall, while another was sprinkled rather than filled with the strangest second-hand clothes—the cast-offs of old age—long petticoats with pockets, high lacy collars with bone supports, routed out of Edwardian drawers and discarded at last for the sake of the free mothers, and corsets that clanked. Baby clothes played only a very small part now that wool was rationed and the second-hand was so much in demand among friends. The third stall was the traditional one—the white elephant—though black might have described it better since many Anglo-Indian families had surrendered their collections of ebony elephants. There were also brass ash-trays, embroidered match-cases which had not held matches now for a very long time, books too shabby for the bookstall, two post-card albums, a complete set of Dickens cigarette-cards, an electro-plated egg-boiler, a long pink cigarette-holder, several embossed boxes for pins from Benares, a signed post-card of Mrs. Winston Churchill, and a plateful of mixed foreign copper coins. . . . Arthur Rowe turned over the books and found with an ache of the heart a dingy copy of *The Little Duke*. He paid sixpence for it and walked on. There was something threatening, it seemed to him, in the very perfection of the day. Between the plane trees which shaded the treasure-ground he could see the ruined section of the square; it was as if Providence had led him to exactly this point to indicate the difference between then and now. These people might have been playing a part in an expensive morality for his sole benefit. . . .

He couldn't, of course, not take part in the treasure-hunt, though it was a sad declension to know the nature of the prize, and afterwards there remained nothing of consequence but the fortune-teller—it was a fortune-teller's booth and not a lavatory. A curtain made of a cloth brought home by somebody from Algiers dangled at the entrance. A lady caught his arm and said, "You must. You really must. Mrs. Bellairs is quite wonderful. She told my son . . ." and clutching another middle-aged lady as she went by, she went breathlessly on, "I was just telling this gentleman about wonderful Mrs. Bellairs and my son."

"Your younger son?"

"Yes. Jack."

The interruption enabled Rowe to escape. The sun was going down: the square garden was emptying: it was nearly time to dig up the treasure and make tracks, before darkness and blackout and siren-time. So many fortunes one had listened to, behind a country hedge, over the cards in a liner's saloon, but the fascination remained even when the fortune was cast by an amateur at a garden fête. Always, for a little while, one could half-believe in the journey overseas, in the strange dark woman, and the letter with good news. Once somebody had refused to tell his fortune at all—it was just an act, of course, put on to impress him—and yet that silence had really come closer to the truth than anything else.

He lifted the curtain and felt his way in.

It was very dark inside the tent, and he could hardly distinguish Mrs. Bellairs, a bulky figure shrouded in what looked like cast-off widow's weeds—or perhaps it was some kind of peasant's costume. He was unprepared for Mrs. Bellairs' deep powerful voice: a convincing voice. He had expected the wavering tones of a lady whose other hobby was water-colours.

"Sit down, please, and cross my hand with silver."

"It's so dark."

But now he could just manage to make her out: it was a peasant's costume with a big head-dress and a veil of some kind tucked back over her shoulder. He found a half-crown and sketched a cross upon her palm.

"Your hand."

He held it out and felt it gripped firmly as though she intended to convey: expect no mercy. A tiny electric nightlight was reflected down on the girdle of Venus, the little crosses which should have meant children, the long, long line of life. . . .

He said, "You're up-to-date. The electric nightlight, I mean."

She paid no attention to his flippancy. She said, "First the character, then the past: by law I am not allowed to tell the future. You're a man of determination and imagination and you are very sensitive—to pain, but you sometimes feel you have not been allowed a proper scope for your gifts. You want to do great deeds, not dream them all day long. Never mind. After all, you have made one woman happy."

He tried to take his hand away, but she held it too firmly: it would have been a tug of war. She said, "You have found the true contentment in a happy marriage. Try to be more patient, though. Now I will tell you your past."

He said quickly, "Don't tell me the past. Tell me the future."

It was as if he had pressed a button and stopped a machine. The silence was odd and unexpected. He hadn't hoped to silence her, though he dreaded what she might say, for even inaccuracies about things which are dead can be as painful as the truth. He pulled his hand again and it came away. He felt awkward sitting there with his hand his own again.

Mrs. Bellairs said, "My instructions are these. What you want is the cake. You must give the weight as four pounds eight and a half ounces."

"Is that the right weight?"

"That's immaterial."

He was thinking hard and staring at Mrs. Bellairs' left hand which the light caught: a square ugly palm with short blunt fingers prickly with big art-and-crafty rings of silver and lumps of stone. Who had given her instructions? Did she refer to her familiar spirits? And if so, why had she chosen him to win the cake? or was it really just a guess of her own? Perhaps she was backing a great number of weights, he thought, smiling in the dark, and expected at least a slice from the winner. Cake, good cake, was scarce nowadays.

"You can go now," Mrs. Bellairs said.

"Thank you very much."

At any rate, Arthur Rowe thought, there was no harm in trying the tip—she might have stable information, and he returned to the cake-stall. Although the garden was nearly empty now except for the helpers, a little knot of people always surrounded the cake, and indeed it was a magnificent cake. He had always liked cakes, especially rich Dundees and dark brown home-made fruit-cakes tasting elusively of Guinness. He said to the lady at the stall, "You won't think me greedy if I have another sixpennyworth?"

"No. Please."

"I should say, then, four pounds eight and a half ounces."

He was conscious of an odd silence, as if all the afternoon they had been waiting for just this, but hadn't somehow expected it from him. Then a stout woman who hovered on the outskirts gave a warm and hearty laugh. "Lawks," she said. "Anybody can tell you're a bachelor."

"As a matter of fact," the lady behind the stall rebuked her sharply, "this gentleman has won. He is not more than a fraction of an ounce out. That counts," she said, with nervous whimsicality, "as a direct hit."

"Four pounds eight ounces," the stout woman said. "Well, you be careful, that's all. It'll be as heavy as lead."

"On the contrary, it's made with real eggs."

The stout woman went away laughing ironically in the direction of the clothing stall.

Again he was aware of the odd silence as the cake was handed over: they all came round and watched—three middle-aged ladies, the clergyman who had deserted the chequer-board, and looking up Rowe saw the gypsy's curtain lifted and Mrs. Bellairs peering out at him. He would have welcomed the laughter of the stout outsider as something normal and relaxed: there was such an intensity about these people as though they were attending the main ceremony of the afternoon. It was as if the experience of childhood renewed had taken a strange turn, away from innocence. There had never been anything quite like this in Cambridgeshire. It was dusk and the stall-holders were ready to pack up. The stout woman sailed towards the gates carrying a corset (no paper wrappings allowed). Arthur Rowe said, "Thank you. Thank you very much." He felt so conscious of being surrounded that he wondered whether anyone would step aside and let him out. Of course the clergyman did, laying a hand upon his upper arm and squeezing gently. "Good fellow," he said, "good fellow."

The treasure-hunt was being hastily concluded, but this time there was nothing for Arthur Rowe. He stood with his cake and *The Little Duke* and watched. "We've left it very late, very late," the lady wailed beneath her floppy hat.

But late as it was, somebody had thought it worth while to pay for entrance at the gate. A taxi had driven up, and a man made hastily for the gypsy tent rather as a mortal sinner in fear of immediate death might dive towards a confessional-box. Was this another who had great faith in wonderful Mrs. Bellairs, or was it perhaps Mrs. Bellairs' husband come prosaically to fetch her home from her unholy rites?

The speculation interested Arthur Rowe, and he scarcely took in the fact that the last of the treasure-hunters was making for the garden gate and he was alone under the great planes with the stall-keepers. When he realised it he felt the embarrassment of the last guest in a restaurant who notices suddenly the focused look of the waiters lining the wall.

But before he could reach the gate the clergyman had intercepted him jocosely. "Not carrying that prize of yours away so soon?"

"It seems quite time to go."

"Wouldn't you feel inclined—it's usually the custom at a fête like this—to put the cake up again—for the Good Cause?"

Something in his manner—an elusive patronage as though he were a kindly prefect teaching to a new boy the sacred customs of the school—offended Rowe. "Well, you haven't any visitors left surely?"

"I meant to auction—among the rest of us." He squeezed Rowe's arm again gently. "Let me introduce myself. My name's Sinclair. I'm supposed, you know, to have a touch—for touching." He gave a small giggle. "You see that lady over there—that's Mrs. Fraser—*the* Mrs. Fraser. A little friendly auction like this gives her the opportunity of presenting a note to the cause—unobtrusively."

"It sounds quite obtrusive to me."

"They're an awfully nice set of people. I'd like you to know them, Mr. . . ."

Rowe said obstinately, "It's not the way to run a fête—to prevent people taking their prizes."

"Well, you don't exactly come to these affairs to make a profit, do you?" There were possibilities of nastiness in Mr. Sinclair that had not shown on the surface.

"I don't want to make a profit. Here's a pound note, but I fancy the cake."

Mr. Sinclair made a gesture of despair towards the others openly and rudely.

Rowe said, "Would you like *The Little Duke* back? Mrs. Fraser might give a note for that just as unobtrusively."

"There's really no need to take that tone."

The afternoon had certainly been spoiled: brass bands lost their associations in the ugly little fracas. "Good afternoon," Rowe said.

But he wasn't to be allowed to go yet; a kind of deputation advanced to Mr. Sinclair's support—the treasure-hunt lady flapped along in the van. She said, smiling coyly, "I'm afraid I am the bearer of ill tidings."

"You want the cake too," Rowe said.

She smiled with a sort of elderly impetuosity. "I must *have* the cake. You see—there's been a mistake. About the weight. It wasn't—what you said." She consulted a slip of paper. "That rude woman was right. The real weight was three pounds seven ounces. And that gentleman," she pointed towards the stall, "won it."

It was the man who had arrived late in the taxi and made for Mrs. Bellairs' booth. He kept in the dusky background by the cake-stall and let the ladies fight for him. Had Mrs. Bellairs given him a better tip?

Rowe said, "That's very odd. He got the exact weight?"

There was a little hesitation in her reply—as if she had been cornered in a witness-box undrilled for that question. "Well, not exact. But he was within three ounces." She seemed to gain confidence. "He guessed three pounds ten ounces."

"In that case," Rowe said, "I keep the cake because you see I guessed three pounds five the first time. Here is a pound for the cause. Good evening."

He'd really taken them by surprise this time; they were wordless, they didn't even thank him for the note. He looked back from the pavement and saw the group from the cake-stall surge forward to join the rest, and he waved his hand. A poster on the railings said: "The Comforts for Mothers of the Free Nations Fund. A fête will be held . . . under the patronage of royalty. . . ."

ii

Arthur Rowe lived in Guilford Street. A bomb early in the blitz had fallen in the middle of the street and blasted both sides, but Rowe stayed on. Houses went overnight, but he stayed. There were boards instead of glass in every room, and the doors no longer quite fitted and had to be propped at night. He had a sitting-room and a bedroom on the first floor, and he was done for by Mrs. Purvis, who also stayed—because it was her house. He had taken the rooms furnished and simply hadn't bothered to make any alterations. He was like a man camping in a desert. Any books there were came from the two-penny or the public library except for *The Old Curiosity Shop* and *David Copperfield*, which he read, as people used to read the Bible, over and over again till he could have quoted chapter and verse, not so much because he liked them as because he had read them as a child, and they carried no adult memories. The pictures were Mrs. Purvis's—a wild water-colour of the Bay of Naples at sunset and several steel engravings and a photograph of the former Mr. Purvis in the odd dated uniform of 1914. The ugly arm-chair, the table covered with a thick woollen cloth, the fern in the window—all were Mrs. Purvis's, and the radio was hired. Only the packet of cigarettes on the man-telpiece belonged to Rowe, and the tooth-brush and shaving tackle in the bedroom (the soap was Mrs. Purvis's), and inside a cardboard box his sleeping pills. In the sitting-room there was not even a bottle of ink or a packet of stationery: Rowe didn't write letters, and he paid his income tax at the post office.

You might say that a cake and a book added appreciably to his possessions.

When he reached home he rang for Mrs. Purvis. "Mrs. Purvis," he said, "I won this magnificent cake at the fête in the square. Have you by any chance a tin large enough?''

"It's a good-sized cake for these days," Mrs. Purvis said hungrily. It wasn't the war that had made her hungry; she had always, she would sometimes confide to him, been like it from a girl. Small and thin and bedraggled, she had let herself go after her husband died. She would be seen eating sweets at all hours of the day: the stairs smelt like a confectioner's shop: little sticky paper-bags would be found mislaid in corners, and if she couldn't be discovered in the house, you might be sure she was standing in a queue for fruit gums. "It weighs two and a half pounds if it weighs an ounce," Mrs. Purvis said.

"It weighs nearly three and a half."

"Oh, it couldn't do that."

"You weigh it."

When she was gone he sat down in the arm-chair and closed his eyes. The fête was over: the immeasurable emptiness of the week ahead stretched before him. His proper work had been journalism, but that had ceased two years ago. He had four hundred a year of his own, and as the saying goes, he didn't have to worry. The army wouldn't have him, and his short experience of civil defence had left him more alone than ever—they wouldn't have him either. There were munition factories, but he was tied to London. Perhaps if every street with which he had associations were destroyed, he would be free to go—he would find a factory near Trumpington. After a raid he used to sally out and note with a kind of hope that this restaurant or that shop existed no longer—it was like loosening the bars of a prison cell one by one.

Mrs. Purvis brought the cake in a large biscuit-tin. "Three and a half!" she said scornfully. "Never trust these charities. It's just under three."

He opened his eyes. "That's strange," he said, "that's very strange." He thought for awhile. "Let me have a slice," he said. Mrs. Purvis hungrily obeyed. It tasted good. He said, "Put it away in the tin now. It's the kind of cake that improves with keeping."

"It'll get stale," Mrs. Purvis said.

"Oh no, it's made with real eggs." But he couldn't bear the yearning way in which she handled it. "You can give yourself a slice, Mrs. Purvis," he said. People could always get things out of him by wanting them enough; it broke his precarious calm to feel that people suffered. Then he would do anything for them. Anything.

iii

It was the very next day that the stranger moved in to Mrs. Purvis's back room on the third floor. Rowe met him in the evening of the second day on the dusk of the stairs; the man was talking to Mrs. Purvis in a vibrant undertone, and Mrs. Purvis stood back against the wall with an out-of-depth scared expression. "One day," the man was saying, "you'll see." He was dark and dwarfish and twisted in his enormous shoulders with infantile paralysis.

"Oh, sir," Mrs. Purvis said to Rowe with relief, "this gentleman wants to hear the news. I said I thought perhaps you'd let him listen . . ."

"Come in," Rowe said, and opened his door and ushered the stranger in—his first caller. The room at this time of the evening was very dim; beaverboard in the windows kept out the last remains of daylight and the single globe was shaded for fear of cracks. The Bay of Naples faded into the wall-paper. The little light that went on behind the radio dial had a homely effect like a nightlight in a child's nursery—a child who is afraid of the dark. A voice said with hollow cheeriness, "Good night, children, good night."

The stranger hunched down in one of the two easy-chairs and began to comb his scalp with his fingers for scurf. You felt that sitting was his natural position; he became powerful then with his big out-of-drawing shoulders in evidence and his height disguised. He said, "Just in time," and without offering his case he lit a cigarette; a black bitter tang of Caporal spread over the room.

"Will you have a biscuit?" Rowe asked, opening his cupboard door. Like most men who live alone, he believed his own habits to be the world's; it never occurred to him that other men might not eat biscuits at six.

"Wouldn't you like the cake?" Mrs. Purvis asked, lingering in the doorway.

"I think we had better finish the biscuits first."

"Cakes," said the stranger, "are hardly worth eating these days."

"But this one," Mrs. Purvis said with vicarious pride, "was made with real eggs. Mr. Rowe won it in a raffle." And just at that moment the news began— "and this is Joseph Macleod reading it." The stranger crouched back in his chair and listened; there was something supercilious in his manner, as though he were listening to stories of which only he was in a position to know the real truth.

"It's a little more cheerful to-night," Rowe said.

"They feed us," the stranger said.

"You won't want the cake?" Mrs. Purvis asked.

"Well, perhaps this gentleman would rather have a biscuit . . . ?"

"I'm very fond of cake," the stranger said sharply, "when it's good cake," as though his taste were the only thing that mattered, and he stamped out his Caporal on the floor.

"Then fetch it, Mrs. Purvis, and a pot of tea."

The stranger hoisted his deformed figure round in the chair to watch the cake brought in. Certainly he was fond of cake: it was as though he couldn't keep his eyes off it. He seemed to hold his breath until it reached the table safely; then he sat impatiently forward in his chair.

"A knife, Mrs. Purvis?"

"Oh dear, oh dear. This time of night," Mrs. Purvis explained, "I always get forgetful. It's the sireens."

"Never mind," Rowe said, "I'll use my own." He brought tenderly out of his pocket his last remaining treasure—a big schoolboy's knife. He couldn't resist displaying its beauties to a stranger—the corkscrew, the tweezers, the blade that shot open and locked when you pressed a catch. "There's only one shop you can get these in now," he said, "a little place off the Haymarket." But the stranger paid him no attention, waiting impatiently to see the knife slide in. Far away on the outskirts of London the sirens began their nightly wail.

The stranger's voice said, "Now you and I are intelligent men. We can talk freely . . . about things." Rowe had no idea what he meant. Somewhere two miles above their heads an enemy bomber came up from the estuary. "Where are you? Where are you?" its uneven engine-beat pronounced over and over again. Mrs. Purvis had left them; there was a scrambling on the stairs as she brought her bedding down, a slam of the front door: she was making for her favourite shelter down the street. "There's no need for people like you and me to get angry," the stranger said, "about things."

He pushed his great deformed shoulder into the light, getting nearer to Rowe, sidling his body to the chair's edge. "The stupidity of this war," he said. "Why should you and I . . . intelligent men . . . ?" He said, "They talk about democracy, don't they. But you and I don't swallow stuff like that. If you want democracy— I don't say you do, but if you want it—you must go to Germany for it. What do you want?" he suddenly inquired.

"Peace," Rowe said.

"Exactly. So do we."

"I don't suppose I mean your kind of peace."

But the stranger listened to nobody but himself. He said, "We can give you peace. We are working for peace."

"Who are we?"

"My friends and I."

"Conscientious objectors?"

The deformed shoulder moved impatiently. He said, "One can worry too much about one's conscience."

"What else could we have done? Let them take Poland too without a protest?"

"You and I are men who know the world." When the stranger leant forward, his chair slid an inch with him, so that he bore steadily down on Rowe like something mechanised. "We know that Poland was one of the most corrupt countries in Europe."

"Who are we to judge?"

The chair groaned nearer. "Exactly. A Government like the one we had . . . and have . . ."

Rowe said slowly, "It's like any other crime. It involves the innocent. It isn't any excuse that your chief victim was . . . dishonest, or that the judge drinks . . ."

The stranger took him up. Whatever he said had an intolerable confidence. "How wrong you are. Why, even murder can sometimes be excused. We've all known cases, haven't we . . . ?"

"Murder . . ." Rowe considered slowly and painfully. He had never felt this man's confidence about anything. He said, "They say, don't they, that you shouldn't do evil that good may come."

"Oh, poppycock," sneered the little man. "The Christian ethic. You're intelligent. Now I challenge you. Have you ever really followed that rule?"

"No," Rowe said. "No."

"Of course not," the stranger said. "Haven't we checked up on you? But even without that, I could have told . . . you're intelligent . . . ." It was as if intelligence was the password to some small exclusive society. "The moment I saw you, I knew you weren't—one of the sheep." He started violently as a gun in a square near-by went suddenly off, shaking the house, and again faintly up from the coast came the noise of another plane. Nearer and nearer the guns opened up, but the plane pursued its steady deadly tenor until again one heard, "Where are you? Where are you?" overhead and the house shook to the explosion of the neighbouring gun. Then a whine began, came down towards them like something aimed deliberately at this one insignificant building. But the bomb burst half a mile away: you could feel the ground dent. "I was saying," the stranger said, but he'd lost touch, he had mislaid his confidence: now he was just a cripple trying not to be frightened of death. He said, "We're going to have it properly to-night. I hoped they were just passing . . ."

Again the drone began.

"Have another piece of cake?" Rowe asked. He couldn't help feeling sorry for the man: it wasn't courage in his own case that freed him from fear so much as loneliness. "It may not be . . ." he waited till the scream stopped and the bomb exploded—very near this time—probably the end of the next street: *The Little Duke* had fallen on its side . . . "much." They waited for a stick of bombs to drop, pounding a path towards them, but there were no more.

"No, thank you—that's to say, please, yes." The man had a curious way of crumbling the cake when he took a slice: it might have been nerves. To be a cripple in wartime, Rowe thought, is a terrible thing; he felt dangerous pity stirring in the bowels. "You say you checked me up, but who are you?" He cut himself a piece of cake and felt the stranger's eyes on him all the time like a starving man watching through the heavy plate-glass window the gourmet in the restaurant. Outside an ambulance screamed by, and again a plane came up. The night's noise and fires and deaths were now in train; they would go on like a routine till three or four in the morning: a bombing pilot's eight-hour day. He said, "I was telling you about this knife . . ." During the intense preoccupation of a raid it was hard to stick to any one line of thought.

The stranger interrupted, laying a hand on his wrist—a nervous bony hand attached to an enormous arm. "You know there's been a mistake. That cake was never meant for you."

"I won it. What do you mean?"

"You weren't meant to win it. There was a mistake in the figures."

"It's a bit late now to worry, isn't it?" Rowe said. "We've eaten nearly half."

But the cripple took no notice of that. He said, "They've sent me here to get it back. We'll pay in reason."

"Who are they?"

But he knew who *they* were. It was comic; he could see the whole ineffective rabble coming across the grass at him: the elderly woman in the floppy hat who almost certainly painted water-colours, the intense whimsical lady who had managed the raffle, and wonderful Mrs. Bellairs. He smiled and drew his hand away. "What are you all playing at?" he asked. Never had a raffle, surely, been treated quite so seriously before. "What good is the cake to you now?"

The other watched him with gloom. Rowe tried to raise the cloud. "I suppose," he said, "it's the principle of the thing. Forget it and have another cup of tea. I'll fetch the kettle."

"You needn't bother. I want to discuss . . ."

"There's hardly anything left to discuss, and it isn't any bother."

The stranger picked at the scurf which had lodged below his finger-nail. He said, "There's no more to say then?"

"Nothing at all."

"In that case . . ." the stranger said: he began to listen as the next plane beat towards them. He shifted uneasily as the first guns fired, far away in East London. "Perhaps I will have another cup."

When Rowe returned the stranger was pouring out the milk—and he had cut himself another piece of cake. He was conspicuously at home with his chair drawn nearer to the gas fire. He waved his hand towards Rowe's chair as if *he* were the host, and he seemed quite to have forgotten the squabble of a moment ago. "I was thinking," he said, "while you were out of the room that it's intellectuals like ourselves who are the only free men. Not bound by conventions, patriotic emotions, sentimentality . . . we haven't what they call a stake in the country. We aren't shareholders and it doesn't matter to us if the company goes on the rocks. That's quite a good image, don't you think?"

"Why do you say 'we'?"

"Well," the cripple said, "I see no sign that you are taking any active part. And of course we know why, don't we?" and suddenly, grossly, he winked.

Rowe took a sip of tea: it was too hot to swallow . . . an odd flavour haunted him like something remembered, something unhappy. He took a piece of cake to drown the taste, and looking up caught the anxious speculative eyes of the cripple, fixed on him, waiting. He took another slow sip and then he remembered. Life struck back at him like a scorpion, over the shoulder. His chief feeling was astonishment and anger, that anybody should do this to *him*. He dropped the cup on the floor and stood up. The cripple trundled away from him like something on wheels: the huge back and the long strong arms prepared themselves . . . and then the bomb went off.

They hadn't heard the plane this time; destruction had come drifting quietly down on green silk cords: the walls suddenly caved in. They were not even aware of noise.

Blast is an odd thing; it is just as likely to have the effect of an embarrassing dream as of man's serious vengeance on man, landing you naked in the street or exposing you in your bed or on your lavatory seat to the neighbours' gaze. Rowe's head was singing; he felt as though he had been walking in his sleep; he was lying in a strange position, in a strange place. He got up and saw an enormous quantity of saucepans all over the floor: something like the twisted engine of an old car turned out to be a refrigerator. He looked up and saw Charles's Wain heeling over an arm-chair which was poised thirty feet above his head: he looked down and saw the Bay of Naples intact at his feet. He felt as though he were in a strange country without any maps to help him, trying to get his position by the stars.

Three flares came sailing slowly, beautifully, down, clusters of spangles off a Christmas tree: his shadow shot out in front of him and he felt exposed, like a jailbreaker caught in a searchlight beam. The awful thing about a raid is that it goes on: your own private disaster may happen early, but the raid doesn't stop. They were ma- chine-gunning the flares: two broke with a sound like cracking plates and the third came to earth in Russell Square; the darkness returned coldly and comfortingly.

But in the light of the flares Rowe had seen several things; he had discovered where he was—in the basement kitchen: the chair above his head was in his own room on the first floor, the front wall had gone and all the roof, and the cripple lay beside the chair, one arm swinging loosely down at him. He had dropped neatly and precisely at Rowe's feet a piece of uncrumbled cake. A warden called from the street, "Is anyone hurt in there?" and Rowe said aloud in a sudden return of his rage, "It's beyond a joke: it's beyond a joke."

"You're telling me," the warden called down to him from the shattered street as yet another raider came up from the south-east muttering to them both like a witch in a child's dream, "Where are you? Where are you? Where are you?"

2

Private Inquiries

"There was a deep scar long after the pain had ceased."
THE LITTLE DUKE

i

Orthotex—the Longest Established Private Inquiry Bureau in the Metro- polis—still managed to survive at the unravaged end of Chancery Lane, close to a book auctioneer's, between a public-house which in peacetime had been famous for its buffet and a legal bookshop. It was on the fourth floor, but there was no lift. On the first floor was a notary public, on the second floor the office of a monthly called *Fitness and Freedom*, and the third was a flat which nobody occupied now.

Arthur Rowe pushed open a door marked Inquiries, but there was no one there. A half-eaten sausage-roll lay in a saucer beside an open telephone directory: it might, for all one knew, have lain there for weeks. It gave the office an air of sudden abandonment, like the palaces of kings in exile where the tourist is shown the magazines yet open at the page which royalty turned before fleeing years ago. Arthur Rowe waited a minute and then explored further, trying another door.

A bald-headed man hurriedly began to put a bottle away in a filing cabinet.

Rowe said, "Excuse me. There seemed to be nobody about. I was looking for Mr. Rennit."

"I'm Mr. Rennit."

"Somebody recommended me to come here."

The bald-headed man watched Rowe suspiciously with one hand on the filing cabinet. "Who, if I may ask?"

"It was years ago. A man called Keyser."

"I don't remember him."

"I hardly do myself. He wasn't a friend of mine. I met him in a train. He told me he had been in trouble about some letters. . . ."

"You should have made an appointment."

"I'm sorry," Rowe said. "Apparently you don't want clients. I'll say good morning."

"Now, now," Mr. Rennit said. "You don't want to lose your temper. I'm a busy man, and there's ways of doing things. If you'll be brief . . ." Like a man who deals in something disreputable—pornographic books or illegal operations— he treated his customer with a kind of superior contempt, as if it was not he who wanted to sell his goods, but the other who was over-anxious to buy. He sat down at his desk and said as an afterthought, "Take a chair." He fumbled in a drawer and hastily tucked back again what he found there; at last he discovered a pad and pencil. "Now," he said, "when did you first notice anything wrong?" He leant back and picked at a tooth with his pencil point, his breath whistling slightly between the uneven dentures. He looked abandoned like the other room: his collar was a little frayed and his shirt was not quite clean. But beggars, Rowe told himself, could not be choosers.

"Name?" Mr. Rennit went on. "Present address?" He stubbed the paper fiercely, writing down the answers. At the name of a hotel he raised his head and said sombrely, "In your position you can't be too careful."

"I think perhaps," Rowe said, "I'd better begin at the beginning."

"My good sir," Mr. Rennit said, "you can take it from me that I know all the beginnings. I've been in this line of business for thirty years. Thirty years. Every client thinks he's a unique case. He's nothing of the kind. He's just a repetition. All I need from you is the answer to certain questions. The rest we can manage without you. Now then—when did you notice anything wrong, wife's coldness?"

"I'm not married," Rowe said.

Mr. Rennit shot him a look of disgust; he felt guilty of a quibble. "Breach of promise, eh?" Mr. Rennit asked. "Have you written any letters?"

"It's not breach of promise either."

"Blackmail?"

"No."

"Then why," Mr. Rennit asked angrily, "do you come to me?" He added his tag, "I'm a busy man," but never had anyone been so palpably unemployed. There were two trays on his desk marked In and Out, but the Out tray was empty and all the In tray held was a copy of *Men Only*. Rowe might perhaps have left if he had known any other address, and if it had not been for that sense of pity which is more promiscuous than lust. Mr. Rennit was angry because he had not been given time to set his scene, and he could so obviously not afford his anger. There was a kind of starved nobility in the self-sacrifice of his rage.

"Doesn't a detective deal with anything but divorces and breaches of promise?"

Mr. Rennit said, "This is a respectable business with a tradition. I'm not Sherlock Holmes. You don't expect to find a man in my position, do you, crawling about floors with a microscope looking for blood-stains?" He said stiffly, "If you are in any trouble of that kind, I advise you to go to the police."

"Listen," Rowe said, "be reasonable. You know you can do with a client just as much as I can do with you. I can pay, pay well. Be sensible and unlock that cupboard and let's have a drink on it together. These raids are bad for the nerves. One has to have a little something . . ."

The stiffness drained slowly out of Mr. Rennit's attitude as he looked cautiously back at Rowe. He stroked his bald head and said, "Perhaps you're right. One gets rattled. I've never objected to stimulants *as* stimulants."

"Everybody needs them nowadays."

"It was bad last night at Purley. Not many bombs, but the waiting. Not that we haven't had our share, and land-mines. . . ."

"The place where I live went last night."

"You don't say," Mr. Rennit said without interest, opening the filing cabinet and reaching for the bottle. "Now last week . . . at Purley . . ." He was just like a man discussing his operations. "Not a hundred yards away. . . ."

"We both deserve a drink," Rowe said.

Mr. Rennit—the ice broken—suddenly became confiding. "I suppose I was a bit sharp. One does get rattled. War plays hell with a business like this." He explained. "The reconciliations—you wouldn't believe human nature could be so contrary. And then, of course, the registrations have made it very difficult. People daren't go to hotels as they used to. And you can't *prove* anything from motor-cars."

"It must be difficult for you."

"It's a case of holding out," Mr. Rennit said, "keeping our backs to the wall until peace comes. Then there'll be such a crop of divorces, breaches of promise. . . ." He contemplated the situation with uncertain optimism over the bottle. "You'll excuse a tea-cup?" He said, "When peace comes an old-established business like this—with connections—will be a gold-mine." He added gloomily, "Or so I tell myself."

Listening Rowe thought, as he often did, that you couldn't take such an odd world seriously, and yet all the time, in fact, he took it with a mortal seriousness. The grand names stood permanently like statues in his mind: names like Justice and Retribution, though what they both boiled down to was simply Mr. Rennit, hundreds and hundreds of Mr. Rennits. But of course if you believed in God— and the Devil—the thing wasn't quite so comic. Because the Devil—and God too—had always used comic people, futile people, little suburban natures and the maimed and warped to serve his purposes. When God used them you talked emptily of Nobility and when the devil used them of Wickedness, but the material was only dull shabby human mediocrity in either case.

". . . new orders. But it will always be the same world, I hope," Mr. Rennit was saying.

"Queer things do happen in it, all the same," Rowe said. "That's why I'm here."

"Ah yes," Mr. Rennit said. "We'll just fill our cups and then to business. I'm sorry I have no soda-water. Now just tell me what's troubling you—as if I was your best friend."

"Somebody tried to kill me. It doesn't sound important when so many of us are being killed every night—but it made me angry at the time."

Mr. Rennit looked at him imperturbably over the rim of his cup. "Did you say you were *not* married?"

"There's no woman in it. It all began," Rowe said, "with a cake." He described the fête to Mr. Rennit, the anxiety of all the helpers to get the cake back, the stranger's visit . . . and then the bomb. "I wouldn't have thought twice about it," Rowe said, "if it hadn't been for the taste the tea had."

"Just imagination, probably."

"But I knew the taste. It was—hyoscine," he admitted reluctantly.

"Was the man killed?"

"They took him to hospital, but when I called to-day he'd been fetched away. It was only concussion and his friends wanted him back."

"The hospital would have the name and address."

"They had a name and address, but the address—I tried the London Directory —simply didn't exist." He looked up across the desk at Mr. Rennit expecting some sign of surprise—even in an odd world it was an odd story, but Mr. Rennit said calmly, "Of course there are a dozen explanations." He stuck his fingers into his waist-coat and considered. "For instance," he said, "it might have been a kind of confidence trick. They are always up to new dodges, those people. He might have offered to take the cake off you—for a large sum. He'd have told you something valuable was hidden in it."

"Something hidden in it?"

"Plans of a Spanish treasure off the coast of Ireland. Something romantic. He'd have wanted you to give him a mark of confidence in return. Something substantial like twenty pounds while he went to the bank. Leaving you the cake, of course."

"It makes one wonder . . ."

"Oh, it would have worked out," Mr. Rennit said. It was extraordinary, his ability to reduce everything to a commonplace level. Even air-raids were only things that occurred at Purley.

"Or take another possibility," Mr. Rennit said. "If you are right about tea. I don't believe it, mind. He might have introduced himself to you with robbery in mind. Perhaps he followed you from the fête. Did you flourish your money about?"

"I did give them a pound when they wanted the cake."

"A man," Mr. Rennit said, with a note of relief, "who gives a pound for a cake is a man with money. Thieves don't carry drugs as a rule, but he sounds a neurotic type."

"But the cake?"

"Pure patter. He hadn't really come for the cake."

"And your next explanation? You said there were a dozen."

"I always prefer the Straightforward," Mr. Rennit said, running his fingers up and down the whisky bottle. "Perhaps there was a genuine mistake about the cake and he had come for it. Perhaps it contained some kind of a prize . . ."

"And the drug was imagination again?"

"It's the straightforward explanation."

Mr. Rennit's calm incredulity shook Rowe. He said with resentment, "In all your long career as a detective, have you never come across such a thing as murder—or a murderer?"

Mr. Rennit's nose twitched over the cup. "Frankly," he said, "no. I haven't. Life, you know, isn't like a detective story. Murderers are rare people to meet. They belong to a class of their own."

"That's interesting to me."

"They are very, very seldom," Mr. Rennit said, "what we call gentlemen. Outside of story-books. You might say that they belong to the lower orders."

"Perhaps," Rowe said, "I ought to tell you that I am a murderer myself."

ii

"Ha-ha," said Mr. Rennit miserably.

"That's what makes me so furious," Rowe said. "That they should pick on me, me. They are such amateurs."

"You are—a professional?" Mr. Rennit asked with a watery and unhappy smile.

Rowe said, "Yes, I am, if thinking of the thing for two years before you do it, dreaming about it nearly every night until at last you take the drug out from the unlocked drawer, makes you one . . . and then sitting in the dock trying to make out what the judge is really thinking, watching each one of the jury, wondering what *he* thinks . . . there was a woman in pince-nez who wouldn't be separated from her umbrella, and then you go below and wait hour after hour till the jury come back and the warder tries to be encouraging, but you know if there's any justice left on earth there can be only one verdict. . . ."

"Would you excuse me one moment?" Mr. Rennit said. "I think I heard my man come back. . . ." He emerged from behind his desk and then whisked through the door behind Rowe's chair with surprising agility. Rowe sat with his hands held between his knees, trying to get a grip again on his brain and his tongue. . . . "Set a watch, O Lord, before my mouth and a door round about my lips. . . ." He heard a bell tinkle in the other room and followed the sound. Mr. Rennit was at the phone. He looked piteously at Rowe and then at the sausage-roll as if that were the only weapon within reach.

"Are you ringing up the police?" Rowe asked, "or a doctor?"

"A theatre," Mr. Rennit said desparingly, "I just remembered my wife. . . ."

"You are married, are you, in spite of all your experience?"

"Yes." An awful disinclination to talk convulsed Mr. Rennit's features as a thin faint voice came up the wires. He said, "Two seats—in the front row," and clapped the receiver down again.

"The theatre?"

"The theatre."

"And they didn't even want your name? Why not be reasonable?" Rowe said. "After all, I had to tell you. You have to have all the facts. It wouldn't be fair otherwise. It might have to be taken into consideration, mightn't it, if you work for me."

"Into consideration?"

"I mean—it might have a bearing. That's something I discovered when they tried me—that everything may have a bearing. The fact that I had lunch on a certain day alone at the Holborn Restaurant. Why was I alone, they asked me. I said I liked being alone sometimes, and you should have seen the way they nodded at the jury. It had a bearing." His hands began to shake again. "As if I really wanted to be alone for life . . ."

Mr. Rennit cleared a dry throat.

"Even the fact that my wife kept love-birds . . ."

"You *are* married?"

"It was my wife I murdered." He found it hard to put things in the right order; people oughtn't to ask unnecessary questions: he really hadn't meant to startle Mr. Rennit again. He said, "You needn't worry. The police know all about it."

"You were acquitted?"

"I was detained during His Majesty's pleasure. It was quite a short pleasure: I wasn't mad, you see. They just had to find an excuse." He said with loathing, "They pitied me, so that's why I'm alive. The papers all called it a mercy killing." He moved his hands in front of his face as though he were troubled by a thread of cobweb. "Mercy to her or mercy to me. They didn't say. And I don't know myself."

"I really don't think," Mr. Rennit said, swallowing for breath in the middle of a sentence and keeping a chair between them, "I can undertake . . . It's out of my line."

"I'll pay more," Rowe said. "It always comes down to that, doesn't it?" and as soon as he felt cupidity stirring in the little dusty room, over the half-eaten sausage-roll and the saucer and the tattered telephone-directory, he knew he had gained his point. Mr. Rennit after all could not afford to be nice. Rowe said, "A murderer is rather like a peer: he pays more because of his title. One tries to travel incognito, but it usually comes out . . ."

3

Frontal Assault

*"It were hard he should not have one faithful
comrade and friend with him."*
THE LITTLE DUKE

i

Rowe went straight from Orthotex to the Free Mothers. He had signed a contract with Mr. Rennit to pay him fifty pounds a week for a period of four weeks to carry out investigations; Mr. Rennit had explained that the expenses would be heavy—Orthotex employed only the most experienced agents—and the one agent he had been permitted to see before he left the office was certainly experienced. (Mr. Rennit introduced him as A.2, but before long he was absent-mindedly addressing him as Jones.) Jones was small and at first sight insignificant, with his thin pointed nose, his soft brown hat with a stained ribbon, his grey suit which might have been quite a different colour years ago, and the pencil and pen on fasteners in the breast pocket. But when you looked a second time you saw experience; you saw it in the small cunning rather frightened eyes, the weak defensive mouth, the wrinkles of anxiety on the forehead—experience of innumerable hotel corridors, of bribed chamber-maids and angry managers, experience of the insult which could not be resented, the threat which had to be ignored, the promise which was never kept. Murder had a kind of dignity compared with this muted second-hand experience of scared secretive passions.

An argument developed almost at once in which Jones played no part, standing close to the wall holding his old brown hat, looking and listening as though he were outside a hotel door. Mr. Rennit, who obviously considered the whole investigation the fantastic fad of an unbalanced man, argued that Rowe himself should not take part. "Just leave it to me and A.2," he said. "If it's a confidence trick . . ."

He would not believe that Rowe's life had been threatened. "Of course," he said, "we'll look into the chemists' books—not that there'll be anything to find."

"It made me angry," Rowe repeated. "He said he'd checked up—and yet he had the nerve." An idea came to him and he went excitedly on, "It was the same drug. People would have said it was suicide, that I'd managed to keep some of it hidden. . . ."

"If there's anything in your idea," Mr. Rennit said, "the cake was given to the wrong man. We've only got to find the right one. It's a simple matter of tracing. Jones and I know all about tracing. We start from Mrs. Bellairs. She told you the weight, but why did she tell you the weight? Because she mistook you in the dark for the other man. There must be some resemblance. . . ." Mr. Rennit exchanged a look with Jones. "It all boils down to finding Mrs. Bellairs. That's not very difficult. Jones will do that."

"It would be easiest of all for me to ask for her—at the Free Mothers."

"I'd advise you to let Jones see to it."

"They'd think he was a tout."

"It wouldn't do at all for a client to make his own investigations, not at all."

"If there's nothing in my story," Rowe said, "they'll give me Mrs. Bellairs' address. If I'm right they'll try to kill me, because, though the cake's gone, I know there was a cake, and that there are people who want the cake. *There's* the work for Jones, to keep his eye on me."

Jones shifted his hat uneasily and tried to catch his employer's eye. He cleared his throat and Mr. Rennit asked, "What is it, A.2?"

"Won't do, sir," Jones said.

"No?"

"Unprofessional, sir."

"I agree with Jones," Mr. Rennit said.

All the same, in spite of Jones, Rowe had his way. He came out into the shattered street and made his sombre way between the ruins of Holborn. In his lonely state to have confessed his identity to someone was almost like making a friend. Always before it had been discovered, even at the warden's post; it came out sooner or later, like cowardice. They were extraordinary the tricks and turns of fate, the way conversations came round, the long memories some people had for names. Now in the strange torn landscape where London shops were reduced to a stone ground-plan like those of Pompeii he moved with familiarity; he was part of this destruction as he was no longer part of the past—the long weekends in the country, the laughter up lanes in the evening, the swallows gathering on telegraph wires, peace.

Peace had come to an end quite suddenly on an August the thirty-first—the world waited another year. He moved like a bit of stone among the other stones—he was protectively coloured, and he felt at times, breaking the surface of his remorse, a kind of evil pride like that a leopard might feel moving in harmony with all the other spots on the world's surface, only with greater power. He had not been a criminal when he murdered; it was afterwards that he began to grow into criminality like a habit of thought. That these men should have tried to kill him who had succeeded at one blow in destroying beauty, goodness, peace—it was a form of impertinence. There were times when he felt the whole world's criminality was his; and then suddenly at some trivial sight—a woman's bag, a face on an elevator going up as he went down, a picture in a paper—all the pride seeped out of him. He was aware only of the stupidity of his act; he wanted to creep out of sight and weep; he wanted to forget that he had ever been happy. A voice would whisper, "You say you killed for pity; why don't you have pity on yourself?" Why not indeed? except that it is easier to kill someone you love than to kill yourself.

ii

The Free Mothers had taken over an empty office in a huge white modern block off the Strand. It was like going into a mechanised mortuary with a separate lift for every slab. Rowe moved steadily upwards in silence for five floors: a long passage, frosted glass, somebody in pince-nez stepped into the lift carrying a file marked "Most Immediate" and they moved on smoothly upwards. A door on the seventh floor was marked "Comforts for Mothers of the Free Nations. Enquiries."

He began to believe that after all Mr. Rennit was right. The stark efficient middle-class woman who sat at a typewriter was so obviously incorruptible and unpaid. She wore a little button to show she was honorary. "Yes?" she asked sharply and all his anger and pride drained away. He tried to remember what the stranger had said—about the cake not being intended for him. There was really nothing sinister in the phrase so far as he could now remember it, and as for the taste, hadn't he often woken at night with that upon his tongue?

"Yes?" the woman repeated briskly.

"I came," Rowe said, "to try and find out the address of a Mrs. Bellairs."

"No lady of that name works here."

"It was in connection with the fête."

"Oh, they were all voluntary helpers. We can't possibly disclose addresses of voluntary helpers."

"Apparently," Rowe said, "a mistake was made. I was given a cake which didn't belong to me . . ."

"I'll inquire," the stark lady said and went into an inner room. He had just long enough to wonder whether after all he had been wise. He should have brought A.2 up with him. But then the normality of everything came back; he was the only abnormal thing there. The honorary helper stood in the doorway and said, "Will you come through, please?" He took a quick glance at her typewriter as he went by; he could read "The Dowager Lady Cradbrooke thanks Mrs. J. A. Smythe-Philipps for her kind gift of tea and flour. . . ." Then he went in.

He had never become accustomed to chance stabs: only when the loved person is out of reach does love become complete. The colour of the hair and the size of the body—something very small and neat and incapable, you would say, of inflicting pain—this was enough to make him hesitate just inside the room. There were no other resemblances, but when the girl spoke—in the slightest of foreign accents—he felt the kind of astonishment one feels at a party hearing the woman one loves talking in a stranger's tone to a stranger. It was not an uncommon occurrence; he would follow people into shops, he would wait at street corners because of a small resemblance, just as though the woman he loved was only lost and might be discovered any day in a crowd.

She said, "You came about a cake?"

He watched her closely: they had so little in common compared with the great difference, that one was alive and the other dead. He said, "A man came to see me last night—I suppose from this office."

He fumbled for words because it was just as absurd to think that this girl might be mixed up in a crime as to think of Alice—except as a victim. "I had won a cake in a raffle at your fête—but there seemed to be some mistake."

"I don't understand."

"A bomb fell before I could make out what it was he wanted to tell me."

"But no one could have come from here," she said. "What did he look like?"

"Very small and dark with twisted shoulders—practically a cripple."

"There is no one like that here."

"I thought perhaps that if I found Mrs. Bellairs . . ." The name seemed to convey nothing. "One of the helpers at the fête."

"They were all volunteers," the girl explained. "I dare say we could find the address for you through the organisers, but is it so—important?"

A screen divided the room in two; he had imagined they were alone, but as the girl spoke a young man came round the screen. He had the same fine features as the girl; she introduced him, "This is my brother, Mr. . . ."

"Rowe."

"Somebody called on Mr. Rowe to ask about a cake. I don't quite understand. It seems he won it at our fête."

"Now let me see, who could that possibly be?" The young man spoke excellent English; only a certain caution and precision marked him as a foreigner. It was as if he had come from an old-fashioned family among whom it was important to speak clearly and use the correct words; his care had an effect of charm, not of pedantry. He stood with his hand laid lightly and affectionately on his sister's shoulder as though they formed together a Victorian family group. "Was he one of your countrymen, Mr. Rowe? In this office we are most of us foreigners, you know." Smiling he took Rowe into his confidence. "If health or nationality prevent us fighting for you, we have to do something. My sister and I are—technically—Austrian."

"This man was English."

"He must have been one of the voluntary helpers. We have so many—I don't know half of them by name. You want to return a prize, is that it? A cake?"

Rowe said cautiously, "I wanted to inquire about it."

"Well, Mr. Rowe, if I were you, I should be unscrupulous. I should just 'hang on' to the cake." When he used a colloquialism you could hear the inverted commas drop gently and apologetically around it.

"The trouble is," Rowe said, "the cake's no longer there. My house was bombed last night."

"I'm sorry. About your house, I mean. The cake can't seem very important now, surely?"

They were charming, they were obviously honest, but they had caught him neatly and effectively in an inconsistency.

"I shouldn't bother," the girl said, "if I were you."

Rowe watched them hesitatingly. But it is impossible to go through life without trust: that is to be imprisoned in the worst cell of all, oneself. For more than a year now Rowe had been so imprisoned—there had been no change of cell, no exercise-yard, no unfamiliar warder to break the monotony of solitary confinement. A moment comes to a man when a prison-break must be made whatever the risk. Now cautiously he tried for freedom. These two had lived through terror themselves, but they had emerged without any ugly psychological scar. He said, "As a matter of fact it wasn't simply the cake which was worrying me."

They watched him with a frank and friendly interest; you felt that in spite of the last years there was still the bloom of youth on them—they still expected life to offer them other things than pain and boredom and distrust and hate. The young man said, "Won't you sit down and tell us . . . ?" They reminded him of children who liked stories. They couldn't have accumulated more than fifty years' experience between them. He felt immeasurably older.

Rowe said, "I got the impression that whoever wanted that cake was ready to be—well, violent." He told them of the visit and the stranger's vehemence and the odd taste in his tea. The young man's very pale blue eyes sparkled with his interest and excitement. He said, "It's a fascinating story. Have you any idea who's behind it—or what? How does Mrs. Bellairs come into it?"

He wished now that he hadn't been to Mr. Rennit—these were the allies he needed, not the dingy Jones and his sceptical employer.

"Mrs. Bellairs told my fortune at the fête, and told me the weight of the cake —which wasn't the right weight."

"It's extraordinary," the young man said enthusiastically.

The girl said, "It doesn't make sense." She added almost in Mr. Rennit's words, "It was probably all a misunderstanding."

"Misunderstanding," her brother said and then dropped his inverted commas round the antiquated slang, " 'my eye.' " He turned to Rowe with an expression of glee. "Count this society, Mr. Rowe, as far as the secretary's concerned at your service. This is really interesting." He held out his hand. "My name—*our* name is Hilfe. Where do we begin?"

The girl sat silent. Rowe said, "Your sister doesn't agree."

"Oh," the young man said, "she'll come round. She always does in the end. She thinks I'm a romantic. She's had to get me out of too many scrapes." He became momentarily serious. "She got me out of Austria." But nothing could damp his enthusiasm for long. "That's another story. Do we begin with Mrs. Bellairs? Have you any idea what it's all about? I'll get our grim volunteer in the next room on the hunt," and opening the door he called through. "Dear Mrs. Dermody, do you think you could find the address of one of our voluntary helpers called Mrs. Bellairs?" He explained to Rowe, "The difficulty is she's probably just the friend of a friend—not a regular helper. Try Canon Topling," he suggested to Mrs. Dermody.

The greater the young man's enthusiasm, the more fantastic the whole incident became. Rowe began to see it through Mr. Rennit's eyes—Mrs. Dermody, Canon Topling . . .

He said, "Perhaps after all your sister's right."

But young Hilfe swept on. "She may be, of course she may be. But how dull if she is. I'd much rather think, until we *know*, that there's some enormous conspiracy . . ."

Mrs. Dermody put her head in at the door and said, "Canon Topling gave me the address. It's 5 Park Crescent."

"If she's a friend of Canon Topling," Rowe began and caught Miss Hilfe's eye. She gave him a secret nod as much as to say—now you're on the right track.

"Oh, but let's 'hang on' to the stranger," Hilfe said.

"There may be a thousand reasons," Miss Hilfe said.

"Surely not a thousand, Anna," her brother mocked. He asked Rowe, "Isn't there anything else you can remember which will convince her?" His keenness was more damping than her scepticism. The whole affair became a game one couldn't take seriously.

"Nothing," Rowe said.

Hilfe was at the window looking out. He said, "Come here a moment, Mr. Rowe. Do you see that little man down there—in the shabby brown hat? He arrived just after you, and he seems to be staying . . . There he goes now, up and down. Pretends to light a cigarette. He does that too often. And that's the second evening paper he's bought. He never comes quite opposite, you see. It almost looks as if you are being trailed."

"I know him," Rowe said. "He's a private detective. He's being paid to keep an eye on me."

"By Jove," young Hilfe said—even his exclamations were a little Victorian— "you do take this seriously. We're allies now you know—you aren't 'holding out' on us, are you?"

"There is something I haven't mentioned." Rowe hesitated.

"Yes?" Hilfe came quickly back and with his hand again on his sister's shoulder waited with an appearance of anxiety. "Something which will wipe out Canon Topling?"

"I think there was something in the cake."

"What?"

"I don't know. But he crumbled every slice he took."

"It may have been habit," Miss Hilfe said.

"Habit!" her brother teased her.

She said with sudden anger, "One of these old English characteristics you study so carefully."

Rowe tried to explain to Miss Hilfe, "It's nothing to do with me. I don't want their cake, but they tried, I'm sure they tried, to kill me. I know it sounds unlikely, now, in daylight, but if you had seen that wretched little cripple pouring in the milk, and then waiting, watching, crumbling the cake. . . ."

"And you really believe," Miss Hilfe said, "that Canon Topling's friend . . ."

"Don't listen to her," Hilfe said. "Why not Canon Topling's friend? There's no longer a thing called a criminal class. *We* can tell you that. There were lots of people in Austria you'd have said couldn't . . . well, do the things we saw them do. Cultured people, pleasant people, people you had sat next to at dinner."

"Mr. Rennit," Rowe said, "the head of the Orthotex Detective Agency, told me to-day that he'd never met a murderer. He said they were rare and not the best people."

"Why, they are dirt cheap," Hilfe said, "nowadays. I know myself at least six murderers. One was a cabinet minister, another was a heart specialist, the third a bank manager, an insurance agent . . ."

"Stop," Miss Hilfe said, "please stop."

"The difference," Hilfe said, "is that in these days it really pays to murder, and when a thing pays it becomes respectable. The rich abortionist becomes a gynaecologist and the rich thief a bank director. Your friend is out of date." He went on explaining gently, his very pale blue eyes unshocked and unshockable. "Your old-fashioned murderer killed from fear, from hate—or even from love, Mr. Rowe, very seldom for substantial profit. None of these reasons is quite—respectable. But to murder for position—that's different, because when you've gained the position nobody has a right to criticise the means. Nobody will refuse to meet you if the position's high enough. Think of how many of your statesmen have shaken hands with Hitler. But, of course, to murder for fear or from love, Canon Topling wouldn't do that. If he killed his wife he'd lose his preferment," and he smiled at Rowe with a blithe innocence of what he was saying.

When he came out of what wasn't called a prison, when His Majesty's pleasure had formally and quickly run its course, it had seemed to Rowe that he had emerged into quite a different world—a secret world of assumed names, of knowing nobody, of avoiding faces, of men who leave a bar unobtrusively when other people enter. One lived where least questions were asked, in furnished rooms. It was the kind of world that people who attended garden fêtes, who went to Matins, who spent week-ends in the country and played bridge for low stakes and had an account at a good grocer's, knew nothing about. It wasn't exactly a criminal world, though eddying along its dim and muted corridors you might possibly rub shoulders with genteel forgers who had never actually been charged or the corrupter of a child. One attended cinemas at ten in the morning with other men in macintoshes who had somehow to pass the time away. One sat at home and read *The Old Curiosity Shop* all the evening. When he had first believed that someone intended to murder him, he had felt a sort of shocked indignation; the act of murder belonged to him like a personal characteristic, and not the inhabitants of the old peaceful places from which he was an exile, and of which Mrs. Bellairs, the lady in the floppy hat and the clergyman called Sinclair were so obviously inhabitants. The one thing a murderer should be able to count himself safe from was murder—by one of these.

But he was more shocked now at being told by a young man of great experience that there was no division between the worlds. The insect underneath the stone has a right to feel safe from the trampling superior boot.

Miss Hilfe told him, "You mustn't listen." She was watching him with what looked like sympathy. But that was impossible.

"Of course," Hilfe said easily, "I exaggerate. But all the same you have to be prepared in these days for criminals—everywhere. They call it having ideals. They'll even talk about murder being the most merciful thing.''

Rowe looked quickly up, but there was no personal meaning in the pale blue theoretical eyes. "You mean the Prussians?" Rowe asked.

"Yes, if you like, the Prussians. Or the Nazis. The Fascists. The Reds, the Whites . . .''

A telephone rang on Miss Hilfe's desk. She said, "It's Lady Dunwoody.''

Hilfe, leaning quickly sideways, said, "We are so grateful for your offer, Lady Dunwoody. We can never have too many woollies. Yes, if you wouldn't mind sending them to this office, or shall we collect? You'll send your chauffeur. Thank you. Good-bye.'' He said to Rowe, with a rather wry smile, "It's an odd way for someone of my age to fight a war, isn't it? collecting woollies from charitable old dowagers. But it's useful, I'm allowed to do it, and it's something not to be interned. Only—you do understand, don't you—a story like yours excites me. It seems to give one an opportunity, well, to take a more violent line.'' He smiled at his sister and said with affection, "Of course she calls me a romantic.''

But the odd thing was she called him nothing at all. It was almost as if she not only disapproved of him, but had disowned him, wouldn't co-operate in any-thing—outside the woollies. She seemed to Rowe to lack her brother's charm and ease; the experience which had given him an amusing nihilistic abandon had left her brooding on some deeper, more unhappy level. He felt no longer sure that they were both without scars. His brother had the ideas, but she felt them. When Rowe looked at her it was as if his own unhappiness recognised a friend and signalled, signalled, but got no reply.

"And now," Hilfe said, "what next?"

"Leave it alone." Miss Hilfe addressed herself directly to Rowe—the reply when it did at last come was simply to say that communication was at an end.

"No, no," Hilfe said, "we can't do that. This is war.''

"How do you know," Miss Hilfe said, still speaking only to Rowe, "that even if there is something behind it, it isn't just—theft, drugs, things like that?''

"I don't know," Rowe said, "and I don't care. I'm angry, that's all.''

"What is your theory, though?" Hilfe asked. "About the cake?"

"It might have contained a message, mightn't it?"

Both the Hilfes were silent for a moment as though that were an idea which had to be absorbed. Then Hilfe said, "I'll go with you to Mrs. Bellairs.''

"You can't leave the office, Willi," Miss Hilfe said. "I'll go with Mr. Rowe. You have an appointment.''

"Oh, only with Trench. You can handle Trench for me, Anna." He said with glee, "This is important. There may be trouble.''

"We could take Mr. Rowe's detective.''

"And warn the lady? He sticks out a yard. No," Hilfe said, "we must very gently drop him. I'm used to dropping spies. It's a thing one has learned since 1933.''

"But I don't know what you want to say to Mr. Trench.''

"Just stave him off. Say we'll settle at the beginning of the month. You'll forgive us talking business, Mr. Rowe.''

"Why not let Mr. Rowe go alone?"

Perhaps, Rowe thought, she does after all believe there's something in it; perhaps she fears for her brother. She was saying, "You don't both of you want to make fools of yourselves, Willi."

Hilfe ignored his sister completely. He said to Rowe, "Just a moment while I write a note for Trench," and disappeared behind the screen.

When they left the office together it was by another door; dropping Jones was as simple as that, for he had no reason to suppose that his employer would try to evade him. Hilfe called a taxi, and as they drove down the street, Rowe was able to see how the shabby figure kept his vigil, lighting yet another cigarette with his eyes obliquely on the great ornate entrance, like a faithful hound who will stay interminably outside his master's door. Rowe said, "I wish we had let him know."

"Better not," Hilfe said. "We can pick him up afterwards. We shan't be long," and the figure slanted out of sight as the taxi wheeled away; he was lost amongst the buses and bicycles, absorbed among all the other loitering seedy London figures, never to be seen again by anyone who knew him.

4

An Evening With Mrs. Bellairs

"There be dragons of wrong here and everywhere,
quite as venomous as any in my Sagas."
THE LITTLE DUKE

i

Mrs. Bellairs' house was a house of character; that is to say it was old and unrenovated, standing behind its little patch of dry and weedy garden among the To Let boards on the slope of Campden Hill. A piece of statuary lay back in a thin thorny hedge like a large block of pumice stone, chipped and grey with neglect, and when you rang the bell under the early Victorian portico, you seemed to hear the sound pursuing the human inhabitants into back rooms as though what was left of life had ebbed up the passages.

The snowy-white cuffs and the snowy-white apron of the maid who opened the door came as a surprise. She was keeping up appearances as the house wasn't, though she looked nearly as old. Her face was talcumed and wrinkled and austere like a nun's. Hilfe said, "Is Mrs. Bellairs at home?"

The old maid watched them with the kind of shrewdness people learn in convents. She said, "Have you an appointment?"

"Why no," Hilfe said, "we were just calling. I'm a friend of Canon Topling's."

"You see," the maid explained, "this is one of her evenings."

"Yes?"

"If you are not one of the group . . ."

An elderly man with a face of extraordinary nobility and thick white hair came up the path. "Good evening, sir," the maid said. "Will you come right in?" He was obviously one of the group, for she showed him into a room on the right and they heard her announce, "Dr. Forester." Then she came back to guard the door.

Hilfe said, "Perhaps if you would take my name to Mrs. Bellairs, we might join the group. Hilfe—a friend of Canon Topling's."

"I'll *ask* her," the maid said dubiously.

But the result was after all favourable. Mrs. Bellairs herself swam into the little jumbled hall. She wore a Liberty dress of shot silk and a toque and she held out both hands as though to welcome them simultaneously. "Any friend of Canon Topling . . ." she said.

"My name is Hilfe. Of the Free Mothers Fund. And this is Mr. Rowe."

Rowe watched for a sign of recognition, but there was none. Her broad white face seemed to live in worlds beyond them.

"If you'd join our group," she said, "we welcome newcomers. So long as there's no settled hostility."

"Oh, none, none," Hilfe said.

She swayed in front of them like a figure-head into a drawing-room all orange curtain and blue cushion, as though it had been furnished once and for all in the twenties. Blue blackout globes made the room dim like an Oriental café. There were indications among the trays and occasional tables that it was Mrs. Bellairs who had supplied the fête with some of its Benares work.

Half a dozen people were in the room, and one of them immediately attracted Rowe's attention—a tall, broad, black-haired man; he couldn't think why, until he realised that it was his normality which stood out. "Mr. Cost," Mrs. Bellairs was saying, "this is . . ."

"Mr. Rowe." Hilfe supplied the name, and the introductions went round with a prim formality. One wondered why Cost was here, in the company of Dr. Forester with his weak mouth and his nobility; Miss Pantil, a dark young-middle-aged woman with blackheads and a hungry eye; Mr. Newey—"Mr. Frederick Newey"—Mrs. Bellairs made a point of the first name—who wore sandals and no socks and had a grey shock of hair; Mr. Maude, a short-sighted young man who kept as close as he could to Mr. Newey and fed him devotedly with thin bread and butter, and Collier, who obviously belonged to a different class and had worked himself in with some skill. He was patronised, but at the same time he was admired. He was a breath of the larger life and they were interested. He had been a hotel waiter and a tramp and a stoker, and he had published a book—so Mrs. Bellairs whispered to Rowe—of the most fascinating poetry, rough but spiritual. "He uses words," Mrs. Bellairs said, "that have never been used in poetry before." There seemed to be some antagonism between him and Mr. Newey.

All this scene became clear to Rowe over the cups of very weak China tea which were brought round by the austere parlourmaid.

"And what," Mrs. Bellairs asked, "do you do, Mr. Rowe?" She had been explaining Collier in an undertone—calling him plain Collier because he was a Player and not a Gentleman.

"Oh," Rowe said, watching her over his tea-cup, trying to make out the meaning of her group, trying in vain to see her in a dangerous rôle, "I sit and think."

It seemed to be the right as well as the truthful answer. He was encircled by Mrs. Bellairs' enthusiasm as though by a warm arm. "I shall call you our philosopher," she said. "We have our poet, our critic . . ."

"What is Mr. Cost?"

"He is Big Business," Mrs. Bellairs said. "He works in the City. I call him our mystery man. I sometimes feel he is a hostile influence."

"And Miss Pantil?"

"She has quite extraordinary powers of painting the inner world. She sees it as colours and circles, rhythmical arrangements, and sometimes oblongs."

It was fantastic to believe that Mrs. Bellairs could have anything to do with crime—or any of her group. He would have made some excuse and gone if it had not been for Hilfe. These people—whatever Hilfe might say—did not belong under the stone with him.

He asked vaguely, "You meet here every week?"

"Always on Wednesdays. Of course we have very little time because of the raids. Mr. Newey's wife likes him to be back at Welwyn before the raids start. And perhaps that's why the results are bad. They can't be driven, you know." She smiled. "We can't promise a stranger anything."

He couldn't make out what it was all about. Hilfe seemed to have left the room with Cost. Mrs. Bellairs said, "Ah, the conspirators. Mr. Cost is always thinking up a test."

Rowe tried out a question tentatively. "And the results are sometimes bad?"

"So bad I could cry . . . if I knew at the time. But there are other times—oh, you'd be surprised how good they are."

A telephone was ringing in another room. Mrs. Bellairs said, "Who can that naughty person be? All my friends know they mustn't ring me on Wednesdays."

The old parlourmaid had entered. She said with distaste, "Somebody is calling Mr. Rowe."

Rowe said, "But I can't understand it. Nobody knows . . ."

"Would you mind," Mrs. Bellairs said, "being very quick?"

Hilfe was in the hall talking earnestly to Cost. He asked, "For you?" He too was discomposed. Rowe left a track of censorious silence behind him: they watched him following the maid. He felt as though he had made a scene in church and was now being conducted away. He could hear behind him nothing but the tinkle of tea-cups being laid away.

He thought: perhaps it's Mr. Rennit, but how can he have found me? or Jones? He leant across Mrs. Bellairs' desk in a small packed dining-room. He said, "Hullo," and wondered again how he could have been traced. "Hullo."

But it wasn't Mr. Rennit. At first he didn't recognise the voice—a woman's. "Mr. Rowe?"

"Yes."

"Are you alone?"

"Yes."

The voice was blurred; it was as if a handkerchief had been stretched across the mouthpiece. She couldn't know, he thought, that there were no other women's voices to confuse with hers.

"Please will you leave the house as soon as you can?"

"It's Miss Hilfe, isn't it?"

The voice said impatiently, "Yes. Yes. All right. It is."

"Do you want to speak to your brother?"

"Please do not tell him. And leave. Leave quickly."

He was for a moment amused. The idea of any danger in Mrs. Bellairs' company was absurd. He realised how nearly he had been converted to Mr. Rennit's way of thinking. Then he remembered that Miss Hilfe had shared those views. Something had converted her—the opposite way. He said, "What about your brother?"

"If you go away, he'll go too."

The dimmed urgent voice fretted at his nerves. He found himself edging round the desk so that he could face the door, and then he moved again, because his back was to a window. "Why don't you tell this to your brother?"

"He would want to stay all the more." That was true. He wondered how thin the walls were. The room was uncomfortably crowded with trashy furniture: one wanted space to move about—the voice was disturbingly convincing—to manœuvre in. He said, "Is Jones still outside—the detective?"

There was a long pause: presumably she had gone to the window. Then the voice sprang at him unexpectedly loud—she had taken away the handkerchief. "There's nobody there."

"Are you sure?"

"Nobody."

He felt deserted and indignant. What business had Jones to leave his watch? Somebody was approaching down the passage. He said, "I must ring off."

"They'll try to get you in the dark," the voice said, and then the door opened. It was Hilfe.

He said, "Come along. They are all waiting. Who was it?"

Rowe said, "When you were writing your note I left a message with Mrs. Dermody, in case anyone wanted me urgently."

"And somebody did?"

"It was Jones—the detective."

"Jones?" Hilfe said.

"Yes."

"And Jones had important news?"

"Not exactly. He was worried at losing me. But Mr. Rennit wants me at his office."

"The faithful Rennit. We'll go straight there—afterwards."

"After what?"

Hilfe's eyes expressed excitement and malice. "Something we can't miss—'at any price.' " He added in a lower voice, "I begin to believe we were wrong. It's lots of fun, but it's not—dangerous."

He laid a confiding hand on Rowe's arm and gently urged him, "Keep a straight face, Mr. Rowe, if you can. You mustn't laugh. She *is* a friend of Canon Topling."

The room when they came back was obviously arranged for something. A rough circle had been formed with the chairs, and everyone had an air of impatience politely subdued. "Just sit down, Mr. Rowe, next Mr. Cost," said Mrs. Bellairs, "and then we'll turn out the lights."

In nightmares one knows the cupboard door will open: one knows that what will emerge is horrible: one doesn't know what it is . . .

Mrs. Bellairs said again, "If you'll just sit down, so that we can turn out the lights."

He said, "I'm sorry. I've got to go."

"Oh, you can't go now," Mrs. Bellairs cried. "Can he, Mr. Hilfe?"

Rowe looked at Hilfe, but the pale blue eyes sparkled back at him without understanding. "Of course, he mustn't go," Hilfe said. "We'll both wait. What did we come for?" An eyelid momentarily flickered as Mrs. Bellairs with a gesture of appalling coyness locked the door and dropped the key down her blouse and shook her fingers at them. "We always lock the door," she said, "to satisfy Mr. Cost."

In a dream you cannot escape: the feet are leaden-weighted: you cannot stir from before the ominous door which almost imperceptibly moves. It is the same in life; sometimes it is more difficult to make a scene than to die. A memory came back to him of someone else who wasn't certain, wouldn't make a scene, gave herself sadly up and took the milk. . . . He moved through the circle and sat down on Cost's left like a criminal taking his place in an identity parade. On his own left side was Miss Pantil. Dr. Forester was on one side of Mrs. Bellairs and Hilfe on the other. He hadn't time to see how the others were distributed before the light went out. "Now," Mrs. Bellairs said, "we'll all hold hands."

The blackout curtains had been drawn and the darkness was almost complete. Cost's hand felt hot and clammy, and Miss Pantil's hot and dry. This was the first séance he had ever attended, but it wasn't the spirits he feared. He wished Hilfe was beside him, and he was aware all the time of the dark empty space of the room behind his back, in which anything might happen. He tried to loosen his hands, but they were firmly gripped. There was complete silence in the room. A drop of sweat formed above his right eye and trickled down. He couldn't brush it away: it hung on his eyelid and tickled him. Somewhere in another room a gramophone began to play.

It played and played—something sweet and onomatopœic by Mendelssohn, full of waves breaking in echoing caverns. There was a pause and the needle was switched back and the melody began again. The same waves broke interminably into the same hollow. Over and over again. Underneath the music he became aware of breathing on all sides of him—all kinds of anxieties, suspenses, excitements controlling the various lungs. Miss Pantil's had an odd dry whistle in it, Cost's was heavy and regular, but not so heavy as another breath which laboured in the dark, he couldn't tell whose. All the time he listened and waited. Would he hear a step behind him and have time to snatch away his hands? He no longer doubted at all the urgency of that warning—"They'll try to get you in the dark." This was danger: this suspense was what somebody else had experienced, watching from day to day his pity grow to the monstrous proportions necessary to action.

"Yes," a voice called suddenly, "yes, I can't hear?" and Miss Pantil's breath whistled and Mendelssohn's waves moaned and withdrew. Very far away a taxi-horn cried through an empty world.

"Speak louder," the voice said. It was Mrs. Bellairs, with a difference: a Mrs. Bellairs drugged with an idea, with an imagined contact beyond the little dark constricted world in which they sat. He wasn't interested in any of that: it was a human movement he waited for. Mrs. Bellairs said in a husky voice, "One of you is an enemy. He won't let it come through." Something—a chair, a table?—cracked, and Rowe's fingers instinctively strained against Miss Pantil's. That wasn't a spirit. That was the human agency which shook tambourines or scattered flowers or imitated a child's touch upon the cheek—it was the dangerous element, but his hands were held.

"There is an enemy here," the voice said. "Somebody who doesn't believe, whose motives are evil. . . ." Rowe could feel Cost's fingers tighten round his. He wondered whether Hilfe was still completely oblivious to what was happening: he wanted to shout to him for help, but convention held him as firmly as Cost's hand. Again a board creaked. Why all this mummery, he thought, if they are all in it? But perhaps they were not all in it. For anything he knew he was surrounded by friends—but he didn't know which they were.

"Arthur."

He pulled at the hands holding him: that wasn't Mrs. Bellairs' voice.

"Arthur."

The flat hopeless voice might really have come from beneath the heavy graveyard slab.

"Arthur, why did you kill . . ." The voice moaned away into silence, and he struggled against the hands. It wasn't that he recognised the voice: it was no more his wife's than any woman's dying out in infinite hopelessness, pain and reproach: it was that the voice had recognised him. A light moved near the ceiling, feeling its way along the walls, and he cried, "Don't. Don't."

"Arthur," the voice whispered.

He forgot everything, he no longer listened for secretive movements, the creak of boards. He simply implored, "Stop it, please stop it," and felt Cost rise from the seat beside him and pull at his hand and then release it, throw the hand violently away, as though it were something he didn't like to hold. Even Miss Pantil let him go, and he heard Hilfe say, "This isn't funny. Put on the light."

It dazzled him, going suddenly on. They all sat there with joined hands watching him; he had broken the circle—only Mrs. Bellairs seemed to see nothing, with her head down and her eyes closed and her breathing heavy. "Well," Hilfe said, trying to raise a laugh, "that was certainly quite an act," but Mr. Newey said, "Cost. Look at Cost," and Rowe looked with all the others at his neighbour. He was taking no more interest in anything, leaning forward across the table with his face sunk on the French polish.

"Get a doctor," Hilfe said.

"I'm a doctor," Dr. Forester said. He released the hands on either side of him, and everyone became conscious of sitting there like children playing a game and surreptitiously let each other go. He said gently, "A doctor's no good, I'm afraid. The only thing to do is to call the police."

Mrs. Bellairs had half-woken up and sat with leery eyes and her tongue a little protruding.

"It must be his heart," Mr. Newey said. "Couldn't stand the excitement."

"I'm afraid not," Dr. Forester said. "He has been murdered." His old noble face was bent above the body; one long sensitive delicate hand dabbled and came up stained like a beautiful insect that feeds incongruously on carrion.

"Impossible," Mr. Newey said, "the door was locked."

"It's a pity," Dr. Forester said, "but there's a very simple explanation of that. One of us did it."

"But we were all," Hilfe said, "holding. . . ." Then they all looked at Rowe.

"He snatched away his hand," Miss Pantil said.

Dr. Forester said softly, "I'm not going to touch the body again before the police come. Cost was stabbed with a kind of schoolboy's knife. . . ."

Rowe put his hand quickly to an empty pocket and saw a room full of eyes noting the movement.

"We must get Mrs. Bellairs out of this," Dr. Forester said. "Any séance is a strain, but this one . . ." He and Hilfe between them raised the turbaned bulk; the hand which had so delicately dabbled in Cost's blood retrieved the key of the room with equal delicacy. "The rest of you," Dr. Forester said, "had better stay here, I think. I'll telephone to Notting Hill police station, and then we'll both be back."

For a long while there was silence after they had gone; nobody looked at Rowe, but Miss Pantil had slid her chair well away from him, so that he now sat alone beside the corpse, as though they were two friends who had got together at a party. Presently Mr. Newey said, "I'll never catch my train unless they hurry." Anxiety fought with horror—any moment the sirens might go—he caressed his sandalled foot across his knee, and young Maude said hotly, "I don't know why *you* should stay," glaring at Rowe.

It occurred to Rowe that he had not said one word to defend himself: the sense of guilt for a different crime stopped his mouth. Besides, what could he, a stranger, say to Miss Pantil, Mr. Newey and young Maude to convince them that in fact it was one of their friends who had murdered? He took a quick look at Cost, half expecting him to come alive again and laugh at them—"one of my tests," but nobody could have been deader than Cost was now. He thought: somebody here *has* killed him—it was fantastic, more fantastic really than that he should have done it himself. After all, he belonged to the region of murder—he was a native of that country. As the police will know, he thought, as the police will know.

The door opened and Hilfe returned. He said, "Dr. Forester is looking after Mrs. Bellairs. I have telephoned to the police." His eyes were saying something to Rowe which Rowe couldn't understand. Rowe thought: I must see him alone, surely he can't believe . . .

He said. "Would anybody object if I went to the lavatory and was sick?"

Miss Pantil said, "I don't think anybody ought to leave this room till the police come."

"I think," Hilfe said, "somebody should go with you. As a formality, of course."

"Why beat about the bush," Miss Pantil said. "Whose knife is it?"

"Perhaps Mr. Newey," Hilfe said, "wouldn't mind going with Mr. Rowe. . . ."

"I won't be drawn in," Newey said. "This has nothing to do with me. I only want to catch my train."

"Perhaps I had better go then," Hilfe said, "if you will trust me." No one objected.

The lavatory was on the first floor. They could hear from the landing the steady soothing rhythm of Dr. Forester's voice in Mrs. Bellairs' bedroom. "I'm all right," Rowe whispered. "But Hilfe, I didn't do it."

There was something shocking in the sense of exhilaration Hilfe conveyed at a time like this. "Of course you didn't," he said. "This is the Real Thing."

"But why? Who did it?"

"I don't know, but I'm going to find out." He put his hand on Rowe's arm with a friendliness that was very comforting, urging him into the lavatory and locking the door behind them. "Only, old fellow, you must be off out of this. They'll hang you if they can. Anyway, they'll shut you up for weeks. It's so convenient for Them."

"What can I do? It's my knife."

"They are devils, aren't they," Hilfe said with the same light-hearted relish he might have used for a children's clever prank. "We've just got to keep you out of the way till Mr. Rennit and I . . . By the way, better tell me who rang you up."

"It was your sister."

"My sister . . ." Hilfe grinned at him. "Good for her, she must have got hold of something. I wonder just where. She warned you, did she?"

"Yes, but I was not to tell you."

"Never mind that. I shan't eat her, shall I?" The pale blue eyes became suddenly lost in speculation.

Rowe tried to recall them. "Where can I go?"

"Oh, just underground," Hilfe said casually. He seemed in no hurry at all. "It's the fashion of our decade. Communists are always doing it. Don't you know how?"

"This isn't a joke."

"Listen," Hilfe said. "The end we are working for isn't a joke, but if we are going to keep our nerve we've got to keep our sense of humour. You see, They have none. Give me only a week. Keep out of the way as long as that."

"The police will be here soon."

Hilfe said, "It's only a small drop from this window to the flower-bed. It's nearly dark outside and in ten minutes the sirens will be going. Thank God, one can set one's clock by them."

"And you?"

"Pull the plug as you open the window. No one will hear you then. Wait till the cistern refills, then pull the plug again and knock me out 'good and hard.' It's the best alibi you can give me. After all, I'm an enemy alien."

5

Between Sleeping and Waking

"They came to a great forest, which seemed to have no path through it."

THE LITTLE DUKE

There are dreams which belong only partly to the unconscious; these are the dreams we remember on waking so vividly that we deliberately continue them, and so fall asleep again and wake and sleep and the dream goes on without interruption, with a thread of logic the pure dream doesn't possess.

Rowe was exhausted and frightened; he had made tracks half across London while the nightly raid got under way. It was an empty London with only occasional bursts of noise and activity. An umbrella shop was burning at the corner of Oxford Street; in Wardour Street he walked through a cloud of grit: a man with a grey dusty face leant against a wall and laughed and a warden said sharply, "That's enough now. It's nothing to laugh about." None of these things mattered. They were like something written; they didn't belong to his own life and he paid them no attention. But he had to find a bed, and so somewhere south of the river he obeyed Hilfe's advice and at last went underground.

He lay on the upper tier of a canvas bunk and dreamed that he was walking up a long hot road near Trumpington scuffing the white chalk-dust with his shoe caps. Then he was having tea on the lawn at home behind the red brick wall and his mother was lying back in a garden chair eating a cucumber sandwich. A bright blue croquet-ball lay at her feet, and she was smiling and paying him the half-attention a parent pays a child. The summer lay all around them, and evening was coming on. He was saying, "Mother, I murdered her . . ." and his mother said, "Don't be silly, dear. Have one of these nice sandwiches."

"But Mother," he said, "I did. I did." It seemed terribly important to him to convince her; if she were convinced, she could do something about it, she could tell him it didn't matter and it would matter no longer, but he had to convince her first. But she turned away her head and called out in a little vexed voice to someone who wasn't there, "You *must* remember to dust the piano."

"Mother, please listen to me," but he suddenly realised that he was a child, so how could he make her believe? He was not yet eight years old, he could see the nursery window on the second floor with the bars across, and presently the old nurse would put her face to the glass and signal to him to come in. "Mother," he said, "I've killed my wife, and the police want me." His mother smiled and shook her head and said, "My little boy couldn't kill anyone."

Time was short; from the other end of the long peaceful lawn, beyond the croquet hoops and out of the shadow of the great somnolent pine, came the vicar's wife carrying a basket of apples. Before she reached them he must convince his mother, but he had only childish words. "I have. I have."

His mother leant back smiling in the deck-chair, and said, "My little boy wouldn't hurt a beetle." (It was a way she had, always to get the conventional phrase just wrong.)

"But that's why," he said. "That's why," and his mother waved to the vicar's wife and said, "It's a dream, dear, a nasty dream."

He woke up to the dim lurid underground place—somebody had tied a red silk scarf over the bare globe to shield it. All along the walls the bodies lay two deep, while outside the raid rumbled and receded. This was a quiet night: any raid which happened a mile away wasn't a raid at all. An old man snored across the aisle and at the end of the shelter two lovers lay on a mattress with their hands and knees touching.

Rowe thought: this would be a dream, too, to her; she wouldn't believe it. She had died before the first great war, when aeroplanes—strange crates of wood—just staggered across the Channel. She could no more have imagined this than that her small son in his brown corduroy knickers and his blue jersey with his pale serious face—he could see himself like a stranger in the yellowing snapshots of her album—should grow up to be a murderer. Lying on his back he caught the dream and held it—pushed the vicar's wife back into the shadow of the pine—and argued with his mother.

"This isn't real life any more," he said. "Tea on the lawn, evensong, croquet, the old ladies calling, the gentle unmalicious gossip, the gardener trundling the wheelbarrow full of leaves and grass. People write about it as if it still went on; lady novelists describe it over and over again in books of the month, but it's not there any more."

His mother smiled at him in a scared way but let him talk; he was the master of the dream now. He said, "I'm wanted for a murder I didn't do. People want to kill me because I know too much. I'm hiding underground, and up above the Germans are methodically smashing London to bits all round me. You remember St. Clement's— the bells of St. Clement's. They've smashed that—St. James's, Piccadilly, the Burlington Arcade, Garland's Hotel, where we stayed for the pantomime, Maples and John Lewis. It sounds like a thriller, doesn't it, but the thrillers are like life—more like life than you are, this lawn, your sandwiches, that pine. You used to laugh at the books Miss Savage read—about spies, and murders, and violence, and wild motor-car chases, but dear, that's real life: it's what we've all made of the world since you died. I'm your little Arthur who wouldn't hurt a beetle and I'm a murderer too. The world has been remade by William Le Queux." He couldn't bear the frightened eyes which he had himself printed on the cement wall; he put his mouth to the steel frame of his bunk and kissed the white cold cheek. "My dear, my dear, my dear. I'm glad you are dead. Only do you know about it? do you know?" He was filled with horror at the thought of what a child becomes, and what the dead must feel watching the change from innocence to guilt and powerless to stop it.

"Why, it's a madhouse," his mother cried.

"Oh, it's much quieter there," he said. "I know. They put me in one for a time. Everybody was very kind there. They made me librarian. . . . ." He tried to express clearly the difference between the madhouse and this. "Everybody in the place was very—reasonable." He said fiercely, as though he hated her instead of loving her, "Let me lend you the History of Contemporary Society. It's in hundreds of volumes, but most of them are sold in cheap editions: *Death in Piccadilly*, *The Ambassador's Diamonds*, *The Theft of the Naval Papers*, *Diplomacy*, *Seven Days' Leave*, *The Four Just Men*. . . ."

He had worked the dream to suit himself, but now the dream began to regain control. He was no longer on the lawn; he was in the field behind the house where the donkey grazed which used to take their laundry to the other end of the village on Mondays. He was playing in a haystack with the vicar's son and a strange boy with a foreign accent and a dog called Spot. The dog caught a rat and tossed it, and the rat tried to crawl away with a broken back, and the dog made little playful excited rushes. Suddenly he couldn't bear the sight of the rat's pain any more; he picked up a cricket-bat and struck the rat on the head over and over again; he wouldn't stop for fear it was still alive, though he heard his nurse call out, "Stop it, Arthur. How can you? Stop it," and all the time Hilfe watched him with exhilaration. When he stopped he wouldn't look at the rat; he ran away across the field and hid. But you always had to come out of hiding some time, and presently his nurse was saying, "I won't tell your mother, but don't you ever do it again. Why, she thinks you wouldn't hurt a fly. What came over you I don't know." Not one of them guessed that what had come over him was the horrible and horrifying emotion of pity.

That was partly dream and partly memory, but the next was altogether dream. He lay on his side breathing heavily while the big guns opened up in North London, and his mind wandered again freely in that strange world where the past and future leave equal traces, and the geography may belong to twenty years ago or to next year. He was waiting for someone at a gate in a lane: over a high hedge came the sound of laughter and the dull thud of tennis-balls, and between the leaves he could see moth-like movements of white dresses. It was evening and it would soon be too dark to play, and someone would come out and he waited dumb with love. His heart beat with a boy's excitement, but it was the despair of a grown man that he felt when a stranger touched his shoulder and said, "Take him away." He didn't wake; this time he was in the main street of a small country town where he had sometimes, when a boy, stayed with an elder sister of his mother's. He was standing outside the inn yard of the King's Arms, and up the yard he could see the lit windows of the barn in which dances were held on Saturday nights. He had a pair of pumps under his arm and he was waiting for a girl much older than himself who would presently come out of her cloakroom and take his arm and go up the yard with him. All the next few hours were with him in the street: the small crowded hall full of the familiar peaceful faces—the chemist and his wife, the daughters of the headmaster, the bank manager and the dentist with his blue chin and his look of experience, the paper streamers of blue and green and scarlet, the small local orchestra, the sense of a life good and quiet and enduring, with only the gentle tug of impatience and young passion to disturb it for the while and make it doubly dear forever after. And then without warning the dream twisted towards nightmare; somebody was crying in the dark with terror—not the young woman he was waiting there to meet, whom he hadn't yet dared to kiss and probably never would, but someone whom he knew better even than his parents, who belonged to a different world altogether, to the sad world of shared love. A policeman stood at his elbow and said in a woman's voice, "You had better join our little group," and urged him remorselessly towards a urinal where a rat bled to death in the slate trough. The music had stopped, the lights had gone, and he couldn't remember why he had come to this dark vile corner, where even the ground whined when he pressed it, as if it had learnt the trick of suffering. He said, "Please let me go away from here," and the policeman said, "Where do you want to go to, dear?" He said, "Home," and the policeman said, "This is home. There isn't anywhere else at all," and whenever he tried to move his feet the earth whined back at him: he couldn't move an inch without causing pain.

He woke and the sirens were sounding the All Clear. One or two people in the shelter sat up for a moment to listen, and then lay down again. Nobody moved to go home: this was their home now. They were quite accustomed to sleeping underground; it had become as much part of life as the Saturday night film or the Sunday service had ever been. This was the world *they* knew.

6

Out of Touch

"You will find every door guarded."
THE LITTLE DUKE

i

Rowe had breakfast in an A.B.C. in Clapham High Street. Boards had taken the place of windows and the top floor had gone; it was like a shack put up in an earthquake town for relief work. For the enemy had done a lot of damage in

Clapham. London was no longer one great city: it was a collection of small towns. People went to Hampstead or St. John's Wood for a quiet week-end, and if you lived in Holborn you hadn't time between the sirens to visit friends as far away as Kensington. So special characteristics developed, and in Clapham where day raids were frequent there was a hunted look which was absent from Westminister, where the night raids were heavier but the shelters were better. The waitress who brought Rowe's toast and coffee looked jumpy and pallid, as if she had lived too much on the run; she had an air of listening whenever gears shrieked. Gray's Inn and Russell Square were noted for a more reckless spirit, but only because they had the day to recover in.

The night raid, the papers said, had been on a small scale. A number of bombs had been dropped, and there had been a number of casualties, some of them fatal. The morning communiqué was like the closing ritual of a midnight Mass. The sacrifice was complete and the papers pronounced in calm invariable words the "Ite Missa Est." Not even in the smallest type under a single headline was there any reference to an "Alleged Murder at a Séance"; nobody troubled about single deaths. Rowe felt a kind of indignation. He had made the headlines once, but his own disaster, if it had happened now, would have been given no space at all. He had almost a sense of desertion; nobody was troubling to pursue so insignificant a case in the middle of a daily massacre. Perhaps a few elderly men in the C.I.D., who were too old to realise how the world had passed them by, were still allowed by patient and kindly superiors to busy themselves in little rooms with the trivialities of a murder. They probably wrote minutes to each other; they might even be allowed to visit the scene of the "crime," but he could hardly believe that the results of their inquiries were read with more interest than the scribblings of those eccentric clergymen who were still arguing about evolution in country vicarages. "Old So-and-So," he could imagine a senior officer saying, "poor old thing, we let him have a few murder cases now and then. In his day, you know, we used to pay quite a lot of attention to murder, and it makes him feel that he's still of use. The results— Oh well, of course, he never dreams that we haven't time to read his reports."

Rowe, sipping his coffee, seeking over and over again for the smallest paragraph, felt a kinship with the detective inspectors, the Big Five, *My Famous Cases*; he was a murderer and old-fashioned, he belonged to their world—and whoever had murdered Cost belonged there too. He felt a slight resentment against Willi Hilfe, who treated murder as a joke with a tang to it. But Hilfe's sister hadn't treated it as a joke; she had warned him, she had talked as if death were still a thing that mattered. Like a lonely animal he scented the companionship of his own kind.

The pale waitress kept an eye on him; he had had no chance of shaving, so that he looked like one of those who leave without paying. It was astonishing what a single night in a public shelter could do to you; he could smell disinfectant on his clothes as though he had spent the night in a workhouse infirmary.

He paid his bill and asked the waitress, "Have you a telephone?" She indicated one near the cash desk, and he dialled Rennit. It was risky, but something had to be done. Of course, the hour was too early. He could hear the bell ringing uselessly in the empty room, and he wondered whether the sausage-roll still lay beside it on the saucer. It was always in these days questionable whether a telephone bell would ring at all, because overnight a building might have ceased to exist. He knew now that part of the world was the same: Orthotex still stood.

He went back to his table and ordered another coffee and some notepaper. The waitress regarded him with increasing suspicion. Even in a crumbling world the conventions held; to order again after payment was unorthodox, but to ask for notepaper was continental. She could give him a leaf from her order pad, that was all. Conventions were far more rooted than morality; he had himself found that it was easier to allow oneself to be murdered than to break up a social gathering. He began to write carefully in a spidery hand an account of everything that had happened. Something had got to be done; he wasn't going to remain permanently in hiding for a crime he hadn't committed, while the real criminals got away with—whatever it was they were trying to get away with. In his account he left out Hilfe's name—you never knew what false ideas the police might get, and he didn't want his only ally put behind bars. He was already deciding to post his narrative straight to Scotland Yard.

When he had finished it, he read it over while the waitress watched; the story was a terribly thin one—a cake, a visitor, a taste he thought he remembered, until you got to Cost's body and all the evidence pointing at himself. Perhaps after all he would do better not to post it to the police, but rather to some friend. . . . But he had no friend, unless he counted Hilfe . . . or Rennit. He made for the door and the waitress stopped him. "You haven't paid for your coffee."

"I'm sorry. I forgot."

She took the money with an air of triumph; she had been right all the time. She watched him through the window from between the empty cake-stands making his uncertain way up Clapham High Street.

Promptly at nine o'clock he rang again—from close by Stockwell Station—and again the empty room drummed on his ear. By nine-fifteen, when he rang a third time, Mr. Rennit had returned. He heard his sharp anxious voice saying, "Yes. Who's there?"

"This is Rowe."

"What have you done with Jones?" Mr. Rennit accused him.

"I left him yesterday," Rowe said, "outside . . ."

"He hasn't come back," Mr. Rennit said.

"Maybe he's shadowing . . ."

"I owe him a week's wages. He said he'd be back last night. It's not natural." Mr. Rennit wailed up the phone, "Jones wouldn't stay away, not with me owing him money."

"Worse things have happened than that."

"Jones is my right arm," Mr. Rennit said. "What have you done with him?"

"I went and saw Mrs. Bellairs . . ."

"That's neither here nor there. I want Jones."

"And a man was killed."

"What?"

"And the police think I murdered him."

There was another wail up the line. The small shifty man was being carried out of his depth; all through his life he had swum safely about among his prickly little adulteries, his compromising letters, but the tide was washing him out to where the bigger fishes hunted. He moaned, "I never wanted to take up your case."

"You've got to advise me, Rennit. I'll come and see you."

"No." He could hear the breath catch down the line. The voice imperceptibly altered. "When?"

"At ten o'clock. Rennit, are you still there?" He had to explain to somebody. "I didn't do it, Rennit. You must believe that. I don't make a habit of murder." He always bit on the word murder as you bite a sore spot on the tongue; he never used the word without self-accusation. The law had taken a merciful view: himself he took the merciless one. Perhaps if they had hanged him he would have found excuses for himself between the trap-door and the bottom of the drop, but they had given him a lifetime to analyse his motives in.

He analysed now—an unshaven man in dusty clothes sitting in the Tube between Stockwell and Tottenham Court Road. (He had to go a roundabout route because the Tube had been closed at many stations.) The dreams of the previous night had set his mind in reverse. He remembered himself twenty years ago day-dreaming and in love; he remembered without self-pity, as one might watch the development of a biological specimen. He had in those days imagined himself capable of extraordinary heroisms and endurances which would make the girl he loved forget the awkward hands and the spotty chin of adolescence. Everything had seemed possible. One could laugh at day-dreams, but so long as you had the capacity to day-dream, there was a chance that you might develop some of the qualities of which you dreamed. It was like the religious discipline: words however emptily repeated can in time form a habit, a kind of unnoticed sediment at the bottom of the mind—until one day to your own surprise you find yourself acting on the belief you thought you didn't believe in. Since the death of his wife Rowe had never day-dreamed; all through the trial he had never even dreamed of an acquittal. It was as if that side of the brain had been dried up; he was no longer capable of sacrifice, courage, virtue, because he no longer dreamed of them. He was aware of the loss—the world had dropped a dimension and become paper-thin. He wanted to dream, but all he could practise now was despair, and the kind of cunning which warned him to approach Mr. Rennit with circumspection.

ii

Nearly opposite Mr. Rennit's was an auction-room which specialised in books. It was possible from before the shelves nearest the door to keep an eye on the entrance to Mr. Rennit's block. The weekly auction was to take place next day, and visitors flowed in with catalogues; an unshaven chin and a wrinkled suit were not out of place here. A man with a ragged moustache and an out-at-elbows jacket, the pockets bulging with sandwiches, looked carefully through a folio volume of landscape gardening: a Bishop—or he might have been a Dean—was examining a set of the

Waverley novels: a big white beard brushed the libidinous pages of an illustrated Brantôme. Nobody here was standardised; in tea-shops and theatres people are cut to the pattern of their environment, but in this auction-room the goods were too various to appeal to any one type. Here was pornography—eighteenth-century French with beautiful little steel engravings celebrating the copulations of elegant over-clothed people on Pompadour couches, here were all the Victorian novelists, the memoirs of obscure pig-stickers, the eccentric philosophies and theologies of the seventeenth century—Newton on the geographical position of Hell, and Jeremiah Whiteley on the Path of Perfection. There was a smell of neglected books, of the straw from packing-cases and of clothes which had been too often rained upon. Standing by the shelves containing lots one to thirty-five Rowe was able to see anyone who came in or out by the door Mr. Rennit used.

Just on the level of his eyes was a Roman missal of no particular value included in Lot 20 with Religious Books Various. A big round clock, which itself had once formed part of an auction, as you could tell from the torn label below the dial, pointed 9:45 above the auctioneer's desk. Rowe opened the missal at random, keeping three-quarters of his attention for the house across the street. The missal was ornamented with ugly coloured capitals; oddly enough, it was the only thing that spoke of war in the old quiet room. Open it where you would, you came on prayers for deliverance, the angry nations, the unjust, the wicked, the adversary like a roaring lion. . . . The words stuck out between the decorated borders like cannon out of a flower-bed. "Let not man prevail," he read—and the truth of the appeal chimed like music. For in all the world outside that room man had indeed prevailed; he had himself prevailed. It wasn't only evil men who did these things. Courage smashes a cathedral, endurance lets a city starve, pity kills . . . we are trapped and betrayed by our virtues. It might be that whoever killed Cost had for that instant given his goodness rein, and Rennit, perhaps for the first time in his life, was behaving like a good citizen by betraying his client. You couldn't mistake the police officer who had taken his stand behind a newspaper just outside the auction-room.

He was reading the *Daily Mirror*. Rowe could see the print over his shoulder with Zec's cartoon filling most of the page. Once, elusively, from an upper window Mr. Rennit peered anxiously out and withdrew. The clock in the auction-room said five minutes to ten. The grey day full of last night's débris and the smell of damp plaster crept on. Even Mr. Rennit's desertion made Rowe feel a degree more abandoned.

There had been a time when he had friends, not many because he was not gregarious—but for that very reason in his few friendships he had plunged deeply. At school there had been three: they had shared hopes, biscuits, measureless ambitions, but now he couldn't remember their names or their faces. Once he had been addressed suddenly in Piccadilly Circus by an extraordinary grey-haired man with a flower in his button-hole and a double-breasted waistcoat and an odd finicky manner, an air of uncertain and rather seedy prosperity. "Why, if it isn't Boojie," the stranger said, and led the way to the bar of the Piccadilly Hotel, while Rowe sought in vain for some figure in the lower fourth—in black Sunday trousers or football shorts, inky or mud-stained—who might be connected with this over-plausible man who now tried unsuccessfully to borrow a fiver, then slid away to the gents and was no more seen, leaving the bill for Boojie to pay.

More recent friends he had had, of course: perhaps half a dozen. Then he married and his friends became his wife's friends even more than his own. Tom Curtis, Crooks, Perry and Vane . . . Naturally they had faded away after his arrest. Only poor silly Henry Wilcox continued to stand by, because, he said, "I know you are innocent. You wouldn't hurt a fly"—that ominous phrase which had been said about him too often. He remembered how Wilcox had looked when he said, "But I'm not innocent. I did kill her." After that there wasn't even Wilcox or his small domineering wife who played hockey. (Their mantelpiece was crowded with the silver trophies of her prowess.)

The plain-clothes man looked impatient. He had obviously read every word of his paper because it was still open at the same place. The clock said five past ten. Rowe closed his catalogue, after marking a few lots at random, and walked out into the street. The plain-clothes man said, "Excuse me," and Rowe's heart missed a beat.

"Yes?"

"I've come out without a match."

"You can keep the box," Rowe said.

"I couldn't do that, not in these days." He looked over Rowe's shoulder, up the street to the ruins of the Safe Deposit, where safes stood about like the above-ground tombs in Latin cemeteries, then followed with his eye a middle-aged clerk trailing his umbrella past Rennit's door.

"Waiting for someone?" Rowe asked.

"Oh, just a friend," the detective said clumsily. "He's late."

"Good morning."

"Good morning, sir." The "sir" was an error in tactics, like the soft hat at too official an angle and the unchanging page of the *Daily Mirror*. They don't trouble to send their best men for mere murder, Rowe thought, touching the little sore again with his tongue.

What next? He found himself, not for the first time, regretting Henry Wilcox. There were men who lived voluntarily in deserts, but they had their God to commune with. For nearly ten years he had felt no need of friends—one woman could include any number of friends. He wondered where Henry was in wartime. Perry would have joined up and so would Curtis. He imagined Henry as an air-raid warden, fussy and laughed at when all was quiet, a bit scared now during the long exposed vigils on the deserted pavements, but carrying on in dungarees that didn't suit him and a helmet a size too large. God damn it, he thought, coming out on the ruined corner of High Holborn, I've done my best to take part too. It's not my fault I'm not fit enough for the army, and as for the damned heroes of civil defence—the little clerks and prudes and what-have-yous—they didn't want me: not when they found I had done time—even time in an asylum wasn't respectable enough for Post Four or Post Two or Post any number. And now they've thrown me out of their war altogether; they want me for a murder I didn't do. What chance would they give me with my record?

He thought: Why should I bother about that cake any more? It's nothing to do with me: it's their war, not mine. Why shouldn't I just go into hiding until everything's blown over (surely in wartime a murder does blow over). It's not my war; I seem to have stumbled into the firing-line, that's all. I'll get out of London and let the fools scrap it out, and the fools die. . . . There may have been nothing important in the cake; it may have contained only a paper cap, a motto, a lucky sixpence. Perhaps that hunchback hadn't meant a thing: perhaps the taste was imagination: perhaps the whole scene never happened at all as I remember it. Blast often did odd things, and it certainly wasn't beyond its power to shake a brain that had too much to brood about already. . . .

As if he were escaping from some bore who walked beside him explaining things he had no interest in, he dived suddenly into a telephone-box and rang a number. A stern dowager voice admonished him down the phone as though he had no right on the line at all, "This is the Free Mothers. Who is that, please?"

"I want to speak to Miss Hilfe."

"Who is that?"

"A friend of hers." A disapproving grunt twanged the wires. He said sharply, "Put me through, please," and almost at once he heard the voice which if he had shut his eyes and eliminated the telephone-box and ruined Holborn he could have believed was his wife's. There was really no resemblance, but it was so long since he had spoken to a woman, except his landlady or a girl behind a counter, that any feminine voice took him back . . . "Please. Who is that?"

"Is that Miss Hilfe?"

"Yes. Who are you?"

He said as if his name were a household word, "I'm Rowe."

There was such a long pause that he thought she had put the receiver back. He said, "Hullo. Are you there?"

"Yes."

"I wanted to talk to you."

"You shouldn't ring me."

"I've nobody else to ring—except your brother. Is he there?"

"No."

"You heard what happened?"

"He told me."

"You had expected something, hadn't you?"

"Not that. Something worse." She explained, "I didn't know *him*."

"I brought you some worries, didn't I, when I came in yesterday?"

"Nothing worries my brother."

"I rang up Rennit."

"Oh no, no. You shouldn't have done that."

"I haven't learnt the technique yet. You can guess what happened."

"Yes. The police."

"You know what your brother wants me to do?"

"Yes."

Their conversation was like a letter which has to pass a censorship. He had an overpowering desire to talk to someone frankly. He said, "Would you meet me somewhere—for five minutes?"

"No," she said. "I can't. I can't get away."

"Just for two minutes."

"It's not possible."

It suddenly became of great importance to him. "Please," he said.

"It wouldn't be safe. My brother would be angry."

He said, "I'm so alone. I don't know what's happening. I've got nobody to advise me. There are so many questions . . ."

"I'm sorry."

"Can I write to you . . . or him?"

She said, "Just send your address here—to me. No need to sign the note—or sign it with any name you like."

Refugees had such stratagems on the tip of the tongue; it was a familiar way of life. He wondered whether if he were to ask her about money she would have an answer equally ready. He felt like a child who is lost and finds an adult hand to hold, a hand that guides him understandingly homewards. . . . He became reckless of the imaginary censor. He said, "There's nothing in the papers."

"Nothing."

"I've written a letter to the police."

"Oh," she said, "you shouldn't have done that. Have you posted it?"

"No."

"Wait and see," she said. "Perhaps there won't be any need. Just wait and see."

"Do you think it would be safe to go to my bank?"

"You are so helpless," she said, "so helpless. Of course you mustn't. They will watch for you there."

"Then how can I live . . . ?"

"Haven't you a friend who would cash you a cheque?"

Suddenly he didn't want to admit to her that there was no one at all. "Yes," he said, "yes. I suppose so."

"Well then. . . . Just keep away," she said so gently that he had to strain his ears.

"I'll keep away."

She had rung off. He put the receiver down and moved back into Holborn, keeping away. Just ahead of him, with bulging pockets, went one of the bookworms from the auction-room.

"Haven't you a friend?" she had said. Refugees had always friends; people smuggled letters, arranged passports, bribed officials; in that enormous underground land as wide as a continent there was companionship. In England one hadn't yet learned the technique. Whom could he ask to take one of his cheques? Not a tradesman. Since he began to live alone he had dealt with shops only through his landlady. He thought for the second time that day of his former friends. It hadn't occurred to Anna Hilfe that a refugee might be friendless. A refugee always has a party—or a race.

He thought of Perry and Vane: not a chance even if he had known how to find them. Crooks, Boyle, Curtis. . . . Curtis was quite capable of knocking him down. He had simple standards, primitive ways and immense complacency. Simplicity in friends had always attracted Rowe: it was a complement to his own qualities. There remained Henry Wilcox. There was just a chance there . . . if the hockey-playing wife didn't interfere. Their two wives had had nothing in common. Rude health and violent pain were too opposed, but a kind of self-protective instinct would have made Mrs. Wilcox hate him. Once a man started killing his wife, she would have ungrammatically thought, you couldn't tell where it would stop.

But what excuse could he give Henry? He was aware of the bulge in his breast pocket where his statement lay, but he couldn't tell Henry the truth: no more than the police would Henry believe that he had been present at a murder as an onlooker. He must wait till after the banks closed—that was early enough in wartime, and then invent some urgent reason.

What? He thought about it all through lunch in an Oxford Street Lyons, and got no clue. Perhaps it was better to leave it to what people called the inspiration of the moment, or, better still, give it up, give himself up. It only occurred to him as he was paying his bill that probably he wouldn't be able to find Henry anyway. Henry had lived in Battersea, and Battersea was not a good district to live in now. He might not even be alive—twenty thousand people were dead already. He looked him up in a telephone book. He was there.

That meant nothing, he told himself; the blitz was newer than the edition. All the same, he dialled the number just to see—it was as if all his contacts now had to be down a telephone line. He was almost afraid to hear the ringing tone, and when it came he put the receiver down quickly and with pain. He had rung Henry up so often—before things happened. Well, he had to make up his mind now: the flat was still there, though Henry mightn't be in it. He couldn't brandish a cheque down a telephone line; this time the contact had got to be physical. And he hadn't seen Henry since the day before the trial.

He would almost have preferred to throw his hand in altogether.

He caught a number 19 bus from Piccadilly. After the ruins of St. James's Church one passed at that early date into peaceful country. Knightsbridge and Sloane Street were not at war, but Chelsea was, and Battersea was in the front line. It was an odd front line that twisted like the track of a hurricane and left patches of peace. Battersea, Holborn, the East End, the front line curled in and out of them . . . and yet to a casual eye Poplar High Street had hardly known the enemy, and there were pieces of Battersea where the public-house stood at the corner with the dairy and the baker beside it, and as far as you could see there were no ruins anywhere.

It was like that in Wilcox's street; the big middle-class flats stood rectangular and gaunt like railway hotels, completely undamaged, looking out over the park. There were To Let boards up all the way down, and Rowe half hoped he would find one outside No. 63. But there was none. In the hall was a frame in which occupants could show whether they were in or out, but the fact that the Wilcox's was marked In meant nothing at all, even if they still lived there, for Henry had a theory that to mark the board Out was to invite burglary. Henry's caution had always imposed on his friends a long tramp upstairs to the top floor (there were no lifts).

The stairs were at the back of the flats looking towards Chelsea, and as you climbed above the second floor and your view lifted, the war came back into sight. Most of the church spires seemed to have been snapped off two-thirds up like sugar-sticks, and there was an appearance of slum clearance where there hadn't really been any slums.

It was painful to come in sight of the familiar 63. He used to pity Henry because of his masterful wife, his conventional career, the fact that his work—chartered accountancy—seemed to offer no escape; four hundred a year of Rowe's own had seemed like wealth, and he had for Henry some of the feeling a rich man might have for a poor relation. He used to give Henry things. Perhaps that was why Mrs. Wilcox hadn't liked him. He smiled with affection when he saw a little plaque on the door marked A.R.P. Warden: it was exactly as he had pictured. But his finger hesitated on the bell.

iii

He hadn't had time to ring when the door opened and there was Henry. An oddly altered Henry. He had always been a neat little man—his wife had seen to that. Now he was in dirty blue dungarees, and he was unshaven. He walked past Rowe as though he didn't see him and leant over the well of the staircase. "They aren't here," he said.

A middle-aged woman with red eyes who looked like a cook followed him out and said, "It's not time, Henry. It's really not time." For a moment—so altered was Henry—Rowe wondered whether the war had done this to Henry's wife too.

Henry suddenly became aware of him—or half aware of him. He said, "Oh, Arthur . . . good of you to come," as though they'd met yesterday. Then he dived back into his little dark hall and became a shadowy abstracted figure beside a grandfather clock.

"If you'd come in," the woman said, "I don't think they'll be long now."

He followed her in and noticed that she left the door open, as though others were expected; he was getting used now to life taking him up and planting him down without his own volition in surroundings where only he was not at home. On the oak chest—made, he remembered, to Mrs. Wilcox's order by the Tudor Manufacturing Company—a pair of dungarees was neatly folded with a steel hat on top. He was reminded of prison, where you left your own clothes behind. In the dimness Henry repeated, "Good of you, Arthur," and fled again.

The middle-aged woman said, "Any friend of Henry's is welcome. I am Mrs. Wilcox." She seemed to read his astonishment even in the dark, and explained, "Henry's mother." She said, "Come and wait inside. I don't suppose they'll be long. It's so dark here. The blackout, you know. Most of the glass is gone." She led the way into what Rowe remembered was the dining-room. There were glasses laid out as though there was going to be a party. It seemed an odd time of day . . . too late or too early. Henry was there; he gave the effect of having been driven into a corner, of having fled here. On the mantelpiece behind him were four silver cups with the names of teams engraved in double entry under a date: to have drunk out of one of them would have been like drinking out of an account book.

Rowe, looking at the glasses, said, "I didn't mean to intrude," and Henry remarked for the third time, as though it were a phrase he didn't have to use his brain in forming, "Good of you . . ." He seemed to have no memory left of that prison scene on which their friendship had foundered. Mrs. Wilcox said, "It's so good the way Henry's old friends are all rallying to him." Then Rowe, who had been on the point of inquiring after Henry's wife, suddenly understood. Death was responsible for the glasses, the unshaven chin, the waiting . . . even for what had puzzled him most of all, the look of youth on Henry's face. People say that sorrow ages, but just as often sorrow makes a man younger—ridding him of responsibility, giving in its place the lost unanchored look of adolescence.

He said, "I didn't know. I wouldn't have come if I'd known."

Mrs. Wilcox said with gloomy pride, "It was in all the papers."

Henry stood in his corner; his teeth chattered while Mrs. Wilcox went remorselessly on—she had had a good cry, her son was hers again. "We are proud of Doris. The whole post is doing her honour. We are going to lay her uniform—her clean uniform—on the coffin, and the clergyman is going to read about 'Greater love hath no man.' "

"I'm sorry, Henry."

"She was crazy," Henry said angrily. "She had no right . . . I told her the wall would collapse."

"But we are proud of her, Henry," his mother said, "we are proud of her."

"I should have stopped her," Henry said. "I suppose," his voice went high with rage and grief, "she thought she'd win another of those blasted pots."

"She was playing for England, Henry," Mrs. Wilcox said. She turned to Rowe and said, "I think we ought to lay a hockey-stick beside the uniform, but Henry won't have it."

"I'll be off," Rowe said. "I'd never have come if . . ."

"No," Henry said, "*you* stay. *You* know how it is. . . ." He stopped and looked at Rowe as though he realised him fully for the first time. He said, "I killed my wife too. I could have held her, knocked her down. . . ."

"You don't know what you are saying, Henry," his mother said. "What will this gentleman think . . . ?"

"This is Arthur Rowe, mother."

"Oh," Mrs. Wilcox said, "oh," and at that moment up the street came the slow sad sound of wheels and feet.

"How dare he . . . ?" Mrs. Wilcox said.

"He's my oldest friend, mother," Henry said. Somebody was coming up the stairs. "Why *did* you come, Arthur?" Henry said.

"To get you to cash me a cheque."

"The impudence," Mrs. Wilcox said.

"I didn't know about this . . ."

"How much, old man?"

"Twenty?"

"I've only got fifteen. You can have that."

"Don't trust him," Mrs. Wilcox said.

"Oh, my cheques are good enough. Henry knows that."

"There are banks to go to."

"Not at this time of day, Mrs. Wilcox. I'm sorry. It's urgent."

There was a little trumpery Queen Anne desk in the room: it had obviously belonged to Henry's wife. All the furniture had an air of flimsiness; walking between it was like walking, in the old parlour game, blindfold between bottles. Perhaps in her home the hockey-player had reacted from the toughness of the field. Now moving to get at the desk Henry's shoulder caught a silver cup and set it rolling across the carpet. Suddenly in the open door appeared a very fat man in dungarees carrying a white steel helmet. He picked up the cup and said solemnly, "The procession's here, Mrs. Wilcox."

Henry dithered by the desk.

"I have the uniform ready," Mrs. Wilcox said, "in the hall."

"I couldn't get a Union Jack," the post warden said, "not a big one. And those little ones they stick on ruins didn't somehow look respectful." He was painfully trying to exhibit the bright side of death. "The whole post's turned out, Mr. Wilcox," he said, "except those that have to stay on duty. And the A.F.S.—they've sent a contingent. And there's a rescue party and four salvage men—and the police band."

"I think that's wonderful," Mrs. Wilcox said. "If only Doris could see it all."

"But she *can* see it, ma'am," the post warden said. "I'm sure of that."

"And afterwards," Mrs. Wilcox said, gesturing towards the glasses, "if you'll all come up here . . ."

"There's a good many of us, ma'am. Perhaps we'd better make it just the wardens. The salvage men don't really expect . . ."

"Come along, Henry," Mrs. Wilcox said. "We can't keep all these brave kind souls waiting. You must carry the uniform down in your arms. Oh dear, I wish you looked more tidy. Everybody will be watching you."

"I don't see," Henry said, "why we shouldn't have buried her quietly."

"But she's a heroine," Mrs. Wilcox exclaimed.

"I wouldn't be surprised," the post warden said, "if they gave her the George Medal—posthumously. It's the first in the borough—it would be a grand thing for the post."

"Why, Henry," Mrs. Wilcox said, "she's not just your wife any more. She belongs to England."

Henry moved towards the door: the post warden still held the silver cup awkwardly—he didn't know where to put it. "Just anywhere," Henry said to him, "anywhere." They all moved into the hall, leaving Rowe. "You've forgotten your helmet, Henry," Mrs. Wilcox said. He had been a very precise man, and he'd lost his precision; all the things which had made Henry Henry were gone. It was as if his character had consisted of a double-breasted waistcoat, columns of figures, a wife who played hockey. Without these things he was unaccountable, he didn't add up. "You go," he said to his mother, "you go."

"But Henry . . ."

"It's understandable, ma'am," the post warden said, "it's feeling that does it. We've always thought Mr. Wilcox a very sensitive gentleman at the post. They'll understand," he added kindly, meaning, one supposed, the post, the police band, the A.F.S., even the four salvage men. He urged Mrs. Wilcox towards the door with a friendly broad hand, then picked up the uniform himself. Hints of the past penetrated the anonymity of the dungarees—the peaceful past of a manservant, or perhaps of a Commissionaire who ran out into the rain carrying an umbrella. War is very like a bad dream in which familiar people appear in terrible and unlikely disguises. Even Henry . . .

Rowe made an indeterminate motion to follow; he couldn't help hoping it would remind Henry of the cheque. It was his only chance of getting any money: there was nobody else. Henry said, "We'll just see them go off and then we'll come back here. You do understand don't you, I couldn't bear to watch . . ." They came out together into the road by the park; the procession had already started: it moved like a little dark trickle towards the river. The steel hat on the coffin lay blackened and unreflecting under the winter sun, and the rescue party didn't keep step with the post. It was like a parody of a State funeral—but this *was* a State funeral. The brown leaves from the park were blowing across the road, and the drinkers coming out at closing time from the Duke of Rockingham took off their hats. Henry said, "I told her not to do it . . ." and the wind blew the sound of footsteps back to them. It was as if they had surrendered her to the people, to whom she had never belonged before.

Henry said suddenly, "Excuse me, old man," and started after her. He hadn't got his helmet: his hair was beginning to go grey: he broke into a trot, for fear after all of being left behind. He was rejoining his wife and his post. Arthur Rowe was left alone. He turned his money over in his pocket and found there wasn't much of it.

7

A Load of Books

"Taken as we are by surprise, our resistance
will little avail."
THE LITTLE DUKE

i

Even if a man has been contemplating the advantages of suicide for two years, he takes time to make his final decision—to move from theory to practice. Rowe couldn't simply go then and there and drop into the river—besides, he would have been pulled out again. And yet watching the procession recede he could see no other solution. He was wanted by the police for murder, and he had thirty-five shillings in his pocket. He couldn't go to the bank and he had no friend but Henry; of course, he could wait till Henry came back, but the cold-blooded egotism of that act repelled him. It would be simpler and less disgusting to die. A brown leaf settled on his coat—that according to the old story meant money, but the old story didn't say how soon.

He walked along the Embankment towards Chelsea Bridge; the tide was low and the sea-gulls walked delicately on the mud. One noticed the absence of perambulators and dogs: the only dog in sight looked stray and uncared for and evasive. A barrage balloon staggered up from behind the park trees: its huge nose bent above the thin winter foliage, and then it turned its dirty old backside and climbed.

It wasn't only that he had no money: he had no longer what he called a home —somewhere to shelter from people who might know him. He missed Mrs. Purvis coming in with the tea; he used to count the days by her: punctuated by her knock they would slide smoothly towards the end—annihilation, forgiveness, punishment or peace. He missed *David Copperfield* and *The Old Curiosity Shop*; he could no longer direct his sense of pity towards the fictitious sufferings of little Nell—it roamed around and saw too many objects—too many rats that needed to be killed. And he was one of them.

Leaning over the Embankment in the time-honoured attitude of would-be suicides, he began to go into the details. He wanted as far as possible to be unobtrusive; now that his anger had died it seemed to him a pity that he hadn't drunk that cup of tea—he didn't want to shock any innocent person with the sight of an ugly death. And there were very few suicides which were not ugly. Murder was infinitely more graceful because it was the murderer's object not to shock—a murderer went to infinite pains to make death look quiet, peaceful, happy. Everything, he thought, would be so much easier if he had only a little money.

Of course, he could go to the bank and let the police get him. It seemed probable that then he would be hanged. But the idea of hanging for a crime he hadn't committed still had power to anger him: if he killed himself it would be for a crime of which he was guilty. He was haunted by a primitive idea of Justice. He wanted to conform: he had always wanted to conform.

A murderer is regarded by the conventional world as something almost monstrous, but a murderer to himself is only an ordinary man—a man who takes either tea or coffee for breakfast, a man who likes a good book and perhaps reads biography rather than fiction, a man who at a regular hour goes to bed, who tries to develop good physical habits but possibly suffers from constipation, who prefers either dogs or cats and has certain views about politics.

It is only if the murderer is a good man that he can be regarded as monstrous.

Arthur Rowe was monstrous. His early childhood had been passed before the first world war, and the impressions of childhood are ineffaceable. He was brought up to believe that it was wrong to inflict pain, but he was often ill, his teeth were bad and he suffered agonies from an inefficient dentist he knew as Mr. Griggs. He learned before he was seven what pain was like—he wouldn't willingly allow even a rat to suffer it. In childhood we live under the brightness of immortality—heaven is as near and actual as the seaside. Behind the complicated details of the world stand the simplicities: God is good, the grown-up man or woman knows the answer to every question, there is such a thing as truth, and justice is as measured and faultless as a clock. Our heroes are simple: they are brave, they tell the truth, they are good swordsmen and they are never in the long run really defeated. That is why no later books satisfy us like those which were read to us in childhood—for those promised a world of great simplicity of which we knew the rules, but the later books are complicated and contradictory with experience; they are formed out of our own disappointing memories—of the V.C. in the police-court dock, of the faked income tax return, the sins in corners, and the hollow voice of the man we despised talking to us of courage and purity. The Little Duke is dead and betrayed and forgotten; we cannot recognise the villain and we suspect the hero and the world is a small cramped place. The two great popular statements of faith are "What a small place the world is" and "I'm a stranger here myself."

But Rowe was a murderer—as other men are poets. The statues still stood. He was prepared to do anything to save the innocent or to punish the guilty. He believed against all the experience of life that somewhere there was justice, and justice condemned him. He analysed his motives minutely and always summed up against himself. He told himself, leaning over the wall, as he had told himself a hundred times, that it was he who had not been able to bear his wife's pain—and not she. Once, it was true, in the early days of the disease, she had broken down, said she wanted to die, not to wait: that was hysteria. Later it was her endurance and her patience which he had found most unbearable. He was trying to escape his own pain, not hers, and at the end she had guessed or half-guessed what it was he was offering her. She was scared and afraid to ask. How could you go on living with a man if you had once asked him whether he had put poison into your evening drink? Far easier when you love him and are tired of pain just to take the hot milk and sleep. But he could never know whether the fear had been worse than the pain, and he could never tell whether she might not have preferred any sort of life to death. He had taken the stick and killed the rat, and saved himself the agony of watching. . . . He had gone over the same questions and the same answers daily, ever since the moment when she took the milk from him and said, "How queer it tastes," and lay back and tried to smile. He would have liked to stay beside her till she slept, but that would have been unusual, and he must avoid anything unusual, so he had to leave her to die alone. And she would have liked to ask him to stay —he was sure of that—but that would have been unusual too. After all, in an hour he would be coming up to bed. Convention held them at the moment of death. He had in mind the police questions, "Why did you stay?" and it was quite possible that she too was deliberately playing his game against the police. There were so many things he would never know. But when the police did ask questions he hadn't the heart or the energy to tell them lies. Perhaps if he had lied to them a little they would have hanged him. . . .

It was about time now to bring the trial to an end.

ii

"They can't spoil Whistler's Thames," a voice said.

"I'm sorry," Rowe said, "I didn't catch . . ."

"It's safe underground. Bomb-proof vaults."

Somewhere, Rowe thought, he had seen that face before: the thin depressed grey moustache, the bulging pockets, out of which the man now took a piece of bread and threw it towards the mud. Before it had reached the river the gulls had risen: one outdistanced the others, caught it and sailed on, down past the stranded barges and the paper mill, a white scrap blown towards the blackened chimneys of Lots Road.

"Come, my pretties," the man said, and his hand suddenly became a landing ground for sparrows. "They know uncle," he said, "they know uncle." He put a bit of bread between his lips and they hovered round his mouth giving little pecks at it as though they were kissing him.

"It must be difficult in wartime," Rowe said, "to provide for all your nephews."

"Yes, indeed," the man said—and when he opened his mouth you saw his teeth were in a shocking condition, black stumps like the remains of something destroyed by fire. He sprinkled some crumbs over his old brown hat and a new flock of sparrows landed there. "Strictly illegal," he said, "I dare say. If Lord Woolton knew." He put a foot up on a heavy suitcase, and a sparrow perched on his knee. He was overgrown with birds.

"I've seen you before," Rowe said.

"I dare say."

"Twice to-day now I come to think of it."

"Come, my pretties," the elderly man said.

"In the auction-room in Chancery Lane."

A pair of mild eyes turned on him. "It's a small world."

"Do you buy books?" Rowe asked, thinking of the shabby clothes.

"Buy and sell," the man said. He was acute enough to read Rowe's thoughts. "Working clothes," he said. "Books carry a deal of dust."

"You go in for old books?"

"Landscape gardening's my speciality. Eighteenth century. Fullove, Fulham Road, Battersea."

"Do you find enough customers?"

"There are more than you'd think." He suddenly opened his arms wide and shooed the birds away as though they were children with whom he'd played long enough. "But everything's depressed," he said, "these days. What they want to fight for I don't understand." He touched the suitcase tenderly with his foot. "I've got a load of books here," he said, "I got from a lord's house. Salvage. The state of some of them would make you weep, but others . . . I don't say it wasn't a good bargain. I'd show them you, only I'm afraid of bird-droppings. First bargain I've had for months. In the old days I'd have treasured them, treasured them. Waited till the Americans came in the summer. Now I'm glad of any chance of a turnover. If I don't deliver these to a customer at Regal Court before five, I lose a sale. He wants to take them down to the country before the raid starts. I haven't a watch, sir. Could you tell me the time?''

"It's only four o'clock."

"I ought to go on," Mr. Fullove said. "Books are heavy though and I feel just tired out. It's been a long day. You'll excuse me, sir, if I sit down a moment." He sat himself down on the suitcase and drew out a ragged packet of Tenners. "Will you smoke, sir? You look a bit done, if I may say so, yourself."

"Oh, I'm all right." The mild exhausted ageing eyes appealed to him. He said, "Why don't you take a taxi?"

"Well, sir, I work on a very narrow margin these days. If I take a taxi that's a dollar gone. And then when he gets the books to the country, perhaps he won't want one of them."

"They are landscape gardening?"

"That's right. It's a lost art, sir. There's a lot more to it, you know, than flowers. That's what gardening means to-day," he said with contempt, "flowers."

"You don't care for flowers?"

"Oh, flowers," the bookseller said, "are all right. You've got to have flowers."

"I'm afraid," Rowe said, "I don't know much about gardening—except flowers."

"It's the tricks they played." The mild eyes looked up with cunning enthusiasm. "The machinery."

"Machinery?"

"They had statues that spurted water at you when you passed, and the grottoes—the things they thought up for grottoes. Why, in a good garden you weren't safe anywhere."

"I should have thought you were meant to feel safe in a garden."

"They didn't think so, sir," the bookseller said, blowing the stale smell of carious teeth enthusiastically in Rowe's direction. Rowe wished he could get away; but automatically with that wish the sense of pity worked and he stayed.

"And then," the bookseller said, "there were the tombs."

"Did they spurt water too?"

"Oh no. They gave the touch of solemnity, sir, the *memento mori*."

"Black thoughts," Rowe said, "in a black shade?"

"It's how you look at it, isn't it, sir?" But there was no doubt that the bookseller looked at it with a kind of gloating. He brushed a little bird-lime off his jacket and said, "You don't have a taste, sir, for the Sublime—or the Ridiculous?"

"Perhaps," Rowe said, "I prefer human nature plain."

The little man giggled. "I get your meaning, sir. Oh, they had room for human nature, believe me, in the grottoes. Not one without a comfortable couch. They never forgot the comfortable couch," and again with sly enthusiasm he blew his carious breath towards his companion.

"Don't you think," Rowe said, "you should be getting on? You mustn't let me rob you of a sale," and immediately he reacted from his own harshness seeing only the mild tired eyes, thinking, poor devil, he's had a weary day, each one to his taste . . . after all, he liked me. That was a claim he could never fail to honour because it astonished him.

"I suppose I ought, sir." He rose and brushed away some crumbs the birds had left. "I enjoy a good talk," he said. "It's not often you can get a good talk these days. It's a rush between shelters."

"You sleep in a shelter?"

"To tell you the truth, sir," he said as if he were confessing to an idiosyncrasy, "I can't bear the bombs. But you don't sleep as you ought in a shelter." The weight of the suitcase cramped him: he looked very old under its weight. "Some people are not considerate. The snores and squabbles . . ."

"Why did you come into the park? It's not your shortest way?"

"I wanted a rest, sir—and the trees invited, and the birds."

"Here," Rowe said, "you'd better let me take that. There's no bus this side of the river."

"Oh, I couldn't bother you, sir. I really couldn't." But there was no genuine resistance in him; the suitcase was certainly very heavy: folios of landscape gardening weighed a lot. He excused himself, "There's nothing so heavy as books, sir—unless it's bricks."

They came out of the park and Rowe changed the weight from one arm to the other. He said, "You know it's getting late for your appointment."

"It's my tongue that did it," the old bookseller said with distress. "I think—I really think I shall have to risk the fare."

"I think you will."

"If I could give you a lift, sir, it would make it more worth while. Are you going in my direction?"

"Oh, in any," Rowe said.

They got a taxi at the next corner, and the bookseller leant back with an air of bashful relaxation. He said, "If you make up your mind to pay for a thing, enjoy it, that's my idea."

But in the taxi with the windows shut it wasn't easy for another to enjoy it; the smell of dental decay was very strong. Rowe talked for fear of showing his distaste. "And have you gone in yourself for landscape gardening?"

"Well, not what you would call the garden part." The man kept peering through the window—it occurred to Rowe that his simple enjoyment rang a little false. He said, "I wonder, sir, if you'd do me one last favour. The stairs at Regal Court— well, they are a caution to a man of my age. And no one offers somebody like me a hand. I deal in books, but to them, sir, I'm just a tradesman. If you wouldn't mind taking up the bag for me. You needn't stay a moment. Just ask for Mr. Travers in number six. He's expecting the bag—there's nothing you have to do but leave it with him." He took a quick sideways look to catch a refusal on the wing. "And afterwards, sir, you've been very kind, I'd give you a lift anywhere you wanted to go."

"You don't know where I want to go," Rowe said.

"I'll risk that, sir. In for a penny, in for a pound."

"I might take you at your word and go a very long way."

"Try me. Just try me, sir," the other said with forced glee. "I'd sell you a book and make it even." Perhaps it was the man's servility—or it may have been only the man's smell—but Rowe felt unwilling to oblige him. "Why not get the commissionaire to take it up for you?" he asked.

"I'd never trust him to deliver—straightaway."

"You could see it taken up yourself."

"It's the stairs, sir, at the end of a long day." He lay back in his seat and said, "If you must know, sir, I oughtn't to have been carrying it," and he made a movement towards his heart, a gesture for which there was no answer.

Well, Rowe thought, I may as well do one good deed before I go away altogether—but all the same he didn't like it. Certainly the man looked sick and tired enough to excuse any artifice, but he had been too successful. Why, Rowe thought, should I be sitting here in a taxi with a stranger promising to drag a case of eighteenth-century folios to the room of another stranger? He felt directed, controlled, moulded, by some agency with a surrealist imagination.

They drew up outside Regal Court—an odd pair, both dusty, both unshaven. Rowe had agreed to nothing, but he knew there was no choice; he hadn't the hard strength of mind to walk away and leave the little man to drag his own burden. He got out under the suspicious eyes of the commissionaire and lugged the heavy case after him. "Have you got a room booked," the commissionaire asked and added dubiously, "sir?"

"I'm not staying here. I'm leaving this case for Mr. Travers."

"Ask at the desk, please," the commissionaire said, and leapt to serve a more savoury carload.

The bookseller had been right; it was a hard pull up the long wide stairs of the hotel. You felt they had been built for women in evening-dress to walk slowly down; the architect had been too romantic—he hadn't seen a man with two days' beard dragging a load of books. Rowe counted fifty steps.

The clerk at the counter eyed him carefully. Before Rowe had time to speak he said, "We are quite full up, I'm afraid."

"I've brought some books for a Mr. Travers in room six."

"Oh yes," the clerk said. "He was expecting you. He's out, but he gave orders"
—you could see that he didn't like the orders—"that you were to be allowed in."

"I don't want to wait. I just want to leave the books."

"Mr. Travers gave orders that you were to wait."

"I don't care a damn what orders Mr. Travers gave."

"Page," the clerk called sharply, "show this man to number six. Mr. Travers. Mr. Travers has given orders that he's to be allowed in." He had very few phrases and never varied them. Rowe wondered on how few he could get through life, marry and have children. He followed at the page's heels down interminable corridors lit by concealed lighting; once a woman in pink mules and a dressing gown squealed as they went by. It was like the corridor of a monstrous Cunarder—one expected to see stewards and stewardesses, but instead a small stout man wearing a bowler hat padded to meet them from what seemed a hundred yards away, then suddenly veered aside into the intricacies of the building. "Do you unreel a thread of cotton?" Rowe asked, swaying under the weight of the case which the page never offered to take, and feeling the strange light-headedness which comes, we are told, to dying men. But the back, the tight little blue trousers and the bumfreezer jacket, just went on ahead. It seemed to Rowe that one could be lost here for a lifetime: only the clerk at the desk would have a clue to one's whereabouts, and it was doubtful whether he ever penetrated very far in person into the enormous wilderness. Water would come regularly out of taps, and at dusk one could emerge and collect tinned foods. He was touched by a forgotten sense of adventure, watching the numbers go backwards, 49, 48, 47; once they took a short cut which led them through the 60's to emerge suddenly among the 30's.

A door in the passage was ajar and odd sounds came through it as though someone were alternately whistling and sighing, but nothing to the page seemed strange. He just went on: he was a child of this building. People of every kind came in for a night with or without luggage and then went away again; a few died here and the bodies were removed unobtrusively by the service lift. Divorce suits bloomed at certain seasons; co-respondents gave tips and detectives out-trumped them with larger tips—because their tips went on the expense account. The page took everything for granted.

Rowe said, "You'll lead me back?" At each corner arrows pointed above the legend AIR RAID SHELTER. Coming on them every few minutes one got the impression that one was walking in circles.

"Mr. Travers left orders you was to stay."

"But I don't take orders from Mr. Travers," Rowe said.

This was a modern building; the silence was admirable and disquieting. Instead of bells ringing, lights went off and on. One got the impression that all the time people were signalling news of great importance that couldn't wait. This silence —now that they were out of earshot of the whistle and the sigh—was like that of a stranded liner; the engines had stopped, and in the sinister silence you listened for the faint depressing sound of lapping water.

"Here's six," the boy said.

"It must take a long time to get to a hundred."

"Third floor," the boy said, "but Mr. Travers gave orders . . ."

"Never mind," Rowe said. "Forget I said it."

Without the chromium number you could hardly have told the difference between the door and the wall; it was as if the inhabitants had been walled up. The page put in a master-key and pushed the wall in. Rowe said, "I'll just put the case down . . ." But the door had shut behind him. Mr. Travers, who seemed to be a much-respected man, had given his orders and if he didn't obey them he would have to find his way back alone. There was an exhilaration in the absurd episode; he had made up his mind now about everything—justice as well as the circumstances of the case demanded that he should kill himself (he had only to decide the method), and now he could enjoy the oddness of existence; regret, anger, hatred, too many emotions had obscured for too long the silly shape of life. He opened the sitting-room door.

"Well," he said, "this beats all."

It was Anna Hilfe.

He asked, "Have you come to see Mr. Travers too? Are you interested in landscape gardening?"

She said, "I came to see you."

It was really his first opportunity to take her in. Very small and thin, she looked too young for all the things she must have seen, and now taken out of the office frame she no longer looked efficient—as though efficiency were an imitative game she could only play with adult properties, a desk, a telephone, a black suit. Without them she looked just decorative and breakable, but he knew that life hadn't been able to break her. All it had done was to put a few wrinkles round eyes as straightforward as a child's.

"Do you like the mechanical parts of gardening too?" he asked. "Statues that spurt water . . ."

His heart beat at the sight of her, as though he were a young man and this his first assignation outside a cinema, in a Lyons Corner House . . . or in an inn yard in a country town where dances were held. She was wearing a pair of shabby blue trousers ready for the night's raid and a wine-coloured jersey. He thought with melancholy that her thighs were the prettiest he had ever seen.

"I don't understand," she said.

"How did you know I was going to cart a load of books here for Mr. Travers —whoever Mr. Travers is? I didn't know myself until ten minutes ago."

"I don't know what excuse they thought up for you," she said. "Just go. Please."

She looked the kind of child you want to torment—in a kindly way; in the office she had been ten years older. He said, "They do people well here, don't they. You get a whole flat for a night. You can sit down and read a book and cook a dinner."

A pale brown curtain divided the living-room in half; he drew it aside and there was the double bed, a telephone on a little table, a bookcase. He asked, "What's through here?" and opened a door. "You see," he said, "they throw in a kitchen, stove and all." He came back into the sitting-room and said, "One could live here and forget it wasn't one's home." He no longer felt care-free; it had been a mood which had lasted minutes only.

She said, "Have you noticed anything?"

"How do you mean?"

"You don't notice much for a journalist."

"You know I was a journalist?"

"My brother checked up on everything."

"On everything?"

"Yes." She said again, "You didn't notice anything?"

"No."

"Mr. Travers doesn't seem to have left behind him so much as a used piece of soap. Look in the bathroom. The soap's wrapped up in its paper."

Rowe went to the front door and bolted it. He said, "Whoever he is, he can't get in now till we've finished talking. Miss Hilfe, will you please tell me slowly—I'm a bit stupid, I think—first how you knew I was here and secondly why you came?"

She said obstinately, "I won't tell you how. As to why—I've asked you to go away quickly. I was right last time, wasn't I, when I telephoned. . . ."

"Yes, you were right. But why worry? You said you knew all about me, didn't you?"

"There's no harm in you," she said simply.

"Knowing everything," he said, "you wouldn't worry . . ."

"I like justice," she said, as if she were confessing an eccentricity.

"Yes," he said, "it's a good thing if you can get it."

"But They don't."

"Do you mean Mrs. Bellairs," he asked, "and Canon Topling?" It was too complicated: he hadn't any fight left. He sat down in the arm-chair—they allowed in the ersatz home one arm-chair and a couch.

"Canon Topling is quite a good man," she said and suddenly smiled. "It's too silly," she said, "the things we are saying."

"You must tell your brother," Rowe said, "that he's not to bother about me any more. I'm giving up. Let them murder whom they like—I'm out of it. I'm going away."

"Where?"

"It's all right," he said. "They'll never find me. I know a place . . . But they won't want to. I think all they were really afraid of was that I should find *them*. I'll never know now, I suppose, what it was all about. The cake . . . and Mrs. Bellairs. Wonderful Mrs. Bellairs."

"They are bad," she said, as if that simple phrase disposed of them altogether. "I'm glad you are going away. It's not your business." To his amazement she added, "I don't want you to be hurt any more."

"Why," he said, "you know everything about me. You've checked up." He used her own childish word. "I'm bad too."

"Mr. Rowe," she said, "I have seen so many bad people where I come from, and you don't fit: you haven't the right marks. You worry too much about what's over and done. People say English justice is good. Well, they didn't hang you. It was a mercy killing, that was what the papers called it."

"You've read all the papers?"

"All of them. I've even seen the pictures they took. You put your newspaper up to hide your face . . ."

He listened to her with dumb astonishment. No one had ever talked to him openly about it. It was painful, but it was the sort of pain you feel when iodine is splashed on a wound—the sort of pain you can bear. She said, "Where I come from I have seen a lot of killings, but they were none of them mercy killings. Don't think so much. Give yourself a chance."

"I think," he said, "we'd better decide what to do about Mr. Travers."

"Just go. That's all."

"And what will you do?"

"Go too. I don't want any trouble either."

Rowe said, "If they are your enemies, if they've made you suffer, I'll stay and talk to Mr. Travers."

"Oh, no," she said. "They are not mine. This isn't my country."

He said, "Who are they? I'm in a fog. Are they your people or my people?"

"They are the same everywhere," she said. She put out a hand and touched his arm tentatively, as if she wanted to know what he felt like. "You think you are so bad," she said, "but it was only because you couldn't bear the pain. But *they* can bear pain—other people's pain—endlessly. They are the people who don't care."

He could have gone on listening to her for hours; it seemed a pity that he had to kill himself, but he had no choice in the matter. Unless he left it to the hangman. He said, "I suppose if I stay till Mr. Travers comes, he'll hand me over to the police."

"I don't know what they'll do."

"And that little smooth man with the books was in it too. What a lot of them there are."

"An awful lot. More every day."

"But why should they think I'd stay—when once I'd left the books?" He took her wrist—a small bony wrist—and said sadly, "You aren't in it too, are you?"

"No," she said, not pulling away from him, just stating a fact. He had the impression that she didn't tell lies. She might have a hundred vices, but not the commonest one of all.

"I didn't think you were," he said, "but that means—it means they meant us both to be here."

She said, "Oh," as if he'd hit her.

"They knew we'd waste time talking, explaining. They want us both, but the *police* don't want you." He exclaimed, "You're coming away with me now."

"Yes."

"If we are not too late. They seem to time things well." He went into the hall and very carefully and softly slid the bolt, opened the door a crack and then very gently shut it again. He said, "Just now I was thinking how easy it would be to get lost in this hotel, in all these long passages."

"Yes?"

"We shan't get lost. There's someone at the end of the passage waiting for us. His back's turned. I can't see his face."

"They do think of everything," she said.

He found his exhilaration returning. He had thought he was going to die to-day—but he wasn't; he was going to live, because he could be of use to someone again. He no longer felt that he was dragging round a valueless and ageing body. He said, "I don't see how they can starve us out. And they can't get in. Except through the window."

"No," Miss Hilfe said. "I've looked. They can't get in there. There's twelve feet of smooth wall."

"Then all we have to do is sit and wait. We might ring up the restaurant and order dinner. Lots of courses, and a good wine. Travers can pay. We'll begin with a very dry sherry."

"Yes," Miss Hilfe said, "if we were sure the right waiter would bring it."

He smiled. "You think of everything. It's the continental training. What's your advice?"

"Ring up the clerk—we know him by sight. Make trouble about something. Insist that he must come along, and then we'll walk out with him."

"You're right," he said. "Of course that's the way."

He lifted the curtain and she followed him. "What are you going to say?"

"I don't know. Leave it to the moment. I'll think of something." He took up the receiver and listened . . . and listened. He said, "I think the line's dead." He waited for nearly two minutes, but there was only silence.

"We *are* besieged," she said. "I wonder what they mean to do." They neither of them noticed that they were holding hands: it was as though they had been overtaken by the dark and had to feel their way. . . .

He said, "We haven't got much in the way of weapons. You don't wear hatpins nowadays, and I suppose the police have got the only knife I've ever had." They came back hand in hand into the small living-room. "Let's be warm, any way," he said, "and turn on the fire. It's cold enough for a blizzard, and we've got the wolves outside."

She had let go his hand and was kneeling by the fire. She said, "It doesn't go on."

"You haven't put in the sixpence."

"I've put in a shilling."

It was cold and the room was darkening. The same thought struck both of them. "Try the light," she said, but his hand had already felt the switch. The light didn't go on.

"It's going to be very dark and very cold," he said. "Mr. Travers is not making us comfortable."

"Oh," Miss Hilfe said, putting her hand to her mouth like a child. "I'm scared. I'm sorry, but I *am* scared. I don't like the dark."

"They can't do anything," Rowe said. "The door's bolted. They can't batter it down, you know. This is a civilised hotel."

"Are you sure," Miss Hilfe said, "that there's no connecting door? In the kitchen. . . ."

A memory struck him. He opened the kitchen door. "Yes," he said. "You're right again. The tradesmen's entrance. These are good flats."

"But you can bolt that too. Please," Miss Hilfe said.

Rowe came back. He said gently, "There's only one flaw in this well-furnished flat. The kitchen bolt is broken." He took her hand again quickly. "Never mind," he said. "We're imagining things. This isn't Vienna, you know. This is London. We are in the majority. This hotel is full of people—on *our* side." He repeated, "On our side. They are all round us. We've only to shout." The world was sliding rapidly towards night; like a torpedoed liner heeling too far over, she would soon take her last dive into darkness. Already they were talking louder because they couldn't clearly see each other's faces.

"In half an hour," Miss Hilfe said, "the sirens will go. And then they'll all go down into the basement, and the only ones left will be us—and them." Her hand felt very cold.

"Then that's our chance," he said. "When the sirens go, we go too with the crowd."

"We are at the end of the passage. Perhaps there won't be a crowd. How do you know there *is* anyone left in this passage? They've thought of so much. Don't you think they'll have thought of that? They've probably booked every room."

"We'll try," he said. "If we had any weapon at all—a stick, a stone." He stopped and let her hand go. "If those aren't books," he said, "perhaps they are bricks. Bricks." He felt one of the catches. "It isn't locked," he said. "Now we'll see. . . ." But they both looked at the suitcase doubtfully. Efficiency is paralysing. *They* had thought of everything, so wouldn't they have thought of this too?

"I wouldn't touch it," she said.

They felt the inertia a bird is supposed to feel before a snake: a snake too knows all the answers.

"They must make a mistake some time," he said.

The dark was dividing them. Very far away the guns grumbled.

"They'll wait till the sirens," she said, "till everybody's down there, out of hearing."

"What's that?" he said. He was getting jumpy himself.

"What?"

"I think someone tried the handle."

"How near they are getting," she said.

"By God," he said, "we aren't powerless. Give me a hand with the couch." They stuck the end of it against the kitchen door. They could hardly see a thing now; they were really in the dark. "It's lucky," Miss Hilfe said, "that the stove's electric."

"But I don't think it is. Why?"

"We've shut them out of here. But they can turn on the gas."

He said, "You ought to be in the game yourself. The things you think of. Here. Give me a hand again. We'll push this couch through into the kitchen." But they stopped almost before they started. He said, "It's too late. Somebody's in there." The tiniest click of a closing door was all they had heard.

"What happens next?" he asked. Memories of *The Little Duke* came incongruously back. He said, "In the old days they always called on the castle to surrender."

"Don't," she whispered. "Please. They are listening."

"I'm getting tired of this cat and mouse act," he said. "We don't even know he's in there. They are frightening us with squeaking doors and the dark." He was moved by a slight hysteria. He called out, "Come in, come in. Don't bother to knock," but no one replied.

He said angrily, "They've chosen the wrong man. They think they can get everything by fear. But you've checked up on me. I'm a murderer, aren't I? You know that. I'm not afraid to kill. Give me any weapon. Just give me a brick." He looked at the suitcase.

Miss Hilfe said, "You're right. We've got to do something, even if it's the wrong thing. Not just let them do everything. Open it."

He gave her hand a quick nervous pressure and released it. Then, as the sirens took up their nightly wail, he opened the lid of the suitcase. . . .

BOOK TWO

The Happy Man

1

Conversations in Arcady

"His guardians would fain have had it supposed that
the castle did not contain any such guest."
THE LITTLE DUKE

i

The sun came into the room like pale green underwater light. That was because the tree outside was just budding. The light washed over the white clean walls of the room, over the bed with its primrose yellow cover, over the big arm-chair and the couch, and the bookcase which was full of advanced reading. There were some early daffodils in a vase which had been bought in Sweden, and the only sounds were a fountain dripping somewhere in the cool out-of-doors and the gentle voice of the earnest young man with rimless glasses.

"The great thing, you see, is not to worry. You've had your share of the war for the time being, Mr. Digby, and you can lie back with an easy conscience."

The young man was always strong on the subject of conscience. His own, he had explained weeks ago, was quite clear. Even if his views had not inclined to pacifism, his bad eyes would have prevented him from being of any active value —the poor things peered weakly and trustfully through the huge convex lenses like bottle-glass; they pleaded all the time for serious conversation.

"Don't think I'm not enjoying myself here. I am. You know it's a great rest. Only sometimes I try to think—who am I?"

"Well, we know that, Mr. Digby. Your identity card. . . ."

"Yes, I know my name's Richard Digby, but who is Richard Digby? What sort of life do you think I led? Do you think I shall ever have the means to repay you all . . . for this?"

"Now that needn't worry you, Mr. Digby. The doctor is repaid all he wants simply by the interest of your case. You're a very valuable specimen under his microscope."

"But he makes life on the slide so very luxurious, doesn't he?"

"He's wonderful," the young man said. "This place—he planned it all, you know. He's a very great man. There's not a finer shell-shock clinic in the country. Whatever people may say," he added darkly.

"I suppose you have worse cases than mine . . . violent cases."

"We've had a few. That's why the doctor arranged the sick bay for them. A separate wing and a separate staff. He doesn't want even the attendants in this wing to be mentally disturbed. . . . You see it's essential that we should be calm too."

"You're certainly all very calm."

"When the time's ripe I expect the doctor will give you a course of psycho-analysis, but it's really much better, you know, that the memory should return of itself—gently and naturally. It's like a film in a hypo bath," he went on, obviously drawing on another man's patter. "The development will come out in patches."

"Not if it's a good hypo bath, Johns," Digby said. He lay back smiling lazily in the arm-chair, lean and bearded and middle-aged. The angry scar on his forehead looked out of place—like duelling cuts on a professor.

"Hold on to that," Johns said—it was one of his favourite expressions. "You went in for photography then?"

"Do you think that perhaps I was a fashionable portrait photographer?" Digby asked. "It doesn't exactly ring a bell, though of course it goes—doesn't it?—with the beard. No, I was thinking of a darkroom on the nursery floor at home. It was a linen cupboard too, and if you forgot to lock the door, a maid would come in with clean pillow slips and bang went the negative. You see, I remember things quite clearly until, say, eighteen."

"You can talk about that time," Johns said, "as much as you like. You may get a clue and there's obviously no resistance—from the Freudian censor."

"I was just wondering in bed this morning which of the people I wanted to become I did in fact choose. I remember I was very fond of books on African exploration—Stanley, Baker, Livingstone, Burton, but there doesn't seem much opportunity for explorers nowadays."

He brooded without impatience. It was as if his happiness were drawn from an infinite fund of tiredness. He didn't want to exert himself. He was comfortable exactly as he was. Perhaps that was why his memory was slow in returning. He said dutifully, because of course one had to make some effort, "One might look up the old Colonial Office lists. Perhaps I went in for that. It's odd, isn't it, that knowing my name, you shouldn't have found any acquaintance. You'd think there would have been inquiries. If I had been married, for instance. That does trouble me. Suppose my wife is trying to find me. . . ." If only that could be cleared up, he thought, I should be perfectly happy.

"As a matter of fact," Johns said and stopped.

"Don't tell me you've unearthed a wife?"

"Not exactly, but I think the doctor has something to tell you."

"Well," Digby said, "it *is* the hour of audience, isn't it?"

Each patient saw the doctor in his study for a quarter of an hour a day, except those who were being treated by psycho-analysis—they were given an hour of his time. It was like visiting a benign headmaster out of school hours to have a chat about personal problems. One passed through the commonroom where the patients could read the papers, play chess or draughts, or indulge in the rather unpredictable social intercourse of shellshocked men. Digby as a rule avoided the place; it was disconcerting, in what might have been the lounge of an exclusive hotel, to see a man quietly weeping in a corner. He felt himself to be so completely normal—except for the gap of he didn't know how many years and an inexplicable happiness as if he had been relieved suddenly of some terrible responsibility—that he was ill at ease in the company of men who all exhibited some obvious sign of an ordeal, the twitch of an eyelid, a shrillness of voice, or a melancholy that fitted as completely and inescapably as the skin.

Johns led the way. He filled with perfect tact a part which combined assistant, secretary and male nurse. He was not qualified, though the doctor occasionally let him loose on the simpler psyches. He had an enormous fund of hero-worship for the doctor, and Digby gathered that some incident in the doctor's past—it might have been the suicide of a patient, but Johns was studiously vague—enabled him to pose before himself as the champion of the great misunderstood. He said, "The jealousies of medical people—you wouldn't believe it. The malice. The lies." He would get quite pink on the subject of what he called the doctor's martyrdom. There had been an inquiry: the doctor's methods were far in advance of his time; there had been talk—so Digby gathered—of taking away the doctor's licence to practise. "They crucified him," he said once with an illustrative gesture and knocked over the vase of daffodils. But eventually good had come out of evil (one felt the good included Johns); the doctor in disgust at the West End world had retired to the country, had opened his private clinic where he refused to accept any patient without a signed personal request—even the more violent cases had been sane enough to put themselves voluntarily under the doctor's care.

"But what about me?" Digby had asked.

"Ah, you are the doctor's special case," Johns said mysteriously. "One day he'll tell you. You stumbled on salvation all right that night. And anyway you did sign."

It never lost its strangeness—to remember nothing of how he had come here. He had simply woken to the restful room, the sound of the fountain, and a taste of drugs. It had been winter then. The trees were black, and sudden squalls of rain broke the peace. Once very far across the fields came a faint wail like a ship signalling departure. He would lie for hours, dreaming confusedly. It was as if then he might have remembered, but he hadn't got the strength to catch the hints, to fix the sudden pictures, he hadn't the vitality to connect. . . . He would drink his medicines without complaint and go off into deep sleep which was only occasionally broken by strange nightmares in which a woman played a part.

It was a long time before they told him about the war, and that involved an enormous amount of historical explanation. What seemed odd to him, he found, was not what seemed odd to other people. For example, the fact that Paris was in German hands appeared to him quite natural—he remembered how nearly it had been so before in the period of his life that he could recall, but the fact that we were at war with Italy shook him like an inexplicable catastrophe of nature.

"Italy," he exclaimed. Why, Italy was where two of his maiden aunts went every year to paint. He remembered too the Primitives in the National Gallery and Caporetto and Garibaldi, who had given a name to a biscuit, and Thomas Cook's. Then Johns patiently explained about Mussolini.

ii

The doctor sat behind a bowl of flowers at his very simple unstained desk and he waved Digby in as if this were a favourite pupil. His elderly face under the snow-white hair was hawk-like and noble and a little histrionic, like the portrait of a Victorian. Johns sidled out, he gave the impression of stepping backwards the few paces to the door, and he stumbled on the edge of the carpet.

"Well, and how are you feeling?" the doctor said. "You look more yourself every day."

"Do I?" Digby asked. "But who knows really if I do? I don't, and you don't, Dr. Forester. Perhaps I look less myself."

"That brings me to a piece of important news," Dr. Forester said. "I have found somebody who *will* know. Somebody who knew you in the old days."

Digby's heart beat violently. He said, "Who?"

"I'm not going to tell you that. I want you to discover everything for yourself."

"It's silly of me," Digby said, "but I feel a bit faint."

"That's only natural," Dr. Forester said. "You aren't very strong yet." He unlocked a cupboard and took out a glass and a bottle of sherry. "This'll put you to rights," he said.

"Tio Pepe," Digby said, draining it.

"You see," the doctor said, "things are coming back. Have another glass?"

"No, it's blasphemy to drink this as medicine."

The news had been a shock. He wasn't sure that he was glad. He couldn't tell what responsibilities might descend on him when his memory returned. Life is broken as a rule to every man gently; duties accumulate so slowly that we hardly know they are there. Even a happy marriage is a thing of slow growth; love helps to make imperceptible the imprisonment of a man, but in a moment, by order, would it be possible to love a stranger who entered bearing twenty years of emotional claims? Now, with no memories nearer than his boyhood, he was entirely free. It wasn't that he feared to face himself; he knew what he was and he believed he knew the kind of man the boy he remembered would have become. It wasn't failure he feared nearly so much as the enormous tasks that success might confront him with.

Dr. Forester said, "I have waited till now, till I felt you were strong enough."

"Yes," Digby said.

"You won't disappoint us, I'm sure," the doctor said. He was more than ever the headmaster, and Digby a pupil who had been entered for a university scholarship; he carried the prestige of the school as well as his own future with him to the examination. Johns would be waiting with anxiety for his return—the form-master. Of course, they would be very kind if he failed. They would even blame the examiners. . . .

"I'll leave the two of you alone," the doctor said.

"He's here now?"

"*She* is here," the doctor said.

iii

It was an immense relief to see a stranger come in. He had been afraid that a whole generation of his life would walk through the door, but it was only a thin pretty girl with reddish hair, a small girl—perhaps too small to be remembered. She wasn't, he felt certain, anybody he needed to fear.

He rose; politeness seemed the wrong thing; he didn't know whether he ought to shake hands—or kiss her. He did neither. They looked at each other from a distance, and his heart beat heavily.

"How you've changed," she said.

"They are always telling me," he said, "that I'm looking quite myself."

"Your hair is much greyer. And that scar. And yet you look so much younger . . . happier."

"I lead a very pleasant easy life here."

"They've been good to you?" she asked with anxiety.

"Very good."

He felt as though he had taken a stranger out to dinner and now couldn't hit on the right conversational move. He said, "Excuse me. It sounds so abrupt. But I don't know your name."

"You don't remember me at all?"

"No."

He had occasionally had dreams about a woman, but it wasn't this woman. He couldn't remember any details of the dream except the woman's face, and that they had been filled with pain. He was glad that this was not the one. He looked at her again. "No," he said. "I'm sorry. I wish I could."

"Don't be sorry," she said with strange ferocity. "Never be sorry again."

"I just meant—this silly brain of mine."

She said, "My name's Anna." She watched him carefully, "Hilfe."

"That sounds foreign."

"I am Austrian."

He said, "All this is so new to me. We are at war with Germany. Isn't Austria . . . ?"

"I'm a refugee."

"Oh, yes," he said. "I've read about them."

"You have even forgotten the war?" she asked.

"I have a terrible lot to learn," he said.

"Yes, terrible. But need they teach it you?" She repeated, "You look so much happier. . . ."

"One wouldn't be happy, not knowing anything." He hesitated and again said, "You must excuse me. There are so many questions. Were we simply friends?"

"Just friends. Why?"

"You are very pretty. I couldn't tell. . . ."

"You saved my life."

"How did I do that?"

"When the bomb went off—just before it went off—you knocked me down and fell on me. I wasn't hurt."

"I'm very glad. I mean," he laughed nervously, "there might be all sorts of discreditable things to learn. I'm glad there's one good one."

"It seems so strange," she said. "All these terrible years since 1933—you've just read about them, that's all. They are history to you. You're fresh. You aren't tired like all the rest of us everywhere."

"1933," he said. "1933. Now 1066, I can give you that easily. And all the kings of England—at least—I'm not sure . . . perhaps not all."

"1933 was when Hitler came to power."

"Of course. I remember now. I've read it all over and over again, but the dates don't stick."

"And I suppose the hate doesn't either."

"I haven't any right to talk about these things," he said. "I haven't lived them. They taught me at school that William Rufus was a wicked king with red hair— but you couldn't expect us to hate him. People like yourself have a right to hate. I haven't. You see I'm untouched."

"Your poor face," she said.

"Oh, the scar. That might have been anything—a motor-car accident. And after all they were not meaning to kill *me*."

"No?"

"I'm not important." He had been talking foolishly, at random. He had assumed something, and after all there was nothing he could safely assume. He said anxiously, "I'm not important, am I? I can't be, or it would have been in the papers."

"They let you see the papers?"

"Oh yes, this isn't a prison, you know." He repeated, "I'm not important?"

She said evasively, "You are not famous."

"I suppose the doctor won't let you tell me anything. He says he wants it all to come through my memory, slowly and gently. But I wish you'd break the rule about just one thing. It's the only thing that worries me. I'm not married, am I?"

She said slowly, as if she wanted to be very accurate and not to tell him more than was necessary, "No, you are not married."

"It was an awful idea that I might suddenly have to take up an old relationship which would mean a lot to someone else and nothing to me. Just something I had been told about, like Hitler. Of course, a new one's different." He added with a shyness that looked awkward with grey hair, "You are a new one."

"And now there's nothing left to worry you?" she asked.

"Nothing," he said. "Or only one thing—that you might go out of that door and not come back." He was always making advances and then hurriedly retreating like a boy who hasn't learned the technique. He said, "You see, I've suddenly lost all my friends except you."

She said rather sadly, "Did you have a great many?"

"I suppose—by my age—one would have collected a good many." He said cheerfully, "Or was I such a monster?"

She wouldn't be cheered up. She said, "Oh, I'll come back. They want me to come back. They want to know, you see, as soon as you begin to remember. . . ."

"Of course they do. And you are the only clue they can give me. But have I got to stay here till I remember?"

"You wouldn't be much good, would you, without a memory—outside?"

"I don't see why not. There's plenty of work for me. If the army won't have me, there's munitions. . . ."

"Do you want to be in it all again?"

He said, "This is lovely and peaceful. But it's only a holiday after all. One's got to be of use." He went on, "Of course, it would be much easier if I knew what I'd been, what I could do best. I can't have been a man of leisure. There wasn't enough money in my family." He watched her face carefully while he guessed. "There aren't so many professions. Army, Navy, Church. . . . I wasn't wearing the right clothes . . . if these are my clothes." There was so much room for doubt. "Law? Was it law, Anna? I don't believe it. I can't see myself in a wig getting some poor devil hanged."

Anna said, "No."

"It doesn't connect. After all, the child does make the man. I never wanted to be a lawyer. I did want to be an explorer—but that's unlikely. Even with this beard. They tell me the beard really does belong. I wouldn't know. Oh," he went on, "I had enormous dreams of discovering unknown tribes in Central Africa. Medicine? No, I never liked doctoring. Too much pain. I hated pain." He was troubled by a slight dizziness. He said, "It made me feel ill, sick, hearing of pain. I remember —something about a rat."

"Don't strain," she said. "It's not good to try too hard. There's no hurry."

"Oh, that was neither here nor there. I was a child then. Where did I get to? Medicine . . . Trade. I wouldn't like to remember suddenly that I was the general manager of a chain store. That wouldn't connect either. I never particularly wanted to be rich. I suppose in a way I wanted to lead—a good life."

Any prolonged effort made his head ache. But there were things he had to remember. He could let old friendships and enmities remain in oblivion, but if he were to make something of what was left of life he had to know of what he was capable. He looked at his hand and flexed the fingers: they didn't feel useful.

"People don't always become what they want to be," Anna said.

"Of course not; a boy always wants to be a hero. A great explorer. A great writer. . . . But there's usually a thin disappointing connexion. The boy who wants to be rich goes into a bank. The explorer becomes—oh, well, some underpaid colonial officer marking minutes in the heat. The writer joins the staff of a penny paper. . . ." He said, "I'm sorry. I'm not as strong as I thought. I've gone a bit giddy. I'll have to stop—work—for the day."

Again she asked with odd anxiety, "They are good to you here?"

"I'm a prize patient," he said. "An interesting case."

"And Dr. Forester—you like Dr. Forester?"

"He fills one with awe," he said.

"You've changed so much." She made a remark he couldn't understand. "This is how you should have been." They shook hands like strangers. He said, "And you'll come back often?"

"It's my job," she said, "Arthur." It was only after she had gone that he wondered at the name.

iv

In the mornings a servant brought him breakfast in bed: coffee, toast, a boiled egg. The Home was nearly self-supporting; it had its own hens and pigs and a good many acres of rough shooting. The doctor did not shoot himself; he did not approve, Johns said, of taking animal life, but he was not a doctrinaire. His patients needed meat, and therefore shoots were held, though the doctor took no personal part. "It's really the idea of making it a sport," Johns explained, "which is against the grain. I think he'd really rather trap. . . ."

On the tray lay always the morning paper. Digby had not been allowed this privilege for some weeks, until the war had been gently broken to him. Now he could lie late in bed, propped comfortably on three pillows, take a look at the news: "Air Raid Casualties this Week are Down to 255," sip his coffee and tap the shell of his boiled egg: then back to the paper—"The Battle of the Atlantic." The eggs were always done exactly right: the white set and the yoke liquid and thick. Back to the paper: "The Admiralty regret to announce . . . lost with all hands." There was always enough butter to put a little in the egg, for the doctor kept his own cows.

This morning as he was reading Johns came in for a chat, and Digby looking up from the paper asked, "What's a Fifth Column?"

There was nothing Johns liked better than giving information. He talked for quite a while, bringing in Napoleon.

"In other words people in enemy pay?" Digby said. "That's nothing new."

"There's this difference," Johns said. "In the last war—except for Irishmen like Casement—the pay was always cash. Only a certain class was attracted. In this war there are all sorts of ideologies. The man who thinks gold is evil. . . . He's naturally attracted to the German economic system. And the men who for years have talked against nationalism . . . well, they are seeing all the old national boundaries obliterated. Pan-Europe. Perhaps not quite in the way they meant. Napoleon too appealed to idealists." His glasses twinkled in the morning sun with the joys of instruction. "When you come to think of it, Napoleon was beaten by the little men, the materialists. Shopkeepers and peasants. People who couldn't see beyond their counter or their field. They'd eaten their lunch under that hedge all their life and they meant to go on doing it. So Napoleon went to St. Helena."

"You don't sound a convinced patriot yourself," Digby said.

"Oh, but I am," Johns said earnestly. "I'm a little man too. My father's a chemist, and how he hates all these German medicines that were flooding the market. I'm like him. I'd rather stick to Burroughs and Wellcome than all the Bayers. . . ."

He went on, "All the same, the other does represent a mood. It's we who are the materialists. The scrapping of all the old boundaries, the new economic ideas . . . the hugeness of the dream. It *is* attractive to men who are not tied—to a particular village or town they don't want to see scrapped. People with unhappy childhoods, progressive people who learn Esperanto, vegetarians who don't like shedding blood."

"But Hitler seems to be shedding plenty."

"Yes, but the idealists don't see blood like you and I do. They aren't materialists. It's all statistics to them."

"What about Dr. Forester?" Digby asked. "He seems to fit the picture."

"Oh," Johns said enthusiastically, "he's sound as a bell. He's written a pamphlet for the Ministry of Information, 'The Psycho-Analysis of Nazidom.' But there was a time," he added, "when there was—talk. You can't avoid witch-hunting in wartime, and, of course, there were rivals to hollo on the pack. You see, Dr. Forester—well, he's so alive to everything. He likes to know. For instance, spiritualism—he's very interested in spiritualism, as an investigator."

"I was just reading the questions in Parliament," Digby said. "They suggest there's another kind of Fifth Column. People who are blackmailed."

"The Germans are wonderfully thorough," Johns said. "They did that in their own country. Card-indexed all the so-called leaders, socialites, diplomats, politicians, labour leaders, priests—and then presented the ultimatum. Everything forgiven and forgotten, or the Public Prosecutor. It wouldn't surprise me if they'd done the same thing over here. They formed, you know, a kind of Ministry of Fear—with the most efficient under-secretaries. It isn't only that they get a hold on certain people. It's the general atmosphere they spread, so that you can't depend on a soul."

"Apparently," Digby said, "this M.P. has got the idea that important plans were stolen from the Ministry of Home Security. They had been brought over from a Service Ministry for a consultation and lodged overnight. He claims that next morning they were found to be missing."

"There must be an explanation," Johns said.

"There is. The Minister says that the honourable member was misinformed. The plans were not required for the morning conference, and at the afternoon conference they were produced, fully discussed and returned to the Service Ministry."

"These M.P.s get hold of odd stories," Johns said.

"Do you think," Digby asked, "that by any chance I was a detective before this happened? That might fit the ambition to be an explorer, mightn't it? Because there seem to me to be so many holes in the statement."

"It seems quite clear to me."

"The M.P. who asked the question must have been briefed by someone who knew about those plans. Somebody at the conference—or somebody who was concerned in sending or receiving the plans. Nobody else could have known about them. Their existence is admitted by the Minister."

"Yes, yes. That's true."

"It's strange that anyone in that position should spread a canard. And do you notice that in that smooth elusive way politicians have the Minister doesn't, in fact, deny that the plans were missing? He says that they weren't wanted, and that when they were wanted they were there."

"You mean there was time to photograph them?" Johns said excitedly. "Would you mind if I smoked a cigarette? Here, let me take your tray." He spilt some coffee on the bed-sheet. "Do you know," he said, "there was a suggestion of that kind made nearly three months ago? It was just after your arrival. I'll look it out for you. Dr. Forester keeps a file of *The Times*. Some papers were missing then for several hours. They tried to hush that up—said it was just a case of carelessness and that the papers had never been out of the Ministry. An M.P. made a fuss— talked about photographs, and they came down on him like a sledge-hammer. Trying to undermine public confidence. The papers had never left the possession—I can't remember whose possession. Somebody whose word you had to take or else one of you would go to Brixton, and you could feel sure that it wouldn't be he. The papers shut down on it right away."

"It would be strange, wouldn't it, if the same thing had happened again."

Johns said excitedly, "Nobody outside would know. And the others wouldn't say."

"Perhaps the first time was a failure. Perhaps the photos didn't come out properly. Someone bungled. And of course they couldn't use the same man twice. They had to wait until they got their hands on a second man. Until they had him carded and filed in the Ministry of Fear." He thought aloud, "I suppose the only men they couldn't blackmail for something shabby would be saints—or outcasts with nothing to lose."

"You weren't a detective," Johns exclaimed, "you were a detective writer."

Digby said, "You know, I feel quite tired. The brain begins to tick and then suddenly I feel so tired I could lie down and sleep. Perhaps I will." He closed his eyes and then opened them again. "The thing to do," he said, "would be to follow up the first case . . . the bungle done, to find the point of failure." Then he slept.

v

It was a fine afternoon, and Digby went for a solitary walk in the garden. Several days had passed since Anna Hilfe's visit, and he felt restless and moody like a boy in love. He wanted an opportunity to show that he was no invalid, that his mind could work as well as another man's. There was no satisfaction in shining before Johns. . . . He dreamed wildly between the box-hedges.

The garden was of a rambling kind which should have belonged to childhood and only belonged to childish men. The apple trees were old apple trees and gave the effect of growing wild; they sprang unexpectedly up in the middle of a rose-bed, trespassed on a tennis-court, shaded the window of a little outside lavatory like a potting-shed which was used by the gardener—an old man who could always be located from far away by the sound of a scythe or the trundle of a wheelbarrow. A high red brick wall divided the flower-garden from the kitchen-garden and the orchard, but flowers and fruit could not be imprisoned by a wall. Flowers broke among the artichokes and sprang up like flames under the trees. Beyond the orchard the garden faded gradually out into paddocks and a stream and a big untidy pond with an island the size of a billiard-table.

It was by the pond that Digby found Major Stone. He heard him first: a succession of angry grunts like a dog dreaming. Digby scrambled down a bank to the black edge of the water and Major Stone turned his very clear blue military eyes on him and said, "The job's got to be done." There was mud all over his tweed suit and mud on his hands; he had been throwing large stones into the water and now he was dragging a plank he must have found in the potting-shed along the edge of the water.

"It's sheer treachery," Major Stone said, "to leave a place like that unoccupied. You could command the whole house. . . ." He slid the plank forward so that one end rested on a large stone. "Steady does it," he said. He advanced the plank inch by inch towards the next stone. "Here," he said, "you ease it along. I'll take the other end."

"Surely you aren't going in?"

"No depth at this side," Major Stone said, and walked straight into the pond. The black mud closed over his shoes and the turn-ups of his trousers. "Now," he said, "push. Steady does it." Digby pushed, but pushed too hard: the plank toppled sideways into the mud. "Damnation," said Major Stone. He bent and heaved and brought the plank up; scattering mud up to his waist, he lugged it ashore.

"Apologise," he said. "My temper's damned short. You aren't a trained man. Good of you to help."

"I'm afraid I wasn't much good."

"Just give me half a dozen sappers," Major Stone said, "and you'd see. . . ." He stared wistfully across at the little bushy island. "But it's no good asking for the impossible. We've just got to make do. We'd manage all right if it wasn't for all this treachery." He looked Digby in the eyes as though he were sizing him up. "I've seen you about here a lot," he said. "Never spoke to you before. Liked the look of you, if you don't mind my saying so. I suppose you've been sick like the rest of us. Thank God, I'll be leaving here soon. Able to be of use again. What's been your trouble?"

"Loss of memory," Digby said.

"Been out there?" the major asked, jerking his head in the direction of the island.

"No, it was a bomb. In London."

"A bad war, this," the major said. "Civilians with shell-shock." It was uncertain whether he disapproved of the civilians or the shell-shock. His stiff fair hair was grizzled over the ears, and his very blue eyes peered out from under a yellow thatch. The whites were beautifully clear; he was a man who had always kept himself fit and ready to be of use. Now that he wasn't fit and wasn't of use, an awful confusion ruled the poor brain. He said, "There was treachery somewhere or it would never have happened," and turning his back abruptly on the island and the muddy remnants of his causeway, he scrambled up the bank and walked briskly towards the house.

Digby strolled on. At the tennis-court a furious game was in progress—a really furious game. The two men leapt and sweated and scowled; their immense concentration was the only thing that looked abnormal about Still and Fishguard, but when the set was over, they would grow shrill and quarrelsome and a little hysterical. The same climax would be reached at chess. . . .

The rose-garden was sheltered by two walls: one the wall of the vegetable-garden, the other the high wall that cut communication—except for one small door—with what Dr. Forester and Johns called euphemistically "the sick bay." Nobody cared to talk about the sick bay—grim things were assumed, a padded room, strait-jackets. You could see only the top windows from the garden, and they were barred. Not one man in the sanatorium was ignorant of how close he lived to that quiet wing. Hysteria over a game, a sense of treachery, in the case of Davis tears that came too easily—they knew those things meant sickness just as much as violence did. They had signed away their freedom to Dr. Forester in the hope of escaping worse, but if worse happened the building was there on the spot—"the sick bay" —there would be no need to travel to a strange asylum. Only Digby felt quite free from its shadow; the sick bay was not there for a happy man. Behind him the voices rose shrilly from the tennis-court: Fishguard's "I tell you it was inside." "Out." "Are you accusing me of cheating?" "You ought to have your eyes seen to"— that was Still. The voices sounded so irreconcilable that you would have said such a quarrel could have no other end than blows—but no blow was ever struck. Fear of the sick bay perhaps. The voices went suddenly off the air like an unpopular turn. When the dusk fell Still and Fishguard would be in the lounge playing chess together.

How far was the sick bay, Digby sometimes wondered, a fantasy of disordered minds? It was there, of course, the brick wing and the barred windows and the high wall; there was even a segregated staff whom other patients had certainly met at the monthly social evening which he had not yet attended. (The doctor believed that these occasions on which strangers were present—the local clergyman, a sprinkling of elderly ladies, a retired architect—helped the shell-shocked brains to adapt themselves to society and the conventions of good behaviour.) But was anybody certain that the sick bay was occupied? Sometimes it occurred to Digby that the wing had no more reality than the conception of Hell presented by sympathetic theologians—a place without inhabitants which existed simply as a warning.

Suddenly Major Stone appeared again, walking rapidly. He saw Digby and veered towards him down one of the paths. Little beads of sweat stood on his forehead. He said to Digby, "You haven't seen me, do you hear? You haven't seen me," and brushed by. He seemed to be making for the paddock and the pond. In another moment he was out of sight among the shrubberies, and Digby walked on. It seemed to him that the time had come for him to leave. He wasn't in place here: he was normal. A faint uneasiness touched him when he remembered that Major Stone, too, had considered himself cured.

As he came in front of the house Johns emerged. He looked ruffled and anxious. He said, "Have you seen Major Stone?" Digby hesitated for a second only. Then he said, "No."

Johns said, "The doctor wants him. He's had a relapse."

The cameraderie of a fellow-patient weakened. Digby said, "I did see him earlier. . . ."

"The doctor's very anxious. He may do himself an injury—or someone else." The rimless glasses seemed to be heliographing a warning—do *you* wish to be responsible?

Digby said uneasily, "You might have a look round the pond."

"Thanks," Johns said, and called out, "Poole. Poole."

"I'm coming," a voice said.

A sense of apprehension moved like a heavy curtain in Digby's mind; it was as though someone had whispered faintly to him so that he couldn't be sure of the words, "Take care." A man stood at the gate from the sick bay wearing the same kind of white coat that Johns wore on duty, but not so clean. He was a dwarfish man with huge twisted shoulders and an arrogant face. "The pond," Johns said.

The man blinked and made no movement, staring at Digby with impertinent curiosity. He had obviously come from the sick bay; he didn't belong in the garden. His coat and fingers were stained with what looked like iodine.

"We've got to hurry," Johns said. "The doctor's anxious. . . ."

"Haven't I met you," Poole said, "somewhere before?" He watched Digby with a kind of enjoyment. "Oh yes I'm sure I have."

"No," Digby said. "No."

"Well, we know each other now," Poole said. He grinned at Digby and said with relish, "I'm the keeper," swinging a long simian arm towards the sick bay.

Digby said loudly, "I don't know you from Adam. I don't want to know you," and had time to see Johns' look of amazement before he turned his back and listened to their footsteps hurrying towards the pond.

It was true: he didn't know the man, but the whole obscurity of his past had seemed to shake—something at any moment might emerge from behind the curtain. He had been frightened and so he had been vehement, but he felt sure that a black mark would be made on his chart of progress and he was apprehensive. . . . Why should he fear to remember anything? He whispered to himself, "After all, I'm not a criminal."

vi

At the front door a servant met him. "Mr. Digby," she told him, "there's a visitor for you," and his heart beat with hope.

"Where?"

"In the lounge."

She was there looking at a *Tatler*, and he had no idea what to say to her. She stood there as he seemed to remember her from very far back, small, tense, on guard, and yet she was part of a whole world of experience of which he was innocent.

"It's good of you," he began and stopped. He was afraid if he once began making the small talk of a stranger, they would be condemned for life to that shadowy relationship. The weather would lie heavily on their tongues, and they would meet occasionally and talk about the theatre. When they passed in the street he would raise his hat, and something which was only just alive would be safely and hopelessly dead.

He said slowly, "I have been longing for this ever since you came. The days have been very long with nothing to do in them but think and wonder. This is such a strange life. . . ."

"Strange and horrible," she said.

"Not so horrible," he said, but then he remembered Poole. He said, "How did we talk before my memory went? We didn't stand stiffly, did we, like this—you holding a paper and I—we were good friends, weren't we?"

"Yes."

He said, "We've got to get back. This isn't right. Sit down here and we'll both shut our eyes. Pretend it's the old days before the bomb went off. What were you saying to me then?" She sat in miserable silence and he said with astonishment, "You shouldn't cry."

"You said shut your eyes."

"They are shut now."

The bright artificial lounge where he felt a stranger, the glossy magazines and the glass ash-trays were no longer visible: there was just darkness. He put out his hand and touched her. He said, "Is this strange?"

After a long time a dried-up voice said, "No."

He said, "Of course I loved you, didn't I?" When she didn't answer, he said, "I must have loved you. Because directly you came in the other day—there was such a sense of relief, of peace, as if I'd been expecting someone different. How could I have helped loving you?"

"It doesn't seem likely," she said.

"Why not?"

"We'd only known each other a few days."

"Too short, of course, for you to care about me."

Again there was a long silence. Then she said, "Yes, I did."

"Why? I'm so much older. I'm not much to look at. What sort of a person was I?"

She replied at once as though this were easy: this was part of the lesson she had really learnt: she had turned this over in her mind again and again. "You had a great sense of pity. You didn't like people to suffer."

"Is that unusual?" he asked, genuinely seeking information; he knew nothing of how people lived and thought outside.

"It was unusual," she said, "where I came from. My brother. . . ." She caught her breath sharply.

"Of course," he said quickly, snatching at a memory before it went again, "you had a brother, hadn't you? He was a friend of mine too."

"Let's stop playing this game," she said. "Please." They opened their eyes simultaneously on the suave room.

He said, "I want to leave here."

"No," she said, "stay. Please."

"Why?"

"You are safe here."

He smiled. "From more bombs?"

"From a lot of things. You are happy here, aren't you?"

"In a way."

"There"—she seemed to indicate the whole external world beyond the garden wall—"you weren't happy." She added slowly, "I would do anything to keep you happy. This is how you should be. This is how I like you."

"You didn't like me out there?" He tried to catch her humorously in a contradiction, but she wouldn't play. She said, "You can't go on seeing someone unhappy all day every day without breaking."

"I wish I could remember."

"Why bother to remember?"

He said simply—it was one of the few things of which he was certain, "Oh, of course, one's got to remember. . . ."

She watched him with intensity, as though she were making up her mind to some course of action. He went on, "If only to remember you, how I talked to you . . ."

"Oh, don't," she said, "don't," and added harshly like a declaration of war, "Dear heart."

He said triumphantly, "That was how we talked."

She nodded, keeping her eyes on him. He said, "My dear . . ."

Her voice was dry like an old portrait: the social varnish was cracking. She said, "You once said you'd do impossible things for me."

"Yes?"

"Do a possible one. Just be quiet. Stay here a few more weeks till your memory comes back. . . ."

"If you'll come often. . . ."

"I'll come."

He put his mouth against hers: the action had all the uncertainty of an adolescent kiss. "My dear, my dear," he said. "Why did you say we were only friends . . . ?"

"I wasn't going to bind you."

"You've bound me now."

She said slowly, as though she were astonished, "And I'm glad."

All the way upstairs to his room, he could smell her. He could have gone into any chemist's shop and picked out her powder, and he could have told in the dark the texture of her skin. The experience was as new to him as adolescent love: he had the blind passionate innocence of a boy: like a boy he was driven relentlessly towards inevitable suffering, loss and despair, and called it happiness.

vii

Next morning there was no paper on his tray. He asked the woman who brought his breakfast where it was, but all she could tell him was that she supposed it hadn't been delivered. He was touched again by the faint fear he had felt the previous afternoon when Poole came out of the sick bay, and he waited impatiently for Johns to arrive for his morning chat and smoke. But Johns didn't come. He lay in bed and brooded for half an hour and then rang his bell. It was time for his clothes to be laid out, but when the maid came she said she had no orders.

"But you don't need orders," he said. "You do it every day."

"I has to have my orders," she said.

"Tell Mr. Johns I'd like to see him."

"Yes, sir"—but Johns didn't come. It was as if a *cordon sanitaire* had been drawn around his room.

For another half an hour he waited doing nothing. Then he got out of bed and went to the bookcase, but there was little that promised him distraction—only the iron rations of learned old men. Tolstoy's *What I Believe*, Freud's *The Psycho-Analysis of Everyday Life*, a biography of Rudolf Steiner. He took the Tolstoy back with him, and opening it found faint indentations in the margin where pencil marks had been rubbed out. It is always of interest to know what strikes another human being as remarkable and he read:

"Remembering all the evil I have done, suffered and seen, resulting from the enmity of nations, it is clear to me that the cause of it all lay in the gross fraud called patriotism and love of one's country. . . ."

There was a kind of nobility in the blind shattering dogma, just as there was something ignoble in the attempt to rub out the pencil-mark. This was an opinion to be held openly if at all. He looked farther up the page: "Christ showed me that the fifth snare depriving me of welfare is the separation we make of our own from other nations. I cannot but believe this, and therefore if in a moment of forgetfulness feelings of enmity towards a man of another nation may rise within me. . . ."

But that wasn't the point, he thought; he felt no enmity towards any individual across the frontier: if he wanted to take part again, it was love which drove him and not hate. He thought: Like Johns, I am one of the little men, not interested in ideologies, tied to a flat Cambridgeshire landscape, a chalk quarry, a line of willows across the featureless fields, a market town . . . his thoughts scrabbled at the curtain . . . where he used to dance at the Saturday hops. His thoughts fell back on one face with a sense of relief: he could rest there. Ah, he thought, Tolstoy should have lived in a small country—not in Russia, which was a continent rather than a country. And why does he write as if the worst thing we can do to our fellow-man is to kill him? Everybody has to die and everybody fears death, but when we kill a man we save him from his fear which would otherwise grow year by year. . . . One doesn't necessarily kill because one hates: one may kill because one loves . . . and again the old dizziness came back as though he had been struck over the heart.

He lay back on his pillow, and the brave old man with the long beard seemed to buzz at him: "I cannot acknowledge any States or nations. . . . I cannot take part. . . . I cannot take part." A kind of waking dream came to him of a man— perhaps a friend, he couldn't see his face—who hadn't been able to take part; some private grief had isolated him and hidden him like a beard—what was it? he couldn't remember. The war and all that happened round him had seemed to belong to other people. The old man in the beard, he felt convinced, was wrong. He was too busy saving his own soul. Wasn't it better to take part even in the crimes of people you loved, if it was necessary hate as they did, and if that were the end of everything suffer damnation with them, rather than be saved alone?

But that reasoning, it could be argued, excused your enemy. And why not? he thought. It excused anyone who loved enough to kill or be killed. Why shouldn't you excuse your enemy? That didn't mean you must stand in lonely superiority, refuse to kill, and turn the intolerable cheek. "If a man offend *thee* . . ." there was the point—not to kill for one's own sake. But for the sake of people you loved, and in the company of people you loved, it was right to risk damnation.

His mind returned to Anna Hilfe. When he thought of her it was with an absurd breathlessness. It was as if he were waiting again years ago outside—wasn't it the King's Arms?—and the girl he loved was coming down the street, and the night was full of pain and beauty and despair because one knew one was too young for anything to come of this. . . .

He couldn't be bothered with Tolstoy any longer. It was unbearable to be treated as an invalid. What woman outside a Victorian novel could care for an invalid? It was all very well for Tolstoy to preach non-resistance: he had had his heroic violent hour at Sebastopol. Digby got out of bed and saw in the long narrow mirror his thin body and his grey hair and his beard. . . .

The door opened: it was Dr. Forester. Behind him, eyes lowered, subdued like someone found out, came Johns. Dr. Forester shook his head and, "It won't do, Digby," he said, "it won't do. I'm disappointed."

Digby was still watching the sad grotesque figure in the mirror. He said, "I want my clothes. And a razor."

"Why a razor?"

"To shave. I'm certain this beard doesn't belong . . ."

"That only shows your memory isn't returning yet."

"And I had no paper this morning," he went weakly on.

Dr. Forester said, "I gave orders that the paper was to be stopped. Johns has been acting unwisely. These long conversations about the war. . . . You've excited yourself. Poole has told me how excited you were yesterday."

Digby, with his eyes on his own ageing figure in the striped pyjamas, said, "I won't be treated like an invalid or a child."

"You seem to have got it into your head," Dr. Forester said, "that you have a talent for detection, that you were a detective perhaps in your previous life. . . ."

"That was a joke," Digby said.

"I can assure you you were something quite different. Quite different," Dr. Forester repeated.

"What was I?"

"It may be necessary one day to tell you," Dr. Forester said, as though he were uttering a threat. "If it will prevent foolish mistakes. . . ." Johns stood behind the doctor looking at the floor.

"I'm leaving here," Digby said.

The calm noble old face of Dr. Forester suddenly crumpled into lines of dislike. He said sharply, "And paying your bill, I hope?"

"I hope so too."

The features reformed, but they were less convincing now. "My dear Digby," Dr. Forester said, "you must be reasonable. You are a very sick man, a very sick man indeed. Twenty years of your life have been wiped out. That's not health . . . and yesterday and just now you showed an excitement which I've feared and hoped to avoid." He put his hand gently on the pyjama sleeve and said, "I don't want to have to restrain you, to have you certified. . . ."

Digby said, "But I'm as sane as you are. You must know that."

"Major Stone thought so too. But I've had to transfer him to the sick bay. . . . He had an obsession which might at any time have led to violence."

"But I . . ."

"Your symptoms are very much the same. This excitement. . . ." The doctor raised his hand from the sleeve to the shoulder: a warm, soft, moist hand. He said, "Don't worry. We won't let it come to that, but for a little we must be very quiet . . . plenty of food, plenty of sleep . . . some very gentle bromides . . . no visitors for a while, not even our friend Johns . . . no more of these exciting intellectual conversations."

"Miss Hilfe?" Digby said.

"I made a mistake there," Dr. Forester said. "We are not strong enough yet. I have told Miss Hilfe not to come again."

The Sick Bay

"Wherefore shrink from me? What have I done that
you should fear me? You have been listening to evil
tales, my child."
THE LITTLE DUKE

i

When a man rubs out a pencil-mark he should be careful to see that the line is quite obliterated. For if a secret is to be kept, no precautions are too great. If Dr. Forester had not so inefficiently rubbed out the pencil-marks in the margins of Tolstoy's *What I Believe*, Mr. Rennit might never have learnt what had happened to Jones, Johns would have remained a hero-worshipper, and it is possible that Major Stone would have slowly wilted into further depths of insanity between the padded hygienic walls of his room in the sick bay. And Digby? Digby might have remained Digby.

For it was the rubbed-out pencil-marks which kept Digby awake and brooding at the end of a day of loneliness and boredom. You couldn't respect a man who dared not hold his opinions openly, and when respect for Dr. Forester was gone, a great deal went with it. The noble old face became less convincing: even his qualifications became questionable. What right had he to forbid the newspapers— above all, what right had he to forbid the visits of Anna Hilfe?

Digby still felt like a schoolboy, but he now knew that his headmaster had secrets of which he was ashamed: he was no longer austere and self-sufficient. And so the schoolboy planned rebellion. At about half-past nine in the evening he heard the sound of a car, and watching between the curtains he saw the doctor drive away. Or rather Poole drove and the doctor sat beside him.

Until Digby saw Poole he had planned only a petty rebellion—a secret visit to Johns' room; he felt sure he could persuade that young man to talk. Now he became bolder; he would visit the sick bay itself and speak to Stone. The patients must combine against tyranny, and an old memory slipped back of a deputation he had once led to his real headmaster because his form against all precedent—for it was a classical form—had been expected by a new master to learn trigonometry. The strange thing about a memory like that was that it seemed young as well as old: so little had happened since that he could remember. He had lost all his mature experience.

A bubble of excited merriment impeded his breath as he opened the door of his room and took a quick look down the corridor. He was afraid of undefined punishments, and for that reason he felt his action was heroic and worthy of someone in love. There was an innocent sensuality in his thought; he was like a boy who boasts of a beating he has risked to a girl, sitting in the sunshine by the cricket-ground, drinking ginger-beer, hearing the pad-pad of wood and leather, under the spell, day-dreaming and in love. . . .

There was a graduated curfew for patients according to their health, but by half-past nine all were supposed to be in bed and asleep. But you couldn't enforce sleep. Passing Davis's door he could hear the strange uncontrollable whine of a man weeping. . . . Farther down the passage Johns' door was open and the light was on. Taking off his bedroom slippers, he passed quickly across the door-way, but Johns wasn't there. Incurably sociable, he was probably chatting with the housekeeper. On his desk was a pile of newspapers; he had obviously picked them out for Digby before the doctor had laid his ban. It was a temptation to stay and read them, but the small temptation didn't suit the mood of high adventure. To-night he would do something no patient had ever voluntarily done before—enter the sick bay. He moved carefully and silently—the words "Pathfinder' and "Indian" came to his mind—downstairs.

In the lounge the lights were off, but the curtains were undrawn and the moonlight welled in with the sound of the plashing fountain and the shadow of silver leaves. The *Tatlers* had been tidied on the tables, the ash-trays taken away, and the cushions shaken on the chairs—it looked now like a room in an exhibition where nobody crosses the ropes. The next door brought him into the passage by Dr. Forester's study. As he quietly closed each door behind him he felt as though he were cutting off his own retreat. His ribs seemed to vibrate to the beat-beat of his heart. Ahead of him was the green baize door he had never seen opened, and beyond that door lay the sick bay. He was back in his own childhood, breaking out of dormitory, daring more than he really wanted to dare, proving himself. He hoped the door would be bolted on the other side; then there would be nothing he could do but creep back to bed, honour satisfied. . . .

The door pulled easily open. It was only the cover for another door, to deaden sound and leave the doctor in his study undisturbed. But that door, too, had been left unlocked, unbolted. As he passed into the passage beyond, the green baize swung to behind him with a long sigh.

ii

He stood stone still and listened. Somewhere a clock ticked with a cheap tinny sound, and a tap had been left dripping. This must once have been the servants' quarters: the floor was stone, and his bedroom slippers pushed up a little smoke of dust. Everything spoke of neglect; the woodwork when he reached the stairs had not been polished for a very long time and the thin drugget had been worn threadbare. It was an odd contrast to the spruce nursing home beyond the door; everything around him shrugged its shoulders and said, "We are not important. Nobody sees us here. Our only duty is to be quiet and not disturb the doctor." And what could be quieter than dust? If it had not been for the clock ticking he would have doubted whether anyone really lived in this part of the house—the clock and the faintest tang of stale cigarette smoke, of Caporal, that set his heart beating again with apprehension.

Where the clock ticked Poole must live. Whenever he thought of Poole he was aware of something unhappy, something imprisoned at the bottom of the brain trying to climb out. It frightened him in the same way as birds frightened him when they beat up and down in closed rooms. There was only one way to escape the fear of another creature's pain. That was to lash out until the bird was stunned and quiet or dead. For the moment he forgot Major Stone, and smelt his way towards Poole's room.

It was at the end of the passage where the tap dripped, a large square, comfortless room with a stone floor divided in half by a curtain—it had probably once been a kitchen. Its new owner had lent it an aggressive and squalid masculinity as if he had something to prove; there were ends of cigarettes upon the floor, and nothing was used for its right purpose. A clock and a cheap brown teapot served as book-ends on a wardrobe to prop up a shabby collection—Carlyle's *Heroes and Hero-Worship*, lives of Napoleon and Cromwell, and numbers of little paper-covered books about what to do with Youth, Labour, Europe, God. The windows were all shut, and when Digby lifted the drab curtain he could see the bed had not been properly made—or else Poole had flung himself down for a rest and hadn't bothered to tidy it afterwards. The tap dripped into a fixed basin and a sponge-bag dangled from a bedpost. A used tin which once held lobster paste now held old razor-blades. The place was as comfortless as a transit camp; the owner might have been someone who was just passing on and couldn't be bothered to change so much as a stain on the wall. An open suitcase full of soiled underclothes gave the impression that he hadn't even troubled to unpack.

It was like the underside of a stone: you turned up the bright polished nursing home and found beneath it this.

Everywhere there was the smell of Caporal, and on the beds there were crumbs, as though Poole took food to bed with him. Digby stared at the crumbs a long while: a feeling of sadness and disquiet and dangers he couldn't place haunted him—as though something were disappointing his expectations—as though the cricket match were a frost, nobody had come to the half-term holiday, and he waited and waited outside the King's Arms for a girl who would never turn up. He had nothing to compare this place with. The nursing home was something artificial, hidden in a garden. Was it possible that ordinary life was like this? He remembered a lawn and afternoon tea and a drawing-room with watercolours and little tables, a piano no one played and the smell of eau-de-Cologne; but was *this* the real adult life to which we came in time? Had he, too, belonged to this world? He was saddened by a sense of familiarity. It was not of this last he had dreamed a few years back at school, but he remembered that the years since then were not few but many.

At last the sense of danger reminded him of poor imprisoned Stone. He might not have long before the doctor and Poole returned, and though he could not believe they had any power over him, he was yet afraid of sanctions he couldn't picture. His slippers padded again up the passage and up the dingy stairs to the first floor. There was no sound here at all: the tick of the clock didn't reach as far: large bells on rusty wires hung outside what might have been the butler's pantry. They were marked Study, Drawing-Room, 1st Spare Bedroom, 2nd Spare Bedroom, Day Nursery. . . . The wires sagged with disuse and a spider had laid its scaffolding across the bell marked Dining-Room.

The barred windows he had seen over the garden wall had been on the second floor, and he mounted unwillingly higher. He was endangering his own retreat with every step, but he had dared himself to speak to Stone, and if it were only one syllable he must speak it. He went down a passage calling softly, "Stone. Stone."

There was no reply and the old cracked linoleum creaked under his feet and sometimes caught his toes. Again he felt a familiarity—as if this cautious walking, this solitary passage, belonged more to his world than the sleek bedroom in the other wing. "Stone," he called, "Stone," and heard a voice answer, "Barnes. Is that you, Barnes?" coming startlingly from the door beside him.

"Hush," he said, and putting his lips close to the key-hole, "It's not Barnes. It's Digby."

He heard Stone sigh. "Of course," the voice said, "Barnes is dead. I was dreaming. . . ."

"Are you all right, Stone?"

"I've had an awful time," Stone said, so low that Digby could hardly hear him, "an awful time. I didn't really mean I wouldn't eat. . . ."

"Come to the door so that I can hear you better."

Stone said, "They've got me in one of these strait-jackets. They said I was violent. I don't think I was violent. It's just the treachery. . . ." He must have got nearer the door, because his voice was much clearer. He said, "Old man, I know I've been a bit touched. We all are in this place, aren't we? But I'm not *mad*. It just isn't right."

"What did you do?"

"I wanted to find a room to enfilade that island from. They'd begun to dig, you see, months ago. I saw them one evening after dark. One couldn't leave it at that. The Hun doesn't let the grass grow. So I came through into this wing and went to Poole's room. . . ."

"Yes?"

"I didn't mean to make them jump. I just wanted to explain what I was after."

"Jump?"

"The doctor was there with Poole. They were doing something in the dark. . . ." The voice broke: it was horrible hearing a middle-aged man sobbing invisibly behind a locked door.

"But the digging?" Digby asked. "You must have dreamed. . . ."

"That tube. . . . It was awful, old man. I hadn't really meant I wouldn't eat. I was just afraid of poison."

"Poison?"

"Treachery," the voice said. "Listen, Barnes. . . ."

"I'm not Barnes."

Again there was a long sigh. "Of course. I'm sorry. It's getting me down. I *am* touched, you know. Perhaps they are right."

"Who's Barnes?"

"He was a good man. They got him on the beach. It's no good, Digby. I'm mad. Every day in every way I get worse and worse."

Somewhere from far away, through an open window on the floor below, came the sound of a car. Digby put his lips to the door and said, "I can't stay, Stone. Listen. You are not mad. You've got ideas into your head, that's all. It's not right putting you here. Somehow I'll get you out. Just stick it."

"You're a good chap, Digby."

"They've threatened me with this too."

"You," Stone whispered back. "But you're sane enough. By God, perhaps I'm not so touched after all. If they want to put you here, it must be treachery."

"Stick it."

"I'll stick it, old man. It was the uncertainty. I thought perhaps they were right."

The sound of the car faded.

"Haven't you any relations?"

"Not a soul," the voice said. "I had a wife, but she went away. She was quite right, old chap, quite right. There was a lot of treachery."

"I'll get you out. I don't know how, but I'll get you out."

"That island, Digby . . . you've got to watch it, old man. I can't do anything here, and I don't matter, anyway. But if I could just have fifty of the old bunch . . ."

Digby reassured him gently, "I'll watch the island."

"I thought the Hun had got hold of it. They don't let the grass grow. . . . But I'm sometimes a bit confused, old man."

"I must go now. Just stick it."

"I'll stick it, old man. Been in worse places. But I wish you didn't have to go."

"I'll come back for you."

But he hadn't the faintest idea of how. A terrible sense of pity moved him; he felt capable of murder for the release of that gentle tormented creature. He could see him walking into the muddy pond . . . the very clear blue eyes and the bristly military moustache and the lines of care and responsibility. That was a thing you learned in this place: that a man kept his character even when he was insane. No madness would ever dim that military sense of duty to others.

His reconnaissance had proved easier than he had any right to expect: the doctor must be taking a long ride. He reached the green baize door safely, and when it sighed behind him, it was like Stone's weary patience asking him to come back. He passed quickly through the lounge and then more carefully up the stairs until he came again within sight of Johns' open door. Johns wasn't there: the clock on his desk had only moved on twelve minutes: the papers lay in the lamplight. He felt as though he had explored a strange country and returned home to find it all a dream—not a single page of the calendar turned during all his wanderings.

iii

He wasn't afraid of Johns. He went in and picked up one of the offending papers. Johns had arranged them in order and marked the passages. He must have been bitten by the passion for detection. The Ministry of Home Security, Digby read, had replied months ago to a question about a missing document in much the same terms as in the later case. It had never been missing. There had been at most a slight indiscretion, but the document had never left the personal possession of— and there was the great staid respected name which Johns had forgotten. In the face of such a statement how could anyone continue to suggest that the document had been photographed? That was to accuse the great staid name not of an indiscretion but of treason. It was perhaps a mistake not to have left the document in the office safe overnight, but the great name had given his personal assurance to the Minister that not for one second had the document been out of his possession. He had slept with it literally under his pillow. . . . *The Times* hinted that it would be interesting to investigate how the calumny had started. Was the enemy trying to sap our confidence in our hereditary leaders by a whisper campaign? After two or three issues there was silence.

A rather frightening fascination lay in these months-old newspapers. Digby had slowly had to relearn most of the household names, but he could hardly turn the page of any newspaper without encountering some great man of whom he had never heard, and occasionally there would crop up a name he did recognise—someone who had been a figure twenty years ago. He felt like a Rip Van Winkle returning after a quarter of a century's sleep; the people of whom he had heard hardly connected better than he did with his youth. Men of brilliant promise had lapsed into the Board of Trade, and of course in one great case a man who had been considered too brilliant and too reckless ever to be trusted with major office was the leader of his country. One of Digby's last memories was of hearing him hissed by ex-servicemen from the public gallery of a law court because he had told an abrupt unpalatable truth about an old campaign. Now he had taught the country to love his unpalatable truths.

He turned a page and read casually under a photograph: "Arthur Rowe whom the police are anxious to interview in connexion . . ." He wasn't interested in crime. The photograph showed a lean shabby clean-shaven man. All photographs of criminals looked much alike—perhaps it was the spots, the pointilliste technique of the newspaper photograph. There was so much of the past he had to learn that he couldn't be bothered to learn the criminals, at any rate of the domestic kind.

A board creaked and he turned. Johns hovered and blinked in the doorway. "Good evening, Johns," Digby said.

"What are you doing here?"

"Reading the papers," Digby said.

"But you heard the doctor say . . ."

"This isn't a prison, Johns," Digby said, "except for poor Stone. It's a very charming nursing home and I'm a private patient with nothing wrong except loss of memory due to a bomb. . . ." He realised that Johns was listening to him with intensity. "Isn't that about it?" he asked.

"It must be, mustn't it," Johns said.

"So we must keep a sense of proportion, and there's no earthly reason why, if I don't feel like sleep, I shouldn't stroll down the passage to your room for a chat and to read. . . ."

"When you put it like that," Johns said, "it sounds so simple."

"The doctor makes you see it differently, doesn't he?"

"All the same a patient ought to follow the treatment. . . ."

"Or change his doctor. You know I've decided to change my doctor."

"To leave?" Johns asked. There was fear in his voice.

"To leave."

"Please don't do anything rash," Johns said. "The doctor's a great man. He's suffered a lot . . . and that may have made him a bit . . . eccentric. But you can't do better than stay here, really you can't."

"I'm going, Johns."

"Just another month," Johns entreated. "You've been doing so well. Until that girl came. Just a month. I'll speak to the doctor. He'll let you have the papers again. Perhaps he'll even let *her* come. Only let me put it to him. I know the way. He's so sensitive: he takes offence."

"Johns," Digby asked gently, "why should you be afraid of my going?"

The unrimmed glasses caught the light and set it flickering along the wall. Johns said uncontrollably, "I'm not afraid of your going. I'm afraid—I'm afraid of his not letting you go." Very far away they both heard the purr-purr of a car.

"What's wrong with the doctor?" Johns shook his head and the reflection danced again upon the wall. "There's something wrong," Digby pressed him. "Poor Stone saw something odd and so he's put away. . . ."

"For his own good," Johns said imploringly. "Dr. Forester knows. He's such a great man, Digby."

"For his own good be damned. I've been to the sick bay and talked to him. . . ."

"You've been *there*?" Johns said.

"Haven't you—ever?"

"It's forbidden," Johns said.

"Do you always do exactly what Dr. Forester tells you?"

"He's a great doctor, Digby. You don't understand: brains are the most delicate mechanisms. The least thing to upset the equilibrium and everything goes wrong. You have to trust the doctor."

"I don't trust him."

"You mustn't say that. If you only knew how skilful he is, the endless care he takes. He's trying to shelter you until you are really strong enough. . . ."

"Stone saw something odd and Stone's put away."

"No, no." Johns put out a weak hand and laid it on the newspapers like a badgered politician gaining confidence from the despatch box. "If you only knew, Digby. They've made him suffer so with their jealousies and misunderstandings, but he's so great and good and kind. . . ."

"Ask Stone about that."

"If you only knew. . . ."

A soft savage voice said, "I think he'll have to know." It was Dr. Forester, and again that sense of possible and yet inconceivable sanctions set Digby's heart beating.

Johns said, "Dr. Forester, I didn't give him leave. . . ."

"That's all right Johns," Dr. Forester said, "you are very loyal, I know. I like loyalty." He began to take off the gloves he had been wearing in the car; he drew them slowly off the long beautiful fingers. "I remember after Conway's suicide how you stood by me. I don't forget a friend. Have you ever told Digby about Conway's suicide?"

"Never," Johns protested.

"But he should know, Johns. It's a case in point. Conway also suffered from loss of memory. Life, you see, had become too much for him—and loss of memory was his escape. I tried to make him strong, to stiffen his resistance, so that when his memory came back, he would be able to meet his very difficult situation. The time I spent, wasted on Conway. Johns will tell you I was very patient—he was unbearably impertinent. But I'm human, Digby, and one day I lost my temper. I do lose my temper—very seldom, but sometimes. I told Conway everything, and he killed himself that night. You see, his mind hadn't been given time to heal. There was a lot of trouble, but Johns stood by me. He realises that to be a good psychologist you sometimes have to share the mental weaknesses of the patient: one cannot be quite sane all the time. That's what gives one sympathy—and the other thing."

He spoke gently and calmly, as though he were lecturing on an abstract subject, but the long surgical fingers had taken up one of the newspapers and was tearing it in long strips.

Digby said, "But my case is different, Dr. Forester. It was only a bomb that destroyed my memory. Not trouble."

"Do you really believe that?" Dr. Forester said. "And I suppose you think it was just gunfire, concussion, which drove Stone out of his mind? That isn't how the mind works. We make our own insanity. Stone failed—shamefully, so now he explains everything by treachery. But it wasn't anybody else's treachery that left his friend Barnes. . . ."

"And you have a revelation up your sleeve for me too, Dr. Forester?" He remembered the pencil-marks in the Tolstoy rubbed out by a man without the courage of his opinions and that heartened him. He asked, "What were you doing with Poole in the dark when Stone found you?" He had meant it only as a piece of impertinent defiance; he had believed that the scene existed only in Stone's persecuted imagination—like the enemy digging on the island. He hadn't expected to halt Dr. Forester in the middle of his soft tirade. The silence was disagreeable. He tailed weakly off, "And digging. . . ."

The noble old face watched him, the mouth a little open: a tiny dribble ran down the chin.

Johns said, "Please go to bed, Digby. Let's talk in the morning."

"I'm quite ready to go to bed," Digby said. He felt suddenly ridiculous in his trailing dressing-gown and his heelless slippers; he was apprehensive too—it was like turning his back on a man with a gun.

"Wait," Dr. Forester said. "I haven't told you yet. When you know you can choose between Conway's method and Stone's method. There's room in the sick bay. . . ."

"You ought to be there yourself, Dr. Forester."

"You're a fool," Dr. Forester said. "A fool in love. . . . I watch my patients. I know. What's the good of you being in love? You don't even know your real name." He tore a piece out of one of the papers and held it out to Digby. "There you are. That's you. A murderer. Go and think about that."

It was the photograph he hadn't bothered to examine. The thing was absurd. He said, "That's not me."

"Go and look in the glass then," Dr. Forester said. "And then begin to remember. You've got a lot to remember."

Johns protested. "Doctor, that's not the way. . . ."

"He asked for it," Dr. Forester said, "just like Conway did."

But Digby heard no more of what Johns had to say: he was running down the passage towards his room; half-way he tripped on his dressing-gown cord and fell. He hardly felt the shock. He got to his feet a little giddy—that was all. He wanted a looking-glass.

The lean bearded face looked out at him in the familiar room. There was a smell of cut flowers. This was where he had been happy. How could he believe what the doctor had said? There must be a mistake. It didn't connect. . . . At first he could hardly see the photograph; his heart beat and his head was confused. This isn't me, he thought, as that lean shaven other face with the unhappy eyes and the shabby suit came into focus. They didn't fit; the memories he had of twenty years ago and Arthur Rowe whom the police wanted to interview in connexion with—but Dr. Forester had torn the paper too carelessly. In those twenty years he couldn't have gone astray as far as this. He thought: Whatever they say, this man standing here is me. I'm not changed because I lose my memory. This photograph and Anna Hilfe didn't fit, he protested, and suddenly he remembered what had puzzled him and he had quite forgotten, Anna's voice saying, "It's my job, Arthur." He put his hand up to his chin and hid the beard; the long twisted nose told its tale, and the eyes which were unhappy enough now. He steadied himself with his hands on the dressing-table and thought: Yes, I'm Arthur Rowe. He began to talk to himself under his breath, But I'm not Conway. I shan't kill myself.

He was Arthur Rowe with a difference. He was next door to his own youth; he had started again from there. He said, In a moment it's going to come back, but I'm not Conway—and I won't be Stone. I've escaped for long enough: my brain will stand it. It wasn't all fear that he felt; he felt also the untired courage and the chivalry of adolescence. He was no longer too old and too habit-ridden to start again. He shut his eyes and thought of Poole, and an odd medley of impressions fought at the gateway of his unconsciousness to be let out: a book called *The Little Duke* and the word Naples—see Naples and die—and Poole again, Poole sitting crouched in a chair in a little dark dingy room eating cake, and Dr. Forester, Dr. Forester stooping over something dark and bleeding. . . . The memories thickened—a woman's face came up for a moment with immense sadness and then sank again like someone drowned, out of sight; his head was racked with pain as other memories struggled to get out like a child out of its mother's body. He put his hands on the dressing-table and held to it; he said to himself over and over again, "I must stand up. I must stand up," as though there were some healing virtue in simply remaining on his feet while his brain reeled with the horror of returning life.

BOOK THREE

Bits and Pieces

1

The Roman Death

"A business that could scarcely have been pleasant."
THE LITTLE DUKE

i

Rowe followed the man in the blue uniform up the stone stairs and along a corridor lined with doors; some of them were open, and he could see that they led into little rooms all the same shape and size like confessionals. A table and three chairs: there was never anything else, and the chairs were hard and upright. The man opened one door—but there seemed no reason why he should not have opened any of the others—and said, "Wait here, sir."

It was early in the morning; the steel rim of the window enclosed a grey cold sky. The last stars had only just gone out. He sat with his hands between his knees in a dull tired patience; he wasn't important, he hadn't become an explorer; he was just a criminal. The effect of reaching this place had exhausted him; he couldn't even remember with any clearness what he had done—only the long walk through the dark countryside to the station, trembling when the cows coughed behind the hedgerows and an owl shrieked, pacing up and down upon the platform till the train came, the smell of grass and steam. The collector had wanted his ticket and he had none nor had he any money to pay with. He knew his name or thought he knew his name, but he had no address to give. The man had been very kind and gentle; perhaps he looked sick. He had asked him if he had no friends to whom he was going, and he replied that he had no friends. . . . "I want to see the police," he said, and the collector rebuked him mildly, "You don't have to go all the way to London for that, sir."

There was a moment of dreadful suspense when he thought he would be returned like a truant child. The collector said, "You are one of Dr. Forester's patients, aren't you, sir? Now if you get out at the next station, they'll telephone for a car. It won't take more than thirty minutes."

"No."

"You lost your way, sir, I expect, but you don't need to worry with a gentleman like Dr. Forester."

He gathered all the energy of which he was capable and said, "I am going to Scotland Yard. I'm wanted there. If you stop me, it's your responsibility."

At the next stop—which was only a halt, a few feet of platform and a wooden shed among dark level fields—he saw Johns; they must have gone to his room and found it empty and Johns had driven over. Johns saw him at once and came with strained naturalness to the door of the compartment; the guard hovered in the background.

"Hullo, old man," Johns said uneasily, "just hop out. I've got the car here—it won't take a moment to get home."

"I'm not coming."

"The doctor's very distressed. He'd had a long day and he lost his temper. He didn't mean half of what he said."

"I'm not coming."

The guard came nearer to show that he was willing to lend a hand if force were necessary. Rowe said furiously, "You haven't certified me yet. You can't drag me out of the train," and the guard edged up. He said softly to Johns, "The gentleman hasn't got a ticket."

"It's all right," Johns said surprisingly, "there's nothing wrong." He leant forward and said in a whisper, "Good luck, old man." The train drew away, laying its steam like a screen across the car, the shed, the figure which didn't dare to wave.

Now all the trouble was over; all that was left was a trial for murder.

Rowe sat on; the steely sky paled and a few taxis hooted. A small fat distrait man in a double-breasted waistcoat opened the door once, took a look at him and said, "Where's Beale?" but didn't wait for an answer. The long wounded cry of a boat came up from the Pool. Somebody went whistling down the corridor outside, once there was the chink-chink of tea-cups, and a faint smell of kipper blew in from a distance.

The little stout man came briskly in again; he had a round over-sized face and a small fair moustache. He carried the slip Rowe had filled in down below. "So you are Mr. Rowe," he said sternly. "We are glad you've come to see us at last." He rang a bell and a uniformed constable answered it. He said, "Is Beavis on duty? Tell him to come along."

He sat down and crossed his neat plump thighs and looked at his nails. They were very well kept. He looked at them from every angle and seemed worried about the cuticle of his left thumb. He said nothing. It was obvious that he wouldn't talk without a witness. Then a big man in a ready-to-wear suit came with a pad and a pencil and took the third chair. His ears were enormous and stuck out straight from his skull and he had an odd air of muted shame like a bull who has begun to realise that he is out of place in a china shop. When he held the pencil to the pad you expected one or the other to suffer in his awkward grasp, and you felt too that he knew and feared the event.

"Well," the dapper man said, sighed, and tucked his nails away for preservation under his thighs. He said, "You've come here, Mr. Rowe, of your own accord to volunteer a statement?"

Rowe said, "I saw a photograph in the paper. . . ."

"We've been asking you to come forward for months."

"I knew it for the first time last night."

"You seem to have lived a bit out the world."

"I've been in a nursing home. You see . . ."

Every time he spoke the pencil squeaked on the paper, making a stiff consecutive narrative out of his haphazard sentences.

"What nursing home?"

"It was kept by a Dr. Forester." He gave the name of the railway station. He knew no other name. He explained, "Apparently there was a raid." He touched the scar on his forehead. "I lost my memory. I found myself at this place knowing nothing—except bits of my childhood. They told me my name was Richard Digby. I didn't even recognise the photograph at first. You see, this beard . . ."

"And your memory has come back now, I hope?" the little man asked sharply, with a touch—a very faint touch—of sarcasm.

"I can remember something, but not much."

"A very convenient sort of memory."

"I am trying," Rowe said with a flash of anger, "to tell you all I know. . . . In English law isn't a man supposed to be innocent until you prove him guilty? I'm ready to tell you everything I can remember about the murder, but I'm not a murderer."

The plump man began to smile. He drew out his hands and looked at his nails and tucked them back again. "That's interesting, Mr. Rowe," he said. "You mentioned murder, but I have said nothing about murder to you, and no paper has mentioned the word murder . . . yet."

"I don't understand."

"We play strictly fair. Read out his statement so far, Beavis."

Beavis obeyed, blushing nervously, as though he were an overgrown schoolboy at a lectern reading Deuteronomy. "I, Arthur Rowe, have made this statement voluntarily. Last night, when I saw a photograph of myself in a newspaper, I knew for the first time that the police wanted to interview me. I have been in a nursing home kept by a Dr. Forester for the last four months, suffering from loss of memory due to an air-raid. My memory is not fully restored, but I wish to tell everything I know in connexion with the murder of . . ."

The detective stopped Beavis. He said, "That's quite fair, isn't it?"

"I suppose it is."

"You'll be asked to sign it presently. Now tell us the name of the murdered man."

"I don't remember it."

"I see. Who told you we wanted to talk to you about a murder?"

"Dr. Forester."

The promptness of the reply seemed to take the detective by surprise. Even Beavis hesitated before the pencil bore down again upon the pad. "Dr. Forester told you?"

"Yes."

"How did he know?"

"I suppose he read it in the papers."

"We have never mentioned murder in the papers."

Rowe leant his head wearily on his hand. Again his brain felt the pressure of associations. He said, "Perhaps . . ." The horrible memory, stirred, crystallised, dissolved. . . . "I don't know."

It seemed to him that the detective's manner was a little more sympathetic. He said, "Just tell us—in any order—in your own words—what you do remember."

"It will have to be in any order. First there's Poole. He's an attendant in Dr. Forester's sick bay—where the violent cases go, only I don't think they are always violent. I know that I met him in the old days—before my memory went. I can remember a little shabby room with a picture of the Bay of Naples. I seemed to be living there—I don't know why. It's not the sort of place I'd choose. So much of what's come back is just feelings, emotion—not fact."

"Never mind," the detective said.

"It's the way you remember a dream when most of it has gone. I remember great sadness—and fear, and, yes, a sense of danger, and an odd taste."

"Of what?"

"We were drinking tea. He wanted me to give him something."

"What?"

"I can't remember. What I do remember is absurd. A cake."

"A cake?"

"It was made with real eggs. And then something happened. . . ." He felt terribly tired. The sun was coming out. People all over the city were going to work. He felt like a man in mortal sin who watches other people go to receive the sacrament—abandoned. If only he knew what *his* work was.

"Would you like a cup of tea?"

"Yes. I'm a bit tired."

"Go and find some tea, Beavis, and some biscuits—or cake."

He asked no more questions until Beavis had returned, but suddenly as Rowe put out his hand to take a piece of cake, he said, "There are no real eggs in that, I'm afraid. Yours must have been home-made. You couldn't have bought it."

Without considering his reply, Rowe said: "Oh no, I didn't buy it, I won it . . ." and stopped. "That's absurd. I wasn't thinking. . . ." The tea made him feel stronger. He said, "You don't treat your murderers too badly."

The detective said, "Just go on remembering."

"I remember a lot of people sitting round a room and the lights going out. And I was afraid that someone was going to come up behind me and stab me or strangle me. And a voice speaking. That's worse than anything—a hopeless pain, but I can't remember a word. And then all the lights are on, and a man's dead, and I suppose that's what you say I've done. But I don't think it's true."

"Would you remember the man's face?"

"I think I would."

"File, Beavis."

It was growing hot in the small room. The detective's forehead was beaded and the little fair moustache damp. He said, "You can take off your coat if you like," and took his own off, and sat in a pearl-grey shirt with silvered armlets to keep the cuffs exactly right. He looked doll-like as though only the coat were made to come off.

Beavis brought a paper-covered file and laid it on the table. The detective said, "Just look through these—you'll find a few loose photographs too—and see if you can find the murdered man."

A police photograph is like a passport photograph; the intelligence which casts a veil over the crude common shape is never recorded by the cheap lens. No one can deny the contours of the flesh, the shape of nose and mouth, and yet we protest: This isn't me. . . .

The turning of the pages became mechanical. Rowe couldn't believe that it was among people like these that his life had been cast. Only once he hesitated for a moment: something in his memory stirred at sight of a loose photograph of a man with a lick of hair plastered back, a pencil on a clip in the lower left-hand corner, and wrinkled evasive eyes that seemed to be trying to escape too bright a photographer's lamp.

"Know him?" the detective asked.

"No. How could I? Or is he a shopkeeper? I thought for a moment, but no, I don't know him." He turned on. Looking up once he saw that the detective had got his hand out from under his thigh; he seemed to have lost interest. There were not many more pages to turn—and then unexpectedly there the face was: the broad anonymous brow, the dark city suit, and with him came a whole throng of faces bursting through the gate of the unconscious, rioting horribly into the memory. He said, "There," and lay back in his chair giddy, feeling the world turn around him. . . .

"Nonsense," the detective said. The harsh voice hardly penetrated. "You had me guessing for a moment . . . a good actor . . . waste any more time. . . ."

"They did it with my knife."

"Stop play-acting," the detective said. "That man hasn't been murdered. He's just as alive as you are."

ii

"Alive?"

"Of course he's alive. I don't know why you picked on him."

"But in that case"—all his tiredness went: he began to notice the fine day outside—"I'm not a murderer. Was he badly hurt?"

"Do you really mean . . . ?" the detective began incredulously; Beavis had given up the attempt at writing. He said, "I don't know what you are talking about. Where did this happen? when? what was it you think you saw?"

As Rowe looked at the photograph it came back in vivid patches: he said, "Wonderful Mrs.—Mrs. Bellairs. It was her house. A séance." Suddenly he saw a thin beautiful hand blood-stained. He said, "Why . . . Dr. Forester was there. He told us the man was dead. They sent for the police."

"The same Dr. Forester?"

"The same one."

"And they let you go?"

"No, I escaped."

"Somebody helped you?"

"Yes."

"Who?"

The past was swimming back to him, as though now that there was nothing to fear the guard had been removed from the gate. Anna's brother had helped him; he saw the exhilarated young face and felt the blow on his knuckles. He wasn't going to betray him. He said, "I don't remember that."

The little plump man sighed. "This isn't for us, Beavis," he said, "we'd better take him across to 59." He put a call through to someone called Prentice. "We turn 'em in to you," he complained, "but how often do you turn them in to us?" Then they accompanied Rowe across the big collegiate court-yard under the high grey block; the trams twanged on the Embankment, and pigeons' droppings gave a farm-yard air to the sandbags stacked around. He didn't care a damn that they walked on either side of him, an obvious escort; he was a free man still and he hadn't committed murder, and his memory was coming back at every step. He said suddenly, "It was the cake he wanted," and laughed.

"Keep your cake for Prentice," the little man said sourly. "He's the surrealist round here."

They came to an almost identical room in another block, where a man in a tweed suit with a drooping grey Edwardian moustache sat on the edge of a chair as though it were a shooting-stick. "This is Mr. Arthur Rowe we've been advertising for," the detective said and laid the file on the table. "At least he says he is. No identity card. Says he's been in a nursing home with loss of memory. We are the lucky fellows who've set his memory going again. Such a memory. We ought to set up a clinic. You'll be interested to hear he saw Cost murdered."

"Now that is interesting," Mr. Prentice said with middle-aged courtesy. "Not *my* Mr. Cost?"

"Yes. And a Dr. Forester attended the death."

"*My* Dr. Forester?"

"It seems likely. This gentleman has been a patient of his."

"Take a chair, Mr. Rowe . . . and you, Graves."

"Not me. You like the fantastic. I don't. I'll leave you Beavis, in case you want any notes taken." He turned at the door and said, "Pleasant nightmares to you."

"Nice chap, Graves," Mr. Prentice said. He leant forward as though he were going to offer a hip flask. The smell of good tweeds came across the table. "Now would you say it was a good nursing home?"

"So long as you didn't quarrel with the doctor."

"Ha, ha . . . exactly. And then?"

"You might find yourself in the sick bay for violent cases."

"Wonderful," Mr. Prentice said, stroking his long moustache. "One can't help admiring. . . . You wouldn't have any complaint to make?"

"They treated me very well."

"Yes, I was afraid so. You see, if only someone would complain—they are all voluntary patients—one might be able to have a look at the place. I've been wanting to for a long time."

"When you get in the sick bay it's too late. If you aren't mad, they can soon make you mad." In his blind flight he had temporarily forgotten Stone. He felt a sense of guilt, remembering the tired voice behind the door. He said, "They've got a man in there now. He's not violent."

"A difference of opinion with our Dr. Forester?"

"He said he saw the doctor and Poole—he's the attendant—doing something in the dark in Poole's room. He told them he was looking for a window from which he could enfilade——" Rowe broke off. "He *is* a little mad, but quite gentle, not violent."

"Go on," Mr. Prentice said.

"He thought the Germans were in occupation of a little island in a pond. He said he'd seen them digging in."

"And he told the doctor that?"

"Yes." Rowe implored him, "Can't you get him out? They've put him in a strait-jacket, but he wouldn't hurt a soul. . . ."

"Well," Mr. Prentice said, "we must think carefully." He stroked his moustache with a milking movement. "We must look all round the subject, mustn't we?"

"He'll go really mad. . . ."

"Poor fellow," Mr. Prentice said unconvincingly. There was a merciless quality in his gentleness. He switched, "And Poole?"

"He came to me once—I don't know how long ago—and wanted a cake I'd won. There was an air-raid on. I have an idea that he tried to kill me because I wouldn't give him the cake. It was made with real eggs. Do you think I'm mad too?" he asked with anxiety.

Mr. Prentice said thoughtfully, "I wouldn't say so. Life can be very odd. Oh, very odd. You should read more history. Silkworms, you know, were smuggled out of China in a hollow walking-stick. One can't really mention the places diamond-smugglers use. And at this very moment I'm looking—oh, most anxiously—for something which may not be much bigger than a diamond. A cake . . . very good, why not? But he didn't kill you."

"There are so many blanks," Rowe said.

"Where was it he came to see you?"

"I don't remember. There are years and years of my life I still can't remember."

"We forget very easily," Mr. Prentice said, "what gives us pain."

"I almost wish I *were* a criminal, so that there could be a record of me here."

Mr. Prentice said gently, "We are doing very well, very well. Now let's go back to the murder of—Cost. Of course that might have been staged to send you into hiding, to stop you coming to us. But what came next? Apparently you didn't go into hiding and you didn't come to us. And what was it you knew . . . or we knew?'' He put his hands flat on the table and said, ''It's a beautiful problem. One could almost put it into algebraic terms. Just tell me all you told Graves.''

He described again what he could remember: the crowded room and the light going out and a voice talking and fear. . . .

''Graves didn't appreciate all that, I dare say,'' Mr. Prentice said, clasping his bony knees and rocking slightly. ''Poor Graves—the passionate crimes of railway porters are his spiritual province. In this branch our interests have to be rather more bizarre. And so he distrusts us—really distrusts us.''

He began turning the pages of the file rather as he might have turned over a family album, quizzically. ''Are you a student of human nature, Mr. Rowe?''

''I don't know what I am.''

''This face for instance. . . .''

It was the photograph over which Rowe had hesitated: he hesitated again.

''What profession do you think *he* followed?'' Mr. Prentice asked.

The pencil clipped in the breast-pocket: the depressed suit: the air of a man always expecting a rebuff: the little lines of knowledge round the eyes—when he examined it closely he felt no doubt at all. ''A private detective,'' he said.

''Right the first time. And this little anonymous man had his little anonymous name. . . .''

Rowe smiled. ''Jones I should imagine.''

''You wouldn't think it, Mr. Rowe, but you and he—let's call him Jones—had something in common. You both disappeared. But you've come back. What was the name of the agency which employed him, Beavis?''

''I don't remember, sir. I could go and look it up.''

''It doesn't matter. The only one I can remember is the Clifford. It wasn't that.''

''Not the Orthotex?'' Rowe asked. ''I once had a friend . . .'' and stopped.

''It comes back, doesn't it, Mr. Rowe. His name was Jones, you see. And he did belong to the Orthotex. What made you go there? We can tell you even if you don't remember. You thought that someone had tried to murder you—about a cake. You had won the cake unfairly at a fair (what a pun!) because a certain Mrs. Bellairs had told you the weight. You went to find out where Mrs. Bellairs lived—from the offices of the Fund for the Mothers of the Free Nations (if I've got the outlandish name correct) and Jones followed, just to keep an eye on them—and you. But you must have given him the slip somehow, Mr. Rowe, because Jones never came back, and when you telephoned next day to Mr. Rennit you said you were wanted for murder.''

Rowe sat with his hand over his eyes—trying to remember? trying not to remember?—while the voice drove carefully and precisely on.

''And yet no murder had been committed in London during the previous twenty-four hours—so far as we knew—unless poor Jones had gone that way. You obviously knew something, perhaps you knew everything: we advertised for you and you didn't come forward. Until today, when you arrive in a beard you certainly used not to wear, saying you had lost your memory, but remembering at least that you had been accused of murder—only you picked out a man we know is alive. How does it all strike you, Mr. Rowe?''

Rowe said, "I'm waiting for the handcuffs," and smiled unhappily.

"You can hardly blame our friend Graves," Mr. Prentice said.

"Is life really like this?" Rowe asked. Mr. Prentice leant forward with an interested air, as though he were always ready to abandon the particular in favour of the general argument. He said, "This is life, so I suppose one can say it's like life."

"It isn't how I had imagined it," Rowe said. He went on, "You see, I'm a learner. I'm right at the beginning, trying to find my way about. I thought life was much simpler and—grander. I suppose that's how it strikes a boy. I was brought up on stories of Captain Scott writing his last letters home. Oates walking into the blizzard, I've forgotten who losing his hands from his experiments with radium, Damien among the lepers. . . ." The memories which are overlaid by the life one lives came freshly back in the little stuffy office in the great grey Yard. It was a relief to talk. "There was a book called the *Book of Golden Deeds* by a woman called Yonge . . . *The Little Duke*. . . ." He said, "If you were suddenly taken from that world into this job you are doing now you'd feel bewildered. Jones and the cake, the sick bay, poor Stone . . . all this talk of a man called Hitler . . . your files of wretched faces, the cruelty and meaninglessness. . . . It's as if one had been sent on a journey with the wrong map. I'm ready to do everything you want, but remember I don't know my way about. Everybody else has changed gradually and learnt. This whole business of war and hate—even that's strange. I haven't been worked up to it. I expect much the best thing would be to hang me."

"Yes," Mr. Prentice said eagerly, "yes, it's a most interesting case. I can see that to you," he became startlingly colloquial, "this is rather a dingy hole. We've come to terms with it of course."

"What frightens me," Rowe said, "is knowing how I came to terms with it before my memory went. When I came in to London to-day I hadn't realised there would be so many ruins. Nothing will seem as strange as that. God knows what kind of a ruin I am myself. Perhaps I *am* a murderer?"

Mr. Prentice reopened the file and said rapidly, "Oh, we no longer think you killed Jones." He was like a man who has looked over a wall, seen something disagreeable and now walks rapidly, purposefully, away, talking as he goes. "The question is—what made you lose your memory? What do you know about that?"

"Only what I've been told."

"And what have you been told?"

"That it was a bomb. It gave me this scar."

"Were you alone?"

Before he could brake his tongue he said, "No."

"Who was with you?"

"A girl." It was too late now; he had to bring her in, and after all if he were not a murderer, why should it matter that her brother had aided his escape? "Anna Hilfe." The plain words were sweet on the tongue.

"Why were you with her?"

"I think we were lovers."

"You think?"

"I don't remember."

"What does she say about it?"

"She says I saved her life."

"The Free Mothers," Mr. Prentice brooded. "Has she explained how you got to Dr. Forester's?"

"She was forbidden to." Mr. Prentice raised an eyebrow. "They wanted—so they told us—my memory to come back naturally and slowly of itself. No hypnotism, no psycho-analysis."

Mr. Prentice beamed at him and swayed a little on his shooting-stick; you felt he was taking a well-earned rest in the middle of a successful shoot. "Yes, it wouldn't have done, would it, if it had come back too quickly. . . . Although of course there was always the sick bay."

"If only you'd tell me what it's all about."

Mr. Prentice stroked his moustache; he had the *fainéant* air of Arthur Balfour, but you felt that he knew it. He had stylised himself—life was easier that way. He had chosen a physical mould just as a writer chooses a technical form. "Now were you ever a habitué of the Regal Court?"

"It's a hotel?"

"You remember that much."

"Well, it's an easy guess."

Mr. Prentice closed his eyes; it was perhaps an affectation, but who could live without affectations?

"Why do you ask about the Regal Court?"

"It's a shot in the dark," Mr. Prentice said. "We have so little time."

"Time for what?"

"To find a needle in a haystack."

iii

One wouldn't have said that Mr. Prentice was capable of much exertion; rough shooting, you would have said, was beyond him. From the house to the brake and from the brake to the butts was about as far as you could expect him to walk in a day. And yet during the next few hours he showed himself capable of great exertion, and the shooting was indubitably rough. . . .

He had dropped his enigmatic statement into the air and was out of the room almost before the complete phrase had formed, his long legs moving stiffly, like stilts. Rowe was left alone with Beavis and the day wore slowly on. The sun's early promise had been false; a cold unseasonable drizzle fell like dust outside the window. After a long time they brought him some cold pie and tea on a tray.

Beavis was not inclined to conversation. It was as though *his* words might be used in evidence, and Rowe only once attempted to break the silence. He said, "I wish I knew what it was all about" and watched Beavis's long-toothed mouth open and clap to like a rabbit snare. "Official secrets," Beavis said and stared with flat eyes at the blank wall.

Then suddenly Mr. Prentice was with them again, rushing into the room in his stiff casual stride, followed by a man in black who held a bowler hat in front of him with both hands like a basin of water and panted a little in the trail of Mr. Prentice. He came to a stop inside the door and glared at Rowe. He said, "That's the scoundrel. I haven't a doubt of it. I can see through the beard. It's a disguise."

Mr. Prentice gave a giggle. "That's excellent," he said. "The pieces are really fitting."

The man with the bowler said, "He carried in the suitcase and he wanted just to leave it. But I had my instructions. I told him he must wait for Mr. Travers. He didn't want to wait. Of course he didn't want to, knowing what was inside. . . . Something must have gone wrong. He didn't get Mr. Travers, but he nearly got the poor girl . . . and when the confusion was over, he'd gone."

"I don't remember ever seeing him before," Rowe said.

The man gesticulated passionately with his bowler, "I'll swear to him in any court of law."

Beavis watched with his mouth a little open and Mr. Prentice giggled again. "No time," he said. "No time for squabbles. You two can get to know each other later. I need you both now."

"If you'd tell me a little," Rowe pleaded. To have come all this way, he thought, to meet a charge of murder and to find only a deeper confusion. . . .

"In the taxi," Mr. Prentice said. "I'll explain in the taxi." He made for the door.

"Aren't you going to charge him?" the man asked, panting in pursuit.

Mr. Prentice without looking round said, "Presently, presently, perhaps . . ." and then darkly, "Who?"

They swept into the court-yard and out into broad stony Northumberland Avenue, policemen saluting: into a taxi and off along the ruined front of the Strand: the empty eyes of an insurance building: boarded windows: sweet-shops with one dish of mauve cachous in the window.

Mr. Prentice said in a low voice, "I just want you two gentlemen to behave naturally. We are going to a city tailor's where I'm being measured for a suit. I shall go in first and after a few minutes you, Rowe, and last you, Mr. Davis," and he touched the bowler hat with the tip of a finger where it balanced on the stranger's lap.

"But what's it all about, sir?" Davis asked. He had edged away from Rowe, and Mr. Prentice curled his long legs across the taxi, sitting opposite them in a tip-up.

"Never mind. Just keep your eyes open and see if there's anyone in the shop you recognise." The mischief faded from his eyes as the taxi looped round the gutted shell of St. Clement Danes. He said, "The place will be surrounded. You needn't be afraid. . . ."

Rowe said, "I'm not afraid. I only want to know . . ." staring out at odd devastated boarded-up London.

"It's really serious," Mr. Prentice said. "I don't know quite how serious. But you might say that we all depend on it." He shuddered away from what was almost an emotional statement, giggled, touched doubtfully the silky ends of his moustache and said, with sadness in his voice, "You know there are always weaknesses that have to be covered up. If the Germans had known after Dunkirk just how weak . . . There are still weaknesses of which if they knew the exact facts . . ." The ruins around St. Paul's unfolded; the obliterated acres of Paternoster Row. He said, "This would be nothing to it. Nothing." He went slowly on, "Perhaps I was wrong to say there was no danger. If we are on the right track, of course, there must be danger, mustn't there? It's worth—oh, a thousand lives to them."

"If I can be of any use," Rowe said. "This is so strange to me. I didn't imagine war was this," staring out at desolation. Jerusalem must have looked something like this in the mind's eye of Christ when he wept. . . .

"I'm not scared," the man with the bowler said sharply, defensively.

"We are looking," Mr. Prentice said, clasping his bony knees and vibrating with the taxi, "for a little roll of film—probably a good deal smaller than a cotton reel. Smaller than those little rolls you put in Leica cameras. You must have read the questions in Parliament about certain papers which were missing for an hour. It was hushed up publicly. It doesn't help anybody to ruin confidence in a big name—and it doesn't help us to have the public and the press muddying up the trail. I tell you two only because—well, we could have you put quietly away for the duration if there was any leakage. It happened twice—the first time the roll was hidden in a cake and the cake was to be fetched from a certain fête. But you won it," Mr. Prentice nodded at Rowe, "the password as it were was given to the wrong man."

"Mrs. Bellairs?" Rowe said.

"She's being looked after at this minute." He went on explaining with vague gestures of his thin useless-looking hands, "That attempt failed. A bomb that hit your house destroyed the cake and everything—and probably saved your life. But they didn't like the way you followed the case up. They tried to frighten you into hiding—but for some reason that was not enough. Of course they meant to blow you into pieces, but when they found you'd lost your memory, that was good enough. It was better than killing you, because by disappearing you took the blame for the bomb—as well as for Jones."

"But why the girl?"

"We'll leave out the mysteries," Mr. Prentice said. "Perhaps because her brother helped you. They aren't above revenge. There isn't time for all that now." They were at the Mansion House. "What we know is this—they had to wait until the next chance came. Another big name and another fool. He had this in common with the first fool —he went to the same tailor." The taxi drew up at the corner of a city street.

"We foot it from here," Mr. Prentice said. A man on the opposite kerb began to walk up the street as they alighted.

"Do you carry a revolver?" the man in the bowler hat asked nervously.

"I wouldn't know how to use it," Mr. Prentice said. "If there's trouble of that kind just lie flat."

"You had no right to bring me into this."

Mr. Prentice turned sharply. "Oh yes," he said, "every right. Nobody's got a right to his life these days. My dear chap, you are conscripted for your country."

They stood grouped on the pavement: bank messengers with chained boxes went by in top hats: stenographers and clerks hurried past returning late from their lunch. There were no ruins to be seen; it was like peace. Mr. Prentice said, "If those photographs leave the country, there'll be a lot of suicides . . . at least that's what happened in France."

"How do you know they haven't left?" Rowe asked.

"We don't. We just hope, that's all. We'll know the worst soon enough." He said, "Watch when I go in. Give me five minutes with our man in the fitting-room, and then you, Rowe, come in and ask for me. I want to have him where I can watch him—in all the mirrors. Then, Davis, you count a hundred and follow. *You* are going to be too much of a coincidence. You are going to be the last straw."

They watched the stiff old-fashioned figure make his way up the street; he was just the kind of man to have a city tailor—somebody reliable and not expensive whom he could recommend to his son. Presently about fifty yards along he turned in; a man stood at the next corner and lit a cigarette. A motor-car drew up next door and a woman got out to do some shopping, leaving a man at the wheel.

Rowe said, "It's time for me to be moving." His pulse beat with excitement; it was as if he had come to this adventure unsaddened, with the freshness of a boy. He looked suspiciously at Davis, who stood there with a nerve twitching at his cheek. He said, "A hundred and you follow." Davis said nothing. "You understand. You count a hundred."

"Oh," Davis said furiously, "this play-acting. I'm a plain man."

"Those were his orders."

"Who's he to give me orders?"

Rowe couldn't stay to argue: time was up.

War had hit the tailoring business hard. A few rolls of grey inferior cloth lay on the counter; the shelves were nearly empty. A man in a frock-coat with a tired, lined, anxious face said, "What can we do for you, sir?"

"I came here," Rowe said, "to meet a friend." He looked down the narrow aisle between the little mirrored cubicles. "I expect he's being fitted now."

"Will you take a chair, sir?" and "Mr. Ford," he called, "Mr. Ford." Out from one of the cubicles, a tape measure slung round his neck, a little bouquet of pins in his lapel, solid, city-like, came Cost, whom he had last seen dead in his chair when the lights went on. Like a piece of a jig-saw puzzle which clicks into place and makes sense of a whole confusing block, that solid figure took up its place in his memory with the man from Welwyn and the proletarian poet and Anna's brother. What had Mrs. Bellairs called him? He remembered the whole phrase "Our business man."

Rowe stood up as though this were someone of great importance who must be greeted punctiliously, but there seemed to be no recognition in the stolid respectable eyes. "Yes, Mr. Bridges?" Those were the first words he had ever heard him speak; his whole function before had been one of death.

"This gentleman has come to meet the other gentleman."

The eyes swivelled slowly and rested; no sign of recognition broke their large grey calm—or did they rest a shade longer than was absolutely necessary? "I have nearly taken the gentleman's measurements. If you would not mind waiting two minutes. . . ." Two minutes Rowe thought, and then the other, the straw which will really break you down.

Mr. Ford—if this was now to be his name—walked slowly up to the counter; everything he did, you felt, was carefully pondered; his suits must always be well-built. There was no room in that precision for the eccentricity, the wayward act, and yet what a wild oddity lay hidden under the skin. He saw Dr. Forester dabbling his fingers in what looked like blood.

A telephone stood on the counter; Mr. Ford picked up the receiver and dialled. The dial faced Rowe. He watched with care each time where the finger fitted. B. A. T. He felt sure of the letters; but one number he missed, suddenly wavering and catching the serene ponderous gaze of Mr. Ford as he dialled. He was unsure of himself; he wished Mr. Prentice would appear.

"Hullo," Mr. Ford said, "hullo. This is Pauling and Crosthwaite."

Along the length of the window towards the door dragged the unwilling form of the man with the bowler hat: Rowe's hands tightened in his lap. Mr. Bridges was sadly straightening the meagre rolls of cloth, his back turned. His listless hands were like a poignant criticism in the *Tailor and Cutter*.

"The suit was despatched this morning, sir," Mr. Ford was saying, "I trust in time for your journey." He clucked his satisfaction calmly and inhumanly down the telephone, "Thank you very much, sir. I felt very satisfied myself at the last fitting." His eyes shifted to the clanging door as Davis looked in with a kind of wretched swagger. "Oh, yes, sir. I think when you've worn it once, you'll find the shoulders will settle. . . ." Mr. Prentice's whole elaborate plot was a failure: that nerve had not broken.

"Mr. Travers," Davis exclaimed with astonishment.

Carefully putting his hand over the mouthpiece of the telephone Mr. Ford said, "I beg your pardon, sir?"

"You are Mr. Travers." Then Davis, meeting those clear calm eyes, added weakly, "Aren't you?"

"No, sir."

"I thought . . ."

"Mr. Bridges, would you mind attending to this gentleman?"

"Certainly, Mr. Ford."

The hand left the receiver and Mr. Ford quietly, firmly, authoritatively continued to speak up the wire. "No, sir. I find at the last moment that we shall not be able to repeat the trousers. It's not a matter of coupons, no. We can obtain no more of that pattern from the manufacturers—no more at all." Again his eyes met Rowe's and wandered like a blind man's hand delicately along the contours of his face. "Personally, sir, I have no hope. No hope at all." He put the receiver down and moved a little way along the counter. "If you can spare these a moment, Mr. Bridges. . . ." He picked up a pair of cutting-shears.

"Certainly, Mr. Ford."

Without another word he passed Rowe, not looking at him again, and moved down the aisle, without hurry, serious, professional, as heavy as stone. Rowe quickly rose: something, he felt, must be done, be said, if the whole plan were not to end in fiasco. "Cost," he called after the figure, "Cost." It was only then that the extreme calm and deliberation of the figure with the shears struck him as strange. He called out "Prentice" sharply in warning as the fitter turned aside into a cubicle.

But it was not the cubicle from which Mr. Prentice emerged. He came bewilderedly out in his silk shirtsleeves from the opposite end of the aisle. "What is it?" he asked, but Rowe was already at the other door straining to get in. Over his shoulder he could see the shocked face of Mr. Bridges, Davis's goggling eyes. "Quick," he said, "your hat," and grabbed the bowler and crashed it through the glass of the door.

Under the icicles of splintered glass he could see Cost-Travers-Ford. He sat in the arm-chair for clients opposite the tall triple mirror, leaning forward, his throat transfixed, with the cutting-shears held firmly upright between his knees. It was a Roman death.

Rowe thought: this time I *have* killed him, and heard that quiet respectful but authoritative voice speaking down the telephone. "Personally I have no hope. No hope at all."

2

Mopping Up

"You had best yield."
THE LITTLE DUKE

i

Mrs. Bellairs had less dignity.

They had driven straight to Campden Hill, leaving Davis with his wrecked bowler. Mr. Prentice was worried and depressed. "It does no good," he said. "We want them alive and talking."

Rowe said, "He must have had great courage. I don't know why that's so surprising. One doesn't associate it with tailors . . . except for that one in the story who killed a giant. I suppose you'd say this one was on the side of the giants. I wonder why."

Mr. Prentice burst suddenly out as they drove up through the Park in the thin windy rain. "Pity is a terrible thing. People talk about the passion of love. Pity is the worst passion of all: we don't outlive it like sex."

"After all, it's war," Rowe said with a kind of exhilaration. The old fake truism like a piece of common pyrite in the hands of a child split open and showed its sparkling core to him. He was taking part. . . .

Mr. Prentice looked at him oddly, with curiosity. "You don't feel it, do you? Adolescents don't feel pity. It's a mature passion."

"I expect," Rowe said, "that I led a dull humdrum sober life, and so all this excites me. Now that I know I'm not a murderer I can enjoy . . ." He broke off at sight of the dimly remembered house like the scene of a dream: that unweeded little garden with the grey fallen piece of statuary and the small iron gate that creaked. All the blinds were down as though somebody had died, and the door stood open; you expected to see auction tickets on the furniture. "We pulled her in," Mr. Prentice said, "simultaneously."

There was silence about the place; a man in a dark suit who might have been an undertaker stood in the hall. He opened a door for Mr. Prentice and they went in. It wasn't the drawing-room that Rowe vaguely remembered, but a small dining-room crammed full with ugly chairs and a too-large table and a desk. Mrs. Bellairs sat in an arm-chair at the head of the table with a pasty grey closed face, wearing a black turban; the man at the door said, "She won't say a thing."

"Well, ma'am," Mr. Prentice greeted her with a kind of gallant jauntiness.

Mrs. Bellairs said nothing.

"I've brought you a visitor, ma'am," Mr. Prentice said and stepping to one side allowed her to see Rowe.

It is a disquieting experience to find yourself an object of terror: no wonder the novelty of it intoxicates some men. To Rowe it was horrible—as though he had suddenly found himself capable of an atrocity. Mrs. Bellairs began to choke, sitting grotesquely at the table-head; it was as if she had swallowed a fish-bone at a select dinner-party. She must have been holding herself in with a great effort, and the shock had upset the muscles of her throat.

Mr. Prentice was the only one equal to the occasion. He wormed round the table and slapped her jovially on the back. "Choke up, ma'am," he said, "choke up. You'll be all right."

"I've never seen the man," she moaned, "never."

"Why, you told his fortune," Mr. Prentice said. "Don't you remember that?"

A glint of desperate hope slid across the old congested eyes. She said, "If all this fuss is about a little fortune-telling. . . . I only do it for charity."

"Of course, we understand that," Mr. Prentice said.

"And I never tell the future."

"Ah, if we could see into the future. . . ."

"Only character."

"And the weight of cakes," Mr. Prentice said, and all the hope went suddenly out. It was too late now for silence.

"And your little séances," Mr. Prentice went cheerily on, as though they shared a joke between them.

"In the interests of science," Mrs. Bellairs said.

"Does your little group still meet?"

"On Wednesdays."

"Many absentees?"

"They are all personal friends," Mrs. Bellairs said vaguely; now that the questions seemed again on safer ground, she put up one plump powdered hand and adjusted the turban.

"Mr. Cost now . . . he can hardly attend any longer."

Mrs. Bellairs said carefully, "Of course, I recognise this gentleman now. The beard confused me. That was a silly joke of Mr. Cost's. I knew nothing about it. I was far, far away."

"Far away?"

"Where the Blessed are."

"Oh yes, yes. Mr. Cost won't play such jokes again."

"It was meant quite innocently, I'm sure. Perhaps he resented two strangers. . . . We are a very compact little group. And Mr. Cost was never a real believer."

"Let's hope he is now." Mr. Prentice did not seem worried at the moment by what he had called the terrible passion of pity. He said, "You must try to get into touch with him, Mrs. Bellairs, and ask him why he cut his throat this morning."

Into the goggle-eyed awful silence broke the ringing of the telephone. It rang and rang on the desk, and there were too many people in the little crowded room to get to it quickly. A memory shifted like an uneasy sleeper . . . this had happened before.

"Wait a moment," Mr. Prentice said. "You answer it, ma'am."

She repeated, "Cut his throat . . ."

"It was all he had left to do. Except live and hang."

The telephone cried on. It was as though someone far away had his mind fixed on that room, working out the reason for that silence.

"Answer it, ma'am," Mr. Prentice said again.

Mrs. Bellairs was not made of the same stuff as the tailor. She heaved herself obediently up, jangling a little as she moved. She got momentarily stuck between the table and the wall, and the turban slipped over one eye. She said, "Hullo. Who's there?"

The three men in the room stayed motionless, holding their breaths. Suddenly Mrs. Bellairs seemed to recover; it was as if she felt her power—the only one there who could speak. She said, "It's Dr. Forester. What shall I say to him?" speaking over her shoulder with her mouth close to the receiver. She glinted at them, maliciously, intelligently, with her stupidity strung up like a piece of camouflage she couldn't be bothered to perfect. Mr. Prentice took the receiver from her hand and rang off. He said, "This isn't going to help you."

She bridled, "I was only asking. . . ."

Mr. Prentice said, "Get a fast car from the Yard. God knows what those local police are doing. They should have been at the house by this time." He told a second man, "See that this lady doesn't cut her throat. We've got other uses for it."

He proceeded to go through the house from room to room as destructively as a tornado; he was white and angry. He said to Rowe, "I'm worried about your friend—what's his name?—Stone." He said, "The old bitch," and the word sounded odd on the Edwardian lips. In Mrs. Bellairs' bedroom he didn't leave a pot of cream unchurned—and there were a great many. He tore open her pillows himself with vicious pleasure. There was a little lubricious book called *Love in the Orient* on a bed-table by a pink-shaded lamp—he tore off the binding and broke the china base of the lamp. Only the sound of a car's horn stopped the destruction. He said, "I'll want you with me—for identifications," and took the stairs in three strides and a jump. Mrs. Bellairs was weeping now in the drawing-room, and one of the detectives had made her a cup of tea.

"Stop that nonsense," Mr. Prentice said. It was as if he were determined to give an example of thoroughness to weak assistants. "There's nothing wrong with her. If she won't talk, skin this house alive." He seemed consumed by a passion of hatred and perhaps despair. He took up the cup from which Mrs. Bellairs had been about to drink and emptied the contents on the carpet. Mrs. Bellairs wailed at him, "You've got no right . . ."

He said sharply, "Is this your best tea-service, ma'am?" wincing ever so slightly at the gaudy Prussian blue.

"Put it down," Mrs. Bellairs implored, but he had already smashed the cup against the wall. He explained to his man, "The handles are hollow. We don't know how small these films are. You've got to skin the place."

"You'll suffer for this," Mrs. Bellairs said tritely.

"Oh no, ma'am, it's you who'll suffer. Giving information to the enemy is a hanging offence."

"They don't hang women. Not in this war."

"We may hang more people, ma'am," Mr. Prentice said, speaking back at her from the passage, "than the papers tell you about."

ii

It was a long and gloomy ride. A sense of failure and apprehension must have oppressed Mr. Prentice; he sat curled in the corner of the car humming lugubriously. It became evening before they had unwound themselves from the dirty edge of London, and night before they reached the first hedge. Looking back, one could see only an illuminated sky—bright lanes and blobs of light like city squares, as though the inhabited world were up above and down below only the dark unlighted heavens.

It was a long and gloomy ride, but all the time Rowe repressed for the sake of his companion a sense of exhilaration: he was happily drunk with danger and action. This was more like the life he had imagined years ago. He was helping in a great struggle, and when he saw Anna again he could claim to have played a part against her enemies. He didn't worry very much about Stone; none of the books of adventure one read as a boy had an unhappy ending. And none of them was disturbed by a sense of pity for the beaten side. The ruins from which they emerged were only a heroic back-cloth to his personal adventure; they had no more reality than the photographs in a propaganda album: the remains of an iron bedstead on the third floor of a smashed tenement only said, "They shall not pass," not "We shall never sleep in this room, in this home, again.'' He didn't understand suffering because he had forgotten that he had ever suffered.

Rowe said, ''After all, nothing can have happened there. The local police . . .''

Mr. Prentice observed bitterly, ''England is a very beautiful country. The Norman churches, the old graves, the village green and the public-house, the policeman's home with his patch of garden. He wins a prize every year for his cabbages . . .''

''But the county police . . .''

''The Chief Constable served twenty years ago in the Indian Army. A fine fellow. Has a good palate for port. Talks too much about his regiment, but you can depend on him for a subscription to any good cause. The superintendent . . . he was a good man once, but they'd have retired him from the Metropolitan Police after a few years' service without a pension, so the first chance he got he transferred to the county. You see, being an honest man, he didn't want to lay by in bribes from bookmakers for his old age. Only, of course, in a small county there's not much to keep a man sharp. Running in drunks. Petty pilfering. The judge at the assizes compliments the county on its clean record.''

''You know the men?''

''I don't know *these* men, but if you know England you can guess it all. And then suddenly into this peace—even in wartime it's still peace—comes the clever, the warped, the completely unscrupulous, ambitious, educated criminal. Not a criminal at all, as the county knows crime. He doesn't steal and he doesn't get drunk—and if he murders, they haven't had a murder for fifty years and can't recognise it.''

''What do you expect to find?'' Rowe asked.

''Almost anything except what we are looking for. A small roll of film.''

''They may have got innumerable copies by this time.''

''They may have, but they haven't innumerable ways of getting them out of the country. Find the man who's going to do the smuggling—and the organiser. It doesn't matter about the rest.''

''Do you think Dr. Forester . . . ?''

''Dr. Forester,'' Mr. Prentice said, ''is a victim—oh, a dangerous victim, no doubt, but he's not the victimiser. He's one of the used, the blackmailed. That doesn't mean, of course, that he isn't the courier. If he is, we are in luck. He couldn't get away . . . unless these country police . . .'' Again the gloom of defeat descended on him.

''He might pass it on.''

''It isn't so easy,'' Mr. Prentice said. ''There are not many of these people at large. Remember, to get out of the country now you must have a very good excuse. If only the country police . . .''

''Is it so desperately important?''

Mr. Prentice thought gloomily, ''We've made so many mistakes since this war began, and they've made so few. Perhaps this one will be the last we'll make. To trust a man like Dunwoody with anything secret . . .''

''Dunwoody?''

''I shouldn't have let it out, but one gets impatient. Have you heard the name? They hushed it up because he's the son of the grand old man.''

''No, I've never heard of him . . . I think I've never heard of him.''

A screech owl cried over the dark flat fields; their dimmed headlights just touched the near hedge and penetrated no farther into the wide region of night: it was like the coloured fringe along the unexplored spaces of a map. Over there among the unknown tribes a woman was giving birth, rats were nosing among sacks of meal, an old man was dying, two people were seeing each other for the first time by the light of a lamp; everything in that darkness was of such deep importance that their errand could not equal it—this violent superficial chase, this cardboard adventure hurtling at seventy miles an hour along the edge of the profound natural common experiences of men. Rowe felt a longing to get back into that world: into the world of homes and children and quiet love and the ordinary unspecified fears and anxieties the neighbour shared; he carried the thought of Anna like a concealed letter promising just that: the longing was like the first stirring of maturity when the rare experience suddenly ceases to be desirable.

"We shall know the worst soon," Mr. Prentice said. "If we don't find it here"—his hunched hopeless figure expressed the weariness of giving up.

Somebody a long way ahead was waving a torch up and down, up and down. "What the hell are they playing at?" Mr. Prentice said. "Advertising. . . . They can't trust a stranger to find his way through their country without a compass."

They drew slowly along a high wall and halted outside big heraldic gates. It was unfamiliar to Rowe; he was looking from the outside at something he had only seen from within. The top of a cedar against the sky was not the same cedar that cast a shadow round the bole. A policeman stood at the car door and said, "What name, sir?"

Mr. Prentice showed a card. "Everything all right?"

"Not exactly, sir. You'll find the superintendent inside."

They left the car and trailed, a little secretive dubious group, between the great gates. They had no air of authority; they were stiff with the long ride and subdued in spirit: they looked like a party of awed sightseers taken by the butler round the family seat. The policeman kept on saying, "This way, sir," and flashing his torch, but there was only one way.

It seemed odd to Rowe, returning like this. The big house was silent—and the fountain was silent too. Somebody must have turned off the switch which regulated the flow. There were lights on in only two of the rooms. This was the place where for months he had lain happily in an extraordinary peace; this scene had been grafted by the odd operation of a bomb on to his childhood. Half his remembered life lay here. Now that he came back like an enemy, he felt a sense of shame. He said, "If you don't mind, I'd rather not see Dr. Forester. . . ."

The policeman with the torch said, "You needn't be afraid, sir, he's quite tidy."

Mr. Prentice had not been listening. "That car," he said, "who does it belong to?"

A Ford V 8 stood in the drive—that wasn't the one he meant, but an old tattered car with cracked and stained windscreen—one of those cars that stand with a hundred others in lonely spoilt fields along the highway—yours for five pounds if you can get it to move away.

"That, sir—that's the reverend's."

Mr. Prentice said sharply, "Are you holding a party?"

"Oh no, sir. But as one of them was still alive, we thought it only right to let the vicar know."

"Things seem to have happened," Mr. Prentice said gloomily. It had been raining and the constable tried to guide them with his torch between the puddles in the churned-up gravel and up the stone steps to the hall door.

In the lounge where the illustrated papers had lain in glossy stacks, where Davis had been accustomed to weep in a corner and the two nervous men had fumed over the chess pieces, Johns sat in an arm-chair with his head in his hands. Rowe went to him; he said, "Johns," and Johns looked up. He said, "He was such a great man . . . such a great man. . . ."

"Was?"

"I killed him."

iii

It had been a massacre on an Elizabethan scale. Rowe was the only untroubled man there—until he saw Stone. The bodies lay where they had been discovered: Stone bound in his strait-waistcoat with the sponge of anaesthetic on the floor beside him and the body twisted in a hopeless attempt to use his hands. "He hadn't a chance," Rowe said. This was the passage he had crept up excited like a boy breaking a school rule; in the same passage, looking in through the open door, he grew up—learned that adventure didn't follow the literary pattern, that there weren't always happy endings, felt the awful stirring of pity that told him something had got to be done, that you couldn't let things stay as they were, with the innocent struggling in fear for breath and dying pointlessly. He said slowly, "I'd like . . . how I'd like . . ." and felt cruelty waking beside pity, its old and tried companion.

"We must be thankful," an unfamiliar voice said, "that he felt no pain." The stupid complacent and inaccurate phrase stroked at their raw nerves.

Mr. Prentice said, "Who the hell are you?" He apologised reluctantly, "I'm sorry. I suppose you are the vicar."

"Yes. My name's Sinclair."

"You've got no business here."

"I *had* business," Mr. Sinclair corrected him. "Dr. Forester was still alive when they called me. He was one of my parishioners." He added in a tone of gentle remonstrance, "You know—we are allowed on a battlefield."

"Yes, yes, I daresay. But there are no inquests on those bodies. Is that your car at the door?"

"Yes."

"Well, if you wouldn't mind going back to the vicarage and staying there till we are through with this. . . ."

"Certainly. I wouldn't want to be in the way."

Rowe watched him: the cylindrical black figure, the round collar glinting under the electric light, the hearty intellectual face. Mr. Sinclair said to him slowly, "Haven't we met . . . ?" confronting him with an odd bold stare.

"No," Rowe said.

"Perhaps you were one of the patients here?"

"I was."

Mr. Sinclair said with nervous enthusiasm, "There. That must be it. I felt sure that somewhere. . . . On one of the doctor's social evenings, I dare say. Good night."

Rowe turned away and considered again the man who had felt no pain. He remembered him stepping into the mud, desperately anxious, then fleeing like a scared child towards the vegetable garden. He had always believed in treachery. He hadn't been so mad after all.

They had had to step over Dr. Forester's body; it lay at the bottom of the stairs. A sixth snare had entangled the doctor: not love of country but love of one's fellow-man, a love which had astonishingly flamed into action in the heart of respectable, hero-worshipping Johns. The doctor had been too sure of Johns: he had not realised that respect is really less reliable than fear: a man may be more ready to kill one he respects than to betray him to the police. When Johns shut his eyes and pulled the trigger of the revolver which had once been confiscated from Davis and had lain locked away for months in a drawer, he was not ruining the man he respected—he was saving him from the interminable proceedings of the law courts, from the crudities of prosecuting counsel, the unfathomable ignorances of the judge, and the indignity of depending on the shallow opinion of twelve men picked at random. If love of his fellow-man refused to allow him to be a sleeping partner in the elimination of Stone, love also dictated the form of his refusal.

Dr. Forester had shown himself disturbed from the moment of Rowe's escape. He had been inexplicably reluctant to call in the police, and he seemed worried about the fate of Stone. There were consultations with Poole from which Johns was excluded, and during the afternoon there was a trunk call to London. . . . Johns took a letter to the post and couldn't help noticing the watcher outside the gate. In the village he saw a police car from the county town. He began to wonder. . . .

He met Poole on the way back. Poole, too, must have seen. All the fancies and resentments of the last few days came back to Johns. Sitting in a passion of remorse in the lounge, he couldn't explain how all these indications had crystallised into the belief that the doctor was planning Stone's death. He remembered theoretical conversations he had often had with the doctor on the subject of euthanasia: arguments with the doctor, who was quite unmoved by the story of the Nazi elimination of old people and incurables. The doctor had once said, "It's what any State medical service has sooner or later got to face. If you are going to be kept alive in institutions run by and paid for by the State, you must accept the State's right to economise when necessary. . . ." He intruded on a colloquy between Poole and Forester, which was abruptly broken off, he became more and more restless and uneasy, it was as if the house were infected by the future: fear was already present in the passages. At tea Dr. Forester made some remark about "poor Stone."

"Why poor Stone?" Johns asked sharply and accusingly.

"He's in great pain," Dr. Forester said. "A tumour. . . . Death is the greatest mercy we can ask for him."

He went restlessly out into the garden in the dusk; in the moonlight the sundial was like a small sheeted figure of someone already dead at the entrance to the rose garden. Suddenly he heard Stone crying out. . . . His account became more confused than ever. Apparently he ran straight to his room and got out the gun. It was just like Johns, that he had mislaid the key and found it at last in his pocket. He heard Stone cry out again. He ran through the lounge, into the other wing, made for the stairs—the sickly confected smell of chloroform was in the passage, and Dr. Forester stood on guard at the foot of the stairs. He said crossly and nervously, "What do you want, Johns?" and Johns, who still believed in the misguided purity of the doctor's fanaticism, saw only one solution: he shot the doctor. Poole, with his twisted shoulder and his malign conceited face, backed away from the top of the stairs—and he shot him, too, in a rage because he guessed he was too late.

Then, of course, the police were at the door. He went to meet them, for apparently the servants had all been given the evening off, and it was that small banal fact of which he had read in so many murder stories that brought the squalid truth home to him. Dr. Forester was still alive, and the local police thought it only right to send for the parson. . . . That was all. It was extraordinary the devastation that could be worked in one evening in what had once seemed a kind of earthly paradise. A flight of bombers could not have eliminated peace more thoroughly than had three men.

The search was then begun. The house was ransacked. More police were sent for. Lights were switched on and off restlessly through the early morning hours in upstairs rooms. Mr. Prentice said, "If we could find even a single print. . . ." but there was nothing. At one point of the long night watch Rowe found himself back in the room where Digby had slept. He thought of Digby now as a stranger—a rather gross, complacent, parasitic stranger whose happiness had lain in too great an ignorance. Happiness should always be qualified by a knowledge of misery. There on the book-shelf stood the Tolstoy with the pencil-marks rubbed out. Knowledge was the great thing . . . not abstract knowledge in which Dr. Forester had been so rich, the theories which lead one enticingly on with their appearance of nobility, of transcendent virtue, but detailed passionate trivial human knowledge. He opened the Tolstoy again: "What seemed to me good and lofty—love of fatherland, of one's own people—became to me repulsive and pitiable. What seemed to me bad and shameful—rejection of fatherland and cosmopolitanism—now appeared to me on the contrary good and noble." Idealism had ended up with a bullet in the stomach at the foot of the stairs; the idealist had been caught out in treachery and murder. Rowe didn't believe they had had to blackmail him much. They had only to appeal to his virtues, his intellectual pride, his abstract love of humanity. One can't love humanity. One can only love people.

"Nothing," Mr. Prentice said. He drooped disconsolately across the room on his stiff lean legs and drew the curtain a little aside. Only one star was visible now: the others had faded into the lightening sky. "So much time wasted," Mr. Prentice said.

"Three dead and one in prison."

"They can find a dozen to take their place. I want the films: the top man." He said, "They've been using photographic chemicals in the basin in Poole's room. That's where they developed the film, probably. I don't suppose they'd print more than one at a time. They'd want to trust as few people as possible, and so long as they have the negative . . ." He added sadly, "Poole was a first-class photographer. He specialised in the life history of the bee. Wonderful studies. I've seen some of them. I want you to come over now to the island. I'm afraid we may find something unpleasant there for you to identify. . . ."

They stood where Stone had stood; three little red lights ahead across the pond gave it in the three-quarter dark an illimitable air as of a harbour just before dawn with the riding lamps of steamers gathering for a convoy. Mr. Prentice waded out and Rowe followed him; there was a thin skin of water over nine inches of mud. The red lights were lanterns—the kind of lanterns which are strung at night where roads are broken. Three policemen were digging in the centre of the tiny island. There was hardly a foothold for two more men. "This was what Stone saw," Rowe said. "Men digging."

"Yes."

"What do you expect . . . ?" He stopped; there was something strained in the attitude of the diggers. They put in their spades carefully as though they might break something fragile, and they seemed to turn up the earth with reluctance. The dark scene reminded him of something: something distant and sombre. Then he remembered a dark Victorian engraving in a book his mother had taken away from him: men in cloaks digging at night in a graveyard with the moonlight glinting on a spade.

Mr. Prentice said, "There's somebody you've forgotten—unaccounted for."

Now as each spade cut down he waited himself with apprehension: he was held by the fear of disgust.

"How do you know where to dig?"

"They left marks. They were amateurs at this. I suppose that was why they were scared of what Stone saw."

One spade made an ugly scrunching sound in the soft earth.

"Careful," Mr. Prentice said. The man wielding it stopped and wiped sweat off his face, although the night was cold. Then he drew the tool slowly out of the earth and looked at the blade. "Start again on this side," Mr. Prentice said. "Take it gently. Don't go deep." The other men stopped digging and watched, but you could tell they didn't want to watch.

The man digging said, "Here it is." He left the spade standing in the ground and began to move the earth with his fingers, gently as though he were planting seedlings. He said with relief, "It's only a box."

He took his spade again, and with one strong effort lifted the box out of its bed. It was the kind of wooden box which holds groceries, and the lid was loosely nailed down. He prised it open with the edge of the blade and another man brought a lamp nearer. Then one by one an odd sad assortment of objects was lifted out: they were like the relics a company commander sends home when one of his men has been killed. But there was this difference: there were no letters or photographs.

"Nothing they could burn," Mr. Prentice said.

These were what an ordinary fire would reject: a fountain-pen clip, another clip which had probably held a pencil.

"It's not easy to burn things," Mr. Prentice said, "in an all-electric house."

A pocket-watch. He nicked open the heavy back and read aloud: "F.G.J., from N.L.J. on our silver wedding, 3.8.15." Below was added: "To my dear son in memory of his father, 1919."

"A good regular time-piece," Mr. Prentice said.

Two plaited metal arm-bands came next. Then the metal buckles off a pair of sock-suspenders. And then a whole collection of buttons—little pearl buttons off a vest, large ugly brown buttons off a suit, brace buttons, pants buttons, trouser buttons—one could never have believed that one man's single change of clothes required so much holding together. Waistcoat buttons. Shirt buttons. Cuff buttons. Then the metal parts of a pair of braces. So is a poor human creature joined respectably together like a doll: take him apart and you are left with a grocery box full of assorted catches and buckles and buttons.

At the bottom there was a pair of heavy old-fashioned boots with big nails worn with so much pavement tramping, so much standing at street corners.

"I wonder," Mr. Prentice said, "what they did with the rest of him."

"Who was he?"

"He was Jones."

3

Wrong Numbers

"A very slippery, treacherous, quaking road it was."
THE LITTLE DUKE

i

Rowe was growing up; every hour was bringing him nearer to hailing distance of his real age. Little patches of memory returned; he could hear Mr. Rennit's voice saying, "I agree with Jones," and he saw again a saucer with a sausage-roll upon it beside a telephone. Pity stirred, but immaturity fought hard; the sense of adventure struggled with common sense as though it were on the side of happiness, and common sense were allied to possible miseries, disappointments, disclosures. . . .

It was immaturity which made him keep back the secret of the telephone number, the number he had so nearly made out in Cost's shop. He knew the exchange was B A T, and he knew the first three numbers were 271: only the last had escaped him. The information might be valueless—or invaluable. Whichever it was, he hugged it to himself. Mr. Prentice had had his chance and failed; now it was his turn. He wanted to boast like a boy to Anna—"I did it."

About four-thirty in the morning they had been joined by a young man called Brothers. With his umbrella and his moustache and his black hat he had obviously modelled himself upon Mr. Prentice. Perhaps in twenty years the portrait would have been adequately copied; it lacked at present the patina of age—the cracks of sadness, disappointment, resignation. Mr. Prentice wearily surrendered the picked bones of investigation to Brothers and offered Rowe a seat in the car going back to London. He pulled his hat over his eyes, sank deep into the seat and said, "We are beaten," as they splashed down a country lane with the moonlight flat on the puddles.

"What are you going to do about it?"

"Go to sleep." Perhaps to his fine palate the sentence sounded over-conscious, for without opening his eyes he added, "One must avoid self-importance, you see. In five hundred years' time, to the historian writing the Decline and Fall of the British Empire, this little episode would not exist. There will be plenty of other causes. You and me and poor Jones will not even figure in a footnote. It will be all economics, politics, battles."

"What do you think they did to Jones?"

"I don't suppose we shall ever know. In time of war, so many bodies are unidentifiable. So many bodies," he said sleepily, "waiting for a convenient blitz." Suddenly, surprisingly and rather shockingly, he began to snore.

They came into London with the early workers; along the industrial roads men and women were emerging from underground; neat elderly men carrying attaché-cases and rolled umbrellas appeared from public shelters. In Gower Street they were sweeping up glass, and a building smoked into the new day like a candle which some late re-veller has forgotten to snuff. It was odd to think that the usual battle had been going on while they stood on the island in the pond and heard only the scrape of the spade. A notice turned them from their course, and on a rope strung across the road already flapped a few hand-written labels. "Barclay's Bank. Please inquire at. . . ." "The Cornwallis Dairy. New address. . . ." "Marquis's Fish Saloon. . . ." On a long, quiet, empty expanse of pavement a policeman and a warden strolled in lazy proprietory conversation like gamekeepers on their estate—a notice read, "Unexploded Bomb." This was the same route they had taken last night, but it had been elaborately and trivially changed. What a lot of activity, Rowe thought, there had been in a few hours—the sticking up of notices, the altering of traffic, the getting to know a slightly different London. He noticed the briskness, the cheerfulness on the faces; you got the impression that this was an early hour of a national holiday. It was simply, he supposed, the effect of finding oneself alive.

Mr. Prentice muttered and woke. He told the driver the address of a small hotel near Hyde Park Corner—"if it's still there," and insisted punctiliously on arranging Rowe's room with the manager. It was only after he had waved his hand from the car—"I'll ring you later, dear fellow'—that Rowe realised his courtesy, of course, had an object. He had been lodged where they could reach him; he had been thrust securely into the right pigeon-hole, and would presently, when they required him, be pulled out again. If he tried to leave it would be reported at once. Mr. Prentice had even lent him five pounds—you couldn't go far on five pounds.

Rowe had a small early breakfast. The gas-main apparently had been hit, and the gas wouldn't light properly. It wasn't hardly more than a smell, the waitress told him—not enough to boil a kettle or make toast. But there was milk and post-toasties and bread and marmalade—quite an Arcadian meal, and afterwards he walked across the Park in the cool early sun and noticed, looking back over the long empty plain, that he was not followed. He began to whistle the only tune he knew; he felt a kind of serene excitement and well-being, for he was not a murderer. The forgotten years hardly troubled him more than they had done in the first weeks at Dr. Forester's home. How good it was, he thought, to play an adult part in life again, and veered with his boy's secret into Bayswater towards a telephone-box.

He had collected at the hotel a store of pennies. He was filled with exhilaration, pressing in the first pair and dialling. A voice said briskly, "The Hygienic Baking Company at your service," and he rang off. It was only then he began to realise the difficulties ahead: he couldn't expect to know Cost's customer by a sixth sense. He dialled again and an old voice said, "Hullo." He said, "Excuse me. Who is that, please?"

"Who do you want?" the voice said obstinately—it was so old that it had lost sexual character and you couldn't tell whether it was a man's or a woman's.

"This is Exchange," Rowe said; the idea came to him at the moment of perplexity, as though his brain had kept it in readiness all the while. "We are checking up on all subscribers since last night's raid."

"Why?"

"The automatic system has been disarranged. A bomb on the district exchange. Is that Mr. Isaacs of Prince of Wales Road?"

"No, it isn't. This is Wilson."

"Ah, you see, according to our dialling you should be Mr. Isaacs."

He rang off again; he wasn't any the wiser; after all, even a Hygienic Bakery might conceal Mr. Cost's customer—it was even possible that his conversation had been a genuine one. But no, that he did not believe, hearing again the sad stoical voice of the tailor, "Personally I have no hope. No hope at all." Personally—the emphasis had lain there. He had conveyed as clearly as he dared that it was for him alone the battle was over.

He went on pressing in his pennies; reason told him that it was useless, that the only course was to let Mr. Prentice into his secret—and yet he couldn't believe that somehow over the wire some sense would not be conveyed to him, the vocal impression of a will and violence sufficient to cause so many deaths—poor Stone asphyxiated in the sick bay, Forester and Poole shot down upon the stairs, Cost with the shears through his neck, Jones . . . The cause was surely too vast to come up the wire only as a commonplace voice saying, "Westminister Bank speaking."

Suddenly he remembered that Mr. Cost had not asked for any individual. He had simply dialled a number and had begun to speak as soon as he heard a voice reply. That meant he could not be speaking to a business address—where some employee would have to be brought to the phone.

"Hullo."

A voice took any possible question out of his mouth. "Oh, Ernest," a torrential voice said, "I knew you'd ring. You dear sympathetic thing. I suppose David's told you Minny's gone. Last night in the raid, it was awful. We heard her voice calling to us from outside, but, of course, there was nothing we could do. We couldn't leave our shelter. And then a land-mine dropped—it must have been a land-mine. Three houses went, a huge hole. And this morning not a sign of Minny. David still hopes of course, but I knew at the time, Ernest, there was something elegiac in her mew. . . ."

It was fascinating, but he had work to do. He rang off.

The telephone-box was getting stiflingly hot. He had already used up a shillings-worth of coppers; surely among these last four numbers a voice would speak and he would know. "Police Station, Mafeking Road." Back on to the rest with the receiver. Three numbers left. Against all reason he was convinced that one of these three. . . . His face was damp with sweat. He wiped it dry, and immediately the beads formed again. He felt suddenly an apprehension; the dryness of his throat, his heavily beating heart warned him that this voice might present too terrible an issue. There had been five deaths already. . . . His head swam with relief when a voice said "Gas Light and Coke Company." He could still walk out and leave it to Mr. Prentice. After all, how did he know that the voice he was seeking was not that of the operator at the Hygienic Baking Company—or even Ernest's friend?

But if he went to Mr. Prentice he would find it hard to explain his silence all these invaluable hours. He was not, after all, a boy: he was a middle-aged man. He had started something and he must go on. And yet he still hesitated while the sweat got into his eyes. Two numbers left: a fifty per cent chance. He would try one, and if that number conveyed nothing at all, he would walk out of the box and wash his hands of the whole business. Perhaps his eyes and his wits had deceived him in Mr. Cost's shop. His finger went reluctantly through the familiar acts: BAT 271: which number now? He put his sleeve against his face and wiped, then dialled.

BOOK FOUR

The Whole Man

1

Journey's End

"Must I—and all alone?"
THE LITTLE DUKE

i

The telephone rang and rang; he could imagine the empty rooms spreading round the small vexed instrument. Perhaps the rooms of a girl who went to business in the city, or a tradesman who was now at his shop: of a man who left early to read at the British Museum: innocent rooms. He held the welcome sound of an unanswered bell to his ear. He had done his best. Let it ring.

Or were the rooms perhaps guilty rooms? The rooms of a man who had disposed in a few hours of so many human existences. What would a guilty room be like? A room, like a dog, takes on some of the characteristics of its master. A room is trained for certain ends—comfort, beauty, convenience. This room would surely be trained to anonymity. It would be a room which would reveal no secrets if the police should ever call; there would be no Tolstoys with pencilled lines imperfectly erased, no personal touches; the common mean of taste would furnish it—a wireless set, a few detective novels, a reproduction of Van Gogh's sunflower. He imagined it all quite happily while the bell rang and rang. There would be nothing significant in the cupboards: no love-letters concealed below the handkerchiefs, no cheque-book in a drawer: would the linen be marked? There would be no presents from anyone at all—a lonely room: everything in it had been bought at a standard store.

Suddenly a voice he knew said a little breathlessly, "Hullo. Who's that?" If only, he thought, putting the receiver down, she had been quite out of hearing when the bell rang, at the bottom of the stairs, or in the street. If only he hadn't let his fancy play so long, he need never have known that this was Anna Hilfe's number.

He came blindly out into Bayswater; he had three choices—the sensible and the honest choice was to tell the police. The second was to say nothing. The third was to see for himself. He had no doubt at all that this was the number Cost had rung; he remembered how she had known his real name all along, how she had said— it was a curious phrase—that it was her "job" to visit him at the home. And yet he didn't doubt that there was an answer, an answer he couldn't trust the police to find. He went back to his hotel and up to his room, carrying the telephone directory with him from the lounge—he had a long job to do. In fact, it was several hours before he reached the number. His eyes were swimming and he nearly missed it. 16, Prince Consort Mansions, Battersea—a name which meant nothing at all. He thought wryly: of course, a guilty room would be taken furnished. He lay down on his bed and closed his eyes.

It was past five o'clock in the afternoon before he could bring himself to act, and then he acted mechanically. He wouldn't think any more: what was the good of thinking before he heard her speak? A 19 bus took him to the top of Oakley Street, and a 49 to Albert Bridge. He walked across the bridge, not thinking. It was low tide and the mud lay up under the warehouses. Somebody on the Embankment was feeding the gulls; the sight obscurely distressed him and he hurried on, not thinking. The waning sunlight lay in a wash of rose over the ugly bricks, and a solitary dog went nosing and brooding into the park. A voice said, "Why, Arthur," and he stopped. A man wearing a beret on untidy grey hair and warden's dungarees stood at the entrance to a block of flats. He said doubtfully, "It is Arthur, isn't it?"

Since Rowe's return to London many memories had slipped into place—this church and that shop, the way Piccadilly ran into Knightsbridge. He hardly noticed when they took up their places as part of the knowledge of a lifetime. But there were other memories which had to fight painfully for admission; somewhere in his mind they had an enemy who wished to keep them out and often succeeded. Cafés and street corners and shops would turn on him a suddenly familiar face, and he would look away and hurry on as though they were the scenes of a road accident. The man who spoke to him belonged to these, but you can't hurry away from a human being as you can hurry away from a shop.

"The last time you hadn't got the beard. You are Arthur, aren't you?"

"Yes. Arthur Rowe."

The man looked puzzled and hurt. He said, "It was good of you to call that time."

"I don't remember."

The look of pain darkened like a bruise. "The day of the funeral."

Rowe said, "I'm sorry. I had an accident: my memory went. It's only beginning to come back in parts. Who are you?"

"I'm Henry—Henry Wilcox."

"And I came here—to a funeral?"

"My wife got killed. I expect you read about it in the papers. They gave her a medal. I was a bit worried afterwards because you'd wanted me to cash a cheque for you and I forgot. You know how it is at a funeral: so many things to think about. I expect I was upset too."

"Why did I bother you then?"

"Oh, it must have been important. It went right out of my head—and then I thought, I'll see him afterwards. But I never saw you."

Rowe looked up at the flats above them. "Was it here?"

"Yes."

He looked across the road to the gate of the park: a man feeding gulls: an office worker carrying a suitcase; the road reeled a little under his feet. He said, "Was there a procession?"

"The post turned out. And the police and the rescue party."

Rowe said, "Yes. I couldn't go to the bank to cash the cheque. I thought the police thought I was a murderer. But I had to find money if I was going to get away. So I came here. I didn't know about the funeral. I thought all the time about this murder.''

"You brood too much," Henry said. "A thing that's done is done, ' and he looked quite brightly up the road the procession had taken.

"But this was never done, you see. I know that now. I'm not a murderer," he explained.

"Of course you aren't, Arthur. No friend of yours—no proper friend—ever believed you were.''

"Was there so much talk?''

"Well, naturally . . .''

"I didn't know." He turned his mind into another track: along the Embankment wall—the sense of misery and then the little man feeding birds, the suitcase . . . he lost the thread until he remembered the face of the hotel clerk, and then he was walking down interminable corridors, a door opened and Anna was there. They shared the danger—he clung to that idea. There was always an explanation. He remembered how she had told him he had saved her life. He said stiffly, "Well, good-bye. I must be getting on.''

"It's no use mourning someone all your life," Henry said. "That's morbid.''

"Yes. Good-bye.''

"Good-bye.''

ii

The flat was on the third floor. He wished the stairs would never end, and when he rang the bell he hoped the flat would be deserted. An empty milk bottle stood outside the door on the small dark landing; there was a note stuck in it; he picked it out and read it—"Only half a pint to-morrow, please." The door opened while he still held it in his hand, and Anna said hopelessly, "It's you.''

"Yes, me.''

"Every time the bell rang, I've been afraid it would be you.''

"How did you think I'd find you?''

She said, "There's always the police. They are watching the office now." He followed her in.

It wasn't the way he had at one time—under the sway of the strange adventure—imagined that he would meet her again. There was a heavy constraint between them. When the door closed they didn't feel alone. It was as if all sorts of people they both knew were with them. They spoke in low voices so as not to intrude. He said, "I got your address by watching Cost's fingers on the dial—he telephoned you just before he killed himself.''

"It's so horrible," she said. "I didn't know you were there.''

" 'I've no hope at all.' '' That's what he said. 'Personally I've no hope.' ''

They stood in a little ugly crowded hall as though it wasn't worth the bother of going any farther. It was more like a parting than a reunion—a parting too sorrowful to have any grace. She wore the same blue trousers she had worn at the hotel; he had forgotten how small she was. With the scarf knotted at her neck she looked heart-breakingly impromptu. All around them were brass trays, warming-pans, knick-knacks, an old oak chest, a Swiss cuckoo clock carved with heavy trailing creeper. He said, "Last night was not good either. I was there too. Did you know that Dr. Forester was dead—and Poole?"

'No.''

He said, "Aren't you sorry—such a massacre of your friends?"

"No," she said, "I'm glad." It was then that he began to hope. She said gently, "My dear, you have everything mixed up in your head, your poor head. You don't know who are your friends and who are your enemies. That's the way they always work, isn't it?"

"They used you to watch me, didn't they, down there at Dr. Forester's, to see when my memory would begin to return? Then they'd have put me in the sick bay like poor Stone."

"You're so right and so wrong," she said wearily. "I don't suppose we'll ever get it straight now. It's true I watched you for them. I didn't want your memory to return any more than they did. I didn't want you hurt." She said with sharp anxiety, "Do you remember everything now?"

"I remember a lot and I've learned a lot. Enough to know I'm not a murderer."

She said, "Thank God."

"But you knew I wasn't?"

"Yes," she said, "of course. I knew it. I just meant—oh, that I'm glad *you* know." She said slowly, "I like you happy. It's how you ought to be."

He said as gently as he could, "I love you. You know that. I want to believe you are my friend. Where are the photographs?"

A painted bird burst raspingly out of the hideous carved clock case and cuckooed the half-hour. He had time to think between the cuckoos that another night would soon be on them. Would that contain horror too? The door clicked shut and she said simply, "He has them."

"He?"

"My brother." He still held the note to the milkman in his hand. She said. "You are so fond of investigation, aren't you? The first time I saw you you came to the office about a cake. You were so determined to get to the bottom of things. You've got to the bottom now."

"I remember. He seemed so helpful. He took me to that house. . . ."

She took the words out of his mouth. "He staged a murder for you and helped you to escape. But afterwards he thought it safer to have you murdered. That was my fault. You told me you'd written a letter to the police, and I told him."

"Why?"

"I didn't want to get him into trouble for just frightening you. I never guessed he could be so thorough."

"But you were in that room when I came with the suitcase?" he said. He couldn't work it out. "You were nearly killed too."

"Yes. He hadn't forgotten, you see, that I telephoned to you at Mrs. Bellairs. *You* told him that. I wasn't on his side any longer—not against you. He told me to go and meet you—and persuade you not to send the letter. And then he just sat back in another flat and waited."

He accused her, "But you are alive."

"Yes," she said, "I'm alive, thanks to you. I'm even on probation again—he won't kill his sister if he doesn't feel it's necessary. He calls that family feeling. I was only a danger because of you. This isn't *my* country. Why should I have wanted your memory to return? You were happy without it. I don't care a damn about England. I want you to be happy, that's all. The trouble is he understands such a lot."

He said obstinately, "It doesn't make sense. Why am I alive?"

"He's economical." She said, "They are all economical. You'll never understand them if you don't understand that." She repeated wryly, like a formula, "The maximum of terror for the minimum time directed against the fewest objects."

He was bewildered: he didn't know what to do. He was learning the lesson most people learn very young, that things never work out in the expected way. This wasn't an exciting adventure, and he wasn't a hero, and it was even possible that this was not a tragedy. He became aware of the note to the milkman. "He's going away?"

"Yes."

"With the photographs, of course."

"Yes."

"We've got to stop him," he said. The "we" like the French *tu* spoken for the first time conveyed everything.

"Yes."

"Where is he now?"

She said, "He's here."

It was like exerting a great pressure against a door and finding it ajar all the time. "Here?"

She jerked her head. "He's asleep. He had a long day with Lady Dunwoody about woollies."

"But he'll have heard us."

"Oh no," she said. "He's out of hearing, and he sleeps so sound. That's economy too. As deep a sleep and as little of it. . . ."

"How you hate him," he said with surprise.

"He's made such a mess," she said, "of everything. He's so fine, so intelligent—and yet there's only this fear. That's all he makes."

"Where is he?"

She said, "Through there is the living-room and beyond that is his bedroom."

"Can I use the telephone?"

"It's not safe. It's in the living-room and the bedroom door's ajar."

"Where's he going?"

"He has permission to go to Ireland—for the Free Mothers. It wasn't easy to get, but your friends have made such a sweep. Lady Dunwoody worked it. You see, he's been so grateful for her woollies. He gets the train tonight." She said, "What are you going to do?"

"I don't know."

He looked helplessly round. A heavy brass candlestick stood on the oak chest; it glittered with polish; no wax had ever sullied it. He picked it up. "He tried to kill me," he explained weakly.

"He's asleep. That's murder."

"I won't hit first."

She said, "He used to be sweet to me when I cut my knees. Children always cut their knees. . . . Life is horrible, wicked."

He put the candlestick down again.

"No," she said. "Take it. You mustn't be hurt. He's only my brother, isn't he?" she asked, with obscure bitterness. "Take it. Please." When he made no move to take it, she picked it up herself; her face was stiff and schooled and childish and histrionic. It was like watching a small girl play Lady Macbeth. You wanted to shield her from the knowledge that these things were really true.

She led the way holding the candlestick upright as though it were a rehearsal: only on the night itself would the candle be lit. Everything in the flat was hideous except herself; it gave him more than ever the sense that they were both strangers here. The heavy furniture must have been put in by a company, bought by an official buyer at cut rates, or perhaps ordered by telephone—suite 56a of the autumn catalogue. Only a bunch of flowers and a few books and a newspaper and a man's sock in holes showed that people lived here. It was the sock which made him pause; it seemed to speak of long mutual evenings, of two people knowing each other over many years. He thought for the first time, "It's her brother who's going to die." Spies, like murderers, were hanged, and in this case there was no distinction. He lay asleep in there and the gallows was being built outside.

They moved stealthily across the anonymous room towards a door ajar. She pushed it gently with her hand and stood back so that he might see. It was the immemorial gesture of a woman who shows to a guest after dinner her child asleep.

Hilfe lay on the bed on his back without his jacket, his shirt open at the neck. He was deeply and completely at peace, and so defenceless that he seemed to be innocent. His very pale gold hair lay in a hot streak across his face as though he had lain down after a game. He looked very young; he didn't, lying there, belong to the same world as Cost bleeding by the mirror, and Stone in the strait-jacket. One was half-impelled to believe, "It's propaganda, just propaganda: he isn't capable . . ." The face seemed to Rowe very beautiful, more beautiful than his sister's, which could be marred by grief or pity. Watching the sleeping man he could realise a little of the force and the grace and the attraction of nihilism—of not caring for anything, of having no rules and feeling no love. Life became simple. . . . He had been reading when he fell asleep; a book lay on the bed and one hand still held the pages open. It was like the tomb of a young student; bending down you could read on the marble page the epitaph chosen for him, a verse:

"Denn Orpheus ists. Seine Metamorphose
in dem und dem. Wir sollen uns nicht mühn

um andre Namen. Ein für alle Male
ists Orpheus, wenn es singt. . . ."

The knuckles hid the rest.

It was as if he were the only violence in the world and when he slept there was peace everywhere.

They watched him and he woke. People betray themselves when they wake; sometimes they wake with a cry from an ugly dream: sometimes they turn from one side to the other and shake the head and burrow as if they are afraid to leave sleep. Hilfe just woke; his lids puckered for a moment like a child's when the nurse draws the curtain and the light comes in; then they were wide open and he was looking at them with complete self-possession. The pale blue eyes held full knowledge of the situation; there was nothing to explain. He smiled and Rowe caught himself in the act of smiling back. It was the kind of trick a boy plays suddenly, capitulating, admitting everything, so that the whole offence seems small and the fuss absurd. There are moments of surrender when it is so much easier to love one's enemy than to remember. . . .

Rowe said weakly, "The photographs. . . ."

"The photographs." He smiled frankly up. "Yes, I've got them." He must have known that everything was up—including life, but he still retained the air of badinage, the dated colloquialisms which made his speech a kind of light dance of inverted commas. "Admit," he said, "I've led you 'up the garden.' And now I'm 'in the cart.' " He looked at the candlestick which his sister stiffly held and said, "I surrender," with amusement, lying on his back on the bed, as though they had all three been playing a game.

"Where are they?"

He said, "Let's strike a bargain. Let's 'swop,' " as though he were suggesting the exchange of foreign stamps for toffee.

Rowe said, "There's no need for me to exchange anything. You're through."

"My sister loves you a lot, doesn't she?" He refused to take the situation seriously. "Surely you wouldn't want to eliminate your brother-in-law?"

"You didn't mind trying to eliminate your sister."

He said blandly and unconvincingly, "Oh, that was a tragic necessity," and gave a sudden grin which made the whole affair of the suitcase and the bomb about as important as a booby-trap on the stairs. He seemed to accuse them of a lack of humour; it was not the kind of thing they ought to have taken to heart.

"Let's be sensible civilised people," he said, "and come to an agreement. Do put down the candlestick, Anna: I can't hurt you here even if I wanted to." He made no attempt to get up, lying on the bed, displaying his powerlessness like evidence.

"There's no basis for an agreement," Rowe said. "I want the photographs, and then the police want you. You didn't talk about terms to Stone—or Jones."

"I know nothing about all that," Hilfe said. "I can't be responsible—can I?—for all my people do. That isn't reasonable, Rowe." He asked, "Do you read poetry? There's a poem here which seems to meet the case. . . ." He sat up, lifted the book and dropped it again. With a gun in his hand he said, "Just stay still. You see there's still something to talk about."

Rowe said, "I've been wondering where you kept it."

"Now we can bargain sensibly. We're both in a hole."

"I still don't see," Rowe said, "what you've got to offer. You don't really imagine, do you, that you can shoot us both, and then get to Ireland. These walls are thin as paper. You are known as the tenant. The police would be waiting for you at the port."

"But if I'm going to die anyway, I might just as well—mightn't I?—have a massacre."

"It wouldn't be economical."

He considered the objection half-seriously and then said with a grin, "No, but don't you think it would be rather grand?"

"It doesn't much matter to me how I stop you. Being killed would be quite useful."

Hilfe exclaimed, "Do you mean your memory's come back?"

"I don't know what that's got to do with it."

"Such a lot. Your past history is really sensational. I went into it all carefully and so did Anna. It explained so much I didn't understand at first when I heard from Poole what you were like. The kind of room you were living in, the kind of man you were. You were the sort of man I thought I could deal with quite easily until you lost your memory. That didn't work out right. You got so many illusions of grandeur, heroism, self-sacrifice, patriotism. . . ." Hilfe grinned at him. "Here's a bargain for you. My safety against your past. I'll tell you who you were. No trickery. I'll give you all the references. But that won't be necessary. Your own brain will tell you I'm not inventing."

"He's just lying," Anna said. "Don't listen to him."

"She doesn't want you to hear, does she? Doesn't that make you curious? She wants you as you are, you see, and not as you were."

Rowe said, "I only want the photographs."

"You can read about yourself in the newspaper. You were really quite famous. She's afraid you'll feel too grand for her when you know."

Rowe said, "If you give me the photographs. . . ."

"And tell you your story?"

He seemed to feel some of Rowe's excitement. He shifted a little on his elbow and his gaze moved for a moment. The wrist-bone cracked as Anna swung the candlestick down, and the gun lay on the bed. She took it up and said, "There's no need to bargain with him."

He was moaning and doubled with pain; his face was white with it. Both their faces were white. For a moment Rowe thought she would go on her knees to him, take his head on her shoulder, surrender the gun to his other hand. . . . "Anna," Hilfe whispered, "Anna."

She said, "Willi," and rocked a little on her feet.

"Give me the gun," Rowe said.

She looked at him as if he were a stranger who shouldn't have been in the room at all; her ears seemed filled with the whimper from the bed. Rowe put out his hand and she backed away, so that she stood beside her brother. "Go outside," she said, "and wait. Go outside." In their pain they were like twins. She pointed the gun at him and moaned, "Go outside."

He said, "Don't let him talk you round. He tried to kill you," but seeing the family face in front of him his words sounded flat. It was as if they were so akin that either had the right to kill the other; it was only a form of suicide.

"Please don't go on talking," she said. "It doesn't do any good." Sweat stood on both their faces: he felt helpless.

"Only promise," he said, "you won't let him go."

She moved her shoulders and said, "I promise." When he went she closed and locked the door behind him.

For a long time afterwards he could hear nothing—except once the closing of a cupboard door and the chink of china. He imagined she was bandaging Hilfe's wrist; he was probably safe enough, incapable of further flight. Rowe realised that now if he wished he could telephone to Mr. Prentice and have the police surround the flat—he was no longer anxious for glory; the sense of adventure had leaked away and left only the sense of human pain. But he felt that he was bound by her promise; he had to trust her, if life was to go on.

A quarter of an hour dragged by and the room was full of dusk. There had been low voices in the bedroom: he felt uneasy. Was Hilfe talking her round? He was aware of a painful jealousy; they had been so alike and he had been shut out like a stranger. He went to the window and drawing the blackout curtain a little aside looked out over the darkening park. There was so much he had still to remember; the thought came to him like a threat in Hilfe's dubious tones.

The door opened, and when he let the curtain fall he realised how dark it had become. Anna walked stiffly towards him and said, "There you are. You've got what you wanted." Her face looked ugly in the attempt to avoid tears; it was an ugliness which bound him to her more than any beauty could have done; it isn't being happy together, he thought as though it were a fresh discovery, that makes one love—it's being unhappy together. "Don't you want them," she asked, "now I've got them for you?"

He took the little roll in his hand: he had no sense of triumph at all. He asked, "Where is he?"

She said, "You don't want him now. He's finished."

"Why did you let him go?" he asked. "You promised."

"Yes," she said, "I promised." She made a small movement with her fingers, crossing two of them—he thought for a moment that she was going to claim that child's excuse for broken treaties.

"Why?" he asked again.

"Oh," she said vaguely, "I had to bargain."

He began to unwrap the roll carefully; he didn't want to expose more than a scrap of it. "But he had nothing to bargain with," he said. He held the roll out to her on the palm of his hand. "I don't know what he promised to give you, but this isn't it."

"He swore that's what you wanted. How do you know?"

"I don't know how many prints they made. This may be the only one or there may be a dozen. But I do know there's only one negative."

She asked sadly, "And that's not it?"

"No."

iii

Rowe said, "I don't know what he had to bargain with, but he didn't keep his part."

"I'll give up," she said. "Whatever I touch goes wrong, doesn't it? Do what you want to do."

"You'll have to tell me where he is."

"I always thought," she said, "I could have both of you. I didn't care what happened to the world. It couldn't be worse than it's always been, and yet the globe, the beastly globe, survives. But people, you, him. . . ." She sat down on the nearest chair—a stiff polished ugly upright chair: her feet didn't reach the floor. She said, "Paddington: the 7:20. He said he'd never come back. I thought you'd be safe then."

"Oh," he said, "I can look after myself," but meeting her eyes he had the impression that he hadn't really understood. He said, "Where will he have it? They'll search him at the port anyway."

"I don't know. He took nothing."

"A stick?"

"No," she said, "nothing. He just put on his jacket—he didn't even take a hat. I suppose it's in his pocket."

He said, "I'll have to go to the station."

"Why can't you leave it to the police now?"

"By the time I get the right man and explain to him, the train will have gone. If I miss him at the station, then I'll ring the police." A doubt occurred. "If he told you that, of course he won't he there."

"He didn't tell me. I didn't believe what he told me. That was the original plan. It's his only hope of getting out of here."

When he hesitated she said, "Why not just let them meet the train at the other end? Why do it all yourself?"

"He might get out on the way."

"You mustn't go like this. He's armed. I let him have his gun."

He suddenly laughed. "By God," he said, "you have made a mess of things, haven't you?"

"I wanted him to have a chance."

"You can't do much with a gun in the middle of England except kill a few poor devils." She looked so small and beaten that he couldn't preserve any anger. She said, "There's only one bullet in it. He wouldn't waste that."

"Just stay here," Rowe said.

She nodded. "Good-bye."

"I'll be back quite soon." She didn't answer, and he tried another phrase. "Life will begin all over again then." She smiled unconvincingly, as though it were he who needed comfort and reassurance, not she.

"He won't kill me."

"I'm not afraid of that."

"What are you afraid of then?"

She looked up at him with a kind of middle-aged tenderness, as though they'd grown through love into its later stage. She said, "I'm afraid he'll talk."

He mocked at her from the door. "Oh, he won't talk *me* round," but all the way downstairs he was thinking again, I didn't understand her.

The searchlights were poking up over the park; patches of light floated like clouds along the surface of the sky. It made the sky seem very small; you could probe its limit with light. There was a smell of cooking all along the pavement from houses where people were having an early supper to be in time for the raid. A warden was lighting a hurricane-lamp outside a shelter. He said to Rowe, "Yellow's up." The match kept going out—he wasn't used to lighting lamps; he looked a bit on edge: too many lonely vigils on deserted pavements; he wanted to talk. But Rowe was in a hurry: he couldn't wait.

On the other side of the bridge there was a taxi-rank with one cab left. "Where do you want to go?" the driver asked and considered, looking up at the sky, the pillows of light between the few stars, one pale just visible balloon. "Oh, well," he said, "I'll take a chance. It won't be worse there than here."

"Perhaps there won't be a raid."

"Yellow's up," the driver said, and the old engine creaked into life.

They went up across Sloane Square and Knightsbridge and into the Park and on along the Bayswater Road. A few people were hurrying home; buses slid quickly past the Request stops; Yellow was up; the saloon bars were crowded. People called to the taxi from the pavement, and when a red light held it up an elderly gentleman in a bowler hat opened the door quickly and began to get in. "Oh," he said, "I beg your pardon. Thought it was empty. Are you going towards Paddington?"

"Get in," Rowe said.

"Catching the 7:20," the stranger said breathlessly. "Bit of luck for me this. We'll just do it."

"I'm catching it too," Rowe said.

"Yellow's up."

"So I've heard."

They creaked forward through the thickening darkness. "Any land-mines your way last night?" the old gentleman asked.

"No, no. I don't think so."

"Three near us. About time for the Red I should think."

"I suppose so."

"Yellow's been up for a quarter of an hour," the elderly gentleman said, looking at his watch as though he were timing an express train between stations. "Ah, that sounded like a gun. Over the estuary, I should say."

"I didn't hear it."

"I should give them another ten minutes at most," the old gentleman said, holding his watch in his hand, as the taxi turned into Praed Street. They swung down the covered way and came to rest. Through the blacked-out station the season-ticket holders were making a quick get-away from the nightly death; they dived in earnest silence towards the suburban trains, carrying little attaché-cases, and the porters stood and watched them go with an air of sceptical superiority. They felt the pride of being a legitimate objective: the pride of people who stayed.

The long train stood darkly along number one platform: the bookstalls closed, the blinds drawn in most of the compartments. It was a novel sight to Rowe and yet an old sight. He had only to see it once like the sight of a bombed street, for it to take up its place imperceptibly among his memories. This was already life as he'd known it.

It was impossible to see who was in the train from the platform; every compartment held its secrets close. Even if the blinds had not been lowered, the blued globes cast too little light to show who sat below them. He felt sure that Hilfe would travel first class; as a refugee he lived on borrowed money, and as the friend and confidant of Lady Dunwoody he was certain to travel in style.

He made his way down the first-class compartments along the corridor. They were not very full; only the more daring season-ticket holders remained in London as late as this. He put his head in at every door and met at once the disquieting return stare of the blue ghosts.

It was a long train, and the porters were already shutting doors higher up before he reached the last first-class coach. He was so accustomed to failure that it took him by surprise, sliding back the door to come on Hilfe.

He wasn't alone. An old lady sat opposite him, and she had made Hilfe's hands into a cat's cradle for winding wool. He was handcuffed in the heavy oiled raw material for seamen's boots. His right hand stuck stiffly out, the wrist bandaged and roughly splinted, and round and round ever so gently the old lady industriously wound her wool. It was ludicrous and it was sad; Rowe could see the weighted pocket where the revolver lay, and the look that Hilfe turned on him was not reckless nor amused nor dangerous: it was humiliated. He had always had a way with old ladies.

Rowe said, "You won't want to talk here."

"She's deaf," Hilfe said, "stone deaf."

"Good evening," the old lady said, "I hear there's a Yellow up."

"Yes," Rowe said.

"She's deaf," Hilfe said, "stone deaf."

"Shocking," the old lady said and wound her wool.

"I want the negative," Rowe said.

"Anna should have kept you longer. I told her to give me enough start. After all," he added with gloomy disappointment, "it would have been better for both. . . ."

"You cheated her too often," Rowe said. He sat down by his side and watched the winding up and over and round.

"What are you going to do?"

"Wait till the train starts and then pull the cord."

Suddenly from very close the guns cracked—once, twice, three times. The old lady looked vaguely up as though she had heard something very faint intruding on her silence. Rowe put his hand into Hilfe's pocket and slipped the gun into his own. "If you'd like to smoke," the old lady said, "don't mind me."

Hilfe said, "I think we ought to talk things over."

"There's nothing to talk about."

"It wouldn't do, you know, to get me and not to get the photographs."

Rowe began, "The photographs don't matter by themselves. It's you. . . ." But then he thought: they do matter. How do I know he hasn't passed them on already? if they are hidden, the place may be agreed on with another agent . . . even if they are found by a stranger, they are not safe. He said, "We'll talk," and the siren sent up its tremendous howl over Paddington. Very far away this time there was a pad, pad, pad, like the noise a fivesball makes against the glove, and the old lady wound and wound. He remembered Anna saying, "I'm afraid he'll talk," and he saw Hilfe suddenly smile at the wool as if life had still the power to tickle him into savage internal mirth.

Hilfe said, "I'm still ready to swop."

"You haven't anything to swop."

"You haven't much, you know, either," Hilfe said. "You don't know where the photos are. . . ."

"I wonder when the sirens will go," the old lady said. Hilfe moved his wrists in the wool. He said, "If you give back the gun, I'll let you have the photographs. . . ."

"If you can give me the photographs, they must be with you. There's no reason why I should bargain."

"Well," Hilfe said, "if it's your idea of revenge, I can't stop you. I thought perhaps you wouldn't want Anna dragged in. She let me escape, you remember. . . ."

"There," the old lady said. "we've nearly done now."

Hilfe said, "They probably wouldn't hang her. Of course that would depend on what I say. Perhaps it would be just an internment camp till the war's over—and then deportation if you win. From my point of view," he explained dryly, "she's a traitor, you know."

Rowe said, "Give me the photographs and then we'll talk." The word "talk" was like a capitulation. Already he was beginning painfully to think out the long chain of deceit he would have to practise on Mr. Prentice if he were to save Anna.

The train rocked with an explosion; the old lady said, "At last we are going to start," and leaning forward she released Hilfe's hands. Hilfe said with a curious wistfulness, "What fun they are having up there." He was like a mortally sick man saying farewell to the sports of his contemporaries: no fear, only regret. He had failed to bring off the record himself in destruction. Five people only were dead: it hadn't been much of an inning compared with what they were having up there. Sitting under the darkened globe, he was a long way away; wherever men killed his spirit moved in obscure companionship.

"Give them to me," Rowe said.

He was surprised by a sudden joviality. It was as if Hilfe after all had not lost all hope—of what? escape? further destruction? He laid his left hand on Rowe's knee with a gesture of intimacy. He said, "I'll be better than my word. How would you like to have your memory back?"

"I only want the photographs."

"Not here," Hilfe said. "I can't very well strip in front of a lady, can I? He stood up. "We'd better leave the train."

"Are you going?" the old lady asked.

"We've decided, my friend and I," Hilfe said, "to spend the night in town and see the fun."

"Fancy," the old lady vaguely said, "the porters always tell you wrong."

"You've been very kind," Hilfe said, bowing. "Your kindness disarmed me."

"Oh, I can manage nicely now, thank you."

It was as if Hilfe had taken charge of his own defeat. He moved purposefully up the platform and Rowe followed like a valet. The rush was over; he had no chance to escape; through the glassless roof they could see the little trivial scarlet stars of the barrage flashing and going out like matches. A whistle blew and the train began to move very slowly out of the dark station; it seemed to move surreptitiously; there was nobody but themselves and a few porters to see it go. The refreshment-rooms were closed, and a drunk soldier sat alone on a waste of platform vomiting between his knees.

Hilfe led the way down the steps to the lavatories; there was nobody there at all—even the attendant had taken shelter. The guns cracked: they were alone with the smell of disinfectant, the greyish basins, the little notices about venereal disease. The adventure he had pictured once in such heroic terms had reached its conclusion in the Gentlemen's. Hilfe looked in an L.C.C. mirror and smoothed his hair.

"What are you doing?" Rowe asked. "Oh, saying good-bye," Hilfe said. He took off his jacket as though he were going to wash, then threw it over to Rowe. Rowe saw the tailor's tag marked in silk, Pauling and Crosthwaite. "You'll find the photographs," Hilfe said, "in the shoulder."

The shoulder was padded.

"Want a knife?" Hilfe said. "You can have your own," and he held out a boy's compendium.

Rowe slit the shoulder up and took out from the padding a roll of film; he broke the paper which bound it and exposed a corner of negative. "Yes," he said. "This is it."

"And now the gun?"

Rowe said slowly, "I promised nothing."

Hilfe said with sharp anxiety, "But you'll let me have the gun?"

"No."

Hilfe suddenly was scared and amazed. He exclaimed in his odd dated vocabulary, "It's a caddish trick."

"You've cheated too often," Rowe said.

"Be sensible," Hilfe said. "You think I want to escape. But the train's gone. Do you think I could get away by killing you in Paddington station? I wouldn't get a hundred yards."

"Why do you want it then?" Rowe asked.

"I want to get further away than that." He said in a low voice, "I don't want to be beaten up." He leant earnestly forward and the L.C.C. mirror behind him showed a tuft of fine hair he hadn't smoothed.

"We don't beat up our prisoners here."

"Oh no?" Hilfe said. "Do you really believe that? Do you think you are so different from us?"

"Yes."

"I wouldn't trust the difference," Hilfe said. "I know what we do to spies. They'll think they can make me talk—they will make me talk." He brought up desperately the old childish phrase, "I'll swop." It was difficult to believe that he was guilty of so many deaths. He went urgently on, "Rowe, I'll give you your memory back. There's no one else will."

"Anna," Rowe said.

"She'll never tell you. Why, Rowe, she let me go to stop me. . . . Because I said I'd tell you. She wants to keep you as you are."

"Is it as bad as that?" Rowe asked. He felt fear and an unbearable curiosity. Digby whispered in his ear that now he could be a whole man again: Anna's voice warned him. He knew that this was the great moment of a lifetime; he was being offered so many forgotten years, the fruit of twenty years' experience. His breast had to press the ribs apart to make room for so much more; he stared ahead of him and read—"Private Treatment Between the Hours of . . ." On the far edge of consciousness the barrage thundered.

Hilfe grimaced at him. "Bad?" he said. "Why—it's tremendously important."

Rowe shook his head sadly: "You can't have the gun."

Suddenly Hilfe began to laugh: the laughter was edged with hysteria and hate. "I was giving you a chance," he said. "If you'd given me the gun, I might have been sorry for you. I'd have been grateful. I might have just shot myself. But now"—his head bobbed up and down in front of the cheap mirror—"now I'll tell you gratis."

Rowe said, "I don't want to hear," and turned away. A very small man in an ancient brown Homburg came rocking down the steps from above and made for the urinal. His hat came down over his ears: it might have been put on with a spirit-level. "Bad night," he said, "bad night." He was pale and wore an expression of startled displeasure. As Rowe reached the steps a bomb came heavily down, pushing the air ahead of it like an engine. The little man hastily did up his flies; he crouched as though he wanted to get farther away. Hilfe sat on the edge of the wash-basin and listened with a sour nostalgic smile, as though he were hearing the voice of a friend going away forever down the road. Rowe stood on the bottom step and waited and the express roared down on them and the little man stooped lower and lower in front of the urinal. The sound began to diminish, and then the ground shifted very slightly under their feet at the explosion. There was silence again except for the tiny shifting of dust down the steps. Almost immediately a second bomb was under way. They waited in fixed photographic attitudes, sitting, squatting, standing: this bomb could not burst closer without destroying them. Then it too passed, diminished, burst a little farther away.

"I wish they'd stop," the man in the Homburg said, and all the urinals began to flush. The dust hung above the steps like smoke, and a hot metallic smell drowned the smell of ammonia. Rowe climbed the steps.

"Where are you going?" Hilfe said. He cried out sharply, "The police?" and when Rowe did not reply, he came away from the wash-basin. "You can't go yet—not without hearing about your wife."

"My wife?" He came back down the steps; he couldn't escape now: the lost years waited for him among the wash-basins. He asked hopelessly, "Am I married?"

"You *were* married," Hilfe said. "Don't you remember now? You poisoned her." He began to laugh again. "Your Alice."

"An awful night," the man in the Homburg said; he had ears for nothing but the heavy uneven stroke of the bomber overhead.

"You were tried for murder," Hilfe said, "and they sent you to an asylum. You'll find it in all the papers. I can give you the dates. . . ."

The little man turned suddenly to them and spreading out his hands in a gesture of entreaty he said in a voice filled with tears, "Shall I ever get to Wimbledon?" A bright white light shone through the dust outside, and through the glassless roof of the station the glow of the flares came dripping beautifully down.

It wasn't Rowe's first raid: he heard Mrs. Purvis coming down the stairs with her bedding: the Bay of Naples was on the wall and *The Old Curiosity Shop* upon the shelf. Guilford Street held out its dingy arms to welcome him, and he was home again. He thought: what will that bomb destroy? Perhaps with a little luck the flower shop will be gone near Marble Arch, the sherry bar in Adelaide Crescent, or the corner of Quebec Street, where I used to wait so many hours, so many years . . . there was such a lot which had to be destroyed before peace came.

"Go along," a voice said, "to Anna now," and he looked across a dimmed blue interior to a man who stood by the wash-basins and laughed at him.

"She hoped you'd never remember." He thought of a dead rat and a policeman, and then he looked everywhere and saw reflected in the crowded court the awful expression of pity: the judge's face was bent, but he could read pity in the old fingers which fidgeted with an Eversharp. He wanted to warn them—don't pity me. Pity is cruel. Pity destroys. Love isn't safe when pity's prowling round.

"Anna . . ." the voice began again, and another voice said with a kind of distant infinite regret at the edge of consciousness, "And I might have caught the 6:15." The horrible process of connexion went on; his Church had once taught him the value of penance, but penance was a value only to oneself. There was no sacrifice, it seemed to him, that would help him to atone to the dead. The dead were out of reach of the guilty. He wasn't interested in saving his own soul.

"What are you going to do?" a voice said. His brain rocked with its long journey; it was as if he were advancing down an interminable passage towards a man called Digby—who was so like him and yet had such different memories. He could hear Digby's voice saying, "Shut your eyes. . . ." There were rooms full of flowers, the sound of water falling, and Anna sat beside him, strung up, on guard, in defence of his ignorance. He was saying, "Of course you have a brother . . . I remember. . . ."

Another voice said, "It's getting quieter. Don't you think it is?"

"What are you going to do?"

It was like one of those trick pictures in a children's magazine: you stare at it hard and you see one thing—a vase of flowers—and then your focus suddenly changes and you see only the outlined faces of people. In and out the two pictures flicker. Suddenly, quite clearly, he saw Hilfe as he had seen him lying asleep— the graceful shell of a man, all violence quieted. He *was* Anna's brother. Rowe crossed the floor to the wash-basins and said in a low voice that the man in the Homburg couldn't hear, "All right. You can have it. Take it."

He slipped the gun quickly into Hilfe's hand.

"I think," a voice behind him said, "I'll make a dash for it. I really think I will. What do you think, sir?"

"Be off," Hilfe said sharply, "be off."

"You think so too. Yes. Perhaps." There was a scuttling on the steps and silence again.

"Of course," Hilfe said, "I could kill you now. But why should I? It would be doing you a service. And it would leave me to your thugs. How I hate you though."

"Yes?" He wasn't thinking of Hilfe; his thoughts swung to and fro between two people he loved and pitied. It seemed to him that he had destroyed both of them.

"Everything was going so well," Hilfe said, "until you came blundering in. What made you go and have your fortune told? You had no future."

"No." He remembered the fête clearly now; he remembered walking round the railings and hearing the music; he had been dreaming of innocence. . . . Mrs. Bellairs sat in a booth behind a curtain. . . .

"And just to have hit on that one phrase," Hilfe said. " 'Don't tell me the past. Tell me the future.' "

And there was Sinclair too. He remembered with a sense of responsibility the old car standing on the wet gravel. He had better go away and telephone to Prentice. Sinclair probably had a copy. . . .

"And then on top of everything Anna. Why the hell should any woman love you?" He cried out sharply, "Where are you going?"

"I've got to telephone to the police."

"Can't you give me just five minutes?"

"Oh no," Rowe said. "No. It's not possible." The process was completed; he was what Digby had wanted to be—a whole man. His brain held now everything it had ever held. Willi Hilfe gave an odd little sound like a retch. He began to walk rapidly towards the lavatory cubicles, with his bandaged hand stuck out. The stone floor was wet and he slipped but recovered. He began to pull at a lavatory door, but of course it was locked. He didn't seem to know what to do: it was as if he needed to get behind a door, out of sight, into some burrow. . . . He turned and said imploringly, "Give me a penny," and everywhere the sirens began to wail the All Clear; the sound came from everywhere: it was as if the floor of the urinal whined under his feet. The smell of ammonia came to him like something remembered from a dream. Hilfe's strained white face begged for his pity. Pity again. He held out a penny to him and then tossed it and walked up the steps; before he reached the top he heard the shot. He didn't go back: he left him for others to find.

iv

One can go back to one's own home after a year's absence and immediately the door closes it is as if one has never been away. Or one can go back after a few hours and everything is so changed that one is a stranger.

This, of course, he knew now, was not his home. Guilford Street was his home. He had hoped that wherever Anna was there would be peace; coming up the stairs a second time he knew that there would never be peace again while they lived.

To walk from Paddington to Battersea gives time for thought. He knew what he had to do long before he began to climb the stairs. A phrase of Johns's came back to mind about a Ministry of Fear. He felt now that he had joined its permanent staff. But it wasn't the small Ministry to which Johns had referred, with limited aims like winning a war or changing a constitution. It was a Ministry as large as life to which all who loved belonged. If one loved one feared. That was something Digby had forgotten, full of hope among the flowers and *Tatlers*.

The door was open as he had left it, and it occurred to him almost as a hope that perhaps she had run out into the raid and been lost forever. If one loved a woman one couldn't hope that she would be tied to a murderer for the rest of her days.

But she was there—not where he had left her, but in the bedroom where they had watched Hilfe sleeping. She lay on the bed face downwards with her fists clenched. He said, "Anna."

She turned her head on the pillow; she had been crying, and her face looked as despairing as a child's. He felt an enormous love for her, enormous tenderness, the need to protect her at any cost. She had wanted him innocent and happy . . . she had loved Digby. . . . He had got to give her what she wanted. . . . He said gently, "Your brother's dead. He shot himself," but her face didn't alter. It was as if none of that meant anything at all—all that violence and gracelessness and youth had gone without her thinking it worth attention. She asked with terrible anxiety, "What did he say to you?"

Rowe said, "He was dead before I could reach him. Directly he saw me he knew it was all up."

The anxiety left her face: all that remained was that tense air he had observed before—the air of someone perpetually on guard to shield him. . . . He sat down on the bed and put his hand on her shoulder. "My dear," he said, "my dear. How much I love you." He was pledging both of them to a lifetime of lies, but only he knew that.

"Me too," she said. "Me too."

They sat for a long while without moving and without speaking; they were on the edge of their ordeal, like two explorers who see at last from the summit of the range the enormous dangerous plain. They had to tread carefully for a lifetime, never speak without thinking twice; they must watch each other like enemies because they loved each other so much. They would never know what it was not to be afraid of being found out. It occurred to him that perhaps after all one could atone even to the dead if one suffered for the living enough.

He tried tentatively a phrase, "My dear, my dear, I am so happy," and heard with infinite tenderness her prompt and guarded reply, "I am too." It seemed to him that after all one could exaggerate the value of happiness. . . .

Our Man in Havana

PART ONE

1

i

"That nigger going down the street," said Dr. Hasselbacher standing in the Wonder Bar, "he reminds me of you, Mr. Wormold." It was typical of Dr. Hasselbacher that after fifteen years of friendship he still used the prefix Mr.— friendship proceeded with the slowness and assurance of a careful diagnosis. On Wormold's death-bed, when Dr. Hasselbacher came to feel his failing pulse, he would perhaps become Jim.

The negro was blind in one eye and one leg was shorter than the other; he wore an ancient felt hat and his ribs showed through his torn shirt like a ship's under demolition. He walked at the edge of the pavement, beyond the yellow and pink pillars of a colonnade, in the hot January sun, and he counted every step as he went. As he passed the Wonder Bar, going up Virdudes, he had reached "1,369." He had to move slowly to give time for so long a numeral. "One thousand three hundred and seventy." He was a familiar figure near the National Square, where he would sometimes linger and stop his counting long enough to sell a packet of pornographic photographs to a tourist. Then he would take up his count where he had left it. At the end of the day, like an energetic passenger on a trans-Atlantic liner, he must have known to a yard how far he had walked.

"Joe?" Wormold asked. "I don't see any resemblance. Except the limp, of course," but instinctively he took a quick look at himself in the mirror marked Cerveza Tropical, as though he might really have been so broken down and darkened during his walk from the store in the old town. But the face which looked back at him was only a little discoloured by the dust from the harbour-works; it was still the same, anxious and criss-crossed and fortyish: much younger than Dr. Hasselbacher's, yet a stranger might have felt certain it would be extinguished sooner— the shadow was there already, the anxieties which are beyond the reach of a tranquilliser. The negro limped out of sight, round the corner of the Paseo. The day was full of bootblacks.

"I didn't mean the limp. You don't see the likeness?"

"No."

"He's got two ideas in his head," Dr. Hasselbacher explained, "to do his job and to keep count. And, of course, he's British."

"I still don't see . . ." Wormold cooled his mouth with his morning daiquiri. Seven minutes to get to the Wonder Bar: seven minutes back to the store: six minutes for companionship. He looked at his watch. He remembered that it was one minute slow.

"He's reliable, you can depend on him, that's all I meant," said Dr. Hasselbacher with impatience. "How's Milly?"

"Wonderful," Wormold said. It was his invariable answer, but he meant it.

"Seventeen on the seventeenth, eh?"

"That's right." He looked quickly over his shoulder as though somebody were hunting him and then at his watch again. "You'll be coming to split a bottle with us?"

"I've never failed yet, Mr. Wormold. Who else will be there?"

"Well, I thought just the three of us. You see, Cooper's gone home, and poor Marlowe's in hospital still, and Milly doesn't seem to care for any of this new crowd at the Consulate. So I thought we'd keep it quiet, in the family."

"I'm honoured to be one of the family, Mr. Wormold."

"Perhaps a table at the Nacional—or would you say that wasn't quite—well, suitable?"

"This isn't England or Germany, Mr. Wormold. Girls grow up quickly in the tropics."

A shutter across the way creaked open and then regularly blew to in the slight breeze from the sea, click clack like an ancient clock. Wormold said, "I must be off."

"Phastkleaners will get on without you, Mr. Wormold." It was a day of uncomfortable truths. "Like my patients," Dr. Hasselbacher added with kindliness.

"People have to get ill, they don't have to buy vacuum cleaners."

"But you charge them more."

"And get only twenty per cent for myself. One can't save much on twenty per cent."

"This is not an age for saving, Mr. Wormold."

"I must—for Milly. If something happened to me . . ."

"We none of us have a great expectation of life nowadays, so why worry?"

"All these disturbances are very bad for trade. What's the good of a vacuum cleaner if the power's cut off?"

"I could manage a small loan, Mr. Wormold."

"No, no. It's not like that. My worry isn't this year's or even next year's, it's a long-term worry."

"Then it's not worth calling a worry. We live in an atomic age, Mr. Wormold. Push a button—piff bang—where are we? Another Scotch, please."

"And that's another thing. You know what the firm has done now? They've sent me an Atomic Pile Cleaner."

"Really? I didn't know science had got that far."

"Oh, of course, there's nothing atomic about it—it's only a name. Last year there was the Turbo Jet; this year it's the Atomic. It works off the light-plug just the same as the other."

"Then why worry?" Dr. Hasselbacher repeated like a theme tune, leaning into his whisky.

"They don't realise that sort of name may go down in the States, but not here, where the clergy are preaching all the time against the misuse of science. Milly and I went to the Cathedral last Sunday—you know how she is about Mass, thinks she'll convert me, I wouldn't wonder. Well, Father Mendez spent half an hour describing the effect of a hydrogen bomb. Those who believe in heaven on earth, he said, are creating a hell—he made it sound that way too—it was very lucid. How do you think I liked it on Monday morning when I had to make a window display of the new Atomic Pile Suction Cleaner? It wouldn't have surprised me if one of the wild boys around here had broken the window. Catholic Action, Christ the King, all that stuff. I don't know what to do about it, Hasselbacher."

"Sell one to Father Mendez for the Bishop's palace."

"But he's satisfied with the Turbo. It was a good machine. Of course this one is too. Improved suction for bookcases. You know I wouldn't sell anyone a machine that wasn't good."

"I know, Mr. Wormold. Can't you just change the name?"

"They won't let me. They are proud of it. They think it's the best phrase anyone has thought up since 'It beats as it sweeps as it cleans.' You know they had something called an air-purifying pad with the Turbo. Nobody minded—it was a good gadget, but yesterday a woman came in and looked at the Atomic Pile and she asked whether a pad that size could really absorb all the radio-activity. And what about Strontium 90? she asked."

"I could give you a medical certificate," said Dr. Hasselbacher.

"Do you never worry about anything?"

"I have a secret defence, Mr. Wormold. I am interested in life."

"So am I, but . . ."

"You are interested in a person, not in life, and people die or leave us—I'm sorry; I wasn't referring to your wife. But if you are interested in life it never lets you down. I am interested in the blueness of the cheese. You don't do crosswords, do you, Mr. Wormold? I do, and they are like people: one reaches an end. I can finish any cross-word within an hour, but I have a discovery concerned with the blueness of cheese that will never come to a conclusion—although of course one dreams that perhaps a time might come . . . One day I must show you my laboratory."

"I must be going, Hasselbacher."

"You should dream more, Mr. Wormold. Reality in our century is not something to be faced."

ii

When Wormold arrived at his store in Lamparilla Street, Milly had not yet returned from her American convent school, and in spite of the two figures he could see through the door, the shop seemed to him empty. How empty! And so it would remain until Milly came back. He was aware whenever he entered the shop of a vacuum that had nothing to do with his cleaners. No customer could fill it, particularly not the one who stood there now looking too spruce for Havana and reading a leaflet in English on the Atomic Pile, pointedly neglecting Wormold's assistant. Lopez was an impatient man who did not like to waste his time away from the Spanish edition of *Confidential*. He was glaring at the stranger and making no attempt to win him over.

"*Buenos días*," Wormold said. He looked at all strangers in the shop with an habitual suspicion. Ten years ago a man had entered the shop, posing as a customer, and he had guilelessly sold him a sheep's wool for the high-gloss finishing on his car. He had been a plausible impostor, but no one could be a less likely purchaser of a vacuum cleaner than this man. Tall and elegant, in his stone-coloured tropical suit, and wearing an exclusive tie, he carried with him the breath of beaches and the leathery smell of a good club: you expected him to say, "The Ambassador will see you in a minute." His cleaning would always be arranged for him—by an ocean or a valet.

"Don't speak the lingo, I'm afraid," the stranger answered. The slang word was a blemish on his suit, like an egg-stain after breakfast. "You are British, aren't you?"

"Yes."

"I mean—really British. British passport and all that."

"Yes. Why?"

"One likes to do business with a British firm. One knows where one is, if you see what I mean."

"What can I do for you?"

"Well, first, I just wanted to look around." He spoke as though he were in a bookshop. "I couldn't make your chap understand that."

"You are looking for a vacuum cleaner?"

"Well, not exactly looking."

"I mean, you are thinking of buying one?"

"That's it, old man, you've hit it on the nail." Wormold had the impression that the man had chosen his tone because he felt it matched the store—a protective colouring in Lamparilla Street; the breeziness certainly didn't match his clothes. One can't successfully follow St. Paul's technique of being all things to all men without a change of suit.

Wormold said briskly, "You couldn't do better than the Atomic Pile."

"I notice one here called the Turbo."

"That too is a very good cleaner. Have you a big apartment?"

"Well, not exactly big."

"Here, you see, you get two sets of brushes—this one for waxing and this for polishing—oh no, I think it's the other way round. The Turbo is air-powered."

"What does that mean?"

"Well, of course, it's . . . well, it's what it says, air-powered."

"This funny little bit here—what's that for?"

"That's a two-way carpet nozzle."

"You don't say so? Isn't that interesting? Why two-way?"

"You push and you pull."

"The things they think up," the stranger said. "I suppose you sell a lot of these?"

"I'm the only agent here."

"All the important people, I suppose, have to have an Atomic Pile?"

"Or a Turbo Jet."

"Government offices?"

"Of course. Why?"

"What's good enough for a government office should be good enough for me."

"You might prefer our Midget Make-Easy."

"Make what easy?"

"The full title is Midget Make-Easy Air-Powered Suction Small Home Cleaner."

"That word air-powered again."

"I'm not responsible for it."

"Don't get riled, old man."

"Personally I hate the words Atomic Pile," Wormold said with sudden passion. He was deeply disturbed. It occurred to him that this stranger might be an inspector sent from the head office in London or New York. In that case they should hear nothing but the truth.

"I see what you mean. It's not a happy choice. Tell me, do you service these things?"

"Quarterly. Free of charge during the period of guarantee."

"I meant yourself."

"I send Lopez."

"The sullen chap?"

"I'm not much of a mechanic. When I touch one of these things it somehow seems to give up working."

"Don't you drive a car?"

"Yes, but if there's anything wrong, my daughter sees to it."

"Oh yes, your daughter. Where's she?"

"At school. Now let me show you this snap-action coupling," but of course, when he tried to demonstrate, it wouldn't couple. He pushed and screwed. "Faulty part," he said desperately.

"Let me try," the stranger said, and in the coupling went as smooth as you could wish.

"How old is your daughter?"

"Sixteen," he said and was angry with himself for answering.

"Well," the stranger said, "I must be getting along. Enjoyed our chat."

"Wouldn't you like to watch a cleaner at work? Lopez here would give you a demonstration."

"Not at the moment. I'll be seeing you again—here or there," the man said with a vague and insolent confidence and was gone out of the door before Wormold thought to give him a trade-card. In the square at the top of Lamparilla Street he was swallowed up among the pimps and lottery sellers of the Havana noon.

Lopez said, "He never intended to buy."

"What did he want then?"

"Who knows? He looked a long time through the window at me. I think perhaps if you had not come in, he would have asked me to find him a girl."

"A girl?"

He thought of the day ten years ago and then with uneasiness of Milly, and he wished he had not answered so many questions. He also wished that the snap-action coupling had coupled for once with a snap.

2

He could distinguish the approach of Milly like that of a police-car from a long way off. Whistles instead of sirens warned him of her coming. She was accustomed to walk from the bus stop in the Avenida de Belgica, but today the wolves seemed to be operating from the direction of Compostella. They were not dangerous wolves, he had reluctantly to admit that. The salute which had begun about her thirteenth birthday was really one of respect, for even by the high Havana standard Milly was beautiful. She had hair the colour of pale honey, dark eyebrows, and her pony-trim was shaped by the best barber in town. She paid no open attention to the whistles, they only made her step the higher—seeing her walk, you could almost believe in levitation. Silence would have seemed like an insult to her now.

Unlike Wormold, who believed in nothing, Milly was a Catholic: he had been made to promise her mother that before they married. Now her mother, he supposed, was of no faith at all, but she had left a Catholic on his hands. It brought Milly closer to Cuba than he could come himself. He believed that in the rich families the custom of keeping a duenna lingered still, and sometimes it seemed to him that Milly too carried a duenna about with her, invisible to all eyes but her own. In church, where she looked more lovely than in any other place, wearing her feather-weight mantilla embroidered with leaves transparent as winter, the duenna was always seated by her side, to observe that her back was straight, her face covered at the suitable moment, the sign of the cross correctly performed. Small boys might suck sweets with impunity around her or giggle from behind the pillars, she sat with the rigidity of a nun, following the Mass in a small gilt-edged missal bound in a morocco the colour of her hair (she had chosen it herself). The same invisible duenna saw to it that she ate fish on Friday, fasted on Ember Days and attended Mass not only on Sundays and the special feasts of the church, but also on her saint's day. Milly was her home-name: her given name was Seraphina—in Cuba "a double of the second class," a mysterious phrase which reminded Wormold of the race-track.

It had been long before Wormold realised that the duenna was not always by her side. Milly was meticulous in her behaviour at meals and had never neglected her night-prayers, as he had good reason to know since, even as a child, she had kept him waiting, to mark him out as the non-Catholic he was, before her bedroom door until she had finished. A light burnt continually in front of the image of Our Lady of Guadalupe. He remembered how he had overheard her at the age of four praying, "Hail Mary, quite contrary."

One day however, when Milly was thirteen, he had been summoned to the convent school of the American Sisters of Clare in the white rich suburb of Vedado. There he learnt for the first time how the duenna left Milly under the religious plaque by the grilled gateway of the school. The complaint was of a serious nature: she had set fire to a small boy called Thomas Earl Parkman, junior. It was true, the Reverend Mother admitted, that Earl, as he was known in the school, had pulled Milly's hair first, but this she considered in no way justified Milly's action which might well have had serious results if another girl had not pushed Earl into a fountain. Milly's only defence of her conduct had been that Earl was a Protestant and if there was going to be a persecution Catholics could always beat Protestants at that game.

"But how did she set Earl on fire?"

"She put petrol on the tail of his shirt."

"Petrol!"

"Lighter-fluid, and then she struck a match. We think she must have been smoking in secret."

"It's a most extraordinary story."

"I guess you don't know Milly then. I must tell you, Mr. Wormold, our patience has been sadly strained."

Apparently, six months before setting fire to Earl, Milly had circulated round her art-class a set of postcards of the world's great pictures.

"I don't see what's wrong in that."

"At the age of twelve, Mr. Wormold, a child shouldn't confine her appreciation to the nude, however classical the paintings."

"They were all nude?"

"All except Goya's Draped Maja. But she had her in the nude version too."

Wormold had been forced to fling himself on Reverend Mother's mercy—he was a poor non-believing father with a Catholic child, the American convent was the only Catholic school in Havana which was not Spanish, and he couldn't afford a governess. They wouldn't want him to send her to the Hiram C. Truman School, would they? And it would be breaking the promise he had made to his wife. He wondered in private whether it was his duty to find a new wife, but the nuns might not put up with that and in any case he still loved Milly's mother.

Of course he spoke to Milly and her explanation had the virtue of simplicity.

"Why did you set fire to Earl?"

"I was tempted by the devil," she said.

"Milly, please be sensible."

"Saints have been tempted by the devil."

"You are not a saint."

"Exactly. That's why I fell." The chapter was closed—at any rate it would be closed that afternoon between four and six in the confessional. Her duenna was back at her side and would see to that. If only, he thought, I could know for certain when the duenna takes her day off.

There had been also the question of smoking in secret.

"Are you smoking cigarettes?" he asked her.

"No."

Something in her manner made him re-phrase the question. "Have you ever smoked at all, Milly?"

"Only cheroots," she said.

Now that he heard the whistles warning him of her approach he wondered why Milly was coming up Lamparilla from the direction of the harbour instead of from the Avenida de Belgica. But when he saw her he saw the reason too. She was followed by a young shop assistant who carried a parcel so large that it obscured his face. Wormold realised sadly that she had been shopping again. He went upstairs to their apartment above the store and presently he could hear her superintending in another room the disposal of her purchases. There was a thump, a rattle and a clang of metal. "Put it there," she said, and, "No, there." Drawers opened and closed. She began to drive nails into the wall. A piece of plaster on his side shot out and fell into the salad; the daily maid had laid a cold lunch.

Milly came in strictly on time. It was always hard for him to disguise his sense of her beauty, but the invisible duenna looked coldly through him as though he were an undesirable suitor. It had been a long time now since the duenna had taken a holiday; he almost regretted her assiduity, and sometimes he would have been glad to see Earl burn again. Milly said grace and crossed herself and he sat respectfully with his head lowered until she had finished. It was one of her longer graces, which probably meant that she was not very hungry, or that she was stalling for time.

"Had a good day, Father?" she asked politely. It was the kind of remark a wife might have made after many years.

"Not so bad, and you?" He became a coward when he watched her; he hated to oppose her in anything, and he tried to avoid for so long as possible the subject of her purchases. He knew that her monthly allowance had gone two weeks ago on some ear-rings she had fancied and a small statue of St. Seraphina.

"I got top marks today in Dogma and Morals."

"Fine, fine. What were the questions?"

"I did best on Venial Sin."

"I saw Dr. Hasselbacher this morning," he said with apparent irrelevance.

She replied politely, "I hope he was well." The duenna, he considered, was overdoing it. People praised Catholic schools for teaching deportment, but surely deportment was intended only to impress strangers. He thought sadly, But I *am* a stranger. He was unable to follow her into her strange world of candles and lace and holy water and genuflections. Sometimes he felt that he had no child.

"He's coming in for a drink on your birthday. I thought we might go afterwards to a night-club."

"A night-club!" The duenna must have momentarily looked elsewhere as Milly exclaimed, "O Gloria Patri."

"You always used to say Alleluia."

"That was in Lower Four. Which night-club?"

"I thought perhaps the Nacional."

"Not the Shanghai Theatre?"

"Certainly not the Shanghai Theatre. I can't think how you've even heard of the place."

"In a school things get around."

Wormold said, "We haven't discussed your present. A seventeenth birthday is no ordinary one. I was wondering . . ."

"Really and truly," Milly said, "there's nothing in the world I want."

Wormold remembered with apprehension that enormous package. If she had really gone out and got everything she wanted . . . He pleaded with her, "Surely there must be something you still want."

"Nothing. Really nothing."

"A new swim-suit," he suggested desperately.

"Well, there is one thing . . . But I thought we might count it as a Christmas present too, and next year's and the year after that . . ."

"Good heavens, what is it?"

"You wouldn't have to worry about presents any more for a long time."

"Don't tell me you want a Jaguar."

"Oh no, this is quite a small present. Not a car. This would last for years. It's an awfully economical idea. It might even, in a way, save petrol."

"Save petrol?"

"And today I got all the etceteras—with my own money."

"You haven't got any money. I had to lend you three pesos for Saint Seraphina."

"But my credit's good."

"Milly, I've told you over and over again I won't have you buying on credit. Anyway it's my credit, not yours, and my credit's going down all the time."

"Poor Father. Are we on the edge of ruin?"

"Oh, I expect things will pick up again when the disturbances are over."

"I thought there were always disturbances in Cuba. If the worst came to the worst I could go out and work, couldn't I?"

"What at?"

"Like Jane Eyre I could be a governess."

"Who would take you?"

"Señor Perez."

"Milly, what on earth are you talking about? He's living with his fourth wife, you're a Catholic. . . ."

"I might have a special vocation to sinners," Milly said.

"Milly, what nonsense you talk. Anyway, I'm not ruined. Not yet. As far as I know. Milly, what have you been buying?"

"Come and see." He followed her into her bedroom. A saddle lay on her bed; a bridle and bit were hanging on the wall from the nails she had driven in (she had knocked off a heel from her best evening shoes in doing it); reins were draped between the light brackets; a whip was propped up on the dressing-table. He said hopelessly, "Where's the horse?" and half expected it to appear from the bathroom.

"In a stable near the Country Club. Guess what she's called."

"How can I?"

"Seraphina. Isn't it just like the hand of God?"

"But, Milly, I can't possibly afford . . ."

"You needn't pay for her all at once. She's a chestnut."

"What difference does the colour make?"

"She's in the stud-book. Out of Santa Teresa by Ferdinand of Castile. She would have cost twice as much, but she fouled a fetlock jumping wire. There's nothing wrong, only a kind of lump, so they can't show her."

"I don't mind if it's a quarter the price. Business is too bad, Milly."

"But I've explained to you, you needn't pay all at once. You can pay over the years."

"And I'll still be paying for it when it's dead."

"She's not an it, she's a she, and Seraphina will last much longer than a car. She'll probably last longer than you will."

"But, Milly, your trips out to the stables, and the stabling alone . . ."

"I've talked about all that with Captain Segura. He's offering me a rock-bottom price. He wanted to give me free stabling, but I knew you wouldn't like me to take favours."

"Who's Captain Segura, Milly?"

"The head police officer in Vedado."

"Where on earth did you meet him?"

"Oh, he often gives me a lift to Lamparilla in his car."

"Does Reverend Mother know about this?"

Milly said stiffly, "One must have one's private life."

"Listen, Milly, I can't afford a horse, you can't afford all this—stuff. You'll have to take it back." He added with fury, "And I won't have you taking lifts from Captain Segura."

"Don't worry. He never touches me," Milly said. "He only sings sad Mexican songs while he drives. About flowers and death. And one about a bull."

"I won't have it, Milly. I shall speak to Reverend Mother, you've got to promise . . ." He could see under the dark brows how the green and amber eyes contained the coming tears. Wormold felt the approach of panic; just so his wife had looked at him one blistering October afternoon when six years of life suddenly ended. He said, "You aren't in love, are you, with this Captain Segura?"

Two tears chased each other with a kind of elegance round the curve of a cheek-bone and glittered like the harness on the wall; they were part of her equipment too. "I don't care a damn about Captain Segura," Milly said. "It's just Seraphina I care about. She's fifteen hands and she's got a mouth like velvet, everybody says so."

"Milly dear, you know that if I could manage it . . ."

"Oh, I knew you'd take it like this," Milly said. "I knew it in my heart of hearts. I said two novenas to make it come right, but they haven't worked. I was so careful too. I was in a state of grace all the time I said them. I'll never believe in a novena again. Never. Never." Her voice had the lingering resonance of Poe's Raven. He had no faith himself, but he never wanted by any action of his own to weaken hers. Now he felt a fearful responsibility; at any moment she would be denying the existence of God. Ancient promises he had made came up out of the past to weaken him.

He said. "Milly I'm sorry . . ."

"I've done two extra Masses as well." She shovelled on to his shoulders all her disappointment in the old familiar magic. It was all very well talking about the easy tears of a child, but if you are a father you can't take risks as a school-teacher can or a governess. Who knows whether there may not be a moment in childhood when the world changes forever, like making a face when the clock strikes?

"Milly, I promise if it's possible next year . . . Listen, Milly, you can keep the saddle till then, and all the rest of the stuff."

"What's the good of a saddle without a horse? And I told Captain Segura . . ."

"Damn Captain Segura—what did you tell him?"

"I told him I had only to ask you for Seraphina and you'd give her to me. I said you were wonderful. I didn't tell him about the novenas."

"How much is she?"

"Three hundred pesos."

"Oh, Milly, Milly." There was nothing he could do but surrender. "You'll have to pay out of your allowance towards the stabling."

"Of course I will." She kissed his ear. "I'll start next month." They both knew very well that she would never start. She said, "You see, they did work after all, the novenas, I mean. I'll begin another tomorrow, to make business good. I wonder which saint is best for that."

"I've heard that St. Jude is the saint of lost causes," Wormold said.

3

i

It was Wormold's day-dream that he would wake some day and find that he had amassed savings, bearer-bonds and share-certificates, and that he was receiving a steady flow of dividends like the rich inhabitants of the Vedado suburb; then he would retire with Milly to England, where there would be no Captain Seguras and no wolf-whistles. But the dream faded whenever he entered the big American bank in Obispo. Passing through the great stone portals, which were decorated with four-leaved clovers, he became again the small dealer he really was, whose pension would never be sufficient to take Milly to the region of safety.

Drawing a cheque is not nearly so simple an operation in an American bank as in an English one. American bankers believe in the personal touch; the teller conveys a sense that he happens to be there accidentally and he is overjoyed at the lucky chance of the encounter. "Well," he seems to express in the sunny warmth of his smile, "who would have believed that I'd meet you here, you of all people, in a bank of all places?" After exchanging with him news of your health and of his health, and after finding a common interest in the fineness of the winter weather, you shyly, apologetically, slide the cheque towards him (how tiresome and incidental all such business is), but he barely has time to glance at it when the telephone rings at his elbow. "Why, Henry," he exclaims in astonishment over the telephone, as though Henry too were the last person he expected to speak to on such a day, "what's the news of you?" The news takes a long time to absorb; the teller smiles whimsically at you: business is business.

"I must say Edith was looking swell last night," the teller said.

Wormold shifted restlessly.

"It was a swell evening, it certainly was. Me? Oh, I'm fine. Well now, what can we do for you today?"

". . . . ."

"Why, anything to oblige, Henry, you know that . . . A hundred and fifty thousand dollars for three years . . . no, of course there won't be any difficulty for a business like yours. We have to get the O.K. from New York, but that's a formality. Just step in any time and talk to the manager. Monthly payments? That's not necessary with an American firm. I'd say we could arrange five per cent. Make it two hundred thousand for four years? Of course, Henry."

Wormold's cheque shrank to insignificance in his fingers. "Three hundred and fifty dollars"—the writing seemed to him almost as thin as his resources.

"See you at Mrs. Slater's tomorrow? I expect there'll be a rubber. Don't bring any aces up your sleeve, Henry. How long for the O.K.? Oh, a couple of days if we cable. Eleven tomorrow? Any time you say, Henry. Just walk in. I'll tell the manager. He'll be tickled to death to see you."

"Sorry to keep you waiting, Mr. Wormold." Surname again. Perhaps, Wormold thought, I am not worth cultivating or perhaps it is our nationalities that keep us apart. "Three hundred and fifty dollars?" The teller took an unobtrusive glance in a file before counting out the notes. He had hardly begun when the telephone rang a second time.

"Why, Mrs. Ashworth, where have you been hiding yourself? Over at Miami? No kidding?" It was several minutes before he had finished with Mrs. Ashworth. As he passed the notes to Wormold, he handed over a slip of paper as well. "You don't mind, do you, Mr. Wormold. You asked me to keep you informed." The slip showed an overdraft of fifty dollars.

"Not at all. It's very kind of you," Wormold said. "But there's nothing to worry about."

"Oh, the bank's not worrying, Mr. Wormold. You just asked, that's all."

Wormold thought, If the overdraft had been fifty thousand dollars he would have called me Jim.

ii

For some reason that morning he had no wish to meet Dr. Hasselbacher for his morning daiquiri. There were times when Dr. Hasselbacher was a little too carefree, so he looked in at Sloppy Joe's instead of at the Wonder Bar. No Havana resident ever went to Sloppy Joe's because it was the rendezvous of tourists; but tourists were sadly reduced nowadays in number, for the President's régime was creaking dangerously towards its end. There had always been unpleasant doings out of sight, in the inner rooms of the Jefatura, which had not disturbed the tourists in the Nacional and the Seville-Biltmore, but one tourist had recently been killed by a stray bullet while he was taking a photograph of a picturesque beggar under a balcony near the palace, and the death had sounded the knell of the all-in tour "including a trip to Varadero beach and the night-life of Havana." The victim's Leica had been smashed as well, and that had impressed his companions more than anything with the destructive power of a bullet. Wormold had heard them talking afterwards in the bar of the Nacional. "Ripped right through the camera," one of them said. "Five hundred dollars gone just like that."

"Was he killed at once?"

"Sure. And the lens—you could pick up bits for fifty yards around. Look. I'm taking a piece home to show Mr. Humpelnicker."

The long bar that morning was empty except for the elegant stranger at one end and a stout member of the tourist police who was smoking a cigar at the other. The Englishman was absorbed in the sight of so many bottles, and it was quite a while before he spotted Wormold. "Well I never," he said, "Mr. Wormold, isn't it?" Wormold wondered how he knew his name, for he had forgotten to give him a trade-card. "Eighteen different kinds of Scotch," the stranger said, "including Black Label. And I haven't counted the Bourbons. It's a wonderful sight. Wonderful," he repeated, lowering his voice with respect. "Have you ever seen so many whiskies?"

"As a matter of fact I have. I collect miniatures and I have ninety-nine at home."

"Interesting. And what's your choice today? A dimpled Haig?"

"Thanks, I've just ordered a daiquiri."

"Can't take those things. They relax me."

"Have you decided on a cleaner yet?" Wormold asked for the sake of conversation.

"Cleaner?"

"Vacuum cleaner. The things I sell."

"Oh, cleaner. Ha ha. Throw away that stuff and have a Scotch."

"I never drink Scotch before the evening."

"You Southerners!"

"I don't see the connexion."

"Makes the blood thin. Sun, I mean. You were born in Nice, weren't you?"

"How do you know that?"

"Oh well, one picks things up. Here and there. Talking to this chap and that. I've been meaning to have a word with you as a matter of fact."

"Well, here I am."

"I'd like it more on the quiet, you know. Chaps keep on coming in and out."

No description could have been less accurate. No one even passed the door in the hard straight sunlight outside. The officer of the tourist police had fallen contentedly asleep after propping his cigar over an ash-tray; there were no tourists at this hour to protect or to supervise. Wormold said, "If it's about a cleaner, come down to the shop."

"I'd rather not, you know. Don't want to be seen hanging about there. Bar's not a bad place after all. You run into a fellow-countryman, have a get together, what more natural?"

"I don't understand."

"Well, you know how it is."

"I don't."

"Well, wouldn't you say it was natural enough?"

Wormold gave up. He left eighty cents on the counter and said, "I must be getting back to the shop."

"Why?"

"I don't like to leave Lopez for long."

"Ah, Lopez. I want to talk to you about Lopez." Again the explanation that seemed most probable to Wormold was that the stranger was an eccentric inspector from headquarters, but surely he had reached the limit of eccentricity when he added in a low voice, "You go to the Gents and I'll follow you."

"The Gents? Why should I?"

"Because I don't know the way."

In a mad world it always seems simpler to obey. Wormold led the stranger through a door at the back, down a short passage, and indicated the toilet. "It's in there."

"After you, old man."

"But I don't need it."

"Don't be difficult," the stranger said. He put a hand on Wormold's shoulder and pushed him through the door. Inside there were two wash-basins, a chair with a broken back, and the usual cabinets and pissoirs. "Take a pew, old man," the stranger said, "while I turn on a tap." But when the water ran he made no attempt to wash. "Looks more natural," he explained (the word "natural' seemed a favourite adjective of his), "if someone barges in. And of course it confuses a mike."

"A mike?"

"You're quite right to question that. Quite right. There probably wouldn't be a mike in a place like this, but it's the drill, you know, that counts. You'll find it always pays in the end to follow the drill. It's lucky they don't run to waste-plugs in Havana. We can just keep the water running."

"Please will you explain . . . ?"

"Can't be too careful even in a Gents, when I come to think of it. A chap of ours in Denmark in 1940 saw from his own window the German fleet coming down the Kattegat."

"What gut?"

"Kattegat. Of course he knew then the balloon had gone up. Started burning his papers. Put the ashes down the lav. and pulled the chain. Trouble was—late frost. Pipes frozen. All the ashes floated up into the bath down below. Flat belonged to an old maiden lady—Baronin someone or other. She was just going to have a bath. Most embarrassing for our chap."

"It sounds like the Secret Service."

"It *is* the Secret Service, old man, or so the novelists call it. That's why I wanted to talk to you about your chap Lopez. Is he reliable or ought you to fire him?"

"Are you in the Secret Service?"

"If you like to put it that way."

"Why on earth should I fire Lopez? He's been with me ten years."

"We could find you a chap who knew all about vacuum cleaners. But of course—naturally—we'll leave that decision to you."

"But I'm not in your Service."

"We'll come to that in a moment, old man. Anyway we've traced Lopez—he seems clear. But your friend Hasselbacher, I'd be a bit careful of him."

"How do you know about Hasselbacher?"

"I've been around a day or two, picking things up. One has to on these occasions."

"What occasions?"

"Where was Hasselbacher born?"

"Berlin, I think."

"Sympathies East or West?"

"We never talk politics."

"Not that it matters—East or West they play the German game. Remember the Ribbentrop Pact. We won't be caught that way again."

"Hasselbacher's not a politician. He's an old doctor and he's lived here for thirty years."

"All the same, you'd be surprised . . . But I agree with you, it would be conspicuous if you dropped him. Just play him carefully, that's all. He might even be useful if you handle him right."

"I've no intention of handling him."

"You'll find it necessary for the job."

"I don't want any job. Why do you pick on me?"

"Patriotic Englishman. Been here for years. Respected member of the European Traders' Association. We must have our man in Havana, you know. Submarines need fuel. Dictators drift together. Big ones draw in the little ones."

"Atomic submarines don't need fuel."

"Quite right, old man, quite right. But wars always start a little behind the times.

Have to be prepared for conventional weapons too. Then there's economic intelligence—sugar, coffee, tobacco.''

"You can find all that in the Government year-books."

"We don't trust them, old man. Then political intelligence. With your cleaners you've got the entrée everywhere."

"Do you expect me to analyse the fluff?"

"It may seem a joke to you, old man, but the main source of the French intelligence at the time of Dreyfus was a charwoman who collected the scraps out of the waste-paper baskets at the German Embassy."

"I don't even know your name."

"Hawthorne."

"But who are you?"

"Well, you might say I'm setting up the Caribbean network. One moment. Someone's coming. I'll wash. You slip into a closet. Mustn't be seen together."

"We *have* been seen together."

"Passing encounter. Fellow-countrymen." He thrust Wormold into the compartment as he had thrust him into the lavatory, "It's the drill, you know," and then there was silence except for the running tap. Wormold sat down. There was nothing else to do. When he was seated his legs still showed under the half door. A handle turned. Feet crossed the tiled floor towards the pissoir. Water went on running. Wormold felt an enormous bewilderment. He wondered why he had not stopped all this nonsense at the beginning. No wonder Mary had left him. He remembered one of their quarrels. "Why don't you do something, act some way, any way at all? You just stand there . . ." At least, he thought, this time I'm not standing, I'm sitting. But in any case what could he have said? He hadn't been given time to get a word in. Minutes passed. What enormous bladders Cubans had, and how clean Hawthorne's hands must be getting by this time. The water stopped running. Presumably he was drying his hands, but Wormold remembered there were no towels. That was another problem for Hawthorne, but he would be up to it. All part of the drill. At last the feet passed towards the door. The door closed.

"Can I come out?" Wormold asked. It was like a surrender. He was under orders now.

He heard Hawthorne tiptoeing near. "Give me a few minutes to get away, old man. Do you know who that was? The policeman. A bit suspicious, eh?"

"He may have recognised my legs under the door. Do you think we ought to change trousers?"

"Wouldn't look natural," Hawthorne said, "but you are getting the idea. I'm leaving the key of my room in the basin. Fifth floor Seville-Biltmore. Just walk up. Ten tonight. Things to discuss. Money and so on. Sordid issues. Don't ask for me at the desk."

"Don't you need your key?"

"Got a pass key. I'll be seeing you."

Wormold stood up in time to see the door close behind the elegant figure and the appalling slang. The key was there in the wash-basin—Room 501.

iii

At half-past nine Wormold went to Milly's room to say good night. Here, where the duenna was in charge, everything was in order—the candle had been lit before the statue of St. Seraphina, the honey-coloured missal lay beside the bed, the clothes were eliminated as though they had never existed, and a faint smell of eau-de-Cologne blew about like incense.

"You've got something on your mind," Milly said. "You aren't still worrying, are you, about Captain Segura?"

"You never pull my leg, do you, Milly?"

"No. Why?"

"Everybody else seems to."

"Did Mother?"

"I suppose so. In the early days."

"Does Dr. Hasselbacher?"

He remembered the negro limping slowly by. He said, "Perhaps. Sometimes."

"It's a sign of affection, isn't it?"

"Not always. I remember at school——" He stopped.

"What do you remember, Father?"

"Oh, a lot of things."

Childhood was the germ of all mistrust. You were cruelly joked upon and then you cruelly joked. You lost the remembrance of pain through inflicting it. But somehow, through no virtue of his own, he had never taken that course. Lack of character perhaps. Schools were said to construct character by chipping off the edges. His edges had been chipped, but the result had not, he thought, been character—only shapelessness, like an exhibit in the Museum of Modern Art.

"Are you happy, Milly?" he asked.

"Oh yes."

"At school too?"

"Yes. Why?"

"Nobody pulls your hair now?"

"Of course not."

"And you don't set anyone on fire?"

"That was when I was thirteen," she said with scorn. "What's worrying you, Father?"

She sat up in bed, wearing a white nylon dressing-gown. He loved her when the duenna was there, and he loved her even more when the duenna was absent: he couldn't afford the time not to love. It was as if he had come with her a little way on a journey that she would finish alone. The separating years approached them both, like a station down the line, all gain for her and all loss for him. That evening hour was real, but not Hawthorne, mysterious and absurd, not the cruelties of police-stations and governments, the scientists who tested the new H-bomb on Christmas Island, Kruschev who wrote notes: these seemed less real to him than the inefficient tortures of a school-dormitory. The small boy with the damp towel whom he had just remembered—where was he now? The cruel come and go like cities and thrones and powers, leaving their ruins behind them. They had no permanence. But the clown whom he had seen last year with Milly at the circus—that clown was permanent, for his act never changed. That was the way to live; the clown was unaffected by the vagaries of public men and the enormous discoveries of the great.

Wormold began to make faces in the glass.

"What on earth are you doing, Father?"

"I wanted to make myself laugh."

Milly giggled. "I thought you were being sad and serious."

"That's why I wanted to laugh. Do you remember the clown last year, Milly?"

"He walked off the end of a ladder and fell in a bucket of whitewash."

"He falls in it every night at ten o'clock. We should all be clowns, Milly. Don't ever learn from experience."

"Reverend Mother says . . ."

"Don't pay any attention to her. God doesn't learn from experience, does He, or how could He hope anything of man? It's the scientists who add the digits and make the same sum who cause the trouble. Newton discovering gravity—he learned from experience and after that . . ."

"I thought it was from an apple."

"It's the same thing. It was only a matter of time before Lord Rutherford went and split the atom. He had learned from experience too, and so did the men of Hiroshima. If only we had been born clowns, nothing bad would happen to us except a few bruises and a smear of whitewash. Don't learn from experience, Milly. It ruins our peace and our lives."

"What are you doing now?"

"I'm trying to waggle my ears. I used to be able to do it. But the trick doesn't work any longer."

"Are you still unhappy about Mother?"

"Sometimes."

"Are you still in love with her?"

"Perhaps. Now and then."

"I suppose she was very beautiful when she was young."

"She can't be old now. Thirty-six."

"That's pretty old."

"Don't you remember her at all?"

"Not very well. She was away a lot, wasn't she?"

"A good deal."

"Of course I pray for her."

"What do you pray? That she'll come back?"

"Oh no, not *that*. We can do without her. I pray that she'll be a good Catholic again."

"I'm not a good Catholic."

"Oh, that's different. You are invincibly ignorant."

"Yes, I expect I am."

"I'm not insulting you, Father. It's only theology. You'll be saved like the good pagans. Socrates, you know, and Cetewayo."

"Who was Cetewayo?"

"He was king of the Zulus."

"What else do you pray?"

"Well, of course, lately I've been concentrating on the horse."

He kissed her good night. She asked, "Where are you going?"

"There are things I've got to arrange about the horse."

"I give you a lot of trouble," she said meaninglessly. Then she sighed with content, pulling the sheet up to her neck. "It's wonderful, isn't it, how you always get what you pray for."

4

i

At every corner there were men who called "Taxi' at him as though he were a stranger, and all down the Paseo, at intervals of a few yards, the pimps accosted him automatically without any real hope. "Can I be of service, sir?" "I know all the pretty girls." "You desire a beautiful woman." "Postcards?" "You want to see a dirty movie?" They had been mere children when he first came to Havana, they had watched his car for a nickel, and though they had aged alongside him they had never got used to him. In their eyes he never became a resident; he remained a permanent tourist, and so they went pegging along—sooner or later, like all the others, they were certain that he would want to see Superman performing at the San Francisco brothel. At least, like the clown, they had the comfort of not learning from experience.

By the corner of Virdudes Dr. Hasselbacher hailed him from the Wonder Bar. "Mr. Wormold, where are you off to in such a hurry?"

"An appointment."

"There is always time for a Scotch." It was obvious from the way he pronounced Scotch that Dr. Hasselbacher had already had time for a great many.

"I'm late as it is."

"There's no such thing as late in this city, Mr. Wormold. And I have a present for you."

Wormold turned in to the bar from the Paseo. He smiled unhappily at one of his own thoughts. "Are your sympathies with the East or the West, Hasselbacher?"

"East or West of what? Oh, you mean *that*. A plague on both."

"What present have you got for me?"

"I asked one of my patients to bring them from Miami," Hasselbacher said. He took from his pocket two miniature bottles of whisky: one was Lord Calvert, the other Old Taylor. "Have you got them?" he asked with anxiety.

"I've got the Calvert, but not the Taylor. It was kind of you to remember my collection, Hasselbacher." It always seemed strange to Wormold that he continued to exist for others when he was not there.

"How many have you got now?"

"A hundred with the Bourbon and the Irish. Seventy-six Scotch."

"When are you going to drink them?"

"Perhaps when they reach two hundred."

"Do you know what I'd do with them if I were you?" Hasselbacher said. "Play checkers. When you take a piece you drink it."

"That's quite an idea."

"A natural handicap," Hasselbacher said. "That's the beauty of it. The better player has to drink more. Think of the finesse. Have another Scotch."

"Perhaps I will."

"I need your help. I was stung by a wasp this morning."

"You are the doctor, not me."

"That's not the point. One hour later, going out on a sick call beyond the airport, I ran over a chicken."

"I still don't understand."

"Mr. Wormold, Mr. Wormold, your thoughts are far away. Come back to earth. We have to find a lottery-ticket at once, before the draw. Twenty-seven means a wasp. Thirty-seven a chicken."

"But I have an appointment."

"Appointments can wait. Drink down that Scotch. We've got to hunt for the ticket in the market." Wormold followed him to his car. Like Milly, Dr. Hasselbacher had faith. He was controlled by numbers as she was by saints.

All round the market hung the important numbers in blue and red. What were called the ugly numbers lay under the counter; they were left for the small fry and the street sellers to dispose of. They were without importance, they contained no significant figure, no number that represented a nun or a cat, a wasp or a chicken. "Look. There's 2 7 4 8 3," Wormold pointed out.

"A wasp is no good without a chicken," said Dr. Hasselbacher. They parked the car and walked. There were no pimps around this market; the lottery was a serious trade uncorrupted by tourists. Once a week the numbers were distributed by a government department, and a politician would be allotted tickets according to the value of his support. He paid $18 a ticket to the department and he resold to the big merchants for $21. Even if his share were a mere twenty tickets he could depend on a profit of sixty dollars a week. A beautiful number containing omens of a popular kind could be sold by the merchants for anything up to thirty dollars. No such profits, of course, were possible for the little man in the street. With only ugly numbers, for which he had paid as much as twenty-three dollars, he really had to work for a living. He would divide a ticket up into a hundred parts at twenty-five cents a part; he would haunt car parks until he found a car with the same number as one of his tickets (no owner could resist a coincidence like that); he would even search for his numbers in the telephone-book and risk a nickel on a call. "Señora, I have a lottery-ticket for sale which is the same number as your telephone."

Wormold said, "Look, there's a 37 with a 72."

"Not good enough," Dr. Hasselbacher flatly replied.

Dr. Hasselbacher thumbed through the sheets of numbers which were not considered beautiful enough to be displayed. One never knew; beauty was not beauty to all men—there might be some to whom a wasp was insignificant. A police siren came shrieking through the dark round three sides of the market, a car rocked by. A man sat on the kerb with a single number displayed on his shirt like a convict. He said, "The Red Vulture."

"Who's the Red Vulture?"

"Captain Segura, of course," Dr. Hasselbacher said. "What a sheltered life you lead."

"Why do they call him that?"

"He specialises in torture and mutilation."

"Torture?"

"There's nothing here," Dr. Hasselbacher said. "We'd better try Obispo."

"Why not wait till the morning?"

"Last day before the draw. Besides, what kind of cold blood runs in your veins, Mr. Wormold? When fate gives you a lead like this one—a wasp and a chicken —you have to follow it without delay. One must deserve one's good fortune."

They climbed back into the car and made for Obispo. "This Captain Segura" —Wormold began.

"Yes?"

"Nothing."

It was eleven o'clock before they found a ticket that satisfied Dr. Hasselbacher's requirements, and then as the shop which displayed it was closed until the morning there was nothing to do but have another drink. "Where is your appointment?"

Wormold said, "The Seville-Biltmore."

"One place is as good as another," Dr. Hasselbacher said.

"Don't you think the Wonder Bar . . . ?"

"No, no. A change will be good. When you feel unable to change your bar you have become old."

They groped their way through the darkness of the Seville-Biltmore bar. They were only dimly aware of their fellow-guests, who sat crouched in silence and shadow like parachutists gloomily waiting the signal to leap. Only the high proof of Dr. Hasselbacher's spirits could not be quenched.

"You haven't won yet," Wormold whispered, trying to check him, but even a whisper caused a reproachful head to turn towards them in the darkness.

"Tonight I have won," Dr. Hasselbacher said in a loud firm voice. "Tomorrow I may have lost, but nothing can rob me of my victory tonight. A hundred and

forty thousand dollars, Mr. Wormold. It is a pity that I am too old for women—
I could have made a beautiful woman very happy with a necklace of rubies. Now
I am at a loss. How shall I spend my money, Mr. Wormold? Endow a hospital?''

"Pardon me," a voice whispered out of the shadows, "has this guy really won
a hundred and forty thousand bucks?"

"Yes, sir, I have won them," Dr. Hasselbacher said firmly before Wormold
could reply, "I have won them as certainly as you exist, my almost unseen friend.
You would not exist if I didn't believe you existed, nor would those dollars. I
believe, therefore you are."

"What do you mean I wouldn't exist?"

"You exist only in my thoughts, my friend. If I left this room . . ."

"You're nuts."

"Prove you exist, then."

"What do you mean, prove? Of course I exist. I've got a first-class business in
real estate: a wife and a couple of kids in Miami: I flew here this morning by Delta:
I'm drinking this Scotch, aren't I?" The voice contained a hint of tears.

"Poor fellow," Dr. Hasselbacher said, "you deserve a more imaginative creator
than I have been. Why didn't I do better for you than Miami and real estate?
Something of imagination. A name to be remembered."

"What's wrong with my name?"

The parachutists at both ends of the bar were tense with disapproval; one shouldn't
show nerves before the jump.

"Nothing that I cannot remedy by taking a little thought."

"You ask anyone in Miami about Harry Morgan . . ."

"I really should have done better than that. But I'll tell you what I'll do," Dr.
Hasselbacher said, "I'll go out of the bar for a minute and eliminate you. Then
I'll come back with an improved version."

"What do you mean, an improved version?"

"Now if my friend, Mr. Wormold here, had invented you, you would have been
a happier man. He would have given you an Oxford education, a name like Pennyfeather . . ."

"What do you mean, Pennyfeather? You've been drinking."

"Of course I've been drinking. Drink blurs the imagination. That's why I thought
you up in so banal a way: Miami and real estate, flying Delta. Pennyfeather would
have come from Europe by K.L.M., he would be drinking his national drink, a
pink gin."

"I'm drinking Scotch and I like it."

"You think you're drinking Scotch. Or rather, to be accurate, I have imagined
you drinking Scotch. But we're going to change all that," Dr. Hasselbacher said
cheerily. "I'll just go out in the hall for a minute and think up some real im-
provements."

"You can't monkey around with me," the man said with anxiety.

Dr. Hasselbacher drained his drink, laid a dollar on the bar, and rose with
uncertain dignity. "You'll thank me for this," he said. "What shall it be? Trust

me and Mr. Wormold here. A painter, a poet—or would you prefer a life of adventure, a gun-runner, a Secret Service agent?''

He bowed from the doorway to the agitated shadow. ''I apologise for the real estate.''

The voice said nervously, seeking reassurance, ''He's drunk or nuts,'' but the parachutists made no reply.

Wormold said, ''Well, I'll be saying good night, Hasselbacher. I'm late.''

''The least I can do, Mr. Wormold, is to accompany you and explain how I came to delay you. I'm sure when I tell your friend of my good fortune he will understand.''

''It's not necessary. It's really not necessary,'' Wormold said. Hawthorne, he knew, would jump to conclusions. A reasonable Hawthorne, if such existed, was bad enough, but a suspicious Hawthorne . . . His mind boggled at the thought.

He made towards the lift with Dr. Hasselbacher trailing behind. Ignoring a red signal light and a warning Mind the Step, Dr. Hasselbacher stumbled. ''Oh dear,'' he said, ''my ankle.''

''Go home, Hasselbacher,'' Wormold said with desperation. He stepped into the lift, but Dr. Hasselbacher, putting on a turn of speed, entered too. He said, ''There's no pain that money won't cure. It's a long time since I've had such a good evening.''

''Sixth floor,'' Wormold said. ''I want to be alone, Hasselbacher.''

''Why? Excuse me. I have the hiccups.''

''This is a private meeting.''

''A lovely woman, Mr. Wormold? You shall have some of my winnings to help you stoop to folly.''

''Of course it isn't a woman. It's business, that's all.''

''Private business?''

''I told you so.''

''What can be so private about a vacuum cleaner, Mr. Wormold?''

''A new agency,'' Wormold said, and the liftman announced, ''Sixth floor.''

Wormold was a length ahead and his brain was clearer than Hasselbacher's. The rooms were built as prison-cells round a rectangular balcony; on the ground floor two bald heads gleamed upwards like traffic globes. He limped to the corner of the balcony where the stairs were, and Dr. Hasselbacher limped after him but Wormold was practised in limping. ''Mr. Wormold,'' Dr. Hasselbacher called, ''Mr. Wormold, I'd be happy to invest a hundred thousand of my dollars . . .''

Wormold got to the bottom of the stairs while Dr. Hasselbacher was still manœuvring the first step; 501 was close by. He unlocked the door. A small table-lamp showed him an empty sitting-room. He closed the door very softly—Dr. Hasselbacher had not yet reached the bottom of the stairs. He stood listening and heard Dr. Hasselbacher's hop, skip and hiccup pass the door and recede. Wormold thought, I feel like a spy, I behave like a spy. This is absurd. What am I going to say to Hasselbacher in the morning?

The bedroom door was closed and he began to move towards it. Then he stopped. Let sleeping dogs lie. If Hawthorne wanted him, let Hawthorne find him without his stir, but a curiosity about Hawthorne induced him to make a parting examination of the room.

On the writing desk were two books—identical copies of Lamb's *Tales from Shakespeare*. A memo pad—on which perhaps Hawthorne had made notes for their meeting—read, "1. Salary. 2. Expenses. 3. Transmission. 4. Charles Lamb. 5. Ink." He was just about to open the Lamb when a voice said, "Put up your hands. *Arriba los manos.*"

"*Las manos,*" Wormold corrected him. He was relieved to see that it was Hawthorne.

"Oh, it's only you," Hawthorne said.

"I'm a bit late. I'm sorry. I was out with Hasselbacher."

Hawthorne was wearing mauve silk pyjamas with a monogram H.R.H. on the pocket. This gave him a royal air. He said, "I fell asleep and then I heard you moving around." It was as though he had been caught without his slang; he hadn't yet had time to put it on with his clothes. He said, "You've moved the Lamb," accusingly as though he were in charge of a Salvation Army chapel.

"I'm sorry. I was just looking round."

"Never mind. It shows you have the right instinct."

"You seem fond of that particular book."

"One copy is for you."

"But I've read it," Wormold said, "years ago, and I don't like Lamb."

"It's not meant for reading. Have you never heard of a book-code?"

"As a matter of fact—no."

"In a minute I'll show you how to work it. I keep one copy. All you have to do when you communicate with me is to indicate the page and line where you begin the coding. Of course it's not so hard to break as a machine-code, but it's hard enough for the mere Hasselbachers."

"I wish you'd get Dr. Hasselbacher out of your head."

"When we have your office here properly organised with sufficient security—a combination-safe, radio, trained staff, all the gimmicks, then of course we can abandon a primitive code like this, but except for an expert cryptologist it's damned hard to break without knowing the name and edition of the book."

"Why did you choose Lamb?"

"It was the only book I could find in duplicate except *Uncle Tom's Cabin*. I was in a hurry and had to get something at the C.T.S. bookshop in Kingston before I left. Oh, there was something too called *The Lit Lamp: A Manual of Evening Devotion*, but I thought somehow it might look conspicuous on your shelves if you weren't a religious man."

"I'm not."

"I brought you some ink as well. Have you got an electric kettle?"

"Yes. Why?"

"For opening letters. We like our men to be equipped against an emergency."

"What's the ink for? I've got plenty of ink at home."

"Secret ink of course. In case you have to send anything by the ordinary mail. Your daughter has a knitting needle, I suppose?"

"She doesn't knit."

"Then you'll have to buy one. Plastic is best. Steel sometimes leaves a mark."

"Mark where?"

"On the envelopes you open."

"Why on earth should I want to open envelopes?"

"It might be necessary for you to examine Dr. Hasselbacher's mail. Of course, you'll have to find a sub-agent in the post office."

"I absolutely refuse . . ."

"Don't be difficult. I'm having traces of him sent out from London. We'll decide about his mail after we've read them. A good tip—if you run short of ink use bird shit, or am I going too fast?"

"I haven't even said I was willing . . ."

"London agrees to $150 a month, with another hundred and fifty as expenses —you'll have to justify those, of course. Payment of sub-agents, etc. Anything above that will have to be specially authorised."

"You are going much too fast."

"Free of income-tax, you know," Hawthorne said and winked slyly. The wink somehow didn't go with the royal monogram.

"You must give me time . . ."

"Your code number is 59200 stroke 5." He added with pride, "Of course *I* am 59200. You'll number your sub-agents 59200 stroke 5 stroke 1 and so on. Got the idea?"

"I don't see how I can possibly be of use to you."

"You are English, aren't you?" Hawthorne said briskly.

"Of course I'm English."

"And you refuse to serve your country?"

"I didn't say that. But the vacuum cleaners take up a great deal of time."

"They are an excellent cover," Hawthorne said. "Very well thought out. Your profession has quite a natural air."

"But it *is* natural."

"Now if you don't mind," Hawthorne said firmly, "we must get down to our Lamb."

ii

"Milly," Wormold said, "you haven't taken any cereals."

"I've given up cereals."

"You only took one lump of sugar in your coffee. You aren't going on a diet, are you?"

"No."

"Or doing a penance?"

"No."

"You'll be awfully hungry by lunch-time."

"I've thought of that. I'm going to eat a terrible lot of potatoes."

"Milly, what's going on?"

"I'm going to economise. Suddenly in the watches of the night I realised what an expense I was to you. It was like a voice speaking. I nearly said, 'Who are you?' but I was afraid it would say, 'Your Lord and your God.' I'm about the age, you know."

"Age for what?"

"Voices. I'm older than St. Thérèse was when she went into the convent."

"Now, Milly, don't tell me you're comtemplating . . ."

"No, I'm not. I think Captain Segura's right. He said I wasn't the right material for a convent."

"Milly, do you know what they call your Captain Segura?"

"Yes. The Red Vulture. He tortures prisoners."

"Does he admit that?"

"Oh, of course with me he's on his best behaviour, but he has a cigarette-case made out of human skin. He pretends it's calf—as if I didn't know calf when I see it."

"You must drop him, Milly."

"I shall—slowly, but I have to arrange my stabling first. And that reminds me of the voice."

"What did the voice say?"

"It said—only it sounded much more apocalyptic in the middle of the night—'You've bitten off more than you can chew, my girl. What about the Country Club?' "

"What about the Country Club?"

"It's the only place where I can get any real riding, and we aren't members. What's the good of a horse in a stable? Of course Captain Segura is a member, but I knew you wouldn't want me to depend on him. So I thought perhaps if I could help you to cut the housekeeping by fasting . . ."

"What good . . . ?"

"Well, then, you might be able to afford to take a family-membership. You ought to enter me as Seraphina. It somehow sounds more suitable than Milly."

It seemed to Wormold that all she said had a quality of sense; it was Hawthorne who belonged to the cruel and inexplicable world of childhood.

Interlude in London

In the basement of the big steel and concrete building near Maida Vale a light over a door changed from red to green, and Hawthorne entered. He had left his elegance behind in the Caribbean and wore a grey flannel suit which had seen better days. At home he didn't have to keep up appearances; he was part of grey January London.

The Chief sat behind a desk on which an enormous green marble paper-weight held down a single sheet of paper. A half-drunk glass of milk, a bottle of grey pills and a packet of Kleenex stood by the black telephone. (The red one was for scrambling.) His black morning coat, black tie and black monocle hiding the left eye gave him the appearance of an undertaker, just as the basement room had the effect of a vault, a mausoleum, a grave.

"You wanted me, sir?"

"Just a gossip, Hawthorne. Just a gossip." It was as though a mute were gloomily giving tongue after the day's burials were over. "When did you get back, Hawthorne?"

"A week ago, sir. I'll be returning to Jamaica on Friday."

"All going well?"

"I think we've got the Caribbean sewn up now, sir," Hawthorne said.

"Martinique?"

"No difficulties there, sir. You remember at Fort de France we are working with the Deuxième Bureau."

"Only up to a point?"

"Oh yes, of course, only up to a point. Haiti was more of a problem, but 59200 stroke 2 is proving energetic. I was more uncertain at first about 59200 stroke 5."

"Stroke five?"

"Our man in Havana, sir. I didn't have much choice there, and at first he didn't seem very keen on the job. A bit stubborn."

"That kind sometimes develops best."

"Yes, sir. I was a little worried too by his contacts. (There's a German called Hasselbacher, but we haven't found any traces of him yet). However he seems to be going ahead. We got a request for extra expenses just as I was leaving Kingston."

"Always a good sign."

"Yes, sir."

"Shows the imagination is working."

"Yes, sir. I was a little worried too by his contacts. (There's a German called Hasselbacher, but we haven't found any traces of him yet.) However he seems to be going ahead. We got a request for extra expenses just as I was leaving Kingston."

"You did right. How are his reports?"

"Well, as a matter of fact, we haven't had any yet, but of course it will take time for him to organise his contacts. Perhaps I rather over-emphasised the need of security."

"You can't. No use having a live wire if it fuses."

"As it happens, he's rather advantageously placed. Very good business contacts —a lot of them with Government officials and leading Ministers."

"Ah," the Chief said. He took off the black monocle and began to polish it with a piece of Kleenex. The eye that he disclosed was made of glass; pale blue and unconvincing, it might have come out of a doll which said "Mama."

"What's his business?"

"Oh, he imports, you know. Machinery, that sort of thing." It was always important to one's own career to employ agents who were men of good social standing. The petty details on the secret file dealing with the store in Lamparilla Street would never, in ordinary circumstances, reach this basement-room.

"Why isn't he already a member of the Country Club?"

"Well, I think he's been rather a recluse of recent years. Bit of domestic trouble."

"Doesn't run after women, I hope?"

"Oh, nothing of that sort, sir. His wife left him. Went off with an American."

"I suppose he's not anti-American? Havana's not the place for any prejudice like that. We have to work with them—only up to a point of course."

"Oh, he's not at all that way, sir. He's a very fairminded man, very balanced. Took his divorce well and keeps his child in a Catholic school according to his wife's wishes. I'm told he sends her greeting-telegrams at Christmas. I think we'll find his reports when they do come in are a hundred per cent reliable."

"Rather touching that, about the child, Hawthorne. Well, give him a prod, so that we can judge his usefulness. If he's all you say he is, we might consider enlarging his staff. Havana could be a key-spot. The Communists always go where there's trouble. How does he communicate?"

"I've arranged for him to send reports by the weekly bag to Kingston in duplicate. I keep one and send one to London. I've given him the book-code for cables. He sends them through the Consulate."

"They won't like that."

"I've told them it's temporary."

"I would be in favour of establishing a radio-unit if he proves to be a good man. He could expand his office-staff, I suppose?"

"Oh, of course. At least—you understand it's not a big office, sir. Old-fashioned. You know how these merchant-adventurers make do."

"I know the type, Hawthorne. Small scrubby desk. Half a dozen men in an outer office meant to hold two. Out-of-date accounting machines. Woman-secretary who is completing forty years with the firm."

Hawthorne now felt able to relax; the Chief had taken charge. Even if one day he read the secret file, the words would convey nothing to him. The small shop for vacuum cleaners had been drowned beyond recovery in the tide of the Chief's literary imagination. Agent 59200/5 was established.

"It's all part of the man's character," the Chief explained to Hawthorne, as though he and not Hawthorne had pushed open the door in Lamparilla Street. "A man who has always learnt to count the pennies and to risk the pounds. That's why he's not a member of the Country Club—nothing to do with the broken marriage. You're a romantic, Hawthorne. Women have come and gone in his life; I suspect they never meant as much to him as his work. The secret of successfully using an agent is to understand him. Our man in Havana belongs—you might say—to the Kipling age. Walking with kings—how does it go?—and keeping your virtue, crowds and the common touch. I expect somewhere in that ink-stained desk of his there's an old penny note-book of black wash-leather in which he kept his first accounts—a quarter gross of india-rubbers, six boxes of steel nibs . . ."

"I don't think he goes quite as far back as steel nibs, sir."

The Chief sighed and replaced the black lens. The innocent eye had gone back into hiding at the hint of opposition.

"Details don't matter, Hawthorne," the Chief said with irritation. "But if you are to handle him successfully you'll have to find that penny note-book. I speak metaphorically."

"Yes, sir."

"This business about being a recluse because he lost his wife—it's a wrong appreciation, Hawthorne. A man like that reacts quite differently. He doesn't show his loss, he doesn't wear his heart on his sleeve. If your appreciation were correct, why wasn't he a member of the club before his wife died?"

"She left him."

"Left him? Are you sure?"

"Quite sure, sir."

"Ah, she never found that penny note-book. Find it, Hawthorne, and he's yours for life. What were we talking about?"

"The size of his office, sir. It won't be very easy for him to absorb many in the way of new staff."

"We'll weed out the old ones gradually. Pension off that old secretary of his . . ."

"As a matter of fact . . ."

"Of course this is just speculation, Hawthorne. He may not be the right man after all. Sterling stuff, these old merchant-kings, but sometimes they can't see far enough beyond the counting-house to be of use to people like ourselves. We'll judge by his first reports, but it's always well to plan a step ahead. Have a word with Miss Jenkinson and see if she has a Spanish speaker in her pool."

Hawthorne rose in the elevator floor by floor from the basement: a rocket's-eye view of the world. Western Europe sank below him: the Near East: Latin America. The filing cabinets stood around Miss Jenkinson like the pillars of a temple round an ageing oracle. She alone was known by her surname. For some inscrutable reason of security every other inhabitant in the building went by a Christian name. She was dictating to a secretary when Hawthorne entered, "Memo to A.O. Angelica has been transferred to C.5 with an increase of salary to £8 a week. Please see that this increase goes through at once. To anticipate your objections I would point out that Angelica is now approaching the financial level of a bus-conductress."

"Yes?" Miss Jenkinson asked sharply. "Yes?"

"The Chief told me to see you."

"I have nobody to spare."

"We don't want anybody at the moment. We're just discussing possibilities."

"Ethel, dear, telephone to D.2 and say I will not have my secretaries kept after 7 p.m. except in a national emergency. If a war has broken out or is likely to break out, say that the secretaries' pool should have been informed."

"We may be needing a Spanish-speaking secretary in the Caribbean."

"There's no one I can spare," Miss Jenkinson said mechanically.

"Havana—a small station, agreeable climate."

"How big is the staff?"

"At present one man."

"I'm not a marriage bureau," Miss Jenkinson said.

"A middle-aged man with a child of sixteen."

"Married?"

"You could call him that," Hawthorne said vaguely.

"Is he stable?"

"Stable?"

"Reliable, safe, emotionally secure?"

"Oh yes, yes, you may be certain of that. He's one of those old-fashioned merchant-types," Hawthorne said, picking up where the Chief had left off. "Built up the business from nothing. Uninterested in women. You might say he'd gone beyond sex."

"No one goes beyond sex," Miss Jenkinson said. "I'm responsible for the girls I send abroad."

"I thought you had nobody available."

"Well," Miss Jenkinson said, "I might possibly, under certain circumstances, let you have Beatrice."

"Beatrice, Miss Jenkinson!" a voice exclaimed from behind the filing cabinets.

"I said Beatrice, Ethel, and I mean Beatrice."

"But, Miss Jenkinson . . ."

"Beatrice needs some practical experience—that is really all that is amiss. The post would suit her. She is not too young. She is fond of children."

"What this station will need," Hawthorne said, "is someone who speaks Spanish. The love of children is not essential."

"Beatrice is half-French. She speaks French really better than she does English."

"I said Spanish."

"It's much the same. They're both Latin tongues."

"Perhaps I could see her, have a word with her. Is she fully trained?"

"She's a very good encoder and she's finished a course in microphotography at Ashley Park. Her shorthand is weak, but her typewriting is excellent. She has a good knowledge of electro-dynamics."

"What's that?"

"I'm not sure, but a fuse box holds no terrors for her."

"She'd be good with vacuum cleaners then?"

"She's a secretary, not a domestic help."

A file drawer slammed shut. "Take her or leave her," Miss Jenkinson said. Hawthorne had the impression that she would willingly have referred to Beatrice as "it."

"She's the only one you can suggest?"

"The only one."

Again a file drawer was noisily closed. "Ethel," Miss Jenkinson said, "unless you can relieve your feelings more silently, I shall return you to D.3."

Hawthorne went thoughtfully away; he had the impression that Miss Jenkinson with considerable agility had sold him something she didn't herself believe in—a gold brick or a small dog—bitch, rather.

PART TWO

1

i

Wormold came away from the Consulate Department carrying a cable in his breast-pocket. It had been shovelled rudely at him, and when he tried to speak he had been checked. "We don't want to know anything about it. A temporary arrangement. The sooner it's over the better we shall be pleased."

"Mr. Hawthorne said . . ."

"We don't know any Mr. Hawthorne. Please bear that in mind. Nobody of the name is employed here. Good morning."

He walked home. The long city lay spread along the open Atlantic; waves broke over the Avenida de Maceo and misted the windscreens of cars. The pink, grey, yellow pillars of what had once been the aristocratic quarter were eroded like rocks; an ancient coat of arms, smudged and featureless, was set over the doorway of a shabby hotel, and the shutters of a night-club were varnished in bright crude colours to protect them from the wet and salt of the sea. In the west the steel skyscrapers of the new town rose higher than lighthouses into the clear February sky. It was a city to visit, not a city to live in, but it was the city where Wormold had first fallen in love and he was held to it as though to the scene of a disaster. Time gives poetry to a battlefield, and perhaps Milly resembled a little the flower on an old rampart where an attack had been repulsed with heavy loss many years ago. Women passed him in the street marked on the forehead with ashes as though they had come up into the sunlight from underground. He remembered that it was Ash Wednesday.

In spite of the school-holiday Milly was not at home when he reached the house—perhaps she was still at Mass or perhaps she was away riding at the Country Club. Lopez was demonstrating the Turbo Suction Cleaner to a priest's housekeeper who had rejected the Atomic Pile. Wormold's worst fears about the new model had been justified, for he had not succeeded in selling a single specimen. He went upstairs and opened the telegram; it was addressed to a department at the British Consulate, and the figures which followed had an ugly look like the lottery tickets that remained unsold on the last day of a draw. There was 2674 and then a string of five-figure numerals: 42811 79145 72312 59200 80947 62533 10605 and so on.

It was his first telegram and he noticed that it was addressed from London. He was not even certain (so long ago his lesson seemed) that he could decode it, but he recognised a single group, 59200, which had an abrupt and monitory appearance as though Hawthorne that moment had come accusingly up the stairs. Gloomily he took down Lamb's *Tales from Shakespeare*—how he had always detested Elia and the essay on Roast Pork. The first group of figures, he remembered, indicated the page, the line and the word with which the coding began. "Dionysia, the wicked wife of Cleon," he read, "met with an end proportionable to her desserts." He began to decode from "desserts." To his surprise something really did emerge. It was rather as though some strange inherited parrot had begun to speak. "No. 1 of 24th January following from 59200 begin paragraph A."

After working for three-quarters of an hour adding and subtracting, he had decoded the whole message apart from the final paragraph where something had gone wrong either with himself or 59200, or perhaps with Charles Lamb. "Following from 59200 begin paragraph A nearly a month since membership Country Club approved and no repeat no information concerning proposed sub-agents yet received stop trust you are not repeat not recruiting any sub-agents before having them properly traced stop begin paragraph B economic and political report on lines of questionnaire left with you should be despatched forthwith to 59200 stop begin paragraph C cursed galloon must be forwarded kingston primary tubercular message ends."

The last paragraph had an effect of angry incoherence which worried Wormold. For the first time it occurred to him that in their eyes—whoever *they* were—he had taken money and given nothing in return. This troubled him. It had seemed to him till then that he had been the recipient of an eccentric gift which had enabled Milly to ride at the Country Club and himself to order from England a few books he had coveted. The rest of the money was now on deposit in the bank; he half believed that some day he might be in a position to return it to Hawthorne.

He thought: I must do something, give them some names to trace, recruit an agent, keep them happy. He remembered how Milly used to play at shops and give him her pocket money for imaginary purchases. One had to play the child's game but sooner or later Milly always required her money back.

He wondered how one recruited an agent. It was difficult for him to remember exactly how Hawthorne had recruited *him*—except that the whole affair had begun in a lavatory, but surely that was not an essential feature. He decided to begin with a reasonably easy case.

"You called me, Señor Vormell." For some reason the name Wormold was quite beyond Lopez' power of pronunciation, but as he seemed unable to settle on a satisfactory substitute, it was seldom that Wormold went by the same name twice.

"I want to talk to you, Lopez."

"Si, Señor Vomell."

Wormold said, "You've been with me a great many years now. We trust each other."

Lopez expressed the completeness of his trust with a gesture towards the heart.

"How would you like to earn a little more money each month?"

"Why, naturally . . . I was going to speak to you myself, Señor Ommel. I have a child coming. Perhaps twenty pesos?"

"This has nothing to do with the firm. Trade is too bad, Lopez. This will be confidential work, for me personally, you understand."

"Ah yes, señor. Personal services I understand. You can trust me. I am discreet. Of course I will say nothing to the señorita."

"I think perhaps you *don't* understand."

"When a man reaches a certain age," Lopez said, "he no longer wishes to search for a woman himself, he wishes to rest from trouble. He wishes to command, 'Tonight yes, tomorrow night no.' To give his directions to someone he trusts . . ."

"I don't mean anything of the kind. What I was trying to say—well, it had nothing to do . . ."

"You do not need to be embarrassed in speaking to me, Señor Vormole. I have been with you many years."

"You are making a mistake," Wormold said. "I had no intention . . ."

"I understand that for an Englishman in your position places like the San Francisco are unsuitable. Even the Mamba Club."

Wormold knew that nothing he could say would check the eloquence of his assistant, now that he had embarked on the great Havana subject; the sexual exchange was not only the chief commerce of the city, but the whole *raison d'être* of a man's life. One sold sex or one bought it—immaterial which, but it was never given away.

"A youth needs variety," Lopez said, "but so too does a man of a certain age. For the youth it is the curiosity of ignorance, for the old it is the appetite which needs to be refreshed. No one can serve you better than I can, because I have studied you, Señor Venell. You are not a Cuban: for you the shape of a girl's bottom is less important than a certain gentleness of behaviour . . ."

"You have misunderstood me completely," Wormold said.

"The señorita this evening goes to a concert."

"How do you know?"

Lopez ignored the question. "While she is out, I will bring you a young lady to see. If you don't like her, I will bring another."

"You'll do nothing of the sort. Those are not the kind of services I want, Lopez. I want . . . well, I want you to keep your eyes and ears open and report to me . . ."

"On the señorita?"

"Good heavens no."

"Report on what then, Señor Vommold?"

Wormold said, "Well, things like . . ." But he hadn't the faintest idea on what subjects Lopez was capable of reporting. He remembered only a few points in the long questionnaire and none of them seemed suitable, "Possible Communist infiltration in the armed forces. Actual figures of sugar- and tobacco-production last year." Of course there were the contents of waste-paper baskets in the offices where Lopez serviced the cleaners, but surely even Hawthorne was joking when he spoke of the Dreyfus case—if those men ever joked.

"Like what, señor?"

Wormold said, "I'll let you know later. Go back to the shop now."

ii

It was the hour of the daiquiri, and in the Wonder Bar Dr. Hasselbacher was happy with his second Scotch. "You are worrying still, Mr. Wormold?" he said.

"Yes, I am worrying."

"Still the cleaner—the Atomic cleaner?"

"Not the cleaner." He drained his daiquiri and ordered another.

"Today you are drinking very fast."

"Hasselbacher, you've never felt the need of money, have you? But then, you have no child."

"Before long you will have no child either."

"I suppose not." The comfort was as cold as the daiquiri. "When the time comes, Hasselbacher, I want us both to be away from here. I don't want Milly woken up by any Captain Segura."

"That I can understand."

"The other day I was offered money."

"Yes?"

"To get information."

"What sort of information?"

"Secret information."

Dr. Hasselbacher sighed. He said, "You are a lucky man, Mr. Wormold. That information is always easy to give."

"Easy?"

"If it is secret enough, you alone know it. All you need is a little imagination, Mr. Wormold."

"They want me to recruit agents. How does one recruit an agent, Hasselbacher?"

"You could invent them too, Mr. Wormold."

"You sound as though you had experience."

"Medicine is my experience, Mr. Wormold. Have you never read the advertisement for secret remedies? A hair tonic confided by the dying Chief of a Red Indian tribe. With a secret remedy you don't have to print the formula. And there is something about a secret which makes people believe . . . perhaps a relic of magic. Have you read Sir James Frazer?"

"Have you heard of a book-code?"

"Don't tell me too much, Mr. Wormold, all the same. Secrecy is not my business—I have no child. Please don't invent me as your agent."

"No, I can't do that. These people don't like our friendship, Hasselbacher. They want me to stay away from you. They are tracing you. How do you suppose they trace a man?"

"I don't know. Be careful, Mr. Wormold. Take their money, but don't give them anything in return. You are vulnerable to the Seguras. Just lie and keep your freedom. They don't deserve truth."

"Whom do you mean by they?"

"Kingdoms, republics, powers." He drained his glass. "I must go and look at my culture, Mr. Wormold."

"Is anything happening yet?"

"Thank goodness, no. As long as nothing happens anything is possible, you agree? It is a pity that a lottery is ever drawn. I lose a hundred and forty thousand dollars a week, and I am a poor man."

"You won't forget Milly's birthday?"

"Perhaps the traces will be bad, and you will not want me to come. But remember, as long as you lie you do not harm."

"I take their money."

"They have no money except what they take from men like you and me."

He pushed open the half-door and was gone. Dr. Hasselbacher never talked in terms of morality; it was outside the province of a doctor.

iii

Wormold found a list of Country Club members in Milly's room. He knew where to look for it, between the latest volume of the *Horsewoman's Year Book* and a novel called *White Mare* by Miss "Pony' Traggers. He had joined the Country Club to find suitable agents, and here they all were in double column, over twenty pages of them. His eye caught an Anglo-Saxon name—Vincent C. Parkman; perhaps this was Earl's father. It seemed to Wormold that it was only right to keep the Parkmans in the family.

By the time he sat down to encode he had chosen two other names—an Engineer Cifuentes and a Professor Luis Sanchez. The professor, whoever he was, seemed a reasonable candidate for economic intelligence, the engineer could provide technical information, and Mr. Parkman political. With the *Tales from Shakespeare* open before him (he had chosen for his key passage—"May that which follows be happy") he encoded "Number 1 of 25th January paragraph A begins I have recruited my assistant and assigned him the symbol 59200/5/1 stop proposed payment fifteen pesos a month stop paragraph B begins please trace the following . . ."

All this paragraphing seemed to Wormold extravagant of time and money, but Hawthorne had told him it was part of the drill, just as Milly had insisted that all purchases from her shop should be wrapped in paper, even a single glass bead. "Paragraph C begins economic report as requested will follow shortly by bag."

There was nothing to do now but wait for the replies and to prepare the economic report. This troubled him. He had sent Lopez out to buy all the Government papers he could obtain on the sugar and tobacco industries—it was Lopez' first mission, and each day now he spent hours reading the local papers in order to mark any passage which could suitably be used by the professor or the engineer; it was unlikely that anyone in Kingston or London studied the daily papers of Havana.

Even he found a new world in those badly printed pages; perhaps in the past he had depended too much on the *New York Times* or *Herald Tribune* for his picture of the world. Round the corner from the Wonder Bar a girl had been stabbed to death; "a martyr for love." Havana was full of martyrs of one kind or another. A man lost a fortune in one night at the Tropicana, climbed on the stage, embraced a coloured singer, then ran his car into the harbour and was drowned. Another man elaborately strangled himself with a pair of braces. There were miracles too; a virgin wept salt tears and a candle lit before Our Lady of Guadalupe burnt inexplicably for one week, from a Friday to a Friday. From this picture of violence and passion and love the victims of Captain Segura were alone excluded—they suffered and died without benefit of Press.

The economic report proved to be a tedious chore, for Wormold had never learnt to type with more than two fingers or to use the tabulator on his machine. It was necessary to alter the official statistics in case someone in the head office thought to compare the two reports, and sometimes Wormold forgot he had altered a figure. Addition and subtraction were never his strong points. A decimal point got shifted and had to be chased up and down a dozen columns. It was rather like steering a miniature car in a slot machine.

After a week he began to worry about the absence of replies. Had Hawthorne smelt a rat? But he was temporarily encouraged by a summons to the Consulate, where the sour clerk handed him a sealed envelope addressed for no reason he could understand to "Mr. Luke Penny." Inside the outer envelope was another envelope marked "Henry Leadbetter. Civilian Research Services"; a third envelope was inscribed 59200/5 and contained three months' wages and expenses in Cuban notes. He took them to the bank in Obispo.

"Office account, Mr. Wormold?"

"No. Personal." But he had a sense of guilt as the teller counted; he felt as though he had embezzled the company's money.

2

i

T en days passed and no word reached him. He couldn't even send his economic report until the notional agent who supplied it had been traced and approved. The time arrived for his annual visit to retailers outside Havana, at Matanzas, Cienfuegos, Santa Clara and Santiago. Those towns he was in the habit of visiting by road in his ancient Hillman. Before leaving he sent a cable to Hawthorne. "On pretext of visiting sub-agents for vacuums propose to investigate possibilities for recruitment port of Matanzas, industrial centre Santa Clara, naval headquarters Cienfuegos and dissident centre Santiago calculate expenses of journey fifty dollars a day.'' He kissed Milly, made her promise to take no lifts in his absence from Captain Segura, and rattled off for a stirrup-cup in the Wonder Bar with Dr. Hasselbacher.

ii

Once a year, and always on his tour, Wormold wrote to his younger sister who lived in Northampton. (Perhaps writing to Mary momentarily healed the loneliness he felt at being away from Milly.) Invariably too he included the latest Cuban postage stamps for his nephew. The boy had begun to collect at the age of six and somehow, with the quick jog-trot of time, it slipped Wormold's memory that his nephew was now long past seventeen and had probably given up his collection years ago. In any case he must have been too old for the kind of note Wormold folded around the stamps; it was too juvenile even for Milly, and his nephew was her senior by several years.

"Dear Mark," Wormold wrote, "here are some stamps for your collection. It must be quite a big collection by now. I'm afraid these ones are not very interesting. I wish we had birds or beasts or butterflies in Cuba like the nice ones you showed me from Guatemala. Your affectionate uncle. P.S. I am sitting looking at the sea and it is very hot.''

To his sister he wrote more explicitly, "I am sitting by the bay in Cienfuegos and the temperature is over ninety, though the sun has been down for an hour. They are showing Marilyn Monroe at the cinema, and there is one boat in the harbour called, oddly enough, the *Juan Belmonte*. (Do you remember that winter in Madrid when we went to the bullfight?) The Chief—I think he's the Chief—is sitting at the next table drinking Spanish brandy. There's nothing else for him to do except go to the cinema. This must be one of the quietest ports in the world. Just the pink and yellow street and a few cantinas and the big chimney of a sugar refinery and at the end of a weed-grown path the *Juan Belmonte*. Somehow I wish I could be sailing in it with Milly, but I don't know. Vacuum cleaners are not selling well—electric current is too uncertain in these troubled days. Last night at Matanzas the lights all went out three times—the first time I was in my bath. These are silly things to write all the way to Northampton.

"Don't think I am unhappy. There is a lot to be said for where we are. Sometimes I fear going home to Boots and Woolworths and cafeterias, and I'd be a stranger now even in the White Horse. The Chief has got a girl with him—I expect he has a girl in Matanzas too: he's pouring brandy down her throat as you give a cat medicine. The light here is wonderful just before the sun goes down: a long trickle of gold and the seabirds are dark patches on the pewter swell. The big white statue in the Paseo which looks in daylight like Queen Victoria is a lump of ectoplasm now. The bootblacks have all packed up their boxes under the arm-chairs in the pink colonnade: you sit high above the pavement as though on library-steps and rest your feet on the back of two little sea-horses in bronze that might have been brought here by a Phoenician. Why am I so nostalgic? I suppose because I have a little money tucked away and soon I must decide to go away forever. I wonder if Milly will be able to settle down in a secretarial-training college in a grey street in north London.

"How is Aunt Alice and the famous wax in her ears? And how is Uncle Edward? or is he dead? I've reached the time of life when relatives die unnoticed."

He paid his bill and asked for the name of the Chief Engineer—it had struck him that he must have a few names checked when he got home, to justify his expenses.

iii

In Santa Clara his old Hillman lay down beneath him like a tired mule. Something was seriously wrong with its innards; only Milly would have known what. The man at the garage said that the repairs would take several days, and Wormold decided to go on to Santiago by coach. Perhaps in any case it was quicker and safer that way, for in the Oriente Province, where the usual rebels held the mountains and Government troops the roads and cities, blocks were frequent and buses were less liable to delay than private cars.

He arrived at Santiago in the evening, the empty dangerous hours of the unofficial curfew. All the shops in the piazza built against the Cathedral façade were closed. A single couple hurried across in front of the hotel; the night was hot and humid, and the greenery hung dark and heavy in the pallid light of half-strength lamps. In the reception office they greeted him with suspicion as though they assumed him to be a spy of one kind or another. He felt like an impostor, for this was a hotel of real spies, real police-informers and real rebel agents. A drunk man talked endlessly in the drab bar, as though he were saying in the style of Gertrude Stein "Cuba is Cuba is Cuba."

Wormold had for his dinner a dry flat omelette, stained and dog-eared like an old manuscript, and drank some sour wine. While he ate he wrote on a picture-postcard a few lines to Dr. Hasselbacher. Whenever he left Havana he despatched to Milly and Dr. Hasselbacher and sometimes even to Lopez bad pictures of bad hotels with a cross against one window like the cross in a detective story which indicates where the crime has been committed. "Car broken down. Everything very quiet. Hope to be back Thursday." A picture-postcard is a symptom of loneliness.

At nine o'clock Wormold set out to find his retailer. He had forgotten how abandoned the streets of Santiago were after dark. Shutters were closed behind the iron grills, and as in an occupied city the houses turned their backs on the passer-by. A cinema cast a little light, but no customer went in; by law it had to remain open, but no one except a soldier or a policeman was likely to visit it after dark. Down a side-street Wormold saw a military patrol go by.

Wormold sat with the retailer in a small hot room. An open door gave on to a patio, a palm tree and a well-head of wrought iron, but the air outside was as hot as the air within. They sat opposite each other in rocking-chairs, rocking towards each other and rocking away, making little currents of air.

Trade was bad—rock rock—nobody was buying electrical goods in Santiago—rock rock—what was the good? rock rock. As though to illustrate the point the electric light went out and they rocked in darkness. Losing the rhythm their heads came into gentle collision.

"I'm sorry."

"My fault."

Rock rock rock.

Somebody scraped a chair in the patio.

"Your wife?" asked Wormold.

"No. Nobody at all. We are quite alone."

Wormold rocked forward, rocked back, rocked forward again, listening to the furtive movements in the patio.

"Of course." This was Santiago. Any house might contain a man on the run. It was best to hear nothing, and to see nothing was no problem, even when the light came half-heartedly back with a tiny yellow glow on the filament.

On his way to the hotel he was stopped by two policemen. They wanted to know what he was doing out so late.

"It's only ten o'clock," he said.

"What are you doing in this street at ten o'clock?"

"There's no curfew, is there?"

Suddenly, without warning, one of the policemen slapped his face. He felt shock rather than anger. He belonged to the law-abiding class; the police were his natural protectors. He put his hand to his cheek and said, "What in God's name do you think . . . ?" The other policeman with a blow in the back sent him stumbling along the pavement. His hat fell off into the filth of the gutter. He said, "Give me my hat," and felt himself pushed again. He began to say something about the British Consul and they swung him sideways across the road and sent him reeling. This time he landed inside a doorway in front of a desk where a man slept with his head on his arms. He woke up and shouted at Wormold—his mildest expression was "pig."

Wormold said, "I am a British subject, my name is Wormold, my address Havana—Lamparilla 37. My age forty-five, divorced, and I want to ring up the Consul."

The man who had called him a pig and who carried on his arm the chevron of a sergeant told him to show his passport.

"I can't. It's in my brief-case at the hotel."

One of his captors said with satisfaction, "Found on the street without papers."

"Empty his pockets," the sergeant said. They took out his wallet and the picture-postcard to Dr. Hasselbacher, which he had forgotten to post, and a miniature whisky bottle, Old Granddad, that he had bought in the hotel-bar. The sergeant studied the bottle and the postcard.

He said, "Why do you carry this bottle? What does it contain?"

"What do you suppose?"

"The rebels make grenades out of bottles."

"Surely not such small bottles." The sergeant drew the cork, sniffed and poured a little on the palm of his hand. "It appears to be whisky," he said and turned to the postcard. He said, "Why have you made a cross on this picture?"

"It's the window of my room."

"Why show the window of your room?"

"Why shouldn't I? It's just—well, it's one of the things one does when travelling."

"Were you expecting a visitor by the window?"

"Of course not."

"Who is Dr. Hasselbacher?"

"An old friend."

"Is he coming to Santiago?"

"No."

"Then why do you want to show him where your room is?"

He began to realise what the criminal class knows so well, the impossibility of explaining anything to a man with power.

He said flippantly, "Dr. Hasselbacher is a woman."

"A woman doctor!" The sergeant exclaimed with disapproval.

"A doctor of philosophy. A very beautiful woman." He made two curves in the air.

"And she is joining you in Santiago?"

"No, no. But you know how it is with a woman, Sergeant? They like to know where their man is sleeping."

"You are her lover?" The atmosphere had changed for the better. "That still does not explain your wandering about the streets at night."

"There's no law . . ."

"No law, but prudent people stay at home. Only mischief-makers go out."

"I couldn't sleep for thinking of Emma."

"Who is Emma?"

"Dr. Hasselbacher."

The sergeant said slowly, "There is something wrong here. I can smell it. You are not telling me the truth. If you are in love with Emma, why are you in Santiago?"

"Her husband suspects."

"She has a husband? *No es muy agradable*. Are you a Catholic?"

"No."

The sergeant picked up the postcard and studied it again. "The cross at a bedroom window—that is not very nice, either. How will she explain that to her husband?''

Wormold thought rapidly. "Her husband is blind.''

"And that too is not nice. Not nice at all.''

"Shall I hit him again?'' one of the policemen asked.

"There is no hurry. I must interrogate him first. How long have you known this woman, Emma Hasselbacher?''

"A week.''

"A week? Nothing that you say is nice. You are a Protestant and an adulterer. When did you meet this woman?''

"I was introduced by Captain Segura.''

The sergeant held the postcard suspended in mid-air. Wormold heard one of the policemen behind him swallow. Nobody said anything for a long while.

"Captain Segura?''

"Yes.''

"You know Captain Segura?''

"He is a friend of my daughter.''

"So you have a daughter. You are married.'' He began to say again, "That is not n . . .'' when one of the policemen interrupted him, "He knows Captain Segura.''

"How can I tell that you are speaking the truth?''

"You could telephone to him and find out.''

"It would take several hours to reach Havana on the telephone.''

"I can't leave Santiago at night. I will wait for you at the hotel.''

"Or in a cell at the station here.''

"I don't think Captain Segura would be pleased.''

The sergeant considered the matter for a long time, going through the contents of the wallet while he thought. Then he told one of the men to accompany Wormold back to the hotel and there to examine his passport (in this way the sergeant obviously thought that he was saving face). The two walked back in an embarrassed silence, and it was only when Wormold had lain down that he remembered the postcard to Dr. Hasselbacher was still on the sergeant's desk. It seemed to him to have no importance; he could always send another in the morning. How long it takes to realise in one's life the intricate patterns of which everything—even a picture-postcard—can form a part, and the rashness of dismissing anything as unimportant. Three days later Wormold took the bus back to Santa Clara; his Hillman was ready; the road to Havana offered him no problems.

3

great many telegrams were waiting for him when he arrived in Havana in the late afternoon. There was also a note from Milly. "What have you been up to? You-know-who" (but he didn't) "very pressing—not in any bad way. Dr. Hasselbacher wants to speak to you urgently. Love. P.S. Riding at Country Club. Seraphina's picture taken by press photographer. Is this fame? Go, bid the soldiers shoot."

Dr. Hasselbacher could wait. Two of the telegrams were marked urgent.

"No. 2 of March 5 paragraph A begins trace of Hasselbacher ambiguous stop use utmost caution in any contact and keep these to minimum message ends."

Vincent C. Parkman was rejected as an agent out of hand. "You are not repeat not to contact him stop probability that he is already employed by American service."

The next telegram—No. 1 of March 4—read coldly, "Please in future as instructed confine each telegram to one subject."

No. 1 of March 5 was more encouraging, "No traces Professor Sanchez and Engineer Cifuentes stop you may recruit them stop presumably men of their standing will require no more than out-of-pocket expenses."

The last telegram was rather an anti-climax. "Following from A.O. recruitment of 59200/5/1"—that was Lopez—"recorded but please note proposed payment below recognised European scale and you should revise to 25 repeat 25 pesos monthly message ends."

Lopez was shouting up the stairs, "It is Dr. Hasselbacher."

"Tell him I'm busy. I'll call him later."

"He says will you come quick. He sounds strange."

Wormold went down to the telephone. Before he could speak he heard an agitated and an old voice. It had never occurred to him before that Dr. Hasselbacher was old. "Please, Mr. Wormold . . ."

"Yes. What is it?"

"Please come to me. Something has happened."

"Where are you?"

"In my apartment."

"What's wrong, Hasselbacher?"

"I can't tell you over the telephone."

"Are you sick . . . hurt?"

"If only that were all," Hasselbacher said. "Please come." In all the years they had known each other, Wormold had never visited Hasselbacher's home. They had met at the Wonder Bar, and on Milly's birthdays in a restaurant, and once Dr. Hasselbacher had visited him in Lamparilla when he had a high fever. There had been an occasion too when he had wept in front of Hasselbacher, sitting on a seat in the Paseo telling him that Milly's mother had flown away on the morning plane to Miami, but their friendship was safely founded on distance—it was always the closest friendships that were most liable to break. Now he even had to ask Hasselbacher how to find his home.

"You don't know?" Hasselbacher asked in bewilderment.

"No."

"Please come quickly," Hasselbacher said, "I do not wish to be alone."

But speed was impossible at this evening hour. Obispo was a solid block of traffic, and it was half an hour before Wormold reached the undistinguished block in which Hasselbacher lived, twelve storeys high of livid stone. Twenty years ago it had been modern, but the new steel architecture to the West outsoared and outshone it. It belonged to the age of tubular chairs, and a tubular chair was what Wormold saw first when Dr. Hasselbacher let him in. That and an old colour print of some castle on the Rhine.

Dr. Hasselbacher like his voice had grown suddenly old. It was not a question of colour. That seamed and sanguine skin could change no more than a tortoise's and nothing could bleach his hair whiter than the years had already done. It was the expression which had altered. A whole mood of life had suffered violence: Dr. Hasselbacher was no longer an optimist. He said humbly, "It is good of you to come, Mr. Wormold." Wormold remembered the day when the old man had led him away from the Paseo and filled him with drink in the Wonder Bar, talking all the time, cauterising the pain with alcohol and laughter and irresistible hope. He asked, "What has happened, Hasselbacher?"

"Come inside," Hasselbacher said.

The sitting-room was in confusion; it was as though a malevolent child had been at work among the tubular chairs, opening this, upsetting that, smashing and sparing at the dictate of some irrational impulse. A photograph of a group of young men holding beer mugs had been taken from the frame and torn apart; a coloured reproduction of the Laughing Cavalier hung still on the wall over the sofa where one cushion out of three had been ripped open. The contents of a cupboard—old letters and bills—were scattered over the floor and a strand of very fair hair tied with black ribbon lay like a washed-up fish among the débris.

"Why?" Wormold asked.

"This does not matter so much," Hasselbacher said, "but come here."

A small room, which had been converted into a laboratory, was now reconverted into chaos. A gas-jet burnt yet among the ruins. Dr. Hasselbacher turned it off. He held up a test tube; the contents were smeared over the sink. He said, "You won't understand. I was trying to make a culture from—never mind. I knew nothing would come of it. It was a dream only." He sat heavily down on a tall tubular adjustable chair, which shortened suddenly under his weight and spilt him on the floor. Somebody always leaves a banana-skin on the scene of a tragedy. Hasselbacher got up and dusted his trousers.

"When did it happen?"

"Somebody telephoned to me—a sick call. I felt there was something wrong, but I had to go. I could not risk not going. When I came back there was *this*."

"Who did it?"

"I don't know. A week ago somebody called on me. A stranger. He wanted me to help him. It was not a doctor's job. I said no. He asked me whether my sympathies were with the East or the West. I tried to joke with him. I said they were in the middle." Dr. Hasselbacher said accusingly, "Once a few weeks ago you asked me the same question."

"I was only joking, Hasselbacher."

"I know. Forgive me. The worst thing they do is making all this suspicion." He stared into the sink. "An infantile dream. Of course I know that. Fleming discovered penicillin by an inspired accident. But an accident has to be inspired. An old second-rate doctor would never have an accident like that, but it was no business of theirs—was it?—if I wanted to dream."

"I don't understand. What's behind it? Something political? What nationality was this man?"

"He spoke English like I do, with an accent. Nowadays, all the world over, people speak with accents."

"Have you rung up the police?"

"For all I know," Dr. Hasselbacher said, "he *was* the police."

"Have they taken anything?"

"Yes. Some papers."

"Important?"

"I should never have kept them. They were more than thirty years old. When one is young one gets involved. No one's life is quite clean, Mr. Wormold. But I thought the past was the past. I was too optimistic. You and I are not like the people here—we have no confessional box where we can bury the bad past."

"You must have some idea . . . What will they do next?"

"Put me on a card-index perhaps," Dr. Hasselbacher said. "They have to make themselves important. Perhaps on the card I will be promoted to atomic scientist."

"Can't you start your experiment again?"

"Oh yes. Yes, I suppose so. But, you see, I never believed in it and now it has gone down the drain." He let a tap run to clear the sink. "I would only remember all this—dirt. That was a dream, this is reality." Something that looked like a fragment of toadstool stuck in the exit-pipe. He poked it down with his finger. "Thank you for coming, Mr. Wormold. You are a real friend."

"There is so little I can do."

"You let me talk. I am better already. Only I have this fear because of the papers. Perhaps it was an accident that they have gone. Perhaps I have overlooked them in all this mess."

"Let me help you search."

"No, Mr. Wormold. I wouldn't want you to see something of which I am ashamed."

They had two drinks together in the ruins of the sitting-room and then Wormold left. Dr. Hasselbacher was on his knees under the Laughing Cavalier, sweeping below the sofa. Shut in his car Wormold felt guilt nibbling around him like a mouse in a prison-cell. Perhaps soon the two of them would grow accustomed to each other and guilt would come to eat out of his hand. People similar to himself had done this, men who allowed themselves to be recruited while sitting in lavatories, who opened hotel doors with other men's keys and received instructions in secret ink and in novel uses for Lamb's *Tales from Shakespeare*. There was always another side to a joke, the side of the victim.

The bells were ringing in Santo Christo, and the doves rose from the roof in the golden evening and circled away over the lottery shops of O'Reilley Street and the banks of Obispo; little boys and girls, almost as indistinguishable in sex as birds streamed out from the School of the Holy Innocents in their black and white uniforms, carrying their little black satchels. Their age divided them from the adult world of 59200 and their credulity was of a different quality. He thought with tenderness, Milly will be home soon. He was glad that she could still accept fairy stories: a virgin who bore a child, pictures that wept or spoke words of love in the dark. Hawthorne and his kind were equally credulous, but what they swallowed were nightmares, grotesque stories out of science fiction.

What was the good of playing a game with half a heart? At least let him give them something they would enjoy for their money, something to put on their files better than an economic report. He wrote a rapid draft, "Number 1 of March 8 paragraph A begins in my recent trip to Santiago I heard reports from several sources of big military installations under construction in mountains of Oriente Province stop these constructions too extensive to be aimed at small rebel bands holding out there stop stories of widespread forest clearance under cover of forest fires stop peasants from several villages impressed to carry loads of stone paragraph B begins in bar of Santiago hotel met Spanish pilot of Cubana air line in advanced stage drunkenness stop he spoke of observing on flight Havana-Santiago large concrete platform too extensive for any building paragraph C 59200/5/3 who accompanied me to Santiago undertook dangerous mission near military H.Q. at Bayamo and made drawings of strange machinery in transport to forest stop these drawings will follow by bag paragraph D have I your permission to pay him bonus in view of serious risks of his mission and to suspend work for a time on economic report in view disquieting and vital nature of these reports from Oriente paragraph E have you any traces Raul Dominguez Cubana pilot whom I propose to recruit as 59200/5/4."

Wormold joyfully encoded. He thought, I never believed I had it in me. He thought with pride, 59200/5 knows his job. His good humour even embraced Charles Lamb. He chose for his passage page 217, line 12: "But I will draw the curtain and show the picture. Is it not well done?"

Wormold called Lopez from the shop. He handed him twenty-five pesos. He said, "This is your first month's pay in advance." He knew Lopez too well to expect any gratitude for the extra five pesos, but all the same he was a little taken aback when Lopez said, "Thirty pesos would be a living wage."

"What do you mean, a living wage? The agency pays you very well as it is."

"This will mean a great deal of work," Lopez said.

"It will, will it? What work?"

"Personal service."

"What personal service?"

"It must obviously be a great deal of work or you wouldn't pay me twenty-five pesos." He had never been able to get the better of Lopez in a financial argument.

"I want you to bring me an Atomic Pile from the shop," Wormold said.

"We have only one in the store."

"I want it up here."

Lopez sighed. "Is that a personal service?"

"Yes."

When he was alone Wormold unscrewed the cleaner into its various parts. Then he sat down at his desk and began to make a series of careful drawings. As he sat back and contemplated his sketches of the sprayer detached from the hose-handle of the cleaner, the needle-jet, the nozzle and the telescopic tube, he wondered: Am I perhaps going too far? He realised that he had forgotten to indicate the scale. He ruled a line and numbered it off: one inch representing three feet. Then for better measure he drew a little man two inches high below the nozzle. He dressed him neatly in a dark suit, and gave him a bowler hat and an umbrella.

When Milly came home that evening he was still busy, writing his first report with a large map of Cuba spread over his desk.

"What are you doing, Father?"

"I am taking the first step in a new career."

She looked over his shoulder. "Are you becoming a writer?"

"Yes, an imaginative writer."

"Will that earn you a lot of money?"

"A moderate income, Milly, if I set my mind to it and write regularly. I plan to compose an essay like this every Saturday evening."

"Will you be famous?"

"I doubt it. Unlike most writers I shall give all the credit to my ghosts."

"Ghosts?"

"That's what they call those who do the real work while the author takes the pay. In my case I shall do the real work and it will be the ghosts who take the credit."

"But you'll have the pay?"

"Oh yes."

"Then can I buy a pair of spurs?"

"Certainly."

"Are you feeling all right, Father?"

"I never felt better. What a great sense of release you must have experienced when you set fire to Thomas Earl Parkman, junior."

"Why do you go on bringing that up, Father? It was years ago."

"Because I admire you for it. Can't you do it again?"

"Of course not. I'm too old. Besides, there are no boys in the senior school. Father, one other thing. Could I buy a hunting flask?"

"Anything you like. Oh, wait. What are you going to put in it?"

"Lemonade."

"Be a good girl and fetch me a new sheet of paper. Engineer Cifuentes is a man of many words."

Interlude in London

"Had a good flight?" the Chief asked.

"A bit bumpy over the Azores," Hawthorne said. On this occasion he had not had time to change from his pale grey tropical suit; the summons had come to him urgently in Kingston and a car had met him at London Airport. He sat as close to the steam radiator as he could, but sometimes he couldn't help a shiver.

"What's that odd flower you're wearing?"

Hawthorne had quite forgotten it. He put his hand up to his lapel.

"It looks as though it had once been an orchid," the Chief said with disapproval.

"Pan American gave it us with our dinner last night," Hawthorne explained. He took out the limp mauve rag and put it in the ash-tray.

"With your dinner? What an odd thing to do," the Chief said. "It can hardly have improved the meal. Personally I detest orchids. Decadent things. There was someone, wasn't there, who wore green ones?"

"I only put it in my button-hole so as to clear the dinner-tray. There was so little room what with the hot cakes and champagne and the sweet salad and the tomato soup and the chicken Maryland and ice-cream . . ."

"What a terrible mixture. You should travel B.O.A.C."

"You didn't give me enough time, sir, to get a booking."

"Well, the matter is rather urgent. You know our man in Havana has been turning out some pretty disquieting stuff lately."

"He's a good man," Hawthorne said.

"I don't deny it. I wish we had more like him. What I can't understand is how the Americans have not tumbled to anything there."

"Have you asked them, sir?"

"Of course not. I don't trust their discretion."

"Perhaps they don't trust ours."

The Chief said, "Those drawings—did you examine them?"

"I'm not very knowledgeable that way, sir. I sent them straight on."

"Well, take a good look at them now."

The Chief spread the drawings over his desk. Hawthorne reluctantly left the radiator and was immediately shaken by a shiver.

"Anything the matter?"

"The temperature was ninety-two yesterday in Kingston."

"Your blood's getting thin. A spell of cold will do you good. What do you think of them?"

Hawthorne stared at the drawings. They reminded him of—something. He was touched, he didn't know why, by an odd uneasiness.

"You remember the reports that came with them," the Chief said. "The source was stroke three. Who is he?"

"I think that would be Engineer Cifuentes, sir."

"Well, even he was mystified. With all his technical knowledge. These machines were being transported by lorry from the army-headquarters at Bayamo to the edge of the forest. Then mules took over. General direction those unexplained concrete platforms.''

"What does the Air Ministry say, sir?''

"They are worried, very worried. Interested too, of course.''

"What about the atomic research people?''

"We haven't shown them the drawings yet. You know what those fellows are like. They'll criticise points of detail, say the whole thing is unreliable, that the tube is out of proportion or points the wrong way. You can't expect an agent working from memory to get every detail right. I want photographs, Hawthorne.''

"That's asking a lot, sir.''

"We have got to have them. At any risk. Do you know what Savage said to me? I can tell you, it gave me a very nasty nightmare. He said that one of the drawings reminded him of a giant vacuum cleaner.''

"A vacuum cleaner!'' Hawthorne bent down and examined the drawings again, and the cold struck him once more.

"Makes you shiver, doesn't it?''

"But that's impossible, sir.'' He felt as though he were pleading for his own career, "It couldn't be a vacuum cleaner, sir. Not a vacuum cleaner.''

"Fiendish, isn't it?'' the Chief said. "The ingenuity, the simplicity, the devilish imagination of the thing.'' He removed his black monocle and his baby-blue eye caught the light and made it jig on the wall over the radiator. "See this one here six times the height of a man. Like a gigantic spray. And this—what does this remind you of?''

Hawthorne said unhappily, "A two-way nozzle.''

"What's a two-way nozzle?''

"You sometimes find them with a vacuum cleaner.''

"Vacuum cleaner again. Hawthorne, I believe we may be on to something so big that the H-bomb will become a conventional weapon.''

"Is that desirable, sir?''

"Of course it's desirable. Nobody worries about conventional weapons.''

"What have you in mind, sir?''

"I'm no scientist,'' the Chief said, "but look at this great tank. It must stand nearly as high as the forest-trees. A huge gaping mouth at the top, and this pipe-line—the man's only indicated it. For all we know, it may extend for miles—from the mountains to the sea perhaps. You know the Russians are said to be working on some idea—something to do with the power of the sun, sea-evaporation. I don't know what it's all about, but I do know this thing is Big. Tell our man we must have photographs.''

"I don't quite see how he can get near enough . . .''

"Let him charter a plane and lose his way over the area. Not himself personally, of course, but stroke three or stroke two. Who is stroke two?''

"Professor Sanchez, sir. But he'd be shot down. They have air-force planes patrolling all that section.''

"They have, have they?''

"To spot for rebels."

"So they say. Do you know, I've got a hunch, Hawthorne."

"Yes, sir?"

"That the rebels don't exist. They're purely notional. It gives the Government all the excuse it needs to shut down a censorship over the area."

"I hope you are right, sir."

"It would be better for all of us," the Chief said with exhilaration, "if I were wrong. I fear these things, I fear them, Hawthorne." He put back his monocle and the light left the wall. "Hawthorne, when you were here last did you speak to Miss Jenkinson about a secretary for 59200 stroke 5?"

"Yes, sir. She had no obvious candidate, but she thought a girl called Beatrice would do."

"Beatrice? How I hate all these Christian names. Fully trained?"

"Yes."

"The time has come to give our man in Havana some help. This is altogether too big for an untrained agent with no assistance. Better send a radio-operator with her."

"Wouldn't it be a good thing if I went over first and saw him? I could take a look at things and have a talk with him."

"Bad security, Hawthorne. We can't risk blowing him now. With a radio he can communicate direct with London. I don't like this tie-up with the Consulate, nor do they."

"What about his reports, sir?"

"He'll have to organise some kind of courier-service to Kingston. One of his travelling salesmen. Send out instructions with the secretary. Have you seen her?"

"No, sir."

"See her at once. Make sure she's the right type. Capable of taking charge on the technical side. You'll have to put her *au fait* with his establishment. His old secretary will have to go. Speak to the A.O. about a reasonable pension until her natural date for retirement."

"Yes, sir," Hawthorne said. "Could I take one more look at those drawings?"

"That one seems to interest you. What's your idea of it?"

"It looks," Hawthorne said miserably, "like a snap-action coupling."

When he was at the door the Chief spoke again. "You know, Hawthorne, we owe a great deal of this to you. I was told once that you were no judge of men, but I backed my private judgment. Well done, Hawthorne."

"Thank you, sir." He had his hand on the door-knob.

"Hawthorne."

"Yes, sir?"

"Did you find that penny note-book?"

"No, sir."

"Perhaps Beatrice will."

PART THREE

1

It was not a night Wormold was ever likely to forget. He had chosen on Milly's seventeenth birthday to take her to the Tropicana. It was a more innocent establishment than the Nacional in spite of the roulette-rooms, through which visitors passed before they reached the cabaret. Stage and dance-floor were open to the sky. Chorus-girls paraded twenty feet up among the great palm-trees, while pink and mauve searchlights swept the floor. A man in bright blue evening clothes sang in Anglo-American about Paree. Then the piano was wheeled away into the undergrowth, and the dancers stepped down like awkward birds from among the branches.

"It's like the Forest of Arden," Milly said ecstatically. The duenna wasn't there: she had left after the first glass of champagne.

"I don't think there were palms in the Forest of Arden. Or dancing girls."

"You are so literal, Father."

"You like Shakespeare?" Dr. Hasselbacher asked.

"Oh, not Shakespeare—there's far too much poetry. You know the kind of thing—Enter a messenger. 'My Lord the Duke advances on the right.' 'Thus make we with glad heart towards the fight.' "

"Is that Shakespeare?"

"It's like Shakespeare."

"What nonsense you talk, Milly."

"All the same the Forest of Arden is Shakespeare too, I think," Dr. Hasselbacher said.

"Yes, but I only read him in Lamb's *Tales from Shakespeare*. He cuts out all the messengers and the sub-Dukes and the poetry."

"They give you that at school?"

"Oh no, I found a copy in Father's room."

"You read Shakespeare in that form, Mr. Wormold?" Dr. Hasselbacher asked with some surprise.

"Oh no, no. Of course not. I really bought it for Milly."

"Then why were you so cross the other day when I borrowed it?"

"I wasn't cross. It was just that I don't like you poking about . . . among things that don't concern you."

"You talk as though I were a spy," Milly said.

"Dear Milly, please don't quarrel on your birthday. You are neglecting Dr. Hasselbacher."

"Why are you so silent, Dr. Hasselbacher?" Milly asked, pouring out her second glass of champagne.

"One day you must lend me Lamb's *Tales*, Milly. I too find Shakespeare difficult."

A very small man in a very tight uniform waved his hand towards their table.

"You aren't worried are you, Dr. Hasselbacher?"

"What should I be worried about, dear Milly, on your birthday? Except about the years of course."

"Is seventeen so old?"

"For me they have gone too quickly."

The man in the tight uniform stood by their table and bowed. His face had been pocked and eroded like the pillars on the sea-front. He carried a chair which was almost as big as himself.

"This is Captain Segura, Father."

"May I sit down?" He inserted himself between Milly and Dr. Hasselbacher without waiting for Wormold's reply. He said, "I am so glad to meet Milly's father." He had an easy rapid insolence you had no time to resent before he had given fresh cause for annoyance. "Introduce me to your friend, Milly."

"This is Dr. Hasselbacher."

Captain Segura ignored Dr. Hasselbacher and filled Milly's glass. He called a waiter. "Bring me another bottle."

"We are just going, Captain Segura," Wormold said.

"Nonsense. You are my guest. It is only just after midnight."

Wormold's sleeve caught a glass. It fell and smashed, like the birthday party. "Waiter, another glass." Segura began to sing softly, "The rose I plucked in the garden," leaning towards Milly, turning his back on Dr. Hasselbacher.

Milly said, "You are behaving very badly."

"Badly? To you?"

"To all of us. This is my seventeenth birthday party, and it's my father's party—not yours."

"Your seventeenth birthday? Then you must certainly be my guests. I'll invite some of the dancers to our table."

"We don't want any dancers," Milly said.

"I am in disgrace?"

"Yes."

"Ah," he said with pleasure, "it was because today I was not outside the school to pick you up. But, Milly, sometimes I have to put police-work first. Waiter, tell the conductor to play 'Happy Birthday to You.' "

"Do no such thing," Milly said. "How can you be so—so vulgar?"

"Me? Vulgar?" Captain Segura laughed happily. "She is such a little jester," he said to Wormold. "I like to joke too. That is why we get on so well together."

"She tells me you have a cigarette-case made out of human skin."

"How she teases me about that. I tell her that her skin would make a lovely . . ."

Dr. Hasselbacher got up abruptly. He said, "I am going to watch the roulette."

"He doesn't like me?" Captain Segura asked. "Perhaps he is an old admirer, Milly? A very old admirer, ha ha!"

"He's an old friend," Wormold said.

"But you and I, Mr. Wormold, know that there is no such thing as friendship between a man and a woman."

"Milly is not yet a woman."

"You speak like a father, Mr. Wormold. No father knows his daughter."

Wormold looked at the champagne bottle and at Captain Segura's head. He was sorely tempted to bring them together. At a table immediately behind the Captain, a young woman whom he had never seen before gave Wormold a grave encouraging nod. He touched the champagne bottle and she nodded again. She must, he thought, be as clever as she was pretty to have read his thoughts so accurately. He was envious of her companions, two pilots from K.L.M. and an air-hostess.

"Come and dance, Milly," Captain Segura said, "and show that I am forgiven."

"I don't want to dance."

"Tomorrow I swear I will be waiting at the convent-gates."

Wormold made a little gesture as much as to say, "I haven't the nerve. Help me." The girl watched him seriously; it seemed to him that she was considering the whole of the situation and any decision she reached would be final and call for immediate action. She siphoned some soda into her whisky.

"Come, Milly. You must not spoil my party."

"It's not your party. It's Father's."

"You stay angry so long. You must understand that sometimes I have to put work even before my dear little Milly."

The girl behind Captain Segura altered the angle of the siphon.

"No," Wormold said instinctively, "no." The spout of the siphon was aimed upwards at Captain Segura's neck. The girl's finger was ready for action. He was hurt that anyone so pretty should look at him with such contempt. He said, "Yes. Please. Yes," and she triggered the siphon. The stream of soda hissed off Captain Segura's neck and ran down the back of his collar. Dr. Hasselbacher's voice called "Bravo' from among the tables. Captain Segura exclaimed "*Coño.*"

"I'm so sorry," the young woman said. "I meant it for my whisky."

"Your whisky!"

"Dimpled Haig," the girl said. Milly giggled.

Captain Segura bowed stiffly. You could not estimate his danger from his size any more than you could a hard drink.

Dr. Hasselbacher said, "You have finished your siphon, madam, let me find you another." The Dutchmen at the table whispered together uncomfortably.

"I don't think I'm to be trusted with another," the girl said.

Captain Segura squeezed out a smile. It seemed to come from the wrong place like toothpaste when the tube splits. He said, "For the first time I have been shot in the back. I am glad that it was by a woman." He had made an admirable recovery; the water still dripped from his hair and his collar was limp with it. He said, "Another time I would have offered you a return match, but I am late at the barracks. I hope I may see you again?"

"I am staying here," she said.

"On holiday?"

"No. Work."

"If you have any trouble with your permit," he said ambiguously, "you must come to me. Good night, Milly. Good night, Mr. Wormold. I will tell the waiter that you are my guests. Order what you wish."

"He made a creditable exit," the girl said.

"It was a creditable shot."

"To have hit him with a champagne bottle might have been a bit exaggerated. Who is he?"

"A lot of people call him the Red Vulture."

"He tortures prisoners," Milly said.

"I seem to have made quite a friend of him."

"I wouldn't be too sure of that," Dr. Hasselbacher said.

They joined their tables together. The two pilots bowed and gave unpronounceable names. Dr. Hasselbacher said with horror to the Dutchmen, "You are drinking Coca-Cola."

"It is the regulation. We take off at 3.30 for Montreal."

Wormold said, "If Captain Segura is going to pay, let's have more champagne. And Coca-Cola."

"I don't think I can drink any more Coca-Cola, can you, Hans?"

"I could drink a Bols," the younger pilot said.

"You can have no Bols," the air-hostess told him firmly, "before Amsterdam."

The young pilot whispered to Wormold, "I wish to marry her."

"Who?"

"Miss Pfunk," or so it sounded.

"Won't she?"

"No."

The elder Dutchman said, "I have a wife and three children." He unbuttoned his breast-pocket. "I have their photographs here."

He handed Wormold a coloured card showing a girl in a tight yellow sweater and bathing-drawers adjusting her skates. The sweater was marked Mamba Club, and below the picture Wormold read, "We guarantee you a lot of fun. Fifty beautiful girls. You won't be alone."

"I don't think this is the right picture," Wormold said.

The young woman, who had chestnut hair and, as far as he could tell in the confusing Tropicana lights, hazel eyes, said, "Let's dance."

"I'm not very good at dancing."

"It doesn't matter, does it?"

He shuffled her around. She said, "I see what you mean. This is meant to be a rumba. Is that your daughter?"

"Yes."

"She's very pretty."

"Have you just arrived?"

"Yes. The crew were making a night of it, so I joined up with them. I don't know anybody here." Her head reached his chin and he could smell her hair; it touched his mouth as they moved. He was vaguely disappointed that she wore a wedding-ring. She said, "My name's Severn. Beatrice Severn."

"Mine's Wormold."

"Then I'm your secretary," she said.

"What do you mean? I have no secretary."

"Oh yes you have. Didn't they tell you I was coming?"

"No." He didn't need to ask who "they' were.

"But I sent the telegram myself."

"There was one last week—but I couldn't make head or tail of it."

"What's your edition of Lamb's *Tales*?"

"Everyman."

"Damn. They gave me the wrong edition. I suppose the telegram *was* rather a mess. Anyway, I'm glad I found you."

"I'm glad too. A bit taken aback, of course. Where are you staying?"

"The Inglaterra tonight, and then I thought I'd move in."

"Move in where?"

"To your office, of course. I don't mind where I sleep. I'll just doss down in one of your staff-rooms."

"There aren't any. It's a very small office."

"Well, there's a secretary's room anyway."

"But I've never had a secretary, Mrs. Severn."

"Call me Beatrice. It's supposed to be good for security."

"Security?"

"It *is* rather a problem if there isn't even a secretary's room. Let's sit down."

A man, wearing a conventional black dinner jacket among the jungle trees like an English district officer was singing:

> *"Sane men surround*
> *You, old family friends.*
> *They say the earth is round—*
> *My madness offends.*
> *An orange has pips, they say,*
> *And an apple has rind.*
> *I say that night is day*
> *And I've no axe to grind.*

> *"Please don't believe . . ."*

They sat at an empty table at the back of the roulette-room. They could hear the hiccup of the little balls. She wore her grave look again—a little self-consciously like a girl in her first long gown. She said, "If I had known I was your secretary I would never have siphoned that policeman—without your telling me."

"You don't have to worry."

"I was really sent here to make things easier for you. Not more difficult."

"Captain Segura doesn't matter."

"You see, I've had a very full training. I've passed in codes and microphotography. I can take over contact with your agents."

"Oh."

"You've done so well they're anxious you should take no risk of being blown. It doesn't matter so much if I'm blown."

"I'd hate to see you blown. Half-blown would be all right."

"I don't understand."

"I was thinking of roses."

She said, "Of course, as that telegram was mutilated, you don't even know about the radio-operator."

"I don't."

"He's at the Inglaterra too. Air-sick. We have to find room for him as well."

"If he's air-sick perhaps . . ."

"You can make him assistant accountant. He's been trained for that."

"But I don't need one. I haven't even got a chief accountant."

"Don't worry. I'll get things straight in the morning. That's what I'm here for."

"There's something about you," Wormold said, "that reminds me of my daughter. Do you say novenas?"

"What are they?"

"You don't know? Thank God for that."

The man in the dinner jacket was finishing his song.

> *"I say that winter's May*
> *And I've no axe to grind."*

The lights changed from blue to rose and the dancers went back to perch among the palm-trees. The dice rattled at the crap-tables, and Milly and Dr. Hasselbacher made their way happily towards the dance-floor. It was as though her birthday had been constructed again out of its broken pieces.

2

i

Next morning Wormold was up early. He had a slight hangover from the champagne, and the unreality of the Tropicana night extended into the office-day. Beatrice had told him he was doing well—she was the mouthpiece of Hawthorne and "those people." He had a sense of disappointment at the thought that she like Hawthorne belonged to the notional world of his agents. His agents. . . .

He sat down before his card-index. He had to make his cards look as plausible as possible before she came. Some of the agents seemed to him now to verge on the improbable. Professor Sanchez and Engineer Cifuentes were deeply committed, he couldn't get rid of them; they had drawn nearly two hundred pesos in expenses. Lopez was a fixture too. The drunken pilot of the Cubana air line had received a handsome bonus of five hundred pesos for the story of the construction in the mountains, but perhaps he could be jettisoned as insecure. There was the Chief Engineer of the *Juan Belmonte* whom he had seen drinking in Cienfuegos—he seemed a character probable enough and he was only drawing seventy-five pesos a month. But there were other characters whom he feared might not bear close inspection: Rodriguez, for example, described on his card as a night-club king, and Teresa, a dancer at the Shanghai Theatre whom he had listed as the mistress simultaneously of the Minister of Defence and the Director of Posts and Telegraphs (it was not surprising that London had found no trace of either Rodriguez or Teresa). He was ready to jettison Rodriguez, for anyone who came to know Havana well would certainly question his existence sooner or later. But he could not bear to relinquish Teresa. She was his only woman spy, his Mata Hari. It was unlikely that his new secretary would visit the Shanghai, where three pornographic films were shown nightly between nude dances.

Milly sat down beside him. "What are all these cards?" she asked.

"Customers."

"Who was that girl last night?"

"She's going to be my secretary."

"How grand you are getting."

"Do you like her?"

"I don't know. You didn't give me a chance to talk to her. You were too busy dancing and spooning."

"I wasn't spooning."

"Does she want to marry you?"

"Good heavens, no."

"Do you want to marry her?"

"Milly, do be sensible. I only met her last night."

"Marie, a French girl at the convent, says that all true love is a *coup de foudre*."

"Is that the kind of thing you talk about at the convent?"

"Naturally. It's the future, isn't it? We haven't got a past to talk about, though Sister Agnes has."

"Who is Sister Agnes?"

"I've told you about her. She's the sad and lovely one. Marie says she had an unhappy *coup de foudre* when she was young."

"Did she tell Marie that?"

"No, of course not. But Marie knows. She's had two unhappy *coups de foudre* herself. They came quite suddenly, out of a clear sky."

"I'm old enough to be safe."

"Oh no. There was an old man—he was nearly fifty—who had a *coup de foudre* for Marie's mother. He was married, like you."

"Well, my secretary's married too, so that should be all right."

"Is she really married or a lovely widow?"

"I don't know. I haven't asked her. Do you think she's lovely?"

"Rather lovely. In a way."

Lopez called up the stairs, "There is a lady here. She says you expect her."

"Tell her to come up."

"I'm going to stay," Milly warned him.

"Beatrice, this is Milly."

Her eyes, he noticed, were the same colour as the night before and so was her hair; it had not after all been the effect of the champagne and the palm-trees. He thought, She looks real.

"Good morning. I hope you had a good night," Milly said in the voice of the duenna.

"I had terrible dreams." She looked at Wormold and the card-index and Milly. She said, "I enjoyed last night."

"You were wonderful with the soda-water siphon," Milly said generously, "Miss . . ."

"Mrs. Severn. But please call me Beatrice."

"Oh, are you married?" Milly asked with phony curiosity.

"I *was* married."

"Is he dead?"

"Not that I know of. He sort of faded away."

"Oh."

"It does happen with his type."

"What was his type?"

"Milly, it's time you were off. You've no business asking Mrs. Severn—Beatrice . . ."

"At my age," Milly said, "one has to learn from other people's experiences."

"You are quite right. I suppose you'd call his type intellectual and sensitive. I thought he was very beautiful; he had a face like a young fledgling looking out of a nest in one of those nature films and fluff-like feathers round his Adam's apple, a rather large Adam's apple. The trouble was when he got to forty he still looked like a fledgling. Girls loved him. He used to go to UNESCO conferences in Venice and Vienna and places like that. Have you a safe, Mr. Wormold?"

"No."

"What happened?" Milly asked.

"Oh, I got to see through him. I mean literally, not in a nasty way. He was very thin and concave and he got sort of transparent. When I looked at him I could see all the delegates sitting there between his ribs and the chief speaker rising and saying, 'Freedom is of importance to creative writers.' It was very uncanny at breakfast."

"And don't you know if he's alive?"

"He was alive last year, because I saw in the papers that he read a paper on 'The Intellectual and the Hydrogen Bomb' at Taormina. You ought to have a safe, Mr. Wormold."

"Why?"

"You can't leave things just lying about. Besides, it's expected of an old-fashioned merchant-king like you."

"Who called me an old-fashioned merchant-king?"

"It's the impression they have in London. I'll go out and find you a safe right away."

"I'll be off," Milly said. "You'll be sensible, won't you, Father? You know what I mean."

ii

It proved to be an exhausting day. First Beatrice went out and procured a large combination-safe, which required a lorry and six men to transport it. They broke the banisters and a picture while getting it up the stairs. A crowd collected outside, including several truants from the school next door, two beautiful negresses and a policeman. When Wormold complained that the affair was making him conspicuous, Beatrice reported that the way to become really conspicuous was to try to escape notice.

"For example, that siphon," she said. "Everybody will remember me as the woman who siphoned the policeman. Nobody will ask questions any more about who I am. They have the answer."

While they were still struggling with the safe a taxi drove up and a young man got out and unloaded the largest suitcase Wormold had ever seen. "This is Rudy," Beatrice said.

"Who is Rudy?"

"Your assistant accountant. I told you last night."

"Thank God," Wormold said, "there seems to be something I've forgotten about last night."

"Come along in, Rudy, and relax."

"It's no earthly use telling him to come in," Wormold said. "Come in where? There's no room for him."

"He can sleep in the office," Beatrice said.

"There isn't enough room for a bed and that safe and my desk."

"I'll get you a smaller desk. How's the air-sickness, Rudy? This is Mr. Wormold, the boss."

Rudy was very young and very pale and his fingers were stained yellow with nicotine or acid. He said, "I vomited twice in the night, Beatrice. They've broken a Röntgen tube."

"Never mind that now. We'll just get the preliminaries fixed. Go off and buy a camp-bed."

"Righto," Rudy said and disappeared. One of the negresses sidled up to Beatrice and said, "I'm British."

"So am I," Beatrice said, "glad to meet you."

"You the gel who poured water on Captain Segura?"

"Well, more or less. Actually I squirted."

The negress turned and explained to the crowd in Spanish. Several people clapped. The policeman moved away, looking embarrassed. The negress said, "You very lovely gel, miss."

"You're pretty lovely yourself," Beatrice said. "Give me a hand with this case." They struggled with Rudy's suitcase, pushing and pulling.

"Excuse me," a man said, elbowing through the crowd, "excuse me, please."

"What do you want?" Beatrice asked. "Can't you see we are busy? Make an appointment."

"I only want to buy a vacuum cleaner."

"Oh, a vacuum cleaner. I suppose you'd better go inside. Can you climb over the suitcase?"

Wormold called to Lopez, "Look after him. For goodness' sake, try and sell him an Atomic Pile. We haven't sold one yet."

"Are you going to live here?" the negress asked.

"I'm going to work here. Thanks a lot for your help."

"We Britishers have to stick together," the negress said.

The men who had been setting up the safe came downstairs spitting on their hands and rubbing them on their jeans to show how hard it had all been. Wormold tipped them. He went upstairs and looked gloomily at his office. The chief trouble was that there was just room for a camp-bed, which robbed him of any excuse. He said, "There's nowhere for Rudy to keep his clothes."

"Rudy's used to roughing it. Anyway there's your desk. You can empty what's in the drawers into your safe and Rudy can keep his things in them."

"I've never used a combination."

"It's perfectly simple. You choose three sets of numbers you can keep in your head. What's your street-number?"

"I don't know."

"Well, your telephone-number—no, that's not secure. It's the kind of thing a burglar might try. What's the date of your birth?"

"1914."

"And your birthday?"

"6th December."

"Well then, let's make it 19-6-14."

"I won't remember that."

"Oh yes, you will. You can't forget your own birthday. Now watch me. You turn the knob anti-clockwise four times, then forward to 19, clockwise three times, then to 6, anti-clockwise twice, forward to 14, whirl it round and it's locked. Now you unlock it the same way—19-6-14 and hey presto, it opens." In the safe was a dead mouse. Beatrice said, "Shop-soiled, I should have got a reduction."

She began to open Rudy's case, pulling out bits and pieces of a radio-set, batteries, camera-equipment, mysterious tubes wrapped up in Rudy's socks. Wormold said, "How on earth did you bring all that stuff through the customs?"

"We didn't. 59200 stroke 4 stroke 5 brought it for us from Kingston."

"Who's he?"

"A Creole smuggler. He smuggles in cocaine, opium and marijuana. Of course he has the customs all lined up. This time they assumed it was his usual cargo."

"It would need a lot of drugs to fill that case."

"Yes. We had to pay rather heavily."

She stowed everything quickly and neatly away after emptying his drawers into the safe. She said, "Rudy's shirts are going to get a bit crushed, but never mind."

"I don't."

"What are these?" she asked, picking up the cards he had been examining.

"My agents."

"You mean you keep them lying about on your desk?"

"Oh, I lock them away at night."

"You haven't got much idea of security, have you?" She looked at a card. "Who is Teresa?"

"She dances naked."

"Quite naked?"

"Yes."

"How interesting for you. London wants me to take over contact with your agents. Will you introduce me to Teresa some time when she's got her clothes on?"

Wormold said, "I don't think she'd work for a woman. You know how it is with these girls."

"I don't. You do. Ah, Engineer Cifuentes. London thinks a lot of him. You can't say he would mind working for a woman."

"He doesn't speak English."

"Perhaps I could learn Spanish. That wouldn't be a bad cover, taking Spanish lessons. Is he as good-looking as Teresa?"

"He's got a very jealous wife."

"Oh, I think I could deal with her."

"It's absurd, of course, because of his age."

"What's his age?"

"Sixty-five. Besides, there's no other woman who would look at him because of his paunch. I'll ask him about the Spanish lessons if you like."

"No hurry. We'll leave it for the moment. I could start with this other one. Professor Sanchez. I got used to intellectuals with my husband."

"He doesn't speak English either."

"I expect he speaks French. My mother was French. I'm bi-lingual."

"I don't know whether he does or not. I'll find out."

"You know, you oughtn't to have all these names written like this *en clair* on the cards. Suppose Captain Segura investigated you. I'd hate to think of Engineer Cifuentes's paunch being skinned to make a cigarette-case. Just put enough details under their symbol to remember them by—59200 stroke 5 stroke 3—jealous wife and paunch. I will write them for you and burn the old ones. Damn. Where are those celluloid sheets?"

"Celluloid sheets?"

"To help burn papers in a hurry. Oh, I expect Rudy put them in his shirts."

"What a lot of knick-knacks you carry around."

"Now we've got to arrange the darkroom."

"I haven't got a darkroom."

"Nobody has nowadays. I've come prepared. Blackout curtains and a red globe. And a microscope, of course."

"What do we want a microscope for?"

"Microphotography. You see, if there's anything really urgent that you can't put in a telegram, London wants us to communicate direct and save all the time it takes via Kingston. We can send a microphotograph in an ordinary letter. You stick it on as a full stop and they float the letter in water until the dot comes unstuck. I suppose you do write letters home sometimes. Business letters . . . ?"

"I send those to New York."

"Friends and relations?"

"I've lost touch in the last ten years. Except with my sister. Of course I send Christmas cards."

"We mightn't be able to wait till Christmas."

"Sometimes I send postage stamps to a small nephew."

"The very thing. We could put a microphotograph on the back of one of the stamps."

Rudy came heavily up the stairs carrying his camp-bed, and the picture-frame was broken all over again. Beatrice and Wormold retired into the next room to give him space and sat on Wormold's bed. There was a lot of banging and clanking and something broke.

"Rudy isn't very good with his hands," Beatrice said. Her gaze wandered. She said, "Not a single photograph. Have you no private life?"

"I don't think I have much. Except for Milly. And Dr. Hasselbacher."

"London doesn't like Dr. Hasselbacher."

"London can go to hell," Wormold said. He suddenly wanted to describe to her the ruin of Dr. Hasselbacher's flat and the destruction of his futile experiments. He said, "It's people like your folk in London . . . I'm sorry. You are one of them."

"So are you."

"Yes, of course. So am I."

Rudy called from the other room, "I've got it fixed."

"I wish you weren't one of them," Wormold said.

"It's a living," she said.

"It's not a real living. All this spying. Spying on what? Secret agents discovering what everybody knows already . . ."

"Or just making it up," she said. He stopped short, and she went on without a change of voice, "There are lots of other jobs that aren't real. Designing a new plastic soap-box, making pokerwork jokes for public-houses, writing advertising slogans, being an M.P., talking to UNESCO conferences. But the money's real. What happens after work is real. I mean, your daughter is real and her seventeenth birthday is real."

"What do you do after work?"

"Nothing much now, but when I was in love . . . we went to cinemas and drank coffee in Espresso bars and sat on summer evenings in the Park."

"What happened?"

"It takes two to keep something real. He was acting all the time. He thought he was the great lover. Sometimes I almost wished he would turn impotent for a while just so that he'd lose his confidence. You can't love and be as confident as he was. If you love you are afraid of losing it, aren't you?" She said, "Oh hell, why am I telling you all this? Let's go and make microphotographs and code some cables." She looked through the door. "Rudy's lying on his bed. I suppose he's feeling airsick again. Can you be air-sick all this while? Haven't you got a room where there isn't a bed? Beds always make one talk." She opened another door. "Table laid for lunch. Cold meat and salad. Two places. Who does all this? A little fairy?"

"A woman comes in for two hours in the morning."

"And the room beyond?"

"That's Milly's. It's got a bed in it too."

3

i

The situation, whichever way he looked at it, was uncomfortable. Wormold was in the habit now of drawing occasional expenses for Engineer Cifuentes and the professor, and monthly salaries for himself, the Chief Engineer of the *Juan Belmonte* and Teresa, the nude dancer. The drunken air-pilot was usually paid in whisky. The money Wormold accumulated he put into his deposit-account—one day it would make a dowry for Milly. Naturally to justify these payments he had to compose a regular supply of reports. With the help of a large map, the weekly number of *Time*, which gave generous space to Cuba in its section on the Western Hemisphere, various economic publications issued by the Government, above all with the help of his imagination, he had been able to arrange at least one report a week, and until the arrival of Beatrice he had kept his Saturday evenings free for homework. The professor was the economic authority, and Engineer Cifuentes dealt with the mysterious constructions in the mountains of Oriente (his reports were sometimes confirmed and sometimes contradicted by the Cubana pilot—a contradiction had a flavour of authenticity). The chief engineer supplied descriptions of labour conditions in Santiago, Matanzas and Cienfuegos and reported on the growth of unrest in the navy. As for the nude dancer, she supplied spicy details of the private lives and sexual eccentricities of the Defence Minister and the Director of Posts and Telegraphs. Her reports closely resembled articles about film stars in *Confidential*, for Wormold's imagination in this direction was not very strong.

Now that Beatrice was here, Wormold had a great deal more to worry about than his Saturday evening exercises. There was not only the basic training which Beatrice insisted on giving him in microphotography, there were also the cables he had to think up in order to keep Rudy happy, and the more cables Wormold sent the more he received. Every week now London bothered him for photographs of the installations in Oriente, and every week Beatrice became more impatient to take over the contact with his agents. It was against all the rules, she told him, for the head of a station to meet his own sources. Once he took her to dinner at the Country Club and, as bad luck would have it, Engineer Cifuentes was paged. A very tall lean man with a squint rose from a table near-by.

"Is that Cifuentes?" Beatrice asked sharply.

"Yes."

"But you told me he was sixty-five."

"He looks young for his age."

"And you said he had a paunch."

"Not paunch—ponch. It's the local dialect for squint." It was a very narrow squeak.

After that she began to interest herself in a more romantic figure of Wormold's imagination—the pilot of Cubana. She worked enthusiastically to make his entry in the index complete and wanted the most personal details. Raul Dominguez certainly had pathos. He had lost his wife in a massacre during the Spanish civil war and had become disillusioned with both sides, with his Communist friends in particular. The more Beatrice asked Wormold about him, the more his character developed, and the more anxious she became to contact him. Sometimes Wormold felt a twinge of jealousy towards Raul and he tried to blacken the picture. "He gets through a bottle of whisky a day," he said.

"It's his escape from loneliness and memory," Beatrice said. "Don't *you* ever want to escape?"

"I suppose we all do sometimes."

"I know what that kind of loneliness is like," she said with sympathy. "Does he drink all day?"

"No. The worst hour is two in the morning. When he wakes then, he can't sleep for thinking, so he drinks instead." It astonished Wormold how quickly he could reply to any questions about his characters; they seemed to live on the threshold of consciousness—he had only to turn a light on and there they were, frozen in some characteristic action. Soon after Beatrice arrived Raul had a birthday and she suggested they should give him a case of champagne.

"He won't touch it," Wormold said, he didn't know why. "He suffers from acidity. If he drinks champagne he comes out in spots. Now the professor on the other hand won't drink anything else."

"An expensive taste."

"A depraved taste," Wormold said without taking any thought. "He prefers Spanish champagne." Sometimes he was scared at the way these people grew in the dark without his knowledge. What was Teresa doing down there, out of sight? He didn't care to think. Her unabashed description of what life was like with her two lovers sometimes shocked him. But the immediate problem was Raul. There were moments when Wormold thought that it might have been easier if he had recruited real agents.

Wormold always thought best in his bath. He was aware one morning, when he was concentrating hard, of indignant noises, a fist beat on the door a number of times, somebody stamped on the stairs, but a creative moment had arrived and he paid no attention to the world beyond the steam. Raul had been dismissed by the Cubana air line for drunkenness. He was desperate; he was without a job; there had been an unpleasant interview between him and Captain Segura, who threatened . . . "Are you all right?" Beatrice called from outside. "Are you dying? Shall I break down the door?"

He wrapped a towel round his middle and emerged into his bedroom, which was now his office.

"Milly went off in a rage," Beatrice said. "She missed her bath."

"This is one of those moments," Wormold said, "which might change the course of history. Where is Rudy?"

"You know you gave him week-end leave."

"Never mind. We'll have to send the cable through the Consulate. Get out the code-book."

"It's in the safe. What's the combination? Your birthday—that was it, wasn't it? December 6?"

"I changed it."

"Your birthday?"

"No, no. The combination, of course." He added sententiously, "The fewer who know the combination the better for all of us. Rudy and I are quite sufficient. It's the drill, you know, that counts." He went into Rudy's room and began to twist the knob—four times to the left, three times thoughtfully to the right. His towel kept on slipping. "Besides, anyone can find out the date of my birth from my registration-card. Most unsafe. The sort of number they'd try at once."

"Go on," Beatrice said, "one more turn."

"This is one nobody could find out. Absolutely secure."

"What are you waiting for?"

"I must have made a mistake. I shall have to start again."

"This combination certainly seems secure."

"Please don't watch. You're fussing me." Beatrice went and stood with her face to the wall. She said, "Tell me when I can turn round again."

"It's very odd. The damn thing must have broken. Get Rudy on the phone."

"I can't. I don't know where he's staying. He's gone to Varadero beach."

"Damn!"

"Perhaps if you told me how you remembered the number, if you can call it remembering. . . ."

"It was my great-aunt's telephone number."

"Where does she live?"

"95 Woodstock Road, Oxford."

"Why your great-aunt?"

"Why not my great-aunt?"

"I suppose we could put through a directory-enquiry to Oxford."

"I doubt whether they could help."

"What's her name?"

"I've forgotten that too."

"The combination really is secure, isn't it?"

"We always just knew her as great-aunt Kate. Anyway she's been dead for fifteen years and the number may have been changed."

"I don't see why you chose her number."

"Don't you have a few numbers that stick in your head all your life for no reason at all?"

"This doesn't seem to have stuck very well."

"I'll remember it in a moment. It's something like 7,7,5,3,9."

"Oh dear, they would have five numbers in Oxford."

"We could try all the combinations of 77539."

"Do you know how many there are? Somewhere around six hundred, I'd guess. I hope your cable's not urgent."

"I'm certain of everything except the 7."

"That's fine. Which seven? I suppose now we might have to work through about six thousand arrangements. I'm no mathematician."

"Rudy must have it written down somewhere."

"Probably on waterproof paper so that he can take it in with him bathing. We're an efficient office."

"Perhaps," Wormold said, "we had better use the old code."

"It's not very secure. However . . ." They found Charles Lamb at last by Milly's bed; a leaf turned down showed that she was in the middle of *Two Gentlemen of Verona*.

Wormold said, "Take down this cable. Blank of March blank."

"Don't you even know the day of the month?"

"Following from 59200 stroke 5 paragraph A begins 59200 stroke 5 stroke 4 sacked for drunkenness on duty stop fears deportation to Spain where his life is in danger stop."

"Poor old Raul."

"Paragraph B begins 59200 stroke 5 stroke 4 . . ."

"Couldn't I just say 'he'?"

"All right. He. He might be prepared under these circumstances and for reasonable bonus with assured refuge in Jamaica to pilot private plane over secret constructions to obtain photographs stop paragraph C begins he would have to fly on from Santiago and land at Kingston if 59200 can make arrangements for reception stop."

"We really are doing something at last, aren't we?" Beatrice said.

"Paragraph D begins stop will you authorise five hundred dollars for hire of plane for 59200 stroke 5 stroke 4 stop further two hundred dollars may be required to bribe airport staff Havana stop paragraph E begins bonus to 59200 stroke 5 stroke 4 should be generous as considerable risk of interception by patrolling planes over Oriente mountains stop I suggest one thousand dollars stop."

"What a lot of lovely money," Beatrice said.

"Message ends. Go on. What are you waiting for?"

"I'm just trying to find a suitable phrase. I don't much care for Lamb's *Tales*, do you?"

"Seventeen hundred dollars," Wormold said thoughtfully.

"You should have made it two thousand. The A.O. likes round figures."

"I don't want to seem extravagant," Wormold said. Seventeen hundred dollars would surely cover one year at a finishing school in Switzerland.

"You're looking pleased with yourself," Beatrice said. "Doesn't it occur to you that you may be sending a man to his death?" He thought, That is exactly what I plan to do.

He said, "Tell them at the Consulate that the cable has to have top priority."

"It's a long cable," Beatrice said. "Do you think this sentence will do? 'He presented Polydore and Cadwal to the king, telling him they were his two lost sons, Guiderius and Arviragus.' There are times, aren't there, when Shakespeare is a little dull."

ii

A week later he took Beatrice out to supper at a fish-restaurant near the harbour. The authorisation had come, though they had cut him down by two hundred dollars so that the A.O. got his round figure after all. Wormold thought of Raul driving out to the airport to embark on his dangerous flight. The story was not yet complete. Just as in real life, accidents could happen; a character might take control. Perhaps Raul would be intercepted before embarking, perhaps he would be stopped by a police-car on his way. He might disappear into the torture-chambers of Captain Segura. No reference would appear in the press. Wormold would warn London that he was going off the air in case Raul was forced to talk. The radio-set would be dismantled and hidden after the last message had been sent, the celluloid sheets would be kept ready for a final conflagration . . . Or perhaps Raul would take off in safety and they would never know what exactly happened to him over the Oriente mountains. Only one thing in the story was certain: he would not arrive in Jamaica and there would be no photographs.

"What are you thinking?" Beatrice asked. He hadn't touched his stuffed langouste.

"I was thinking of Raul." The wind blew up from the Atlantic. Morro Castle lay like a liner gale-bound across the harbour.

"Anxious?"

"Of course I'm anxious." If Raul had taken off at midnight, he would refuel just before dawn in Santiago, where the ground-staff were friendly, everyone within the Oriente province being rebels at heart. Then when it was just light enough for photography and too early for the patrol planes to be up, he would begin his reconnaissance over the mountains and the forest.

"He hasn't been drinking?"

"He promised me he wouldn't. One can't tell."

"Poor Raul."

"Poor Raul."

"He's never had much fun, has he? You should have introduced him to Teresa."

He looked sharply up at her, but she seemed deeply engaged over her langouste.

"That wouldn't have been very secure, would it?"

"Oh, damn security," she said.

After supper they walked back along the landward side of the Avenida de Maceo. There were few people about in the wet windy night and little traffic. The rollers came in from the Atlantic and smashed over the sea-wall. The spray drove across the road, over the four traffic-lanes, and beat like rain under the pock-marked pillars where they walked. The clouds came racing from the east, and he felt himself to be part of the slow erosion of Havana. Fifteen years was a long time. He said, "One of those lights up there may be him. How solitary he must feel."

"You talk like a novelist," she said.

He stopped under a pillar and watched her with anxiety and suspicion.

"What do you mean?"

"Oh, nothing in particular. Sometimes I think you treat your agents like lay figures, people in a book. It's a real man up there—isn't it?"

"That's not a very nice thing to say about me."

"Oh, forget it. Tell me about someone you really care about. Your wife. Tell me about her."

"She was pretty."

"Do you miss her?"

"Of course. When I think of her."

"I don't miss Peter."

"Peter?"

"My husband. The UNESCO man."

"You're lucky then. You're free." He looked at his watch and the sky. "He should be over Matanzas by now. Unless he's been delayed."

"Have you sent him that way?"

"Oh, of course he decides his own route."

"And his own end?"

Something in her voice—a kind of enmity—startled him again. Was it possible she had begun to suspect him already? He walked quickly on. They passed the Carmen Bar and the Cha Cha Club—bright signs painted on the old shutters of the eighteenth-century façade. Lovely faces looked out of dim interiors, brown eyes, dark hair, Spanish and high yellow: beautiful buttocks leant against the bars, waiting for any life to come along the sea-wet street. To live in Havana was to live in a factory that turned out human beauty on a conveyor-belt. He didn't want beauty. He stopped under a lamp and looked directly back at the direct eyes. He wanted honesty. "Where are we going?"

"Don't you know? Isn't it all planned like Raul's flight?"

"I was just walking."

"Don't you want to sit beside the radio? Rudy's on duty."

"We won't have any news before the early morning."

"You haven't planned a late message then—the crash at Santiago?"

His lips were dry with salt and apprehension. It seemed to him that she must have guessed everything. Would she report him to Hawthorne? What would be "their" next move? They had no legal remedy, but he supposed they could stop him ever returning to England. He thought: She will go back by the next plane, life will be the same as before, and, of course, it was better that way; his life belonged to Milly. He said, "I don't understand what you mean." A great wave had broken against the sea-wall of the Avenida, and now it rose like a Christmas-tree covered with plastic frost. Then it sank out of sight, and another tree rose further down the driveway towards the Nacional. He said, "You've been strange all the evening." There was no point in delay; if the game were coming to an end, it was better to close it quickly. He said, "What are you hinting at?"

"You mean there isn't to be a crash at the airport—or on the way?"

"How do you expect me to know?"

"You've been behaving all the evening as if you did. You haven't spoken about him as though he were a living man. You've been writing his elegy like a bad novelist preparing an effect."

The wind knocked them together. She said, "Aren't you ever tired of other people taking risks? For what? For a *Boy's Own Paper* game?"

"You play the game."

"I don't believe in it like Hawthorne does." She said furiously, "I'd rather be a crook than a simpleton or an adolescent. Don't you earn enough with your vacuum cleaners to keep out of all this?"

"No. There's Milly."

"Suppose Hawthorne hadn't walked in on you?"

He joked miserably, "Perhaps I'd have married again for money."

"Would you ever marry again?" She seemed determined to be serious.

"Well," he said, "I don't know that I would. Milly wouldn't consider it a marriage, and one can't shock one's own child. Shall we go home and listen to the radio?"

"But you don't expect a message, do you? You said so."

He said evasively, "Not for another three hours. But I expect he'll radio before he lands." The odd thing was he began to feel the tension. He almost hoped for some message to reach him out of the windy sky.

She said, "Will you promise me that you haven't arranged—anything?"

He avoided answering, turning back towards the President's palace with the dark windows where the President had never slept since the last attempt on his life, and there, coming down the pavement with head bent to avoid the spray, was Dr. Hasselbacher. He was probably on his way home from the Wonder Bar.

"Dr. Hasselbacher," Wormold called to him.

The old man looked up. For a moment Wormold thought he was going to turn tail without a word. "What's the matter, Hasselbacher?"

"Oh, it's you, Mr. Wormold. I was just thinking of you. Talk of the devil," he said, making a joke of it, but Wormold could have sworn that the devil had scared him.

"You remember Mrs. Severn, my secretary?"

"The birthday party, yes, and the siphon. What are you doing up so late. Mr. Wormold?"

"We've been out to supper . . . a walk . . . and you?"

"The same thing."

Out of the vast tossing sky the sound of an engine came spasmodically down, increased, faded again, died out into the noise of wind and sea. Dr. Hasselbacher said, "The plane from Santiago, but it's very late. The weather must be bad in Oriente."

"Are you expecting anyone?" Wormold asked.

"No. No. Not expecting. Would you and Mrs. Severn care to have a drink at my apartment?"

Violence had come and gone. The pictures were back in place, the tubular chairs stood around like awkward guests. The apartment had been reconstructed like a man for burial. Dr. Hasselbacher poured out the whisky.

"It is nice for Mr. Wormold to have a secretary," he said. "Such a short time ago you were worried, I remember. Business was not so good. That new cleaner . . ."

"Things change for no reason."

He noticed for the first time the photograph of a young Dr. Hasselbacher in the dated uniform of an officer in the First World War; perhaps it had been one of the pictures the intruders had taken off the wall. "I never knew you had been in the army, Hasselbacher."

"I had not finished my medical training, Mr. Wormold, when the war came. It struck me as a very silly business—curing men so that they could be killed sooner. One wanted to cure people so that they could live longer."

"When did you leave Germany, Dr. Hasselbacher?" Beatrice asked.

"In 1934. So I can plead not guilty, young lady, to what you are wondering."

"That was not what I meant."

"You must forgive me then. Ask Mr. Wormold—there was a time when I was not so suspicious. Shall we have some music?"

He put on a record of *Tristan*. Wormold thought of his wife; she was even less real than Raul. She had nothing to do with love and death, only with the *Woman's Home Journal*, a diamond engagement ring, twilight-sleep. He looked across the room at Beatrice Severn, and she seemed to him to belong to the same world as the fatal drink, the hopeless journey from Ireland, the surrender in the forest. Abruptly Dr. Hasselbacher stood up and pulled the plug from the wall. He said, "Forgive me. I am expecting a call. The music is too loud."

"A sick call?"

"Not exactly." He poured out more whisky.

"Have you started your experiments again, Hasselbacher?"

"No." He looked despairingly around. "I am sorry. There is no more soda water."

"I like it straight," Beatrice said. She went to the bookshelf. "Do you read anything but medical books, Dr. Hasselbacher?"

"Very little. Heine, Goethe. All German. Do you read German, Mrs. Severn?"

"No. But you have a few English books."

"They were given me by a patient instead of a fee. I'm afraid I haven't read them. Here is your whisky, Mrs. Severn."

She came away from the bookcase and took the whisky. "Is that your home, Dr. Hasselbacher?" She was looking at a Victorian coloured lithograph hanging beside young Captain Hasselbacher's portrait.

"I was born there. Yes. It is a very small town, some old walls, a castle in ruins . . ."

"I've been there," Beatrice said, "before the war. My father took us. It's near Leipzig, isn't it?"

"Yes, Mrs. Severn," Dr. Hasselbacher said, watching her bleakly, "it is near Leipzig."

"I hope the Russians left it undisturbed."

The telephone in Dr. Hasselbacher's hall began to ring. He hesitated a moment. "Excuse me, Mrs. Severn," he said. When he went into the hall he shut the door behind him. "East or west," Beatrice said, "home's best."

"I suppose you want to report that to London? But I've known him for fifteen years, he's lived here for more than twenty. He's a good old man, the best friend . . ." The door opened and Dr. Hasselbacher returned. He said, "I'm sorry. I don't feel very well. Perhaps you will come and hear music some other evening." He sat heavily down, picked up his whisky, put it back again. There was sweat on his forehead, but after all it was a humid night.

"Bad news?" Wormold asked.

"Yes."

"Can I help?"

"You!" Dr. Hasselbacher said. "No. *You* can't help. Or Mrs. Severn."

"A patient?" Dr. Hasselbacher shook his head. He took out his handkerchief and dried his forehead. He said, "Who is not a patient?"

"We'd better go."

"Yes, go. It is like I said. One ought to be able to cure people so that they can live longer."

"I don't understand."

"Was there never such a thing as peace?" Dr. Hasselbacher asked. "I am sorry. A doctor is always supposed to get used to death. But I am not a good doctor."

"Who has died?"

"There has been an accident," Dr. Hasselbacher said. "Just an accident. Of course an accident. A car has crashed on the road near the airport. A young man . . ." He said furiously, "There are always accidents, aren't there, everywhere. And this must surely have been an accident. He was too fond of the glass."

Beatrice said, "Was his name by any chance Raul?"

"Yes," Dr. Hasselbacher said. "That was his name."

PART FOUR

1

i

Wormold unlocked the door. The street-lamp over the way vaguely disclosed the vacuum cleaners standing around like tombs. He started for the stairs. Beatrice whispered, "Stop, stop. I thought I heard . . ." They were the first words either of them had spoken since he had shut the door of Dr. Hasselbacher's apartment.

"What's the matter?"

She put out a hand and clutched some metallic part from the counter; she held it like a club and said, "I'm frightened."

Not half as much as I am, he thought. Can we write human beings into existence? And what sort of existence? Had Shakespeare listened to the news of Duncan's death in a tavern or heard the knocking on his own bedroom door after he had finished the writing of *Macbeth*? He stood in the shop and hummed a tune to keep his courage up.

> *"They say the earth is round—*
> *My madness offends."*

"Quiet," Beatrice said. "Somebody's moving upstairs."

He thought he was afraid only of his own imaginary characters, not of a living person who could creak a board. He ran up and was stopped abruptly by a shadow. He was tempted to call out to all his creations at once and have done with the lot of them—Teresa, the chief, the professor, the engineer.

"How late you are," Milly's voice said. It was only Milly standing there in the passage between the lavatory and her room.

"We went for a walk."

"You brought her back?" Milly asked. "Why?"

Beatrice cautiously climbed the stairs, holding her improvised club on guard.

"Is Rudy awake?"

"I don't think so."

Beatrice said, "If there'd been a message, he would have sat up for you."

If one's characters were alive enough to die, they were surely real enough to send messages. He opened the door of the office. Rudy stirred.

"Any message, Rudy?"

"No."

Milly said, "You've missed all the excitement."

"What excitement?"

"The police were dashing everywhere. You should have heard the sirens. I thought it was a revolution, so I rang up Captain Segura."

"Yes?"

"Someone tried to assassinate someone as he came out of the Ministry of the Interior. He must have thought it was the Minister, only it wasn't. He shot out of a car window and got clean away."

"Who was it?"

"They haven't caught him yet."

"I mean the—the assassinee."

"Nobody important. But he looked like the Minister. Where did you have supper?"

"The Victoria."

"Did you have stuffed langouste?"

"Yes."

"I'm so glad you don't look like the President. Captain Segura said poor Dr. Cifuentes was so scared he went and wet his trousers and then got drunk at the Country Club."

"Dr. Cifuentes?"

"You know—the engineer."

"They shot at him?"

"I told you it was a mistake."

"Let's sit down," Beatrice said. She spoke for both of them.

He said, "The dining-room . . ."

"I don't want a hard chair. I want something soft. I may want to cry."

"Well, if you don't mind the bedroom," he said doubtfully, looking at Milly.

"Did you know Dr. Cifuentes?" Milly asked Beatrice sympathetically.

"No. I only know he has a ponch."

"What's a ponch?"

"Your father said it was a dialect word for a squint."

"He told you that? Poor Father," Milly said. "You *are* in deep waters."

"Look, Milly, will you please go to bed? Beatrice and I have work to do."

"Work?"

"Yes, work."

"It's awfully late for work."

"He's paying me overtime," Beatrice said.

"Are you learning all about vacuum cleaners?" Milly asked. "That thing you are holding is a sprayer."

"Is it? I just picked it up in case I had to hit someone."

"It's not well suited for that," Milly said. "It has a telescopic tube."

"What if it has?"

"It might telescope at the wrong moment."

"Milly, please . . ." Wormold said. "It's nearly two."

"Don't worry. I'm off. And I shall pray for Dr. Cifuentes. It's no joke to be shot at. The bullet went right through a brick wall. Think of what it could have done to Dr. Cifuentes."

"Pray for someone called Raul too," Beatrice said. "They got *him*."

Wormold lay down flat on the bed and shut his eyes. "I don't understand a thing," he said. "Not a thing. It's a coincidence. It must be."

"They're getting rough—whoever they are."

"But why?"

"Spying is a dangerous profession."

"But Cifuentes hadn't really . . . I mean he wasn't important."

"Those constructions in Oriente are important. Your agents seem to have a habit of getting blown. I wonder how. I think you'll have to warn Professor Sanchez and the girl."

"The girl?"

"The nude dancer."

"But how?" He couldn't explain to her he had no agents, that he had never met Cifuentes or Dr. Sanchez, that neither Teresa nor Raul even existed: Raul had come alive only in order to be killed.

"What did Milly call this?"

"A sprayer."

"I've seen something like it before somewhere."

"I expect you have. Most vacuum cleaners have them." He took it away from her. He couldn't remember whether he had included it in the drawings he had sent to Hawthorne.

"What do I do now, Beatrice?"

"I think your people should go into hiding for a while. Not here, of course. It would be too crowded and anyway not safe. What about that Chief Engineer of yours—could he smuggle them on board?"

"He's away at sea on the way to Cienfuegos."

"Anyway he's probably blown too," she said thoughtfully. "I wonder why they've let you and me get back here."

"What do you mean?"

"They could easily have shot us down on the front. Or perhaps they're using us for bait. Of course you throw away the bait if it's no good."

"What a macabre woman you are."

"Oh no. We're back into the *Boy's Own Paper* world, that's all. You can count yourself lucky."

"Why?"

"It might have been the *Sunday Mirror*. The world is modelled after the popular magazines nowadays. My husband came out of *Encounter*. The question we have to consider is to which paper *they* belong."

"They?"

"Let's assume they belong to the *Boy's Own Paper* too. Are they Russian agents,

German agents, American, what? Cuban very likely. Those concrete platforms must be official, mustn't they? Poor Raul. I hope he died quickly.''

He was tempted to tell her everything, but what was ''everything''? He no longer knew. Raul had been killed. Hasselbacher said so.

''First the Shanghai Theatre,'' she said. ''Will it be open?''

''The second performance won't be over.''

''If the police are not there before us. Of course they didn't use the police against Cifuentes. He was probably too important. In murdering anyone you have to avoid scandal.''

''I hadn't thought of it in that light before.''

Beatrice turned out the bedside light and went to the window. She said, ''Don't you have a back door?''

''No.''

''We'll have to change all that,'' she said airily, as though she were an architect too. ''Do you know a nigger with a limp?''

''That will be Joe.''

''He's going slowly by.''

''He sells dirty postcards. He's going home, that's all.''

''He couldn't be expected to follow you with that limp, of course. He may be their tictac man. Anyway we'll have to risk it. They are obviously making a sweep tonight. Women and children first. The professor can wait.''

''But I've never seen Teresa at the theatre. She probably has a different name there.''

''You can pick her out, can't you, even without her clothes? Though I suppose we do look a bit the same naked, like the Japanese.''

''I don't think you ought to come.''

''I must. If one is stopped the other can make a dash for it.''

''I meant to the Shanghai. It's not exactly *Boy's Own Paper*.''

''Nor is marriage,'' she said, ''even in UNESCO.''

ii

The Shanghai was in a narrow street off Zanja surrounded by deep bars. A board advertised *Posiciones*, and the tickets for some reason were sold on the pavement outside, perhaps because there was no room for a box-office, as the foyer was occupied by a pornographic bookshop for the benefit of those who wanted entertainment during the *entr'acte*. The black pimps in the street watched them with curiosity. They were not used to European women here.

''It feels far from home,'' Beatrice said.

The seats all cost one peso twenty-five and there were very few empty ones left in the large hall. The man who showed them the way offered Wormold a packet of pornographic postcards for a peso. When Wormold refused them, he drew a second selection from his pocket.

"Buy them if you want to," Beatrice said. "If it embarrasses you I'll keep my eye on the show."

"There's not much difference," Wormold said, "between the show and the postcards."

The attendant asked if the lady would like a marijuana cigarette.

"*Nein, danke,*" Beatrice said, getting her languages confused.

On either side of the stage, posters advertised clubs in the neighbourhood where the girls were said to be beautiful. A notice in Spanish and bad English forbade the audience to molest the dancers.

"Which is Teresa?" Beatrice asked.

"I think it must be the fat one in the mask," Wormold said at random.

She was just leaving the stage with a heave of her great naked buttocks, and the audience clapped and whistled. Then the lights went down and a screen was lowered. A film began, quite mildly at first. It showed a bicyclist, some woodland scenery, a punctured tyre, a chance encounter, a gentleman raising a straw hat; there was a great deal of flicker and fog.

Beatrice sat silent. There was an odd intimacy between them as they watched together this blue print of love. Similar movements of the body had once meant more to them than anything else the world had to offer. The act of lust and the act of love are the same; it cannot be falsified like a sentiment.

The lights went on. They sat in silence. "My lips are dry," Wormold said.

"I haven't any spit left. Can't we go behind and see Teresa now?"

"There's another film after this and then the dancers come on again."

"I'm not tough enough for another film," Beatrice said.

"They won't let us go behind until the show's over."

"We can wait in the street, can't we? At least we'll know then if we've been followed."

They left as the second film started. They were the only ones to rise, so if somebody had tailed them he must be waiting for them in the street, but there was no obvious candidate among the taxi-drivers and the pimps. One man slept against the lamp-post with a lottery-number slung askew round his neck. Wormold remembered the night with Dr. Hasselbacher. That was when he had learnt the new use for Lamb's *Tales from Shakespeare*. Poor Hasselbacher had been very drunk. Wormold remembered how he had sat slumped in the lounge when he came down from Hawthorne's room. He said to Beatrice, "How easy is it to break a book-code if once you've got the right book?"

"Not hard for an expert," she said, "only a question of patience." She went across to the lottery-seller and straightened the number. The man didn't wake. She said, "It was difficult to read it sideways."

Had he carried Lamb under his arm, in his pocket, or in his brief-case? Had he laid the book down when he helped Dr. Hasselbacher to rise? He could remember nothing, and such suspicions were ungenerous.

"I thought of a funny coincidence," Beatrice said. "Dr. Hasselbacher reads

Lamb's *Tales* in the right edition.'' It was as though her basic training had included telepathy.

"You saw it in his flat?"

"Yes."

"But he would have hidden it," he protested, "if it meant anything at all."

"Or he wanted to warn you. Remember, he brought us back there. He told us about Raul."

"He couldn't have known that he would meet us."

"How do you know?"

He wanted to protest that nothing made sense, that Raul didn't exist, and Teresa didn't exist, and then he thought of how she would pack up and go away and it would all be like a story without a purpose.

"People are coming out," Beatrice said.

They found a side-door that led to the one big dressing-room. The passage was lit by a bare globe that had burned far too many days and nights. The passage was nearly blocked by dustbins and a negro with a broom was sweeping up scraps of cotton-wool stained with face powder, lipstick and ambiguous things; the place smelled of pear-drops. Perhaps after all there would be no one here called Teresa, but he wished that he had not chosen so popular a saint. He pushed a door open and it was like a medieval inferno full of smoke and naked women.

He said to Beatrice, "Don't you think you'd better go home?"

"It's you who need protection here," she said.

Nobody even noticed them. The mask of the fat woman dangled from one ear and she was drinking a glass of wine with one leg up on a chair. A very thin girl with ribs like piano-keys was pulling on her stockings. Breasts swayed, buttocks bent, cigarettes half finished fumed in saucers; the air was thick with burning paper. A man stood on a stepladder with a screwdriver fixing something.

"Where is she?" Beatrice asked.

"I don't think she's here. Perhaps she's sick, or with her lover."

The air flapped warmly round them as someone put on a dress. Little grains of powder settled like ash.

"Try calling her name."

He shouted "Teresa" half-heartedly. Nobody paid any attention. He tried again and the man with the screwdriver looked down at him.

"*Paso algo?*" he asked.

Wormold said in Spanish that he was looking for a girl called Teresa. The man suggested that Maria would do just as well. He pointed his screwdriver at the fat woman.

"What's he saying?"

"He doesn't seem to know Teresa."

The man with the screwdriver sat down on top of the ladder and began to make a speech. He said that Maria was the best woman you could find in Havana. She weighed one hundred kilos with nothing on.

"Obviously Teresa is not here," Wormold explained with relief.

"Teresa. Teresa. What do you want with Teresa?"

"Yes. What do you want with me?" the thin girl demanded, coming forward holding out one stocking. Her little breasts were the size of pears.

"Who are you?"

"*Soy* Teresa."

Beatrice said, "Is that Teresa? You said she was fat—like that one with the mask."

"No, no," Wormold said. "That's not Teresa. She's Teresa's sister. *Soy* means sister." He said, "I'll send a message by her." He took the thin girl's arm and moved her a little away. He tried to explain to her in Spanish that she had to be careful.

"Who are you? I don't understand."

"There has been a mistake. It is too long a story. There are people who may try to do you an injury. Please stay at home for a few days. Don't come to the theatre."

"I have to. I meet my clients here."

Wormold took out a wad of money. He said, "Have you relations?"

"I have my mother."

"Go to her."

"But she is in Cienfuegos."

"There is plenty of money there to take you to Cienfuegos." Everybody was listening now. They pressed close around. The man with the screwdriver had come down from the ladder. Wormold saw Beatrice outside the circle; she was pushing closer, trying to make out what he was saying.

The man with the screwdriver said, "That girl belongs to Pedro. You can't take her away like that. You must talk to Pedro first."

"I do not want to go to Cienfuegos," the girl said.

"You will be safe there."

She appealed to the man. "He frightens me. I cannot understand what he wants." She exhibited the pesos. "This is too much money." She appealed to them. "I am a good girl."

"A lot of wheat does not make a bad year," the fat woman said with solemnity.

"Where is your Pedro?" the man asked.

"He is ill. Why does the man give me all this money? I am a good girl. You know that my price is fifteen pesos. I am not a hustler."

"A lean dog is full of fleas," said the fat woman. She seemed to have a proverb for every occasion.

"What's happening?" Beatrice asked.

A voice hissed, "Psst, psst!" It was the negro who had been sweeping the passage. He said, "*Policia!*"

"Oh hell," Wormold said, "that tears it. I've got to get you out of here." No one seemed unduly disturbed. The fat woman drained her wine and put on a pair of knickers; the girl who was called Teresa pulled on her second stocking.

"It doesn't matter about me," Beatrice said. "You've got to get *her* away."

"What do the police want?" Wormold asked the man on the ladder.

"A girl," he said cynically.

"I want to get this girl out," Wormold said. "Isn't there some back way?"

"With the police there's always a back way."

"Where?"

"Got fifty pesos to spare?"

"Yes."

"Give them to him. Hi, Miguel," he called to the negro. "Tell them to stay asleep for three minutes. Now who wants to be treated to freedom?"

"I prefer the police-station," the fat woman said. "But one has to be properly clothed." She adjusted her bra.

"Come with me," Wormold said to Teresa.

"Why should I?"

"You don't realise—they want you."

"I doubt it," said the man with the screwdriver. "She's too thin. You had better hurry. Fifty pesos do not last forever."

"Here, take my coat," Beatrice said. She wrapped it round the shoulders of the girl, who had now two stockings on but nothing else. The girl said, "But I want to stay."

The man slapped her bottom and gave her a push. "You have his money," he said. "Go with him." He herded them into a small and evil toilet and then through a window. They found themselves in the street. A policeman on guard outside the theatre ostentatiously looked elsewhere. A pimp whistled and pointed to Wormold's car. The girl said again, "I want to stay," but Beatrice pushed her into the rear seat and followed her in. "I shall scream," the girl told them and leant out of the window.

"Don't be a fool," Beatrice said, pulling her inside. Wormold got the car started.

The girl screamed but only in a tentative way. The policeman turned and looked in the opposite direction. The fifty pesos seemed to be still effective. They turned right and drove towards the sea-front. No car followed them. It was as easy as all that. The girl, now that she had no choice, adjusted the coat for modesty and leant comfortably back. She said, *"Hay mucha corriente."*

"What's she saying?"

"She's complaining of the draught," Wormold said.

"She doesn't seem a very grateful girl. Where's her sister?"

"With the Director of Posts and Telegraphs, at Cienfuegos. Of course I could drive her there. We'd arrive by breakfast time. But there's Milly."

"There's more than Milly. You've forgotten Professor Sanchez."

"Surely Professor Sanchez can wait."

"They seem to be acting fast, whoever they are."

"I don't know where he lives."

"I do. I looked him up in the Country Club list before we came."

"You take this girl home and wait there."

They came out on to the front. "You turn left here," Beatrice said.

"I'm taking you home."

"It's better to stay together."

"Milly . . ."

"You don't want to compromise *her*, do you?"

Reluctantly Wormold turned left. "Where to?"

"Vedado," Beatrice said.

iii

The skyscrapers of the new town stood up ahead of them like icicles in the moonlight. A great H.H. was stamped on the sky, like the monogram on Hawthorne's pocket, but it wasn't royal either—it only advertised Mr. Hilton. The wind rocked the car, and the spray broke across the traffic-lanes and misted the seaward window. The hot night tasted of salt. Wormold swung the car away from the sea. The girl said, "*Hace demasiado calor.*"

"What's she saying now?"

"She says it's too hot."

"She's a difficult girl," Beatrice said. "Better turn down the window again."

"Suppose she screams?"

"I'll slap her."

They were in the new quarter of Vedado: little cream-and-white houses owned by rich men. You could tell how rich a man was by the fewness of the floors. Only a millionaire could afford a bungalow on a site that might have held a skyscraper. When he lowered the window they could smell the flowers. She stopped him by a gate in a high white wall. She said, "I can see lights in the patio. Everything seems all right. I'll guard your precious bit of flesh while you go in."

"He seems to be very wealthy for a professor."

"He's not too rich to charge expenses, according to your accounts."

Wormold said, "Give me a few minutes. Don't go away."

"Am I likely to? You'd better hurry. So far they've only scored one out of three, and a near miss, of course."

He tried the grilled gate. It was not locked. The position was absurd. How was he to explain his presence? "You are an agent of mine without knowing it. You are in danger. You must hide." He didn't even know of what subject Sanchez was a professor.

A short path between two palm-trees led to a second grilled gate, and beyond was the little patio where the lights were on. A gramophone was playing softly and two tall figures revolved in silence cheek to cheek. As he limped up the path a concealed alarm-bell rang. The dancers stopped and one of them came out on to the path to meet him.

"Who is that?"

"Professor Sanchez?"

"Yes."

They both converged into the area of light. The professor wore a white dinner-jacket, his hair was white, he had white morning stubble on his chin, and he carried a revolver in his hand which he pointed at Wormold. Wormold saw that the woman behind him was very young and very pretty. She stooped and turned off the gramophone.

"Forgive me for calling on you at this hour," Wormold said. He had no idea how he should begin, and he was disquieted by the revolver. Professors ought not to carry revolvers.

"I am afraid I don't remember your face." The professor spoke politely and kept the revolver pointed at Wormold's stomach.

"There's no reason why you should. Unless you have a vacuum cleaner."

"Vacuum cleaner? I suppose I have. Why? My wife would know." The young woman came through from the patio and joined them. She had no shoes on. The discarded shoes stood beside the gramophone like mousetraps. "What does he want?" she asked disagreeably.

"I'm sorry to disturb you, Señora Sanchez."

"Tell him I'm not Señora Sanchez," the young woman said.

"He says he has something to do with vacuum cleaners," the professor said. "Do you think Maria, before she went away . . . ?"

"Why does he come here at one in the morning?"

"You must forgive me," the professor said with an air of embarrassment, "but this *is* an unusual time." He allowed his revolver to move a little off target. "One doesn't as a rule expect visitors . . ."

"You seem to expect them."

"Oh, this—one has to take precautions. You see, I have some very fine Renoirs."

"He's not after the pictures. Maria sent him. You are a spy, aren't you?" the young woman asked fiercely.

"Well, in a way."

The young woman began to wail, beating at her own long slim flanks. Her bracelets jangled and glinted.

"Don't, dear, don't. I'm sure there's an explanation."

"She envies our happiness," the young woman said. "First she sent the cardinal, didn't she, and now this man . . . Are you a priest?" she asked.

"My dear, of course, he's not a priest. Look at his clothes."

"You may be a professor of comparative education," the young woman said, "but you can be deceived by anyone. Are you a priest?" she repeated.

"No."

"What are you?"

"As a matter of fact I sell vacuum cleaners."

"You said you were a spy."

"Well, yes, I suppose in a sense . . ."

"What have you come here for?"

"To warn you."

The young woman gave an odd bitch-like howl. "You see," she said to the professor, "she's threatening us now. First the cardinal and then . . ."

"The cardinal was only doing his duty. After all he's Maria's cousin."

"You're afraid of him. You want to leave me."

"My dear, you know that isn't true." He said to Wormold, "Where is Maria now?"

"I don't know."

"When did you see her last?"

"But I've never seen her."

"You do rather contradict yourself, don't you?"

"He's a lying hound," the young woman said.

"Not necessarily, dear. He's probably employed by some agency. We had better sit down quietly and hear what he has to say. Anger is always a mistake. He's doing his duty—which is more than can be said of us." The professor led the way back to the patio. He had put his revolver back in his pocket. The young woman waited until Wormold began to follow and then brought up the rear like a watchdog. He half expected her to bit his ankle. He thought, Unless I speak soon, I shall never speak.

"Take a chair," the professor said. What *was* comparative education?

"May I give you a drink?"

"Please don't bother."

"You don't drink on duty?"

"Duty!" the young woman said. "You treat him like a human being. What duty has he got except to his despicable employers?"

"I came here to warn you that the police . . ."

"Oh come, come, adultery is not a crime," the professor said. "I think it has seldom been regarded as that except in the American colonies in the seventeenth century. And in the Mosaic Law, of course."

"Adultery has got nothing to do with it," the young woman said. "She didn't mind us sleeping together, she only minded our being together."

"You can hardly have one without the other, unless you are thinking of the New Testament," the professor said. "Adultery in the heart."

"You have no heart unless you turn this man out. We sit here talking as though we had been married for years. If all you want to do is to sit up all night and talk, why didn't you stick to Maria?"

"My dear, it was your idea to dance before bed."

"You call what you did dancing?"

"I told you that I would take lessons."

"Oh yes, so as to be with the girls at the school."

The conversation seemed to Wormold to be reeling out of sight. He said desperately, "They shot at Engineer Cifuentes. You are in the same danger."

"If I wanted girls, dear, there are plenty at the university. They come to my lectures. No doubt you are aware of that, since you came yourself."

"You taunt me with it?"

"We are straying from the subject, dear. The subject is what action Maria is likely to take next."

"She ought to have given up starchy foods two years ago," the young girl said rather cheaply, "knowing you. You only care for the body. You ought to be ashamed at your age."

"If you don't wish me to love you . . ."

"Love. Love." The young woman began to pace the patio. She made gestures in the air as though she were dismembering love. Wormold said, "It's not Maria you have to worry about."

"You lying hound," she screamed at him. "You said you'd never seen her."

"I haven't."

"Then why do you call her Maria?" she cried and began to do triumphant dance-steps with an imaginary partner.

"You said something about Cifuentes, young man?"

"He was shot at this evening."

"Who by?"

"I don't know exactly, but it's all part of the same round-up. It's a bit difficult to explain, but you really seem to be in great danger, Professor Sanchez. It's all a mistake, of course. The police have been to the Shanghai Theatre too."

"What have I to do with the Shanghai Theatre?"

"What indeed?" cried the young woman melodramatically. "Men," she said, "men! Poor Maria. She hasn't only one woman to deal with. She'll have to plan a massacre."

"I've never had anything to do with anybody at the Shanghai Theatre."

"Maria is better informed. I expect you walk in your sleep."

"You heard what he said, it's a mistake. After all, they shot at Cifuentes. You can't blame her for that."

"Cifuentes? Did he say Cifuentes? Oh, you Spanish oaf. Just because he talked to me one day at the Club while you were in the shower you go and hire desperadoes to kill him."

"Please, dear, be reasonable. I only heard of it just now when this gentle-man . . ."

"He's not a gentleman. He's a lying hound." They had again come full circle in the conversation.

"If he's a liar we need pay no attention to what he says. He's probably slandering Maria too."

"Ah, you would stick up for her."

Wormold said with desperation—it was his last fling, "This has got nothing to do with Maria—with Señora Sanchez, I mean."

"What on earth has Señora Sanchez to do with it?" the professor asked.

"I thought you thought that Maria . . ."

"Young man, you aren't seriously telling me that Maria is planning to do some-thing to my wife as well as to my . . . my friend here? It's too absurd."

Until now the mistake had seemed to Wormold fairly simple to deal with. But now it was as though he had tugged a stray piece of cotton and a whole suit had begun to unwind. Was this Comparative Education? He said, "I thought I was doing you a favour by coming to warn you, but it looks as if death for you might be the best solution."

"You are a very mystifying young man."

"Not young. It's you, Professor, who are young by the look of things." In his anxiety he spoke aloud, "If only Beatrice were here."

The professor said quickly, "I absolutely assure you, dear, that I know nobody called Beatrice. Nobody."

The young woman gave a tigerish laugh.

"You seem to have come here," the professor said, "with the sole purpose of making trouble." It was his first complaint and it seemed a very mild one under the circumstances. "I cannot think what you have to gain by it," he said and walked into the house and closed the door.

"He's a monster," the girl said. "A monster. A sexual monster. A satyr."

"You don't understand."

"I know that tag—to know all is to forgive all. Not in this case, it isn't." She seemed to have lost her hostility to Wormold. "Maria, me, Beatrice—I don't count his wife, poor woman. I've got nothing against his wife. Have you a gun?"

"Of course not. I only came here to save him," Wormold said.

"Let them shoot," the young woman said, "in the belly—low down." And she too went into the house with an air of purpose.

There was nothing left for Wormold to do but go. The invisible alarm gave another warning as he walked towards the gate, but no one stirred in the little white house. I've done my best, Wormold thought. The professor seemed well prepared for any danger and perhaps the arrival of the police might be a relief to him. They would be easier to cope with than the young woman.

iv

Walking away through the smell of the night-flowering plants he had only one wish: to tell Beatrice everything. I am no secret agent, I'm a fraud, none of these people are my agents, and I don't know what's happening. I'm lost. I'm scared. Surely somehow she would take control of the situation; after all she was a professional. But he knew that he would not appeal to her. It meant giving up security for Milly. He would rather be eliminated like Raul. Did they, in his service, give pensions to offspring? But who was Raul?

Before he had reached the second gate Beatrice called to him, "Jim. Look out. Keep away." Even at that urgent moment the thought occurred to him, my name is Wormold, Mr. Wormold, Señor Vomel, nobody calls me Jim. Then he ran— hop and skip—towards the voice and came out to the street, to a radio-car, and to three police-officers, and another revolver pointing at his stomach. Beatrice stood on the sidewalk and the girl was beside her, trying to keep a coat closed which hadn't been designed that way.

"What's the matter?"

"I can't understand a word they say."

One of the officers told him to get into their car.

"What about my own?"

"It will be brought to the station." Before he obeyed they felt him down the breast and side for arms. He said to Beatrice, "I don't know what it's all about, but it looks like the end of a bright career." The officer spoke again. "He wants you to get in too."

"Tell him," Beatrice said, "I'm going to stay with Teresa's sister. I don't trust them."

The two cars drove softly away among the little houses of the millionaires, to avoid disturbing anyone, as though they were in a street of hospitals; the rich need sleep. They had not far to go: a courtyard, a gate closing behind them, and then the odour of a police-station like the ammoniac smell of zoos all the world over. Along the whitewashed passage the portraits of wanted men hung, with the spurious look of bearded old masters. In the room at the end Captain Segura sat playing draughts. "Huff," he said, and took two pieces. Then he looked up at them. "Mr. Wormold," he said with surprise, and rose like a small tight green snake from his seat when he saw Beatrice. He looked beyond her at Teresa; the coat had fallen open again, perhaps with intention. He said, "Who in God's name . . . ?" and then to the policeman with whom he had been playing, "*Anda!*"

"What's the meaning of all this, Captain Segura?"

"You are asking me that, Mr. Wormold?"

"Yes."

"I wish you would tell me the meaning. I had no idea I should see you—Milly's father. Mr. Wormold, we had a call from a Professor Sanchez about a man who had broken into his house with vague threats. He thought it had something to do with his pictures; he has very valuable pictures. I sent a radio-car at once and it is you they pick up, with the señorita here (we have met before) and a naked tart." Like the police-sergeant in Santiago he added, "That is not very nice, Mr. Wormold."

"We had been at the Shanghai."

"That is not very nice either."

"I'm tired of being told by the police that I am not nice."

"Why did you visit Professor Sanchez?"

"That was all a mistake."

"Why do you have a naked tart in your car?"

"We were giving her a lift."

"She has no right to be naked on the streets." The police-officer leant across the desk and whispered. "Ah," Captain Segura said. "I begin to understand. There was a police-inspection tonight at the Shanghai. I suppose the girl had forgotten her papers and wanted to avoid a night in the cells. She appealed to you . . ."

"It wasn't that way at all."

"It had better be that way, Mr. Wormold." He said to the girl in Spanish, "Your papers. You have no papers."

She said indignantly, "*Si, yo tengo.*" She bent down and pulled pieces of crumpled paper from the top of her stockings. Captain Segura took them and examined them. He gave a deep sigh. "Mr. Wormold, Mr. Wormold, her papers are in order. Why do you drive about the streets with a naked girl? Why do you break into the house of Professor Sanchez and talk to him about his wife and threaten him? What is his wife to you?" He said "Go" sharply to the girl. She hesitated and began to take off the coat.

"Better let her keep it," Beatrice said.

Captain Segura sat wearily down in front of the draughts board. "Mr. Wormold, for your sake I tell you this: do not get mixed up with the wife of Professor Sanchez. She is not a woman you can treat lightly."

"I am not mixed up . . ."

"Do you play checkers, Mr. Wormold?"

"Yes. Not very well, I'm afraid."

"Better than these pigs in the station, I expect. We must play together sometimes, you and I. But in checkers you must move very carefully, just as with the wife of Professor Sanchez." He moved a piece at random on the board and said, "Tonight you were with Dr. Hasselbacher."

"Yes."

"Was that wise, Mr. Wormold?" He didn't look up, moving the pieces here and there, playing against himself.

"Wise?"

"Dr. Hasselbacher has got into strange company."

"I know nothing about that."

"Why did you send him a postcard from Santiago marked with the position of your room?"

"What a lot of unimportant things you know, Captain Segura."

"I have a reason to be interested in you, Mr. Wormold. I don't want to see you involved. What was it that Dr. Hasselbacher wished to tell you tonight? His telephone, you understand, is tapped."

"He wanted to play us a record of *Tristan*."

"And perhaps to speak of this?" Captain Segura reversed a photograph on his desk—a flashlight picture with the characteristic glare of white faces gathered round a heap of smashed metal which had once been a car. "And this?" A young man's face unflinching in the flashlight: an empty cigarette-carton crumpled like his life: a man's foot touching his shoulders.

"Do you know him?"

"No."

Captain Segura depressed a lever and a voice spoke in English from a box on his desk. "Hullo. Hullo. Hasselbacher speaking."

"Is anyone with you, H-Hasselbacher?"

"Yes. Friends."

"What friends?"

"If you must know, Mr. Wormold is here."

"Tell him Raul's dead."

"Dead? But they promised . . ."

"You can't always control an accident, H-Hasselbacher." The voice had a slight hesitation before the aspirate.

"They gave me their word . . ."

"The car turned over too many times."

"They said it would be just a warning."

"It is still a warning. Go in and tell h-him that Raul is dead."

The hiss of the tape went on a moment; a door closed.

"Do you still say you know nothing of Raul?" Segura asked.

Wormold looked at Beatrice. She made a slight negative motion of her head. Wormold said, "I give you my word of honour, Segura, that I didn't even know he existed until tonight."

Segura moved a piece. "Your word of honour?"

"My word of honour."

"You are Milly's father. I have to accept it. But stay away from naked women and the professor's wife. Good night, Mr. Wormold."

"Good night."

They had reached the door when Segura spoke again. "And our game of checkers, Mr. Wormold. We won't forget that."

The old Hillman was waiting in the street. Wormold said, "I'll leave you with Milly."

"Aren't you going home?"

"It's too late to sleep now."

"Where are you going? Can't I come with you?"

"I want you to stay with Milly in case of accidents. Did you see that photograph?"

"Yes."

They didn't speak again before Lamparilla. Then Beatrice said, "I wish you hadn't given your word of honour. You needn't have gone as far as that."

"No?"

"Oh, it was professional of you, I can see that. I'm sorry. It's stupid of me. But you are more professional than I ever believed you were." He opened the street-door for her and watched her move away among the vacuum cleaners like a mourner in a cemetery.

2

At the door of Dr. Hasselbacher's apartment house he rang the bell of a stranger on the second floor whose light was on. There was a buzz and the door unlatched. The lift stood ready and he took it up to Dr. Hasselbacher's flat. Dr.

Hasselbacher too had apparently not found sleep. A light shone under the crack of the door. Was he alone or was he in conference with the taped voice?

He was beginning to learn the caution and tricks of his unreal trade. There was a tall window on the landing which led to a purposeless balcony too narrow for use. From this balcony he could see a light in the doctor's flat and it was only a long stride from one balcony to another. He took it without looking at the ground below. The curtains were not quite drawn. He peered between.

Dr. Hasselbacher sat facing him wearing an old *pickel-haube* helmet, a breast-plate, boots, white gloves, what could only be the ancient uniform of a Uhlan. His eyes were closed and he seemed to be asleep. He was wearing a sword, and he looked like an extra in a film-studio. Wormold tapped on the window. Dr. Hasselbacher opened his eyes and stared straight at him.

"Hasselbacher."

The doctor gave a small movement that might have been panic. He tried to whip off his helmet, but the chinstrap prevented him.

"It's me, Wormold."

The doctor came reluctantly forward to the window. His breeches were far too tight. They had been made for a younger man.

"What are you doing there, Mr. Wormold?"

"What are you doing there, Hasselbacher?"

The doctor opened the window and let Wormold in. He found that he was in the doctor's bedroom. A big wardrobe stood open and two white suits hung there like the last teeth in an old mouth. Hasselbacher began to take off his gloves. "Have you been to a fancy-dress dance, Hasselbacher?"

Dr. Hasselbacher said in a shamed voice, "You wouldn't understand." He began piece by piece to rid himself of his paraphernalia—first the gloves, then the helmet, the breastplate, in which Wormold and the furnishings of the room were reflected and distorted like figures in a hall of mirrors. "Why did you come back? Why didn't you ring the bell?"

"I want to know who Raul is."

"You know already."

"I've no idea."

Dr. Hasselbacher sat down and pulled at his boots.

"Are you an admirer of Charles Lamb, Dr. Hasselbacher?"

"Milly lent it me. Don't you remember how she talked of it . . . ?" He sat forlornly in the bulging breeches. Wormold saw that they had been unstitched along a seam to allow room for the contemporary Hasselbacher. Yes, he remembered now the evening at the Tropicana.

"I suppose," Hasselbacher said, "this uniform seems to you to need an explanation."

"Other things need one more."

"I was a Uhlan officer—oh, forty-five years ago."

"I remember a photograph of you in the other room. You were not dressed like that. You looked more—practical."

"That was after the war started. Look over there by my dressing-table—1913, the June manœuvres, the Kaiser was inspecting us.'' The old brown photograph with the photographer's indented seal in the corner showed the long ranks of the cavalry, swords drawn, and a little Imperial figure with a withered arm on a white horse riding by. "It was all so peaceful," Dr. Hasselbacher said, "in those days."

"Peaceful?"

"Until the war came."

"But I thought you were a doctor."

"I became one later. When the war was over. After I'd killed a man. You kill a man—that is so easy," Dr. Hasselbacher said, "it needs no skill. You can be certain of what you've done, you can judge death, but to save a man—that takes more than six years of training, and in the end you can never be quite sure that it was you who saved him. Germs are killed by other germs. People just survive. There is not one patient whom I know for certain that I saved, but the man I killed—I know him. He was Russian and he was very thin. I scraped the bone when I pushed the steel in. It set my teeth on edge. There was nothing but marshes around, and they called it Tannenberg. I hate war, Mr. Wormold."

"Then why do you dress up like a soldier?"

"I was not dressed up in this way when I killed a man. This was peaceful. I love this." He touched the breastplate beside him on the bed. "But there we had the mud of the marshes on us." He said, "Do you never have a desire, Mr. Wormold, to go back to peace? Oh no, I forget, you're young, you've never known it. This was the last peace for any of us. The trousers don't fit any more."

"What made you—tonight—want to dress up like this, Hasselbacher?"

"A man's death."

"Raul?"

"Yes."

"Did you know him?"

"Yes."

"Tell me about him."

"I don't want to talk."

"It would be better to talk."

"We were both responsible for his death, you and I," Hasselbacher said. "I don't know who trapped you into it or how, but if I had refused to help them they would have had me deported. What could I do out of Cuba now? I told you I had lost papers."

"What papers?"

"Never mind that. Don't we all have something in the past to worry about? I know why they broke up my flat now. Because I was a friend of yours. Please go away, Mr. Wormold. Who knows what they might expect me to do if they knew you were here?"

"Who are they?"

"You know that better than I do, Mr. Wormold. They don't introduce themselves." Something moved rapidly in the next room.

"Only a mouse, Mr. Wormold. I keep a little cheese for it at night."

"So Milly lent you Lamb's *Tales*."

"I'm glad you have changed your code," Dr. Hasselbacher said. "Perhaps now they will leave me alone. I can't help them any longer. One begins with acrostics and crosswords and mathematical puzzles and then, before you know, you are employed . . . Nowadays we have to be careful even of our hobbies."

"But Raul—he didn't even exist. You advised me to lie and I lied. They were nothing but inventions, Hasselbacher."

"And Cifuentes? Are you telling me he didn't exist either?"

"He was different. I invented Raul."

"Then you invented him too well, Mr. Wormold. There's a whole file on him now."

"He was no more real than a character in a novel."

"Are they always invented? I don't know how a novelist works, Mr. Wormold. I have never known one before you."

"There was no drunk pilot in the Cubana air line."

"Oh, I agree, you must have invented that detail. I don't know why."

"If you were breaking my cables you must have realised there was no truth in them, you know the city. A pilot dismissed for drunkenness, a friend with a plane, they were all inventions."

"I don't know your motive, Mr. Wormold. Perhaps you wanted to disguise his identity in case we broke your code. Perhaps if your friends had known he had private means and a plane of his own, they wouldn't have paid him so much. How much of it all got into his pocket, I wonder, and how much into yours?"

"I don't understand a word you're saying."

"You read the papers, Mr. Wormold. You know he had his flying-licence taken away a month ago when he landed drunk in a child's playground."

"I don't read the local papers."

"Never? Of course he denied working for you. They offered him a lot of money if he would work for them instead. They too want photographs, Mr. Wormold, of those platforms you discovered in the Oriente hills."

"There are no platforms."

"Don't expect me to believe too much, Mr. Wormold. You referred in one cable to plans you had sent to London. They needed photographs too."

"You must know who They are."

"*Cui bono?*"

"And what do they plan for me?"

"At first they promised me they were planning nothing. You have been useful to them. They knew about you from the very beginning, Mr. Wormold, but they didn't take you seriously. They even thought you might be inventing your reports. But then you changed your codes and your staff increased. The British Secret Service would not be so easily deceived as all that, would it?" A kind of loyalty to Hawthorne kept Wormold silent. "Mr. Wormold, Mr. Wormold, why did you ever begin?"

"You know why. I needed the money." He found himself taking to truth like a tranquilliser.

"I would have lent you money. I offered to."

"I needed more than you could lend me."

"For Milly?"

"Yes."

"Take good care of her, Mr. Wormold. You are in a trade where it is unsafe to love anybody or anything. They strike at that. You remember the culture I was making?"

"Yes."

"Perhaps if they hadn't destroyed my will to live, they wouldn't have persuaded me so easily."

"Do you really think . . . ?"

"I only ask you to be careful."

"Can I use your telephone?"

"Yes."

Wormold rang up his house. Did he only imagine that slight click which indicated that the tapper was at work? Beatrice answered. He said, "Is everything quiet?"

"Yes."

"Wait till I come. Is Milly all right?"

"Fast asleep."

"I'm coming back."

Dr. Hasselbacher said, "You shouldn't have shown love in your voice. Who knows who was listening?" He walked with difficulty to the door because of his tight breeches. "Good night, Mr. Wormold. Here is the Lamb."

"I won't need it any more."

"Milly may want it. Would you mind saying nothing to anyone about this—this—costume? I know that I am absurd, but I loved those days. Once the Kaiser spoke to me."

"What did he say?"

"He said, 'I remember you. You are Captain Müller.' "

Interlude in London

When the Chief had guests he dined at home and cooked his own dinner, for no restaurant satisfied his meticulous and romantic standard. There was a story that once when he was ill he refused to cancel an invitation to an old friend, but cooked the meal from his bed by telephone. With a watch before him on the bed-table he would interrupt the conversation at the correct interval, to give directions to his valet. "Hallo, hallo, Brewer, hallo, you should take that chicken out now and baste it again."

It was also said that once when he had been kept late at the office and had tried to cook the meal from there, dinner had been ruined because from force of habit he had used his red telephone, the scrambler, and only strange noises resembling rapid Japanese had reached the valet's ears.

The meal which he served to the Permanent Under-Secretary was simple and excellent: a roast with a touch of garlic. A Wensleydale cheese stood on the sideboard and the quiet of Albany lay deeply around them like snow. After his exertions in the kitchen the Chief himself smelt faintly of gravy.

"It's really excellent. Excellent."

"An old Norfolk recipe. Granny Brown's Ipswich Roast."

"And the meat itself . . . it really melts . . ."

"I've trained Brewer to do the marketing, but he'll never make a cook. He needs constant supervision."

They ate for a while reverently in silence; the clink of a woman's shoes along the Rope Walk was the only distraction.

"A good wine," the Permanent Under-Secretary said at last.

" '55 is coming along nicely. Still a little young?"

"Hardly."

With the cheese the Chief spoke again. "The Russian note—what does the F.O. think?"

"We are a little puzzled by the reference to the Caribbean bases." There was a crackling of Romary biscuits. "They can hardly refer to the Bahamas. They are worth about what the Yankees paid us, a few old destroyers. Yet we've always assumed that those constructions in Cuba had a Communist origin. You don't think they could have an American origin after all?"

"Wouldn't we have been informed?"

"Not necessarily, I'm afraid. Since the Fuchs case. They say we keep a good deal under our own hat too. What does your man in Havana say?"

"I'll ask him for a full assessment. How's the Wensleydale?"

"Perfect."

"Help yourself to the port."

"Cockburn '35, isn't it?"

" '27."

"Do you believe they intend war eventually?" the Chief asked.

"Your guess is as good as mine."

"They've become very active in Cuba—apparently with the help of the police. Our man in Havana has had a difficult time. His best agent, as you know, was killed, accidentally of course, on his way to take aerial photographs of the constructions—a very great loss to us. But I would give much more than a man's life for those photographs. As it was, we had given fifteen hundred dollars. They shot at another of our agents in the street and he's taken fright. A third's gone underground. There's a woman too, they interrogated her, in spite of her being the mistress of the Director of Posts and Telegraphs. They have left our man alone so far, perhaps to watch. Anyway he's a canny bird."

"Surely he must have been a bit careless to lose all those agents?"

"At the beginning we have to expect casualties. They broke his book-code. I'm never happy with these book-codes. There's a German out there who seems to be their biggest operator and an expert at cryptography. Hawthorne warned our man, but you know what these old merchants are like; they have an obstinate loyalty. Perhaps it was worth a few casualties to open his eyes. Cigar?"

"Thanks. Will he be able to start again if he's blown?"

"He has a trick worth two of that. Struck right home into the enemy-camp. Recruited a double agent in the police-headquarters itself."

"Aren't double agents always a bit—tricky? You never know whether you're getting the fat or the lean."

"I trust our man to huff him every time," the Chief said. "I say huff because they are both great draughts players. Checkers they call it there. As a matter of fact, that's their excuse for contacting each other."

"I can't exaggerate how worried we are about the constructions, C. If only you had got the photographs before they killed your man. The P.M. is pressing us to inform the Yankees and ask their help."

"You mustn't let him. You can't depend on their security."

PART FIVE

1

Huff," said Captain Segura. They had met at the Havana Club. At the Havana Club, which was not a club at all and was owned by Bacardi's rival, all rum-drinks were free, and this enabled Wormold to increase his savings, for naturally he continued to charge for the drinks in his expenses—the fact that the drinks were free would have been tedious, if not impossible, to explain to London. The bar was on the first floor of a seventeenth-century house and the windows faced the Cathedral where the body of Christopher Columbus had once lain. A grey stone statue of Columbus stood outside the Cathedral and looked as though it had been formed through the centuries under water, like a coral reef, by the action of insects.

"You know," Captain Segura said, "there was a time when I thought you didn't like me."

"There are other motives for playing draughts than liking a man."

"Yes. for me too," Captain Segura said. "Look! I make a king."

"And I huff you three times."

"You think I did not see that, but you will find the move is in my favour. There, now I take your only king. Why did you go to Santiago, Santa Clara and Cienfuegos two weeks ago?"

"I always go about this time to see the retailers."

"It really looked as though that *was* your reason. You stayed in the new hotel at Cienfuegos. You had dinner alone in a restaurant on the waterfront. You went to a cinema and you went home. Next morning . . ."

"Do you really believe I'm a secret agent?"

"I'm beginning to doubt it. I think our friends have made a mistake."

"Who are our friends?"

"Oh, let's say the friends of Dr. Hasselbacher."

"And who are they?"

"It's my job to know what goes on in Havana," said Captain Segura, "not to take sides or to give information." He was moving his king unchecked up the board.

"Is there anything in Cuba important enough to interest a Secret Service?"

"Of course we are only a small country, but we lie very close to the American coast. And we point at your own Jamaica base. If a country is surrounded, as Russia is, it will try to punch a hole through from inside."

"What use would I be—or Dr. Hasselbacher—in global strategy? A man who sells vacuum cleaners. A retired doctor."

"There are unimportant pieces in any game," said Captain Segura. "Like this one here. I take it and you don't mind losing it. Dr. Hasselbacher, of course, is very good at crosswords."

"What have crosswords to do with it?"

"A man like that makes a good cryptographer. Somebody once showed me a cable of yours with its interpretation, or rather they let me discover it. Perhaps they thought I would run you out of Cuba." He laughed. "Milly's father. They little knew."

"What was it about?"

"You claimed to have recruited Engineer Cifuentes. Of course that was absurd. I know him well. Perhaps they shot at him to make the cable sound more convincing. Perhaps they wrote it because they wanted to get rid of you. Or perhaps they are more credulous than I am."

"What an extraordinary story." He moved a piece. "How are you so certain that Cifuentes is not my agent?"

"By the way you play checkers, Mr. Wormold, and because I interrogated Cifuentes."

"Did you torture him?"

Captain Segura laughed. "No. He doesn't belong to the torturable class."

"I didn't know there were class-distinctions in torture."

"Dear Mr. Wormold, surely you realise there are people who expect to be tortured and others who would be outraged by the idea. One never tortures except by a kind of mutual agreement."

"There's torture and torture. When they broke up Dr. Hasselbacher's laboratory they were torturing . . . ?"

"One can never tell what amateurs may do. The police had no concern in that. Dr. Hasselbacher does not belong to the torturable class."

"Who does?"

"The poor in my own country, in any Latin American country. The poor of Central Europe and the Orient. Of course in your welfare states you have no poor, so you are untorturable. In Cuba the police can deal as harshly as they like with émigrés from Latin America and the Baltic States, but not with visitors from your country or Scandinavia. It is an instinctive matter on both sides. Catholics are more torturable than Protestants, just as they are more criminal. You see, I was right to make that king, and now I shall huff you for the last time."

"You always win, don't you? That's an interesting theory of yours."

"One reason why the West hates the great Communist states is that they don't recognise class-distinctions. Sometimes they torture the wrong people. So too of course did Hitler and shocked the world. Nobody cares what goes on in our prisons, or the prisons of Lisbon or Caracas, but Hitler was too promiscuous. It was rather as though in your country a chauffeur had slept with a peeress."

"We're not shocked by that any longer."

"It is a great danger for everyone when what is shocking changes."

They had another free daiquiri each, frozen so stiffly that it had to be drunk in tiny drops to avoid a sinus-pain. "And how is Milly?" Captain Segura asked.

"Well."

"I'm very fond of the child. She has been properly brought up."

"I'm glad you think so."

"That is another reason why I would not wish you to get into any trouble, Mr. Wormold, which might mean the loss of your residence-permit. Havana would be poorer without your daughter."

"I don't suppose you really believe me, Captain, but Cifuentes was no agent of mine."

"I do believe you. I think perhaps someone wanted to use you as a stalking-horse, or perhaps as one of those painted ducks which attract the real wild ducks to settle." He finished his daiquiri. "That of course suits my book. I too like to watch the wild duck come in, from Russia, America, England, even Germany once again. They despise the poor local dago marksman, but one day, when they are all settled, what a shoot I will have."

"It's a complicated world. I find it easier to sell vacuum cleaners."

"The business prospers, I hope?"

"Oh yes, yes."

"I was interested that you had enlarged your staff. That charming secretary with the siphon and the coat that wouldn't close. And the young man."

"I need someone to superintend accounts. Lopez is not reliable."

"Ah, Lopez. Another of your agents." Captain Segura laughed. "Or so it was reported to me."

"Yes. He supplies me with secret information about the police-department."

"Be careful, Mr. Wormold. He is one of the torturable." They both laughed, drinking daiquiris. It is easy to laugh at the idea of torture on a sunny day. "I must be going, Mr. Wormold."

"I suppose the cells are full of my spies."

"We can always make room for another by having a few executions."

"One day, Captain, I am going to beat you at draughts."

"I doubt it, Mr. Wormold."

From the window he watched Captain Segura pass the grey pumice-like figure of Columbus on the way to his office. Then he had another free daiquiri. The Havana Club and Captain Segura seemed to have taken the place of the Wonder Bar and Dr. Hasselbacher—it was like a change of life and he had to make the best of it. There was no turning time back. Dr. Hasselbacher had been humiliated in front of him, and friendship cannot stand humiliation. He had not seen Dr. Hasselbacher again. In the club he felt himself, as in the Wonder Bar, a citizen of Havana; the elegant young man who brought him a drink made no attempt to sell him one of the assorted bottles of rum arranged on his table. A man with a grey beard read his morning paper as always at this hour; as usual a postman had interrupted his daily round for his free drink: all of them were citizens too. Four tourists left the bar carrying woven baskets, containing bottles of rum; they were flushed and cheerful and harboured the illusion that their drinks had cost them nothing. He thought, They are the foreigners, and of course untorturable.

Wormold drank his daiquiri too fast and left the Havana Club with his eyes aching. The tourists leant over the seventeenth-century well; they had flung into it enough coins to have paid for their drinks twice over: they were ensuring a happy return. A woman's voice called him and he saw Beatrice standing between the pillars of the colonnade among the gourds and rattles and negro-dolls of the curio-shop.

"What are you doing here?"

She explained, "I'm always unhappy when you meet Segura. This time I wanted to be sure . . ."

"Sure of what?" He wondered whether at last she had begun to suspect that he had no agents. Perhaps she had received instructions to watch him, from London or from 59200 in Kingston. They began to walk home.

"Sure that it's not a trap, that the police aren't waiting for you. A double agent is tricky to handle."

"You worry too much."

"And you have so little experience. Look what happened to Raul and Cifuentes."

"Cifuentes has been interrogated by the police." He added with relief, "He's blown, so he's no use to us now."

"Then aren't you blown too?"

"He gave nothing away. It was Captain Segura who chose the questions, and Segura is one of us. I think perhaps it's time we gave him a bonus. He's trying to compile a complete list for us of foreign agents here—American as well as Russian. Wild duck—that's what he calls them."

"It would be quite a coup. And the constructions?"

"We'll have to let those rest a while. I can't make him act against his own country."

Passing the Cathedral he gave his usual coin to the blind beggar who sat on the steps outside. Beatrice said, "It seems almost worth while being blind in this sun." The creative instinct stirred in Wormold. He said, "You know, he's not really blind. He sees everything that goes on."

"He must be a good actor. I've been watching him all the time you were with Segura."

"And he's been watching you. As a matter of fact he's one of my best informers. I always have him stationed here when I meet Segura. An elementary precaution. I'm not as careless as you think."

"You've never told H.Q."

"There's no point. They could hardly have traces of a blind beggar, and I don't use him for information. All the same if I had been arrested you'd have known of it in ten minutes. What would you have done?"

"Burnt all records and driven Milly to the Embassy."

"What about Rudy?"

"I'd have told him to radio London that we were breaking off and then to go underground."

"How does one go underground?" He didn't probe for an answer. He said slowly as the story grew of itself, "The beggar's name is Miguel. He really does all this for love. You see, I saved his life once."

"How?"

"Oh, it was nothing. An accident to the ferry. It just happened that I could swim and he couldn't."

"Did they give you a medal?" He looked at her quickly, but in her face he could see only innocent interest.

"No. There was no glory. As a matter of fact they fined me for bringing him to shore in a defence zone."

"What a very romantic story. And now of course he would give his life for you."

"Oh, I wouldn't go as far as that."

"Do tell me—have you somewhere a small penny account-book in black wash-leather?"

"I shouldn't think so. Why?"

"With your first purchases of pen-nibs and india-rubbers?"

"Why on earth pen-nibs?"

"I was just wondering, that's all."

"You can't buy account-books for a penny. And pen-nibs—nobody uses pen-nibs nowadays."

"Forget it. Just something Henry said to me. A natural mistake."

"Who's Henry?" he asked.

"59200," she said. He felt an odd jealousy, for in spite of security rules she had only once called him Jim.

The house was empty as usual when they came in; he was aware that he no longer missed Milly, and he felt the sad relief of a man who realises that there is one love at least that no longer hurts him.

"Rudy's out," Beatrice said. "Buying sweets, I suppose. He eats too many. He must consume an awful lot of energy, because he gets no fatter, but I don't see how."

"We'd better get down to work. There's a cable to send. Segura gave some valuable information about Communist infiltration in the police. You'd hardly believe . . ."

"I can believe almost anything. Look at this. I've just discovered something fascinating in the code-book. Did you know there was a group for 'eunuch'? Do you think it crops up often in cables?"

"I expect they need it in the Istanbul office."

"I wish we could use it. Can't we?"

"Are you ever going to marry again?"

Beatrice said, "Your free associations are rather obvious sometimes. Do you think Rudy has a secret life? He can't consume all that energy in the office."

"What's the drill for a secret life? Do you have to ask permission from London before you start one?"

"Well, of course, you would have to get traces before going very far. London prefers to keep sex inside the department."

2

i

I must be getting important," Wormold said. "I've been invited to make a speech."

"Where?" Milly asked, looking politely up from the *Horsewoman's Year Book*. It was the evening hour when work was over and the last gold light lay flat across the roofs and touched the honey-coloured hair and the whisky in his glass.

"At the annual lunch of the European Traders' Association. Dr. Braun, the President, has asked me to make one—as the oldest member. The guest of honour is the American Consul-General," he added with pride. It seemed such a short time ago that he had come to Havana and met with her family in the Floridita bar the girl who was Milly's mother; now he was the oldest trader there. Many had retired: some had gone home to fight in the last war—English, German, French—but he had been rejected because of his bad leg. None of these had returned to Cuba.

"What will you talk about?"

He said sadly, "I shan't. I wouldn't know what to say."

"I bet you'd speak better than any of them."

"Oh no. I may be the oldest member, Milly, but I'm the smallest too. The rum-exporters and the cigar-men—they are the really important people."

"You are you."

"I wish you had chosen a cleverer father."

"Captain Segura says you are pretty good at checkers."

"But not as good as he is."

"Please accept, Father," she said. "I'd be so proud of you."

"I'd make a fool of myself."

"You wouldn't. For my sake."

"For your sake I'd turn cartwheels. All right. I'll accept."

Rudy knocked at the door. This was the hour when he listened in for the last time; it would be midnight in London. He said, "There's an urgent cable from Kingston. Shall I fetch Beatrice?"

"No, I can manage it myself. She's going to a movie."

"Business does seem brisk," Milly said.

"Yes."

"But you don't seem to *sell* any more cleaners."

"It's all long-term promotion," Wormold said.

He went into his bedroom and deciphered the cable. It was from Hawthorne. Wormold was to come by the first possible plane to Kingston and report. He thought: So they know at last.

ii

The rendezvous was the Myrtle Bank Hotel. Wormold had not been to Jamaica for many years, and he was appalled by the dirt and the heat. What accounted for the squalor of British possessions? The Spanish, the French and the Portuguese built cities where they settled, but the English just allowed cities to grow. The poorest street in Havana had dignity compared with the shanty-life of Kingston—huts built out of old petrol-tins roofed with scrap-metal purloined from some cemetery of abandoned cars.

Hawthorne sat in a long chair in the veranda of Myrtle Bank drinking a planter's punch through a straw. His suit was just as immaculate as when Wormold had met him first; the only sign of the great heat was a little powder caked under his left ear. He said, "Take a pew." Even the slang was back.

"Thanks."

"Had a good trip?"

"Yes, thank you."

"I expect you're glad to be at home."

"Home?"

"I mean here—having a holiday from the dagoes. Back in British territory." Wormold thought of the huts he had seen along the harbour and a hopeless old man asleep in a patch of shade and a ragged child nursing a piece of driftwood. He said, "Havana's not so bad."

"Have a planter's punch. They are good here."

"Thanks."

Hawthorne said, "I asked you to come over because there's a spot of trouble."

"Yes?" He supposed that the truth was coming out. Could he be arrested now that he was on British territory? What would the charge be? Obtaining money on false pretences perhaps or some obscurer charge heard *in camera* under the Official Secrets Act.

"About these constructions."

He wanted to explain that Beatrice knew nothing of all this; he had no accomplice except the credulity of other men.

"What about them?" he asked.

"I wish you'd been able to get photographs."

"I tried. You know what happened."

"Yes. The drawings are a bit confusing."

"They are not by a skilled draughtsman."

"Don't get me wrong, old man. You've done wonders, but, you know, there was a time when I was—almost suspicious."

"What of?"

"Well, some of them sort of reminded me—to be frank, they reminded me of parts of a vacuum cleaner."

"Yes, that struck me too."

"And then, you see, I remembered all the thingummies in your shop."

"You thought I'd pulled the leg of the Secret Service?"

"Of course it sounds fantastic now, I know. All the same, in a way I was relieved when I found that the others have made up their minds to murder you."

"Murder me?"

"You see, that really proves the drawings are genuine."

"What others?"

"The other side. Of course I'd luckily kept these absurd suspicions to myself."

"How are they going to murder me?"

"Oh, we'll come to that—a matter of poisoning. What I mean is that next to having photographs one can't have a better confirmation of your reports. We had been rather sitting on them, but we've circulated them now to all the Service Departments. We sent them to Atomic Research as well. They weren't helpful. Said they had no connexion with nuclear fission. The trouble is we've been bemused by the atom-boys and have quite forgotten that there may be other forms of scientific warfare just as dangerous."

"How are they going to poison me?"

"First things first, old man. One mustn't forget the economics of warfare. Cuba can't afford to start making H-bombs, but have they found something equally effective at short range and *cheap*? That's the important word—cheap."

"Please would you mind telling me how they are going to murder me? You see, it interests me personally."

"Of course I'm going to tell you. I just wanted to give you the background first and to tell you how pleased we all are—at the confirmation of your reports, I mean. They plan to poison you at some sort of business lunch."

"The European Traders' Association?"

"I think that's the name."

"How do you know?"

"We've penetrated their organisation here. You'd be surprised how much we know of what goes on in your territory. I can tell you for instance that the death of stroke four was an accident. They just wanted to scare him as they scared stroke three by shooting at him. You are the first one they've really decided to murder."

"That's comforting."

"In a way, you know, it's a compliment. You are dangerous now." Hawthorne made a long sucking noise, draining up the last liquid between the layers of ice and orange and pineapple and the cherry on top.

"I suppose," Wormold said, "I'd better not go." He felt a surprising disappointment. "It will be the first lunch I've missed in ten years. They'd even asked me to speak. The firm always expects me to attend. Like showing the flag."

"But of *course* you've got to go."

"And be poisoned?"

"You needn't eat anything, need you?"

"Have you ever tried going to a public lunch and not eating anything? There's also the question of drink."

"They can't very well poison a bottle of wine. You could give the impression of being an alcoholic, somebody who doesn't eat but only drinks."

"Thank you. That would certainly be good for business."

"People have a soft spot in their hearts for alcoholics," Hawthorne said. "Besides, if you don't go they'll suspect something. It puts my source in danger. We have to protect our sources."

"That's the drill I suppose."

"Exactly, old man. Another point: we know the plot, but we don't know the plotters, except their symbols. If we discover who they are, we can insist on having them locked up. We'll disrupt the organisation."

"Yes, there aren't any perfect murders, are there? I dare say there'll be a clue at the post-mortem on which you can persuade Segura to act."

"You aren't afraid, are you? This is a dangerous job. You shouldn't have taken it unless you were prepared . . ."

"You're like a Spartan mother, Hawthorne. Come back victorious or stay beneath the table."

"That's quite an idea, you know. You could slip under the table at the right moment. The murderers would think you were dead and the others would just think you were drunk."

"This is not a meeting of the Big Four at Moscow. The European Traders don't fall under the table."

"Never?"

"Never. You think I'm unduly concerned, don't you?"

"I don't think there's any need for you to worry yet. They don't serve you, after all. You help yourself."

"Of course. Except that there's always a Morro crab to start with at the Nacional. That's prepared in advance."

"You mustn't eat that. Lots of people don't eat crab. When they serve the other courses never take the portion next to you. It's like a conjuror forcing a card on you. You just have to reject it."

"But the conjuror usually manages to force the card just the same."

"I tell you what—did you say the lunch was at the Nacional?"

"Yes."

"Then why can't you use stroke seven?"

"Who's stroke seven?"

"Don't you remember your own agents? Surely he's the head waiter at the Nacional? He can help to see your plate isn't tampered with. It's time he did something for his money. I don't remember you sending a single report from him."

"Can't you give me any idea who the man at the lunch will be? I mean the man who plans to . . ." he boggled at the word "kill" . . . "to do it."

"Not a clue, old man. Just be careful of everyone. Have another planter's punch."

iii

The plane back to Cuba had few passengers: a Spanish woman with a pack of children—some of them screamed and some of them were air-sick as soon as they left the ground; a negress with a live cock wrapped in her shawl; a Cuban cigar-exporter with whom Wormold had a nodding acquaintance, and an Englishman in a tweed jacket who smoked a pipe until the air-hostess told him to put it out. Then he sucked the empty pipe ostentatiously for the rest of the journey and sweated heavily into the tweed. He had the ill-humoured face of a man who is always in the right.

When lunch was served he moved back several places and sat down beside Wormold. He said, "Can't stand those screaming brats. Do you mind?" He looked at the papers on Wormold's knee. "You with Phastkleaners?" he said.

"Yes."

"I'm with Nucleaners. The name's Carter."

"Oh."

"This is only my second trip to Cuba. Gay spot, they tell me," he said, blowing down his pipe and laying it aside for lunch.

"It can be," Wormold said, "if you like roulette or brothels."

Carter patted his tobacco-pouch as though it were a dog's head—"my faithful hound shall bear me company." "I didn't exactly mean . . . though I'm not a Puritan, mind. I suppose it would be interesting. Do as the Romans do." He changed the subject. "Sell many of your machines?"

"Trade's not so bad."

"We've got a new model that's going to wipe the market." He took a large mouthful of sweet mauve cake and then cut himself a piece of chicken.

"Really."

"Runs on a motor like a lawn-mower. No effort by the little woman. No tubes trailing all over the place."

"Noisy?"

"Special silencer. Less noise than your model. We are calling it the Whisper-Wife." After taking a swig of turtle soup he began to eat his fruit salad, crunching the grape stones between his teeth. He said, "We are opening an agency in Cuba soon. Know Dr. Braun?"

"I've met him. At the European Traders' Association. He's our President. Imports precision-instruments from Geneva."

"That's the man. He's given us very useful advice. In fact I'm going to your bean-feast as his guest. Do they give you a good lunch?"

"You know what hotel-lunches are like."

"Better than this anyway." he said, spitting out a grape-skin. He had overlooked the asparagus in mayonnaise and now began on that. Afterwards he fumbled in his pocket. "Here's my card." The card read: "William Carter B. Tech. (Nottwich)" and in the corner, "Nucleaners Ltd." He said, "I'm staying at the Seville-Biltmore for a week."

"I'm afraid I haven't a card on me. My name's Wormold."

"Met a fellow called Davis?"

"I don't think so."

"Shared digs with him at college. He went into Gripfix and came out to this part of the world. It's funny—you find Nottwich men everywhere. You weren't there yourself, were you?"

"No."

"Reading?"

"I wasn't at a University."

"I couldn't have told it," Carter told him kindly. "I'd have gone to Oxford, you know, but they are very backward in technology. All right for schoolmasters, I suppose." He began to suck again at his empty pipe like a child at a comforter, till it whistled between his teeth. Suddenly he spoke again, as though some remains of tannin had touched his tongue with a bitter flavour. "Outdated," he said, "relics, living on the past. I'd abolish them."

"Abolish what?"

"Oxford and Cambridge." He took the only food that was left in the tray, a roll of bread, and crumbled it like age or ivy crumbling a stone.

At the Customs Wormold lost him. He was having trouble with his sample Nucleaner, and Wormold saw no reason why the representative of Phastkleaners should assist him to enter. Beatrice was there to meet him with the Hillman. It was many years since he had been met by a woman.

"Everything all right?" she asked.

"Yes. Oh yes. They seem pleased with me." He watched her hands on the wheel; she wore no gloves in the hot afternoon; they were beautiful and competent hands. He said, "You aren't wearing your ring."

She said, "I didn't think anyone would notice. Milly did too. You are an observant family."

"You haven't lost it?"

"I took it off yesterday to wash and I forgot to put it back. There's no point, is there, wearing a ring you forget?"

It was then he told her about the lunch.

"You won't go?" she said.

"Hawthorne expects me to. To protect his source."

"Damn his source."

"There's a better reason. Something that Dr. Hasselbacher said to me. They like to strike at what you love. If I don't go, they'll think up something else. Something worse. And we shan't know what. Next time it mightn't be me—I don't think I love myself enough to satisfy them—it might be Milly. Or you." He didn't realise the implication of what he had said until she had dropped him at his door and driven on.

3

i

Milly said, "You've had a cup of coffee, and that's all. Not even a piece of toast."

"I'm just not in the mood."

"You'll go and over-eat at the Traders' lunch today, and you know perfectly well that Morro crab doesn't agree with your stomach."

"I promise you I'll be very very careful."

"You'd do much better to have a proper breakfast. You need a cereal to mop up all the liquor you'll be drinking." It was one of her duenna days.

"I'm sorry, Milly, I just can't. I've got things on my mind. Please don't pester me. Not today."

"Have you prepared your speech?"

"I've done my best, but I'm no speaker, Milly. I don't know why they asked me." But he was uneasily conscious that perhaps he did know why. Somebody must have brought influence to bear on Dr. Braun, somebody who had to be identified at any cost. He thought, I am the cost.

"I bet you'll be a sensation."

"I'm trying hard not to be a sensation at this lunch."

Milly went to school and he sat on at the table. The cereal company which Milly patronised had printed on the carton of Weatbrix the latest adventure of Little Dwarf Doodoo. Little Dwarf Doodoo in a rather brief instalment encountered a rat the size of a St. Bernard dog and he frightened the rat away by pretending to be a cat and saying miaou. It was a very simple story. You could hardly call it a preparation for life. The company also gave away an air-gun in return for twelve lids. As the packet was almost empty Wormold began to cut off the lid, driving his knife carefully along the dotted line. He was turning the last corner when Beatrice entered. She said, "What are you doing?"

"I thought an air-gun might be useful in the office. We only need eleven more lids."

"I couldn't sleep last night."

"Too much coffee?"

"No. Something you told me Dr. Hasselbacher said. About Milly. Please don't go to the lunch."

"It's the least I can do."

"You do quite enough. They are pleased with you in London. I can tell that from the way they cable you. Whatever Henry may say, London wouldn't want you to run a silly risk."

"It's quite true what he said—that if I don't go they will try something else."

"Don't worry about Milly. I'll watch her like a lynx."

"And who's going to watch you?"

"I'm in this line of business; it's my own choice. You needn't feel responsible for me."

"Have you been in a spot like this before?"

"No, but I've never had a boss like you before. You seem to stir them up. You know, this job is usually just an office desk and files and dull cables; we don't go in for murder. And I don't want you murdered. You see, you are real. You aren't *Boy's Own Paper*. For God's sake put down that silly packet and listen to me."

"I was re-reading Little Dwarf Doodoo."

"Then stay at home with him this morning. I'll go out and buy you all the back cartons so that you can catch up."

"All Hawthorne said was sense. I only have to be careful what I eat. It *is* important to find out who they are. Then I'll have done something for my money."

"You've done plenty as it is. There's no point in going to this damned lunch."

"Yes, there is a point. Pride."

"Who are you showing off to?"

"You."

ii

He made his way through the lounge of the Nacional Hotel between the show-cases full of Italian shoes and Danish ash-trays and Swedish glass and mauve British woollies. The private dining-room where the European Traders always met lay just beyond the chair where Dr. Hasselbacher now sat, conspicuously waiting. Wormold approached with slowing steps; it was the first time he had seen Dr. Hasselbacher since the night when he had sat on the bed in his Uhlan's uniform talking of the past. Members of the Association, passing in to the private dining-room, stopped and spoke to Dr. Hasselbacher; he paid them no attention.

Wormold reached the chair where he sat. Dr. Hasselbacher said, "Don't go in there, Mr. Wormold." He spoke without lowering his voice, the words shivering among the show-cases, attracting attention.

"How are you, Hasselbacher?"

"I said, don't go in."

"I heard you the first time."

"They are going to kill you, Mr. Wormold."

"How do you know that, Hasselbacher?"

"They are planning to poison you in there."

Several of the guests stopped and stared and smiled. One of them, an American, said, "Is the food that bad?" and everyone laughed.

Wormold said, "Don't stay here, Hasselbacher. You are too conspicuous."

"Are you going in?"

"Of course, I'm one of the speakers."

"There's Milly. Don't forget her."

"Don't worry about Milly. I'm going to come out on my feet, Hasselbacher. Please go home."

"All right, but I had to try," Dr. Hasselbacher said. "I'll be waiting at the telephone."

"I'll call you when I leave."

"Good-bye, Jim."

"Good-bye, Doctor." The use of his first name took Wormold unawares. It reminded him of what he had always jokingly thought: that Dr. Hasselbacher would use the name only at his bedside when he had given up hope. He felt suddenly frightened, alone, a long way from home.

"Wormold," a voice said, and turning he saw that it was Carter of Nucleaners, but it was also for Wormold at that moment the English midlands, English snobbery, English vulgarity, all the sense of kinship and security the word England implied to him.

"Carter!" he exclaimed, as though Carter were the one man in Havana he wanted most to meet, and at that instant he was.

"Damned glad to see you," Carter said. "Don't know a soul at this lunch. Not even my—not even Dr. Braun." His pocket bulged with his pipe and his pouch; he patted them as though for reassurance, as though he too felt far from home.

"Carter, this is Dr. Hasselbacher, an old friend of mine."

"Good day, Doctor." He said to Wormold, "I was looking all over the place for you last night. I don't seem able to find the right spots."

They moved in together to the private dining-room. It was quite irrational, the confidence he had in a fellow-countryman, but on the side where Carter walked he felt protected.

iii

The dining-room had been decorated with two big flags of the United States in honour of the Consul-General, and little paper flags, as in an airport-restaurant, indicated where each national was to sit. There was a Swiss flag at the head of the table for Dr. Braun, the President; there was even the flag of Monaco for the Monegasque Consul who was one of the largest exporters of cigars in Havana. He was to sit on the Consul-General's right hand in recognition of the Royal alliance. Cocktails were circulating when Wormold and Carter entered, and a waiter at once approached them. Was it Wormold's imagination or did the waiter shift the tray so that the last remaining daiquiri lay nearest to Wormold's hand?

"No. No thank you."

Carter put out his hand, but the waiter had already moved on towards the service-door.

"Perhaps you would prefer a dry Martini, sir?" a voice said. He turned. It was the head-waiter.

"No, no, I don't like them."

"A Scotch, sir? A sherry? An Old-Fashioned? Anything you care to order."

"I'm not drinking." Wormold said, and the headwaiter abandoned him for another guest. Presumably he was stroke seven; strange if by an ironic coincidence he was also the would-be assassin. Wormold looked around for Carter, but he had moved away in pursuit of his host.

"You'd do better to drink all you can," said a voice with a Scotch accent. "My name is MacDougall. It seems we're sitting together."

"I haven't seen you here before, have I?"

"I've taken over from McIntyre. You'd have known McIntyre surely?"

"Oh yes, yes." Dr. Braun, who had palmed off the unimportant Carter upon another Swiss who dealt in watches, was now leading the American Consul-General round the room, introducing him to the more exclusive members. The Germans formed a group apart, rather suitably against the west wall; they carried the superiority of the deutschmark on their features like duelling scars: national honour which had survived Belsen depended now on a rate of exchange. Wormold wondered whether it was one of them who had betrayed the secret of the lunch to Dr. Hasselbacher. Betrayed? Not necessarily. Perhaps the doctor had been blackmailed to supply the poison. At any rate he would have chosen, for the sake of old friendship, something painless, if any poison were painless.

"I was telling you," Mr. MacDougall went energetically on like a Scottish reel, "that you would do better to drink now. It's all you'll be getting."

"There'll be wine, won't there?"

"Look at the table." Small individual milk-bottles stood by every place. "Didn't you read your invitation? An American blue-plate lunch in honour of our great American allies."

"Blue-plate?"

"Surely you know what a blue-plate is, man? They shove the whole meal at you under your nose, already dished up on your plate—roast turkey, cranberry sauce, sausages and carrots and French fried. I can't bear French fried, but there's no pick and choose with a blue-plate."

"No pick and choose?"

"You eat what you're given. That's democracy, man."

Dr. Braun was summoning them to the table. Wormold had a hope that fellow-nationals would sit together and that Carter would be on his other side, but it was a strange Scandinavian who sat on his left scowling at his milk-bottle. Wormold thought, Someone has arranged this well. Nothing is safe, not even the milk. Already the waiters were bustling round the board with the Morro crabs. Then he saw with relief that Carter faced him across the table. There was something so secure in his vulgarity. You could appeal to him as you could appeal to an English policeman, because you knew his thoughts.

"No," he said to the waiter, "I won't take crab."

"You are wise not to take those things," Mr. MacDougall said. "I'm refusing them myself. They don't go with whisky. Now if you will drink a little of your iced water and hold it under the table, I've got a flask in my pocket with enough for the two of us."

Without thinking, Wormold stretched out his hand to his glass, and then the doubt came. Who was MacDougall? He had never seen him before, and he hadn't heard until now that McIntyre had gone away. Wasn't it possible that the water was poisoned, or even the whisky in the flask?

"Why did McIntyre leave?" he asked, his hand round the glass.

"Oh, it was just one of those things," Mr. MacDougall said, "you know the way it is. Toss down your water. You don't want to drown the Scotch. This is the best Highland malt."

"It's too early in the day for me. Thank you all the same."

"If you don't trust the water, you are right not to," Mr. MacDougall said ambiguously. "I'm taking it neat myself. If you don't mind sharing the cap of the flask . . ."

"No, really. I don't drink at this hour."

"It was the English who made hours for drinking, not the Scotch. They'll be making hours for dying next."

Carter said across the table, "I don't mind if I do. The name's Carter," and Wormold saw with relief that Mr. MacDougall was pouring out the whisky; there was one suspicion less, for no one surely would want to poison Carter. All the same, he thought, there is something wrong with Mr. MacDougall's Scottishness. It smelt of fraud like Ossian.

"Svenson," the gloomy Scandinavian said sharply from behind his little Swedish flag; at least Wormold thought it was Swedish: he could never distinguish with certainty between the Scandinavian colours.

"Wormold," he said.

"What is all this nonsense of the milk?"

"I think," Wormold said, "that Dr. Braun is being a little too literal."

"Or funny," Carter said.

"I don't think Dr. Braun has much sense of humour."

"And what do you do, Mr. Wormold?" the Swede asked. "I don't think we have met before, although I know you by sight."

"Vacuum cleaners. And you?"

"Glass. As you know, Swedish glass is the best in the world. This bread is very good. Do you not eat bread?'' He might have prepared his conversation beforehand from a phrase-book.

"Given it up. Fattening, you know.''

"I would have said you could have done with fattening.'' Mr. Svenson gave a dreary laugh like jollity in a long northern night. "Forgive me. I make you sound like a goose.''

At the end of the table, where the Consul-General sat, they were beginning to serve the blue-plates. Mr. MacDougall had been wrong about the turkey; the main course was Maryland chicken. But he was right about the carrots and the French fried and the sausages. Dr. Braun was a little behind the rest; he was still picking at his Morro crab. The Consul-General must have slowed him down by the earnestness of his conversation and the fixity of his convex lenses. Two waiters came round the table, one whisking away the remains of the crab, the other substituting the blue-plates. Only the Consul-General had thought to open his milk. The word "Dulles" drifted dully down to where Wormold sat. The waiter approached carrying two plates; he put one in front of the Scandinavian, the other was Wormold's. The thought that the whole threat to his life might be a nonsensical practical joke came to Wormold. Perhaps Hawthorne was a humorist, and Dr. Hasselbacher. . . . He remembered Milly asking whether Dr. Hasselbacher ever pulled his leg. Sometimes it seems easier to run the risk of death than ridicule. He wanted to confide in Carter and hear his common-sense reply; then looking at his plate he noticed something odd. There were no carrots. He said quickly, "You prefer it without carrots,'' and slipped the plate along to Mr. MacDougall.

"It's the French fried I dislike,'' said Mr. MacDougall quickly and passed the plate on to the Luxemburg Consul. The Luxemburg Consul, who was deep in conversation with a German across the table, handed the plate with absent-minded politeness to his neighbour. Politeness infected all who had not yet been served, and the plate went whisking along towards Dr. Braun, who had just had the remains of his Morro crab removed. The head-waiter saw what was happening and began to stalk the plate up the table, but it kept a pace ahead of him. The waiter, returning with more blue-plates, was intercepted by Wormold, who took one. He looked confused. Wormold began to eat with appetite. "The carrots are excellent,'' he said.

The head-waiter hovered by Dr. Braun. "Excuse me, Dr. Braun,'' he said, "they have given you no carrots.''

"I don't like carrots,'' Dr. Braun said, cutting up a piece of chicken.

"I am so sorry,'' the head-waiter said and seized Dr. Braun's plate. "A mistake in the kitchen.'' Plate in hand like a verger with the collection he walked up the length of the room towards the service-door. Mr. MacDougall was taking a sip of his own whisky.

"I think I might venture now,'' Wormold said. "As a celebration.''

"Good man. Water or straight?''

"Could I take your water? Mine's got a fly in it.''

"Of course.'' Wormold drank two-thirds of the water and held it out for the whisky from Mr. MacDougall's flask. Mr. MacDougall gave him a generous double.

"Hold it out again. You are behind the two of us," he said, and Wormold was back in the territory of trust. He felt a kind of tenderness for the neighbour he had suspected. He said, "We must see each other again."

"An occasion like this would be useless if it didn't bring people together."

"I wouldn't have met you or Carter without it."

They all three had another whisky. "You must both meet my daughter," Wormold said, the whisky warming his cockles.

"How is business with you?"

"Not so bad. We are expanding the office."

Dr. Braun rapped the table for silence.

"Surely," Carter said in the loud irrepressible Nottwich voice as warming as the whisky, "they'll have to serve drinks with the toast."

"My lad," Mr. MacDougall said, "there'll be speeches, but no toasts. We have to listen to the bastards without alcoholic aid."

"I'm one of the bastards," Wormold said.

"You speaking?"

"As the oldest member."

"I'm glad you've survived long enough for that," Mr. MacDougall said.

The American Consul-General, called on by Dr. Braun, began to speak. He spoke of the spiritual links between the democracies—he seemed to number Cuba among the democracies. Trade was important because without trade there would be no spiritual links, or was it perhaps the other way round. He spoke of American aid to distressed countries which would enable them to buy more goods and by buying more goods strengthen the spiritual links. . . . A dog was howling somewhere in the wastes of the hotel and the head-waiter signalled for the door to be closed. It had been a great pleasure to the American Consul-General to be invited to this lunch today and to meet the leading representatives of European trade and so strengthen still further the spiritual links. . . . Wormold had two more whiskies.

"And now," Dr. Braun said, "I am going to call upon the oldest member of our Association. I am not of course referring to his years, but to the length of time he has served the cause of European trade in this beautiful city where, Mr. Minister"—he bowed to his other neighbour, a dark man with a squint—"we have the privilege and happiness of being your guests. I am speaking, you all know, of Mr. Wormold." He took a quick look at his notes. "Mr. James Wormold, the Havana representative of Phastkleaners."

Mr. MacDougall said, "We've finished the whisky. Fancy that now. Just when you need your Dutch courage most."

Carter said, "I came armed as well, but I drank most of it in the plane. There's only one glass left in the flask."

"Obviously our friend here must have it," Mr. MacDougall said. "His need is greater than ours."

Dr. Braun said, "We may take Mr. Wormold as a symbol for all that service means—modesty, quietness, perseverance and efficiency. Our enemies picture the salesman often as a loud-mouthed braggart who is intent only on putting across some product which is useless, unnecessary, or even harmful. That is not a true picture. . . .''

Wormold said, "It's kind of you, Carter. I could certainly do with a drink."

"Not used to speaking?"

"It's not only the speaking." He leant forward across the table towards that common-or-garden Nottwich face on which he felt he could rely for incredulity, reassurance, the easy humour based on inexperience: he was safe with Carter. He said, "I know you won't believe a word of what I'm telling you," but he didn't want Carter to believe. He wanted to learn from him how not to believe. Something nudged his leg and looking down he saw a black dachshund-face pleading with him between the drooping ringlet ears for a scrap—the dog must have slipped in through the service-door unseen by the waiters and now it led a hunted life, half hidden below the table-cloth.

Carter pushed a small flask across to Wormold. "There's not enough for two. Take it all."

"Very kind of you, Carter." He unscrewed the top and poured all that there was into his glass.

"Only a Johnnie Walker. Nothing fancy."

Dr. Braun said, "If anyone here can speak for all of us about the long years of patient service a trader gives to the public, I am sure it is Mr. Wormold, whom now I call upon . . .''

Carter winked and raised an imaginary glass.

"H-hurry," Carter said. "You've got to h-hurry."

Wormold lowered the whisky. "What did you say, Carter?"

"I said drink it up quick."

"Oh no, you didn't, Carter." Why hadn't he noticed that stammered aspirate before? Was Carter conscious of it and did he avoid an initial "h" except when he was preoccupied by fear or h-hope?

"What's the matter, Wormold?"

Wormold put his hand down to pat the dog's head and as though by accident he knocked the glass from the table.

"You pretended not to know the doctor."

"What doctor?"

"You would call him H-Hasselbacher."

"Mr. Wormold," Dr. Braun called down the table.

He rose uncertainly to his feet. The dog for want of any better provender was lapping at the whisky on the floor.

Wormold said, "I appreciate your asking me to speak, whatever your motives." A polite titter took him by surprise—he hadn't meant to say anything funny. He said, "This is my first and it looked at one time as though it was going to be my last public appearance." He caught Carter's eye. Carter was frowning. He felt guilty of a solecism by his survival as though he were drunk in public. Perhaps he was drunk. He said, "I don't know whether I've got any friends here. I've certainly got some enemies." Somebody said "Shame" and several people laughed. If this went on he would get the reputation of being a witty speaker. He said, "We hear a lot nowadays about the cold war, but any trader will tell you that the war between two manufacturers of the same goods can be quite a hot war. Take Phastkleaners and Nucleaners. There's not much difference between the two machines any more than there is between two human beings, one Russian—or German—and one British. There would be no competition and no war if it wasn't for the ambition of a few men in both firms; just a few men dictate competition and invent needs and set Mr. Carter and myself at each other's throats."

Nobody laughed now. Dr. Braun whispered something into the ear of the Consul-General. Wormold lifted Carter's whisky-flask and said, "I don't suppose Mr. Carter even knows the name of the man who sent him to poison me for the good of his firm." Laughter broke out again with a note of relief. Mr. MacDougall said, "We could do with more poison here," and suddenly the dog began to whimper. It broke cover and made for the service-door. "Max," the head-waiter exclaimed. "Max." There was silence and then a few uneasy laughs. The dog was uncertain on its feet. It howled and tried to bite its own breast. The head-waiter overtook it by the door and picked it up, but it cried as though with pain and broke from his arms. "It's had a couple," Mr. MacDougall said uneasily.

"You must excuse me, Dr. Braun," Wormold said, "the show is over." He followed the head-waiter through the service-door. "Stop."

"What do you want?"

"I want to find out what happened to my plate."

"What do you mean, sir? Your plate?"

"You were very anxious that my plate should not be given to anyone else."

"I don't understand."

"Did you know that it was poisoned?"

"You mean the food was bad, sir?"

"I mean it was poisoned and you were careful to save Dr. Braun's life—not mine."

"I'm afraid, sir, I don't understand you. I am busy. You must excuse me." The sound of a howling dog came up the long passage from the kitchen, a low dismal howl intercepted by a sharper burst of pain. The head-waiter called, "Max!" and ran like a human being down the passage. He flung open the kitchen-door. "Max!"

The dachshund lifted a melancholy head from where it crouched below the table, then began to drag its body painfully towards the head-waiter. A man in a chef's cap said, "He ate nothing here. The plate was thrown away." The dog collapsed at the waiter's feet and lay there like a length of offal.

The waiter went down on his knees beside the dog. He said, "*Max mein Kind. Mein Kind.*" The black body was like an elongation of his own black suit. The kitchen-staff gathered around.

The black tube made a slight movement and a pink tongue came out like toothpaste and lay on the kitchen floor. The head-waiter put his hand on the dog and then looked up at Wormold. The tear-filled eyes so accused him of standing there alive while the dog was dead that he nearly found it in his heart to apologise, but instead he turned and went. At the end of the passage he looked back: the black figure knelt beside the black dog and the white chef stood above and the kitchen-hands waited, like mourners round a grave, carrying their troughs and mops and dishes like wreaths. My death, he thought, would have been more unobtrusive than that.

iv

"I have come back," he said to Beatrice, "I am not under the table. I have come back victorious. The dog it was that died."

4

i

C aptain Segura said, "I'm glad to find you alone. Are you alone?"

"Quite alone."

"I'm sure you don't mind. I have put two men at the door to see that we aren't disturbed."

"Am I under arrest?"

"Of course not."

"Milly and Beatrice are out at a cinema. They'll be surprised if they are not allowed in."

"I will not take up much of your time. There are two things I have come to see you about. One is important. The other is only routine. May I begin with what is important?"

"Please."

"I wish, Mr. Wormold, to ask for the hand of your daughter."

"Does that require two policemen at the door?"

"It's convenient not to be disturbed."

"Have you spoken to Milly?"

"I would not dream of it before speaking to you."

"I suppose even here you *would* need my consent by law."

"It is not a matter of law but of common courtesy. May I smoke?"

"Why not? Is that case really made from human skin?"

Captain Segura laughed. "Ah, Milly, Milly. What a tease she is!" He added ambiguously, "Do you really believe that story, Mr. Wormold?" Perhaps he had an objection to a direct lie; he might be a good Catholic.

"She's much too young to marry, Captain Segura."

"Not in this country."

"I'm sure she has no wish to marry yet."

"But you could influence her, Mr. Wormold."

"They call you the Red Vulture, don't they?"

"That, in Cuba, is a kind of compliment."

"Aren't you rather an uncertain life? You seem to have a lot of enemies."

"I have saved enough to take care of my widow. In that way, Mr. Wormold, I am a more reliable support than you are. This establishment—it can't bring you in much money and at any moment it is liable to be closed."

"Closed?"

"I am sure you do not intend to cause trouble, but a lot of trouble has been happening around you. If you had to leave this country, would you not feel happier if your daughter were well established here?"

"What kind of trouble, Captain Segura?"

"There was a car which crashed—never mind why. There was an attack on poor Engineer Cifuentes—a friend of the Minister of the Interior. Professor Sanchez complained that you broke into his house and threatened him. There is even a story that you poisoned a dog."

"That I poisoned a dog?"

"It sounds absurd, of course. But the head-waiter at the Hotel Nacional said you gave his dog poisoned whisky. Why should you give a dog whisky at all? I don't understand. Nor does he. He thinks perhaps because it was a German dog. You don't say anything, Mr. Wormold."

"I am at a loss for words."

"He was in a terrible state, poor man. Otherwise I would have thrown him out of the office for talking nonsense. He said you came into the kitchen to gloat over what you had done. It sounded very unlike you, Mr. Wormold. I have always thought of you as a humane man. Just assure me there is no truth in this story . . ."

"The dog *was* poisoned. The whisky came from my glass. But it was intended for me, not the dog."

"Why should anyone try to poison you?"

"I don't know."

"Two strange stories—they cancel out. Probably there was no poison and the dog just died. I gather it was an old dog. But you must admit, Mr. Wormold, that a lot of trouble seems to go on around you. Perhaps you are like one of those innocent children I have read about in your country who set poltergeists to work."

"Perhaps I am. Do you know the names of the poltergeists?"

"Most of them. I think the time has come to exorcise them. I am drawing up a report for the President."

"Am I on it?"

"You needn't be. I ought to tell you, Mr. Wormold, that I have saved money, enough money to leave Milly in comfort if anything were ever to happen to me. And of course enough for us to settle in Miami if there were a revolution.''

"There's no need for you to tell me all this. I'm not questioning your financial capacity.''

"It is customary, Mr. Wormold. Now for my health—that is good. I can show you the certificates. Nor will there be any difficulty about children. That has been amply proved.''

"I see.''

"There is nothing in that which need worry your daughter. The children are provided for. My present encumbrance is not an important one. I know that Protestants are rather particular about these things.''

"I'm not exactly a Protestant.''

"And luckily your daughter is a Catholic. It would really be a most suitable marriage, Mr. Wormold.''

"Milly is only seventeen.''

"It is the best and easiest age to bear a child, Mr. Wormold. Have I your permission to speak to her?''

"Do you need it?''

"It is more correct.''

"And if I said no . . .''

"I would of course try to persuade you.''

"You said once that I was not of the torturable class.''

Captain Segura laid his hand affectionately on Wormold's shoulders. "You have Milly's sense of humour. But seriously, there is always your residence-permit to consider.''

"You seem very determined. All right. You may as well speak to her. You have plenty of opportunity on her way from school. But Milly's got sense. I don't think you stand a chance.''

"In that case I may ask you later to use a father's influence.''

"How Victorian you are, Captain Segura. A father today has no influence. You said there was something important . . .''

Captain Segura said reproachfully, "This was the important subject. The other is a matter of routine only. Would you come with me to the Wonder Bar?''

"Why?''

"A police matter. Nothing for you to worry about. I am asking you a favour, that is all, Mr. Wormold.''

They went in Captain Segura's scarlet sports-car with a motor-cycle policeman before and behind. All the bootblacks from the Paseo seemed to be gathered in Virdudes. There were policemen on either side of the swing-doors of the Wonder Bar and the sun lay heavy overhead.

The motor-cycle policemen leapt off their machines and began to shoo the bootblacks away. Policemen ran out from the bar and formed an escort for Captain Segura. Wormold followed him. As always at that time of day, the jalousies above the colonnade were creaking in the small wind from the sea. The barman stood on the wrong side of the bar, the customers' side. He looked sick and afraid. Several broken bottles behind him were still dripping single drops, but they had spilt their main contents a long while ago. Someone on the floor was hidden by the bodies of the policemen, but the boots showed—the thick over-repaired boots of a not-rich old man. "It's just a formal identification," Captain Segura said. Wormold hardly needed to see the face, but they cleared a way before him so that he could look down at Dr. Hasselbacher.

"It's Dr. Hasselbacher," he said. "You know him as well as I do."

"There is a form to be observed in these matters," Segura said. "An independent identification."

"Who did it?"

Segura said, "Who knows? You had better have a glass of whisky. Barman!"

"No. Give me a daiquiri. It was always a daiquiri I used to drink with him."

"Someone came in here with a gun. Two shots missed. Of course we shall say it was the rebels from Oriente. It will be useful in influencing foreign opinion. Perhaps it was the rebels."

The face stared up from the floor without expression. You couldn't describe that impassivity in terms of peace or anguish. It was as though nothing at all had ever happened to it: an unborn face.

"When you bury him put his helmet on the coffin."

"Helmet?"

"You'll find an old uniform in his flat. He was a sentimental man." It was odd that Dr. Hasselbacher had survived two world wars and had died at the end of it in so-called peace much the same death as he might have died upon the Somme.

"You know very well it had nothing to do with the rebels," Wormold said.

"It is convenient to say so."

"The poltergeists again."

"You blame yourself too much."

"He warned me not to go to the lunch, Carter heard him, everybody heard him, so they killed him."

"Who are They?"

"You have the list."

"The name Carter wasn't on it."

"Ask the waiter with the dog, then. You can torture *him* surely. I won't complain."

"He is German and he has high political friends. Why should he want to poison you?"

"Because they think I'm dangerous. Me! They little know. Give me another daiquiri. I always had two before I went back to the shop. Will you show me your list, Segura?"

"I might to a father-in-law, because I could trust him."

They can print statistics and count the populations in hundreds of thousands, but to each man a city consists of no more than a few streets, a few houses, a few people. Remove those few and a city exists no longer except as a pain in the memory, like the pain of an amputated leg no longer there. It was time, Wormold thought, to pack up and go and leave the ruins of Havana.

"You know," Captain Segura said, "this only emphasises what I meant. It might have been you. Milly should be safe from accidents like this."

"Yes," Wormold said. "I shall have to see to that."

ii

The policemen were gone from the shop when he returned. Lopez was out, he had no idea where. He could hear Rudy fidgeting with his tubes and an occasional snatch of atmospherics beat around the apartment. He sat down on the bed. Three deaths: an unknown man called Raul, a black dachshund called Max and an old doctor called Hasselbacher; he was the cause—and Carter. Carter had not planned the death of Raul nor the dog, but Dr. Hasselbacher had been given no chance. It had been a reprisal: one death for one life, a reversal of the Mosaic Code. He could hear Milly and Beatrice talking in the next room. Although the door was ajar he only half took in what they were saying. He stood on the frontier of violence, a strange land he had never visited before; he had his passport in his hand. "Profession: Spy." "Characteristic Features: Friendlessness." "Purpose of Visit: Murder." No visa was required. His papers were in order.

And on this side of the border he heard the voices talking in the language he knew.

Beatrice said, "No, I wouldn't advise deep carnation. Not at your age."

Milly said, "They ought to give lessons in make-up during the last term. I can just hear Sister Agnes saying, 'A drop of *Nuit d' Amour* behind the ears.' "

"Try this light carnation. No, don't smear the edge of your mouth. Let me show you."

Wormold thought, I have no arsenic or cyanide. Besides I will have no opportunity to drink with him. I should have forced that whisky down his throat. Easier said than done off the Elizabethan stage, and even there he would have needed in addition a poisoned rapier.

"There. You see what I mean."

"What about rouge?"

"You don't need rouge."

"What smell do you use, Beatrice?"

"*Sous Le Vent.*"

They have shot Hasselbacher, but I have no gun, Wormold thought. Surely a gun should have been part of the office-equipment, like the safe and the celluloid sheets and the microscope and the electric kettle. He had never in his life so much as handled a gun, but that was no insuperable objection. He had only to be as close to Carter as the door through which the voices came.

"We'll go shopping together. I think you'd like *Indiscret*. That's Lelong."

"It doesn't sound very passionate," Milly said.

"You are young. You don't have to put passion on behind the ears."

"You must give a man encouragement," Milly said.

"Just look at him."

"Like this?" Wormold heard Beatrice laugh. He looked at the door with astonishment. He had gone in thought so far across the border that he had forgotten he was still here on this side with them.

"You needn't give them all that encouragement," Beatrice said.

"Did I languish?"

"I'd call it smoulder."

"Do you miss being married?" Milly asked.

"If you mean do I miss Peter, I don't."

"If he died would you marry again?"

"I don't think I'd wait for that. He's only forty."

"Oh yes. I suppose *you* could marry again, if you call it marriage."

"I do."

"But it's terrible, isn't it. *I* have to marry for keeps."

"Most of us think we are going to do that—when we do it."

"I'd be much better off as a mistress."

"I don't believe your father would like that very much."

"I don't see why not. If he married again it wouldn't be any different. She'd really be his mistress, wouldn't she? He wanted to stay with Mother always. I know. He told me so. It was a real marriage. Even a good pagan can't get round that."

"I thought the same about Peter. Milly, Milly, don't let them make you hard."

"They?"

"The nuns."

"Oh. They don't talk to me that way. Not that way at all."

There was always, of course, the possibility of a knife. But for a knife you had to be closer to Carter than he could ever hope to get.

Milly said, "Do you love my father?"

He thought: One day I can come back and settle these questions. But now there are more important problems; I have to discover how to kill a man. Surely they produced handbooks to tell you that? There must be treatises on unarmed combat. He looked at his hands, but he didn't trust them.

Beatrice said, "Why do you ask that?"

"A way you looked at him."

"When?"

"When he came back from that lunch. Perhaps you were just pleased because he'd made a speech?"

"Yes."

"It wouldn't do," Milly said. "I mean, you loving him."

Wormold said to himself, At least if I could kill him, I would kill for a clean reason. I would kill to show that you can't kill without being killed in your turn. I wouldn't kill for my country. I wouldn't kill for capitalism or Communism or social democracy or the welfare state—whose welfare? I would kill Carter because he killed Hasselbacher. A family-feud had been a better reason for murder than patriotism or the preference for one economic system over another. If I love or if I hate, let me love or hate as an individual. I will not be 59200/5 in anyone's global war.

"If I loved him, why shouldn't I?"

"He's married."

"Milly, dear Milly. Beware of formulas. If there's a God, he's not a God of formulas."

"Do you love him?"

"I never said so."

A gun is the only way; where can I get a gun?

Somebody came through the door; he didn't even look up. Rudy's tubes gave a high shriek in the next room. Milly's voice said, "We didn't hear you come in."

He said, "I want you to do something for me, Milly."

"Were you listening?"

He heard Beatrice say, "What's wrong? What's happened?"

"There's been an accident, a kind of accident."

"Who?"

"Dr. Hasselbacher."

"Serious?"

"Yes."

" You are breaking the news, aren't you?" Milly said.

"Yes."

"Poor Dr. Hasselbacher."

"Yes."

"I'll get the chaplain to say a Mass for every year we knew him." There hadn't, he realised, been any need to break a death gently, so far as Milly was concerned. All deaths to her were happy deaths. Vengeance was unnecessary when you believed in a heaven. But he had no such belief. Mercy and forgiveness were scarcely virtues in a Christian; they came too easily.

He said, "Captain Segura was here. He wants you to marry him."

"That old man. I'll never ride in his car again."

"I'd like you to once more, tomorrow. Tell him I want to see him."

"Why?"

"A game of draughts. At ten o'clock. You and Beatrice must be out of the way."

"Will he pester me?"

"No. Just tell him to come and talk to me. Tell him to bring his list. He'll understand."

"And afterwards?"

"We are going home. To England."

When he was alone with Beatrice, he said, "That's that. The end of the office."

"What do you mean?"

"Perhaps we'll go down gloriously with one good report—the list of secret agents operating here."

"Including us?"

"Oh no. We've never operated."

"I don't understand."

"I've got no agents, Beatrice. Not one. Hasselbacher was killed for no reason. There are no constructions in the Oriente mountains."

It was typical of her that she showed no incredulity. This was a piece of information like any other information to be filed for reference. Any assessment of its value would be made, he thought, by the head-office.

He said, "Of course it's your duty to report this immediately to London, but I'd be grateful if you'd wait till after tomorrow. We may be able to add something genuine then."

"If you are alive, you mean."

"Of course I'll be alive."

"You are planning something."

"Segura has the list of agents."

"That's not what you are planning. But if you are dead," she said with what sounded like anger, "*de mortuis* I suppose."

"If something did happen to me I wouldn't want you to learn for the first time from these bogus files what a fraud I'd been."

"But Raul . . . there must have been a Raul."

"Poor man. He must have wondered what was happening to him. Taking a joy-ride in his usual way. Perhaps he was drunk in his usual way too. I hope so."

"But he existed."

"One has to get a name from somewhere. I must have picked his up without remembering it."

"Those diagrams?"

"I drew them myself from the Atomic Pile Cleaner. The joke's over now. Would you like to write out a confession for me to sign? I'm glad they didn't do anything serious to Teresa."

She began to laugh. She put her head in her hands and laughed. She said, "Oh, how I love you."

"It must seem pretty silly to you."

"London seems pretty silly. And Henry Hawthorne. Do you think I would ever have left Peter if once—just once—he'd made a fool of UNESCO? But UNESCO was sacred. Cultural conferences were sacred. He never laughed . . . Lend me your handkerchief."

"You're crying."

"I'm laughing. Those drawings . . ."

"One was a nozzle-spray and another was a double-action coupling. I never thought they would pass the experts."

"They weren't seen by experts. You forget—this is a Secret Service. We have to protect our sources. We can't allow documents like that to reach anyone who really knows. Darling . . ."

"You said darling."

"It's a way of speaking. Do you remember the Tropicana and that man singing? I didn't know you were my boss and I was your secretary, you were just a nice man with a lovely daughter and I knew you wanted to do something crazy with a champagne bottle and I was so deadly bored with sense . . .''

"But I'm not the crazy type."

> " *'They say the earth is round—*
> *My madness offends.'* "

"I wouldn't be a seller of vacuum cleaners if I were the crazy type."

> " *'I say that night is day*
> *And I've no axe to*
> *grind.'* "

"Haven't you any more loyalty than I have?"

"You are loyal."

"Who to?"

"To Milly. I don't care a damn about men who are loyal to the people who pay them, to organisations . . . I don't think even my country means all that much. There are many countries in our blood, aren't there, but only one person. Would the world be in the mess it is if we were loyal to love and not to countries?"

He said, "I suppose they could take away my passport."

"Let them try."

"All the same," he said, "it's the end of a job for both of us."

5

i

Come in, Captain Segura.''

Captain Segura gleamed. His leather gleamed, his buttons gleamed, and there was fresh pomade upon his hair. He was like a well-cared-for weapon. He said. "I was so pleased when Milly brought the message."

"We have a lot to talk over. Shall we have a game first? Tonight I am going to beat you."

"I doubt it, Mr. Wormold. I do not yet have to show you filial respect."

Wormold unfolded the draughts board. Then he arranged on the board twenty-four miniature bottles of whisky: twelve Bourbon confronted twelve Scotch.

"What is this, Mr. Wormold?"

"An idea of Dr. Hasselbacher's. I thought we might have one game to his memory. When you take a piece you drink it."

"A shrewd idea, Mr. Wormold. As I am the better player I drink more."

"And then I catch up with you—in the drinks also."

"I think I would prefer to play with ordinary pieces."

"Are you afraid of being beaten, Segura? Perhaps you have a weak head."

"My head is as strong as another man's, but sometimes with drink I lose my temper. I do not wish to lose my temper with my future father."

"Milly won't marry you, Segura."

"That is what we have to discuss."

"You play with the Bourbon. Bourbon is stronger than Scotch. I shall be handicapped."

"That is not necessary. I will play with the Scotch."

Segura turned the board and sat down.

"Why not take off your belt, Segura? You'll be more comfortable."

Segura laid his belt and holster on the ground beside him. "I will fight you unarmed," he said jovially.

"Do you keep your gun loaded?"

"Of course. The kind of enemies I possess do not give me a chance to load."

"Have you found the murderer of Hasselbacher?"

"No. He does not belong to the criminal class."

"Carter?"

"After what you said, naturally I checked. He was with Dr. Braun at the time. And we cannot doubt the word of the President of the European Traders' Association, can we?"

"So Dr. Braun is on your list?"

"Naturally. And now to play."

There is an imaginary line in draughts, as every player knows, that crosses the board diagonally from corner to corner. It is the line of defence. Whoever gains control of that line takes the initiative; when the line is crossed the attack has begun. With an insolent ease Segura established himself with a Defiance opening, then moved a bottle across through the centre of the board. He didn't hesitate between moves; he hardly looked at the board. It was Wormold who paused and thought.

"Where is Milly?" Segura asked.

"Out."

"And your charming secretary?"

"With Milly."

"You are already in difficulties," Captain Segura said. He struck at the base of Wormold's defence and captured a bottle of Old Taylor. "The first drink," he said and drained it. Wormold recklessly began a pincer-movement in reply and almost at once lost a bottle—of Old Forester this time. A few beads of sweat came out on Segura's forehead and he cleared his throat after drinking. He said, "You play recklessly, Mr. Wormold." He indicated the board. "You should have taken that piece."

"You can huff me," Wormold said.

For the first time Segura hesitated. He said, "No. I prefer you to take my piece."

It was an unfamiliar whisky called Cairngorm and it found a raw spot on Wormold's tongue.

They played for a while with exaggerated care, neither taking a piece.

"Is Carter still at the Seville-Biltmore?" Wormold asked.

"Yes."

"Do you keep him under observation?"

"No. What is the use?"

Wormold was clinging to the edge of the board with what was left of his foiled pincer-movement, but he had lost his base. He made a false move which enabled Segura to thrust a protected piece into square 22 and there was no way left of saving his piece on 25 and preventing Segura from reaching the back row and gaining a king.

"Careless," Segura said.

"I can make it an exchange."

"But I have the king."

Segura drank a Four Roses and Wormold at the other end of the board took a dimpled Haig. Segura said, "It is a hot evening." He crowned his king with a scrap of paper. Wormold said, "If I capture him I have to drink two bottles. I have spares in the cupboard."

"You have thought everything out," Segura said. Was it with sourness?

He played now with great caution. It became difficult to tempt him to a capture and Wormold began to realise the fundamental weakness of his plan, that it is possible for a good player to defeat an opponent without capturing his pieces. He took one more of Segura's and was trapped. He was left without a move.

Segura wiped the sweat from his forehead. "You see," he said, "you cannot win."

"You must give me my revenge."

"This Bourbon is strong. 85 proof."

"We will switch the whiskies."

This time Wormold was black, with the Scotch. He had replaced the three Scotch he had drunk and the three Bourbon. He started with the Old Fourteenth opening, which is apt to lead to a long-drawn-out game, for he knew now that his only hope was to make Segura lose his caution and play for pieces. Again he tried to be huffed, but Segura would not accept the move. It was as though Segura had recognised that his real opponent was not Wormold but his own head. He even threw away a piece with no tactical advantage and forced Wormold to take it—a Hiram Walker. Wormold realised that his own head was in danger; the mixture of Scotch and Bourbon was a deadly one. He said, "Give me a cigarette." Segura leant forward to light it and Wormold was aware of the effort he had to make to keep the lighter steady. It wouldn't snap and he cursed with unnecessary violence. Two more drinks and I have him, Wormold thought.

But it was as difficult to lose a piece to an unwilling antagonist as to capture one. Against his own will the battle was swaying to his side. He drank one Harper's and made a king. He said with false joviality, "The game's mine, Segura. Do you want to pack up?"

Segura scowled at the board. It was obvious that he was torn in two, between the desire to win and the desire to keep his head, but his head was clouded by anger as well as whisky. He said, "This is a pig's way of playing checkers." Now that his opponent had a king, he could no longer play for a bloodless victory, for the king had freedom of movement. This time when he sacrificed a Kentucky Tavern it was a genuine sacrifice and he swore at the pieces. "The damned shapes," he said, "they are all different. Cut-glass, whoever heard of a checker-piece of cut-glass?" Wormold felt his own brain fogged with the Bourbon, but the moment for victory—and defeat—had come.

Segura said, "You moved my piece."

"No, that's Red Label. Mine."

"How in God's name can I tell the difference between Scotch and Bourbon? They are all bottles, aren't they?"

"You are angry because you are losing."

"I never lose."

Then Wormold made his careful slip and exposed his king. For a moment he thought that Segura had not noticed and then he thought that deliberately to avoid drinking Segura was going to let his chance go by. But the temptation to take the king was great and what lay beyond the move was a shattering victory. His own piece would be made a king and a massacre would follow. Yet he hesitated. The heat of the whisky and the close night melted his face like a wax doll's; he had difficulty in focusing. He said, "Why did you do that?"

"What?"

"You lose your king an' the game."

"Damn. I didn't notice. I must be drunk."

"You drunk?"

"A little."

"I'm drunk too. You know I'm drunk. You are trying to make me drunk. Why?"

"Don't be a fool, Segura. Why should I want to make you drunk? Let's stop the game, call it a draw."

"God damn a draw. I know why you want to make me drunk. You want to show me that list—I mean you want me to show you."

"What list?"

"I have you all in the net. Where is Milly?"

"I told you, out."

"Tonight I go to the Chief of Police. We draw the net tight."

"With Carter in it?"

"Who is Carter?" He wagged his finger at Wormold. "You are in it—but I know you are no agent. You are a fraud."

"Why not sleep a bit, Segura? A drawn game."

"No drawn game. Look. I take your king." He opened the little bottle of Red Label and drank it down.

"Two bottles for a king," Wormold said and handed him a Dunosdale Cream.

Segura sat heavily in his chair, his chin rocking. He said, "Admit you are beaten. I do not play for pieces."

"I admit nothing. I have the better head and look, I huff you. You could have gone on.'' A Canadian rye had got mixed with the Bourbons, a Lord Calvert, and Wormold drank it down. He thought, it must be the last. If he doesn't pass out now, I'm finished. I won't be sober enough to pull a trigger. Did he say it was loaded?

"Matters nothing," Segura said in a whisper. "You are finished anyway." He moved his hand slowly over the board as though he were carrying an egg in a spoon. "See?" He captured one piece, two pieces, three . . .

"Drink this, Segura.'' A George IV, a Queen Anne, the game was ending in a flourish of royalty, a Highland Queen.

"You can go on, Segura. Or shall I huff you again? Drink it down.'' Vat 69. "Another. Drink it, Segura.'' Grant's Standfast. Old Argyll. "Drink them, Segura. I surrender now." But it was Segura who had surrendered. Wormold undid the captain's collar to give him air and eased his head on the back of the seat, but his own legs were uncertain as he walked towards the door. He had Segura's gun in his pocket.

ii

At the Seville-Biltmore he went to the house-phone and called up Carter. He had to admit that Carter's nerves were steady—far steadier than his own. Carter's mission in Cuba had not been properly fulfilled and yet he stayed on, as a marksman or perhaps as a decoy duck. Wormold said, "Good evening, Carter."

"Why, good evening, Wormold." The voice had just the right chill of injured pride.

"I want to apologise to you, Carter. That silly business of the whisky. I was tight I suppose. I'm a bit tight now. Not used to apologising."

"It's quite all right, Wormold. Go to bed."

"Sneered at your stammer. Chap shouldn't do that." He found himself talking like Hawthorne. Falsity was an occupational disease.

"I didn't know what the H-hell you meant."

"I shoon—soon—found out what was wrong. Nothing to do with you. That damned head-waiter poisoned his own dog. It was very old, of course, but to give it poisoned scraps—that's not the way to put a dog to sleep."

"Is that what h-happened? Thank you for letting me know, but it's late. I'm just going to bed, Wormold."

"Man's best friend."

"What's that? I can't h-hear you."

"Caesar, the King's friend, and there was the rough-haired one who went down at Jutland. Last seen on the bridge beside his master."

"You are drunk, Wormold." It was so much easier, Wormold found, to imitate drunkenness after—how many Scotch and Bourbon? You can trust a drunk man—*in vino veritas*. You can also more easily dispose of a drunk man. Carter would be a fool not to take the chance. Wormold said, "I feel in the mood for going round the spots."

"What spots?"

"The spots you wanted to see in Havana."

"It's getting late."

"It's the right time." Carter's hesitation came at him down the wire. He said, "Bring a gun." He felt a strange reluctance to kill an unarmed killer—if Carter should ever chance to be unarmed.

"A gun? Why?"

"In some of these places they try to roll you."

"Can't *you* bring one?"

"I don't happen to own one."

"Nor do I," and he believed he caught in the receiver the metallic sound of a chamber being checked. Diamond cut diamond, he thought, and smiled. But a smile is dangerous to the act of hate as much as to the act of love. He had to remind himself of how Hasselbacher had looked, staring up from the floor under the bar. They had not given the old man one chance, and he was giving Carter plenty. He began to regret the drinks he had taken.

"I'll meet you in the bar," Carter said.

"Don't be long."

"I have to get dressed."

Wormold was glad now of the darkness of the bar. Carter, he supposed, was telephoning to his friends and perhaps making a rendezvous, but in the bar at any rate they couldn't pick him out before he saw them. There was one entrance from the street and one from the hotel, and at the back a kind of balcony which would give support if he needed it to his gun. Anyone who entered was blinded for a while by the darkness, as he himself was. When he entered he couldn't for a moment see whether the bar held one or two customers, for the pair were tightly locked on a sofa by the street-door.

He asked for a Scotch, but he left it untasted, sitting on the balcony, watching both doors. Presently a man entered; he couldn't see the face; it was the hand patting the pipe-pocket which identified Carter.

"Carter."

Carter came to him.

"Let's be off," Wormold said.

"Take your drink first and I'll h-have one to keep you company."

"I've had too much, Carter. I need some air. We'll get a drink in some house."

Carter sat down. "Tell me where you plan to take me."

"Any one of a dozen whore-houses. They are all the same, Carter. About a dozen girls to choose from. They'll do an exhibition for you. Come on, we'll go. They get crowded after midnight."

Carter said anxiously, "I'd like a drink first. I can't go to a show like that stone sober."

"You aren't expecting anyone, are you, Carter?"

"No, why?"

"I thought—the way you watched the door . . ."

"I don't know a soul in this town. I told you."

"Except Dr. Braun."

"Oh yes, of course, Dr. Braun. But he's not the kind of companion to take to a h-house, is he?"

"After you, Carter."

Reluctantly Carter moved. It was obvious that he was searching for an excuse to stay. He said, "I just want to leave a message with the porter. I'm expecting a telephone call."

"From Dr. Braun?"

"Yes." He hesitated. "It seems rude going out like this before h-he rings. Can't you wait five minutes, Wormold?"

"Say you'll be back by one—unless you decide to make a night of it."

"It would be better to wait."

"Then I'll go without you. Damn you, Carter, I thought you wanted to see the town." He walked rapidly away. His car was parked across the street. He never looked back, but he heard steps following him. Carter no more wanted to lose him than he wanted to lose Carter.

"What a temper you've got, Wormold."

"I'm sorry. Drink takes me that way."

"I h-hope you are sober enough to drive straight."

"It would be better, Carter, if you drove."

He thought, That will keep his hands from his pockets.

"First right, first left, Carter."

They came out into the Atlantic drive: a lean white ship was leaving harbour, some tourist-cruiser bound for Kingston or for Port au Prince. They could see the couples leaning over the rail, romantic in the moonlight, and a band was playing a fading favourite—"*I could have danced all night.*"

"It makes me homesick," Carter said.

"For Nottwich?"

"Yes."

"There's no sea at Nottwich."

"The pleasure-boats on the river looked as big as that when I was young."

A murderer had no right to be homesick; a murderer should be a machine, and I too have to become a machine, Wormold thought, feeling in his pocket the handkerchief he would have to use to clean the fingerprints when the time came. But how to choose the time? What side-street or what doorway? and if the other shot first . . . ?

"Are your friends Russian, Carter? German? American?"

"What friends?" He added simply, "I have no friends."

"No friends?"

"No."

"To the left again, Carter, then right."

They moved at a walking pace now in a narrow street, lined with clubs; orchestras spoke from below ground like the ghost of Hamlet's father or that music under the paving stones in Alexandria when the god Hercules left Antony. Two men in Cuban night-club uniform bawled competitively to them across the road. Wormold said, "Let's stop. I need a drink badly before we go on."

"Are these whore-houses?"

"No. We'll go to a house later." He thought, If only Carter when he left the wheel had grabbed his gun, it would have been so easy to fire. Carter said, "Do you know this spot?"

"No. But I know the tune." It was strange that they were playing that—"my madness offends."

There were coloured photographs of naked girls outside and in night-club Esperanto one neon-lighted word, Strippteese. Steps painted in stripes like cheap pyjamas led them down towards a cellar foggy with Havanas. It seemed as suitable a place as any other for an execution. But he wanted a drink first. "You lead the way, Carter." Carter was hesitating. He opened his mouth and struggled with an aspirate; Wormold had never before heard him struggle for quite so long. "I h-h-h-hope . . ."

"What do you hope?"

"Nothing."

They sat and watched the stripping and both drank brandy and soda. A girl went from table to table ridding herself of clothes. She began with her gloves. A spectator took them with resignation like the contents of an In tray. Then she presented her back to Carter and told him to unhook her black lace corsets. Carter fumbled in vain at the catches, blushing all the time while the girl laughed and wriggled against his fingers. He said, "I'm sorry, I can't find . . ." Round the floor the gloomy men sat at their little tables watching Carter. No one smiled.

"You haven't had much practice, Carter, in Nottwich. Let me."

"Leave me alone, can't you?"

At last he got the corset undone and the girl rumpled his thin streaky hair and passed on. He smoothed it down again with a pocket-comb. "I don't like this place," he said.

"You are shy with women, Carter." But how could one shoot a man at whom it was so easy to laugh?

"I don't like horseplay," Carter said.

They climbed the stairs. Carter's pocket was heavy on his hip. Of course it might be his pipe he carried. He sat at the wheel again and grumbled. "You can see that sort of show anywhere. Just tarts undressing."

"You didn't help her much."

"I was looking for a zip."

"I needed a drink badly."

"Rotten brandy too. I wouldn't wonder if it was doped."

"Your whisky was more than doped, Carter." He was trying to heat his anger up and not to remember his ineffective victim struggling with the corset and blushing at his failure.

"What's that you said?"

"Stop here."

"Why?"

"You wanted to be taken to a house. Here is a house."

"But there's no one about."

"They are all closed and shuttered like this. Get out and ring the bell."

"What did you mean about the whisky?"

"Never mind that now. Get out and ring."

It was as suitable a place as a cellar (blank walls too had been frequently used for this purpose): a grey façade and a street where no one came except for one unlovely purpose. Carter slowly shifted his legs from under the wheel and Wormold watched his hands closely, the ineffective hands. It's a fair duel, he told himself, he's more accustomed to killing than I am, the chances are equal enough; I am not even quite sure my gun is loaded. He has more chance than Hasselbacher ever had.

With his hand on the door Carter paused again. He said, "Perhaps it would be more sensible—some other night. You know, I h-h-h-h . . ."

"You are frightened, Carter."

"I've never been to a h-h-h-house before. To tell you the truth, Wormold, I don't h-have much need of women."

"It sounds a lonely sort of life."

"I can do without them," he said defiantly. "There are more important things for a man than running after . . ."

"Why did you want to come to a house then?"

Again he startled Wormold with the plain truth. "I try to want them, but when it comes to the point . . ." He hovered on the edge of confession and then plunged. "It doesn't work, Wormold. I can't do what they want."

"Get out of the car."

I have to do it, Wormold thought, before he confesses any more to me. With every second the man was becoming human, a creature like oneself whom one might pity or console, not kill. Who knew what excuses were buried below any violent act? He drew Segura's gun.

"What?"

"Get out."

Carter stood against the whore-house door with a look of sullen complaint rather than fear. His fear was of women, not of violence. He said, "You are making a mistake. It was Braun who gave me the whisky. I'm not important."

"I don't care about the whisky. But you killed Hasselbacher, didn't you?"

Again he surprised Wormold with the truth. There was a kind of honesty in the man. "I was under orders, Wormold. I h-h-h-h——" He had manoeuvred himself so that his elbow reached the bell, and now he leant back and in the depths of the house the bell rang and rang its summons to work.

"There's no enmity, Wormold. You got too dangerous, that was all. We are only private soldiers, you and I."

"Me dangerous? What fools you people must be. I have no agents, Carter."

"Oh yes, you h-have. Those constructions in the mountains. We have copies of your drawings."

"The parts of a vacuum cleaner." He wondered who had supplied them: Lopez? or Hawthorne's own courier, or a man in the Consulate?

Carter's hand went to his pocket and Wormold fired. Carter gave a sharp yelp. He said, "You nearly shot me," and pulled out a hand clasped round a shattered pipe. He said, "My Dunhill. You've smashed my Dunhill."

"Beginner's luck," Wormold said. He had braced himself for a death, but it was impossible to shoot again. The door behind Carter began to open. There was an impression of plastic music. "They'll look after you in there. You may need a woman now, Carter."

"You—you clown."

How right Carter was. He put the gun down beside him and slipped into the driving seat. Suddenly he felt happy. He might have killed a man. He had proved conclusively to himself that he wasn't one of the judges; he had no vocation for violence. Then Carter fired.

6

i

He said to Beatrice, "I was just leaning forward to switch on the engine. That saved me, I imagine. Of course it was his right to fire back. It was a real duel, but the third shot was mine."

"What happened afterwards?"

"I had time to drive away before I was sick."

"Sick?"

"I suppose if I hadn't missed the war it would have seemed much less serious a thing killing a man. Poor Carter."

"Why should you feel sorry for him?"

"He was a man. I'd learnt a lot about him. He couldn't undo a girl's corset. He was scared of women. He liked his pipe and when he was a boy the pleasure-steamers on the river at home seemed to him like liners. Perhaps he was a romantic. A romantic is usually afraid, isn't he, in case reality doesn't come up to expectations. They all expect too much."

"And then?"

"I wiped my prints off the gun and brought it back. Of course Segura will find that two shots have been fired. But I don't suppose he'll want to claim the bullets. It would be a little difficult to explain. He was still asleep when I came in. I'm afraid to think what a head he'll have now. My own is bad enough. But I tried to follow your instructions with the photograph."

"What photograph?"

"He had a list of foreign agents he was taking to the Chief of Police. I photographed it and put it back in his pocket. I'm glad to feel there's one real report that I've sent before I resign."

"You should have waited for me."

"How could I? He was going to wake at any moment. But this micro business is tricky."

"Why on earth did you make a microphotograph?"

"Because we can't trust any courier to Kingston. Carter's people—whoever they are—have copies of the Oriente drawings. That means a double agent somewhere. Perhaps it's your man who smuggles in the drugs. So I made a microphotograph as you showed me and I stuck it on the back of a stamp and I posted off an assorted batch of five hundred British colonials, the way we arranged for an emergency."

"We'll have to cable them which stamp you've stuck it to."

"Which stamp?"

"You don't expect them to look through five hundred stamps, do you, looking for one black dot."

"I hadn't thought of that. How very awkward."

"You must know which stamp . . ."

"I didn't think of looking at the front. I think it was a George V, and it was red—or green."

"That's helpful. Do you remember any of the names on the list?"

"No. There wasn't time to read it properly. I know I'm a fool at this game, Beatrice."

"No. They are the fools."

"I wonder whom we'll hear from next. Dr. Braun . . . Segura . . ."

But it was neither of them.

ii

The supercilious clerk from the Consulate appeared in the shop at five o'clock the next afternoon. He stood stiffly among the vacuum cleaners like a disapproving tourist in a museum of phallic objects. He told Wormold that the Ambassador wanted to see him. "Will tomorrow morning do?" He was working on his last report, Carter's death and his resignation.

"No, it won't. He telephoned from his home. You are to go there straight away."

"I'm not an employee," Wormold said.

"Aren't you?"

Wormold drove back to Vedado, to the little white houses and the bougainvillias of the rich. It seemed a long while since his visit to Professor Sanchez. He passed the house. What quarrels were still in progress behind those doll's-house walls?

He had a sense that everyone in the Ambassador's home was on the look-out for him and that the hall and the stairs had been carefully cleared of spectators. On the first floor a woman turned her back and shut herself in a room; he thought it was the Ambassadress. Two children peered quickly through the banisters on the second floor and ran off with a click of little heels on the tiled floor. The butler showed him into the drawing-room, which was empty, and closed the door on him stealthily. Through the tall windows he could see a long green lawn and tall sub-tropical trees. Even there somebody was moving rapidly away.

The room was like many Embassy drawing-rooms, a mixture of big inherited pieces and small personal objects acquired in previous stations. Wormold thought he could detect a past in Teheran (an odd-shaped pipe, a tile), Athens (an icon or two), but he was momentarily puzzled by an African mask—perhaps Monrovia?

The Ambassador came in, a tall cold man in a Guards tie, with something about him of what Hawthorne would have liked to be. He said, "Sit down, Wormold. Have a cigarette?"

"No thank you, sir."

"You'll find that chair more comfortable. Now it's no use beating about the bush, Wormold. You are in trouble."

"Yes."

"Of course I know nothing—nothing at all—of what you are doing here."

"I sell vacuum cleaners, sir."

The Ambassador looked at him with undisguised distaste. "Vacuum cleaners? I wasn't referring to them." He looked away from Wormold at the Persian pipe, the Greek icon, the Liberian mask. They were like the autobiography in which a man has written for reassurance only of his better days. He said, "Yesterday morning Captain Segura came to see me. Mind you, I don't know how the police got this information, it's none of my business, but he told me you had been sending a lot of reports home of a misleading character. I don't know whom you sent them to: that's none of my business either. He said in fact that you had been drawing money and pretending to have sources of information which simply don't exist. I thought it my duty to inform the Foreign Office at once. I gather you will be receiving orders to go home and report—who to I have no idea, that sort of thing has nothing to do with me." Wormold saw two small heads looking out from behind one of the tall trees. He looked at them and they looked at him, he thought sympathetically. He said, "Yes, sir?"

"I got the impression that Captain Segura considered you were causing a lot of trouble here. I think if you refused to go home you might find yourself in serious trouble with the authorities, and under the circumstances of course I could do nothing to help you. Nothing at all. Captain Segura even suspects you of having forged some kind of document which he says you claim to have found in his possession. The whole subject is distasteful to me, Wormold. I can't tell you how distasteful it is. The correct sources for information abroad are the embassies. We have our attachés for that purpose. This so-called secret information is a trouble to every ambassador."

"Yes, sir."

"I don't know whether you've heard—it's been kept out of the papers—but an Englishman was shot the night before last. Captain Segura hinted that he was not unconnected with you."

"I met him once at lunch, sir."

"You had better go home, Wormold, on the first plane you can manage—the sooner the better for me—and discuss it with your people—whoever they are."

"Yes, sir."

iii

The K.L.M. plane was due to take off at three-thirty in the morning for Amsterdam by way of Montreal. Wormold had no desire to travel to Kingston, where Hawthorne might have instructions to meet him. The office had been closed with a final cable and Rudy and his suitcase were routed to Jamaica. The code-books were burnt with the help of the celluloid sheets. Beatrice was to go with Rudy. Lopez was left in charge of the vacuum cleaners. All the personal possessions he valued Wormold got into one crate, which he arranged to send by sea. The horse was sold—to Captain Segura.

Beatrice helped him pack. The last object in the crate was the statue of St. Seraphina.

"Milly must be very unhappy." Beatrice said.

"She's wonderfully resigned. She says like Sir Humphrey Gilbert that God is just as close to her in England as in Cuba."

"It wasn't quite what Gilbert said."

There was a pile of unsecret rubbish left to be burnt.

Beatrice said, "What a lot of photographs you had tucked away—of *her*."

"I used to feel it was like killing someone to tear up a photograph. Of course I know now that it's quite different."

"What's this red box?"

"She gave me some cuff-links once. They were stolen, but I kept the box. I don't know why. In a way I'm glad to see all this stuff go."

"The end of a life."

"Of two lives."

"What's this?"

"An old programme."

"Not so old. The Tropicana. May I keep it?"

"You are too young to keep things," Wormold said. "They accumulate too much. Soon you find you have nowhere left to live among the junk-boxes."

"I'll risk it. That was a wonderful evening."

Milly and Wormold saw her off at the airport. Rudy disappeared unobtrusively following the man with the enormous suitcase. It was a hot afternoon and people stood around drinking daiquiris. Ever since Captain Segura's proposal of marriage Milly's duenna had disappeared, but after her disappearance the child, whom he had hoped to see again, who had set fire to Thomas Earl Parkman, junior, had not returned. It was as though Milly had outgrown both characters simultaneously. She said with grown-up tact, "I want to find some magazines for Beatrice," and busied herself at a bookstall with her back turned.

"I'm sorry," Wormold said. "I'll tell them when I get back that you know nothing. I wonder where you'll be sent next."

"The Persian Gulf perhaps. Basra."

"Why the Persian Gulf?"

"It's their idea of purgatory. Regeneration through sweat and tears. Do Phast-kleaners have an agency at Basra?"

"I'm afraid Phastkleaners won't keep me on."

"What will you do?"

"I've got enough, thanks to poor Raul, for Milly's year in Switzerland. After that I don't know."

"You could open one of those practical joke shops—you know, the bloodstained thumb and the spilt ink and the fly on the lump of sugar. How ghastly goings-away are. Please don't wait any longer."

"Shall I see you again?"

"I'll try not to go to Basra. I'll try to stay in the typists' pool with Angelica and Ethel and Miss Jenkinson. When I'm lucky I shall be off at six and we could meet at the Corner House for a cheap snack and go to the movies. It's one of those ghastly lives, isn't it, like UNESCO and modern writers in conference? It's been fun here with you."

"Yes."

"Now go away."

He went to the magazine stall and found Milly. "We're off," he said.

"But, Beatrice—she hasn't got her magazines."

"She doesn't want them."

"I didn't say good-bye."

"Too late. She's passed the emigration now. You'll see her in London. Perhaps."

iv

It was as if they spent all their remaining time in airports. Now it was the K.L.M. flight and it was three in the morning and the sky was pink with the reflection of neon-lighted stands and landing-flares, and it was Captain Segura who was doing the "seeing off." He tried to make the official occasion seem as private as possible, but it was still a little like a deportation. Segura said reproachfully, "You drove me to this."

"Your methods are gentler than Carter's or Dr. Braun's. What are you doing about Dr. Braun?"

"He finds it necessary to return to Switzerland on a matter to do with his precision-instruments."

"With a passage booked on to Moscow?"

"Not necessarily. Perhaps Bonn. Or Washington. Or even Bucharest. I don't know. Whoever they are they are pleased, I believe, with your drawings."

"Drawings?"

"Of the constructions in Oriente. He will also take the credit for getting rid of a dangerous agent."

"Me?"

"Yes. Cuba will be a little quieter without you both, but I shall miss Milly."

"Milly would never have married you, Segura. She doesn't really like cigarette-cases made of human skin."

"Did you ever hear whose skin?"

"No."

"A police-officer who tortured my father to death. You see, he was a poor man. He belonged to the torturable class."

Milly joined them, carrying *Time*, *Life*, *Paris-Match* and *Quick*. It was nearly 3:15 and there was a band of grey in the sky over the flare-path where the false dawn had begun. The pilots moved out to the plane and the air-hostesses followed. He knew the three of them by sight; they had sat with Beatrice at the Tropicana weeks ago. A loudspeaker announced in English and Spanish the departure of flight 396 to Montreal and Amsterdam.

"I have a present for each of you," Segura said. He gave them two little packets. They opened them while the plane wheeled over Havana; the chain of lights along the marine parade swung out of sight and the sea fell like a curtain on all that past. In Wormold's packet was a miniature bottle of Grant's Standfast, and a bullet which had been fired from a police-gun. In Milly's was a small silver horseshoe inscribed with her initials.

"Why the bullet?" Milly asked.

"Oh, a joke in rather doubtful taste. All the same, he wasn't a bad chap," Wormold said.

"But not right for a husband," the grown-up Milly replied.

Epilogue in London

i

They had looked at him curiously when he gave his name, and then they had put him into a lift and taken him, a little to his surprise, down and not up. Now he sat in a long basement-corridor watching a red light over a door; when it turned green, they had told him, he could go in, but not before. People who paid no attention to the light went in and went out; some of them carried papers and some of them brief-cases, and one was in uniform, a colonel. Nobody looked at him; he felt that he embarrassed them. They ignored him as one ignores a malformed man. But presumably it was not his limp.

Hawthorne came down the passage from the lift. He looked rumpled as though he had slept in his clothes; perhaps he had been on an all-night plane from Jamaica. He too would have ignored Wormold if Wormold had not spoken.

"Hullo, Hawthorne."

"Oh, you, Wormold."

"Did Beatrice arrive safely?"

"Yes. Naturally."

"Where is she, Hawthorne?"

"I have no idea."

"What's happening here? It looks like a court-martial."

"It *is* a court-martial," Hawthorne said frostily and went into the room with the light. The clock stood at 11:25. He had been summoned for eleven.

He wondered whether there was anything they could do to him beyond sacking him, which presumably they had already done. That was probably what they were trying to decide in there. They could hardly charge him under the Official Secrets Act. He had invented secrets, he hadn't given them away. Presumably they could make it difficult for him if he tried to find a job abroad, and jobs at home were not easy to come by at his age, but he had no intention of giving them back their money. That was for Milly; he felt now as though he had earned it in his capacity as a target for Carter's poison and Carter's bullet.

At 11:35 the Colonel came out; he looked hot and angry as he strode towards the lift. There goes a hanging judge, thought Wormold. A man in a tweed jacket emerged next. He had blue eyes very deeply sunk and he needed no uniform to mark him as a sailor. He looked at Wormold accidentally and looked quickly away again like a man of integrity. He called out "Wait for me, Colonel" and went down the passage with a very slight roll as though he were back on a bridge in rough weather. Hawthorne came next, in conversation with a very young man, and then Wormold was suddenly breathless because the light was green and Beatrice was there.

"You are to go in," she said.

"What's the verdict?"

"I can't speak to you now. Where are you staying?"

He told her.

"I'll come to you at six. If I can."

"Am I to be shot at dawn?"

"Don't worry. Go in now. He doesn't like to be kept waiting."

"What's happening to you?"

She said, "Jakarta."

"What's that?"

"The end of the world," she said. "Further than Basra. Please go in."

A man wearing a black monocle sat all by himself behind a desk. He said, "Sit down, Wormold."

"I prefer to stand."

"Oh, that's a quotation, isn't it?"

"Quotation?"

"I'm sure I remember hearing that in some play—amateur theatricals. A great many years ago, of course."

Wormold sat down. He said, "You've no right to send her to Jakarta."

"Send who to Jakarta?"

"Beatrice."

"Who's she? Oh, that secretary of yours. How I hate these Christian names. You'll have to see Miss Jenkinson about that. She's in charge of the pool, not me, thank God."

"She had nothing to do with anything."

"Anything? Listen, Wormold. We've decided to shut down your post, and the question arises—what are we to do with you?" It was coming now. Judging from the face of the Colonel who had been one of his judges, he felt that what came would not be pleasant. The Chief took out his black monocle and Wormold was surprised by the baby-blue eye. He said, "We thought the best thing for you under the circumstances would be to stay at home—on our training staff. Lecturing. How to run a station abroad. That kind of thing." He seemed to be swallowing something very disagreeable. He added, "Of course, as we always do when a man retires from a post abroad, we'll recommend you for a decoration. I think in your case— you were not there very long—we can hardly suggest anything higher than an O.B.E."

ii

They greeted each other formally in a wilderness of sage-green chairs in an inexpensive hotel near Gower Street called the Pendennis. "I don't think I can get you a drink," he said. "It's Temperance."

"Why did you come here then?"

"I used to come with my parents when I was a boy. I hadn't realised about the temperance. It didn't trouble me then. Beatrice, what's happened? Are they mad?"

"They are pretty mad with both of us. They thought I should have spotted what was going on. The Chief had summoned quite a meeting. His liaisons were all there, with the War Office, the Admiralty, the Air Ministry. They had all your reports out in front of them and they went through them one by one. Communist infiltration in the Government—nobody minded a memo to the Foreign Office cancelling that one. There were economic reports—they agreed they should be disavowed too. Only the Board of Trade would mind. Nobody got really touchy until the Service reports came up. There was one about disaffection in the navy and another about refuelling bases for submarines. The Commander said, 'There must be some truth in these.'

"I said, 'Look at the source. He doesn't exist.'

" 'We shall look such fools,' the Commander said. 'They are going to be as pleased as Punch in Naval Intelligence.'

"But that was nothing to what they felt when the constructions were discussed."

"They'd really swallowed those drawings?"

"It was then they turned on poor Henry."

"I wish you wouldn't call him Henry."

"They said first of all that he had never reported you sold vacuum cleaners but that you were a kind of merchant-king. The Chief didn't join in *that* hunt. He looked embarrassed for some reason, and anyway Henry—I mean Hawthorne— produced the file and all the details were on it. Of course that had never gone further than Miss Jenkinson's pool. Then they said he ought to have recognised the parts of a vacuum cleaner when he saw them. So he said he had, but there was no reason why the *principle* of a vacuum cleaner might not be applied to a weapon. After that they really howled for your blood, all except the Chief. There were moments when I thought he saw the funny side. He said to them, 'What we have to do is quite simple. We have to notify the Admiralty, the War Office and the Air Ministry that all reports from Havana for the last six months are totally unreliable.' ''

"But, Beatrice, they've offered me a job."

"That's easily explained. The Commander crumbled first. Perhaps at sea one learns to take a long view. He said it would ruin the Service as far as the Admiralty was concerned. In future they would rely only on Naval Intelligence. Then the Colonel said, 'If I tell the War Office, we may as well pack up.' It was quite an impasse until the Chief suggested that perhaps the simplest plan was to circulate one more report from 59200/5—that the constructions had proved a failure and had been dismantled. There remained of course you. The Chief felt you had had valuable experience which should be kept for the use of the department rather than for the popular press. Too many people had written reminiscences lately of the Secret Service. Somebody mentioned the Official Secrets Act, but the Chief thought it might not cover your case. You should have seen them when they were balked of a victim. Of course they turned on me, but I wasn't going to be cross-examined by that gang. So I spoke out."

"What on earth did you say?"

"I told them even if I'd known I wouldn't have stopped you. I said you were working for something important, not for someone's notion of a global war that may never happen. That fool dressed up as a Colonel said something about 'your country.' I said, 'What do you mean by his country? A flag someone invented two hundred years ago? The Bench of Bishops arguing about divorce and the House of Commons shouting Ya at each other across the floor? Or do you mean the T.U.C. and British Railways and the Co-op? You probably think it's your regiment if you ever stop to think, but we haven't got a regiment—he and I.' They tried to interrupt and I said, 'Oh, I forgot. There's something greater than one's country, isn't there? You taught us that with your League of Nations and your Atlantic Pact, NATO and UNO and SEATO. But they don't mean any more to most of us than all the other letters, U.S.A. and U.S.S.R. And we don't believe you any more when you say you want peace and justice and freedom. What kind of freedom? You want your careers.' I said I sympathised with the French officers in 1940 who looked after their families; they didn't anyway put their careers first. A country is more a family than a Parliamentary system."

"My God, you said all that?"

"Yes. It was quite a speech."

"Did you believe it?"

"Not all of it. They haven't left us much to believe, have they?—even disbelief. I can't believe in anything bigger than a home, or anything vaguer than a human being."

"Any human being?"

She walked quickly away without answering among the sage-green chairs and he saw that she had talked herself to the edge of tears. Ten years ago he would have followed her, but middle-age is the period of sad caution. He watched her move away across the dreary room and he thought: Darling is a manner of speech, fourteen years between us, Milly—one shouldn't do anything to shock one's child or to injure the faith one doesn't share. She had reached the door before he joined her.

He said, "I've looked up Jakarta in all the reference-books. You can't go there. It's a terrible place."

"I haven't any choice. I tried to stay in the pool."

"Did you want the pool?"

"We could have met at the Corner House sometimes and gone to a movie."

"A ghastly life—you said it."

"You would have been part of it."

"Beatrice, I'm fourteen years older than you."

"What the hell does that matter? I know what really worries you. It's not age, it's Milly."

"She has to learn her father's human too."

"She told me once it wouldn't do my loving you."

"It's got to do. I can't love you as a one-way traffic."

"It won't be easy telling her."

"It may not be very easy to stay with me after a few years."

She said, "My darling, don't worry about that any longer. You won't be left twice."

As they kissed, Milly came in carrying a large sewing basket for an old lady. She looked particularly virtuous; she had probably started a spell of doing good deeds. The old lady saw them first and clutched at Milly's arm. "Come away, dear," she said. "The idea, where anyone can see them!"

"It's all right," Milly said, "it's only my father."

The sound of her voice separated them.

The old lady said, "Is that your mother?"

"No. His secretary."

"Give me my basket," the old lady said with indignation.

"Well," Beatrice said, "that's that."

Wormold said, "I'm sorry, Milly."

"Oh," Milly said, "it's time she learnt a little about life."

"I wasn't thinking of her. I know this won't seem to you like a real marriage . . ."

"I'm glad you are being married. In Havana I thought you were just having an affair. Of course it comes to the same thing, doesn't it, as you are both married already, but somehow it will be more dignified. Father, do you know where Tattersall's is?"

"Knightsbridge, I think, but it will be closed."

"I just wanted to explore the route."

"And you don't mind, Milly?"

"Oh, pagans can do almost anything, and you are pagans. Lucky you. I'll be back for dinner."

"So you see," Beatrice said, "it was all right after all."

"Yes. I managed her rather well, don't you think? I can do some things properly. By the way, the report about the enemy agents—surely that must have pleased them."

"Not exactly. You see, darling, it took the laboratory an hour and a half floating each stamp in water to try to find your dot. I think it was on the four hundred and eighty-second stamp, and then when they tried to enlarge it—well, there wasn't anything there. You'd either overexposed the film or used the wrong end of the microscope."

"And yet they are giving me the O.B.E.?"

"Yes."

"And a job?"

"I doubt whether you'll keep it long."

"I don't mean to. Beatrice, when did you begin to imagine that you were . . . ?"

She put her hand on his shoulder and forced him into a shuffle, among the dreary chairs. Then she began to sing, a little out of tune, as though she had been running a long way in order to catch him up.

> *"Sane men surround*
> *You, old family friends.*
> *They say the earth is round—*
> *My madness offends.*
> *An orange has pips, they say,*
> *And an apple has rind . . ."*

"What are we going to live on?" Wormold asked.

"You and I can find a way."

"There are three of us," Wormold said, and she realised the chief problem of their future—that he would never be quite mad enough.